FOLLOWING THE SNOW

To those of you who've toed the line and to those who ran screeching past it. To those who need to remain hidden and to those who've been told to hush. For those who've clawed their way out and for those still within trauma's grip. To those who feel less than, too much, or not enough.

And to my Momma who taught me to give a damn.

For a list of trigger warnings visit www.Fortneaux.com

ACKNOWLEDGEMENTS

Deciding to write a book at 40 with no formal creative writing training was an experience! Thank you to Josiah of JD Book Services for the coaching and to Emily for taking on the job of editing for a new author. To my wonderful friends who took on the task of giving me their authentic feedback, doing sensitivity reads, and watching out for the grammar mistakes that are so easy to miss, you have my sincerest gratitude. Finally, to my husband, you encouraged me to take a chance; you read every word and every time you told me, "It's not my genre, but I think it's good!" I was able to keep going. You put so much of yourself and your time into this endeavor and truly believed and supported me. You have my eternal thanks. I could not have found a better partner.

EXTRA READER CONTENT

If you find yourself curious, all of the songs sung throughout the novel have been recorded and linked to the website www.Fortneaux.com. Click on the FTS Song page and enter this password: Obligate

CONTENTS

CHAPTER ONE

THE LITTLE THINGS

The long trip to Verus Temple was trying my already thin patience.

Our party, which had begun in my homeland to the far north, had picked up other Troth along our journey south. With each additional retinue that joined on, it became apparent how woefully unprepared the other kingdoms' Honored Women were. After traveling for four days, we had merged with the Troth contingent from Monwyn, a kingdom located in a mountainous region to the far west of the continent. From the moment we connected, I knew the days ahead would be taxing.

By evening on our eighth day of travel, the constant whining about gowns ruined by mud splatters and laments of long hours in the saddle had sapped my composure entirely—and composure wasn't a trait I had in abundance to begin with. I swear I had counted to ten before speaking... at *least* nine times so far. The last time I was this incensed, I'd been wrongly accused of springing a mess of hares from their pen back home.

Things were just... different than I thought they would be. Before setting out on this journey, our Primus had led me to believe that the women representing the Obligation were raised to be paragons of virtue, the inspiration of courts, the brightest stars illuminating the night sky. But the dark-haired Troth riding next to me had proven that notion irrefutably wrong. Come to think of it, every Troth I'd encountered so far had done their best to squash my naïveté.

The small bundle to my right was wrapped in a voluminous gray cloak and rode low in her saddle, hunkered over her mount. She'd been rhythmically leaning back, then forward, then back again for the better part of the morning and into the afternoon, trying to get more comfortable. I had hoped after breaking from our leisurely luncheon she would have been rested enough to resume our ride with less issue, but the discomfort in her backside had been the only topic of conversation for the last two hours. She spoke of it incessantly, to everyone and to no one.

Doing my best not to openly gawk at her inexpert equestrian skills, I took a quick glance in her direction. The sad thing was pressing her cheek into her horse's neck, standing straight-legged in her stirrups, butt thrust into the air. She wept into the red roan's pinned-back left ear, murmuring words I couldn't understand. I wasn't sure of her intention, but it looked like she was aiming to lay belly down, flat on the horse's back. The miserable Troth turned her head, and I caught a better glimpse of her tiny face peeking from the circle of her tightly cinched hood. Her lips were screwed into a compactly pinched pout and her sparse brows had knit together in such an agonizing frown that a deep furrow appeared on her forehead. I wanted to feel sorry for her since she wasn't used to riding such long distances, but if she could yowl more quietly and not spread her discomfort to everyone who passed by, it would make the journey more pleasant.

I ventured another discreet glance in her direction to see if she'd mastered the double-handed butt rub she'd tried moments before and—

Damn! I'm caught.

I made a mental note to work on my composure *and* subtlety.

Her dark gaze was brimming with desperation. I shifted to look away but heard her pathetic little whimper. As if I'd found a seal pup that had strayed too far from its mother, my eyes were physically pulled back to her predicament by some unrelenting force.

Guilt. It was guilt.

And now I was an unwilling prisoner trapped in her ordeal.

"This simply will not do!" she shouted. I barely stopped myself from whipping around to see if there was a guard or servant behind me. "I require a salve to be immediately applied to my flesh!" She snapped her fingers twice in my direction.

My eyes went wide. *There was no way she—*

"You!" she cried. I pointed to my chest and this time did a wide sweep of the area. "Yes, you. If I am able to acquire a Feverfew tincture, would you mind?"

"W-would I mind... rubbing medicated oil into your ass? Your bare ass?" I had always held confident women in high regard, but this Troth—who just asked me to oil her buns—hadn't at any point in the last three days even bothered to share her name with me. "Am I wrong in thinking the exchange of pleasantries typically precedes physical intimacy?"

Okay, so, ten times in four days. *One. Two. Three... Breathe. Four. Five.* There. I was level-headed... tranquil, even.

"This is the nether, the actual nether!" she wailed. Tears fell down her cheeks and ran into the tight neck of her cloak. She hung her head and let out a pained, high-pitch squeal before kicking her horse into a haphazard trot. The shrill noise startled my mount, but with a calm hand, I was able to bring her back to head without disrupting our retinue any further.

I looked to the sky. *Goddess? If this is to be my test of perseverance, I beg of you, please heal this unhinged Troth before she becomes a bigger pain in my own backside.*

I was happy to finally ride in silence.

When my companions were not pitiful, they were sniveling, and if asked to choose, I supposed I'd take the wailer over the shrewish one who acted like a spoiled princess. She had literally turned her nose up at the preserved meats and lavender tea the guards offered us the previous evening. Then, she'd had the audacity to complain of hunger and demand a man-at-arms procure her a light repast after he had bedded down for the night.

This morning, the same guard managed to down a few fowl. He'd roasted them over the sooty orange coals of our previous night's communal fire and offered them to all. The meat was bland but well-cooked and had been the first offering in days not to have been preserved in heavy layers of salt. Many of the Troth had outright rejected the fare, citing the unmet requirements of their complex palettes. I was happy to pocket several extra cuts. It wouldn't be the first time my unrefined taste buds had won me a snack—and with my healthy appetite, I was pleased to get something to tide me over.

The waxed linen pouches my mother had insisted on packing in my trousseau had come in handy. We'd argued over their necessity until my father had gotten tired of hearing our squabbling and, like always, sided with her. I unwrapped two of the rejected drumsticks and ate one with one hand while using my other to shoo away the tiny green flies that kept landing on my mount's neck.

Despite its flavorlessness, this grouse leg was doing wonders to stave off the hunger that accompanied so many hours in the saddle. Our dietary choices were not the only differences I had noticed—the lives of the other Troth must have been very different from mine. Maybe in their homelands, they had lived with teams of servants. In Nortia, noble or not, their little pleas for grilled fruits and hot stews would have been met with silence, or more likely, meals—meager or not—would have stopped altogether. *A week's worth of deprivation is no hardship.*

A strained series of yelps, reminding me of a fox's bark, shattered my calm. The but-thurt Troth had fallen in the ranks and was now back at my side, passionately expressing her sorrow. She clutched the neck of her cloak which caused her reins to shake back and forth.

My eyebrows shot to my forehead. *Did I ever finish my count to ten?*

"Have you tried anything else? Can you solve your problem?" I said snapping my head in her direction while my mother's advice slipped from my lips. "Sit up straight, tuck in your pelvis, quit trying to shove your ankles into your stirrups, and put the balls of your feet on them instead. Now, stop yanking on the reins! This was part of our early Troth training—have you been on a horse since then?"

The crunching of dried leaves under the horse's hoof falls were deafening in the silence that followed my remarks. Wide-eyed and mouth agape, she wrapped herself tighter into her heavy cloak and sat up straight. There were tears again, though this time they didn't spill. She just raised her delicate chin, which popped out from the drawn hood, and met my eyes squarely.

"I will find another servant to administer my salve!" The slight figure urged her horse forward, and I watched as she bobbed in her saddle, a little less chaotically, all the way to the front of our long line.

Eight... Nine. Breathe. Ten.

Our caravan would grow again tomorrow. *Goddess help me.* According to our armed escorts, the last contingent of northern Troth, all representatives of the Kingdom of Gaea, would arrive by mid-morning, completing our collective. Together, we would begin the upward climb of Mount Gammond, the final leg of our journey. I needed to endure just one more day of ridiculousness, and then I would start my life in service to the Ærtan continent.

In the distance, I could see the first third of our party begin to slow and our guide's fist hit the air. We were stopping again. *Looks like the little Troth got what she wanted.*

An escort, dressed in a bright red surcoat with three amber-colored triangles appliquéd across the back, eased from his saddle and walked back three or four horse lengths to aid a woman in dismounting from her horse.

Fucking Monwyns.

I had no idea what metric our guardians used to gauge time, or how they stuck to any kind of schedule, but this would be the second stop of the day to allow my now least favorite Monwyn Troth to take a break. Last time, one of them had to retrieve an elixir from her belongings, and given how she'd been tottering in her saddle after the last stop, my guess was the brew she consumed had more to do with freeing her mind of boredom than staving off the 'oncoming cold,' as she had claimed. *Maybe butthurt Troth could find her salve now, or she could ask drinky Troth to share her "medication."* At this pace, we'd be lucky to reach the temple before nightfall tomorrow.

I watched the Troth head to the back of our line. The woman had an abundance of auburn hair and the largest set of breasts I'd ever seen on a human. As she rummaged through the luggage wagon, they seemed to move like they were two entirely separate entities that had somehow gotten stuck to her body. Eventually, after upturning all manner of baggage, she pulled a honey-colored elixir from a large trunk and drained it. The soon-to-be-soused Obligate ambled over to her horse, stopping once to scratch at her copper-colored locks and again to stare at her red shoes. With her fists on her hips, she sized up her steed, then seemed to realize that returning to her saddle was going to prove tricky. Try as she might, she couldn't throw a leg over her mount, as she needed both her feet to remain standing upright.

How proud her kingdom would have been to bear witness to, not one, but two sets of hands now shoving at her rump while another pair gripped her shoulders and pulled.

Leaning down, I braced my forearm on the black leather saddle and ran my free hand through the stringy, rust-colored mane of the horse who had easily been the best company available this last week. At this moment, idly twisting the horse's hair around my finger, it was my fervent hope that the guards would leave the sloth—I mean the Troth—hanging over her saddle, belly down. The image of her entering the most hallowed grounds of Verus Temple with her arms and legs bobbing to the horse's gait had me grinning, and despite my aggravation about losing time, it was highly amusing to watch her lecherous smile deepen every time a guard shoved his hands against her rear.

At long last, however, a steely-faced protector gained enough traction on the leaf-covered ground to heft the Troth home. He tucked himself under the indigo-clad lady and heaved while his brother-in-arms grabbed and shifted her pliant leg. When she finally gained her seat, I felt like I'd witnessed a miracle.

Our journey continued.

Once we reached our destination, my hope was to separate myself from this shameful collective and focus entirely on the magnanimity of the gift I had been given. Perhaps it was wrong, but I thought compared to the women I had been observing, I had a wholly different sense of respect for the process of Obligation.

A once-in-a-lifetime pilgrimage to our most holy site was considered the ultimate display of piety—becoming a part of its very functioning, like I was soon to do, was as rare as a hot day in Nortia. The reality was, tomorrow we would not only enter the gates of the Goddess's mortal home on the Great Sphere, but we would also begin the most pivotal training of our lives. The doors shuttering our current ways of living would be flung wide, and then we would step over the threshold to our new existences. Tomorrow held promise, and I was netherbent on keeping that thought in the forefront of my mind... mostly to distract me from the guttural hiccups coming from the, *fully* inebriated, Troth ahead.

We were far enough south now that the ground was no longer frozen or sloppy with mud, and the chill winds that had followed us for so long had mellowed to a comfortably warm breeze. The mild temperatures reminded me of the warmest days spent in my homeland, and though I wouldn't say I was homesick for the sight of my perpetually frozen town, I closed my eyes tightly and breathed deeply through my nose, remembering the proud faces of the loved ones I had left behind.

The knots in my stomach, my constant companion since the moment I rode away from the Glass Palace's courtyard, intensified. Being chosen for the Obligation was seen as one of the highest honors in all of Ærta, in part because of its rarity, but also because of the opportunity it provided. As Troth, I could bring prosperity and renown to my kingdom and family.

Troth and Scion were thought to have been touched by the Goddess herself. We were born when her constellation—an oval ring of seven stars—met with the crescent moon of her paramour high in the night sky. That constellation appeared at most twice per year, and the odds of bearing a child... was even rarer. By law, all records of those births were to be sent to the Devotees of Verus Temple within weeks of delivery, though decisions about the child's future could take years to be determined.

If chosen as Obligate, your life's mission became working with kingdom leaders to aid in the maintenance of peace, ensuring the continent's prosperity. You would give your life over to Ærta and in return be sculpted into the ultimate exemplar, an authority legitimized by She Who Is Most Divine.

Since the moment I was accepted and appointed Troth, my whole young life had become focused on preparing for the leafy path I trod at this moment, and though I hadn't understood it as a child, after two and a half decades of devotion, I felt truly ready.

Verus had sent me my first instructor at around the age of five, two years or so after I'd been named Troth. When I first met her, and for months after, I thought that Olena was the meanest person. She reminded me of the hag in the children's tale used to scare all the Nortian littles into bathing—the wrinkled and wire-haired old woman could smell your foul stench, which she craved, and if she sniffed you out with her bulbous, misshapen nose you became her dinner! Olena fit the story's description perfectly and also happened to be incredibly strict and stern.

For two years she lived in a small home near my own, and every morning she'd rise before light to teach me my letters. While the other children my age were playing on the snow mounds outside of the town, I was spending my days perfecting my P's and memorizing the prayers and creeds of our faith. I resented the schooling, and her, until we began reading from the most frivolous of books. Entitled *Magika and Menagerie*, it was so well-loved that I carried it with me, even now.

My playmates, who had been quick to leave me to my parchments, just as quickly returned to me when I could read to them the tales of the Oracles of Lyster or scare them to bits with the story of the Mountain Monster whose body was made of stone and who could eat goats whole! They had never tired of the stories the tome contained and neither had I. It almost became a ritual; after my schooling was done for the day, the evenings were reserved for sitting around the hearth, snacking on fish jerky, and reading, or re-reading, the tales of vile mages and mythical beasts.

I foggily remember the day Olena left, exactly three years from the date she'd arrived. Her departure had crushed me. By the end of her tenure, my resentment of her had been replaced by reverence. Her constancy had been the source of her strictness but also the strength of her method. Her high expectations were paired with endless patience and commitment to my path, and I knew without a doubt that she wished for my success. By now, the pain of her leaving had faded, replaced by the gifts she had left me: the ability to think and to wonder... and her worn-out copy of *Magika*.

Okay, so maybe I was looking backward and not forward *right now*, but I could never remember Olena without thinking of who had followed her. Kan Keagan had traveled to us from the farthest kingdom from my own, the sunbaked court of Solnna. He was my language tutor, chosen by the Primus of Nortia. It was common for a monarch or Primus to encourage learning a talent or attribute that would set us apart from other Obligates. My Primus had decided I would learn the traditional Solnnan tongue, as our Assignments oftentimes included travel and cross-kingdom diplomacy.

Kan was the first man, other than my father, that I'd ever loved. With rich brown skin and dark eyes, he was all warmth and comfort compared to Olena's exacting personality. Together, we spent our days on adventures, never once trapped in the house. We visited all the temples and shrines within a day's walk, including those in the capital only a few miles away. We'd made stops into all manner of shops and immersed ourselves in the language, identifying everything we could, from foods to housewares to animals—speaking only in Solnnan, of course!

No other villagers I knew spoke the language, so Kan Keagan and I had made a game out of telling inside jokes and poking fun at the town's more colorful citizens right under their noses. Once, while visiting the butcher shop, I'd accidentally lapsed into the common language and pointed at the merchant, loudly asking who the "real pig" was. The sharp cleaver, which had been rhythmically turning pork into chops, had gone silent for a moment as it dawned on the butcher what I'd said. Then, he had unleashed his anger, yelling and brandishing his blade in the air. A grim-faced Kan had grabbed my hand and stalked out the door. Fearful of the trouble I was sure to be in, I remember burying my face into his side, awaiting the tongue-lashing I knew I deserved. To my relief, he'd wiped at my tear-stained face and hugged away my shame, and I loved him for it. My days spent with him were the happiest of my youth, and when he died of an intestinal ailment after three and a half years of being in my life, my innocent heart broke. Ten years removed, *that* memory remained as fresh as—

"Halt!" our guide bellowed, cutting short my reminiscence.

Following their stringent daily protocol, the guards who had escorted us this entire journey leapt from their saddles and secured their horses to small trees and old, broken fence posts, likely once a corral.

I watched our guide slowly ease off his horse, the motion reminding me of lumps of snow oozing out of a boat's drainage port. When riding, his large girth had piled around him and hung over both sides of the swell of his saddle, very much how I imagined a polar bear riding a horse would look. Eight days ago, the round fellow had picked us up in Nortia, and for eight days he'd proceeded to be totally disengaged and fully removed from the rest of the group. He seemed content to converse with his old spotted mare and no other. I only knew his name was Fionn because he had introduced himself to my father the day we'd met. He only said two words to us per day: "halt," which meant our encampment had been chosen for the night, and "forward," meaning we were on our way to the next stop.

Perhaps his preference for solitude helped him choose ideal locations for our camps—he had to be quite alert despite his detached demeanor. Generally, our campsites had been near some form of water—a partially frozen lake or a small brook—and almost all locations had several areas of cover for privacy, though I assume that was more for himself than us. I had no clue where he slept, and he hadn't joined us for any meals.

Today's stop met his criteria and may well have been the loveliest of his sites yet.

We were making camp in the shadows of the Sinnon Mountains, the natural border and barrier between Nortia and the rest of the continent. The range was so monstrous that it was divided into three separate chains and touched each of the four kingdoms in some capacity. Mount Gammond had been visible for the last day and would be the ending point of our journey—it marked the dead center of the *Y*-shaped chain that chopped up our continent.

The guards worked quickly to remove their steel gauntlets, then replaced them with the buttery soft, cream-colored, leather gloves they all kept in their matching tanned pouches. They went from mount to mount, inquiring about the state of each Troth and her personal needs for the evening—except for mine. They didn't even attempt with me anymore. This daily ritual took forever, so I'd chosen days ago not to partake.

Tossing a leg over the saddle, I scanned the tree line for a place to relieve myself and spotted a tall oak nestled between two shorter ones. There were enough semi-leafed lower branches to keep me sheltered, so I didn't worry too much about offending anyone's sensibilities while I leaned back onto the rough bark. I remembered this time to hike my gown around my waist, I released the pressure in my bladder and watched a now familiar scene unfold before me.

With little thought for our protector's comforts, the mounted Troth gracefully twisted themselves sideways in their saddles and placed their damp and often dust-covered boots onto the guard's thighs, leaving dirty footprints on their living stepstools. The first time a guard insisted I use his leg as a mounting block, I laughed, thinking it was a joke. I came to find out the guards don't joke, or laugh, or smile, but I was the first Troth they had picked up, so I'd had no reference point for proper protocol.

Shaking my head at the silliness, I used a few leaves to wipe up and remembered *this time* to step out widely before dropping my skirts. It irked me that every night, instead of getting to their dinners, the guards had to spend at least a half hour scrubbing at the dirt that caked around the tightly peened rivets of their splinted leather cuisses, especially knowing that basic horsemanship was required for all Troth. *Every woman here should be able to mount and dismount a horse of her own accord.*

After all Troth were safely deposited on the ground, the guards went to work clearing grassy patches of sticks and stones so they could erect canvas tents. Each took about twenty minutes to raise. I'd noticed over the days we had camped rough that clearing the area well served two purposes. Most importantly, the stones were piled into a ring shape and the smaller sticks were tossed in its center, forming a large firepit. It also lessened the frequency of our guardians being woken at night to move pallets around for an uncomfortable Troth.

Like chicks pecking after a mother hen, I watched as two Monwyn Troth trailed a guard who was in the middle of setting up a particularly large tent. The cloaked women were demanding a spot for their garments to be aired. That spot needed to have sun and adequate airflow, and the garments could not touch the ground, so a method of hanging was required as well. Those women were interrupted by the rump-rubbing Troth, who pleaded with the guard to carry her to the nearby stream so she could soak her bruised bottom. Without even the slightest change to his neutral expression, the guard very calmly listened to each woman, and then systematically carried out their bidding. *I wonder how many years of consistent aggravation it took to acquire the unflappable, stone-faced countenance that all of the guards seem to share?*

We didn't always sleep under the stars, but tonight's site had me looking forward to it. On our fourth night, our guide had "halt"-ed us in a small village and we had stayed at a travelers' inn. Our hosts had seemed more than happy to put us up, and our provided space had been tidy and clean, despite the number of straw beds that had been stuffed into the rooms. Furniture had been scattered around, as well as basins of hot water and towels to clean off the travel grime, but as thankful as I was for the walls, I'd had to share a bed with Cinden, a pinkish-haired Gaean who had cried well into the night, complaining about her lack of feathered pillows. Tonight, I'd have peace and quiet on my own, free from Troth tears.

Well, there might still be tears, but they won't be in my ear all night.

Chuckling to myself, I located my personal spot to make camp. I preferred something at my back, so I found a ridge of densely packed bushes that formed a pseudo wall of vegetation. While inspecting the underbrush for little animals who might be making their home there, I heard the roar of water in the distance and noticed a decent-sized, clear-running stream.

My favorite thing about sleeping outside thus far had been lying down and enjoying the shiny leaves catching the tree-filtered light of the evening's last rays. In the northernmost region of Nortia, our trees stayed green year-round and had no leaves at all, only needles. Flinging out my blankets with a sharp snap, I made a small pallet and arranged the few necessities I had grabbed from the wagon. One of the items was a cream I could apply to my skin to keep it from drying out as we rode through changing climates. My mother had drilled it into my head early on that it must be used religiously. Otherwise, the freezing winds or the hot sun or heavy rains or basically any weather I encountered would render me wrinkly as a walrus's nose. The other item was a thin linen shirt that came almost to my knees. Most everyone slept fully clothed at night and piled on every available layer from their wardrobe as well, but I personally couldn't bear it. Three days into our journey the temperatures had warmed enough that I hadn't needed my cloak again. Even in the coolness of the evening, light perspiration clung to my skin.

Shoving at the heel of my boot, I thought of how different the southern portion of Nortia was compared to its uppermost point. Same kingdom, but Silverstep, the village where I lived, was as far north as you could go, and even during Nortia's warmest season, a thin, fragile film of ice covered the surface of the freshwater lakes. In our cold season, even the drums of drinking water stored in our kitchen would become slushy by morning.

The guards were still occupied running Troth tasks as I readied for bed. After pulling the clinging outer layer of wool over my head and slipping from my underdress and binding, I put on the finely woven linen that had once belonged to my father, before he'd become too large for it. With the stream playing its constant song and the campfires casting their warm glow, I laid atop my blankets and found what my mother called "my calm place," crossing my arms behind my head, I closed my eyes, and let slumber come.

One more sleep until my life truly begins.

··· ✦)(✦ ···

"My Assignment better be stellar or I *will* refuse it!" Jolting me from half-sleep, two Troth, who clearly couldn't find their calm, chattered together at the fire nearest my bed. They voiced their displeasure in high-pitched tones, the noise infiltrating my cozy haven.

"Well, my mother sent a missive to the Mantle last year. She won't settle for just any appointment."

I rolled to my side, searching the near darkness for the loudmouth whose *Assignment* seemed to be keeping me awake.

"They don't think we have opinions on the matter, but I intend to make them aware of my—"

"Can you all shut up?" I followed with a quick, "Please."

In the flickering firelight, I recognized one of their faces. I recalled the day this particular woman had joined us. She was called Kairus by her companions, and her group had met us after what I imagine was an extremely long journey from the western kingdom of Monwyn. Astride her velvety black horse, she had been wrapped in a crimson cloak that matched the red tip of her frozen nose. Currently, that same nose was scrunched up in indignation and her top lip was drawn up in a fine display of exasperation. *Great.* This was not the Troth I wanted to go toe-to-toe with. I'd seen the way she had lorded over her advisor twice now, so I wasn't surprised she was inconsiderate enough to gripe loudly right next to someone trying to sleep.

Her eyes narrowed, and the dancing flames of the fire reflected off their unique shade of blue. Gearing up for the fight, she pursed her lips into a perfect pink heart that still managed to be lovely despite the expression she made.

"Are you always so nasty, *Nortian?*" she sneered, inclining her chin as she spoke.

Propping myself up on my elbows, I prepared for the ensuing spat, but she didn't say another word, just turned away from me and continued to speak to her companion in low whispers.

That works for me.

I couldn't fall back to sleep immediately, having geared myself up, so instead, I stared off into the star-studded sky. Nortian nights weren't conducive to spotting constellations. It was too bitterly cold to remain outside for long. Here, I relished the chance to see the Divine Twins or the Great Whale of Derros. Stargazing was a nice alternative to sleeping, though tonight the trees blocked out all but the Mossius Flame and what I thought might be half of Cynder, the many-headed dog.

I watched the smoky patterns my breath made in the chill and pondered my future until the nervous feeling in the pit of my stomach returned. I didn't think I was scared exactly... *Well, that was a lie.* I was scared, but it was more like if terror introduced herself to excitement and they decided to take a stroll through my belly together. No matter though, anticipation or anxiety, I was committed to whatever Assignment I received after my appraisal. I would do my utmost to meet the Mantle's challenges head-on and try not to let the unknown aspects of my future frighten me.

Before allowing sleep to claim me again, I thought of the image that gave me strength when I needed it most. *Was it only a week or so ago when I last saw my parents' faces?*

There was my father, standing in the king's courtyard, arm wrapped around my mother's shoulders, beaming with pride. His smile was so wide that his teeth showed through his heavily whiskered face, and he hadn't bothered trying to hold back the tears that fell from his eyes.

'Ulltan, you'll upset her.' My mother had told him while patting his arm.

I saw her clearly in my memory, dipping her head, letting me know it was time to go.

Chapter Two

LEMONS SMELL LIKE LOVE

The smell of expensive perfumes—jasmine and rose—tangled with the scent of frying eggs. Crinkling my nose at the unpleasant combination, I tugged at the blankets, forming a better pillow under my head, and sank back into the bliss of near slumber. The tightly woven layer I wrapped myself in during the early morning hours provided the perfect cocoon of insulation, and with one foot exposed to the morning breeze, I was perfectly content to remain as I was. The camp, however, was coming alive around me and the clanking of guards' armoring infiltrated my peace, but even through the clatter and scrapes of metal, I made out a familiar sound. The friction of linen skirts sliding against heavy woolens made a uniquely sonorous noise, one that was rapidly approaching.

"Eira?" I pretended to sleep. "My girl?" I fought to keep my face placid.

A firm jab to the cheek sent my head rocking to the side, and I knew my ruse was over. I heard a long-winded rumble above me. Cracking my eyes open just a sliver, I beheld the vexed face of my Nan, who again prodded me with her slippered foot. Nan was a woman who expected her orders to be carried out immediately. She was so amusingly quick to provoke that there were times I couldn't help but poke the polar bear. Her wide-set eyes, the color of a seal's wet skin, were narrowing dangerously in my direction, and her ruddy complexion was rapidly changing from pinks and reds to deep purple. I knew I was close to setting off her glacier-sized temper.

"Up, Eira, lazy shit!" she barked. Having removed her shoe, she smooshed her chubby little digits into my temple. I smacked at the offending foot, but Nan quickly jerked it back and my hand met air.

"Up, up! Pack your bedroll and get about it!" She clapped her hands emphasizing each word. My mouth tugged into a smile. Despite being surly and deafeningly loud, I loved the woman solidly. I'd known her my whole life, and, poking toes and all, I didn't want to know a time without her.

"I'm up. Alright?" I laughed and grabbed her shoe, tossing it behind her.

Every Obligate was allowed a single companion on their journey to Verus, and that person would be there to serve or guide them in whatever capacity their monarch or Primus had chosen.

Nan was my companion and would be with me until my Assignment became official. When their charge was placed, they'd return to their kingdom and rejoin their normal life, albeit with more prestige than before. Chambermaids or trusted political advisors seemed to be the preferred flavors of counterparts on this journey, which made sense. One could take care of your immediate needs; the other could give wise counsel. My parents, who must have been thinking in a different direction, strayed from the norm and sent me with our family friend.

Nan had come to live with us after being widowed early in her marriage. She'd been in her late teens when she made her vows, but her husband had died a month later, according to my mother. Her husband had been a fisherman who worked for my father, the overseer of our town's docks and shipyards at the time. As I understood it, a boat crew, that included Nan's young man, left the Penumbrean Gulf and ventured into the open sea, never to return. It was a sad story, but a common one in our area of the world. The weather could change rapidly up north, and even minor accidents could turn deadly in rough waters. My parents offered her a place to stay, as she couldn't afford to live on her own so young. She'd planned to stay for a month, but she ended up staying a lifetime. She and my mother became the best of friends. I think it was actually harder for the two of them to part than it was for my mother to say goodbye to her only child.

Propping myself up on my elbow, I watched Nan shuffle away and surveyed our encampment. The three Monwyn Troth, including Kairus, the woman I no doubt offended last night, were huddled together, speaking quietly to each other while applying kohl to their eyelids. The women of Monwyn always appeared put together, and their confident carriage, combined with their face-enhancing abilities, made them seem more worldly and mature. They woke early to ensure they presented themselves with polished and expertly painted faces, and they all moved with a grace that I could only hope to emulate. Funnily though, when I first encountered them, I assumed incorrectly that the daily makeup and jewelry routine meant the ladies would be inclined to the superficial. After spending days with them on the road, I actually found them to be more sharp-witted and sly than conceited.

Under the guise of brushing out the silky auburn curls of drinky Troth, whose actual name was Yemailrys, the women spoke to each other in hushed tones and surveyed their surroundings. They were always more alert than they let on and often could be found watching people's comings and goings through the veil of their lowered lashes. Currently, they focused their shielded gaze on a younger guard—who admittedly was quite handsome. Their tinkling laughter was barely audible, and the guard had no idea he was being sized up.

I continued watching as they moved on to their next prey. Had I not been observing them observing others, I wouldn't have noticed at all. Following their subtle line of vision, I saw what now captured their attention: The Gaean Troth. Dressed in an earthy-green day dress, she knelt in prayer with her face turned toward the mountain. With her hands resting lightly against her brows, she chanted and spoke her prayers loud enough that her voice reverberated off the mountainside. Unlike Nortia, where we kept the religion, but didn't tend to go all out on the rituals, the people of Gaea were known to be deeply devout, which she proved every morning and night.

When we reached the temple, I hoped to build up my knowledge base of cultural customs. I dreamed that perhaps we would be taught by some renowned Ærtan historians. I loved learning about how the continent functioned but was limited by both my access to materials and the fact I'd never traveled more than four hours from Silverstep. What I did know came from a mix of reading *Ærta: Comparative Perspectives and Histories of the Seven Great Kingdoms* and meeting a handful of foreigners over the last few years.

That particular book was a gift from my kingdom's Primus, who had been in her position overseeing our economy, since before my father was born. When I had turned nineteen, she'd invited me to the Glass Palace as an honored guest at Nortia's annual Whaling Festival. During the festivities, I'd been led to her office, where she spoke to me at length concerning the economic ramifications of being born Troth. She counseled that learning about the intricacies and complexities of a people's origin and not focusing solely on the current systems of government would be a most valuable lesson for an Obligate. Then she gave me the volume and told me to study its contents until I had memorized its pages. To this day, I could recite the driest detail of the establishment and development of the seven kingdoms, even if the book was so outdated that it didn't account for the fact there were only four kingdoms in Ærta now.

I took a few moments to observe the Gaean Troth, still at her prayers. It was common knowledge that Gaean Obligates styled their hair the same way, pulled back in three braids that were interwoven with gold fibers. It was also a tradition in their small kingdom to dye their hair red when officially named Troth or Scion. It was done as a tribute to the Goddess who shed her blood giving birth to our world. A merchant I met at a formal dinner once told me that the red coloring came from a plant grown in their kingdom, but the exact formulation for the stain was kept secret. She also mentioned the dye was applied on top of their natural hair color, which produced various hues of red tresses. This Troth's hair was quite pink.

Nortian Troth didn't have customs like that—I didn't know about Solnna or Monwyn. My tutors and Primus never focused on other Obligates. They kept their sights on securing relationships, even ones that may not prove fruitful for many years. Because of that, I was introduced to foreign merchants and emissaries from all over the continent. Every time I met someone new, they gifted me exotic treats or fragrant spices and generally regaled me with some anecdote about their homeland. The Gaean merchant, Rizellan, the one who had told me of their Troth's customs, had brought me a basket of exotic sour fruits and a bolt of silk so fine you could see through it. In addition, she gave me a scroll containing Gaean prayers which she said would come in handy, were I Assigned to her lands.

When I was younger, I thought the frequent gifting was out of kindness, but as I grew, I realized that it was more likely a calculated effort, a payment of tribute, to the Troth that could very well be placed in their court one day. Even having come to that conclusion, I'd met with Rizellan several times over the years and had enjoyed our conversations each time.

I watched a few puffy clouds race across an otherwise clear sky and realized I needed to get going. Used to a land whose primary colors were white and gray—with the occasional yellow thrown in—I was just so taken by the bright orange and red leaves that fluttered to the ground. Rising to my feet, I reached to the sky and stretched my travel-fatigued muscles.

This is it. Today's the day!

My belongings packed up fast. Unless it was drizzling, a tent was just a canvas oven, so mine remained in the wagon most days. If my future job took me to Solnna, the southernmost kingdom on the continent, I'd sell or trade it to a local. I'd been told that it was so hot there that the men often carried out their daily tasks shirtless and the women's gowns had hems above their knees. I couldn't imagine what it would be like to live in a place much warmer than it was here, but I wouldn't scorn the potential adventure if sent there.

Leaving my bedroll on the ground behind the wagon, I spotted Nan sitting across the way. She had her skirts hitched up around her knees and her sleeves rolled up, shoveling eggs into her mouth. She caught my eye and pointed to the stream behind her with her spoon, never pausing in her chews. In Nan's world, beauty began and ended with cleanliness. In order to showcase your naturally given assets, bathing was not optional, which meant not a day went by that I wasn't sponged or scoured. If no water source could be found, she would wake me early to rub almond oil into my skin and scrape it off with a flat piece of whalebone. It did the trick, but I much preferred the use of soap and water to avoid her overzealous handling. She also theorized that makeup was a scam and told me if I scrubbed hard enough it would leave behind all the extra color I might want. *I wonder what she thinks of the Monwyn women's full-face application?*

"Yes, Majesty, I will do your bidding, Majesty," I curtsied before sweeping low and snatching a fried egg from her plate.

"And wash between your stinky hams, girl!" she bellowed, loud enough for Verus to have heard. *Nan!*

The clear stream swirled and bubbled around a wide boulder sitting in its middle. The water wasn't particularly deep—as I could make out the flat stones and mossy greenery of its bottom—but it would be high enough to take some weight off my travel-weary bones. Shedding my linen undershirt and tossing it onto a dry rock, I peeked around to make sure I was alone. I was, though there was a guard far off in the distance.

Sitting on the grassy bank, I dipped a tentative toe in the water before slipping in. The first time I had bathed in a river, I hadn't been prepared for how slick the stones of its floor would be, and I ended up drinking more water than I washed with. This stream's bottom wasn't nearly as treacherous, and the temperature was pure bliss. It was cool enough to make you wade in slowly but warm enough that once submerged, you adjusted quickly. I kicked out and let an arching splash fly and watched the ripples the droplets created. Further out, the water rose just past my hips, and at its deepest point, I squished my feet into the mud, relishing the feel of it between my toes.

Fully aware that I needed to hurry, I tilted my head back until it met the water's surface and let the water run over my shoulders.

Somewhere in the distance, a Troth began to sing.

"She laid her hand upon his chest, her lover's time grew near,
She whispered of their union, lips pressed against his ear,

'Go wait upon the blade, my love. Our journey never ends.
I'll meet you there, I'll find you there, eternity will we spend..."

I lost a few of the remaining lyrics in the sloshing sounds around me, but the song's verses spoke of lovers who had suffered in their lifelong quest to be together. After his father deemed her an unworthy bride, she was banished. She ended up having to fight off attackers and in doing so, was maimed by a multitude of magical curses. The woman eventually made her way back to her lover, but he had been mortally wounded by his own cousin in an attempted escape. *I wonder if the woman could've avoided all that insanity by having stayed away. I mean, I understand love, and I've fought against my mother's rules plenty, but was all that worth it in the end?*

I stopped to watch a school of tiny brown fish scatter wildly and then quickly re-form—I was mostly positive that Nan wouldn't let the party leave without me.

Once I'd shaken a little powder into my palm, I laid the tin carefully on a flat rock that broke the water's surface. Lathering my wet hair and piling it onto the top of my head, I stood still, simply inhaling the scent of lemon and vanilla. The soap had been my mother's gift to me before the journey. She'd made the powder using the peels of the fruits gifted to me, and it immediately became my favorite fragrance. I mixed the soap with water and ran the sudsy mixture over my torso and arms until silky trails of iridescent foam coated my limbs.

After washing all my other parts, I dunked my head under water and felt my hair twist in the water's currents. I tried my best to finger-comb the knots while I was under, but while raking at the strands, a strange feeling tugged at me, causing me to pause and surface. An uneasy weight settled in my stomach. It was similar to what I would feel a few days before my courses, but counting in my head, that didn't add up. Maybe it was my nerves catching up again, or possibly Nan's egg settling poorly... Whatever it was, it continued to rapidly worsen.

I pawed at the shanks of hair plastered to my face, feeling like I was going to be sick. *Maybe the fowl I pocketed wasn't as well cooked as I thought. That would be my luck.* I rubbed my eyes and flung off the moisture that clung to my lashes, then dropped my hands to cover my mouth. I didn't want to vomit in the same water people drank from, but I could feel the bile rising, so I quickly turned to walk toward the water's edge. I breathed deeply along the way and tilted my head towards the sun's rays, focusing on the warmth on my forehead, instead of the churning in my guts.

Ugh, I forgot my soap. Sick or not, I wouldn't leave that behind. I executed a quick about-face and headed back to the rock as fast as I could. Sure enough, it was right where I—

There was a man standing on the other side of the stream.

He was no guard.

Shadows danced in my periphery as cold, blue eyes darted between my face and naked chest. One corner of his mouth hitched up in a broken-toothed smile and soundlessly he entered the water.

Raising one finger to his smirking mouth, he puckered his lips: *shhhhh*. The darkness seemed to expand, cutting off more of my vision. My stomach lurched, needing to empty, but now was not the time to pass out or be ill—it was the time to run. I willed my legs to move, to turn, to do *anything*, but I was frozen, as if under a spell. I stood stock-still, watching him move forward. My mouth opened and closed, trying to form words, but I couldn't let out the scream that would alert the others to his presence. My feet were rooted in place, and now the man was only an arm's length away. He reached to his right side, never dropping his gaze from mine. His hand disappeared momentarily but then reemerged, holding a fraying length of thin rope.

His mouth was moving, but I heard no words. If he was giving me orders, I couldn't comprehend them over the roar that filled my ears. Terror was holding me here. *Get away!* A tight pressure squeezed at the center of my chest as I watched him reach a dripping hand in my direction. Tears stung my eyes when his nails bit into the skin of my wrist, and he squeezed my arm so hard that blood ran between his fingers and down into the water.

And still, I did nothing to save myself.

"AWAY! Get away from her!"

Nan.

The darkness fell away from my sight, and my mind reconnected with my body. It felt like being startled awake from a nightmare and suddenly realizing you are whole.

Life surged back into my legs.

I pivoted hard but couldn't fight the pressure of the waist-high water combined with the man's grip. My head snapped backward as my attacker captured a fistful of my hair and pulled me to him. He yanked my head close to his own, ripping hairs from my scalp in the process. The warmth of his pungent breath crawled down my neck, and his elbow pushed painfully between my shoulder blades as he jerked my head again.

"Deliver h-he–"

A sharp hiss split the air and cut his words short.

Sickening pops crackled in my ear as a wooden bolt found its target, striking deeply, sinking its way through flesh and tissue. Still entangled in my hair, the man tried in vain to dislodge the projectile, clawing at the protruding shaft. A thick, wet, gurgle came from his mouth as he attempted to pull air past his torn throat. I was able to free my wrist as his grip loosened but had to turn and face him full-on in order to rip my hair from his hand. Nothing could have prepared me for the unspeakably gruesome scene. A syrupy rivulet of blood made its way down his chest, becoming more viscous as he continued in vain to dislodge the bolt.

The stream in which we stood turned scarlet.

His life's blood permeated the water, twisting and swirling, like dark pigment added to a dye bath.

"Get her out, fools!" Nan's voice cut through the air. "Fucking idiots, go now!" she screamed.

My attacker's body slumped into the water and caught on my legs, while the current tried to sweep it downstream. Still trying to make sense of the last five seconds, my eyes searched for my companion, who had jumped into the water and was making her way to my side. Behind her, several guards fished their gloves from their pockets. They could be punished for touching a Troth with their bare hands. *I imagine the punishment for letting one die is worse.*

The crossbow that fired the bolt hung loosely in the captain of the guard's hand.

"Nan?" I whimpered, finally able to speak.

"Eira, eyes on me, walk to me, girl. Fucking bastard!" She kicked at the lifeless body bowing itself around my hips.

Nan wrapped my linen shirt around my shoulders and steadily moved us toward the bank. My legs, now unable to support me, shook so hard that when we reached the edge, it took two guards to help me regain my footing. Three steps on my own and I doubled over, vomiting on the grass-covered ground.

"It's a typical response, Troth Nortia. Don't be overly concerned," the nearest guard assured me.

Was that supposed to make me feel better? Puking was literally the least of my concerns.

Two additional guards came and flanked my sides. One covered me with a cloak, and the other assisted Nan in steering me to the nearest fire pit. She pressed me to sit on a mossy patch of ground next to the charred embers that still emanated warmth, but my shivering had nothing to do with the cold.

"Lady Chulainn." The captain of the guard approached. "We checked the body and the perimeter, and it seems to be an isolated incident. We leave soon. Dress quickly."

Nodding my head in understanding, I squinted up at the captain, whose head was framed in the sun's light.

"Who was it. Do you know?"

"A drunk from town," the captain replied, turning to leave.

"But why?"

He pivoted and faced me again.

"He thought to steal a glimpse of a naked woman after imbibing too much drink—it happens all too often," he said and marched away.

All too often? And were they all dismissed as easily?

"Disgusting drunk! Spying on my beauty and thinking with his prick—the shit stain! He deserved the arrow, filthy blood, filthy man!" Nan hollered, still soaked to her chest. Her wool tunic hung heavily, stretching all around her form. I could hear her curses plainly, while she walked to and from the wagon to retrieve a bowl and sponge.

"Eira?" She tilted my face looking for damage. "Don't you dwell on that nasty lout. Touch my girl, will he? No sir! Are you alright, my pup?"

"Nan I'm–"

"Of course not! And how could you be? Filthy pig, fat swine!" Her rant continued, "I'll stick him again, I will—"

"Nan!" I captured the hand scrubbing my arm raw. "Nan, I'll be okay," *Maybe. Sort of.* "Can you find me a dress?"

Violence was not something I'd been subjected to before, especially directed at my person. Sure, I'd seen scuffles break out, but being the object of intended harm?

Never.

Sharp-footed pixies marched their way down my spine, and I shuddered, thinking of what the man may have intended.

The other Troth and their companions were in the distance, all looking in my direction. A flood of embarrassment caused my cheeks to flush hotly. I didn't know how I was supposed to just get back on my horse and continue on as if I'd not seen a man die, as if I couldn't feel the sting of the crescents that marred my skin. Patting my hand after another string of curse-laden threats, Nan looked me squarely in the eyes.

"You have the strength of the north, girl. Don't you forget it."

Chapter Three

And Yet We Move On

Hours into our ascent, the rocking of my speckled gray was lulling me to sleep. At first, the excitement of the new Troth's arrival had kept my mind occupied. She had quickly found Cinden, the other Gaean Troth, and they'd been inseparable since. *It's just me and my thoughts again.*

The new Troth—she hadn't bothered to introduce herself—and her companion had joined us exactly on time. Their journey from the northern point of Gaea had gone smoothly, according to the chatter of the guards who accompanied them. The trail they had taken was fascinating, geographically speaking. Their kingdom was bisected by the tail end of the Sinnon range. The southern parts of their lands were lush and forested, while the northern parts, located just below the Great Rift, were much like southern Nortia. The rift was a massive tear in the earth formed thousands of years ago when Gammond, consort of the Goddess, had raged so intensely that he split the land in two. *If you believe everything the priests say.* Kan Keagan told me it had been caused by the kind of quakes that happened naturally near the mountains, but on a massive scale not seen since.

It struck me that no one in our contingent interacted with anyone who was not from their own kingdom—our party had split into factions on day one. *Alliance building is literally the point of being a Troth!* The red-haired ladies rode far in the front, and the refined women of Monwyn congregated together in the middle of our group. Maybe it was the comfort of kinship or shared traditions that drew them together, or maybe I was making too much of it, riding solitarily, the only Nortian Troth in our band.

By our midday rest, my stomach had calmed, and I was able to eat without ill effects. Nan used the downtime to wash and redress the tiny wounds on my wrist. I used the change in scenery to distract myself from the traumatic events of the morning. Our path had been surrounded by a forest of oaks and elms for the last day, but the higher we went, the more the evergreens began to dominate the landscape.

That was until everything transformed.

We broke through a tree line of heavily scented pines and moved into an open area that gave us an unobstructed view of the summit. The transition was so abrupt it was as if the forest had just vanished, cut off in a line of demarcation so startling, it was like entering another realm. Having never been up a mountain before, I reasoned that the high altitude could cause the lack of vegetation here, but what I couldn't figure out was why the very color of the terrain had shifted as well.

For hours on end, I had been looking up at the peak, enjoying the shadowy patterns made by the rocky crevices and fissures, but standing here, facing the summit now, it became clear that the rocks and boulders were not the normal washed-out gray stone that had made up the rest of the mountain. They had not been shadowed at all... They *were* the shadow! The mountain's rocks were a deep, dark gray that looked nearly obsidian in cloud cover and shimmered ever so slightly in direct sunlight.

I rotated in my saddle to see the phenomenon from another perspective.

Oh. Poor Nan...

She was riding far to the back of our envoy, even past the other companions. Her face was tense, her mouth drawn in a tight line, and her normally high-arched brows furrowed deeply in concern. I knew she must have been feeling as dumbfounded as I was. Nothing about this place felt normal. Catching her eye, I jerked my head, imploring her to join me. She nodded hesitantly and rode cautiously ahead of the others, white-knuckled, clutching her reins the entire way.

"Eira, say your prayers," she murmured while holding her hands to the sky. "This is unnatural, girl. It's not right I'm telling you. The work of demons, work of spirits, of—"

"Put your hands down, Nan. *This*," I gestured to the expanse in front of us, "is where the holiest temple of the Goddess lies. If demons claim a mountain, it probably isn't this one. Look at the others; they're fine." The others really did seem unaffected. If they were as bewildered as the two of us, they didn't show it as they rode straight ahead, nonplussed.

Nan spat on the ground and tapped her brows with both hands. I rolled my eyes skyward. *Father Gammond, she spits not with the intention of offending you.*

I knew where this was going.

Nan was a superstitious sort, which made her very untrusting of anything that was out of her typical experience. To this day she wouldn't touch anything a white fulmar landed on because, apparently, the bird secreted dark energy. She'd once holed up for two days in our town's temple after our priestess spotted one. She stayed there until my mother came and coaxed her out.

"Quit your witching, Nan." I tried to hold back the laughter in my voice, "They'll think we're more backward than they already do!"

Sure enough, right on cue, Kairus turned in her saddle.

Letting a wide grin crack my face, I shrugged my shoulders and leaned over to pat the hand of my dear, apprehensive companion, who responded by spitting on the ground again, doing her damnedest to protect us from all things unholy. Kairus's eyes opened so wide I could see their aqua-blue from several horse lengths away.

Over the course of the next few hours, with Nan stuck close to my side, I ended up being the one who prayed the most. At one point, I begged the gods for Nan's dehydration. The irrational woman had spat all the way to Gammond's summit, swinging back and forth in her saddle, aiming for the targets she thought were bad luck—a flower here, a skittering insect there, and as many blades of grass as she could reach.

The laughter from the front of our entourage had started as intermittent chuckles but, with the ongoing efforts of our savior, became unbridled brays and snorts. I was just thankful they found her antics to be entertaining and not an attempt at sorcery, and that despite my embarrassment, Nan couldn't give two shits about what the others thought.

··· +)(+ ···

My stomach resumed its churning the moment a group of temple escorts, resplendent in brass-trimmed plate armor, met up with our party. They were the first sign of our journey's end.

I watched Fionn raise a hand, greeting the new unit's commander before he peeled off from our group without so much as a goodbye.

Veering left, with soldiers on both sides, we rode toward an intricately carved arch in the distance. The structure was so large that two wagons could easily pass through its opening at once and never worry about colliding. I was better able to make out the scenes depicted on the monument the nearer we came. The Divine Twins, the shared children of the Goddess and Gammond, were featured prominently, as well as two knotted flames that entwined at the structure's keystone—the symbols of Mossius, the god of healing and vitality. The large daggers that framed the inner columns of the arch portrayed the weapon associated with his sister, Merrias. She wielded the blade when meting out judgment, sending the dead on their way to the afterlife.

The path curved sharply after passing under the archway, and all at once, I could see the entire expanse of the back of Gammond's peak. As if sat upon the mountain by a divine hand, Verus Temple came into view, and it was spectacular! There was nothing at home or described in any book I had read, that touched on the scale or majesty of what stood before me. All I had been told was that it was triangular in shape and that it made the Glass Palace look small, but this? This was otherworldly.

The temple was enormous, huge by any measure, and it had been shaped into a Reuleaux triangle, one that looked both circular and angular at once. If you peered straight at the structure, you could see the entirety of its triangulation and pointed tip, but both its visible sides and the front plane had been plumped out so far that it almost looked spherical. I had no explanation for how the shape had been created out of the natural terrain, but whoever, or whatever, had built this temple had the ability to carve away a majority of the mountain's face, creating a single structure from solid stone.

I sat atop my mare, staring.

The three sides that comprised the front of the deep-gray, almost black temple had been polished until they gleamed. Were it not dusk, its reflective surface may have been difficult to look at. A little more than halfway to the temple's back, the shining stones melted seamlessly into the inconsistent mountain rock. It was almost as if the Goddess herself had taken the side of an earthly mountain and combined it with half of a celestial one.

Our contingent rode into the complex's shrine-speckled grounds, where two tall statues came into view. Located at the corners of the structure, the Twin Gods, Mossius and Merrias, had been immortalized in excruciating detail. Merrias wore a chest plate identical to the ones the temple guards wore, and she had a stone dog sitting at her side. In her hand, extending out over the courtyard, was The Arbiter, the blade of judgment. It was believed that when we passed, we would stand on its razor edge and she would twist the blade, casting us into an afterlife of either salvation or the nether, dependent on how well we lived our lives.

Mossius stood like his sister but was cloaked in a long robe that didn't quite touch his sandaled feet. His right hand clutched the strings of a healer's pouch that hung to the middle of his thigh, and his left arm was also outstretched with his palm facing the sky. The children of the Goddess, who shared the same face, looked straight ahead as if protecting the temple. Their gazes were strong and unwavering.

As we rode further into the courtyard, I followed the direction of their unblinking eyes. My breath caught in my throat.

"Goddess be damned," Yemailrys, cursed behind me, having just seen the view for herself.

I must have been looking upon half of Ærta, or at least, that's how it felt. The sun was larger than I had ever seen it, a blazing ball of orange in the purple vastness of the setting sky. Beneath the lavender horizon was its inverse: a sea of grass and trees made from a thousand shades of green. It was so far-reaching I couldn't measure it with my eyes. It struck me that here, on top of Mount Gammond, I was just an insignificant mote in a world so much bigger than I had known.

There was a sharp cough to my left.

A guard, who had clearly been trying to get my attention, stood rigidly at the side of my mount. My cheeks warmed.

"Welcome to Verus. As you dismount, follow the stationed guards into the temple and have your lineage papers prepared for registration." He lifted a gloved hand after finishing the rehearsed speech.

"Thanks, but no need, I can hop d—"

"*Ahem*," he interrupted politely and sank down to one knee.

"If you insist," I grabbed the hand and drew my leg over the saddle, "but this is kind of silly. How often do you scrub your armor? Everyd—"

A thunderous jet of fire erupted from Mossius's outstretched hand. The Troth behind me screamed, and I jerked backward, surprised by the blaze surging high into the air. The flames illuminated the stone face of the deity—it was as if Mossius had come to life.

I tilted my head back to take in the statue's full majesty and unintentionally threw the guard off balance, causing me to wobble in the air. I would have fallen if not for the fast hand that braced my knee. As the guard strained to right himself, I was struck again that his face never betrayed even a hint of emotion, not even with me dancing atop his thigh. With a sheepish grin, I thanked him for his assistance but received no response.

"Lineage papers, right." I nodded crisply. "And our companions, where will they go?" I asked wondering where Nan and the others had gone.

"They have been taken to your chambers to prepare your rooms."

I nodded again and went to grab my papers from my horse's pack.

Kairus had just dismounted behind me. She would never have wavered atop a guard. One look from her, and I was positive Mossius would have quit his flames. My mother was that way as well: never flustered, always controlled. She would have made an ideal Troth. I was more like my father, prone to worry and overly expressive.

I snuck a peak at Kairus, wanting to mimic her proud stance, but standing alone next to her mount, she looked different than normal, somehow smaller. Her head was held high, and her back was as straight as a knife, but her expression had gone blank. She looked exhausted, stripped bare. I could detect nothing but bleakness in her countenance.

"You ready?" I asked, walking nearer to her.

It took her a second to respond, but when she finally did, she looked down her nose and sparked back to life.

"I was raised for this moment, Nortia."

With an audible pop, I smacked my lips. *I guess reaching out was the wrong move.*

"Got your papers?" I asked, trying to change the course of the conversation.

She held up a leather-bound tome that had been tooled with intricate knotwork. At the top of its sapphire cover, the title, *Septimus*, had been burnished to a gleaming gold.

"Yes, and an extensive and *spotless* record of ancestry—You?" she smirked and turned to walk away.

One. Two. Breathe. The eight sheets of vellum, tucked into the pages of my favorite book, burned in my hands, but much less so than the rising fury building within me. It was one thing to act aloof when dealing with the difficulties of leaving your home, but slighting my family to make yourself feel superior? *That crossed the line. Three. Four. Breathe.*

Nope!

Rage replaced my embarrassment, and I shot my hand up in Nan's favorite gesture. *Monwyn ass!*

The effort was wasted.

Kairus never saw what she deserved. I was cut off by a team of draft horses and our heavily laden wagon rambling by. I sneered at its wooden side, sucking in a tense breath, willing my indignation to simmer down. When the wagon finally cleared, Kairus was gone, and no one else was around... except, of course, the same guard I'd nearly felled. He stared at me meanly. Even if his face wasn't moving his eyes told me—*Oh!*

I had yet to pull my hoisted finger from the air! Jerking my hand down as fast as I could, I made a show of smoothing the invisible wrinkles from the skirts of my gown and threw many apologetic looks at the man.

I need to get it together.

In my best imitation of Kairus, I pulled my shoulders back, plastered a serene expression on my face, and strode toward the open doors of the magnificence in front of me.

Chapter Four

WELP.

"Name, documents, kingdom." The priestess held her hands out, not bothering to look up.

"Eira Chulainn, Nortia." I handed over the small stack of parchment. Beyond her, several large and impressively decorated volumes, containing the generational stories of the other Troth, were laid out. The priestesses' eyebrows snapped together, and she blinked rapidly. Making a show of hefting her hands up and down, she discerned the weight of the folded pages I had given her.

"Lady Chulainn, I have you listed, but are these partial documents? Have you misplaced the others or left the rest with your companion?" she asked.

"These are complete. It's all there... I didn't see a need to bind them," I answered more tersely than I should have, still bristling from my earlier interaction.

"Mmmhmm, well." She flipped the papers open with a snap, "I'll just take a quick look."

Several minutes passed, and her silence caused me to grow even antsier at the close inspection of my family's history. I could hear the people behind me sighing in their frustration at being held up. I did my best to ignore them and used the awkwardly spent time to take in my new home.

All of the priestesses I could see in the vestibule—like the guards who brought us here—wore variations of red or gold. The priestess sitting behind the large wooden desk wore flowing, ruby robes that danced with the subtle movements of her finger as it skimmed across a line of surnames and dates. Around her neck, she wore an elegant collar of linked iridescent shards. The woven scales covered her from just beneath her chin to the tips of her shoulders, and the unusual garment reflected purple and blue as it bent the light of the oil lamps that dotted the blackened stone walls.

The temple's center, located directly behind her, was a massive open atrium with stairways located at each side and another in its middle. I couldn't see how many floors there were to the very top of the temple, but judging from the size of the outside, I'd guess at least four or five.

"Rise, all! The Scions of the great Kingdom of Monwyn have entered!" a voice loudly announced, breaking me from my rumination. The priestess shoved out of her chair and shot to her feet, and I watched my papers scatter across her desk.

I turned toward the source of the sound.

The entire crowd reacted. Heads swiveled, and people throughout the room strained their necks to look at the entryway behind me. Curious as to who could cause such a reaction from so many, I followed suit.

You could feel the energy shift when four men strode purposefully into the cramped space. They seemed to take up all of the remaining air in the room, and their physical presence was so striking that they all but demanded the attention of everyone in the chamber.

With the eyeful I got, it was immediately evident what had caused the stir. The men of Monwyn were every bit as striking as their women and seemed at least twice as self-assured.

The man at the head of the unit oozed an almost palpable confidence. Just standing there, you knew he'd been blessed by the divine.

He was a dark god.

His cobalt tunic fit him to perfection and highlighted his muscular arms and wide shoulders. The woolen fabric stretched so snugly across his chest that it was nearly indecent, and his thick thighs were encased in leather breeches so tight that I could see the definition of the muscles beneath... *among other things.* Tall boots skimmed the bottoms of his knees and—*Oh, Father Gammond, his face.* If I could just keep staring at that face, I'd forget all about the river and forget to give a shit about bratty Kairus and the other self-centered Troth.

His mossy-green eyes were surrounded by thick, black lashes, and his heavy brows matched the color of his midnight-hued hair, which he wore swept back into a single braid that began at his forehead and ended in a heavy tail past his shoulders. The sides of his head had been shaved closely, and his jaw was covered by a beard so crisply defined it—*Oh, Goddess, his mouth.* I'm fairly certain the room itself groaned when his full lips parted into a heartbreakingly endearing smile.

He stood among his escorts—and a shorter man I assumed to be another Scion—taking in his surroundings and grinning at the people who gawked at him. Warmly, he nodded to a young man who scurried by with his hands full of luggage and then raised a hand in salutation to an older priestess, who smiled up at him as if she'd known him forever.

The Scion, who stood well above six feet tall, whispered something to his hooded companion, who moved dutifully away to stand against a nearby wall. I watched the encounter closely, appreciating how his big body moved so elegantly despite its size.

He made his way around the room shaking hands with a group I didn't recognize and stopped briefly to make small talk with a priest. This continued for some time until, ready to move on, he pivoted quickly and turned his gorgeous face in my direction.

I swallowed hard.

He was staring right at me.

Striding forward, he closed the distance between us, and my body went rigid. Another step and my head swam from lack of air. He was getting so near to me now my heart picked up speed.

Goddess, divine creator, your son blesses me with his presence.

He breezed right past me and stepped up to the large desk, addressing the enraptured priestess who stood beaming behind it. *Fucking Scion asshole.*

"Madam, would this be where I sign in?" He said in a tone dripping with kindness. I glared at his big back and felt my ears burning from the sting of disrespect.

"Oh, oh no!" the priestess stammered. "No, your registration isn't located here, but I would be delighted to show you to the correct area, *personally*, Lord Scion."

"A kindness, madam. I would so hate to interrupt your work, so simply point and we shall be on our way."

Rankling at each courteous word they shared, I silently mocked his stupid voice. *A kindness, madam, blah blah blah!* My eyes rolled to the back of my head, and I clenched my jaw tightly.

One... two... I was tired of counting.

I tapped on his shoulder, wanting nothing more than to finish the business that was already in progress. I was ignored.

"As *such* esteemed emissaries, I must insist!" The priestess simpered. "After all I am..." her voice faded away when I knocked on the broad back like it was the ironbound door to a fortress.

The big, beautiful asshole sighed loudly but now had no choice but to acknowledge me. Turning around stiffly, he let his eyes glaze over in boredom before deigning to even look at me.

"She was working with me," I stated, "and *you*," I pointed at the middle of his chest, "cut the line." The Monwyn's lips tightened at one corner, and as if I'd not said a single word to him, he stared off and slowly blinked his uncaring eyes.

The priestess rushed around her desk tossing my documents atop a stack of books.

"We are done, Lady Chulainn; all is well. Head up the eastern stairway and you will find your dormitory to the left. Here is your key. Welcome!"

Still denying my existence, the Scion offered an elbow to the priestess, who was suddenly all laughs and smiles as he wheeled her around. With a quick flick of the wrist, the jerk motioned forward his escorts and took off across the gleaming marble floors.

I stared at a now empty desk. Indignant at having been snubbed for the second time today. I gripped the key tightly in my fisted hand, happy to feel its metal bite. *A reset... that's what I need. I am supposed to be here. I'm just as valuable as the others in this room. Take a breath and shake it off, Eira.*

I nearly collided with the Scion's hooded escort as he passed.

He came so close to me that his deep-blue cloak brushed my gown. *Did all Monwyns lack manners?* It seemed the men were just as insufferable as their women!

A twisting ball of aggravation formed in my chest. Words that would make Nan blush threatened to erupt from my mouth.

ONE! TWO! BREATHE!

I launched myself forward to escape the scene I was about to make, just as the shrouded figure took a single ill-timed step backward, causing me to plow directly into his side. His dirt-covered boots pressed against the toes of my leather riding shoes, forcing me to stumble in place. Face obscured, he cocked his head to the side like a mongrel dog and leaned toward me until his hood nearly touched my hair. *Nobody has the right to come this close to me without my approval!*

I was ready for battle.

The quick hiss of a deep inhale came from the man as I watched his chest rise and fall. The man had sniffed me.

He.

Sniffed.

Me.

How fucking gross! What in all of Ærta was wrong with these people? Had I really left a perfectly sane existence only a week ago to come here, to the holiest grounds on the continent, and surround myself with freaks! Freaks and snobs! And who was worse? The nasty Troth, all snide and conceited, with their stupid, perfect faces and... and stupid, perfect pedigree! Or was it the pompous men striding in like they were the only Obligate in the room AND having that confirmed by an ogling audience of panting bitches!

My angry footsteps pounded against the floor.

I didn't give a damn what anyone thought about me as I passed them by, not looking at their faces or offering greetings. I narrowly missed shoving into a startled priestess but managed to sidestep her without casualty. *How are these people so good at being in the way? Is it in the curriculum?*

Not slowing my steps, I finally faced the entryway to the corridor where my room should be. Scanning the walls, I located the chamber appointments, posted near a long hallway. My name had been exquisitely printed in a loopy flourishing hand and next to it a number twelve was written in black ink. In the mood I was in, I wanted nothing more than to rip the beautiful parchment in half and stomp all over its perfect penmanship.

Tears began to sting my eyes. I'd let my anger go too far.

I made my way down the hallway, fighting to not let a single tear drop fall.

Up ahead, a small cluster of Troth I'd not seen on our journey—probably Solnnans—were standing around door number eight. I wasn't about to let them see me cry. I'd imagine they'd be just like the others, belittling me or mistaking me for a servant.

The tears continued to well up.

I made it safely past the group by murmuring a quick hello and finally arrived at my door. Knowing that Nan was on the other side gave me the measure of comfort I needed. She'd tell me to get my shit together while surrounding me in her bear hug of an embrace, and quite possibly give me some solid advice about not letting others dictate my existence. Right now, that's all I wanted.

The key caught briefly, stiff in the locking mechanism, and the tears spilled at last, this last barrier proving to be too much for me to handle. As I clamped my lips against the threatening sobs, to my eternal relief, the lock clicked open, and the door swung free. I rolled myself around its solidness, using my hands as a guide as my vision blurred with tears. The door closed, and I pressed my back against it and swiped at my eyes with both hands. The stress of travel, of leaving home, of the Goddess-awful attack, all of it, had finally boiled up and over, leaving me a vulnerable, emotional mess. Sniffing loudly, I drew in a shuddering breath.

"Are you going to make it?"

Just damn it all to the nether.

I recognized the voice.

The fine annunciation of each and every word made my stomach clench tightly. *How absurd is life?*

A belt of laughter bubbled up in my throat and exploded out in a mixture of tinkling giggles and resonant snorts. My shoulders quaked and the tears resumed, a river whose flow was impossible to control.

"No?" She paused for an answer. "Okay. So, when you regain your sanity, get rid of the plate your maid brought in—it smells awful—and you look disgusting."

"Th-thank you, *Kairus*." I managed the sarcastic reply.

CHAPTER FIVE

FAMILIAL LOVE

An hour or so later, sitting on a tiny three-legged stool next to a fireplace, it became clear that the Goddess was most certainly testing me. I munched on the dried fish and crackers Nan had left and watched Kairus drape lush gowns and a rainbow of wool hoods and stockings over every surface of the room... including the bed that, at this point, I only assumed I'd get to sleep in.

The room to which I'd been appointed was really lovely. I just wish I'd realized it was a shared space. That's what my lack of composure got me, though. Had I not been so affected by the actions of others, I probably would have seen Kairus's name next to the number twelve. *Oh, well, hindsight and all that.*

Our space had been set up symmetrically. Two wooden wardrobes had been situated on either side of the chamber, and they reached almost all the way to the ceiling. Their bottoms consisted of three drawers and their tops formed a double closet that would store our hanging gowns nicely. Our beds had been snugged up to the sides of the wardrobes and ran longwise against the wall. *Small mercies. The wall would be a better view than Kairus's face.* One of the short sides of the rectangular room featured an inset fireplace, currently stoked so high sweat was running down my back. The opposite wall boasted a floor-to-ceiling tapestry that featured an intricately detailed sun, mountain, whale, and tree, all woven into a red background.

On either side of the long tapestry were two separate doors. My guess was they led to our companions' rooms. I was still feeling too dejected to explore, so I instead sat in silence, running my feet over the edge of a room-sized rug. It was probably the most ostentatious thing in the chamber, even beyond the shining, brocaded blankets that covered each bed. It depicted the story of Goddess Merrias's only daughter who unknowingly overcame the malevolent Magis Raephin many centuries ago. It was one of my most favorite stories, especially as told by my grandmother, who never left out the more adult details.

As she told it, the Magis had stolen the Arbiter Blade, the only object known that could sever a god's lifeline. Raephin, a sorcerer bent on enslaving the continent, had discovered a way to defeat Cynder the many-headed dog who had, for an age, guarded the weapon for its master. While Merrias had been laying with her consort Derros, the Magis, through vile witchcraft, ensnared the four heads of Merrias's beloved pet and delivered to it a lethal surge of dark magic. When the goddess found Cynder, the animal was dying and there was nothing in her powers that could save her darling pet. Fueled by an endless rage, Derros spent fifty years after the incident hunting the Magis who had stolen the joy of his still mourning lover. Raephin had cloaked himself from the eyes of the gods, but eventually, Derros found him anyway. He had made himself a king in a faraway land, his reign enabled by enslavement and depravity. Merrias, desperate to find her dagger and avenge her pet, transformed herself into a human and set about seducing Raephin. He succumbed to her charms, and she lived as his partner for many mortal years, building his trust and love. She bore him a child—his only child—whom he loved more than life itself, more even than his insatiable need for dominion.

After three years of this double life, Merrias located the Arbiter. On the eve of their daughter's naming celebration, as Raephin settled himself on his throne, Merrias slid a dagger from under her cloak and pulled it across their child's throat. Frantic and filled with despair, the Magis poured his power into their child's body attempting to save her. He utilized all of his abilities and all of his dark tricks in an effort to bring his child back, but he was unable to draw her soul from the æther. In his attempt, he turned his daughter's mortal frame into a vessel that would ultimately contain the world's dark forces. Merrias was finally able to wound the Magis as deeply as he had her, those many years before. Weakened and without sorcery, she easily took his life.

Once she had been collected by Derros and returned to their home, Merrias implored the Goddess to give her child life again. The Goddess, loving her own daughter, breathed new life into her grandchild and restored her soul to the realm of the living. It was a fitting reward for Merrias, the Goddess of Balance: a new child and minor god from the death of the most powerful mortal to have lived. Known in the pantheon as just "The Child," Merrias' daughter became the guardian of innocence.

The rug I sank my toes into depicted The Child, her arms flung around the scruff of a vicious-looking dog. The background was a motif of daggers and swirls representing the magic that became a part of her legend. My friends and I loved the story, even with its violent bits. In our minds, Merrias was the toughest of the gods, having sought out and carried through such a profound plan of vengeance.

A knock sounded at the door and Kairus ushered in Nan along with her advisor.

The older gentleman walked in and sat on the edge of her bed and spoke to her in hushed tones. He completely ignored the two other people in the room.

Out of the corner of my eye, I saw Nan's hands go to her hips while her head shook back and forth. I realized that bear-hugging Nan had been wishful thinking on my part. Looking around the room, lips pursed in distaste, she went to work tossing Kairus's strewn-about clothing back onto the bed where the pair sat talking. I grinned at their muffled huffs when a thick cloak and several gowns flew across the room, landing on top of their fair heads.

"Madam, cease your assault at once!" the man's voice cut in and out, as fabric hit him squarely in the face.

"What kind of roommate are you, Eira? Get off that servant's stool and clear out your bags. This pretty Troth has had to work around your luggage strewn all about. Look at her, she's distraught with the disarray you've forced her to create. She's practically wrinkled up like a raisin not knowing what to do," Nan reprimanded. She continued on, whirling about the room, tossing all manner of items at the pair. Kairus's advisor, who was dressed in a smart, bright-blue short coat began to snatch flying garments out of the air, causing his fine, straw-colored hair to muss with the effort.

"There we are." Nan thrust the last of Kairus's items into the Troth's hands. "For the next few months, you girls will be sharing this space and *will* get along like two kits in a burrow. Now, introductions." She looked pointedly at the advisor's gawping face.

Hefting a small mountain of material from his lap and heaving it onto the bed, he swiped at the tight-fitting legs of his black pants and stood to his full height.

"But of course, Madam... Lady." He bowed stiffly, first to Nan and then myself. "You stand in the presence of Tussi Ivo Obbus, fourth advisor to the great Ahdmundus, the seventh son of His former Majesty of Monwyn. He who ranks high in the line of succession, who sired the radiant beauty that sits here before you." Bowing toward Kairus, he waved his hand in a flurry of tight circles.

"Wait, what? You sired that child?" Nan blinked, darting her eyes between the two.

"W-what, I... no! Of course not! That is not at all–"

"You cannot sire a child then?" Nan interrupted, looking at the ruffled advisor compassionately. *Ha! Tussi might do well in the courts of Monwyn, but he isn't equipped to deal with my Nortian Nan!*

Nan tossed her head toward me expectantly.

"I... I am Eira Verras Chulainn, daughter of Ulltan, overseer of His Majesties docks in the Kingdom of Nortia. It's a pleasure to make your acquaintance."

"And I'm Nan, Eira's companion."

She threw Kairus a look.

"Kairus. I'm just Kairus." The Troth leveled her gaze at Tussi Ivo Obbus, whose prideful countenance dimmed at her blasé response. "Could you get to the purpose of your intrusion, Tussi?"

Nan answered for him, "The purpose is that dinner will be served to you in your rooms tonight, and you are expected to be bathed, dressed, and ready for the Congregation by seven in the morning, *sharp*. I'll not have either of you girls showing up late or with travel filth behind your ears." She directed the last comment at Kairus, who blanched and reached a hand to her head.

"Come on Tubby, the girls have one hour to clean this pigsty if they wish to be fed." Nan grabbed the arm of the sputtering advisor and led him to the door.

Remaining on my stool a little longer than I should have, I glanced at a silent Kairus, who still sat on the bed clutching her ear.

"She means it... about getting fed. I once got into a mud fight with the town boys and for *three days*, every time she found a speck of muck in the house, I wasn't allowed to find dinner."

Kairus rose from her perch, bleakly surveying the mess. A substantial pile of clothing dropped to her feet.

"You want help?" I threw out the lifeline, steeling myself for the backlash that never came.

Kairus nodded her acceptance.

···*)(*···

We sat together in silence munching on a meal of poached salmon and sauteed squash. After more than a week of meals on the road, the spiced and herbed fare was an exquisite change. It was a treat for me; fresh produce wasn't as readily available in Nortia as it was here, closer to warmer lands. In between tiny bites, I noticed that Kairus still seemed to be as down as she was when we entered the temple. Her eyes had lost their sparkle, and so much food remained on her plate, I thought she might be faking her chews. After another half hour of sitting and staring, the silence itself began to overwhelm me. I'd rather have faced her wicked tongue than her sadness, or ennui, or whatever it was going on with her.

"Do you want to explore a little?" I asked, hoping she'd take me up on the outing.

She shook her head and laid down on her side, facing the wall.

"If you need something, let me know, okay?" Seconds ticked by with no answer, so I collected our dishes and turned to the door to head out.

"Thank you," she murmured in a small voice.

"You're welcome," I replied, and I meant it. I hoped she could pull out of whatever was keeping her down.

In the hallway, plates and bowls were stacked outside the other rooms. I unloaded my arms similarly and decided to search for the toilets. I pushed at a few unnumbered doors, but none opened, so I figured the facilities were probably at the end of the hallway or right outside of the main entryway like they were at the Glass Palace. Had I not acted like a petulant child earlier, sobbing my way down the corridor, I surely would have made note of their location.

Lamps, placed at even intervals along the walls, had been turned low for the evening, causing long shadows to dance cozily along the flecked jet walls. Taking a left at the end of the Troth's wing, I walked in the opposite direction of the staircase. I trailed a hand along the darkened stone as I went, not immediately seeing any doorways or signs. The walls were as smooth as river rocks, and so far were seamless, having no cement or mud used to join them. Was it possible that this place had been carved from a single gigantic chunk of stone? It was hard to fathom the level of planning it would take to accomplish such a feat.

After walking halfway around the second level, I found myself standing in front of a splendid balustrade. A series of complex columns had been cut through the stone, which allowed light to pass through, complementing the natural beauty of the structure. I skimmed my fingers along it, searching for nails or other joints. I found none. *Simply spectacular.*

I looked out over the balcony's railing, struck again by the magnitude of the gift I'd been given in being here. Not many could say they had ever seen Verus, and fewer still had been invited to take part in the blessed function of Obligation.

The embarrassment from this evening's emotional episode burned hotly across my cheeks. This was the Goddess' temple and surely she surrounded me even now. *I need to do better. I will do better.*

Placing my hands on the banister, I hoisted myself up and craned my head until I could see the very center of the temple's point. Low light was streaming through an opening at the apex, and it looked to be covered with some type of crystalline glass that threw rainbows around the top third of the building. Despite it being night outside, the multicolored rays bent and bounced in hues of blue, green, and violet, reminding me of the collar the registrant had worn earlier that day. Stepping up on the jutting base of the short wall, I was afforded another six inches of height, and with thighs pressed into the top of the low wall, I was able to lean out a little further, gaining a clear view of the temple's otherworldly projections. I gazed at the magnificence for so long that my hands began to go numb. I rubbed my palms together until I could feel my fingertips and—

An intense ray of white light beamed down from the temple's point, seeming to ignite the swirling specks of dust captured in its illumination. I leaned low over the railing, following its trajectory.

A tremendous oval ring, with a seven-pointed star at its center, dominated the floor of the atrium below. My gasp echoed off the walls. It was the Goddess' sign. A representation of the womb from which all life had come. Tears stung my eyes for the second time today... or maybe the third. I'd never experienced firsthand the divine, and this moment was defining. I was here... because of her.

"Beautiful, is it not?" a low whisper came from behind me.

I gasped and jolted forward, having lost the careful balance of my footing. Frantically, I threw my hands out, hoping to catch myself, but found nothing but air. My body plunged downward, and in an effort to regain equilibrium, I desperately twisted and flailed.

Two strong hands braced themselves on either side of my thighs and held firmly, preventing my fall. Unintentionally, they also turned my rump into a fulcrum, which caused my upper body to hinge dramatically at the hips. I managed to guard my face when I came crashing down, but my stomach hit the far edge of the wall and knocked the air from my lungs. I struggled to inhale, while the hands pulled at my rear until my backside lay firmly against a solid form.

When the pain in my stomach subsided long enough for me to move again, I looked over my shoulder.

It was the dark god.

The beautiful jerk from Monwyn.

"Get *off* me! I pushed against the wall, squirming in my attempt to shake off the hands that lingered too long.

"Lady, it would seem to me—"

"I don't give a damn what it *seems* to you! Why the nether did you sneak up on me? Do you often lurk around in the dark like a creep?"

I smacked at his hands, freeing myself enough to swing around and hop to the floor, my balance restored.

"Not the thanks I expected, but rudeness does seem to be your forte. As I recall, you are the little harpy from this morning," he smirked.

A harpy? Does he see me as the problem? Well, pretty doesn't mean intelligent.

"If I'm such a creature, it's solely because your pretentious, self-righteous, egotistical self is allowed to behave poorly, all because of that handsome face sitting on top of your bull neck!" I stuck my finger into his chest and walked him back across the floor.

"You think I am handsome then?" he cooed while taking a step forward, pushing against the finger leveled at his chest.

Oh, please, you know you are.

I retreated, realizing my words didn't have their intended effect.

Seeking a swift exit, I moved fast and skirted around him, but the Scion's hand shot out and snaked around my waist. He used my momentum against me, and in just a few steps my back made contact with the cool surface of a wall, a stark contrast to the warmth of his body that was now only a whisper away.

I knew I should be angry, and I knew I should've lashed out, but his closeness was kind of exhilarating. Unfamiliar for sure, but not in an entirely uncomfortable way.

Eira, this is like falling-for-your-captor bullshit!

I was puzzled by my reaction.

I was aware that I was allowing his handsomeness to override my good senses, but I was also finding it hard to look away from the bewitching rise and fall of his solid-looking chest.

"I think you are handsome, too," he whispered intimately, bending so that his mouth was close to my ear.

Well damn, I'm one of the panting bitches too.

My eyes closed when he ran the tip of his nose along the column of my neck, and when the end of his braid swept over my bared clavicle, I hummed my delight. His touch elicited a sensation that ran the length of my chest.

I breathed in deeply.

Like the spices traded by visiting merchants, he smelled exotic and warm, and his very scent sent shivers dancing down my spine. I did my best to mull over my response to his touch, but I found it difficult to concentrate. Before this, the most masculine man I had known was my uncle, who stayed out in the tundra for months at a time. *This was in no way like being near my uncle.*

"What are you thinking of, pretty harpy?" His voice turned as thick as honey.

"My Uncle Inis," I whispered breathily. My own voice sounded foreign to my ears.

"Pardon me?" He stood up quickly and I immediately mourned the loss of contact. "You are right now, right here, at *this* very moment, thinking of an uncle?"

Drunk on the sensual feelings, my heavy eyelids opened slowly, just in time to see him throw back his head and launch into a full-bellied laugh.

"You are an amusing Troth to be sure. Come, I'll escort you to your room," he chuckled good-naturedly.

The moment had most definitely passed.

"Not necessary!" I declared in a high-pitched tone. After dipping under the arm that he had rested against the side of my head, I scurried in the direction of the dormitories, hearing his laughter fade as I rushed back to my room.

After fumbling to unlock my door, I bounded in and woke a sleeping Kairus who bolted upright with a hand to her chest.

"Eira! What's—"

"WHERE'S THE BATHROOM?" I yelled.

Confused, she pointed to the doors at the back of our chamber.

"Of course." I lunged toward the far wall and flung the door wide.

Gasping for air, I made my way to the mirror that hung over a dainty white sink and stared at my disheveled reflection.

My uncle? I covered my face with both hands, attempting to shield myself from my own mortification. It didn't work, but looking around the well-appointed bathing chamber, I figured I could do worse than staying in here for the rest of my life.

CHAPTER SIX

SOME LIKE IT HOT

AND SOME THEY DO NOT.

"Should I expect this every morning?" asked Kairus, who snuggled deeply under a mound of covers.

At some point while I slept, she'd gotten up to stoke the dimming fire, which made me sweat uncontrollably. With no windows to open, my only recourse had been to remove my clothes and lay naked on top of the thick bed coverings—even then I'd been uncomfortable.

"I saw you sleeping on the bedding when we traveled here. I assumed it to be some strange Nortian custom. Now that you have actually *seen* the way a bed functions—do you comprehend how they work?" *Is that amusement I detect?* "Should I endeavor to explain the finer points of bed rest after the evening meal? I am *positive* I can work up the basics for you quickly."

"If you didn't keep the room as hot as Mossius's bonfire, you'd no longer have to gaze upon my impeccably and clearly superior form," I joked, sweeping a dramatic hand down the length of my very much *not* impeccable figure.

"Your superior... HA!" The pile she was under shook along with her cackles, until she tossed the mound of blankets aside and sat up in her heavy nightgown. "Come on, get up, we have two hours to prepare." Kairus, who'd been so forlorn yesterday, popped up and headed to her wardrobe.

"I can dress in fifteen minutes," I groaned, wanting nothing more than to catch another hour of sleep.

"The Congregation is our first meeting with the High Mantle. It will also be the first time the Troth and Scion will assemble. Did your advisor not fill you in? It's an outlandishly fancy meet-up."

Shit.

"Well, I don't have an advisor—I have a Nan," I said, feeling sheepish all of a sudden. *I wonder what other information I'm missing.*

"Don't worry," Kairus smiled. "She had some of it figured out." She nodded her head in the direction of my wardrobe, where a single door had been propped open. Hugging a pillow to cover myself, I walked over and peered into the closet. The most beautiful gown I'd ever seen was hanging from a silk-wrapped hanger and a little piece of parchment had been pinned to its hem. I flipped the folded paper and angled it toward the lamp light.

From Momma.

···+)(+···

If the rest of the morning was as strange as the bathtubs, I was doomed. At home, during the warm season, homemade soaps would have been melted down into a liquid and added into one of the round metal tubs that every family had. Children, or servants if you had them, would then fill it up with tepid buckets of water to create sudsy cleansing foam. You'd wash up in the basin, step out over the drain and toss a bucket of fresh water over your head to rinse. *Simple.*

After I gave up and asked, Kairus informed me that all I had to do was turn a knob and water would pour into the sunken pool, which took up a majority of the chamber's space. We didn't need to heat it, and if we wanted more, we just turned it on again. After tossing a few sweet-smelling chunks of soap into the tub, I flipped up the single handle on the wall and watched, quite impressed, at the amount of steamy water flowing from a single spigot that was shaped like the curving neck of a great egret. This had to be another of the Goddess' miracles. I knew that systems of drains and pipes could easily remove water from a raised location, but I had no clue how they could get water to come up the mountain and into this room.

I submerged myself into what I thought would be the most overheated and uncomfortable bathing experience of my life. To my surprise, however, the toasty bath didn't make me break into a sweat, but did wonders to ease the tension that knotted in my shoulders. The water hadn't produced a rich foam on its surface like the baths at home, but I could easily fish the bars from the floor and scrub myself with a well-soaped cloth.

Nan had been beside herself with worry, thinking the nail marks on my wrist would become infected and made me swear I'd scrub the already fading crescents twice per day. Considering how icky just looking at them made me feel, I had already washed them a third and fourth time.

With a little less than two hours to go, I enjoyed the temporary calm of my little private room. The combined scents of lavender and something wonderfully spicy filled the air, and like I was reliving the moment, I could feel the Scion's silky hair tickling my chest again. After last night's encounter, I'm sure he took me to be some inexperienced weakling. I mean, I was babbling incoherently about my uncle and all, but I absolutely placed some of the blame right back on him. First, don't scare someone who's leaning over a railing. Second, I *guarantee* he knows the effect he has on people, and I bet I wasn't the only human he'd turned into a simpering puddle.

He would be at the Congregation. I would see him today. There was no avoiding it, and quite frankly, I didn't want to avoid him. He could play his game, whatever it may be, but I had a choice in whether or not I'd play back.

"SO YOU CAN DRESS IN FIFTEEN BUT CANNOT WASH IN UNDER AN HOUR? GET OUT!" Kairus hollered from outside the door.

"Shit, Kairus! You scared me to death. I'm coming!"

I watched my roommate fiddle with a multitude of vials and tins while I patted my hair dry. She had so many little pots of cream and shells filled with pigment that her lap couldn't contain them all and they spilled onto the floor. Kairus, uncaring about that fact, was looking into a hand mirror with her mouth pulled tightly in a little *O*. How quickly she was able to transform herself with a few small brushes was amazing. She darkened her lashes with a dampened powder and swiped a brown kohl across her upper and lower lids. Like magic, her fair-colored, youthful face was remade into one of bold maturity.

We peered into the wall mirror in Kairus's bathroom and, turning back and forth, she appraised her appearance. She was resplendent in an indigo charmeuse gown. The fabric of the richly colored garment was shot through with silver fibers, which made the material glimmer. The effect was stunning, adding an even more eye-catching luminescence to the already striking woman. Her sleeves were long and fit tightly down to her first knuckle, and each wrist was stacked with thin silver bands that had been studded with rubies. The most captivating part of her gown, though, was the daring neckline that plunged from her clavicle to her navel, where a silver ring pierced her flesh.

"You look amazing, seriously. You've got hair the color of... of moonbeams," I said, meaning every word.

"Moonbeams?" she laughed and shared a happy little smile.

"You heard me—take the compliment!" She caught the hand I batted at her and pulled me front and center.

I looked at my own reflection, twisting around as Kairus had. In twenty and five years I'd never felt so pretty.

My gown was made from a fabric that I had immediately recognized. A Solnnan merchant had visited our capital last year, and it was among the other bolts and sewing notions he was selling. My father, who had escorted me that evening, must have remembered how I'd squealed in delight as I ran my hands over the pure white material. The merchant called it silk velvet, it was glowy and smooth, reminiscent of how a horse muzzle felt on your fingertips.

The long, sleeveless garment covered me from neck to floor, where it pooled at my feet. Two slits ran from the point below my natural waist to the ground, revealing not only my legs but the full curve of both hips. The style was far out of my comfort zone. I was used to heavy layers and fur and leather, and you simply didn't walk around with any parts of your body uncovered in my kingdom. Frostbite was a painful reality if you weren't careful.

I ran my hands over my hips while I rocked back and forth on my feet.

"Men like thick hips, Eira. Actually, they like any hips as long as they are smacking up against theirs."

"Yeah, okay, but my real fear is my woolybush popping out of its burrow."

"Y-your WHAT?" Kairus bent double laughing so hard her face turned an alarming shade of pink. "Oh, my Goddess, I ca-cannot breathe! Your wooly—ha!"

It was another minute until she grabbed my arm and stood up.

"Here, wait," she got out between giggles. Turning my head with her hand, she dipped a tiny brush into a dark powder and ran it through my lashes. Hurriedly but precisely, she painted my lips with a peachy-colored cream and rubbed a light pink balm onto both my cheeks. I caught Kairus's smug smile in the mirror, she was quite pleased with her handiwork, and I had to admit, I was too.

"Now, let's go!"

CHAPTER SEVEN

FAMILY RESEMBLANCE

B y the time we reached the twin doors that led into the Congregation hall, Kairus's new warmth had cooled. She set her jaw and angled her head back slightly, giving off that I'm-better-than-you half-scowl that had irked me so much on our journey. Behind the grand staircase, which connected the first through third levels of the temple, was a series of large rooms that had been carved deep into the body of the mountain. I paused for a moment to steel my nerves, while Kairus swept past me and across the threshold without so much as a nod or wave.

Well, that ended quickly.

As more people arrived, I found myself caught up in self-doubt. At home, I'd been so sure of the quality of my preparations, but now, I was growing concerned that maybe too much confidence had led me down the path of arrogance. And, if that were the case, I needed to reflect on how I'd been viewing others.

I made it through the doorway.

This was no ordinary room—could you even call it a room if it were the most splendid space you'd ever seen? The word "room" just seemed an inadequate description. It was the largest indoor area I'd ever seen, and it was just magnificent. We were surrounded by the smooth temple stone, but heavy and ornately carved moldings capped the ceiling and ran along the bottom of each wall, their sparkling white finish a stark contrast to the familiar deep gray. Grand partitions allowed the space to be divided into multiple rooms or to be precisely shaped for utility or effect. The back of the second level was a modular masterwork.

I walked across the white marble floor and headed toward a cluster of plush chairs that were upholstered in crimson. In front of them, a raised platform jutted out from the back of the room, and at its end stood a white altar, covered partly by a golden cloth.

A lovely, black-haired Troth breezed past me and walked toward a group of others. I stopped short to examine the small assemblage she met up with and was struck by how impressive they all were. They could easily have been the muses of the great masters.

Each garment stood out, clearly tailor-made for the wearer; their fit and form were too perfect to be otherwise. I recognized the Gaean from our trip south. She was covered from breasts to ankles in sage feathers whose tips had been dipped in glistening gold. Another, who I'd yet to formally meet, wore a gown whose hem began well above her knees and then swooped down in a train of rose and violet flowers that flowed down her legs like a waterfall. And there was another who—

A gilded door opened, admitting a group of Scion and their attendants. The males had certainly known to come well dressed. Some wore smart military uniforms, highly decorated with baldrics and badges that displayed their merits. Many had their swords swinging lightly at their hips. Others filled out impeccably fitted coats, both short and floor length, trimmed in silk brocades or furs or even jewels.

I wonder if any of their fathers are fishermen or farmers or bakers. They all looked royal to me.

I spotted a table of refreshments to the side of the group and decided to help myself to a plate of colorful confections. Each of the sweets, adorably, reflected a particular kingdom. There was a Nortian shortbread with black and white icing drizzled over the top, and what I assumed to be a Monwyn layer cake, made to look like a tiny mountain, complete with spun-sugar clouds. I chose to sample the Solnnan dessert, which was covered in fruits I'd not tasted before. Its base was a lightly flavored cream that was topped with purple berries and a slice of a pink-fleshed fruit that was speckled with black dots.

I really hoped no one saw my eyes roll. The flavor was purely—no, *profoundly* delectable, a mix of honied sweetness with a tart and—

Every single head swung to the door.

Just like yesterday, when the Scion stepped into the room, the entire crowd shifted their focus. The same aggravation I'd felt last night tiptoed back in. My first inclination was to think of an excuse to stay away from him, but that was quickly replaced by the desire to remind him this was *my* temple too.

I stuffed the remaining half of the treat in my mouth.

Here I come, sir! I held my breath while I marched in his direction. Already, a ring of admirers had formed around him. A tight cluster of men and women vied for his attention, waving their hands around and laughing so falsely it set my teeth on edge. As a few new faces joined in the praise party, they blocked any chance I had to catch his eye. But I already knew how to deal with this. I pivoted around a Scion who was as bald as an egg and moved past another who had the most remarkable skin I'd ever seen, a captivating marbling of both deep brown and alabaster. Finally, sidestepping a servant, I arrived at the broad back of my foe.

I lifted my arm high up to his shoulder blade... and knocked.

He chuckled and as he turned to me, I immediately felt the lure of his sexy smirk.

Gammond's gonads! I'd like to feed that mouth a little dessert...

"I had hoped to meet again, Lady," he said in a voice so alluring that I had to consciously stop myself from licking my lips.

"I'm sure you did. May we speak privately?"

The ears of both Scion and Troth alike perked up around us, reminding me of the small white foxes back home whose ears darted back and forth while listening for the skitters of their prey.

"But of course, I relish the opportunity to spend *any* moment in your presence." Ignoring all the others, he tucked my hand into the crook of his arm, and together we walked toward the corner of the large hall.

"*Look,*" I spun on him, severing our physical contact, "we need to get things straight. First, I don't even know your name, and yet *you* took the liberty of trying to get snuggly with me in the dead of night after *you* caused me to almost fall and break my neck. Was it on purpose? If it was, I'd have serious concerns regarding any future interactions we may have, *and* I'd be hard-pressed to not see you as dangerously warped. Second, if you'd like to get to know me, I'd suggest opening your mouth and starting a conversation. Attempting to trap me in some childish flirtation will end poorly for you, *and* I will not jeopardize my chances of success here because you like to play around."

Watching the Scion's face change from confusion to shock to confusion again, I knew I had hit my mark. Awaiting his response, I tapped my foot and assumed a cross-armed stance, mimicking my mother at her most righteous. He stared at me through narrowed eyes, but before he could muster a response, he was cut off by a throat clearing behind him. Saved by the interruption, he turned away momentarily and motioned forward another exquisitely formed Scion. *The Goddess must've tossed in a few extra muscles and a whole lot of good-looking when she made these men.*

"Lady, uh...?" asked the tall Scion, whose name I *still* didn't know.

"It's Eira," I said, flicking my eyes back to the new addition.

"Troth Eira of Nortia, I would like to introduce you to my advisor, Tommand, of Basillia, Royal Emissary of Monwyn, and great Protector of our Kingdom."

A companion? Huh.

With a curt bow, the advisor bent at the waist and extended an arm in my direction. I quirked a brow at his Scion.

"What's this, a Monwyn with manners? How refreshing." I just couldn't resist the slight.

I placed my hand into the upturned palm and was struck by the juxtaposition of the egoist Scion and his cultured advisor. That is until I felt the barest of contacts against my skin. A breath? His lips? Maybe the tickle of a whisker?

Straightening, the emissary looked at me blankly and mumbled some indifferent greeting. He seemed so unaffected by the pomp around him, he managed to look even more unimpressed than Kairus had. I watched as he placed his hand on the Scion's back, shifting him to discuss some matter more privately. While rapidly becoming irritated at being left alone in the corner, I used the moment to study both men.

Where the Scion was astonishingly handsome, carefully coiffed, and expertly manicured, his advisor was more *potent*. He was quite a bit shorter than the Scion, but where the taller man was leaner in his muscularity, Tommand was broad and thickly built, so much so, the swell of his biceps couldn't be hidden by the plain woolen coat he wore. His hair was closely shorn, so I couldn't make out its color, but the coarse shadow on his jaw was fairly dark. His lips were full but firm and his aquiline nose countered his ruggedness, giving him a rather regal appearance. Without outright gawking, I thought his eyes were a rich cinnamony brown which would certainly compliment his beautiful olive complexion.

"Where would you set my price, Lady Chulainn, after such a... thorough appraisal?" he spoke without turning to face me. His voice was low, his tone precisely modulated, and it felt like every clipped word he spoke was an insult directed at my person.

So Monwyn does mean asshole.

"Leave her alone, Tommand. Shoo now..." the Scion chided, again tucking my hand into the crook of his elbow. "He can be so boorish," he inclined his head in Tommand's direction, "and please, call me Ambrose."

·· •)(•··

So much for trying to focus on the Goddess's gift. What I really wanted to do was ogle every man in the temple. The smooth-talking Scion, his good-looking servant, and now the slice of divinity sitting next to me. The excuse I'd given myself for the last five minutes was that it was because Nortia wasn't exactly a hotbed of handsome, mostly on account of having to wear concealing furs and knitted scarves around all but your eyes for most of the year.

The assemblage had been directed to the chairs, which had been set up in semicircular rows. There had been no seating arrangements so Ambrose, still stuck to my side, had taken up residence to my left, and another Scion, Greggen, sat to my right. Tall and thin, Greggen was gracefully built, and his sleeveless, floor-length overcoat allowed for ample views of his sinewy arms, which looked like they had been carved from granite. Two gold bands set with large yellow stones sat on the top and bottom of his well-toned bicep, emphasizing his arm in the most appealing way.

Situated as I was right now, enveloped in a cloak of masculinity, I was feeling quite warm... quite pleasant indeed. Ambrose was so close that his arm kept coming in contact with my shoulder, and I kept glancing down waiting for Greggen's thigh to touch my own.

"All rise! All rise in the presence of the exalted High Mantle, Holiest of Holies, They Who Serve the Blessed Goddess, They Who Keep with the Divine, Caretaker of Humanity, Defender of Ærta!"

All at once, the lamps on the walls' perimeters dimmed, effectively drawing attention to the dais and altar. Murmurs rose around me, and I noticed, without surprise, that at this moment, many shed silent tears. We were in the presence of They Who Intercede With the Goddess, her representative on the mortal plane.

The Obligates stood at once, and together we placed our fingertips to our brows.

Through parted fingers, I watched the High Mantle appear in an open doorway located behind the dais. They stood unmoving, and the stillness was somehow more poignant than words could have ever been.

Before walking to the altar, Their arms raised in a prayer, a silent homage to She Who'd Given All. The Mantle's movements were so graceful, so fluid, that I was reminded of the rolling mists that appeared on the hillsides at home when an infrequent warm breeze encountered the frozen ground. Cloaked in silken robes of garnet and gold, the High Mantle laid Their delicate hands on the altar at the end of the platform.

"A hundred years ago," the Mantle gestured for everyone to be seated, "our world was nearly shattered by corruption—by a poison that worked so deeply into the hearts of mankind that our very existence was threatened. There were those who did not heed the gifts our Goddess provided, who, in their desire for dominance, learned to conjure a force

so potent that wielding it tainted their souls, twisting them to malevolence and greed."
The light veil that obscured the Mantle's face fluttered with each of Their words. "It was
the unity of the seven kingdoms that stopped the bloodshed that would have taken our
world. The loss of life was so great and the destruction so wanton, that only four of our
original kingdoms remain. We remember the citizens who've for a century slept under the
ruins of their homelands. To the people of Hain, Inglis, and Taleer, we commend your
souls to Merrias and will do so until our feet no longer touch the soil. The gates were flung
open to receive your refugees. Your children, born of the deserts and isles, were taken in
and taught to thrive in the icescapes of Nortia—in the deep woods of Gaea, the rolling
hills of Monwyn, and in the warmth of Solnna." The Mantle paused and inclined Their
head. "It is for those thousands of faceless martyrs that you, children of the Goddess, are
called to give your lives over in service to the Obligation. You are charged with continuing
the process that has maintained accord among humanity all these years. We have come
too far as a people to allow our efforts to wane. Our futures and those of all Ærta begin
again, in this room, at this very moment."

The High Mantle turned and walked unhurriedly back through the doors from which
They came. I could feel the very weight of my blessing pressing down upon me.

This was why. This was why we came.

Two new people entered through the doorway, one of whom moved forward to the
altar, the other sat in the empty chair to its side. The speaker wore a floor-length tunic
of violet and a buttoned hood made from the same luminescent material as the Mantle's
robes. He was a large man, in both height and weight, with an exquisitely smooth black
complexion and laugh lines that wrinkled around his eyes when he grinned. He reminded
me so much of—

"I am Devotee Mariad Keagan. Welcome, all, to this most blessed assembly! We are
rewarded by the Goddess for our good works and for the peace this Congregation will
bring to her lands and people. Embrace the fortune of your circumstances and give praise
to she who has given you another year and a greater purpose!" He lifted his fingers to
his silvery eyes and then gestured to the audience of Scion and Troth, who mimicked his
actions.

Except for me.

My hands were pressed firmly to my mouth, where they'd been from the moment he
spoke his name.

Though my eyes had remained dry in the presence of Their Holiness, they now spilled
hot tears down my cheeks.

Kan Keagan. He must have had a family. It was like staring into the face I had memorized over a decade ago.

My heart raced in my chest. If Kan had a family, then not only did his memory live on... but so did a piece of him. I tried unsuccessfully to squash the sob that left my mouth, and I could feel my shoulders begin to quiver. I was at once overcome by a swirling storm of emotions: sorrow, hope... relief. I'd always felt such guilt because his body had been buried in the sea and not sent to his homeland. Even now, just the thought of it spiked my anxiety to the point I needed to get out of the room. I buried my face tighter in my hands.

There was a soft touch at my side.

I wiped at my eyes, and as my blurry vision cleared, I turned to Ambrose, who tilted his head in concern. He dipped his chin and drew his brows together, silently mouthing "You okay?" I nodded, just once, smiling weakly, and leaned into the arm that he'd tucked close by my side. Maybe it shouldn't, but it felt right to borrow some of his strength in such an affecting moment, even though I'd known him less than a single day.

"Today, Troth and Scion alike will begin the final training to advance their skills and knowledge base. Every conference you attend will aid you in your Assignment and increase your odds of prosperity." Smiling broadly, Devotee Keagan swept an upturned hand across the hall.

"For our Troth, the following curriculum will be taught by temple instructors and emissaries from each of our continent's kingdoms. The first session is Matters of the Court. This two-day course will provide intense instruction surrounding the high levels of etiquette expected from our Troth. Their placements will require them to effectively navigate the upper echelons of society, master the dos-and-do-nots of each Kingdom and be able to contend successfully in any court in which they shall serve."

His remarks brought me back to the present.

"Matters of the State is a course based on the understanding and study of political conventions and trade dynamics which work to facilitate partnerships between the four kingdoms. Troth often become advocates for not only their new homes, but their kingdoms of origin as they navigate the complex waters of state diplomacy."

I felt a feather-light touch on my thigh, but kept my eyes forward, listening to our speaker.

"Finally, Matters of Unity and Matters of Domestic Art will round out our Troth's experience. The Matters of Unity will be steeped in..."

Ambrose ran the pad of his thumb along my exposed hip, working his way further under the material of my gown with every stroke. *Not an accidental contact after all.* I sat up straighter, worried we'd be seen.

He stilled his motions.

I glanced at him through lowered lashes and caught a little half-smile. I found myself grinning, partly because he was so unabashedly flirty, and partly because, if I was being honest, I enjoyed the attention.

When he began again, I convinced myself that nobody could see us. His arm was caught between us and the navy short cloak he wore, spilled out behind my chair. I closed my eyes enjoying the caresses that were now nearing the sensitive fold of my hip and took a cleansing breath when he skimmed his nails along my skin. I let myself sink into the intimate sensation that had suddenly become more noteworthy than the curriculum.

He probably thinks I'm easy prey. I'm inclined to let him believe it.

"Oh!" His fingers woke me from my contemplation, smartly pinching the skin of my thigh. I turned my head in his direction, not bothering to shield it this time.

My breath caught.

Goddess alive! The look he gave me couldn't be mistaken for anything other than desire... and I mean, full-on licking-his-lips, smoldering-eyed lust. My chest tightened and tingled in response, but now was not the time to add kindling to the fire. I found his hand and moved it judiciously away.

"—Domestic Arts will be of the utmost importance to our Troth. You will be taught to manage a multitude of differing factions, learn to lead with grace and wisdom, and to become a mediator when the need arises. Being able to problem solve is paramount to your growth and productivity," Keagan finished.

As the Devotee took his seat, I hoped with all my heart I'd have the opportunity to discover if my hunch about his relation to Kan Keagan was correct.

The remaining speaker came forward. She moved slowly, her gait heavy and uneven. It seemed the cause of her difficult movements was the leg that dragged slightly behind her. Her black and white regalia marked her as Nortian, and she was similarly covered from chin to middle chest by the same style of hood Devotee Keagan wore.

"Our Scion will be expected to present themselves at every planned session. Not doing so will result in punishment. The elevated status of your gender, which you assume gives you power over others, is no more than a happenstance of nature. What hangs betwixt your legs does not, at any juncture, become a valid excuse when you yourself make poor choices."

Stifled feminine laughter could be heard over the murmuring of male voices. *She is not messing around.* Her tone led me to believe that skipping lectures had been an issue in the past, and considering the actions of the Scion next to me, I could only imagine the reasons for why.

"Scion, your instruction will consist of the following: First, Overseeing Trade and Economic Provisions. If you cannot secure and hold merchanting relations, you will fail. Second, in Adjudicating Regional Disputes, if you waiver in your ability to make sound decisions or provide advice to others that leads them to folly, you will have failed. Likewise, if the power to make decisions goes to your head and thoughts of prestige and influence overcome your abilities and cloud your decency, it will be left to your brother Scion to ensure you are permanently removed from your Assignment."

I hope that doesn't mean as permanent as she made it sound.

"That leads me directly to the gravity of the last course you will undertake. Personal Skill at Arms and Small Unit Command could very well be the course to break you. I would venture to say, by the puffed-up way in which you all now sit, that you are confident in your abilities to protect yourselves. *Your* Assignments are not measured by the dependability of your keeping yourself alive. After all, you can be readily replaced. They are, however, measured upon your skill at keeping safe the most vulnerable of the courts in which you will serve. If you were to perish but had honorably done your duty, you could expect your kingdom to survive. If you are weak and unmindful of your preparations, significant portions of your people will be preyed upon, and so too would your kingdom suffer."

The solemnity of her words hung in the air.

"Expect to receive your schedules at this evening's meal... you are dismissed."

The unnamed Devotee turned to the exit.

CHAPTER EIGHT

A PLEASURE TO MEET YOU

O bligates and their companions were invited to dinner that evening. Nan, who sat to my left, looked as lovely as I'd ever seen her, wearing a gown she and my mother had sewn while working on the new dresses I needed here. Her hair had been arranged in soft curls, pulled to one side, and clasped in a pearled barrette. The style showed off her constantly pink, smooth, and unlined skin. Her long-sleeved gown was such a dark gray it appeared black, and the material hugged her ample chest, nipped in at her waist, and flared out over her full hips. She had pearled the square neckline of her dress, which drew attention to her décolletage and a shocking swell of cleavage. *Well, shocking to me. I'd never seen her neck before and deer skins would have made a strange impression at the meal.*

We shared a round table, swathed in gold cloth, with two Solnnan Troth and their companions. One Troth, by the name of Richelle, had the most inviting personality. She welcomed us like kin who had been gone too long, and immediately I felt an affinity for the plump little woman. She was shorter than me and dressed in a purple cowl-necked gown that was made of extremely heavy brushed wool. It occurred to me that the Solnnans, so used to life in the heat, probably felt perpetually frozen on the high mountain.

"My mother says I could charm the hairs off a hippo!" She wagged a finger at the Scion who sat with us. She gestured animatedly with every other word she said, and it caused the fluff of her thick, orange-red hair to bounce against her shoulders.

"Lady, I was under the impression that the hippopotamus was not a creature covered in fur." Sitting on Nan's left, a handsome, older gentleman spoke while looking confusedly at Richelle.

Her eyes sparkled, and her lips pressed together in a tight line.

"They're not! No hair at all" She burst into an uproarious howl that set the entire table to laughter.

Richelle had brought with her a maid, who right now looked like she'd rather be anywhere else than next to her vivacious Troth. The slight woman fidgeted with her napkin and rotated her silverware in a shaky hand. When I asked her how she had enjoyed her two days in the temple so far, she had answered in a voice so faint I ended up just nodding and smiling, hoping she hadn't said something like, "I would prefer repeatedly stabbing my foot to staying here another night."

"Young man, I'm surprised they didn't make that beard of yours beam like a beet!" Nan let a joke fly. Richelle thumped her hands wildly on the table in glee.

Amias, who sat straight across from me, was a Scion from Gaea whose bald head was a fascinating contrast to the red-hued braids of the other Obligates from his kingdom. He had a dense, multicolored beard of browns and black that reminded me of my father's, and when he laughed, his small round eyes disappeared.

"Luckily that was never a written requirement. Rest assured until thirty or so I dutifully colored even the last whisp, until it shed and joined Merrias." Amias laughed. If I had to guess his age, I would put him near year thirty-five, maybe older.

Tonight was the first time in days that I'd felt relaxed enough to fully let my guard down. The group chatted with ease, and there was no pressure for any of the Obligates to act as if the High Mantle were sitting at the next table. It *was* strange having Nan here, though. Not in a bad way, but she usually took on a parental role in my life or acted like an aunt with more authority. But tonight, she was my equal... and she was stealing the show. She kept the conversations going and the topics interesting, never once letting awkward silences plague our group. By the middle of dinner, even the uncomfortable maid, Abben, was relaxed enough to share a little about herself, albeit very quietly. Nan may not have been the wittiest or even the best listener, but she knew how to bring out the best of those around her.

"You told him to put his man parts on ice?" Richelle hollered after Nan recalled the first time she had been alone with her future husband.

Nan quirked her mouth in a kittenish expression and scrunched her shoulders to her ears. She was so different tonight. I'd never thought of her as particularly effervescent, but here she was, full of energy, injecting humor and life into a situation that could have easily been downright awful.

I squinted, trying to see her through the eyes of our dinner friends, and attempted to forget the stories I'd heard at least twenty times, or that I'd known her for longer than I'd known how to walk. Right now she was flashing her pearly smile at the man to her left, and in this instant, she seemed much younger than I'd ever thought her to be. I actually didn't know how old Nan was, but I concluded that right here, in her element, perhaps I'd put her in a little box that deserved to be much bigger.

"No doubt, a woman as fetching as yourself drew the attention of many a suitor, and your husband, is he..." coolly remarked the well-dressed gentlemen making eyes at Nan.

"He finds himself quite dead at the moment," she breathed in a sultry tone.

Amias's escort—who was unashamedly pursing his lips—was a political advisor who went only by his surname, Marcyn. His first name was Radley, but as he explained, his father, also Radley, had named all four of his sons the same, so that his eventual heir would bear his name, no matter how many died before their prime. Nan wasted no time telling him she thought it was a horrific practice and that his father should be ashamed, and he agreed with her, or maybe he just acted like he did so he could continue bobbing his head up and down with the movement of her heaving bosom.

I swear, if I catch Nan and Marcyn in some dark hall, ha! Smiling over my glass, I pictured Nan in a passionate embrace with the advisor. I didn't think it was gross to do so, but it certainly gave me the giggles. My mother had always taught me that great pleasure could be gained from physical intimacy and that, if I was inclined to feel that way, I would eventually want to join with others. She also counseled that being selective was a good idea.

I was certainly open to the idea of intimacy and had shared in a few moments of groping and heavy breathing in the past, but the thought of Nan "joining" with Marcyn made me feel like I had when I'd accidentally come upon a couple passionately kissing in the shadows of the apothecary's store. I remember being so shocked by their closeness that I scream-laughed and pointed, causing one of the young men to jump so hard he hit the other's nose with his forehead. Thankfully they had just laughed it off and made their way into the shop. I chuckled all the way home, where my mother met me at the door, arms crossed and foot tapping. Daydreaming about kisses, I'd forgotten to pick up her order.

I'm sure Nan had been kissed like that before though, and glancing at her and Marcyn, it looked like she may want to be again. If she did, I'd want it for her too. I would never begrudge someone their happiness.

I brought the tart red wine to my mouth, savoring its bold flavor. All the thoughts of kisses started my insides tingling, reminding me of the proximity I'd shared with a certain Scion. I snuck a peek at Ambrose, using the stemware to conceal the tongue that darted out to moisten my lips. *I'd like to find myself in a dark hallway with that one.*

Of course, I'd noticed him immediately when we arrived; his head had risen easily above those of his adoring fans.

He was currently bent down, engrossed in his conversation with Cinden, the pillow-sobbing Troth. She stared at him invitingly while chewing on her plump bottom lip. The big buffoon clearly liked what he saw. He wagged his dark brows and shot her a teasing smile, all the while inching closer. *He looks ridiculous.* Cinden pushed her breasts up with her folded arms and leaned over the table, acting like whatever stupid story he'd told was interesting. *Yes, my gorgeous Troth, let me tell you all about how I keep my hair so shiny and thick.* Actually, it was probably something wildly suggestive and she was trying to fan the flames of his ardor. I wasn't about to be jealous though. If you were charming *and* looked like the Goddess created you for the sole purpose of copulation, I bet all kinds of opportunities fell into your lap.

I wondered what it would be like to share a kiss with such a virile and appealing man. It had to be better than the kiss Gen Makerly had given me years ago, which had been all bumping faces and overzealous tongue. Perhaps with Ambrose, it would be like the one I witnessed at the apothecary: potent and impassioned, shared between those who knew what they wanted.

I sighed into my glass and took a too-large gulp of wine. I knew, of course, that his teasing and toying were not exclusive to me and that when compared, I firmly fell in the average category on the Troth scale of attractiveness, but I'd welcome the flirtation. That wasn't forbidden, I didn't think, but anything more would be unwise, as our Assignments would surely take us in different directions. *Stupid Cinden.* Ambrose tilted his head back, laughing so prettily at whatever the Troth had told him. His hand lay so close to hers that their fingers touched. *Stupid Ambrose.*

Taking another sip, I willed his image out of my head and purposefully shifted to cut him out of view... just to collide right into the serious stare of Emissary Tommand. The broad-shouldered advisor was leaning back, pushed away from the table, one arm crossed over the other. He thumbed at the material of his dark blue jacket, looking every bit the pretentious king presiding over his court. I bet he never tired of lording over a room filled with his subjects. He drew down both corners of his mouth. I'd been caught eyeing his charge, and the look on his face said *back off*. It raised my hackles that he hadn't shot daggers at Cinden's breasts out on the table. I suppose he found the Gaean more worldly than a Nortian bumpkin. *Whatever.*

The surly Tommand flicked his head towards the door, ending our erstwhile stare-off. *Surely I'd misunderstood the gesture. Did he really just command me to leave my table?*

He caught my eyes again and repeated the motion, narrowing his eyes disapprovingly when I didn't snap to his bidding. *One, two... three. Breathe. Fucking Monwyns.*

I considered staying put, but the need to make him understand that I wasn't another subordinate in his weird game of superiority won out. This ass was going to be aware of *exactly* the role he played in my life.

Nan, a few shades pinker than she was ten minutes ago, was still engrossed in a conversation with her admirer, so I pushed out from the table and marched out, smacking the double doors open with both hands. Two minutes hadn't passed when I heard the noise of the chattering crowd swell only to be cut off again.

Positioning myself in front of the balcony, I prepared to execute a dramatic turn and stare coolly into the haughty-faced advisor as I told him off. Unfortunately, the goon was too fast and grabbed my elbow so quickly that I had no time for the planned theatrics.

Jerking my arm back, I tried in vain to free myself from his grasp, but the unphased Tommand held firm and steered us away from the dining hall.

He paused to greet an acolyte, nodding his head and bowing curtly, and I used the opportunity to pinch the inside of his arm with my free hand. He gave no indication that he'd even felt my fingers. *Fine, let's see where this goes, he couldn't kidnap a Troth from the heavily secured temple, and besides, plenty of witnesses were milling about.* Abruptly, he pivoted and pulled us both into the shadow created by the staircase overhang.

"Are you aware of the rules to the game you are so willfully trying to play?" His pupils dilated as he spat out the words. "I could all but smell envy seeping from your pores." I turned to face him squarely, and our eyes locked. *Definitely cinnamon-brown.* No amount of counting would slow the burn of indignation he'd made me feel.

"What games I play are the games *I* choose! I and I alone dictate how I play them and how *you*, a man I have met twice, thinks he has any say in what I do is beyond the pale. You can fuck right off if you think you can speak to me as if you own me!" Conviction burned in my every word.

"Yes, let us speak of *fucking*," came his sharp reply.

Through narrowed eyes, I raked my gaze from his head to his toes, momentarily disconcerted by my loss of words.

"Are you intact?"

I blinked wildly, my indignation turning to biting fury. I'd never hit anyone before. I'd never had a reason to, but my fists seemed to curl of their own accord. *Count, now! One. Think. Two. Breathe.* I needed to focus and take back the dominant role in this conversation. He was baiting me, and I was falling for the worm. *Am I intact? What a piece of shit.*

"Tommand. Does anyone call you Tom?" It was a start, not a strong one, but here I was, turning things around.

"They do not."

"Really? Nobody? May I call you Tom?"

"You may not."

"Oh, okay, *Tom.*"

He clenched his jaw but said nothing, the muscle there ticking rapidly as he ground his teeth together.

"What's your concern? You afraid your sexy Scion is going to get taken in by the wicked ole un-*intact* slut of Nortia? Is that your issue? That I have ensnared him so completely in a single day that he will forgo his Assignment and you and he will become Monwyn's biggest disappointment?" I walked towards him, hips swaying, arms tucked behind my back, mimicking what I had seen my mother do to my father. "'Are you intact?' Are you an *asshole?*" *That's what I should have started with.*

"Your lack of purity is neither here nor there, but what you must—" I cut him off.

"What I *must* is for me to decide, or have you already forgotten that? You don't strike me as a slow man, *Tom.*" I paused briefly, watching his jaw work, the flicker quickening. His mouth opened to speak, but I shushed him quickly, a bold new plan of action forming in my mind. "Or is this something else then?" I sauntered forward until my chest brushed lightly against his. Had he pushed away or indicated discomfort, I would have backed off, but he remained, unmoving, jaw ticking.

I had him.

Emboldened by the rush of outsmarting my target, I pushed tighter against him, which caused my breasts to swell up above the neckline of my dress.

"Not so immune yourself, I see." Wantonly, I looked down at my breasts and then up into his eyes, pulling the side of my lip into my mouth like I had seen Cinden do.

He looked... covetous.

"What I think, *Tom*, is that you'd like to switch places with your Scion. Did he tell you about our meeting last night?"

His stubble-covered jaw relaxed and a single eyebrow shot up. "Actually, yes, he told me it ended before any real fun began," he replied smugly. I watched the side of his mouth rise in a secretive grin.

Damn! Not the response I expected.

"Hmmm, would you have been able to finish what your strapping Scion did not?" I placed two fingertips on the side of his neck just under his ear and ran them down the exposed skin to the top of his neckline. He moved under my touch, rolling his shoulders like a contented cat. Continuing my experimental exploration, I hooked a finger in the collar of his shirt and popped open its first button.

"More?" I questioned, testing the waters.

"Yes." There was no hesitation in his blunt admission.

Hypocrite.

Glancing down, I didn't dare let him see my eyes narrow in triumph. I could play along. I slid my hands into his coat and felt the hardness of his prominent pectorals before drifting down to his stomach. He may be a jerk, but I could still appreciate the Monwyn characteristic for a well-built body.

His eyes closed in response, and feeling as bold as a polar bear in a blizzard, I slid my hands further down the plane of his stomach and flared my fingers out over his hips, tucking them into the waistband of his pants. Tommand let out a shaky breath.

"I'm sorry, what was that?" I purred. His response was a low rumble in the back of his throat. The sound sent a charged thrill through me, and my own breathing quickened. *Is this what playing with fire feels like?*

Alight with the courage that came with these new feelings, my fingertips, still ensconced, tugged at the waistband of his pants, pulling his lower half closer. His soft moan was a song to my ears. Goosebumps skated down my neck and shoulders, and a familiar pulsing took up between the juncture of my thighs. I slid my greedy hands together, intending to pull at the leather thongs that laced his pants and call it a night. But as my fingers came together, I realized all too slowly that they rested around the very tip of his arousal, warm and rigid, nestled at the top of his pants. He jerked his hips which caused his erection to glide between my hands, brushing my knuckles. *Oh, fuck.*

"Oh, fuck," he groaned.

Retreat!

I tried not to panic. This was a little *too* bold and hadn't factored into my power play. Especially the part where I was enjoying it. I had gone too far, and Goddess strike me to ash, this is not how I intended things to go. *Could he not turn that thing off while I thought this through?*

Tom grabbed my hips tightly and let his hands roam to the small of my back. Heading lower, he palmed and squeezed each cheek of my bottom and pulled me forcefully against him. I could hear the sounds of his enjoyment vibrating in his chest when he ground his hips against me again. *Shit, shit, shit!*

"So you are aware, had it been me, I would have fucked you so thoroughly the only sound echoing off the walls would have been my name on your lips." Tom, nipped at my ear, and like a dog betraying their master, my nipples tightened and strained against his chest. I couldn't think. I could barely remember how I got here.

None too gently, he caught my waist in his hands and twisted our bodies around, pressing my back against the closest wall. Two days, *two*, and I had found myself in this position twice.

"You do respond just as beautifully as he said..."

There was a brief pause. I opened the eyes I'd squeezed shut. Tommand's head was bent, and he was watching his own hands as he ran them over the curve of my breasts and down the side of my rib cage.

It was time to stop the game that was turning too risky. I tilted his chin up.

"Tommand, I..."

Goddess, you created your daughter to know pleasure, would it defile your temple to take him right here?

The longing I saw in his eyes stripped me bare. His mouth had slackened, parting ever so slightly, and his lips, so enticingly sensual, drew me further down the path I'd mistakenly thought I could navigate. Ambrose had looked at me with half the intensity of what I saw on Tommand's face.

"You what?" he asked while trailing his fingers along the edge of my jaw.

"I what?" I said, not having understood the question. Right now, the only part of me that worked was sending out delicious little pulses of desire. I could feel the heaviness of my own arousal.

I leaned my head against the wall and breathed in deeply. He took a steadying breath as well, as I slicked my skirts down with both hands. More in control now, I stepped forward to push past Tommand, who had turned to the side to straighten his coat. My hand brushed against his still-hard length, and a raspy moan escaped me, recharging the already static air.

"More?" his eyes danced in anticipation.

I nodded, unable to speak the words.

I knew I could have ended this. I could have just shaken my head "no," but... I didn't.

Tommand stepped in closely, moving us further into the concealing shadows. I closed my eyes as I anticipated his fevered response. What I hadn't anticipated was the feather-light caress of his lips against mine. My little whimpers mingled with his deep and throaty hum.

"How *much* more, Nortia?" He scooped his hips upwards, grinding them into my own. My small cries amped into a lusty sob. Catching my chin in his hand, lips still on mine, he pulled down, forcefully parting my mouth. "Is this what you want?"

I'll show you what I want.

Abandoning all thoughts of gentleness, my inquisitive tongue found his, and instantly I forgave Gen Makerly for her overeagerness.

For the briefest moment I worried Tommand would find my enthusiasm distasteful, but his hand wrapped around the base of my neck and he practically purred into my mouth. His other hand came to my breast, cupping its weight while his thumb circled its peak. Waves of pleasure inundated me, and everywhere he touched was left tingling. His greedy tongue rubbed and tasted mine, and I sucked lightly at the tip of his, coaxing it between my lips.

He pulled away.

He took a single step back and reached down to adjust the straining bulge in his pants.

"I'm guessing intact." He shrugged a shoulder.

I watched him pull at the cuffs of his jacket and straighten his collar. And then, as if nothing had ever happened—as if I wasn't panting like a snow fox in the desert—he glanced down at his timepiece and strode back toward the dining hall.

My own ill-planned maneuver had been used against me.

My trap turned into an ambush!

Maybe tomorrow I'd be able to laugh off being so thoroughly duped, but right now I had to figure out how to walk back into the dining hall, all too aware of the moisture that clung to my undergarments.

Head up. Shoulders back and here we go. I strutted into the room and waved at Greggen, who'd been sitting at the next table over. Fully intent on grabbing my schedule and feigning a headache, I downed the rest of my drink and turned tail. Too bad I wasn't fast enough to escape an over-exuberant Nan who had other plans.

Leading me around the room, she introduced me to all her new acquaintances: a massive red-headed Gaean and a statuesque Solnnan Troth. Each of them smiled broadly and talked to us at length.

"Oh! And this is Ambrose of Monwyn, I think you sat next to him at the Congregation." The Scion bowed low over my outstretched hand.

"Indeed, we exchanged *pleasantries* just yesterday," he said gaily.

All the heat that had dissipated after my earlier activities threatened to rise up and scald my cheeks. *We surely had exchanged pleasantries... and then I'd exchanged them with his help!*

"You beware of this one, Eira. An expert flirt he is!" Nan's eyes twinkled as she swatted at the hand that still held mine. A wide grin split her face.

"And you remember the Monwyn emissary?"

The man in question walked forward.

"I believe so. *Tom*, isn't it?"

I smiled with the confidence of ten Monwyn Troth.

CHAPTER NINE

I'LL HAVE WHAT HE'S HAVING

Welp, I touched a penis... and managed to orchestrate the unsuccessful seduction of a man I don't like... who was literally the closest person to the man I sorta liked... all because I wanted to shove his arrogant smirk down his throat. Why I couldn't fall asleep was a total mystery. That same mystery drove my all-consuming need to count the tiny chips and irregularities in the stone ceiling above. I'd committed to the ciphering for the last couple of hours and had a real shot of finishing my calculations before the sun rose.

My first training session was hours away, and besides not sleeping, all I'd managed to do was debate whether Tommand's reactions to me were fake or not. I mean, clearly, there was a *solid* piece of evidence that couldn't have been... *I think.* After a brain-befuddling back and forth, the only conclusion I'd come to was that a master manipulator had called my bluff and found me lacking.

"I'm guessing intact."

Had I been so amateur a seductress? Had he been clenching that stern jaw so tightly to avoid laughing at me? And on top of that, how embarrassing was it that my body sang right along to his cocky tune. *Pull it together. How often have you accused males of thinking with their lower half? You're no better!*

In my mind, I imagined shoving all the Monwyns I'd met behind a door and turning the key in the lock. I snatched up the parchment beside me to reread tomorrow's—or more accurately—today's schedule. My first course would be Matters of the Court, and Kairus's was Matters of Unity. I closed my eyes and pulled a pillow over my face. *I've gone to lessons sleepy before. I guess I'll be doing it again.*

Two days ago, I wouldn't have thought I'd need a course on good manners, but after some self-reflection, I couldn't deny that it was *me* who'd left a perfectly nice dinner to go tell a man off but ended up touching his meat-sickle instead.

Tomorrow, exhaustion would be my penance.

After stepping off the fifth-floor staircase, I walked past a row of wooden doors with several alcoves dotted in between. Each little recess had a statue or painting in its center and a low kneeler placed to afford the devout some comfort and privacy. I had a little bit of time before my class began, so I popped into each of the small sanctuaries to see which of the divine was venerated. On this floor, so far, I'd seen a statue of Lykksun, which was surrounded by a halo of tiny golden suns, and another of Gammond, sitting on a throne of books. I nearly collided with a man in the last alcove who was deep in prayer but was able to stop myself before running him over. Slowly and as soundlessly as possible, I tiptoed backward, not wishing to disturb the aged believer.

"Lord Mossius... hear me. Th-thy divinity... knows no b-bounds... your healing touch is infinite, let m-my name... be a whisper in your mouth... S-Son of She... " a wet cough strangled his voice and his words trailed.

"Son of She Who Bore Us All, your presence alleviates all fear as my time draws near. I ask that my suffering be brief." I finished the intercession and laid a hand on his quivering shoulder. I'd learned the prayer from Olena—a rite for the dying. The man's hand found mine. His skin was parchment-thin. With great effort, he turned his head, and his rheumy eyes met mine.

Oh, my heart.

This man wasn't an old-timer at all. He was likely no older than Nan. His gauntness must have been caused by some progressive illness.

I was paralyzed, briefly, by the agonizing despair that accompanied grief. It didn't matter that I didn't know him. I mourned the loss of his future, of the life I'm sure he'd planned, never expecting it to be cut short. He curled his cold hand around mine and weakly rested them together on his forehead. It was a common benediction amongst the priestly class, and I was honored to receive the touch. He inhaled an obviously painful breath before another coughing fit doubled him over. I held him up and felt his brow for fever. Luckily, there was none.

"Thank you... ch-child." The priest returned my hand and slumped further onto his knees.

"Can I help you get somewhere?" I offered, worried he'd not be able to make it anywhere on his own.

"No, I a-am... where I... belong," he struggled out.

I hesitated, not wanting to leave him alone, but nodded my understanding before leaving him to his prayers. In a perhaps futile attempt to bring him some comfort, I wrapped my short cloak around his shoulders, adding another layer to his too-thin homespun covering. I remembered the disease that lay waste to Kan Keagan and how quickly it had taken him. I couldn't imagine the trepidation that even the most devout must endure when facing life's end.

Goddess, please watch over him.

Moving closer to the low-walled balcony, my steps were slower and heavier than before.

I peeked over the banister and became a little disoriented. I'd never been up this high before, and it made me queasy looking down into the enormous open space. At this height, I could just make out the edge of the floor below me, but after that... nothing. It felt way too much like floating in the sky. I closed my eyes to center myself, and when I opened them...

Ambrose.

He was speaking to the other Monwyn Scion, whose name was Evandr. I'd not been formally introduced to him but knew who he was on account of his unusual features. He was quite short, and he was also extremely pale—like snow drift pale. His hair would make Kairus' look dull. The two wrestled, practicing their feints and dodges. To their right, Tommand leaned over the banister, resting his weight on crossed arms.

His eyes met mine.

I waved a hand in greeting and managed a smile that I knew didn't reach my eyes. He tilted his head in acknowledgment, and I turned and made my way along the railing. I could feel his gaze on my back until I found the doorway for my first lecture.

There was a handwritten missive to the left of the doorframe: *Welcome, esteemed guests, to Matters of the Court.* The solid white door looked oddly out of place set in the dark stone walls. I tried the handle, but the door didn't budge. After jostling the mechanism, I tried again and got the same result. Channeling my father, I gave the door a shove with my shoulder, thinking the wood may have expanded in the changing season. Nothing.

I double-checked the time and location on my schedule. This was it. This was where I was supposed to be. Finding someone who'd be able to help meant walking down a million flights of stairs *and* being late. I absolutely hated being late, but there was no other recourse. I turned to leave and made it a few feet down the hallway when my ears caught a sound. A faint scratching noise had come from beyond the alabaster door. *Shit. Maybe I woke up late. I bet they lock the doors on tardy Obligates!* A mild panic set in. I was faced with two choices: I could leave and go back to my room and pray they didn't take attendance, or I could knock and possibly piss off the instructor in the middle of their lesson.

Damnit. I figured the scolding I'd get for interrupting would be milder than the punishment for not showing up.

I rapped twice on the door.

Instantly it swung open, revealing a severe-looking man. He stood almost exactly the same height as me, which made it extremely disconcerting when he stared for several seconds, scrutinizing every detail of my face.

"It took you two and a quarter minutes to figure out that it was polite to knock on a closed door, and I am sure you were the picture of grace when you tried shoving your way through a solid piece of wood." The disapproving eyes finally left mine and glanced down at the pocket watch that lay across the open pages of a leather-bound notebook. "Chin up, you were not nearly the most uncouth," he said, shooting a look at Cinden. She was standing in the corner of the room brooding, and I could hear the angry little huffs of air she took from here. I just barely managed to stifle my laughter as each of her exhalations caused the furious little curls of her pinkish bangs to fly.

"That one screamed for the door to be opened for a solid thirty seconds before lifting a fist," he scoffed. "Enjoy the refreshments while we wait on those who made *no* effort at making themselves known."

Not one to shy away from snacks, I filled a little plate with hard cheeses and fruit and found a small but well-padded chair on the right side of the mostly bare room.

I watched the man I assumed to be our instructor. He never stopped moving, not once. He constantly circled Cinden, myself, and the table of food, only to start his circuit again, investigating things that I'd swear hadn't changed. His eyes flicked back and forth continually, and any time someone picked at the refreshments, he re-counted each of the offerings and jotted something in his book.

When I finished with the snacks, I sat my plate at the low table beside me and leaned back in my chair, watching him watch everything else. He was rather unusual looking, incredibly slight of build, but not skeletal like the priest had been. He wore aubergine pants that flowed around his legs and paired them with a ruby tunic, whose collar was pinned together with a silver dagger brooch.

"Get up!"

I startled awake to the sound of loud clapping next to my ear. *Fuck, I fell asleep.*

"We are fully assembled. Pass through the door at the back."

I hopped up from my chair and moved quickly away from him.

The room on the other side was about the same size as the one we'd just left, but that's where the comparison stopped. In this chamber, the floors were covered in a chevron-patterned carpet of violet and black. The walls were covered in ebony wooden panels that were carved into columns and arches. Between each column, a depiction of each of the phases of the Goddess's lifecycle had been masterfully painted on canvas. At the rooms center, a marble dining table, which looked to seat twelve, was topped with a lavender-and-gold runner which was woven to show large sunbursts and beautiful birds with their wings outstretched. Two floral arrangements, overstuffed with flowers of purple and yellow, sat on either side of a gold candelabra whose white tapers circled an extravagantly brilliant base.

Three people were already seated around the table. I exchanged a nod with a priestess and then caught the grass-green eyes of another guest between the candelabra's wide-set arms. I smiled a close-lipped smile at them, but it quickly turned into a full-on beam as the excitement of starting my first course caught up with me. The guest grinned back and fanned a wave of fingers. The motion made their tiered earrings sway and twinkle in a wash of glittering multi-colored stones.

A loud clap sounded, drawing everyone's attention to the front of the room.

"I am Lord Gotwig, your instructor, and so far, you are all failing this course."

He closed his gold watch with a snap! With the flick of a finger, he motioned those standing to take their seats.

"I wasn't aware the class had begun," whined the Solnnan Troth to my right, annoyed by his demeanor.

"It's obvious you aren't aware of much, madam," Gotwig retorted while flinging out his arm and pointing to a chair at the end of the table. The Troth moved silently toward the indicated spot. I seated myself in the chair nearest me before an insult could be hurled my way. I'd prefer being ignored over capturing his attention.

Damn, too late. As if reading my mind, he rotated toward me, never lifting his feet from the floor. I realized my mistake too late. I'd even *seen* the servants pulling out the chairs and pushing them in for the Troth as they sat. My impulse earned me a stern look and a full thirty seconds of furious scribbling.

"So sorry!" I apologized, hoping to make him aware that I understood my error.

"It's not that you lack the understanding of how to properly be seated—well, actually, you do." He rolled his eyes. "More importantly, however, it is that you sat in *my* chair." The tips of his graying mustache practically touched with the extremity of his grimace.

"Extract yourself, *now*." Gotwig fixed me with a sharp stare and didn't look away until I shoved backward in my chair. "My guess is you are the Nortian Troth?" I nodded. "I expected as much. They tend to be a people who give no thought to proper protocol, happy to blame their unrefined actions on the weather."

My eyebrows rose, but instead of firing off a quick retort, I shuffled around to the right, trying to put as much distance between me and Gotwig as possible. I dropped into a chair and reached between my legs to pull myself more snugly to the table and—*Fuck!*

Gotwig glowered. He compressed his already thin lips into a white line and darted his eyes to a spot behind my head. I already knew what I'd find, but I turned anyway–I couldn't look at him any longer.

"Again, I'm so sorry for my lack of... of... *refinement*," I apologized profusely to the liveried servant. His arms were still extended from where I'd yanked the chair from his hands. Graciously, he inclined his head.

"Don't apologize to the help." Gotwig rolled his eyes again, this time so dramatically his irises completely disappeared. "First lesson: do not *ever* sit at either head of the table unless you are hosting the soiree or you are the *reason* for the occasion. Of course, if you find yourself in the Monwyn court, the waitstaff will show you to your location and inform you of the order in which you are allowed to take your ease."

Opening his watch, he checked the time and snapped it closed so fast it startled the guest seated next to him.

"Second, as Troth, it is not only your kingdom you represent. Maybe even more importantly, you are the embodiment of this temple and the process of Obligation, that which holds the continent together and secures it from darkness. Do *not* embarrass us."

Still listening, I saw a set of servants bending down to speak to each Troth. I didn't want to mess up the next step in whatever this process was, so I paid close attention to their interactions. When the voice whispered in my ear, it asked which wine I'd prefer.

"Water, please," I said kindly. I couldn't blame the single glass of wine for how I acted under the stairs last night, but I wanted to keep sharp today.

"The current options are a dry red from the Rifted Monks or a fruity white from the vineyards of former Primus Monwyn," the servant replied.

Hoping to make up for my earlier faux pas, I asked for the white and thanked the servant. He cleaned the rim of my drinking vessel with a napkin and poured a full glass. I sipped the crisp liquid, thankful to have something in my hands. The wine's scent was sweet, a bouquet of apples and pears. I was used to the bold, warmed wines my grandmother served when she was alive. She'd always kept a large stock for when water was more difficult to come by.

"From this moment on, every movement you make should distinguish you from others, highborn or low. Every word that passes from your lips should receive careful consideration before being spoken." Gotwig motioned to a servant, who filled his goblet to the halfway point. *He chose the white!* It shouldn't have excited me so much to have chosen the same, but I needed a win.

A team of acolytes entered through the back of the room, and delicious smells wafted through the air. Plates laden with fragrant sausages and toasted loaves of bread were laid about the table, and a salad of root vegetables and leafy greens was tonged into the fine white bowls of our place settings. Half slices of what I thought might be grapefruit were served alongside tiny, three-footed crystal ramekins.

This was a challenge I was prepared for! I knew exactly what each of the four forks and three knives were used for and remembered which glasses and cups to use and which to avoid throughout the course of the meal. *Bless the Primus for those dinner invites.* Relief poured through me as the rest of the meal continued without complication... for me, at least. A burgundy-haired Troth puckered her lips after tasting what *did* turn out to be grapefruit, and she was admonished and told never to show any feelings about what was served unless they were complimentary. That's when we also learned that sugar from the small pots was meant to be sprinkled on the pretty pink fruit, lessening the bitter flavor. We were also told *twice* that had we been observant *at all*, we could have figured that out on our own.

I listened in on the conversation between Cinden and a non-Troth guest. Through that, I learned that one was a Solnnan emissary, here for the purpose of teaching Matters of Domestic Arts, and the other was a visiting priestess on pilgrimage, having come from Nortia a little over four months ago.

"Are you enjoying your time here?" I turned at the sound of a soft voice. In my earnest quest to be more observant, I'd all but forgotten the person sitting next to me. It was the guest with the stunning jewels and bright eyes.

"That's a loaded question," I smiled. "To be honest, it's a lot different than what I expected, and I'm finding it challenging to adapt to my surroundings."

"How so?"

"Well," I stared at their pink-painted lips while considering my words, "I think in my mind, I was coming to Verus a pre-made paragon of the Obligate process, and that's totally not the case. For example, I've insulted my very first instructor twice, oh no, *three times* since walking through the door." I chuckled and tossed my head toward Gotwig. "Also, in the last three days, I've had more eye-opening experiences than I had over a lifetime in

Nortia. I've decided I'm going to minimize those kinds of adventures and instead focus on why I'm here in the first place."

The perfectly manicured brows of my tablemate shot up and their burst of laughter filled me with friendly warmth.

"The Goddess wouldn't begrudge you having experiences while here. Life is about partaking in her gifts. Have you enjoyed your *dalliances*?" Those eyes lit up knowingly.

It was my turn to laugh now. Bashfully, I exchanged glances with my neighbor, whose wavy brown hair fell over their shoulder as they leaned in.

"In some ways, I have." I could feel my cheeks burn. "Nortia could be less than stimulating, so I feel a little behind the other Troth in terms of emotional maturity," my neighbor nodded their understanding, "and I've been putting myself into complicated situations before thinking them all the way through... which is pretty much the opposite of mature, you know?"

"I think all experiences are valuable, no matter how small or how impactful they may be. Ultimately, they add up to the total sum of who we are the moment we stand upon Merrias's blade." My neighbor twisted a gold ring around their delicate finger. "Don't fear life's experiences, instead seek to understand how they will harm or help you in becoming the self of your choosing."

The self of my choosing.

I mulled over the advice as I bit into a segment of grapefruit. There were parts of me, experiences I'd had, that I *knew* I was choosing to ignore. I'd not even *started* to process the attack in the stream and its emotional aftermath, though it kept popping into my mind when I least expected it. How could I use that experience to become the self of my choosing? I knew next time I didn't want to freeze. I wanted to take action—any sort of action—to try and protect myself from the violence used against me. Gammond forbid, if something like it ever occurred again, I may not be able to rely on others to deliver me.

Then there were the experiences I'd shared with the Monwyn men. On one hand, I absolutely wanted to continue exploring my sensuality, but I also didn't want it to be a game to get some invisible upper hand, as it had been with Tommand. And though I might very well like becoming the plaything of the big flirt, Ambrose, I would need to establish clear boundaries up front.

"Everyone, listen up." Gotwig clinked the side of his glass with a spoon, "This ends today's session, but a few notes before you leave." His predatory smile alarmed me.

Class was over? What did we learn? I wasn't the only Troth looking around confused. I glanced at Cinden, who shrugged and blew out her cheeks.

"As Troth, you will be dissected by everyone you encounter. Perhaps they wish to *be* you... perhaps they wish to use you. Many will seek closeness as a way to bind you to them. Others will shun you or praise you publicly in an effort to manipulate the opinions of those around you. You do not know them or their agenda, and they are *not* your allies." He flipped open his notebook and glanced down. "Remember these words: in all instances practice neutrality."

Gotwig rose and walked around the table.

"Luræna of Solnna, work to negate your over-animated body language. Your constant slumping and finger-tapping are a straightforward indication of your lack of engagement. Any host would be appalled at your reception of their hospitality and seek to cut ties with you."

The Troth openly blanched.

"Close your mouth. The word was *neutrality*."

Luræna's mouth snapped close so hard that her chin-length hair swung back from her face.

"Cinden of Gaea, you knew easily where I was at all times and tracked me to every location I moved. This is commendable. Keep sharp and observant above all." A look of triumph spread across her face, quickly replaced by a look of apprehension as Gotwig began again, "You will, however, issue an apology to my servant at once. He made me aware that you referred to him as a 'lowborn dog' when he didn't know which rift vineyard the wine came from. It will do you well to remember that people of lower status, especially those that serve another, don't owe you their silence... but do owe their masters loyalty. This level of childishness will impact the quality of your Assignment. Consider your actions."

Hearing Cinden squeak out an apology might have made me chuckle on another day, but right now, I felt too bad for her.

It went like this for two more Troth until I was nauseated beyond belief.

Finally, it was my turn.

His squinty blue eyes nailed me to the back of my plush seat.

"Eira of Nortia, from the moment you knocked upon the door, you have avoided people and excluded yourself from almost all table conversations. This may be because you were too busy observing the others around you or because you feel you are above mixing with the rest of the rabble. It truly does not matter which; either could harm your ability to make connections." He fingered the watch while he spoke, picking at its twisted chain. "When you did deign to engage in conversation, you divulged all manner of personal detail and used your dinner partner like a personal diary or childhood friend.

Do you even know to whom you spoke? Blind trust in others will set you up for not only personal scandal, but potential political failure. What you choose to tell others can be used to create a strong narrative. It is your duty to make sure it is *you* and not *them* in control of the content."

I didn't know where to look, so I stared at the hands folded in my lap. I had never felt this level of shame.

"Lastly," *My Goddess, he's not done,* "I had thought Cinden and potentially Eira were astute enough, but alas, they too will feel the effects of their deficiency. Not a single one of you noticed the differences in the way I or our three guests were served. There will be those who wish to harm, incapacitate, or simply intoxicate you enough to make you babble. Dried ipecacuanha was wiped onto the rims of your glasses right in front of your faces. In about an hour, every Troth in this room will become quite ill. Let this be a lesson. Think about the *why* of what you are seeing. Why would they clean your glasses and leave out those of the guests? What are the chances of you *all* receiving smudged glasses? If something seems off, even in the slightest, question it. Had you simply noticed without fully deducing, you could have just chosen not to consume the drink. The only agenda you will ever know is your own. Return to your rooms."

Still focused on the hands in my lap, I heard my stomach bubbling loudly. *What had I told my neighbor?* Shoving my anxiety aside, I stood and reached out to the person who'd gotten up to leave.

"Please, wait." My hand met their elbow. "If I was offensive, please forgive my foolishness."

"Oh, young one, there was no offense. Nothing I told you was an untruth and anything you told me I will keep to myself. It's just another experience to reflect upon."

I stuttered out my thanks and apologized again, truly remorseful.

"May I ask your name? It was rude of me to have not performed even the most basic rule of politeness!" I removed my hand from their elbow, to rest it against my churning stomach.

"Of course, I am most often referred to as... Them."

With one last gentle smile, they turned and walked out the door.

Too stunned to move, a servant, *bless them*, came to my aid and retrieved my chair, lightly pushing it against the back of my knees. They tucked me snugly into the edge of the table, and without missing a beat, pressed a clean napkin into my hand a split second before hot tears rolled down my cheeks.

This whole time, the Holiest of Holies, the High Mantle Themself, had been my dinner partner.

CHAPTER TEN

MORE SHITS, LESS GIGGLES

Perhaps, the most memorable of lessons are learned during the intense reflection you experience when both ends of your anatomy race to expel the contents of your stomach.

An hour after being poisoned, I found myself lying in a puddle of my own sweat.

"Nan, it's... again... it's... OH!"

Staring into the low bowl of water for the sixth time, I begged the Goddess to end my toxin-induced vomiting by whatever means she could provide: passing out, lighting strike... sudden death.

"Hush, my pup, the yammering makes it worse."

Nan hadn't left my side for a moment unless she was rewetting a cloth to blot my forehead. In between those times, she'd been pacing the room, distressed by how my first lesson had been carried out. That was until Marcyn stopped by to check on her. He'd been searching for honey to stem the stinging burn that Amias had acquired at *his* first session, and while he visited, he shared a stomach remedy with her. Now, a more chipper Nan consoled herself by breaking up mint leaves and muddling them into a cold, citrus infused glass of water.

"My girl, I've had time to think. I don't like the trickery that went on, but it's a lesson you won't soon forget, yes?" I squished my face against the cold stone wall and nodded.

"I'll be the most... observant fucking Troth they've created," I murmured.

"Shame on that mouth of yours!" she scolded. Nan hated when I cussed, so I rarely let it slip. "Your brain must be addled as well."

My nausea began to taper off after two hours or so, and though I dared not leave the bathroom, Nan deemed me well enough to recover alone. Before leaving, she braided my hair into a crown on the top of my head and soaped up the scabs on my wrist. They were almost completely healed over.

Recalling the Mantle's advice, I used the forced downtime for reflecting. Before coming here, I had been confident that I understood the role of an Obligate. I was to work on cementing relationships and overseeing negotiations that would lead to alliances that ultimately would help maintain order in the kingdoms. Not once did I assume that nefarious acts or purposeful manipulations would be a part of it... *I just wanted Nortia to have more oranges.*

The Mantle had witnessed everything in the session, which meant They condoned the methods used to teach us. I'd be a fool to ignore the message that intrigue and subterfuge would play a part in my future. I just wasn't sure I was right for the job now. I rolled onto my butt and sat against the wall. During tomorrow's lesson, I'd need to be as observant as Cinden and as calculating as Kairus.

Nan knocked and entered without waiting for a response and proceeded to pull the yellow dress I wore over my head. I didn't fight it; I just raised my hands above my head like a toddler being undressed.

"You stink, love. Roll into that tub while I send this to be cleaned."

Doing as she bade, I crawled to the tub and washed and scrubbed until I felt refreshed enough to toss on my too-big linen shirt and make my way into the room.

Kairus, who'd gotten back a while ago, sat on her bed, staring wide-eyed into the abyss. She looked like she'd been told the world was coming to an end or her father had gone missing or something equally as disturbing.

"So... how was *Matters of Unity*, Kairus?"

"I would rather not discuss it," she deflected, nodding her head up and down long after having answered.

"That bad?"

"Mmhmm, their methods of familiarizing us with *unity* are quite unorthodox."

More unorthodox than back-to-back episodes of puking and hours of cataclysmic diarrhea? The thought made my heart pound. If the sassiest Troth I knew had been dazed by the content, I didn't stand a chance.

A light tapping sounded at the door, and two folded parchments slid into the room. Kairus, still stupefied, didn't move, so I staggered off the bed, holding my woozy head, and picked up the missive with her name on it.

"Kairus Septimus, Troth of Monwyn, you are cordially invited to your First Maneuvering. We will begin promptly at seven-thirty in the courtyard."

Mine read the same.

I couldn't believe we were tasked with something else after the day we'd endured. Deciding we should nap before our first combined Obligate Maneuvering, I prayed that whatever was ahead of us didn't involve food.

··· ✦ ⟩)(✦ ···

Together, we walked out of the temple's main entrance and down the ramp that led to the courtyard. Surprisingly, despite the grandeur of the architecture behind us, the prayer yard was a simple, mostly dust-covered rectangle, sprinkled with shrines. I could count nine or ten altars from where I stood, and on each of the white stone structures were large metal bowls that contained offering fires. Acolytes and priestesses tossed prayers written on wood or paper scraps into the flames, and the smoke rose to the celestial planes, lifting their prayers to the gods' ears. Solid, round-top steles had also been erected between the altars and if they were like the ones back home, prayers would be carved onto their large flat sides.

I looked to the right of the field, where an assemblage of uniformed guards stood at attention. In the middle of their unit was Tommand. He was dressed in the darkest blue from head to toe and had the mightier-than-thou expression he favored plastered on his handsome face. The side of his keyhole neckline fluttered in the mountain winds, and my fingertips tingled, remembering the wavy hair I'd touched below his collar.

I heard another group of rowdy Obligates exiting the temple.

"Zotikos, I'm just glad it didn't take *my* eyebrows, I'd have nothing left if it had." Amias joked with the Scion who was not only missing a patch at his hairline but who, sure enough, only had half of his right brow remaining.

"Tell that to your tits, Amias!" Zotikos laughed and pointed at his bound chest; one of the pale markings on his multihued skin had turned an angry red above his bandage. The two of them walked out nearer the field and loudly greeted Greggen and Evandr, the Scion that Ambrose had been play-fighting with this morning.

It didn't take long for the other Obligates to gather, and when all were accounted for, Tommand strode forward, ever the commander, and motioned for everyone to sit on the large stone ramp. A few Scion remained standing, but most did what they were told without issue. I sat next to Kairus, and Greggen sat on my other side, cracking his knuckles. I saw many dour faces as I looked around and suspected a great deal of the people here had also received their comeuppances during the day.

"Set it there and rejoin your formation," Tommand addressed the guard at his side. Quickly, the guard set up a three-legged easel in front of our group, and working fast, he rolled out a large sheet of parchment and attached it to the flat surface using pins. Tommand strode forward and began sketching a diagram that looked like multiple *V's* that attached to each other—four at the top, two in the middle, and one at the bottom.

Was he leading this Maneuvering? I wasn't surprised to see an emissary with the group, I knew they could instruct as well as make their case for Obligate Assignments. I would've just assumed he'd taught something like, *Keeping Your Accounts up to Date* or *How Not to Change Your Expression for Days at a Time.*

"Obligates must work together to solve the host of issues that can and do arise in all kingdoms," he began, still focused on the board. "Threats to your people and selves can be both physical and political. They may come in the form of manipulation or as an all-out assault. I have worked to protect the King of Monwyn for fourteen years, and throughout those, I have been set upon by highwaymen, political rivals, and those whose only motivations seem to be reintroducing darkness into the world." He turned, studying our faces as he spoke, pacing back and forth, like some predatory feline.

"To protect themselves and their kingdoms, Scions must hone their abilities to make split decisions and build adequate forces out of anyone around them—young or old, frail or in good health. There are situations where you will need others to aid you." As if summoned, a handful of advisors, including Marcyn, and a larger crowd of acolytes dressed in plain robes walked into the courtyard.

Tommand walked back to the board and raised his hand to write. "Today's Maneuvering will go as follows. The eight Scion will serve as their team's commanders." He wrote the names of a Scion above each of the eight points of the *V's* on the top row. "Ambrose, Amias, Castor, Evandr, Greggen, Lok, Ozius and Zotikos."

"Your teams will consist of a mixture of Troth, guards, acolytes, and companions." As each passed in front of him, Tommand pointed at their chests and gave each a number, one through eight. He then did the same for each Troth. I was assigned four, placing me under the command of Evandr. Kairus had been given a two, which placed her on Amias's team.

"The rules and purpose of this Maneuvering are as follows. In the first round, your team of eight will be given two padded polearms, a rope that measures six feet in length, and a pitcher of water. Any of these items can be used in any capacity your team sees fit. The objective will be to successfully move specific items across the field of play."

Tommand's hand swept the courtyard in front of us. "The items must remain unscathed and must be taken past the gates where your opposing team begins. Lastly, the losing team will join the winning team after each match, forming a new, larger unit, led by the victorious Scion. Questions?"

"The women are expected to have polearms used against them?" Greggen asked, shaking his head in disbelief. "Surely not!"

"Thieves and madmen will spare no thought to the gender of their adversaries. They will mow them down like the rest... or treat them far worse," Tommand responded matter-of-factly, leaving "far worse" to be determined by the audience.

I swallowed a lump of fear and hoped the atmosphere would soon become more game-like.

"You will have fifteen minutes to discuss strategy with your teams, and then I will deliver the first item into your care."

Teams began to form and then peel off, distancing themselves from the others. I followed Evandr who stopped behind a stele on which was written a prayer to Gammond.

"Listen up, we gotta divide ourselves into units. Who here has fighting experience?" The two guards and a single companion, who introduced herself as Evon, raised their hands.

"Take these." Evandr thrust two long poles into the hands of the guards, "the rest of you, if their weapons fall, pick them up and strike with the padded end. Got it?" Tommand walked into our circle not long after the advice was given and listened to our commander continue his plan.

"Anyone in a dress or long robe, tie up everything that hangs and secure the extra material with your belts. You don't want to give the other team anything to grab onto or have the extra cloth slowing you down."

Seeing them struggle, I introduced myself and offered my aid to the two acolytes on my team. Lyta and Silinas were their names. Both had close-shaved heads and wore identical robes that split to their hips in the front and back.

"Here, we can pull the garment's sections around your waists and tie them behind your back. Are you okay with your... short pants showing?" I asked, looking at their brown-clad legs. I honestly didn't know what to make of the shapeless garments that cut off at their knees.

"Yes, it's fine. Surely the Goddess will forgive the sin of our bare legs this once," said Silinas.

"I'm sure there is something else we c—"

"I'm joking, I promise! We could go around naked if we wanted. Now, what if we split your dress up the front and back? Or rolled it above your hips?" Lyta leaned in and gathered my skirts in her hands. Evandr drew closer, sensing we were at a loss.

"Do you mind?" He pointed a finger at my legs. I shook my head, hoping our leader could figure something out. I didn't want to be a weak link. The Scion, who was even broader than Tommand, was built like a square, but despite that, he dropped nimbly to his knees and reached right between my legs.

"You—" Tommand stopped. "You have five minutes to head to the far left of the field. Your team will be in the first round of challenges, competing against team Ozius." After digging into a leather satchel that crossed over his chest, his hand emerged holding a delicate white teacup, decorated with red and gold triangles.

Evandr, still holding my skirts, unbuckled his belt and whipped it off with one hand. He secured it around my waist and then yanked the very back of my skirts forward, pulling them between my thighs and tucking them through the thin leather. It created what looked like a pair of puffy pants that stopped right above my ankles. I patted my hips and jumped up and down to test their security. Our commander nodded, pleased with his ingenuity. It definitely minimized the volume of fabric I'd have to deal with otherwise.

Walking into the small circle of our group, Tommand held out the dainty cup.

"Scion Evandr, your team will need to transport the object past your challenger's gate, fully *intact*."

"ARE YOU S—" I coughed loudly, covering my outburst. "Oh, goodness, excuse me." I thumped myself on the chest to sell the fake. "Are you...um, supposed to... keep the cup in plain view the entire time?" *Whew. Good on the fly.*

Tommand moved closer, looking at me in feigned concern and ignoring my question.

"Are you alright, Troth Nortia? If the *game* we play is too much, you can sit out."

"Thank you, Emissary... but I'm ready for *more*."

"Hmm." With a curt nod, Tommand walked away.

"I'm making the assumption that as a Scion of Gaea, Ozius spent more time in prayer than he did at martial practice." Evandr bade us follow him, and we moved toward our starting gate. "Therefore, I feel he will be conservative and play defense. We will take the opposite stance, striking at their hearts and charging directly through them." Forming the top of a triangle with the tips of his fingers he showed us how to line up. "Our two guards will stand at the front, clearing our path, using the weapons they've been given. Behind them will go Troth Farai, who I am putting in charge of the cup. Evon and I will flank her sides and if need be, meet additional threats in hand-to-hand combat." He bent to Evon to discuss their plan and handed her a fraying length of rope.

"Our two acolytes, Lyta and Silinas, will run with Eira, acting as our decoys. When I give the signal, you will find an opening and run toward the other team's starting gate. If we can draw their attention to the three of you, the rest of us can focus on getting Farai across."

My heart thundered as we walked together to the far side of the field. I was equally terrified and thrilled to be a part of this scenario but wasn't certain I had the physical stamina it required. On the other hand, with the amount of adrenaline rushing through me at the moment, I felt like I could run to the top of the temple.

The Troth next to me was tucking our teacup under her shirt, settling the delicate glass between her breasts for safekeeping.

"Can you see it sticking out?" My teammate turned to me, pushing out her chest and waving her arms about.

"I think we're good, you can see the handle stick out just a little when you move, but I don't think it's enough to draw attention," I told her honestly.

"Good enough for me. I'm Farai, by the way; we traveled here together." The Troth walked toward me, extending her hand. "Your advice to improve my horsemanship came in quite handy. I wanted to say thank you." She smiled widely, showing off a gap between her front teeth. The effect was enchanting on her slim, freckled face.

Butthurt Troth.

"You... you're welcome. I'm sorry I was so harsh that day. I have no excuse for it," I said, recalling the terse words I'd thrown her way and immediately regretting how I acted.

"Apologies accepted... as long as we get this cup across the gate." She winked.

I returned her infectious smile.

Gods, Eira, you were such a hag that day. She'd been struggling, and I'd shown her no sympathy.

I would've liked to continue speaking with her, but Evandr began to deliver more directives.

"Don't move into formation until we are halfway across the field. If we are ambushed before that, scatter and then regroup at the Shrine of Derros." Assessing our readiness, Evandr delivered this last command while striking us each sharply on the shoulder as he walked by.

From our vantage point, we could see the enemy team far off in the distance, standing between the upright poles of their home gate. Near the ramp, an audience gathered. I could only really make out Ambrose and Greggen, who stood a head higher than everyone else. Tommand and another man, who looked vaguely familiar, appeared on the top of an altar to better view the competition.

With a raised arm, the emissary hoisted a red banner in the air.

"Get ready..." Evandr's voice was steady but did nothing to calm me. Taking a cursory glance at Farai, I saw her face had gone green and she looked to be on the verge of illness. I reached out and squeezed her hand. She turned to me, sucking in a breath so deep the teacup's little handle became visible. I nodded at her assuredly, not at all confident myself.

Tommand's hand dropped.

"Run!" Evandr's barked order spurred the team to action.

The game had begun.

Following Evandr's lead, our unit wove in and out of the shrines that peppered the temple's front yard. It felt like our commander was testing the reactions of the other team, who had, as he had guessed, come out slowly. Their leader, Ozius, set his eyes on Evandr, and they never once left him.

Leading us to the far right of the field, our opponents hesitated briefly as a portion of their team split off. One unit headed toward the right side, away from us, and the others, cautiously, moved in our direction.

"That can't go unanswered. Left guard pursue!" Our nameless guard peeled off and dropped back. Like a herding dog, he rounded on the two who had separated from their flock and pressured them back. We slowed our pace from an all-out run to a jog, allowing Evandr to scope out our adversaries and their weaknesses. We were just approaching the middle of the yard when Ozius turned briefly to take measure of his team members' locations.

In that same moment, Evandr burst forward in an all-out sprint, and our team followed his lead. At the midpoint, still running, he held his hands up in the wedge shape, and we arranged ourselves into our triangular formation, barreling directly toward our competitors. My eyes stung and my lungs burned from the exertion, but I was too afraid to blink. I understood now that our opponents could easily exploit any advantage, no matter how slight or short-lived.

The closer we came, the more I was able to make out the faces of the other team. Some jerked their heads back and forth, confused as to their next move, and others looked determined, standing as solidly as the stone shrines that surrounded us. Veering right, Evandr aimed the point of our wedge at the gate and drove us even faster forward.

As if he had forced our opponents to make a premature choice, a companion darted out from behind a cluster of guards and acolytes. The woman went running in the opposite direction as we closed in tightly on their group. Evandr shouted to the guard in front of him to again break formation and give chase. Like a bolt, the armored man shot out, heading straight toward the fleeing woman. Just steps before making physical contact with the other team, I saw our guard swing his staff at the companion's legs, landing a blow with enough force to send her sprawling to the ground. *Shit! I thought he'd go easier.*

We encountered Ozius, whose wine-red hair was dripping with sweat. Weapon in hand, he stood at the head of his unit with an entirely confident expression on his face. When he realized the coming clash was unavoidable, he motioned his people forward, and they ran at us, preparing for engagement.

"EIRA, GO!" Evandr shouted.

This was it.

I pivoted hard.

I'd just seen Ozius take out our remaining front guard with a single, magnificent hit to the stomach, and the fear that spiked within me seemed to force my feet to move faster. I pushed off the ground with the balls of my feet. My steps felt strong. I saw Evon, with a rope-wrapped fist, momentarily engaging with the opposing Scion but didn't get a chance to see the outcome as I hauled ass away from the active fighting.

The two acolytes ran at my sides, having no trouble keeping up the pace, but all too quickly the sound of muffled grunts and shouts came from behind me. I shifted directions and was briefly afforded a peek at the small mob who pursued me on my new trajectory. I pivoted again and ran as fast as I could towards the enemy's gate, determined not to look back again.

Lyta disappeared from my peripheral vision.

The footfalls were closer now, and I could feel them pounding the ground at my back. A sinking feeling hit at the pit of my stomach when, to my right, Silinas's head snapped forward as she took a thrust to the back.

She crumpled.

I was alone.

Roughly twenty feet in front of me, and closer to their goal, I spotted Farai running hard with Evon acting as her shield.

Please let this end, please let this end.

A hand skimmed my cheek and then locked onto my shoulder.

I was back in the river.

I could hear the ripping of my hair and smell the foulness of his breath. The shadows danced in my vision.

Don't freeze, don't freeze, MOVE! He'll...

I fell to the ground but found my voice.

"GET AWAY!" I screamed until my ears hurt. "DON'T TOUCH ME! GET OFF!" I went hoarse. "DO NOT FUCKING TOUCH ME!" I threatened the darkness.

"Hey," a solid, but not brutal hand shook my shoulder, "Eira, you can stop now... you won." The words cut through the haze of fear that had trapped my mind.

I was safe.

I was in the prayer yard, curled into myself.

My throat was raw and I could taste blood, but I was safe. I looked up at Ozius, who wore a big smile, seemingly unaffected by what he had witnessed. "Your defense tactic was good, Troth Nortia. I stopped the moment I thought you were hurt." He held out his hand to help me up and then took my chin between his fingers. "Your lip's busted, but otherwise you'll heal."

"Thank you, Ozius." He saw me to the sideline, and on shaking legs, I made my way to the temple's ramp, where I watched three more scenarios play out.

The victors of the first rounds were Ambrose, Castor, Evandr, and Lok.

The losers joined with their conquerors, and we became teams of sixteen. I honestly didn't know if I could make it through another round, the first one having ended as it did, but all too soon we were called to take on Scion Lok.

Evandr had already formed a plan for this round, and in it, I was to play a much smaller role, *thank the Goddess*. The shorter team members were to run behind the taller ones and duck in and out of different shrines to throw off our challengers. It worked, and we won by bringing a small statue of a bowhead whale, the god Derros's symbol, across the opposing gate.

The final round was to be Monwyn versus Monwyn.

Ambrose had led his team to a second victory, and he and Evandr now stood on opposing sides of the field, thirty-one people at each of their backs.

The flag waved, and the last game was afoot. This time the objective was to move a wagon across the field, again passing between the gates where the other team started.

Now, armed with eight polearms, four ropes, and four pitchers of water apiece, the teams faced off. Evandr had broken our large team into units again, one to move the wagon, one to defend it, which he called a striker unit, and another to be used as scouts.

"Find out who has the weapons and report back. Stay far away." After issuing the order, the scouts left and then returned every few minutes to bring Evandr up to speed.

"Ozius and Lok are armed, as are several guards."

Evandr nodded and surveyed the field while the rest of us continued to push the slow-moving wagon.

For the longest time, it seemed like both teams were in a stalemate, solely focused on keeping the wheels turning.

"The enemy approaches!" yelled Scion Castor. He'd been our rear lookout.

"Strikers at the ready!" Evandr bellowed.

Our defenders flared out, surrounding the back of the wagon. They were made up of three squads of three people, each outfitted with a polearm and rope. I continued pushing the cart's back edge but wasn't sure I was being helpful at all. Regardless, I drove forward until my muscles burned.

The battle began behind me: grunts of pain and the thud of poles against flesh. I glanced over my shoulder and saw that a few members of our own unit had been tied together and dumped uselessly to the ground. Ambrose had chosen his attack team well, and in the distance, his grouping of Troth and companions were left alone, freely rolling their wagon, advancing their chances of victory. Our progression was slow, and we lost momentum every time we sent out new fighters to reform our dwindling striker supply.

"Damnit! Left side is stuck. Everyone to the front now. Roll it backward on three and then shove it to the right." We had become stuck on a rock, but under the guidance of Evon, the remaining wagon team was able to clear the stone that had impeded us.

"Everything okay?" Evandr asked, checking in.

"We lost a little water, but the pitchers survived," I reported.

Evandr's head snapped in the direction of the fighters, and he went running. Luræna, who'd taken a short break from pushing, returned to my side and resumed her efforts.

"I think we've been outfought," she mumbled.

"You might be right. Their wagon hasn't stopped once."

I looked around and surveyed the carnage. It wasn't good. Our numbers had continued to dwindle, and our fighters were rapidly tiring. Exhausted, I took a short break myself and watched a little drip of water roll off the back of the wagon and settle in the dirt.

"Luræna, I have an idea."

Evandr was being chased across the field, or I would have sought permission. I told the Troth my plan instead.

"Why not? It's better than waiting to get pummeled."

I went quickly to the rest of our unit and filled them in. They agreed that the loss of two of the remaining eight pushers didn't amount to a lot of muscle and they could keep the vehicle rolling.

"You ready?" I asked Luræna.

Her answer was to start grabbing pitchers from the wagon and handing them off to me. Together, we moved out, hiding behind the shrines, trying to keep away from the fights. It was slow going, trying to not spill any liquid as we went, but we didn't have much time to execute what would likely end up being a failed plan.

"When we get there, we have to move fast. I'm betting Ambrose keeps a close watch," I whispered.

"Okay, but keep telling me what to do. I'm not brave, Eira."

"You don't have to be brave, just... resolute."

"Alright," she swallowed.

Our home gate came into view, and the other team's wagon was still a solid forty feet away.

"Thank Goddess it's getting dark. That should help us a little. Now, once we get there, pour these out as quickly as you can. Come, on." Luræna and I hunched over as low as we could and ran to a spot about ten feet from the front of the gate. We poured the water onto the dirt-covered ground, but instead of sinking in and causing mud to form, it pooled on top and ran away in rivulets. "Fuck, fuck, FUCK!" I cursed while watching my plan fail.

Luræna dropped to her knees.

"Eira, come on, we're resolute." She started pawing at the ground, digging her fingers in, creating the thickest mud she could. I spotted the other team's pitchers near the gates, and though many of them had been drained, two remained quite full. I added the water to Luræna's mud trenches and joined her on the ground, putting all of my energy into expanding the channel.

"Let's shatter the pitchers and inset the shards in an arch around the gate," I managed to say between panted breaths.

"Yes! Do it," she replied. Her encouragement bolstered me.

I snatched a pitcher close by and slammed it onto the ground.

"Shoot, that was loud," I grabbed a sharp sliver and hacked at my makeshift pants until I'd cut away almost all the material of one leg. Trying again, I grabbed another pitcher and wrapped it loosely in the cloth before smashing it. "That's better." Four pitchers later, a good-sized line of jagged clay was laid out.

"PEOPLE AT THE GATE!" cried a voice in the distance.

No amount of darkness could hide us now.

Their armed combatants came running back to the wagon's defense and discovered our makeshift barrier.

I spotted Ambrose. He barely looked winded at all, but instead of running at us himself, he motioned three men to give chase and turned back to the fray.

"Luræna, run!"

She shot off without hesitation while I jammed a few of the remaining fragments into the ground. Finally satisfied, I got to my feet and ran, only to find myself intercepted by a guard who jumped out from behind a nearby stele.

He had no weapons that I could see, but he moved in ways that told me he didn't need them. We circled each other, and I mimicked his stance, not knowing what else to do. His right hand struck out quickly, but he couldn't keep his grasp on my forearm. I was more prepared for his next strike and met his hand as it struck out like a snake. My knuckles collided with his, and he managed to grab my bicep, but again, he wasn't able to keep hold of my mud-slicked arm when I yanked it back.

The guard froze.

He stared blankly at me for a few seconds before looking down at his naked hand. His glove had come off in the scuffle. There was a sudden, unexpected stillness and before he had time to register my intent, I lunged at him and snatched at his other glove, which came off with no resistance.

"Lady Troth," as if burned, he pulled his naked hand away, "come no closer."

In my best impression of Ambrose, I threw my head back and laughed more freely than I had in weeks... and then I gave chase.

The guard backed up, both hands raised in a plea, before turning on his heel.

"These stupid gloves are useful after all!" I sang out.

I knew I was running toward the enemy, but I didn't care. I chased the guard past his wagon, past a handful of fighters, and right past Ambrose, who flung his arms wide and tugged me flush against his torso.

"I barely touch you and already you throw yourself at me. How utterly scandalous."

I tilted my head back and smiled into his amused face.

"You want a real scandal? Look over there." From my position, I could see that our trenches hadn't worked to trap the wagon's wheels as I had intended, but they did make the other team's pushers slip around in the mud while the pottery shards kept them on their toes. They lost just enough time to give team Evandr the ten-second lead they needed.

"Well done, clever harpy. Have you thought of my consolation prize? I do hope it involves more *physical* conditioning." I heard the whoops and hollers from my teammates in the distance and beamed. "Congratulations," Ambrose whispered in my ear.

"Thanks!" I reached up and grabbed his already bent head and planted a sloppy, muddy kiss on one side of his face and then the other.

Still holding me in his arms, he tossed his head back and burst into howling laughter... and I didn't stop myself from joining in.

CHAPTER ELEVEN

TO THE VICTOR

The demeanor of the Obligates I knew yesterday had changed in a single evening. Somewhere out on the field, our formalities had been tossed off and left to die. We gathered under the light cast by the outstretched arm of Mossius, while it burned through the night.

Kairus was lying on her side, her head cradled in a thoughtful-looking Amias's lap. Her dress had ripped from shoulder to hip, but she didn't seem to care. She'd made no attempt to fix it or the makeup that had smeared down her face. I searched the crowd for Farai and found her with Evon. The freckled Troth was plucking blood-matted hair from a gash that started at the companion's lip and extended down to her chin. I made a mental note to revisit our conversation from earlier, wanting to again apologize for judging her at a time when I should have rendered aid... like she was doing now.

"Evon only got away because *you* busted up my eye." Ozius barked. Evandr's mouth fell open. I could hear the boom of his laughter from the other side of the ramp. Both Scion sported the telltale purpling blotches of what would tomorrow be black eyes, but for now, competition forgotten, they laid on their backs resting their heads on their arms.

"Come on man, you doubted her strength, and *that* was your downfall. She popped you so hard your daddy saw Derros," Evandr joked.

"And you all thought the water was for drinking." Greggen teased Ambrose, whose beard was so full of dirt it had turned light brown.

He hadn't left my side since crushing me into his arms during the final match, and now I sat between his outstretched legs, reclining on his chest. I closed my eyes against the exhaustion but still managed a satisfied smile while listening to their banter.

"Fighting is thirsty work," Ambrose claimed. "And do not even think about taking credit for the harpy's idea. It was fucking brilliant!" My head bounced against his chest with the rhythm of his laughter.

"You think you could have done better, Emissary?" I heard Lok's acerbic comment and opened my eyes to find him and Tommand walking toward us.

"This is not about my capabilities, Scion Lok. This is about your ability to listen to an expert's advice and apply it where necessary." Tommand's reply was met with a sneer from the young Scion.

"An expert? Until I've seen you in action you will remain, in my mind, a *tutor*." Lok spat out the last word as if teachers were a people to be looked down upon.

"Tommand would toss you on your ass before you could raise your hand, Lok. Watch yourself," Ambrose said, suddenly going stiff.

Tommand remained silent and began to walk away.

"Show me then, *tutor*." The challenge hung in the air. Every Obligate in a fifteen-foot radius turned their attention to where the two men faced off.

"Perhaps if you were at full capacity. It would not be fair to accept a—"

"Take us all on, *Tom*," Ambrose instigated.

I smacked my hand down on the big thigh that cradled my hip.

"He's one man, asshole. Why would you do that?" I sat up and swiveled so I could look him in the eye.

"One man can do more damage than you think, beautiful harpy." He wrapped an arm around me and pulled me against his chest. I obliged the possessive touch and snuggled closer to his warmth

"Yes, and eight ca—" my retort was cut off by a low rumble. Angling my head, I shifted back just before his bloodied knuckles came to rest on my cheek.

"Wiggle those again and your clothes come off," he whispered.

"It was an innocent snuggle, I'm sleepy," I scoffed.

"Bullshit." Ambrose slid his hand to the base of my neck and jerked my head forward. Before I could protest the treatment, he brought his mouth crushing down on mine and pressed his tongue against my lips seeking entry.

Instinctively, I opened to him.

A rush of warmth spread throughout my body. His tongue rubbed my own, flicking lightly in and out of my mouth. *Is everyone watching this? Do I care?* He licked at the stinging cut I'd received in the Maneuvering and let out a low growl.

"Be careful. If you fuck on the temple floor, the Goddess gifts you triplets!" Zotikos hollered.

"Oh... ohhh, Ambrose you big-dicked bull, take me here on this ramp!" Someone in the crowd teased. Others panted heavily or screamed out obscenities. Egged on by the commotion, Ambrose tilted my head further back, granting himself better access.

I sighed against his mouth. Chills raced down my arms, and a luscious tightness snaked its way through my stomach and lower.

"I accept."

The statement barely penetrated the fogginess of my thoroughly preoccupied mind.

Ambrose smiled against my mouth and all around whistles and whoops could be heard. I wasn't sure if they were intended for the steamy display or the promise of entertainment to come. Either way, my breathing was erratic from both possibilities.

"When I win, we will move this back to my chamber." He didn't wait for a response but jumped up with the other excited Scion.

"Why do men like to fight so much?" Cinden asked from somewhere behind me.

"According to my mother, they like swinging their fists as much as their dicks." Yemail-rys crowed while sliding nearer.

I laughed along with the others until Kairus dropped down next to me, having lost her comfy pillow.

"What was *that*?" she questioned in an overly eager voice. She took my hand in hers and placed them on her fevered face. "I didn't know where to look, but I couldn't look away!" She laughed out loud and drew closer while pushing the strap of her underdress back on her shoulder. "Has that happened before?" she asked, nudging me with her arm.

"Not like that," I giggled. "I'm not sure I'll be able to look at him again."

"No problem... just have him mount you from the back."

"Kairus!"

We put our heads together, sharing in a fit of giggles.

The scene in front of us began to unfold and, kiss forgotten, all eyes were glued to the men who stood on the field. Yelling the objective at the top of his lungs, Lok dared Tommand to get from where he stood—approximately twenty feet from the others—to the altar directly behind where the eight Scion were milling about.

"Fine," Tommand said blandly as he tightened the laces of his boots and stretched down to touch his toes.

"Do you always stretch before apprehending highwaymen, *Protector*?" Castor heckled. Tommand ignored him and went about pulling his shirt over his head.

Oh, glorious Gammond.

Given an unimpeded view of what my hands had so scandalously touched before, my body sparked to flame. *If Ambrose is an appetizer, Tommand is the main course.*

Tommand stretched his neck from side to side and rolled his well-muscled shoulders backward. He wasn't the chiseled, carved perfection you knew Ambrose would be, instead, he was something entirely different—where Ambrose's body was a display, Tommand's was a tool. From the lip-smacking going on behind me, I knew the others saw it too. I could barely resist the urge to walk out on that field and run my hands down the heavy biceps that had been hidden by his shirt. My mouth went dry at the sight of the wavy hair that began at his collarbone and trailed down the plane of his stomach... and then below the waist of his pants. Hearing the reactions of the other women, I felt oddly proud to have touched what they seemed to covet. His olive-toned skin was bathed in the firelight of a nearby altar.

"Gross, he's got a hole in his side."

"I think it's sexy," Luræna said to the gaggle of Troth.

Me too, Lu, me too. Standing illuminated, I saw two large scars on his torso. One was newer, still pink but healed, and the other much older. Someone whispered the word "mutilated" nearby, but to me... I saw nothing but a survivor. The longest of his scars began at the point of his shoulder and slashed diagonally across his chest, stopping at the center of his breastbone. The other looked as if something had tried to gouge out his insides. The wound hadn't knit together well, and the angry mark reminded me of a knot in a tree's trunk. It started below his left ribcage and flared out in an oval that extended down past the waist of the loose pants he wore.

"So, both of the Monwyn men?" Kairus questioned.

"Don't be ridiculous."

"You are *actually* panting, Eira." Kairus leaned into my side. "I find Monwyn men to be the least attractive. They are conceited and act like animals. I prefer a stoic man who doesn't need to be the center of attention." Her head drifted in Amias's direction where he spoke with Castor.

"I didn't know *that* was under his shirt! can I surrender now?" Greggen directed the jibe at Tommand.

"Let's do this!" A hubris-high Lok yelled while twisting his shoes into the dirt to gain traction.

Tommand inclined his chin.

All at once, Greggen and Ozius shot forward, running at full speed.

I expected Tommand to evade, but instead, he raised both fists and moved calmly to intercept the faster of the two charging men.

Ozius never stood a chance.

As he reached out to grab his would-be prey, Tommand lazily slapped his hand away, and then, fast as a shark's jaw could snap, he surged forward, hooking a foot behind the taller man's knee. With his left arm, Tommand pushed at Ozius' chest, and with his right, he drove a fist into the man's jaw, sending him to the ground.

Greggen, only a step behind, used the opportunity to loop his arm under Tommand's and twisted it roughly in an attempt to restrain him. The emissary made no attempt to wrestle free. Instead, he snapped his head back with such force I feared Greggen's nose would shatter. After sinking to his knees, the tree-tall Scion covered his face, trying to staunch the flow of blood that had begun gushing from both nostrils.

Tommand shot off, now the aggressor.

His third adversary was Amias. With arms out in front, palms open, Amias crouched down lower than seemed comfortable. He struck fast, landing a heel strike to Tommand's stomach and another to his face. The emissary's head snapped to the side, absorbing most of the impact, and he recovered quickly.

The light that showed in Tommand's face made the others seem less alive. His broad, blood-stained grin turned his face into nothing short of a masterpiece. Ambrose may have been born to serve the Goddess, but Tommand would be the one who'd storm the realms to protect her. He was feral, powerful... a warrior-king.

I held my breath.

My choice was made.

His smile deepened, revealing a dimple near the left side of his mouth, and it was like the tiny divot had a direct connection to the cluster of nerves between my thighs.

Ambrose who?

Tommand's hand flashed at Amias's face, forcing him to lean away, but as the Gaean regained his center of gravity, his head connected with the forearm side of a well-timed elbow. Amias went down hard.

As Tommand turned toward his goal, Ambrose snuck up from behind and tackled him, knocking them both to the ground. They grappled fiercely, doing their best to gain a solid handhold on one another, but Ambrose couldn't manage to grasp the sweat-slicked skin of his companion.

In an effort to regain the upper hand, Tommand gathered his legs under himself and wrapped his arms around the Scion's thighs. He leveraged his weight and thrust forward, dumping Ambrose backward. The giant Scion smacked the ground so hard that white clouds of dust swirled in the air around him. Hands up in defeat, he stayed down, laughing between his gasps for air.

The remaining Scion formed a unit and approached the still grinning, now more bloodied Tommand. They attacked at once, throwing shots left and right. They tried to surround him, but Tommand moved so fast and fluidly that he was unable to be pinned.

Zotikos' arm was caught, and a well-placed kick took out his knee. Castor rained heavy blows upon Tommand's back, but with a twist of his torso, Tommand grabbed the Gaean's red braids and snapped his hand so forcefully it bent the Scion double. Tommand's knee met Castor's rapidly dropping head and Castor met the ground.

"Damn, he moves fast," Luræna exclaimed. She was right. Tommand never stopped. He moved around constantly and stayed light on his feet.

Balling his fists, Tommand drilled into Lok's stomach so hard that the wide-eyed Scion staggered two steps before folding onto himself and dropping into a heap.

Evandr was the only one left standing.

Tommand whirled in his direction and prowled toward him like a predator stalking his prey. Evandr bravely held his position as Tommand approached.

Time slowed to a standstill.

The grounds were so silent, it seemed even Mossius had hushed his roaring flame.

As quickly as the eye could blink, Tommand shot out and snatched Evandr's hand.

The square-shaped Scion flinched and quickly pulled a knee across his leg to defend his crotch. It was a wasted movement—Tommand had stopped his attack and was now shaking Evandr's arm up and down as if the two had just met.

Screaming their approval, the crowd went wild!

The participants, in various states of discomfort, made their way back to us. Greggen's nose had stopped bleeding and, though puffy, didn't look worse for wear, and Ozius's lip was purpling nicely to match his right eye. Ambrose limped slightly as he came to sit in front of me.

"Tommand?" I questioned the half-dressed man casually strolling back to the sideline. He turned to hear me. "Forgive me if I'm wrong, but were you not supposed to make it past the altar?"

"She's right!" hollered Lok.

I just couldn't help myself. I knew it was petty to one-up him after he so handily destroyed my attempts at seduction, but I really wanted to watch those magnificent muscles rippling while he ran.

There was only a brief pause before eight angry Scion began chasing a half-clothed dignitary across the field.

··· ✳)(✦ ···

The scent of apples clung to my skin after scrubbing away the blood and dirt that had caked onto every surface of my body. I'd found dried mud sticking to the backs of my knees, and in the creases of my thighs, and enough of it had seeped into the stitching of my shoes that they were ruined.

My calves were on fire and burned and pinched every time I flexed my toes. I could feel the outline of my biceps, inflamed and swollen, and the level of pain I felt when stretching the tight tendons in the back of my thighs made me think of Farai and how, were she here, I'd be begging her to rub oil into my muscles, pleading for her forgiveness. Keeping as still as possible, I balanced on the edge of the immersed bench, trying to think of something, anything, other than the discomfort that came with movement.

The Maneuvering had been extreme, and so had my first session. Had I made the same choices in real-world scenarios, I'm not sure I would have survived either of today's encounters. With no indication I'd been duped, the poison would have taken me out, and were Ambrose a true enemy, I'd be dead or captured, or worse. Going forward, I needed to be more focused on my surroundings and more thoughtful about who I trusted. That applied not only to my Obligate responsibilities but also to what Kairus had dubbed the "Monwyn Situation" as well.

I mean, what are the chances that two incredibly attractive men who come from the same kingdom would be interested in the same random woman? Tommand had confirmed he was aware of the moment Ambrose and I had shared, and yet, he had touched me anyway. *That didn't seem like the healthiest of Advisor and Scion relationships. I wonder if Tommand had told Ambrose about dinner?*

My first explanation for how they acted was jealousy, but I shut that down as a potential because it made *me* seem like too big of a deal.

Competition, that's what this is about. They were clearly both competitors and odds were I was being used for sport. *Maybe I could become the third competitor in our little game... maybe?* With my luck though, I'd screw something up and get kicked out. I could just see my mother's shock and disappointment when I handed her the note that read, *Madam, we regret to inform you that your child has become too horny to continue her Obligate training.*

Were I not an Obligate, maybe then I'd be up to the task of taking them both on.

Ambrose appeared in my mind's eye. I felt so small and feminine in his arms, and I could just imagine the delight I'd have in loosening his dark braid and letting it fall around his shoulders. He'd bend down to take my mouth, and that skilled tongue would part my lips again.

I ran my hands along my collarbone and down my breasts, lightly skimming my rosy nipples, imagining a pair of larger hands replacing my own. Drifting lower over my hips and lower still, I let myself explore beneath the water's surface. Remembering the flick of his tongue, I touched the cluster of nerves at my apex and drew little circles around the sensitive skin. What would it be like if his hand were here? Would his touch be as possessive as his mouth had been? My nipples hardened at just the thought. He would look down at me with those mossy colored eyes or... or... were the eyes brown? *Oh, yes...* they were cinnamon-brown, with pupils ringed in a beautiful golden sunburst.

I inched my hand lower and dipped a finger into my passage, sliding it in until it could go no further. Working my finger slowly in and even more slowly out, I remembered the thickness of Tommand's arousal. When I touched him there, his skin had felt as smooth as the fabric of my velvet dress, but his erection was remarkably hard, like it was carved from wood.

Delicious pressure built between my legs.

I remembered the feeling of Tommand grinding his hips into me, and how it felt knowing I'd been the cause of his frustration. I slid another finger alongside my first and moaned softly. Laying my head on the stone ledge of the tub, I pumped firmer and faster until I felt myself clenching around my digits. Tommand's bloody smile appeared in my mind, but he wasn't chasing after the Scion, he was thrusting himself into me, telling me that nothing felt as good as my body tightening around him.

My passage tensed and spasmed while I stroked that delightful spot within, and with one last inhale, my climax surged. Wave after wave of pleasure coursed through me, making every inch of my skin feel gloriously sensitive. Chest still heaving, I found myself quite satisfied and much more relaxed than I had been.

Maybe now I can get them off my mind.

As I dried and dressed, I had to laugh at myself. I knew very well that a few moments of my own handiwork wouldn't be enough to evict them entirely from my thoughts.

A skittering noise sounded at the door the moment I lay down.

Familiar enough at this point, I turned my sore neck and saw that sure enough, a missive had been slid under the threshold. I tried not to wake Kairus as I lumbered stiffly across the floor.

To Eira Chulainn, Troth of Nortia, do we send greetings! Your presence is required two days from today. Fourth level, room twenty-three, seven in the evening.

I laid the parchment on a low stand at the end of my bed, where I kept the other notes I'd received and crawled back into bed.

CHAPTER TWELVE

EXPERIENCES

I was thirsty.

I was so parched I thought I might pass out. But if I did, I didn't know what nefariousness would befall my unconscious form.

I stared at the crystalline pitcher that sat in front of me. The lecture had now spanned into its sixth hour. I flicked my eyes to Cinden, honing in on the weary expression she wore. Her eyebrows hung low on her forehead, and she chewed her bottom lip, staring as if entranced at the vessel that mocked us both. I pointed at the pitcher and shrugged, scrunching my face in question. The Troth shook her head and placed a hand on her stomach. My sandpapery tongue dragged across the roof of my mouth, and I prayed for the moisture that I knew wasn't coming.

I nodded my head ever so slightly. She was right. After yesterday, trusting any of the instructors was risky. Even now my eyes tracked our teacher, who was repeatedly tapping her index finger on a hand-drawn map of the most southern kingdom. So far, Former Primus Meridett, had been an outstanding orator and magnificent font of knowledge... which concerned me all the more. *She had means, motive, and opportunity.*

"Alright! So, Solnna's major exports include—but are not limited to—fine items and luxury goods. They are known for their fabric districts and fine woven materials, and you won't find better silks and linens anywhere on the continent!"

I watched our teacher clap her hands happily together. *Totally faking it.*

"Due to their warm climate, a variety of natural dyestuffs are grown there, giving them the ability to turn basic fabrics into colorful works of art. Their formulas are state secrets effectively creating a monopoly on many sought-after materials. You know, a Troth once divulged a single ingredient to a visiting merchant, and they found her corpse a few days later, bound in a blanket of the same periwinkle hue she'd blabbed about."

Meridett flung her arms wide and shook her head remorsefully. "I'm joking. Look at all of you!"

Are you, though? Are you actually joking, you... energetic little bundle of terror.

She went and stood in front of a wide board that stretched across the entire back wall. Four polar-bear-sized parchments were hung from it, and on each she'd written the name of a kingdom in a heavy, sprawling hand. For the past hour, maybe two, the tiny woman had diagrammed the overland and maritime trade routes of the continent, shifting a small riser almost constantly to reach any blank spaces that she'd yet to fill.

Unlike Gotwig's short-lived lesson, she gave no indication that her lecture was near its end, and if I was being honest, minus the thirst and newfound paranoia, I could have listened to her all day.

I studied the former Primus, observing her closely. I watched the way she moved and listened to the way she spoke, trying to discern what her mannerisms and idiosyncrasies could tell me about who she chose to present herself as. From the way she talked about it, I deduced that the interconnectedness of the continent's kingdoms was her area of expertise, and without a doubt, she had a keen eye for what was worth trading and to whom. She often offered up advice as to what bargaining chips could be used to clinch deals, and which should never be used in economic matters. For example, I took extensive notes on marriage proposals and betrothals. You could absolutely use those types of agreements to secure arrangements, but any form of enslavement or servitude without an indenture contract was a hard no.

One thing I noticed and liked about our instructor was that when asked a question, she would pause, and really think, formulating her answer before she spoke. The habit made for a few awkward minutes of silence, but her answers were masterfully crafted, and each word she chose provided us with an abundance of clarity and context. I also liked the way she inflected her voice when she spoke. It gave her an air of true enthusiasm and it made me feel that her true passion was the acquisition of knowledge. *Shit, I'm falling under her spell.*

This morning, I woke up physically ill, thinking about who we would encounter after yesterday's attempted murder. So far though, from everything I'd seen, she seemed Gotwig's antithesis. The only apparent similarity they shared was their noticeably small statures. While he was older, I'd place her in her fourth decade, as she had only the beginnings of light webbing around her eyes. Where he reminded me of a pale rodent, Primus Meridett was a vibrant and intelligent lemming, the most adorable and industrious of creatures from back home.

Currently, I watched her struggle to swap out the nib of her pen. She'd been wrestling with it for a few minutes now and seemed totally immune to the fact her endeavors had coated her hands in black ink.

"There!" she shouted triumphantly, holding the repaired stylus in the air. The skirts of her dress danced around, and I noticed both new and old ink stains on the blue-striped fabric. Back at it, she bounded, literally jumping, back and forth between parchments, drawing connections and regaling us with what relationships tied the kingdoms together and what could, in the span of a conversation, tear them apart.

"A Gaean will find it incredibly rude if you attempt to press an offer before they have been given ample time to reflect on the eventuality through prayer." She placed her hands on her brow, which left a dark smudge on her forehead. "Hear me well, make your offer in the morning, and then allow them time for reflection. After a few hours' time, let them know that you would be so very pleased to continue the discussion *after* their evening rituals. You may even offer to join them in their daily ablutions and services if you are so inclined. Piety goes a long way in gaining their favor, but be forewarned: they *will* recognize insincerity."

I closed my eyes in an effort to convince myself that my eyelids weren't sticking to my eyeballs from dehydration. I was so close to just jumping off the blade and taking whatever consequence came.

"Oh! Have you all been told not to touch the hair of a Gaean Obligate? Troth or Scion, their hair is considered a prayer, off limits to anyone, barring their life mates. Now, I'm not saying that you would, but it has happened and ended up costing the Monwyns a major economic opportunity."

Of course it was the Monwyns. Just last night Tommand snatched Castor's braids so violently it felled the man.

What's that noise? Don't do it, Cinden!

A heavy slosh turned into a steady pour.

I peeked opened my left eye to see Primus Meridett standing directly in front of me filling a glass with water.

"Now, on to the subject of Nortia." The woman continued pouring until the glass was full. "In this kingdom, the exports do *not* tend to be considered luxuries." She lifted the glass to her mouth and took a fast swig. "Instead, they deal in items of industry and agriculture, as well as many products from their fishing fleets." Without stopping her lecture, she set the glass in front of me and winked a walnut-wood colored eye.

I was going to trust her. Maybe she conned me into it, or maybe I was stupidly gullible, but, the choice made, I brought the glass to my mouth and drank deeply, listening to her between loud gulps.

Cinden turned unblinking eyes on me. For a solid minute, she stared, I assume to ensure I didn't drop to the ground or start foaming at the mouth.

"This very temple procures its lamp oil from the Nortian whalers, and similarly, many of the combs, plates, knitting needles, and netting shuttles used around the continent are made from the whalebone sourced there," Meridett continued.

From the corner of my eye, I watched Cinden pour a glass so full she had to slide it across the table and lean over the vessel to drink the water down. Like a thirsty kitten, she made joyful little mewls in the back of her throat.

"Monwyn is a kingdom with truly unique economic customs, largely due to its geographic isolation. The mountain ranges that surround their capital make travel difficult and its most eastern side borders the sea, which becomes effectively cut off due to snow and sea ice that forms in the north. Now, they *are* able to consistently trade with Solnna by water, as the kingdom lies due south, but they find themself cut off entirely from the north for at least six months out of the year, meaning they have to stockpile and monitor their oil reserves closely."

It was odd to hear someone speak so candidly about Nortia, but it was wonderful hearing that my homeland was integral to the continent. I loved living on the eastern side of the gulf, even though it could be inhospitable to travelers. Watching the crashing waves and the freezing sea spray coat the shore was a favorite pastime of mine. Massive curling icicles as tall as Ambrose would form all over the lighthouses and piers, making Silverstep look like something straight out of *Magika*.

"Despite the fact that Monwyn is isolated, their reserves of marble, malachite, quartz, and gold make them the wealthiest kingdom on the continent."

At just the mention of malachite, the Gaeans in the room sat up straighter and leaned toward the Primus. Rizellan had told me that the people of her kingdom practically lived for the variegated green rock. They wore it, used it in their rituals, and Cult Mossius relied upon it heavily in their medical practices.

"I've written several primers detailing the economic functionings of each kingdom and have copies for you. Please take volume one from this pile," she hefted the stack in her left hand, "as well as volume two, which contains a valuable bit of information on the more eccentric cultural habits of each," she lifted the other stack. "It's never too early to learn that if you want to make friends with a Solnnan, you greet them with a kiss on the lips!"

Luræna sputtered behind me, filling the room with her rich laughter.

"I'm kidding again." Meridett's face split into a grin. "But you *will* want to treat them like a member of your own family and not with the detachment some other kingdoms seem to value in their diplomatic relations."

I took a copy of each pamphlet as she walked by.

"Troth Chulainn, stay after for a moment. Everyone else, I truly appreciate your willingness to learn about our world... you may leave." She shifted the remaining journals to one hand to wave at each Troth as they made their exit. Luræna, eyes crinkling, glanced over her shoulder and mouthed "You're in trouble" and then stuck out her tongue.

Primus Meridett waved me over.

"Have a seat." She straddled a chair and rested her chin on its high back. "How is Adrielle? Well, I hope?" she inquired.

"I'm sorry, who—"

"Oh! Of course... How is the Primus of Nortia?" She ran her hand through her hair, and a wide grin broke over her face.

"Well, she seems to be... good. Maybe? I saw her the day I left, and she seemed as she always did, focused, immersed in her duties." And that was the truth. Our Primus had to be one of the most focused humans I'd ever known. She was in work mode at all times, constantly digging into what needed to be done to ensure the success of her post.

"Good, that's when she's at her best." Tinkering with the gold hoops in her earlobes, Meridett paused. "She was my mentor before I was elected to the Gaean Primerate... I miss her guidance often."

I nodded, wondering how the strict northern Primus had dealt with this life-filled, ball of energy.

"Anyhow, you are the first Nortian Troth, or Scion for that matter, that I've seen in at least three years, maybe four. Are the whale populations increasing after their last migration? I know there were concerns about the number of calves being born. Oh! And the fur trappers? I still have a pair of fur-lined trousers that Adri—the Primus gave me. That must have been twenty years ago—couldn't fit them now if I tried!"

···✦)(✦···

"You missed dinner. You love dinner!"

Back in our room, Kairus was changing out of a slinky purple gown that had golden mountain-like triangles sewn to its hem.

"We ended up just eating in her office. She had little pouches of snacks and treats from all around the continent, and, by the way, I know where I want my Assignment to be. I'll have to get used to the zealots, but the Gaeans have the most delicious... everything. Fruits and nuts and have you ever had a persimmon? So sweet and soft and bright."

"Eira, your Nortian is showing." She rolled her eyes and smirked. "Of course I've had a persimmon."

I threw my finger into the air, right in front of her face and she dramatically clutched at her chest feigning injury.

"Have you ever thought of becoming a Primus?" Her profoundly blue eyes met mine. "You would be free to make your own schedule, you could talk about whales for hours... and no one would ever question you for missing dinner." Her playful grin didn't quite reach her eyes.

"Kairus?"

"Hmm?"

"Do you not want to be here? As a Troth?" The room felt smaller the moment the question passed my lips.

Kairus laid back and stared at the ceiling. "Frankly, I have never felt called, and sometimes this whole thing just seems ridiculous. To think that a person born under some random sky is to be considered greater than another has always felt wrong to me." She rolled over on her side and propped her head up. "Also... I just feel like it is *not* okay that we are expected to give up our own autonomy. Eira, we have *no* input."

"But the Goddess gave—"

"The Goddess gave us lives to live and minds to think. Why would she want others to choose what we are allowed to become... to do?" Her mouth tightened.

I sat up on the edge of the bed but stayed silent. I hadn't been prepared for Kairus's honesty, not really. I expected her typical backhanded comment, but her unfiltered answer hit me harder than a jibe ever could. Her viewpoint was sobering.

"Maybe it will shock you, but before coming here I decided to experience as many things as I could, knowing it would all end when I received my Assignment. She waved her outstretched arm above her head. "I expect I will never again make the memories *I* want to make."

I had no words to offer.

For me, the Obligation was the greatest gift I'd ever been given, the only future I had thought of. It was an opportunity for this dockworker's daughter to change the world.

The walls were smothering me.

"Let's take a walk. I need some air."

Kairus nodded and shoved her toes into the red leather short boots by the corner of her bed.

Together we made a lap around the second level and spent time looking out over the balcony. We spotted and waved at Amias, who was headed toward the temple's main entrance, and continued our stroll.

"What did you choose to experience back home?"

Kairus stopped in her tracks.

"I'm sorry, you... you don't have to tell me," I said, meaning it sincerely.

"No, it's okay. I am not ashamed." She smiled and leaned her head against mine in a sweet and comforting gesture. "Well... I sang to a bunch of drunks in a tavern. I climbed a fire mountain just to see what was inside... and I slept with two men who I really liked," my eyes turned to saucers at her last comment. "Not at the same time, Eira!" She smacked at our joined hands and laughed so hard it echoed off the walls. "And I learned to play caid."

"Caid! Who taught you to play?" The rough-and-tumble game was enjoyed in all kingdoms today. Originally, the sport had made its way to us from another continent, well before the isolation. By Ærtan rules, only men of noble birth could play the game, which could span across a kingdom and last for days.

"That I will not tell." Kairus shrugged, keeping her secret her own.

"I guess what I don't understand, Kairus, is why you think your adventures will stop after you're given an Assignment. You'll still be you, right? That won't change, and you'll have a position of rank, surely that will allow for some freedom?"

She didn't provide answers, and I didn't press further.

We found ourselves walking down the ramp and into the front lawn where we sat together on the ground. A group of Scion were out practicing their swordsmanship, pressing each other in exaggeratedly slowed attacks and countering each other's movements at a snail's pace.

"Your muscles have memory." Tommand explained at the same time he was pushing Lok's elbow closer to his side. "If you practice these movements, perfectly and repeatedly, you will eventually be able to perform them without conscious effort."

My fingertips tingled.

"If you like one of them, I would suggest a good coupling." Kairus looked at me seriously. "Purity is not a big deal at Verus. You know that, right? It is not a requirement or whatever, like it is in Gaea. There's nothing mystical about sex, you are not more holy for not having it." She squeezed my hand.

I didn't bother to deny the fact that I'd not gone all the way. I'd had a few trysts, but, despite my partner's enthusiasm, they'd never ended in my completion, so I chose to go no further.

"Who took your purity? Was it good?" I asked, knowing she'd be truthful.

"I did," came her reply. "The idea that someone *takes* something from us like a prize or sacred object is gross. *I* made the choice to have sex with a man I had known most of my life... and really enjoyed the experience. It was on my terms and now my *purity*," she spat the word, "will not be used as some extra incentive in a depraved political arrangement."

Goddess! If Kairus blasted me with many more lightning bolts of truth, my hair would singe off before nightfall.

I laid back and shielded my eyes from the sun.

"So, which one would it be?"

I knew she was asking about the "Monwyn Situation." I turned my head and looked to where they were wrestling in the yard with the other bare-chested Scion.

"Well, Kairus," I stared off into the distance and dramatically placed the back of my hand on my forehead. "Neither of them could possibly live up to the sizzling moments of passion that I shared with the ever determined Gen Makerly. I've never been able to forget the fat tongue that filled my mouth or the clumsy fingers that pinched at my clitoris like lobster claws."

The twinkle in Kairus's eyes returned, and for the second time that evening, we broke into a fit of giggles.

"Troth Chulainn." I knew without looking who'd snuck up on us. My name on his lips sent my heart racing.

"Emissary Tommand," I greeted him a little too breathily.

"This one? Really?" Kairus inclined her head towards the sweat-soaked man and with a practiced swing of her skirt stood up quickly.

And then she left.

"What was that?" Tommand asked, arching a confused brow.

I shrugged, doing my best to seem unaffected by the oh-so-inviting chest in front of me.

"Anyhow," he placed his fists on his hips, "I wanted to discuss the Maneuvering with you. Are you available in two hours' time?" He reached for the cloth that had been tucked into a belt loop and wiped the sweat from his face and neck.

"What would we need to discuss? Combat skills fall under the purview of the Scion, yes?" I managed to steadily hold his gaze.

"Yes... and no, but I would speak with you in private."

My mouth went dry. *Private, sounds perfect.*

"Where will we meet?"

"Fourth floor, room sixteen."

Turning his back to me, he jogged back toward the training field but stopped short.

"Do you own pants?" He correctly interpreted my bewildered expression. "You can wear mine."

CHAPTER THIRTEEN

IT COULD BE WORSE

IT COULD BE BETTER

S tanding in the bathtub, fully aware that I was blowing this out of proportion, I washed under the assumption I was going to get naked tonight. In my sane mind, I knew that whatever Tommand wanted to discuss was likely not an illicit rendezvous, but I was still going in prepared.

Lathering the soap in my cloth, I scoured my armpits, washed the crack of my butt twice, and scrubbed the curls between my legs and all parts below, making sure not to miss a single crevice or indentation. I sudsed between my toes, scraped the dirt from under my nails, and remembered to wash behind my ears. I thought about dabbing a little lavender and vanilla oil onto the creases of my thighs but wondered if that would seem a little too forward. *If he's smelling your thighs, forward won't be an issue, Eira.* I did it, and then added some to my neck as well. Recalling my last attempt at seduction, tonight couldn't get any worse than the "I'm guessing intact" incident.

I brushed out my hair and braided it into two plaits that fell over my shoulders and took a moment to stare at my reflection in the mirror. I liked what I saw. I wasn't a Kairus or Cinden, but I appreciated my strong features. My lips were full, and I thought the pronounced bow of my top lip was attractive. They weren't the perfectly heart-shaped set like Richelle's, but they were expressive nonetheless. I rubbed a sweet-smelling yellow cream into the skin of my face and felt a measure of calm in the familiar action.

I knew I was doing the "Eira thing" by jumping right in, or maybe overboard, but after Kairus had voiced her concerns about her future... how could I do anything but?

As I brushed my teeth and chewed a few leaves of mint, I forced myself to think rationally, having let myself go a little too far. The real deal was that the emissary, brought here to teach Scion to fight, wished to speak to me privately about the Maneuvering. My guess was he saw something I'd done wrong or wished to address the fact that I had acted without direct orders from my commander. *But maybe it was for sex.*

"I can hear you giggling!" Kairus shouted from the bedroom.

Shutting the door behind me I encountered the silly-faced Troth standing in the middle of our room. Her pink lips were sucked into her mouth and her eye were opened wider than a startled snow owl's. I held my head up, looked down my nose, and strode right past her. She caught my arm and swung me around.

"Take this just in case," she giggled and handed me a little ring of... paper? Leather? Sensing my confusion she continued, "it's a sheath of animal intestine. You unroll it over his *appendage,* and it keeps you from getting stuff."

"'Stuff'? And really, Kairus... you can't say penis?" I made to give the roll back to her, but she closed my fist, making me promise to take it.

"Wish me luck!"

"Good fuck!" she yelled as I walked out the door.

· · · ✦)(✦ · · ·

I knocked on door sixteen and was greeted by a fully dressed and freshly shaved Tommand. I was struck again by how handsome I found him and how jittery I became when I was near him. It bordered on ridiculous, really. Even the masculine scent of the soap he used lured me nearer—he smelled of cedarwood and warmed cloves. I hadn't recognized it then, but it was the same tantalizing smell that had surrounded us while taking our liberties under the staircase.

Wordlessly, Tommand stepped back and motioned me into the room.

The door shut with a click.

A part of me expected to walk into an office, the other, a bedroom. I was wrong on both accounts. Instead of the massive bed I had imagined him to sleep in, there were just two chairs. The plush rug where we were supposed to make love was a pile of compressed straw mats. The two huge mirrors that hung from ceiling to the floor... Well, they weren't in my daydream, but they could stay.

"Come sit." I moved to join Tommand, who was already sitting in a chair across the room. "Troth Chulainn, I'd like to discuss a particular moment during the First Maneuvering."

I knew it. Would it be the mud trick or chasing the guard?

"Violence has unfortunately been a frequent occurrence in my life, and I believe what I witnessed during the first match indicated it may also be a part of yours."

Sobering instantly, I swallowed the lump in my throat. I knew exactly the incident he referred to. I felt the heated prickle of embarrassment that always seemed to accompany my thoughts of that day in the river. I looked up at Tommand. His face didn't look judgmental, didn't look surprised, or accusatory. I could only detect concern.

"Troth Nortia, if you have had violence used against you, it is no fault of your own. If you are able, will you describe the situation you encountered? I may be able to offer advice on how to react if you ever find yourself in a similar predicament." His eyes searched mine, and he didn't press me. He simply waited for my answer.

Just the image of Ozius's hand—the attacker's hand—reaching out for me turned my stomach. I couldn't bring myself to meet Tommand's gaze again. I wanted to trust him, I wanted to face my fear, but it felt so impossible to say the words. I felt like it was *I* who hadn't been careful enough that day.

"I have found that in some situations, giving voice to your trauma can help with the memories that catch you off guard." He rubbed his shoulder unconsciously.

His subtle vulnerability gave me the push to move past my discomfort and recount the events. Leaving out no detail, I began from the very beginning.

"...and now, I see his face in my dreams, and just like it was in the moment, I'm unable to move away, unable to help myself." I choked out the last of my words, suppressing a sob. I hadn't processed that day with anyone else, not even Nan, and speaking the words made me feel almost as vulnerable as I had in the hours after the incident.

"Would you feel comfortable enough to continue speaking to someone? There are priestesses trained to help people, but it can be a long, sometimes lifetime, process."

"Thank you, Tom." His nostrils flared slightly at the accidental use of his shortened name. "I'm sure I'll be fine, though. This type of thing is not uncommon and—"

"And it was an act that made you feel helpless. Someone attacking an innocent should never be considered the norm... which is why I need to apologize for my actions the other evening." He reached out to my hand but then dropped his arm to rest on his knee. "It was my intent to speak to you of the burgeoning attraction I had detected between you and Scion Ambrose but—"

"Before you continue," I interrupted, "I don't see any relation between the attack on my person and your... *our* actions at dinner. As I recall, questions were asked and consent given, and it was *I* who approached you in a way I shouldn't have."

He shook his head, not wanting the apology, and the silence stretched between us until he abruptly cleared his throat.

"I would like to offer you lessons in defense. It is not traditionally an area in which a Troth participates, but because of the nature of your duties, you will come upon those who may attempt to threaten you, or more directly, use your safety as a bargaining chip." He stood and walked confidently to the middle of the padded floor. "Freezing or feeling helpless is a natural reaction for some, but it will not help you out of those situations."

I never *ever* wanted to feel as weak as I had that day, and here was my chance to learn from someone who I had seen with my own eyes rip through a group of eight grown men.

"I would like to learn."

"Good." He motioned to the clothing hanging over the chair he had occupied. "Put on the pants."

Okay. Pants. I'd never worn them, but after seeing the men practicing in the yard, I could understand why the garment was suited to learning combat. I tugged off my wool over-gown and linen underlayer and tossed them over the chair. It missed and landed in a heap, but I ignored it and snatched up the buff-colored linen. I put one leg in and teetered unsteadily until I followed it with the other. At mid-thigh, they became quite tight, but determined, I shimmied and wiggled to get them up over my hips. By some miracle, they stretched enough that they laced together, albeit just barely.

Straightening, I lifted each leg and bent low, testing the feel and getting accustomed to having both legs encased in fabric. *If I don't bust the ass out of these, it's because the Goddess took pity.* I tightened up the closure of my chest binding and looked down for one final inspection.

I was ready. *Breathe deep Eira, this is for the "you of your choosing."*

I turned.

"Tommand?" He was bent over his shoes but instead of tying them he'd become frozen in place. "Tommand?" I walked towards him, concerned.

"I... I intended the pants to go under your gown." He still hadn't stood upright.

Well, fuck.

"The Scions practiced this way, so..." I wasn't about to feel bad, I practically painted on the stupid things. "Next time you intend something try making it clear."

He shook his head like a wet dog and rubbed his jaws with both hands, seeming to have snapped out of his stupor.

"Will you be removing your shirt as well?" I asked innocently.

"I will not," he responded quickly.

"Alright then." I held my palms up in an apologetic gesture. "Let's get to it."

"Come forward and attempt to strike me here." He smacked his hand against his scarred shoulder. It struck me as funny that in our last private encounter, I had desperately wanted to hit him and now I had my chance. Tom must have seen the amusement on my face because he rolled his eyes and began tapping his foot like I was taking too long.

Standing an arm's length away, I balled up my fist and took a swing. The contact made a thud that sounded solid to my ears but didn't even seem to register for him.

"That was not terrible, but you can improve." He grabbed my hand and moved my thumb to rest under my knuckles, and then pushed his palm against the flat area between my curled pointer and middle fingers. "You will want to strike using this part of your hand, and instead of swinging that arm around your body, strike straight forward using the momentum that comes from your hips. Use the power generated there to add strength to your strike." He took a step back. "Do it again."

Squaring up like I had seen him do, I closed my eyes and thought about how to punch from my hips, how the motions should look, and how they might feel. I opened my eyes and struck. Though his shoulder only moved maybe a half inch, I could immediately feel the difference in my power.

"Better. Again." He signaled me forward.

Over the next hour I felt like I threw a thousand punches, and with each one, he'd adjust something or add another piece of advice.

Eventually, I dropped to the mat, exhausted beyond even that of the Maneuvering. Sweat dripped into my eyes and I didn't care what I looked like crumpled on the ground at his feet.

"You need to practice your form daily to continue to improve, but let's move on. I'm going to put my arms around you, and I want you to attempt to break free. Are you okay with that? If you feel afraid at any time, say 'stop' and I *will* let go." He waited for my answer, and I nodded my affirmation. "Let's start with you facing me."

I stood and walked my sweat-drenched self to stand in front of him.

His solid arms circled my shoulders and squeezed, clamping all the way around my back. I was entombed in a dome of cedar and could feel the thump of his heartbeat against my temple.

"Are you going to try... at all?" he grumbled. As if to spur me on, he tightened his grip twofold.

I made a move to dislodge him.

Nothing.

I strained against him and struggled to free my arms. I twisted and pushed and didn't budge an inch.

"Nortia, I want you to think about the parts of your body that are free. Do not waste your energy struggling against my strength." He increased the pressure further.

"Okay, okay," I replied, trying to think through my next move. I could use my head as he had against Greggen, but positioned as I was, I didn't think I could reach anything vital. *Maybe I could hit his chin?* I tried to jump, but he brought me quickly back into place. The hop gave me an idea though. I raised my foot and stomped on his toes.

"Yes, what else?" he praised. "What else can you do?"

Encouraged, I kicked out at Tommand's legs and then hauled a knee to his groin, which he quickly defended with his thigh. My actions broke enough of his hold for me to free a single arm, and when he let me out of his embrace, I felt like I could take on the whole of Ærta!

"How'd it taste? Not as sweet as my victory!" I hopped up and down and smiled up at Tommand, who grinned back.

"We will meet again at the end of this week. What I want you to think about until then is how you can combine the instruction you are learning in the temple with the instruction I am providing. Focus on how you can avoid or preempt confrontations."

"Tommand, thank you." I threw all of the sincerity I could into my voice and turned to dress. I attempted to shimmy out of the loaned pants but found it much more difficult trying to pull them down over my sweaty legs.

"Keep them, just... keep them," he said from behind me. He sounded aggravated. I reached for my gown, tossed the material over my head, and covered myself, pants and all. I'd deal with them in my room, even if I had to get Kairus to help me pull them off.

"You dropped something." Tommand made his way to my side and bent low. I finished fiddling with the arms of my underlayer and tried without luck to smooth the fabric over the bulge created by the pant's front lacings.

Tommand cleared his throat.

"Troth Chulainn, you should leave... *now*," he said in a gritty voice.

Confused by his sudden change in tone, I looked up and straightened.

He extended his arm and placed the rolled sheath into my palm.

"To the door, Troth Chulainn."

CHAPTER FOURTEEN

THINGS I WISH TO UNLEARN

"You did WHAT?" Flipping onto her stomach, Kairus shoved her face into a fluffy down pillow and proceeded to scream-laugh at the tale I'd told her twice already.

"Last time, *okay?*" I pursed my lips and forced her to scoot over on the bed. "*Ahem...* I got naked and put on his pants... are you following me?" I lifted her blonde curls and moved closer to her ear. "So that I could *wrestle* with him." I dropped the hair and placed my hands on her back, shoving her up and down into the mattress. "And then... I tossed your penis sheath in front of him... and he told me to GET OUT!"

My roommate howled for the next ten minutes until finally sneaking a peek at me from beneath her pillow. I snapped my head in her direction and stared her down. That was all it took. She snorted so loudly that I feared a herd of pigs would come crashing into our room, seeking their porcine queen.

There was a heavy knock at the door.

"Oh my Goddess, little piggy, who'd you call?"

I leapt off the bed. Recently, Tussi had taken to calling around this time of night to school Kairus on what he called "ignoble nasties." If scratching her elbow in public had caused his most recent etiquette-derived apoplexy, then her deafening snorts were sure to send him over the edge.

I swung the door wide.

"Obligates Chulainn, Septimus, your presence at the Second Maneuvering is required. I will escort you to the location."

I'd not expected a temple guard.

"The next Maneuvering is tonight?" I glanced back at Kairus. "It has to be near midnight."

"These people don't sleep." She rolled off of her bed and made to pull a gown from her wardrobe.

"You come as you are," ordered the man.

"A moment, sir!" A quickly escalating Kairus dressed him down. "We will dress and *then* follow you without issue."

Without a word, the guard entered our room and grabbed Kairus by the arm.

"Remove your hand!" Kairus clawed at his fingers, trying in vain to loosen his grip. The guard leveraged his body against the doorframe and with little effort forced her into the hallway.

Another guard appeared.

"I'm coming. Don't touch me." I threw my hands up and made to follow, wearing nothing but my oversized linen shirt and underclothes.

They escorted us to the second-level ballroom, which looked nothing like it had when the Congregation took place. The wooden partitions had been moved forward on both sides of the enormous room, transforming it into a long, narrow hall. Around the space, chairs had been placed in pods of three and the lamps had been turned up to full brightness. I surveyed the Obligates who stood or sat in various states of dress. A flustered Farai had distanced herself far from the others, wearing only a low-cut, sleeveless nightgown and hugging her freckled arms close to her chest. Luræna was still clothed in the gown she'd worn during the day, though her brightly colored makeup had been removed and she wore no shoes. Amias, who didn't seem to care at all, leaned back in a chair and was snoozing with his head propped against a wall. He wore only his small clothes leaving his torso and legs bare. Evandr was in nothing but his knee-length stockings and the tiniest black underwear I'd ever seen.

"You like what you see?" The conceited Monwyn blew kisses in my direction.

"I am overcome with a near-tortuous need," I said in the most monotone voice I could muster. "I'm also desperately curious as to why you even bother with underwear." We both fell into easy laughter while the brawny Scion made a show of rapidly flexing his pecs.

"Not to intrude, but I believe I heard a few of my favorite words falling from that lush mouth?" Ambrose approached me from behind. "I find myself quite available to assuage even the most tortuous of needs."

Out of the corner of my eye, I saw Evandr covering his nipples with his fingertips.

"Is that so? It seems Evandr is in desperate need of something at the moment."

Ambrose narrowed his eyes and looked me up and down.

"But... what is this?" he asked while slipping a finger into the wide neckline of the shirt I wore, drawing it slowly over my shoulder, "Have I been bested? Is there another?" His eyes darkened and his lips turned down. "Whose shirt graces your silken skin, scandalous one?"

"Well... *Ambrose*." I walked my fingers up his muscular arm and tweaked the edge of his tunic. It's my... *father's*." I drew out the last word in a low, seductive voice.

"Disgusting. I guess winters *are* long in the frozen north. I find myself rapidly deflating!" He made a scene of pushing the fabric back over my shoulder and knocking my hand away from his arm.

"Don't bash Nortia because you neither grow nor show... and at least she's more fashionably dressed than you. What is *that*?" He pointed to the oddly tall and exceptionally snug undergarment Ambrose had tucked his shirt into.

"Fuck off, it keeps this body tight."

"And here we have Troth Nortia in a stunning ensemble! Is she poorly mimicking the Solnnan short dress, or has she been rummaging through *my* drawers?" sang Evander.

Ambrose grabbed my hand and spun me around his finger to the delicate applause of Farai, who had finally joined us, our playful antics making her feel a bit more comfortable.

A commotion in the direction of the doorway interrupted our revelry.

Straining, I listened, trying to discern the source of what sounded like a series of high-pitched shrieks.

"Are we going to fight a coyote in our undies?" joked Yemailrys. There were a few odd chuckles, but for the most part, the room had quieted, our gaiety rapidly replaced by apprehension.

The shrill wails cut off, and the room went silent.

I looked to Ambrose. He shook his head, not understanding what was happening himself, and defensively, he moved between me and the door. My anxiety surged, and I left our small group in search of Kairus.

I was relieved to find her sitting in a chair tucked behind Greggen, who, like me, wore only a shirt. With legs crossed at the ankles and his hands folded neatly in his lap, he kept himself decent.

The noises came again, long desperate sobs. Something had been hurt—something felt fear.

I went to stand closer to Greggen, who instinctively moved to shield Kairus, his partial nudity forgotten. The tension in the room became a physical presence, the air so brittle I feared it would fracture the moment someone spoke. Lok padded to the door, his chin-length ringlets shifting over his ear as he cocked his head to the side. Farai shrank back into the farthest corner.

With a loud *crack*, the door slammed open with a force so great, the wooden panel bounced off the stone wall, nearly shuttering it again. I momentarily caught sight of tangled bodies, but the door swung back again before I could discern whose. A hand reached around the doorframe and held tightly, struggling to stay anchored against an unseen force.

With a frustrated cry, the hand disappeared but was replaced by an armored leg that pushed the door wide.

The air hitched in my throat.

A sharp gasp sounded behind me.

"What the fuck is this?" Greggen cursed.

Two guards flung Cinden to the floor.

She wore no clothing, and after the initial impact of hitting the ground, she curled herself into a ball, doing what she could to hide herself.

Behind her, an enraged Ozius was being held against his will. He too stood naked other than the dozen or more bleeding cuts and scrapes on his body. Unlike Cinden, there was no shame in his stance, only fury. His wine-colored hair was coming unbound, and his every muscle was under tension. The black eye he'd received at the First Maneuvering made his pale irises glow, giving him an almost demonic appearance. The two guards flanking him struggled to maintain their hold. Each had seized one of Ozius's arms and had pulled them back, forcing his elbows to straighten unnaturally. Their gloved palms rested above the joints, locking his arms into place, but if the Scion was in pain, he hid it well. I watched as a third armored man rushed forward and wrapped his arms around Ozius's chest, squeezing the Scion so tightly it looked to be impacting his ability to breathe.

I was horrified.

This couldn't be happening in the very temple committed to Ærta's peace!

It wasn't their nudity that made my stomach churn, or the fact they had probably been found nude together. I just couldn't fathom any reason why the two were being so thoroughly debased. The temple was a sanctuary for love and accord. Its very mission was to spread and maintain harmony; this was meant to shame.

Cinden remained on the ground, her hands wrapped around the top of her head. She pulled her legs tightly against her bottom, trying to cover her private areas. Her needless humiliation provoked my outrage.

Surging forward, I pushed past Greggen, sending him slightly off balance.

A guard placed himself in my way.

"BACK UP!" I shouted.

He made no motion to move, so I continued forward. I planted my foot and squatted slightly just before jamming my shoulder into the soft flesh above his hip. I was angling for the spot right below his leather-covered chest like I had seen Tommand do when he took on the Scion collective. Other than the guard, I was probably the most surprised person in the room when he lost his footing and toppled onto his side.

I moved as fast as I could and sank to my knees next to the fallen Troth, putting my arms protectively around her.

"Cinden, it's Eira. It's me..." Allowing my touch, she wrapped herself in my embrace and clung, softly weeping into my shoulder.

"Come on." I tugged at her gently. "Come with me, Cinden." I hugged her to my chest with one arm while trying to remove my shirt. I still had my binding and small clothes, and it would afford her cover. I tugged at its hem but was stopped before the material rose over my hips.

"She will remain in the state she was found for the duration of the Maneuvering."

The burning rage coursing through my veins turned to ice.

Gotwig.

"In your Assignments, you will be forced into vulnerability. Some of those circumstances will be manufactured exploitation. Other times, your *own* choices will lead you into situations that are... distressing." The nasty little man glanced briefly at Cinden.

"Distressing? Distressing is figuring out which gown to wear!" I flung back at him, "*This* is sick! What makes you—"

I felt a presence at my back and the gentle squeeze of a hand on my shoulder. I twisted sharply, ready to face the guard again, but instead found Ambrose. He bent down and ever so delicately dislodged Cinden from my arms, taking her up like she was a doll made of glass. I could still make out her choking cries, even when he stowed her behind Greggen and Kairus.

"Mmmm, yes, there's always some display of heroism at this point." Gotwig smoothed his pale mustache and checked the time on his watch. "Not often as grandiose, however." He looked down his nose at the guard who had since regained his feet.

"Are you able to control yourself now?" he asked Ozius, who had calmed with Cinden's release.

The Scion nodded sharply and ripped his arms free of the guards, who took up their places on either side of Gotwig. Straightening, Ozius proudly inclined his chin and sauntered into the room, looking as unaffected as if he were walking into dinner. He stood between Greggen and Ambrose, making no attempt to hide his nakedness.

Gaining my feet, I glared at Gotwig, who'd just rolled his small, red-rimmed eyes in my direction.

"I think control may be *your* issue," I hissed, my anger still burning. He pressed his lips into a line of disdain. "Do you enjoy the suffering of others? Does humiliation make you feel powerful?"

"Quite the opposite, in fact," he responded blandly.

"And yet you orchestrated this horseshit!"

"Mind your mouth, Troth." He peered down his nose and stepped toward me, "This is why I prefer the company of servants. You can't even begin to imagine true suffering."

I wanted to step backward as he approached but fought the urge.

"I have suffered debasements your simple mind couldn't comprehend. I have been brutalized beyond what most humans could endure. But you see, I learned to conquer myself, to control *me*... You would not have survived." Again he stepped closer, focusing on me as if the others in the room had ceased to exist. *So fucking twisted.*

His arm reached up between us, and his cool hand settled on my chin.

"Hmmm." He twisted my head from side to side and, while still holding my face, stuck a finger into my mouth and pulled at my bottom lip. I flinched hard and jerked backward. "I gave you no consent to touch me."

"Your consent was nullified the moment you slipped from your mother's thighs."

With his inspection complete, he walked away and into the middle of the room.

"A demonstration!" Gotwig yelled. The guard positioned behind him moved to his side. "Strike!" The guard lashed out with not a speck of hesitation, smashing his fist into Gotwig's face.

Our instructor didn't so much as blink. He made no reaction at all, just stood there, not a squint, not a twitch.

"*Again*, and put your gauntlet on. This little show gets tiresome when it takes too long." The guard reached for the armor that had been tied to his belt and flexed his fingers into the metal glove. He struck again, throwing his whole body into the fist that landed with an audible crack. The impact snapped Gotwig's head around, and a line of crimson bloomed across his jaw. The metal that shielded the guard's knuckles had caught his flesh, and the gash welled and spilled over. Gotwig reached into his vest pocket and produced a handkerchief that he used to dab at the dark flow. He continued on as if nothing had occurred.

"Now, if we may, I'd like to start tonight's Maneuvering." Weaving in and out of the assembled Obligates he continued. "As a group, we will learn to identify ways in which a body responds to certain stimuli, and then in small clusters, we will test our self-control... and yes, that was painful, but you *can* learn to perfect your detachment. Now sit."

Choosing a triad of chairs toward the back, Kairus and I placed Cinden between us and covered her as much as we could with our own clothing. Ozius sat in the grouping to our front, helping to block her from view.

"We will need a volunteer... You there." Gotwig motioned to a Gaean Troth.

She rose from her chair, pausing briefly before joining him at the front of the room. She wore only her green stockings and a short undergown. One of her three auburn braids was undone, the tresses waving far past her shoulders.

"That's Chentel. We took Unity together," Kairus whispered over Cinden's bowed head. "Her father is the Arch Healer of Temple Mossius."

As Chentel moved forward, the perimeter of the room darkened, and three acolytes holding bright oil lamps rushed to stand near Gotwig. He bade the Troth to stand still and went to work positioning each light. He hung two lamps by either side of her face, and another just below her chin. When satisfied, he tipped Chentel's head and pressed it to the side before maneuvering himself behind her.

"My dear, your job is a simple one. Let nothing change from how you are at this moment," he said loudly enough for the assembly of Obligates to hear.

Gotwig's skeletal hand snaked around the Troth's throat, the arm it attached to brushing her unbound hair. At the contact, Chentel's eyes, almost as blue as Kairus's, widened ever so slightly.

"No, no. You must remain as stone. Do not let your emotions show. I feel the change in you, and we've just begun." The hand tightened around her neck. His fingers dug into her light-beige flesh.

"You are feeling fear." With one hand on her neck, the other went to her loosened hair. "Obligates, watch for the pulse in the hollow of her neck. You will begin to notice a flicker and a quickening as she increases her respirations. These short inhalations are an indicator of panic or stress. That is, to anyone competent enough to notice."

In a fluid movement, Gotwig shifted to the Troth's side and clutched a handful of Chentel's locks. I fought back the curse on my tongue, appalled that he would dare take the liberty of touching her hair.

"You will notice the slight tremble in her chest, just the smallest vibration, as she fights to stay calm." Reaching to his side, a knife appeared in our instructor's hand. He slashed the blade into the unbound section of her hair, and a red lock rode the air, coasting down to her feet.

"See the fine sheen on her forehead. She has almost peaked in her response. Were you able to see the tightening of her stomach as her hair was severed? You may not have, but I was able to feel the subtle clench." As his words ended, a tear rolled down the Troth's upturned face. "Obligate, hear me well: there is nothing more sacred than the life you were chosen for. Not that hair upon the ground, not the tear on your cheek. You may sit. Your performance was below adequate, but you'll learn." Gotwig pocketed his blade as Chentel bent to reclaim her shorn hair. She made her way back to her seat and hung her head.

Kairus's expression had gone cold. Her gaze was locked straight ahead, and I could feel her contempt. Yet another choice taken from its rightful owner. She took Cinden's hand in her own and the three of us waited for what would come next.

"Though fear is an easy response to elicit, it is not the most commonly used when trying to secure or maintain a profitable arrangement. Fear is powerful but unpredictable, and nakedly obvious in its use. Lust is a much more effective tool when one needs the attention of a particular target and not the whole court. You will all eventually have it used against you. You may even choose to employ it yourself." The man repositioned the acolytes once more. "*You*," he pointed a finger at Amias, "come here."

The Scion walked forward, and I noticed the double flame brand on his back. When he made it to the center of the floor, Gotwig took hold of his arm and spun him so that his side could be viewed by the audience.

"Arousal can be detected in stages, and there are telltale signs of someone responding to a stimulus... though it does vary based on one's natural libido and of course the nature of the liaison."

I fought to still the tremor in my hand.

"Lady Septimus, you will make a decision. Will it be Troth Cinden or Troth Eira to partner with Scion Amias in this example?"

Kairus's mask held firmly in place as she glanced briefly at the woman between us.

"Troth Eira." She turned, affixing her cold stare on Gotwig.

"Come forward, Obligate Nortia. Position your back to Amias's front." I moved as he bade, maintaining the notion that I was keeping Cinden safe. She had already endured too much to be violated again.

I spared Amias a glance before turning my back.

"You will notice the color rising on the Troth's neck and cheeks. It's subtle, but what you are seeing now is most likely embarrassment or shame. Flushing of pink or orange or bronze can be detected in both paler and richer skin tones as blood surfaces. It can appear on the nose, ears, and chest. Now, shift your attention to the fair-skinned Scion. A change of color should be particularly easy to observe. Troth Eira, bend at your hips."

I couldn't make myself move.

"Notice the twitch in our Scion's penis." Gotwig positioned an acolyte's arm so near my backside that I could feel the heat of the lamp. "With the mere mention of a potential sexual encounter, you will see a response begin in our male specimen. Troth Nortia, bend as asked." A guard took a step forward, and not wishing to be handled as Cinden had, I complied, bending forward and resting my elbows on my knees.

"People with vaginas do not tend to have *as* noticeable reactions as those with penises, so you will need to pay closer attention to see the effects of their arousal. That can also help you in your delivery of pleasure as well. Inattentive lovers do not secure contracts." He smirked.

"Move them out of the way." I saw the acolyte walk past and felt her hand near my bottom. She tugged at my underwear, untying the right side.

I focused on my anger to keep from crying, I imagined what it would be like to wrap my hands around Gotwig's thin neck or what it would feel like to hoist him over the fourth-level banister.

"See here, the red blotches appearing at the male's neck and chest. He is becoming desirous. Note the rigidity of his nipples, females will experience the same, and will often be more pronounced. Walk forward, Scion." I couldn't see him, but Amias cleared his throat at about the same time his semi-rigid erection settled onto my exposed backside.

My face was on fire. *One. Two. Three. Four. Five. Breathe. Breathe. BREATHE!*

"I would expect at this time for a full erection to be achieved, as the male's breathing has become more rapid." Someone jerked the hem of my shirt back over my hips and two acolytes came to stand near my head. "But alas, we have an example of a man who has either worked on his ability to control his responses... or he has found the female's body so repugnant it has stopped the sexual process."

I'll kill the fucker.

"You may both sit."

I spun on the little rodent, intent on punching the nose I knew would feel the pain, even if he didn't show it. Drawing upon every ounce of energy I had, from my feet to my hips, I reared back and let loose, only to have Amias gently redirect my arm mid-swing.

"He's not worth it." The Scion's calm eyes searched mine, tempering a little of the fury I felt.

I threw myself back into the chair so hard its front legs left the ground.

"Thank you, Eira... I would have wished for death," Cinden whispered in my ear.

"You know what the issue was." Kairus peeked over the pink head that had gone back to the cradle of her arms. "It was those thick thighs of yours."

Chapter Fifteen

SHALL WE PLAY A GAME?

G otwig's nasty games continued through the night.

The little wretch lined everyone up on the back wall and called each of the Obligates forward to retrieve a folded parchment. Our names were emblazoned across them in a fine hand of light-purple ink. My heart went out to Cinden, who had to step forward unclothed, but at least she no longer shed tears. On the back of each folded paper was a number. I was given the number three.

"Once you have identified your group, head to the chairs," Gotwig instructed us.

I was grouped with Ambrose, Ozius, and the Solnnan Troth, Kymor. Ambrose took up position behind the three of us, allowing Ozius to be seated, for which I was grateful. He sat with his arms crossed, leaning back in the chair, and the pose left his member laying against his thigh in plain view. It shouldn't have made me so uncomfortable, knowing he had been forced to be as he was, but I found it difficult to focus sitting next to a fully naked man.

"The next exercise will go as follows: the parchments in your possession contain information about the various members of your group. Scion Greggen, please stand up for a demonstration." Greggen rose and stood in the middle of his grouping.

"Seated Obligates, you will read the recorded statements or perform the action it details for each specimen. Watch for the most minute changes occurring and discuss them as they happen." Gotwig strode purposefully towards Greggen, who'd been partnered with Lok, Yemailrys, and Luræna. "When you find *yourself* the specimen in question, your task will be to veil your body's responses and emotes. Hold your breathing steady and push pain or surprise out of your consciousness. Troth Luræna, read the statement marked *Greggen* loud enough for the room to hear."

Scanning her note, Luræna visibly paled.

"Greggen, you have twice stolen the property of the High Mantle. If the items located in the bottom drawer of your wardrobe were to be discovered, you would be taken into the custody of the guards and punished. You are a criminal." The Troth turned her apologetic eyes to Greggen.

"What changes were seen as you watched the male?" he asked Yemailrys. The Troth stared at her model, her eyebrows drawn.

"Nothing, he was as if made of rock," she replied.

"And you, Troth Eira?" He walked to where I sat.

"I... I saw his eyes change, but I can't entirely explain how. They didn't move, but their intensity became... more?" My voice wavered with Gotwig in such close proximity.

"You are correct. His eyes did betray his otherwise nonplussed reaction." Gotwig moved again, pointing at Greggen's face with the pen he used to take notes.

"With certain emotions, your pupils will become larger or smaller, changing the dispersion of color in the iris. Watch for this to happen as an indicator of emotional response." He stepped to Greggen's other side and lifted his hand to pull at the man's cheek. "As you become adept at recognizing bodily responses, you may find the tiniest of movements occurring in the facial muscles, even down to something as small as the eye's waterline. Scion Lok, what did you perceive?"

"His neck," the uncomfortable Scion shared.

"What about his neck?" Gotwig wafted his hand in front of his face, imploring the Scion to elaborate.

"The long muscle moved," Lok's bass voice answered.

"Not as dumb as you look then?"

Fists clenching, Lok shot out of his seat, growling at the insult.

Several obligates flinched, startled by his swift lunge, but not Gotwig. He pivoted so swiftly he seemed to magically appear behind the Scion, who went crashing to his knees. Our instructor pulled a knife from his waist as casually as one might draw a pen from a pouch and placed it at the juncture of Lok's neck and shoulder.

"There are animals trained to have more self-control than yourself."

Lok's eyes enlarged as Gotwig pressed the knife slowly into his flesh. "Pain is generally an easy response to spot. Note the flare of his nostrils, the quiver of his eye as the stimulus is further introduced. If I press harder, you will see the body involuntarily move away and the flesh itself may even warm or constrict." Lok's body did just as Gotwig said it would. "I do, however, think our Scion is ready to rejoin his group." He pulled the knife out, slowly, and a tendril of blood fell into Lok's shirt collar where it absorbed and spread quickly through its fibers.

"Now, begin." Gotwig cleaned his blade on his already bloodied handkerchief. He then began circling around the groups, advising the Obligates on how to properly mask their responses.

"I will go first," Ambrose volunteered. He stood at ease, legs spread slightly and back held straight, the ever-amused expression he wore pasted across his face.

"Ambrose, you... you enjoy taking men to your bed just as much as women," Kymor read, stumbling over her words, unable to maintain eye contact with the handsome Scion. "My apologies, that is private and should have remained such."

"Apologize again and I will reveal what you most fear, Troth. What of his reaction, Kymor?"

Startled, my hand flew to my throat. Gotwig had joined us, approaching silently from behind.

"I saw nothing," she said.

A brief nod affirmed her answer, and he turned to Ozius who looked down at his parchment.

"Ambrose, I know that your mother was a whore and your lineage is questionable." Ozius raised his eyebrows as he read.

Again, Ambrose made no response that I could discern.

"Well done, Scion, I see someone has put work into the dominion of himself. You may be seated."

Gotwig rested his fingers lightly on my shoulder. Feeling a sense of disgust, the hair on my arms rose "Troth Nortia, you interest me... stand."

The last thing I wanted was to be interesting to him. Shaking off his touch, I stood, and Ambrose slid into the seat I'd occupied.

"Scion Monwyn, begin."

"Hmmm," Ambrose rumbled, a half-smile on his lips. "Animals in heat tend to rut with the most robust males, yet you are favoring the smaller of two Monwyns." He looked to Gotwig and inclined his chin, almost respectfully, for the well-placed low blow.

"Oh! Her eyebrow twitched, just the end of the left one." Chentel pointed a finger to where I stood, almost excitedly calling out my failure.

"Indeed she did, no doubt wondering how I go about collecting information. Next." Gotwig remained with our group. Ozius fidgeted with his parchment, looking more uncomfortable now than he had been standing nude in a room full of near strangers.

"*Ozius.*" Gotwig said the name like a warning. The Scion flattened his mouth defiantly and met Ambrose's eyes. With a flick of the wrist, Gotwig summoned two guards, who bounded forward to flank the reluctant man. "Recognize that this is a single moment and an exercise for her greater good. She must have the ability to protect herself from true predators."

My stomach knotted listening to the exchange. Not knowing what was to come made me feel horrifically vulnerable but I tried my damnedest to hide it. The naked Ozius inhaled deeply and briefly closed his eyes before vacating his seat. Walking to me, concern openly written on his features, he held my gaze. I could sense his preemptive apology. Whatever was coming, I needed to steel myself. I had to become as stoic as one of the stone-faced guards, two of which I could see still standing behind the Scion. I would survive this, and tomorrow I would reexamine my commitment to the path of Obligation. Ozius reached his hand toward my face and slid his fingers along the right side of my head. So it was to be another sexual humiliation. I realized though, with some surprise, that my embarrassment over the Scion's nakedness had vanished, replaced by the hatred I felt for he who had put us in this situation. I'd like to shove my first into the little man's thro—

Ozius' hand snatched closed around the top of my braid. He sunk his fingers deeply into the rope of hair and jerked his arm back.

A searing pain ripped at my scalp.

I went momentarily blind, blackness overtaking my vision.

"No, not this, no... please!" My own voice shouted in my ears. Hot tears rolled down my face, and suddenly the eyes I gazed into didn't belong to the Scion anymore. They were blue, cold.

"Fight Eira, fight this!" I heard another voice in the darkness.

"Troth Nortia, return to the present. Make a choice... control or casualty, decide!"

I was drowning, suffocating,

Decide. I heard him. *Decide.*

I lunged at my attacker, knowing I couldn't run. I shifted my hips and planted my feet. I looked into the blue depths and saw the mouth working, the words incomprehensible.

And then something changed.

I called upon those who had been violated, those who had suffered at the hands of others, and asked to borrow their strength. I rose, twisting my body, and with an explosive force, slammed my knee into the soft flesh of my attacker... who released me.

He released me.

"Eira." A hand shook my shoulder. "Eira!" Slowly the haze lifted. I opened my eyes and saw Ozius laying beside me, sprawled on the floor in a puddle of his own vomit. Chentel was still seated, frozen in place, clutching her parchment to her chest. Ambrose was kneeling by my side, and Gotwig... he was smiling as if the Goddess herself lit him from within.

"Nortia, you have the makings of a formidable Obligate, but we do need to work on your poise. Come to my office in three days."

Chapter Sixteen

AND THREE MAKES COMPANY

I needed to speak with someone in charge.

What happened at the Second Maneuvering went against human decency. I'd been raised to believe the Obligates were the moral compasses of Ærta, not cruel political agents who could kick a puppy without shedding a tear. So I'd been born under the Goddess's sky—how that translated into a life of humiliation and torture, I wasn't sure, but I needed to get answers. I simply couldn't believe this had been allowed for the last hundred years.

Back in my room, I sobbed.

Tears ran down my cheeks and neck, soaking the top of my shirt. Two or three hours of broken sleep hadn't eased my exhaustion or turned off the disgust I was feeling for these walls.

"Kairus, I… I don't think I'm meant to be here. Four days in and each of them has made me rethink everything." I patted the wetness from my face with my too-long sleeves.

"That is because Troth life is court life, and you haven't experienced that before." We sat on the floor, arms pressed together.

"You're telling me that's how you grew up? LIKE THAT?"

"I grew up locked away unless my father was called to the palace. Sometimes I would be summoned with him and other times not. When he went alone, his guards would watch my mother's every move, but when she would come to wish me a good night, she would counsel me to always present myself as a good girl who followed the rules. I was raised to be some man's prize, even though most of the men I encountered at court were revolting. So maybe it wasn't *just* like that, but I was very aware of the realities of Obligation."

"What he did was sick, Kairus, and it sounds like maybe the men of your kingdom are sick as well." I pulled my knees into my chest. "I can't even wrap my head around the Mantle condoning this, but They must."

"Eira, everything that happened last night was calculated. It was *meant* to make us vulnerable. We were sleep deprived and forced into discomfort so that Gotwig could ensure he got the responses he needed to show us what we will face." Her tone was gentle, but her words held conviction, "We must learn to conquer ourselves, to be stronger than our opponents... so that we can look out for those who are powerless."

There was wisdom in her words.

I could hear their truth, but I wasn't ready to accept this as the "life of my choosing."

"Also, Kairus, I feel for Amias, and for you. I know you enjoy his company. We were both forced into accepting what amounts to an assault, and I'm not sure if it was worse for the person playing the victim or the perpetrator."

"Do *not* be sorry on my account. I don't have any claim on Amias, and right or wrong, I maintain that it was done to prepare us for what lies ahead." Kairus pulled back, turning to face me. "Eira, life at court is a constant struggle between superiors and subordinates. Every move you make is watched, is used against you, and whoever is the strongest wins until the next victor topples them. Maybe in Nortia it's different, but I highly doubt it." She pulled me into an embrace. "The true mission of the Obligation is not to parade around like a holy Devotee, inspiring people with your presence, it's to go head-to-head with would-be despots. It's to bring to heel the perverse and the greedy. Eira, we will be soldiers fighting, not on the front lines, but in the bedrooms, in the throne rooms... and you must be ready."

I remained silent.

I couldn't—didn't—want to respond. Kairus only knew about her homeland. Perhaps it was only Monwyn that teamed with wickedness. I'd met the King of Nortia once and never detected any sort of foulness, and I had certainly never been asked to take part in untoward actions or nefarious dealings.

Would I have recognized if he had?

"I have a meeting this evening, fourth level. I'm going to explore a little before then." I had to get out of the room. I smiled weakly. "I hear you, Kairus. I promise I do."

···◆)〕〔(◆···

I tried running up the steps to burn off my anxious energy, but I didn't make it far, my goal had been the fifth floor and currently, I sat on a bench between the third and fourth levels gasping for air. The exertion aided in calming my mind, but I was also drawing attention. Several people stopped to make sure I was okay. One such was a priestess, a jolly middle-aged woman, who sat with me for a few minutes discussing the more interesting features of the temple. The fifth floor, as it turned out, housed a public study and a prayer room. There were two more flights to go, but that sounded like just the thing to satisfy my need for contemplation.

But first, I needed to ensure I'd make it up the remaining flights.

Priestesses and acolytes passed by me frequently, and I found myself noticing many differences among them. One wore the elaborately scaled collar I had seen on my first day here. I imagined they must have had some high-level occupation or type of advanced training due to their rarity. Another group boasted short red hoods that barely covered their shoulders. The garment looked to be home-spun and made of coarse wool, nothing like the opulent silks worn by the Devotees. A third type, like the priestess who stopped and spoke with me, wore a floor-length amber tunic, heavily embroidered in crimson, that split on both sides revealing baggy red pants. Maybe the study would have information regarding the priestess' designations. If it did, there might also be material on the origins of the Obligation.

Part of me was ready to sign my name to resignation papers... if that was even a thing. The other part of me wanted to test my resiliency, to see if I could grow into what the Mantles of the last hundred years thought I could.

"Lyta!" The acolyte who'd been on my team in the First Maneuvering appeared at the top of the staircase. It took a second for recognition to set in, but she found her way to me, smiling warmly.

"Troth Nortia, it's nice to see you. Are you well since the field?" She sat down next to me and folded her hands in her lap.

"I am... alive since the field." I shrugged.

Knowingly, Lyta leaned into my shoulder with her own.

"I've lived here for four years now, and I still find myself surprised by what the Obligates go through. Yours was the first Maneuvering I was picked to perform in, though I've watched a couple of others."

"Were you scared?" I questioned.

"Yes and no. I feared the strength of the Scion and worried over the pain that might come from the physical aspects of the exercise," she rubbed at the wrappings that bound her wrist, "but when praying for guidance, I realized that any temporary discomfort would be offset by Ærta's future leaders gaining new skills."

"Has a... has a Troth ever... given back the gift, taken a different path?" I murmured.

She settled her bandaged hand on my own.

"Not that I've heard of, and Eira, what would be gained by working against what the Goddess created you for?"

I drummed my fingers against the seat of the bench.

"I'm headed to the study. Are you free to join me?"

"I have my duties to attend to, but I'm assuming you don't know where it is?" she concluded correctly. "I'll show you."

We walked together up the stairs, and Lyta led me across the landing to a door on our right. She opened it to reveal a long, dimly lit hallway.

"This must go into the middle of the mountain."

"It surely does. The study and the prayer hall are the center of the temple, the very heart of Verus. Walk the hall to its end and take the door on the right." She waved her hand and turned to leave but glanced back once more. "Eira... Troth Nortia, try to see beyond what happens here, look beyond the trials, the uncertainty, and think about why you were called."

I nodded and watched the back of Lyta's shorn head as she went on her way.

Unlike the temple proper, the stone of the hallway had been left rough and unpolished. I ran my hand along the cool surface, the scratchy texture on my palm somehow grounding me. I counted twelve lamps before two doors appeared. The one on the left was stained crimson, its grain swirling in darker gyres. The other was a light wood with a relief of an oil lamp carved in its center. The simple half-circle basin with two flames dancing from entwined wicks was the symbol that represented the consort Gammond, the god of wisdom and divine counsel.

There appeared to be no handle or locking mechanism on the door, and with a tentative touch it swung forward easily.

The room I entered was a welcome contrast to the dark, imposing aesthetic of the rest of the temple, and calling it a study was criminal. Where the parts of Verus I'd seen were opulent and mysterious, the area devoted to Gammond was bright, as if natural light somehow illuminated its contents. The study's walls were covered in massive white tiles veined with gold. Light-colored wooden shelves had been built into both sides of the airy central space. The left side rose up at least three levels and contained more books than I'd ever imagined existed.

Every shelf was awash in a rainbow of leather-bound tomes. Rolled parchments in tubular containers cluttered the lowest levels of the shelving, and angled ladders were scattered about for book retrieval. I remember thinking once that the Primus's library in Nortia must have been the greatest on the continent, but her entire office would have fit in this space at least five times. It was incredible.

I moved past a priestess deep in study. She sat alone, leafing through a giant volume at one of the many white marble-topped tables that had been placed in perfectly straight rows down the middle of the floor. I could happily lose hours sitting beside her.

Walking deeper into the room, a tall glittering cylinder caught my attention. It appeared to house a staircase that twisted up, almost to the ceiling. I thought I was done with stairs today, but I had to see if the study contained more books than what I saw from the first level.

Rushing forward, I quashed the need to run my hands along the bookcases I passed and quickly reached the spiral's narrow entrance. Excitedly, I stepped into the golden, filigreed cage that surrounded the steps, eager to see what other treasures this wonderful library was hiding. I wound my way to the next floor and looked out through the shaped metal. I felt like I'd been magically made tiny and had been placed inside the elaborate goldwork brooch my grandmother used to wear at her neck.

The second-floor landing opened in two directions. To the left, the rows of books from the first floor continued their climb, and a wrought iron balcony provided access to this layer of multistoried shelves. To the right, I could see a single massive table upon which lay piles of what looked to be hundreds of maps. This would be a floor I'd come back to soon. After the shock of the obsidian-colored mountain, I wanted to find out what else was out there before being Assigned to another kingdom... if I chose to continue. I knew of the Rift, I knew there were chains of islands and a fire mountain on the continent as well. But when it came down to it, I knew little other than their names or basic formation.

Continuing my climb, I came to the third floor where the walls reverted back to the dark gray natural stone of the hallway that led me here. I wandered out of the stairwell and entered a dimly lit chamber with a single orb-shaped lamp hung from the middle of the ceiling. Seven open archways lined the small room's perimeter, two of which glowed faintly from within.

Making my way through the first lighted doorway I peered around the corner and was greeted by a short hallway that had paintings hung on both sides of the wall. One depicted the birth of the world where the Goddess, drawn as a faceless woman, held a globe of indigo and green to her heart. The other was a grotesque scene of the raised dead that had been spawned during the Awakening. So many lives were lost in the war, and even a hundred years later I couldn't fully comprehend the enormity of the conflict. The only world I'd ever known was one of four kingdoms, living together and working towards a common good.

I entered the small passageway, hunting for more of the temple's hidden treasures. Heading further in, I found a matching set of leather-wrapped spears mounted to the back wall and a handleless door to the left. Imbued with a mix of curiosity and excitement, I placed my palm against the wood and held my breath in anticipation of the bounty I would behold—another of the Goddess' surprises.

Muffled noises intruded on my almost meditative state. I paused to weigh my options. The entire study had been open and inviting and I'd seen no locks or latches. I'd hate to burst in on a conference of Devotees, but I just had to know what was on the other side. What exploration ends at a closed door?

Holding my breath, I pushed gently.

Cinden was straddling Ozius, who sat atop a black chaise, her folded legs holding him closely on either side. His long braids were pressed into the wall at his back, and his kiss-swollen lips smiled up at the Troth who moved on him rhythmically. The man, so much paler than the rose-flushed, tawny-skinned, Troth above him, looked at her like he beheld the Goddess herself. The Scion's gray leathers spilled into a pool at his ankles, and the knees of his hair-covered legs were bent, making a seat for his still-clothed lover.

"How long have we waited?" Ozius asked in a husky voice, "I should have taken you on the front grounds." He pulled at her skirts, hitching them up around her waist, the light green of her gown a beautiful compliment to her long, pink braids.

"It doesn't matter," the statuesque Troth murmured while undoing the cloth buttons of his shirt. "And it's not like we didn't do other things before this."

One of Ozius' hands captured the light folds of her gown and held them against the small of her back, and he used the fingers of his other hand to trace circles around one of the twin indentions at the top of her behind.

"But this," she ran both hands over the hair-covered chest at her front and pushed her fingers through the coarse brown curls, "is easily the best thing." She tilted her head backward until her gold-glinting braids brushed the hands cupping her bottom. Ozius moaned deeply and tugged at the left plait. Encouraged by his touch, Cinden responded by lifting herself further on her knees and slowly sliding herself down his length.

Ozius grabbed the Troth by her hips, stilling her movements.

"I'm not likely to last long this way." His love-filled, amber eyes were only for her.

"I know." Her tinkling laughter filled the tiny room, and thrusting her chest forward, she reached into her dress, freeing an upturned breast from the neckline.

A warm heat spread through my stomach and then lower. *I should leave.*

I should have left the moment I registered what was occurring, but my curiosity begged me not to turn away. I had seen animals in the act before, a common sight during Nortia's warmer season, but I had precious little experience of what it could be like between a man and a woman, even if I understood its mechanics. Squeezing my thighs together I tried in earnest to slow my breathing by pulling smooth, consistent breaths through my nose.

I watched as Cinden bent forward, pressing her breasts against his chest before taking his mouth with her own. She murmured her delight as his tongue flicked out and touched her full bottom lip.

My chest constricted, and my own blossoming arousal heightened at the sound. She ground her hips against him and then, ending their kiss, reached behind his head to gently pull his braids forward, resting them on his chest. She slid her hands from the top of his head to the leather-bound tips of their bottoms, and Ozius turned into her touch, laying his lips against her open palm.

Lifemates.

The act, which I had initially thought to be a spontaneous coupling after a horrific trial the day before, was in actuality a tender moment between lovers. My heart expanded in my chest.

I want this.

I watched Ozius's hands roam and finally tuck under Cinden's round backside. He splayed his fingers widely and assisted her with the movements that were becoming more frenzied and less rhythmic by the second. He thrust his hips, meeting her descent, and the added movement opened the view between their bodies, allowing me to glimpse the erection she'd mounted. Ozius was long and hard, a deeper color than the rest of his body, and slick from her wetness. He shifted, lifting his head and bringing his mouth closed over Cinden's earthy-topaz nipple. He swirled his tongue in circles around her areola and nipped at her peaked flesh before flicking his tongue over the sensitive spot. Holding her nipple between his teeth, he smiled a teasing smile and bucked his hips from below. Cinden strained and sighed sweetly as she reached between their two bodies, placing her hand between her legs.

His eyes closed.

Her head fell back... and the three of us groaned in unison.

Shit, shit, SHIT! Tearing myself away, I fled, running as fast as I could down the hall.

I grabbed the wall and pivoted around it, the momentum aiding me in shooting across the entryway floor and into one of the unlit hallways. I fervently prayed to the Goddess I would make it to a door before Ozius got his pants up. My face was on fire and mentally chiding myself, I closed the distance undiscovered. With both hands raised, I bolted through with enough force to smack painfully into a stone wall.

A stone wall with hands.

I was spun around roughly, and my arms were twisted painfully behind my back. A scream tore from my throat, but it never escaped the heavy hand that struck and sealed my mouth, muffling the sound.

"Ambrose, enough," whispered a voice, somehow forceful and quiet at the same time. A lamp on the corner table illuminated, and the room brightened just enough to reveal a deeply concerned Tommand. The hands binding me released at his words, and a grim-faced Ambrose stepped round my side.

"Are you pursued?" he questioned.

Tommand hurried to the door, pressing the side of his head against the wood. Crouching, he motioned for silence and then reached into his knee-high leather boot to unsheathe a blade the length of my forearm. The low light reflected off the wicked-looking blade and made the brass of the compact crossguard gleam. I was mortified. I feared he'd use the weapon unknowingly against an innocent Cinden or Ozius who might, righteously, come after the person who'd spied upon their intimate moment.

The Monwyns looked like two crossbow prods, drawn and taught, awaiting their deadly release.

"No, stop!" I gasped.

Neither paid attention. "I became startled in the dark!" *I mean, it wasn't an untruth.* Without moving his eyes from the door, Tommand visibly relaxed.

"You are behaving like you encountered a wraith... because of the dark?" Tommand murmured, in a tone that implied I'd taken leave of my senses.

"I... yes." The lie rang false.

"So I could walk out... right now?" He shifted his eyes to mine. "And all would be well?"

He made to open the door, but I shoved forward and leaned into the frame, knocking his raised hand out of the way. Tommand's eyebrows shot up, and the tip of his tongue flicked to the corner of his lips. He watched me intently.

"I'll keep you safe, my frightened one," said Ambrose who looked quite menacing, cracking his knuckles in the shadows.

"What are *you two* doing here in the dark?" I desperately tried to deflect.

The two men straightened and glanced at each other.

"Reading," Tommand said innocently, gesturing to a stack of books on the corner table. "That is until you shot in like a sea serpent after its dinner." He quirked a brow and gave me a once-over.

"Slimy scales and tentacles are better than a bulbous-nosed troll I suppose?" I mimicked his stance and slowly looked him up and then down.

"You know very well that is not what I meant and—I look nothing like a troll."

Tommand began moving toward the door.

"Fine, it's fine. Let's just read! What do we have?" I pushed myself off of the doorframe and dashed to the corner where I sank into one of the chaise lounges, staring back at the entirety of the "Monwyn Situation."

"*Fire Mountains: Location and Extraction Techniques for Precious Gems and Stone.* That sounds horrendous. Um..." I picked up the next book and read the title aloud, "*A Children's Guide to Growing up Gaean.*" The corners of my mouth twitched, amused by the reading choices of the two who had to be nearing their third decades. Ever so gently, I placed the book back on the table and gave it's cover a little tap.

Reaching for the last volume, I patted my hand invitingly on the empty space beside me.

Ambrose came to sit and slid so close that our thighs and arms snugged together.

"*Ahem*," I cleared my throat and poked at his thickly muscled arm. He had the audacity to look offended and peered at me from the corners of his eyes, like a child who'd just been scolded. With a huff, he moved to the end of the lounge and crossed his big arms over his chest. I grabbed the last book and tilted its gray cover towards the light "*Finding Pleasure in Groups of Two, Three, or More.*"

Oh, boy.

Tommand chuckled as he sank down at the head of the lounge on the other side of the table. It put him closer to me than Ambrose currently was.

"I will gift you a castle if you read a single page of that book aloud," Ambrose said while twisting his legs onto the chaise and laying back. He forced his head under my arm and laid it down in my lap. "One paragraph for a small cabin?" He batted his sinfully long lashes at me.

"*Growing up Gaean* it is. And we don't get castles in this job, so I would be quite hurt when you couldn't deliver... but let's keep the cabin on the table." I dropped the book, though I was *more* than a little curious about its contents. Tommand picked up the green and gold book and passed it to me. I noticed a series of raised scars on the back of his hand. Yet another testament to the violence that had occurred in his life.

"Come on then," Ambrose snuggled his head deeper into my thighs, the friction pulling little hairs loose from his thick, black braid.

In my best impression of Olena, I began, "Possibly the most important part of growing up Gaean is committing yourself to daily prayers. In the morning before you break your fast it is imperative that you give thanks to the Goddess for allowing you another day. During the prayer ritual, find a quiet space to reflect on the gifts that today might bring, and don't forget to cover your eyes lightly with the fingertips of both hands. Even sight unseen, we still walk the path chosen for us by the Goddess."

A series of light snores interrupted my reading.

Ambrose was fast asleep, and his fully relaxed face was adorable. The dark crescents of his eyelashes lay lightly on his cheeks, and his mouth parted innocently. Even his mussed whiskers, normally combed to perfection, made him look as sweet as a toddling babe.

"He told me about last night."

My eyes met Tommand's.

"Do you share everything with each other?" The question came out sharper than I had intended, but it prickled me knowing that an accounting of my public degradation had made it to his ears.

"Mostly," he responded quietly. "How do you feel about what happened?"

I was angry. I was lost.

My deep emotional fatigue compelled me to tell him that I was fine, but I had trusted him once before, and he'd given no indication that he judged me then. Quite the opposite, in fact. I decided to put my faith in him again.

"Right now... I don't want to be part of this." I turned my head from him when tears began to moisten my lashes. "I don't have the strength to become the viper this place wants me to be." Closing the book with one hand, I set it aside.

"From what I understand, your strength isn't the problem. It's not so often that a temple guard loses his footing." He smiled faintly and crossed his legs at the ankles.

"*That* was my lack of impulse control and good fortune. Impulsiveness seems to be at the heart of all my issues. You will recall last evening." No use in hiding from what happened after training. I fiddled with the knob of the brass lamp, turning it a hair to the left and then right. "I don't have control when I need it, and when I think I have it, I usually don't."

"I thought it was brave of you to aid the Gaean. You put the needs of the downtrodden above your own, a response very much in line with what this temple would expect from their Obligate."

I couldn't deal with praise right now.

"Tommand? What's your favorite animal?" He blinked rapidly at the random question and the corner of his mouth curved up.

"It's, well... I like turtles."

A smile tugged at one side of his mouth, and I beamed. The thought of him petting a tiny green turtle in his big nicked-up palm made my heart feel floppy.

"Nortia?"

"Mmhmm?"

"What's your favorite food?" He questioned, propping his elbow on the raised side of the chaise.

"Tom, a better question would be, 'Eira, what's the only food you don't like?'" A giggle escaped me, and I bit my bottom lip against the noise while placing a gentle hand against Ambrose's uncovered ear.

"Eira, what is the only food you don't like?" He touched his booted foot to my toe. I beckoned him closer, crooking my finger, all the while doing my best not to disturb the snoring Scion.

He was so close I could feel the warmth of his breath on my hand.

"The only food I don't like... is the food not in my mouth." Tapping my index finger to the tip of his nose, I was rewarded with a charmingly lopsided grin.

It changed his whole face.

The gold in his copper-brown eyes seemed to respond to his laughter, glowing heavily around his pupil. His beard had grown out a little and the dark shadow made his strong mouth stand out more prominently. There was something so attractive about his lips. They tipped up ever so slightly on their outer corners, belying the scowl he preferred. It felt silly. I'd known him for only a week, but I'd never experienced this level of magnetism.

Tommand's hand captured mine unexpectedly.

"Do you feel this too?" He looked at me with expectant eyes and rubbed the pad of his thumb in the middle of my palm.

"I do," I breathed.

He pulled our entwined hands to his face and down his scratchy cheek before bringing my wrist to his lips. He inhaled deeply, and his chest rose steadily. The touch of his mouth made my pulse quicken and the skin of my arms break out in gooseflesh. We sat like this while time ticked by, simply content to be in each other's presence. Warm lips nuzzled at the base of my hand sporadically, and Tommand's eyes sought mine each time I adjusted the head in my lap, smiling contentedly before drifting back to the geology text in his other hand. I cherished the odd moment of peace and connection.

"Tommand?"

"Yes," he said in barely a whisper.

"Would you teach me to use a knife?"

"Do you have reason to believe you must arm yourself?" He dropped my hand like it burned him and returned immediately to Protector mode.

"I... no? Maybe? I just want to be prepared if..."

Trailing off, I watched his hand extend towards mine and waited for the contact that never came. Instead, he dropped it and drummed his fingers against the table's surface like I'd become an annoyance. It hurt my feelings more than it should have.

"Tommand, about yesterday. Though it wasn't intended, I put you in an awkward situation, and there's no need to continue to force yourself to aid me," I glanced at the hand he'd pulled back, "We've both gone through unfortunate circumstances, but I'm not your issue."

"You think—" he managed before a grumbling Ambrose cut in.

"The two of you have nothing to argue over. Me, however... what I want to know," Ambrose turned his head, nudging my stomach with his nose, "is why you flung that sheath at *him* and not me?"

I took his strong chin between my fingers and moved his face away from my body.

"It's because he's much better looking than you," I leaned down and whispered.

The giant of a man shoved off me faster than I'd ever seen him move. He pressed a hand to my forehead.

"She's ill, Tommand. A healer at once!" He snapped his fingers at his companion who, with an amused look in my direction, sat back and crossed a leg over one knee. Ambrose stood, snatching at the bottom of his untucked brown shirt, bristling from the sting of my insult. Tommand, ignoring his Scion's command, sat forward, surveying his charge.

The tips of Tommand's lashes were lighter than the rest of their length, and his profile was elegant, even with the slight bump in the bridge of his nose.

"I have someplace to be, Troth Nortia." I started, jumping just a little. He'd caught me staring. "Is it safe to go out?" He reached into his coat pocket, withdrew a timepiece, and dangled the watch in front of me.

"Shit!" It was five till seven. "Ambrose, quit sulking, thanks for the company."

I ran out the door.

Chapter Seventeen

WARMTH

D oor twenty-three was just ahead, and I was only a minute late. I made to grab the handle and plow right through but stopped short, remembering Gotwig's first chastisement. I paused briefly to smooth the hair at the crown of my head and straighten the gray overdress I'd chosen to wear this afternoon. In hindsight, the wool dress with sleeves that split from wrist to shoulder would not have been my first choice for running through hallways or down steps, but here I was. I pulled at the crisp white undersleeves, to ensure I was presentable. To me, the gown represented my homeland, and it felt right to be dressed as such when summoned to official Troth business. I stilled my fist before knocking on the door. I'd been so caught up in the craziness of the Maneuvering and lessons that I'd forgotten to ask Nan what this meeting was about... *time management, yet another area I'd need to address in my personal reflections.* The butterflies returned. I knew it wasn't Tommand... I prayed it wasn't Gotwig.

I sent a silent prayer to the Goddess and rapped twice.

"Enter," a muffled, but masculine voice called from within.

The door swung wide, revealing a quaint office. The walls were covered in paneling and painted a rich yellowy-cream, and large tapestries hung from all four sides. Mismatched furniture, chairs, and short side tables were scattered about, and brilliantly patterned purple and white pillows were strewn in front of a roaring fireplace to my right. An unsettling amount of heat poured out of the open door.

The smell of something familiar wafted in the air—the bright, and sharp scent of lemons and spearmint that reminded me of... Kan. I looked to my left, and sitting at a fine desk was the Solnnan I'd hoped for the opportunity to meet. His face came alive, and his silvery, smokey-quartz-hued eyes gleamed. Dressed in a scarlet fur-lined coat, Mariad Keagan stood up and flung his arms wide.

"Troth Nortia! I've waited years!" He circled the desk and stood in his stocking feet. I kicked off my shoes, remembering the custom that Kan couldn't keep in Nortia as his feet were always too cold, and ran to the stout-chested man, who surrounded me in his arms.

"Here, here, little Nortia," he cooed. I felt the wetness of my tears seeping into the brushed wool of his soft garment, "I see Meridett has taught you how to properly greet a Solnnan." I felt his chuckle rumble throughout his barrel-sized chest.

"Oh, oh! I'm so sorry, here we are, perfect strangers, I just, do you... did you know Kan Keagan?" I wiped at my face and slipped from his arms, embarrassed by my too-big-to-contain emotions. The Devotee didn't seem to mind, though, and continued lightly holding the sides of my shoulders. It felt like greeting a beloved family member you hadn't seen in years.

"Yes, child, Kan was my uncle," Mariad motioned to a set of chairs that sat on either side of an ornate tapestry that showed the Goddess watching over the famed Gilded Palace of Solnna.

Mariad began to rummage through the drawers of his desk. Behind him, on a shelf, was a statue of the Goddess Lykksun. She brought good fortune to the world and also happened to be the mother of Derros, Master of the Seas. Finally, pulling a hanky from a set of drawers, the Devotee sat with me and held my palm between his two warm hands.

"I've never cried as much in my life as I have here... well, except when we lost him." Mariad nodded his head knowingly.

"He loved you a great deal, little one. Twice a year he'd write to us back home, and the whole family would gather and wait for my father to regale us with Uncle's newest tale from the ice lands." Mariad pulled the top off a small jar that sat on a table between us. "Here, I've been told you can't cry and eat tarted sweets at the same time." He pushed the little jar toward me and urged me to take a treat. As childish as it seemed, I needed the coddling right now and gratefully plucked two candies from the jar.

"With every missive, Uncle would tell us of your progress and... and I distinctly recall a story where a little girl snuck a parcel of Gaean chickens into his room because she didn't want them eaten," he laughed while smacking the table so hard the jar of sweets danced across its top. "He was confident that your caring heart would be a blessing in the righteous path you would walk. And here you are, the first Obligate from Nortia to have arrived at the temple in years!"

And here I am, thinking about quitting. The tears threatened again, and I popped the tarted sweets in my mouth.

"Ohh!" All at once I was hit with a taste so sour I couldn't speak. My whole face froze in a pucker, and I couldn't pull back the arms that stood out straight from my body.

Saliva bombarded my mouth. I slurped repeatedly to keep it from poring down my chin.

"There it is! There can be no tears squeezed up as you are." A dazzling smile split his face, and laughter bubbled between us both. The flavor of the tart began to mellow to a delightful honied sweetness, and my body slowly resumed its normal functioning.

"I'm sorry for all the weeping. Truly, it's not my normal disposition." I grabbed the hanky again and patted at the corners of my eyes and lips.

"Tears are often the same size as your love for someone, little Nortia," he shared while offering more sweets. "Now, to the business at hand. Feeling like I have known you for much of my life, I called you here to ensure you were getting along comfortably. Obligation can be a peculiar experience, and it is my understanding that even before you arrived, there was an incident during your travels."

"Yes, there was." Even though it had been difficult to share before, I decided to immediately trust the Devotee. *Apparently, I was going to trust everyone.* The accounting of that day poured from my mouth again. My previous apprehension didn't plague me. This was different, like speaking to my father, or Kan... someone I knew would keep me safe.

"It was a villager who had imbibed too much drink. He spotted me bathing and attempted to come after me."

"A villager? That is most unfortunate. What did this person look like? I would have our units made aware that someone capable of grossly violent actions could be about." Mariad's expression was quite serious.

"Well... I imagine he won't be a problem any longer. He was killed by the captain of the guard who—"

"Describe him nonetheless, and I will speak to the captain. This simply can't be something that happens in the future, and the miscreants in all the nearby villages should be made aware of the consequences of assaulting one of the temple's chosen."

"Or anyone else... chosen or not," I chimed in.

"Chosen or not," he agreed.

I really didn't want to picture him again, but for Mariad, and for others, I would endure the discomfort.

"He was..." I tried to push past the sick feeling that overwhelmed me in order to recall the man's appearance. I closed my eyes and thought back, endeavoring to recollect the image I'd done my best to lock away. "He was... blue-eyed, an icy blue-gray, and the whites of his eyes... were deeply yellowed. When he dragged me backward... the smell of him, was pungent, like vinegar."

"What did he wear?" asked Mariad.

"The man," His image became crisper. There he was... knee-deep in the water. "He wore... what did he wear? It was... His shirt was faded, a faded green maybe? The color was darker, yes, a darker green where it met the water." I could feel my chest rising heavily with each inhalation, but it was like my breaths hadn't fully circulated when I exhaled. It always started here. I knew the terror was waiting to creep in. "He... he said something."

"What did he say, child? What were his words?" The Devotee's voice infiltrated the rendering, becoming a part of the scenario. "Speak them, Eira."

"Divulge, *something*... deliver up? Us? I can't–"

The bolt struck deep, the gristle popped and crunched, and blood pooled, spreading around my submerged hips. His voice in my ear, the slurring, the smell.

"His mouth... it moved, unnaturally." My attacker walked toward me. "No, please, don't touch me again," I pleaded with the figment. "Please don't..."

"Child, come back now. Don't go farther, return little one."

Kan was with me. It was his firm and comforting voice bringing me back... No, not Kan, it was Mariad. I opened my eyes and saw him studying my face. It struck me as odd, but instead of the intense panic that normally accompanied my return to reality, I came back more calmly than I had before. No screaming, no disassociating.

"Do not dwell any longer, child. You are safe within these walls."

"Am I, though?" The exhaustion of the day caught up with me and loosened my tongue. His thick brows shot up and an amused smile played on his lips.

I covered my mouth to stifle a wry laugh. "You do know what happens in these classes? Yes? It's nuts. This whole place is around the fucking bend somewhere."

"My, but you *are* every bit the girl in the letters!" he asserted mirthfully. Mariad tensed just slightly, and he nodded his head affirmatively. "And I do, yes."

His demeanor changed, and he sat back looking contemplative.

"When I was made Devotee some nine years ago, I tendered my resignation in my second month of service. The methods used to instruct the Obligates settled poorly on me, and I found it difficult to reconcile what I knew happened in the process and what I knew must be carried out across the four kingdoms. I couldn't see the greater good or condone the methods being taught... even for the sake of the disadvantaged." He leaned forward and placed his elbows on his knees.

"How did you overcome it? How did you see beyond it all? The things we've done—the things done to us this last week. These were not at all what I thought the Obligation would be. I'm not sure I could ever commit undue violence or lure someone to my bed to take advantage. I thought the Obligation centered around trade and negotiations between aggrieved nobles... but I'm learning that those dealings are just the sideshow." We sat together in thoughtful silence. "I thought I'd be meeting emissaries and merchants in a little office decorated with paintings of seal pups and sweet puffins."

"Would you have come if you *had* known?" he asked, his silver eyes peering earnestly into my own.

"I... I don't know if I would have," I whispered looking down at my lap.

"Don't be ashamed to speak honestly with me, little one. I understand truthfulness to be one of your most becoming habits."

"You say 'becoming'; my Nan would say ill-mannered... but she's worse than me, always blurting out." I giggled.

"Your Nan? Is this the same Nannetta that Uncle had been so smitten with?" he said, surprise registering on his face.

"Smitten? With Nan!" I tucked one leg under my bottom and grabbed both of Mariad's hands.

"I believe they were an item, little Nortia, until his end."

"*My* Nan and *my* Kan Keagan!" I shouted to the room. "Had I known it at the time I would never have forgiven her." I tossed back my head and let out a bark so loud it made Mariad hop in his seat. "I'm so sorry. It's just, I thought I'd marry him one day."

"Marry that old man? He must have been reaching sixty years," he howled, the sound of his roaring laughs booming off the walls.

Mariad wiped at his eyes and patted himself on the chest.

"By the way, your Solnnan is still quite proficient."

We had lapsed into the language a while back without skipping a beat. It still fit like a second skin and comfortably flowed off my tongue. I'd missed its lilting sound... its musical quality.

Devotee Keagan placed a tarted sweet in his mouth, and I eyeballed him with a one-eyed squint, waiting for his face to pucker. He looked at me quizzically for a moment and then burst into laughter again. He was entirely unaffected by the little ball of massive flavor.

"Little Troth, having you here before me, I can see why Uncle remained in that frozen land so long... what a delight you are."

We talked for an hour or more, sharing tales and memories. My cheeks hurt from smiling, but I blossomed in the feeling of genuine happiness.

"Allow me to be blunt for a moment. You are a highly valuable asset to my people back home. If you are placed in Solnna, I am sure both of our kingdoms will benefit massively from the negotiations you will be able to arrange. Likewise, if you are placed in Gaea or Monwyn, you would have the ability to act as a checkpoint for both sets of our kingdom's merchants. Having someone with your level of fluency could only be beneficial. Would you feel comfortable acting on behalf of my people? Kan's people?"

Well, that took a turn.

"I would have concerns that the leaders of other kingdoms might see it as showing allegiance to Solnna over their own people. If the 'checkpoints' were not constantly shown to be above board, issues would be sure to present themselves... but if the Primuses *and* royals approved of the arrangement, I could see it being mutually beneficial."

"And you doubt your ability to be a Troth, Madam Nortia?" he winked.

"Devotee Keagan? Can I do this? Become what this temple wants?" I laid my hand in his proffered palm. "Will I be able to work through what feels like the forced restructuring of my morality?"

He observed me while mulling over his thoughts.

"I think, little one, that you should not worry about what this temple wants and should instead focus on what our people need." He slid a gold bracelet studded with purple stones from his wrist to my own. "You will always have your own moral compass, and though it may change over time, as is natural, it is not something anyone can take from you. If at some point, you choose to act against your own nature, it is a choice I know you will not make lightly, and"—he paused, while I studied his gift—"not all issues will require you to behave in a way that you feel is indecent, but if the moment comes, you must be versed in all the tools available to solve your problem."

Can you solve your problem? My mother's words echoed.

Though my concern had not been completely assuaged, his advice was profound. Maybe I *could* make it another day.

"Thank you, Devotee Keagan," I breathed, "and truth be told, I'd like to be placed in Solnna, if for the sweets alone... am I allowed to say that?"

"You can say and do as you please in this temple. Just remember, even the walls have ears." As he spoke, his breath feathered the fur at his collar, which waved like the dried wheat fields we'd passed on our journey.

"Is *that* how Gotwig does it?" I teased.

Had anyone been passing by door twenty-three they would have heard the unmistakable roar of the laughter-filled Devotee.

CHAPTER EIGHTEEN

FINE, IT'S FINE.

The toll of the day weighed heavily on my mind and body. I shuffled my way down what felt like a dozen flights of stairs and, shoes in hand, made it back to the second level. A hot bath was calling me, and I was sure I heard the bed whispering my name.

Turning down the Troth's wing, I saw Evon in the hallway. She'd recently trimmed her hair, transforming the bronzy blonde whisps that hung below her ears into delightfully pointed spikes. The short style looked good on Greggen's companion, whom I was beginning to idolize. She'd jumped into the fray of the Maneuvering like no other woman I'd ever seen before and didn't even blink an eye when she'd gone hand-to-hand with a Scion. We waved our hellos as she approached, and I was struck by how much her musculature resembled Greggen's. Like him, she was tall and lean, and I could see the outlines of the muscles that rippled across her stomach. I thought her biceps rivaled the statue of Merrias outside.

"Troth Nortia, how are you?" Evon inquired.

"I'm well, thank you. What brings you to the Troth side?" I asked. I'd not seen her here before.

"Greggen's feeling puny, and I was hoping to find Marcyn to see if he has something to help... he mentioned that if I found Nan, I'd increase the likelihood of locating Marcyn as well."

I smiled knowingly and nodded my head.

"Hang on. I'll see if she's in."

Smiling to myself, now less aggravated at the key catching in the stupid lock, I popped into my room. *Nan and Marcyn.* Tomorrow, I still wanted to corner her and make inquiries about her "little fling" with my childhood crush, but I was really happy that what I'd seen between Nan and the dashing advisor at dinner had budded.

"She's not here. Maybe check the kitchens? They're probably swapping recipes or something." I could just imagine the two smiling into each other's eyes while grinding up ingredients for poultices.

"I'll head there now. Thanks." Evon laughed.

Kairus was still out, which wasn't unusual, and, bless her, she hadn't left her usual roaring fire for me to smother. I pulled off my gown and underclothes and stifled a yawn before laying them both neatly over the opened top drawer of my wardrobe. Were I to crumple this silk underdress, I'd wake to all my others missing... probably for days. *Nan can sure make a point.*

My breasts had been bound up the whole day, and I rubbed them both, massaging their sore tissue until they felt a little better. They'd been this way for a couple of days now, so I knew my cycle would begin soon. I'd never been exactly regular, but the symptoms I had were always consistent: sore boobs, horrific cramps, and a hatred for anything with a heartbeat. I'd start right before the next super physical Maneuvering, most likely. Granted, my no-nonsense period attitude might come in handy.

The light scent of lavender soap had disappeared when I released my hair from its tight braid. I wanted nothing more than to crawl onto my covers and sleep, but I knew a hot bath would ease the strain of today's stair-filled adventures. Plus, I couldn't go another day without washing or I'd look like I was coated in rendered whale fat. I grabbed the newly delivered soaps from my side table and brought the little tin of waxy bars to my nose, sampling each one as I walked to the bathroom. One of my favorite things about living here was getting these little packages every other day. I loved to guess at their combinations. Today's were... not citrus or floral, or even the familiar vanilla. I stuck my face into the mix again. These were woodsy and spicy and—

"We need to talk."

I jumped back, sending the handful of toiletries clattering to the floor.

"Gammond's balls, Ambrose!" I hissed through clenched teeth. "How'd you get in here and what are you doing?" Dropping to my knees to retrieve the cleansers, I selected a particularly weighty bar and launched it. Even when the soap struck him square in the chest, he just lay there, all cozy and relaxed in a steaming tub of bubble-topped water.

"Goddess, Eira, I knew they'd be magnificent, but I wasn't at all accurate when I imagined the color of those mouthwateringly mauve tips."

On all fours, like I was, it dawned on me that every inch of my body was bared to the Scion, and that, looking down between my arms, gravity was pulling everything it could toward the ground. Indignation and self-consciousness were battling in my mind, and I couldn't decide between crawling back through the door or yelling for a guard. *Oh, wait.* Like a jolt to the brain, a more enjoyable option presented itself.

I crawled over to the spigot on the wall and turned the lever to the hottest temperature possible.

"I appreciate your attempt to scald me, but honestly, I'd like to remain. The Scion are not given this luxury. Do you know that four of us share a bathing chamber? It is absolutely revolting." He lazily dropped his head back, which drew my attention to the neatly folded pile of clothing on the back of the chamber floor.

"Ambrose, get out." I snatched up his shirt from the pile and covered myself.

"Really, Eira? You are being rather immature," he closed his eyes, "I bet you'd show Tommand those dark curls... or are you one of those people who finds fault in every part of their body?"

"The issue I have is not with my body, *Ambrose*. The issue is I didn't choose for you to see me this way," I fumed, smacking at the handle that turned off the water.

"It was you who *chose* to come parading in here on those gloriously thickset thighs of yours. I certainly did not intend for you to be naked... and it is obvious you do have an issue with yourself, hiding like you are."

"We can't all be built like a god, Ambrose, and this fake flirtation... it needs to stop."

"What's fake? I cannot wait to push myself between those legs, bite that roll at your hip." He gnashed his teeth in emphasis.

"That little roll? Ambrose, are you calling me fa—"

"Fascinating... yes, Eira, you certainly are... and would you not agree with me that all bodies are *delicious* bodies? I've not found one yet, large or small, she, him, or they, that did not satisfy me... and I them. I am just stumped as to why, you, the current object of my desire, are playing keep away." He rolled his head in my direction.

"Eira, let's play together... just a little." He stared at me through half-closed eyes and raised his arms to rest on the back edge of the bath. "I've felt your passion and would very much like teaching you to enjoy the next step."

The Ambrose in the tub was not at all the petulant man-baby he'd been in the study, and Goddess, after witnessing Cinden and Ozius, I'd felt such pent-up desire all day. *Wait, am I considering this? And what about Tommand?*

"Do you really think Tommand is more handsome than me? More appealing than all of this?" he said thickly, running a lazy hand across his muscular chest.

It's like he'd known I was thinking about his advisor.

"I'm more attracted to him, yes, and you needn't go back and share that with him," I murmured, already regretting the overshare.

"Tommand thinks you are attractive, too. He mentioned your eyes. What did he call them? The color of an angry ocean."

Hearing that Tommand found me attractive made little fairies dance in my head, but something still didn't feel right.

"Ambrose, clear something up for me. You want to 'get between my legs,' Tommand finds me 'attractive,' I've done stuff with the both of you. Is this a contest? Do you go after the same person for sport... or are you friends who don't actually like each other?"

He let out a long breath and smiled faintly while he swirled his fingertips in the thick, sudsy foam.

"Here's the deal: Tommand made a choice a long time ago not to *be* with anyone if you get my meaning. I mean, sure, he fucked plenty when he was younger, but with his job being what it is, he's not keen on having the person he loves murdered in front of his eyes as vengeance, or them being kidnapped for ransom, or having them be disemboweled to make a point, or waking up to find the parts of their dismembered body scattered—"

"Okay. I get it. Please stop."

"*You* just happened to pique his interest, probably because he likes them succulent, but I'm afraid it's just him and his hand until he's retired." Ambrose rolled his shoulders as he spoke, which caused the muscles of his chest to tense and relax.

"I think that's awfully sad... but reasonable. I couldn't imagine what it would be like to constantly worry that I was endangering someone I loved... I kind of regret touching his penis now."

"You did what? And we haven't even..." Ambrose pursed his lips.

"Oh, he didn't share *that* with you?" A coy smile pulled at my mouth, and I hugged his cardamom-smelling shirt closer.

"No. No, he didn't... Eira, get in the tub."

My mind may have been empathizing with Tommand, but my body was certainly reacting to Ambrose's command. Would it be problematic to have a little fun with the man I'd imagined in this very bath a few days ago?

"You will stop if I ask you to?" I quizzed.

"I will... but you won't."

"And you won't have any emotional hang-ups or anything like that afterward?"

"I'm not really the commitment type, Eira, so no."

"And are you... clean." The last thing I wanted was an itchy crotch and a trip to the healer.

"I am and have always been fastidious in my safety."

I decided.

Tossing his shirt to the side, I slid myself towards the tub, increasingly aware of the cold stone under my hot skin. I lowered myself into the heated water, thankful for the bubbles that gave me *some* cover. I crossed an arm over my chest as a comfort against Ambrose's unwavering gaze and felt my face become as red as the Mantle's robes.

"Eira, I meant what I said; your body was designed to entice. Those big, beautiful breasts belong in someone's hands, and the soft curve of your stomach is divine, the image of the Goddess herself. I imagine you will fit flawlessly around my cock."

I dropped my arms and felt the little pulses start below the water's surface.

"Walk to me." His voice dropped low.

My nipples hardened into tight buds, and he watched their transformation appreciatively as he drew the corner of his lower lip between his teeth.

"How do you feel about watching me make myself come?" he asked.

I feel like that would be insanely scandalous. I swallowed my nerves and nodded, wanting him to continue. He dropped an arm under the water, and his bicep began tensing and relaxing in a steady rhythm. My mouth watered. Watching him pleasure himself spiked my own arousal surprisingly high. The way he moved, the delight on his face, it was all rather appealing.

"I believe I have identified the flush of your desire... Gotwig would be impressed don't you think? Now, replace my hand with yours, Nortia. Work me up, then down."

I half-walked, half-floated to him, and sunk my hand into the sudsy water where I felt the currents shifting as he stroked himself. When I found Ambrose's hand, he took my fingers in his own and closed them around his length. He groaned deeply, and a wonderfully heavy sensation settled in my passage. I was becoming slick and wet, preparing for the pleasure I hoped he could give.

"There is nothing like the touch of the uninitiated. No, it is not an insult." He lifted his hand to my cheek. "Watching you... feeling you discover me, is a pleasure all its own."

I *had* been moving tentatively at first, shyly feeling the different parts of him, but fortified by his words and my own growing need, I sent my other hand under the water to cup his testicles, which were weightier than I assumed they would be.

"Made for this," he whispered. "Nortia, sit on my lap, facing me."

Remembering Cinden doing the same with Ozius, I obeyed, wanting so badly to feel his chest on mine. Grasping his elbows for support I moved forward placing my knees on either side of his thighs. I rose up and poised my opening on the tip of his erection.

"Not yet, greedy harpy... too soon," he ground out the words as he reached around to cup my backside. Extra buoyant in the water, he pulled me tightly against him, where his arousal stood proudly between us. I ran my hands down his flawless fair-skinned chest.

"Have you pleasured yourself before?"

I nodded, not caring if I seemed brazen. His hand moved to my entrance, parting me expertly.

"Outstanding." Ambrose used his legs to raise my hips just above the water and began to insert a single finger slowly into me. I almost climaxed on contact. His single finger was close to the size of two of mine, and in this position, I could take in every inch he fed me.

"You feel perfect to me... but tell me what feels best." He hooked his finger, just a little, and moved it in and out.

"A little further in, and... slower." I reached behind his head, found the soap that had deflected off of him earlier, and slicked up my hands. This was something that made stimulating my own clitoris more fun, and I figured he might like it as well. Wrapping my hand around his length, I squeezed and glided my fingers over him, following the rhythm his finger had set.

"Exquisite... Tommand will have my head when I tell him—"

"That *I've* had *your* head?" I squeezed him harder.

Green eyes narrowed wickedly, my comment earning me a deep thrust.

"You may end up... *yes*, now faster... my masterwork, Nortia."

"Ambrose, what's it like when you're with a man?" I conjured an image of him and a faceless other. "In my mind, it's all hard planes and big hands and—"

"It's delicious. And I can take as well as I can give."

"Mmm, I bet you can." Just the thought nearly put me over the edge.

"And you, would you like a pair of fine tits at your lips?"

My head fell back and rolled to my shoulder. "Yes, I would. That... Ambrose, I like *that*," I breathed while pumping him more quickly.

A crash sounded in the other room.

Fuck! The door wasn't closed!

"My girl, are you here?" Wide-eyed, I untangled from the Scion and motioned for him to duck under the bubbly water. He scoffed at my face.

"You will *die* here," I whispered, drawing a finger across my neck. "Yes, Nan... just about done. I'll be right out!"

Ambrose dunked his body under the water, tucking himself into the corner of the tub. I stood in front of him, frantically piling up suds.

"Eira, tomorrow is the Grooming for all Troth," Nan said, peering around the door. Ambrose's hand nudged my thigh, and I squeezed my legs tightly shut. "You are expected on the third level by eleven in the morning. Now get out, go on; I'll fetch you a drink from the kitchen before bed."

A soap-slicked finger pushed right through my curls.

"Thank you! Nan, can you please see if they have the honied milk?" I tried my best to keep the alarm from my voice.

"I will love, back in a moment."

The door in the next room shut, and with the strength of fifteen Scion, I pulled an impressively aroused Ambrose to his feet.

"Get out, get your clothes, and go. I bought us ten minutes max."

"We were in the middle of—"

"—signing our death notices if she or Tussi catches you here. Mossius forbid Tussi walks in! The mood has passed. Thank you and goodbye."

"Troth Nortia, the state I find myself in—"

"—can be remedied with your own hand. Get out!" I grabbed the shirt he was pulling over his head and jerked it down quickly. The clock was already ticking, and the Scion was fumbling, trying to step into his underclothes. Snatching the small shorts from his hands, I thrust his pants at him.

"Pants, now. Put those in your pocket." I began shoving a half-dressed Ambrose into the other room.

The door opened, and we froze.

Kairus's expression transformed from shock to pure amusement, her smile curling up like a cat's whiskers.

"That's not the right one, Eira." She looked at Ambrose and back at me, her eyes sparkling as she watched him struggle to get his tight pants over his wet thighs.

"Well," I shrugged, "he was the one that was available."

"I am not sure my ego can take more of this," Ambrose lamented while closing the buttons at his waist.

Silently, Kairus leaned over and reopened the door.

"You'll be fine." I pushed him through the threshold, and Kairus slammed the door home.

Naked, dripping in the middle of our room, I glanced at my tight-lipped friend whose shoulders were already shaking from repressed laughter.

"I am *literally* the best Troth ever." I grinned and headed back to the bath to wash.

Chapter Nineteen

THE GROOMING

"**Y**ou would not have pried that man from my room!" Richelle blurted, brandishing her butter-covered knife.

"I'm just glad it was you who walked in," I stuffed a piece of cheese and a handful of grapes in my mouth. "Who do you think would have been worse, Tussi or Nan?" I plucked another fruit and turned toward Kairus.

"Oh. Well, let us think." Dramatically, Kairus tossed out her hands and then balled them under her chin, like she was ready to tell a story to a group of toddlers. "Tussi, upon witnessing you wanking Ambrose, would likely have torn out the remaining two hairs from his head and passed clear out... but not before wailing something like 'ignoble Nortian trollop' before he hit the ground." She perfectly mimicked Tussi by thrusting a pointed finger in the air. "Nan? I wouldn't put it past her to have pulled him out of that tub by the big ole dick—and it was huge you all, like... " she grasped her tall glass of juice, milking the vessel with both hands, "about like this... right, Eira?"

Luræna dissolved into fits of laughter so intense she sagged across Richelle for support, only to be furiously jostled by the orange-haired Troth bouncing merrily in her seat.

Grabbing the purple liquid from my blonde friend, I hefted the glass one-handed and eyed it closely.

"Kairus, I'm not sure what *you* saw, but I promise, ladies, I only needed one hand." I quipped. Luræna's high-pitched shrieks startled a nearby acolyte who'd been refilling mugs of steaming hot tea at the next table over. She didn't attempt to conceal her annoyance at the boisterous behavior.

"Okay, but I can grasp a jug the size of a baby's head with these paws. I need accurate details, Eir—Oh! Speaking of... your paramour just walked in looking worse for wear." Richelle tipped a mug to her mouth and wiggled her sparse brows. Not one of them covert, every Troth at the table swiveled around to catch an eyeful of an exceptionally rough-looking Ambrose.

"Eira? Do you think the same person who busted his lip also gave him that nasty cut?" Kairus inspected her fingernails at arm's length. "It appears his nose is also one size too big for his pretty face this morning."

"My bet's on Nan," Luræna teased, tucking one side of her blue-black hair behind her ear.

I chuckled behind my hand but was actually quite concerned about the man I'd kicked out of my bedroom. He still wore his perpetually amused expression, but he looked ragged. He looked lost-a-fight-with-an-orca-and-got-gored-by-a-moose bad.

Noticing his enraptured audience, Ambrose snapped to attention and saluted like a soldier would his captain, his left fist placed on his right shoulder. He blew a kiss before making his way to a table with Greggen and Evandr, who had no visible injuries. My guess was, whatever happened, it had nothing to do with Scion training.

"L-la-ladies, I am so... sorry to disturb you," stammered Abben, who approached our table, "Richelle, uh, T-Troth Solnna, we must head to the Grooming."

"Thank you, Abben. Let's get going. My mother told me the Grooming would be all manner of interesting!" She rose from her seat and tucked her arm into her companion's elbow. "Come on, girls!"

···+)⚊(+···

On our way to the third level, Kairus explained that Tussi had told her that the Grooming was a day devoted to bettering ourselves and learning the social customs of the four kingdoms. Richelle's mother told her it was all makeup and fun. Having spent my entire life as the always hygienic but no-frills Eira, I was hoping her mom's explanation was more true-to-life. I was looking forward to the opportunity to enhance my appearance. I wanted to see if I'd be treated differently like the Monwyns often were.

I didn't think that a person's appearance was a prime factor in being a successful Obligate, but I was keenly aware of how different Troth were treated. A few days ago, on the way to dinner, Yemailrys had tried to push past a slow-walking Zotikos on the stairs. It ended with him stumbling backward and sprawling across the last couple of steps. She had rushed to his side, batting her beautifully outlined eyes and letting her locks fall over her shoulder and onto his arm. His response, legs askew and his arm awkwardly bent, was to look up into her face and say, "It was entirely my fault, lovely lady." She'd flounced off afterward, smiling secretively at Luræna as she passed. Weaponizing my looks was a skill I *wanted* to learn.

Kairus had shown me there were other uses for cosmetics as well. Having lived with her for the week, I'd noticed she could fall into dark spells rather quickly. She would go silent, blank-faced, and often glassy-eyed and stare into the room as if she was no longer on our plane. She always managed to overcome what bore down on her, though, and putting on her pigments, creams, and oils was a ritual that seemed to aid her in feeling more alive. It didn't seem to matter to her if others noticed or appreciated the effort—she was doing it so that she felt better, more confident, and more in control.

After stepping off the third-floor staircase, we made our way around the balcony and came to a set of free-swinging double doors.

"Did you see Cinden yesterday? We were supposed to meet with Chentel last evening, but she never showed up," Kairus asked as we followed behind a group of our sister Troth.

"Nope, didn't see her at—whoa!" The air behind the doors struck me, heavy and wet, and as we proceeded forward to another double set, my light-pink linen day dress became sodden and sagged from my body.

"I'm glad I didn't wear silk today," Kairus exclaimed while patting gently under her eyes.

A second set of doors swung open, and a thick fog rolled out surrounding us. An acolyte wrapped in a short length of sopping red cloth appeared from the mists and handed us each a loosely woven basket.

"Welcome, Obligates, in the next room, you are to remove your clothing, including all bindings, brassieres, or slips. Nothing is to remain on your feet, and all cosmetics must be scrubbed from your body. Place your personal belongings in the baskets, where they will remain until the Grooming has ended." The acolyte, whose head was shaved close like Lyta's, pointed us through the door and to the right.

Along with the Troth in front of us, we entered a short hallway and walked into a small changing room that would only fit three or four comfortably. Its walls were painted in stripes of cream and gold and it smelled strongly of woodsmoke. I glimpsed a Solnnan Troth removing her undergarments and then placing her basket on one of the four-tiered shelves built into the back wall. Each had been labeled with the name of a kingdom. I sat and pulled off my shoes and stockings and took a moment to dig the dirt from my toenail—*stupid Maneuvering*—before pulling my gown over my head. Kairus hadn't moved.

"You okay?"

"I will be... maybe... I just have to get used to this." She dropped her dress to the ground and stepped out with her back to me. I watched her move her arms to her stomach and then her legs, unsure of where they would offer the most protection. She settled on crossing them over her chest.

"Do Monwyns not wear bindings?" I asked, curious as to why she was bare under her garment. I untied the linen small clothes from either side of my hips and tossed them in to meet my other belongings.

"Not that I am aware of. We have a type of chemise, though, that laces at the sides and front... but I am much less endowed than many so have no need to wear one." She shrugged and tucked her hands into her underarms.

"I've not known a day without my binding. The moment you hit thirteen in Nortia, every woman wears one at all times unless you're sleeping. Did you see what that Solnnan Troth was wearing before she left?" The item in question had been made with two wide straps at the shoulder that connected to a structured garment that cupped her breasts and hugged the Troth from her ribcage to her natural waist. "It didn't look like it squished her like my wraps do." I massaged my chest, happy to be unencumbered.

"Uh oh, Kairus." My short burst of laughter bounced off the walls. "Your powdered blacks run all over your cheeks. You look... like a wild little imp! Please don't turn me to stone, or milk my muskoxen dry, sneaky demon!"

"Stupid wet air! I bet my hair looks as flat as Gotwig's ass too!" She snatched up a square of cloth from a stack on the shelf and rubbed the smeared mess from her eyes.

"It's going to take more than that, imp-friend." I grabbed another cloth and together we scraped and rubbed till her skin glowed red—Nan would have approved.

Still laughing at the sight of our bedraggled selves, we hurried back into the main room, where the steam did quite a bit to conceal the bodies of the present Troth. Kairus was able to relax enough to carry on a conversation but continued hugging herself around the waist.

"Eira," she whispered into my ear, "Yemailrys's breasts are bigger than your giant head... you think she could spare some for me?"

Now I had to look.

I glanced to the side, doing my best to look natural.

"I heard that, Kairus!" Yemailrys's honied voice sang out, "And you can have all you want. These grain sacks made me both the laughingstock of my friends and the object of too many nasty old men's desire." She hefted the two mounds to her neck and let them fall with a meaty thwack. "These have been with me since my twelfth year, can you imagine?"

Amid a flurry of laughter, three more Troth arrived, and if I'd counted right, the total number of honored women added up to an even ten. Up to this point, I'd only interacted with a handful of them personally but was looking forward to officially meeting them, even if doing so unclothed.

"Obligates, head to the steam room's back door." Three acolytes entered the room and ushered us to our next destination.

We walked through and entered a room that was shaped like an octagon. It was bright and airy, and quite cold. Four sides had entryways that led to additional spaces. The entire surface of the room was covered in small white tiles, including the expanse of the vaulted ceiling. Dozens of small mirrors hung on the walls at differing heights, and the majority of the floor's space was taken up by a ring of raised platforms.

"Welcome to your Grooming, ladies." I turned around to see who spoke. "You find yourselves standing in the presence of Cyra Fabia, world traveler, and personal wardrobe attendant to the grand Queen Jessum of Solnna and four of the lesser Queens Gaea! I bear rights of admittance to every court on the continent, and I can tell immediately from the look and smell of you, I am in for a challenge!"

Dressed in a light-gold ensemble that bared her shoulders and flowed free from her bust, a striking older woman walked so gracefully toward us that she seemed to glide across the floor. She was willowy and tall and had hawkish features that seemed to have been molded from finely polished clay. Her slightly hooked nose gave her an air of dignity, and the shimmering gold painted on her eyes complemented her smooth, almost buttery complexion.

"Please move into the circle. You may sit on the platforms individually but make sure to face the inside of our ring."

Richelle sat on the platform to my left, and Kairus occupied the one to my right, with Cinden and Kymor seated beyond her.

"I've traversed the kingdoms more often than anyone alive. More than the merchants and certainly more than the priests. I have learned to navigate the upper echelons of each distinct society," she smoothed a stray steel-gray lock at her temple, returning it to her swept-back length of her hair, "and were any of those snobby socialites as clever as I, perhaps they would have recognized they dined with a cheesemonger's daughter, but, as our luck would have it... humans only tend to see what you show them."

Cyra Fabia, moved in a tight circle, surveying each Troth as she rotated on an invisible axis at the center of our stations. "Today we will reduce ourselves to blank slates and then rebuild our images anew, all in preparation for tomorrow's Third Maneuvering."

She turned and her gaze landed on Farai.

"Monwyns, assist each other in removing your artificial hair. Gaeans, we have on staff a healer of Cult Mossius. They will reform your styles and perform the proper ritual the day after tomorrow. For now, undo your braids and remove the gold fibers. Ensure your spoken permission is given to each of the acolytes who are working with you... and do not cross me on this."

Chentel openly blanched at the demand, and a watery-eyed Cinden clutched at the bottom of her leather-encased braid. The three Monwyn women gathered together and began pulling out thick falls of each other's hair that had somehow been attached to their scalps. My mouth fell open as I watched Kairus's moonbeam-colored curls get heaped into a pile. She was left with much thinner shoulder-length coils. Yemailrys' auburn locks followed suit as did Farai's multi-tonal brunette and gold-tinged ringlets. I was stunned. I thought the magnificent locks of the Monwyns must have been some trait passed down for generations or maybe they were so stunning because they bathed in magical mountain water. When the three rejoined us after completing their task, they looked so much more vulnerable than they had when they were only nude. My heart went out to them. Yemailrys crossed her legs and arms, and Farai, who I now suspected had been using her long locks to shield herself, was on the verge of tears. I recalled how she'd shied away from the crowd before Gotwig's nasty Maneuvering and knew this had to be even more difficult for her, as she'd been almost fully covered then.

"Well done. Now, stand up on your platforms, ladies, hands on your hips. Don't look so sullen, dear this is a safe space," Fabia clucked at Luræna.

Our instructor began walking the inner ring as I heard little sniffles coming from my left. I saw that the most spirited Troth among us had been reduced to pouring tears.

"Richelle?" I asked, concerned about my friend.

"Goddess, Eira, I'm as plump as a pig... two pigs!" More tears fell from her hazel eyes and ran down her neck. "Father says I have no control, my brother says no husband would ever mount an elephant so fat, and here I am about to take on a job that requires me to *entice* people."

Hear me, Goddess, if I ever cross her brother, for every tear she's cried, he'll earn a punch to his nasty fucking throat.

"Your brother sounds like a real fucking catch, Richelle." I couldn't and didn't want to hide the anger in my voice.

"Oh, he is," she said earnestly. "He's high born and handsome and does everything well."

"Seems to me he doesn't *brother* all that well." She nodded her agreement while running a hand across her tear-stained cheeks. "Richelle, I think you are enchanting just as you are, and you know what, Ambrose actually managed to teach me something of value last night." I held out my open palm and she sat hers gingerly in mine. "*All* bodies are delicious bodies."

A little smile cracked her mouth.

"*He* said that? Really?"

"Mmhmm and he also said he wanted to bite my fat roll, so he must have meant it." I cocked my head at her and pulled a face.

"He wanted to... ha! Well, I have plenty to feast on." She managed a smile. "If I'm good enough for the Scion of Sensuality, I guess I can at least try to be okay in front of my sisters." Simultaneously, she took my hand and a deep breath. Together, we stood, bearing our perfect imperfections to everyone in the room.

"Eira?" She bit at a fingernail on her other hand. "You have very nice breasts. They are shapely and a great size for your body," Richelle said with a matter-of-fact nod of her head.

"Richelle, you should know... your butt is shaped like one of those fantastically round Solnnan cakes, and I think it's delightful."

I felt fingers lace through mine on my opposite hand and I turned to Kairus.

"Eira, I saw you looking at the marks on your thighs the other day. They don't take away from the fact that you are a uniquely beautiful human... not even a single ounce," she squeezed my hand.

Kymor jumped in.

"Kairus, I think you are the most stunning woman I've ever seen. With or without the extra hair, you make people stop in their tracks when you walk by." Kymor took Kairus's hand in hers.

"Even though one of my nipples is crooked?"

"I stand by what I said." Kymor, whose dark-blonde curls rose high around her crown, raised Kairus's hand and planted a kiss right on the top like the most devoted courtier.

I looked beyond to Cinden, whose hair tumbled in crimpy waves down her back.

"Cinden–"

"I know *you* know I'm a feast for the eyes; I've seen you *study* me." She winked and turned away.

Ouch. I'd been caught after all. I guess I'd need to figure out how to apologize to the two Gaeans sooner rather than later, and how embarrassing was that going to be? *I'm sorry I watched you sex each other up. You were performing so well I had to take notes.* I needed to calm myself before everyone mistook my mortal embarrassment for sex flush. *Stupid Gotwig.*

"Ladies, if you are done with your rather absurd praise party, I find I would like to begin *my* session. Hands to your hips." At our instructor's words, we silenced and dutifully stood still on our platforms.

"There are differing standards of beauty in each of the kingdoms." She leisurely made her way around the circle and stopped next to Luræna. "You will note the Solnnan women remove the hair from their arms, underarms, mons pubis, and legs. I've been told the custom is about combating the hot climate, but more likely the custom was born of sexual preference. Solnnan males will often remove the hair from their faces and chests... and like their women, they do enjoy the use of cosmetics, though more sparingly."

She made her next stop at Cinden.

"My, aren't we lovely?" She looked the Troth up then down and motioned for her to spin around until she faced front again. "Troth Gaea, please open your mouth wide." Cinden obeyed, dropping her jaw and tilting her head backward. "When a Gaean child's permanent teeth are nascent, the back molars are capped in gold. If you are of the royal class, the caps will be set with a flurry of tiny malachite gemstones. The gold honors Mossius, and the green stone is said to speed the healing processes of those who wear it. Some Gaeans will bear an inked or scarred marking of the double flames on their bodies. More often than not, it seems to appeal to the more devout members of the healer's cult."

Fabia passed over me, and her gaze landed on Kairus. "Please drop your arms, Lady Monwyn."

Kairus hesitated just briefly before lowering the arms that had covered her chest again.

"Lady Monwyn. I see the scar, but where is your Progression Ring?" Our instructor's smooth voice warbled.

"Well, uh... I removed it and used it to pierce my navel." Kairus, looking sheepish for the first time since we'd met, shrugged and folded her hands together at her stomach.

"That will be remedied before you leave this temple." Cyra Fabia, who was taller than Kairus on her pedestal, leveled her gaze at the Troth, leaving no room for challenge.

"Monwyn women of high status or great wealth, upon beginning their menses, have a thin ring of gold placed around their left nipple, and a bar is pierced through the flesh, keeping the ring secure. Women with this piercing are highly sought after on the marriage market and are generally betrothed through political arrangement." Our instructor changed her course and stood with her back to me. "The upper class and all royal males of Monwyn have a single or double piercing in the very top of their ear as well. One piercing indicates a boy having come of age, and the second denotes a man who has taken a wife."

"Lastly, we have Nortia." She never turned to face me but spoke at the assembled Troth. "Nortia's women spend their days wrapped in furs. Their hairstyles tend toward function over fashion. There are no truly unique customs of body modification... just... women as they are. They do bind their chests tightly as a measure of sexual modesty."

"Wait, what? It's so they can bow hunt. That's what my Gram told us."

"Your *Gram* was wrong."

One... two... hide it Eira, choke it back! Women of means do hunt, and it just makes it easier to move unimpeded. You know this.

"The men follow no clothing restrictions but can be heavily decorated with permanent ink. This is generally found across the outer thighs and shoulders." Spinning on her heel, she walked toward me, not stopping until we were uncomfortably close. "Want a little fun fact? Those who are exceptionally perceptive can identify a Nortian by their slightly fishy scent. Consuming seafood almost exclusively leads to the ever-so-faint aroma. Not to mention, angling is a favorite pastime for the young and old, and odors do sink into leather and fur." Fabia came towards me, sniffing rapidly. "Yes... just ever so slightly."

"I smell like fish? A lot of people smell like fish after they eat it. It's natural, plus the fish and whale industry keeps my people fed, so I hope people continue eating *and* smelling like fish," I bristled, feeling heat flood my face.

"Troth Nortia, you will *know* if I mean to insult you. This is just a piece of knowledge that may be useful in the future. So touchy, another very Nortian quality." She turned and floated gracefully back to the middle of the circled platforms.

"Today, ladies, you will assume new identities. Each of you will be transformed into an upper-class woman from a kingdom not your own, and at tomorrow's Maneuvering, you will present yourself thusly, *never* dropping from character. After today's Grooming, I will provide primers and props for you to study. I will be amongst your judges at tomorrow evening's performance, and I *will* know if you have shirked your readings."

"Silinas, my list!" The acolyte ran forward, unrolling a parchment. "The following Troth will play the role of Gaeans: Kairus, Luræna, and Richelle. The Solnnans will be Chentel and Farai. Our Monwyns are Eira, Kymor, and Kol. Finally, our Nortians—Cinden, and Yemailrys.

"Gaeans pass through the door to my right. Monwyns, the left. Nortians, proceed forward through the double doors, and Solnnans, you will walk back into the steam chamber and take in the vapors until called."

We all moved slowly from our stands. Becoming Monwynified was going to be interesting. I'd somehow have to discover and master poise overnight. *Shit!* I backtracked quickly to the Monwyn door, having just followed the "Nortian" group to their destination. The three of us huddled just inside the doorway.

"Hello, I'm Eira. I saw you at the First Maneuvering, but we haven't been introduced."

"Kol," the stout woman waggled her fingers in greeting.

Kol was interesting. She looked a lot older than the average Troth. Her skin seemed more mature and her light brown hair was frosted with strands of white at the top of her crown.

"I waited to make my journey," she grinned. I got the impression that was how she started off most of her conversations here. I was curious to hear what Kol's story was. I knew a Primus or king made the ultimate choice on when a Troth was sent to the temple, but she seemed to be in the latter end of her third decade, nearly twice the age of the youngest Troth here.

"Well, I'm glad to meet you. Ready to become a mountain woman?"

"Obligates, hurry now. Please lay on the tables, face down." A priestess flanked by two shorn acolytes waved us further in. "We are on a strict timetable!"

This room was very much like the one we had just come from but was full of clashing smells. Sweet, citrus, floral, and medicinal, all tangled into a heady and jarring aroma. I hopped up on a table next to Kymor. Kol took the table on my other side. Twisting onto my stomach, I laid flat, ready for the next steps in our transformations.

"Monwyn women keep themselves pristine. The skin is soft and youthful and will remain so well into their older years. The three of you come from places where harsh extremes are the norm and can age the skin before its time. We will work to mitigate the damage that has already been done," said the priestess.

One of the acolytes moved next to my table, but I couldn't make out what she was doing positioned as I was. The only indication of what was coming was a sucking, squelching noise, like digging out a glob of jam from a brand-new jar.

A massive blob plopped down on the middle of my back.

"We will first scour your bodies to remove impurities that cause a multitude of skin ailments." I turned my head to watch the acolyte who was working on Kymor. With both hands, she began to rub a thick green gel into the Troth's back and waist. The acolyte at my side began working the mixture into my shoulders a moment later. The blob's texture was gritty, but the smell of the abrasive goo was divine.

"Crushed walnut shells have been finely ground into a grit that will slough off the overabundance of oil that collects and cakes the skin, causing unsightly eruptions and other imperfections on the body. The honey you smell will cleanse and calm inflammation, and the mint will even out your complexions and reduce the redness caused by the abrasive scrub."

The process was quite pleasant. It was like finally having an itch scratched that you couldn't reach on your own. I closed my eyes and enjoyed the acolyte's ministrations.

The cooling sensation from the mint left me feeling fresh. That is, until the acolyte made her third pass over my now super-sensitive skin. The massage began to feel less like a relieved itch and more like having glass ground into my flesh. The stinging started as a mild irritation and amplified until I felt like I was burning from within.

"This is seriously painful," Kol said through gritted teeth.

"I feel like I've been sitting on coals," I agreed.

"You be thankful someone taught you about moisturizing cream. You still have some dry spots, but those two were scrubbed way harder than you. Now, flip," The priestess commanded. *Thank you, Momma.* I twisted to my back, wincing at the sting between my shoulder blades. I'd not even had a chance to lay back when another cold blob was slapped between my breasts.

"Troth Nortia, a recommendation: if you don't want your breasts flattened out like lily pads before you are in your third decade, I'd suggest trying the undergarment worn by the Solnnans. For overabundant, slightly drooping chests like yours, they do wonders for maintaining a youthful figure." The priestess walked through the tables as the scrubbing continued. *This is Nan's ideal afterlife.*

"Kymor and Eira will require extractions," said the priestess who examined my face. She looked to her left. "Kol will need her sunspots lightened."

By the time our scrub was finished, I was raw and nauseous from the torture. The cool burn didn't subside until we were doused with buckets of warm water.

"It's a wonder the Monwyn women aren't *more* peevish than they are," murmured Kymor, who bent at the waist trying to remove a speck of stubborn green. Her lightly tanned skin was splotched with a maze of angry, reddening streaks.

While the priestess instructed the acolytes, commenting often on their techniques, the women squeezed and picked at my face and Kymor's chest and back. I didn't have any blemishes that *I* noticed, but they were clearly mining for ore. I saw welts and fingernail indentations scattered across Kymor's body, and the acolyte in charge of her patted a cloth on the spots that bled. Kol sat patiently on her table and watched us while a thick, white paste dried on her face and hands.

"Eira, having hair of a deeper hue means the light dusting of hair on your face tends to be darker as well. Monwyn women shape their brows meticulously and would find it unseemly to have even a single stray hair on their upper lip or chin."

The acolyte produced metal tweezers from under the table and began plucking at my brows, first below their natural arch and then above. The hair removal wasn't so bad, but when she moved to pull out the few hairs from my top lip, my eyes watered profusely with every sharp tug.

"Well done, Troth! Your skin is glowing and any nicks or marks that are left should disappear by morning." She produced a small mirror and held it up to my face. "Though you can resume your normal grooming habits after the Maneuvering, I would venture to say you may wish to keep up with at least part of this new regimen."

I didn't think my features would change much from the hair removal process, but the face I saw reflected looked more angular... more refined. The arches of my brows were more distinct than they had been, and their tails seemed sharper and more elongated. The look was quite reminiscent of Yemailrys and Farai, whereas Kairus' brows were too light a color to look shabby.

"You may stand and follow." They marched us across the tile floor where we stood shoulder to shoulder. The acolytes then toweled off Kymor and me, while another removed the paste from Kol's skin. I could smell the pungent poultice from where I stood and saw that it had turned the flesh underneath an alarmingly pale color.

"Does it hurt?" Kymor whispered.

"Quite badly," the stoic Kol whispered back.

"In Monwyn, skin lotions are applied to your persons twice per day and to your hands four times." We were handed jars of lotion and began applying them all over as instructed. "Take these with you and follow the protocol until tomorrow evening." The jar I received was purple and smelled of jasmine.

"In the next area, your hair will be modified and styled to reflect the Monwyn sense of fashion. Please walk out the way you entered."

Passing under the threshold, my group of three encountered a morose-looking Cinden and a shockingly flat-chested Yemailrys, who looked like she was having trouble drawing her breath. Flashing a tight smile, I waved at the pair as we crossed the hall.

"You're as red as an apple," Cinden scoffed, looking downright alarmed.

"Because Monwyn women practice self-mutilation!" Kymor joked.

I smacked playfully at Cinden's leg as she passed but failed to dodge the well-timed slap of Yemailrys's palm against my bare butt. The cackles of naughty Troth filled the room.

"Ladies, do come now!" A stern-faced priestess waved us through the door across the main chamber. "Sit quickly." A row of low chairs with blue cushions lined the wall at the back of the room.

"We will begin by adding plant-based fibers into your existing hair. They have been prepared, combed, and dyed into colors slightly bolder than your natural locks. Kol, we will apply a walnut and sage stain to your crown, removing the gray, before we begin." She pointed Kol in the direction of a drainage hole in the floor, telling her to sit on the tile floor next to it. The priestess took stock of the more seasoned Troth, scrunching up her nose and turning down the sides of her mouth. "Monwyn women do their best to preserve their youth for as long as possible, so your current configuration of colors would be unacceptable to any noble woman below her sixth decade."

"I'm thirty-and-nine, priestess... in case you were wondering," Kol sighed but didn't look upset.

"I do admit to being curious about your advanced age. It's not common to receive a Troth after her third decade has begun." The priestess swept up her robes, moving closer to Kol. "Do you still have your courses?"

"I do."

"And are they regular? We often have trouble controlling the menses of the older Obligate."

"I'm sorry, you what?" I butt in. This was the first I'd heard of this.

"You've yet to attend Matters of Unity I presume? Since you began your journey to the temple, the liquids you have been given have contained herbs used to control one's cycle. It would be poor form for the temple to send you to your Assignments with a babe in your belly, and given the way you Obligates rut, it's quite the necessary step. According to this morning's charting, you should all get your bleed in the next three days... you may close your mouth, Troth Nortia."

One... two... breathe... breathe... three.

"Perhaps telling us immediately that we were to be drugged would be better?" I piped up.

"Calm yourself. You will find it to relieve certain afflictions, and all of the priestesses and acolytes follow the same protocol." She flippantly dismissed my concern. "It is quite safe."

"In three days' time, I'll be locked in my bathing chamber. Can you imagine every woman in this temple starting her monthlies at once?" Kol mused. "Have the Scion been warned? Someone should probably tell them."

"Or not," I said dryly.

As we continued to converse, acolytes used a dark, sticky substance and flat bone scrapers to secure bundles of hair near our scalps. Sure enough, the thinly woven strands were a shade different from our hair colors. They were richer and shinier than what grew naturally from our heads. As section after section was applied, I felt my head become heavier and my hair fuller. I reached down beside me and pulled a handful of the waist-length fibers to my face, impressed by how much they looked and felt like my own.

Kol, who had finished her first treatment, was now having her hair lengthened, and I was able to watch the process. After one Troth applied the fibers, the other wetted and wrapped the new strands around a mess of fabric-covered dowels and rolled them up, securing them around her forehead and ears.

"To the last room, ladies!" the priestess clapped, drawing our attention. "The curling rods won't be removed until after your last Grooming session, and your ringlets should remain intact for several days if they are taken care of."

We were again escorted into the main chamber, where I saw Farai coming out of her room. Her hair had been straightened and rolled under itself, giving her a look similar to Luræna's short, sleek style. I didn't even recognize Chentel, who walked with her, until we met in the middle of the room.

"That one is the worst." The now short-haired brunette scratched at her hairless arm.

"I guess I can say I tried it once, but I won't be doing it again." Farai pointed to her vulva, now smooth, red, and irritated. "It looks like one of those bald cats now." Our small group shared a conciliatory chuckle. "Welp, Goddess be with you!" A humorous smile danced across her face.

Several tall tables and a little rolling cart were positioned on the left side of the much smaller third room, with a sizable, recessed fireplace occupying the back wall. The massive hearth housed two separate flames, and a multitude of vessels and bowls hung suspended from its mantel. Below those, dozens of three-legged pots were scattered around the blazes. A priestess, whose features were obscured by her hood, was mixing a brown powder into a bowl of thin, yellow liquid, and a cloying smell permeated the air, joined almost immediately by a faint smell of alcohol.

"Come forward." A woman dressed in a forest-green wrap waved over our group. She sat next to the cart I'd spotted earlier, but I was just now seeing that it was covered in blades and metal tools of various sizes. She went to work, laying out needles of differing lengths and thicknesses, and spoke to us without looking up from her task.

"The following will alter you semi-permanently, but you get to decide your level of commitment." She picked up a pair of metal tongs. "Your job is to become an elite Monwyn woman. The most coveted Monwyn women wear the Progression Ring. It's a permanent sign that the person in question has reached adulthood and is able to reproduce spawn that will come from a quality background. After the gold ring is measured, shaped, and placed around the base of your left nipple, a hollowed needle will be passed through the flesh, creating a hole. From there, a thin hammered bar will be placed into said hole and kept secure with fixtures attached on either side."

Kymor's eyes blinked rapidly, and she shuffled uncomfortably from side to side. The thought of having anything stabbed through one of the most sensitive parts of me made me balk. My palms began to sweat.

"Kymor?"

"No, not worth it." The Troth shook her head, sending the little rods dancing around her unamused face. I looked at Kol and raised my brows in question.

"I can't say I am particularly interested in the adornment, as I have quite visibly reached adulthood... but if you do it... I will." There was a mischievous glint in her eyes, and the corners of her thin lips pulled back in a conspirator's grin.

"Challenge accepted, Madam Sol—Monwyn!" Striding forward with not an ounce of real confidence, I thought of my conversation with Mariad. I wanted to keep the mission of the Obligation in the forefront of my mind, and maybe this would be a tangible reminder of my recommitment.

"Relax and take a few deep breaths. You will need to keep the area clean if you choose to keep the ring after the Third Maneuvering. If you wish to remove it, come back here and I will take it out for you, understand?"

I laid back on the table and closed my eyes, regret instantly sneaking its way in. Resisting the urge to grab my unadorned boobs and run away, I did as was recommended and took a few steady inhalations, which, honestly, made me feel more anxious than calm. *Don't bolt, Eira. You can handle anything for ten seconds. Breathe in, breathe out.*

A hand curved around my own, wrapping around my palm and squeezing firmly. It was Kol. I could smell the lavender on her skin and didn't need to open my eyes.

I squeezed back.

Jumping as the cold ring of metal slid over my nipple, I almost called it quits, but I did my best to settle and mentally prepare for the next step.

I could handle anything.

Pain is fleeting.

Oh, shit!

Metal tongs clamped down on me, and the pressure they created bordered on painful. I sent up a silent prayer.

"Hold tight. In three, two, there we go."

"Whoa! Whoa!" I felt the needle slide the entire way through my nipple and sting painfully before coming out on the other side. Sweat broke out all over my body and my heart palpitated oddly. Clamp still in place, I opened my eyes, surprised when I found there was no bloody stream running down my chest.

"I can't believe I just did that, Kol." I looked up at the Troth, who smiled down at me serenely. I felt another squeeze. *Wow, she truly did look much younger now.* "Thank you, Kol. I needed the support."

Passing the bar through the fresh piercing was uncomfortable but nowhere near as painful as the puncture. It did, however, produce a small bead of blood.

"Kol?" I searched her face and watched her eyes glaze over. "Kol, are you okay?" I squeezed at her hand which had gone completely slack. I sat up quickly and reached out, just in time for her to slide through my hands and hit the floor.

"Kol!" Kymor ran to her side.

"She'll be okay," our piercer muttered. "It's easier to work on her like this anyhow." She moved toward the downed Solnnan, who had passed out cold. She measured a set of rings against Kol's breast.

"You're cult Mossius?" I asked, seeing the double-flamed scar on her upper back.

"I'm a healer, yes, studied under the Gaean priests. I'll have an herb rinse and cooling cream for your recovery. I'll pack two and you can give her the directions." She never looked up from her work. "Return to the main room. You'll have help with taking out those curling rods and be given the needed cosmetics and powders along with your primer."

The healer pointed to the door, and Kymor and I walked out, but only after we double-checked on Kol.

By the time we made our way down to the second floor, I'd decided to take my meal in my room and read up on the Monwyn way of life. The crude pasta and deliciously peppery chicken that had been delivered washed down well with a refreshingly tall glass of lemon water, and I couldn't resist taking the leftover half of Kairus's cake. She had slipped out to see Amais after Tussi had come by for the evening.

I dutifully applied my lotions for the second time and picked up the bracelet I'd sat on the low table the night before. I already cherished the gold cuff that Mariad had slipped onto my wrist and closely examined its craftsmanship. This was the first piece of jewelry I'd ever been gifted, and it meant the world to me. He was the reason I'd been able to make it through the day, and knowing that Kan Keagan had been proud of me—had believed in me—made me realize that perhaps I was made of sterner stuff than I thought.

A soft knock sounded at the door, and more than a little weary, I grabbed the wrap I'd kept on hand ever since Tussi had walked in on me in my usual sleeping attire. Kairus told me it had been the best two minutes of her life. It *was* pretty funny hearing him scream.

"Just a moment," I called out while belting the black silk at my waist.

I opened the door.

"You look... I was afraid that..."

CHAPTER TWENTY

SHOW ME YOURS

"Tommand?" I grabbed his hand and pulled him inside, checking both directions of the hallway before softly closing the door. "Tommand, what's happened?" I searched his distraught face and clutched his hand tighter.

"Ambrose. He walked in looking like... another human. The thought of them altering you..." He reached out, capturing one of my new curls between his fingers. "I couldn't stand the thought of not seeing *you* anymore."

I was dreaming.

I was fast asleep, and the ruffled Tommand standing in front of me would soon turn into the spotted narwhal that often sang to me in slumber.

He dropped the lock he held and let his hand drift from my shoulder to the point right above my elbow. His touch left a tingling trail of raised hair in its wake. He sensed my reaction and dropped his arm to his side, clenching his jaw tightly.

"Have a seat, Tommand," I motioned for him to sit on the edge of the bed, and he complied. He sat and harshly rubbed his face between his hands. The gesture was so... un-Tommand-like.

"I owe you an explanation for everything." He sat up tall, looking straight ahead. "Last night, I lost it, and I hurt my brother. I have never, *ever*, struck someone out of jealousy or without due cause—even if Ambrose had been taunting me to provoke my aggression." Tom was rattled, visibly angry with himself. "I have always maintained strict control over my actions. Shit, we've handled the same women... but when he *regaled* me with the tale of the bath, *your* bath"—he swallowed deeply—"about his hands on you... in you," Tommand's voice dropped low.

I watched the struggle play out in his mind and saw his physical responses become more pronounced. His pupils turned to pinpricks, and he slid his palms down his thighs while he breathed deeply through his nose and slowly out of his mouth.

"One of the issues I see, Tommand, is that you and Ambrose continually feel the need to share every little detail of your lives with each other. You were *both* aware of our shared intimacy. Maybe learn to leave out a few tidbits here and there."

Tommand glanced up and he pressed his lips together.

You know I'm right.

"Lady Chulainn, it may come as a surprise, but before you left the study, I was seconds away from telling you that... that you were right, you are not my issue—"

"No surprise there," I interrupted.

"But... I *want* you to be my issue... and *my* issue alone." He made to take my hand but stopped short of contact.

Oh.

Oh, my.

It took a few seconds to sink in, but all at once I felt like I'd been struck by the frigid wave of a winter ocean.

"I... I... um..." I stammered.

"When you prayed with that old priest, I felt the good in you. When you championed Troth Gaea, shielding her from degradation, I wanted to pull you in my arms and shelter *you* from any harm." He paused, closing his eyes. "When I watched you send Troth Farai away while you continued your mission... you were courage incarnate." Tommand inhaled a shaky breath, and I stared at the wall, frozen, listening to what I never expected to hear.

"I find with every passing day that I grow further in my need to be near you... but I am keenly aware that our lives are on different trajectories. Troth Nortia—"

He stopped briefly when I sat next to him, my legs suddenly not providing adequate support.

"Just Eira," I whispered.

"I cannot." His mouth set in a firm line, and he continued. "We are on two separate paths, both of which have greater purpose."

His rejection—which I ultimately knew was coming—still felt like a physical blow. I was almost angry that he'd simply not kept his feelings to himself.

I like you... but can't like you... just wanted you to know.

"Here's what I think Tommand. The future will continue to be the future. Why would we not take advantage of the right now?" I murmured, surprised by my daring.

"Because taking advantage of you is *not* okay," he asserted, his tone heavy with emotion. *Back off, Eira.*

"Tommand, let's read." He glanced at me sideways and shook his head, already starting to relax.

"By all means, Nortia, let's read." His eyes rolled toward the sky, but he smiled tightly.

"Lie back."

"Troth Nortia, I don't think th—"

"*Emissary* Tommand, hear my vow," I intoned dramatically. "You are safe from my advances from now... until at least tomorrow."

His head snapped to face me.

"But you are *not* safe from mine."

My stomach tightened. I ached to touch him, to explore the body that made my own react as nothing ever had. The gold ring in his rich brown eyes reflected the intensity of his desire.

The person I wanted... wanted me too.

Like the fast-moving flame of a wildfire, a pulsing pressure flared, coiling between my legs, but I suppressed the feelings, understanding it wasn't the time.

"I've never felt safer," I reassured him, resting my hand softly on his shoulder. Tommand tensed but eventually shifted.

His body made my bed look so small and cozy. He laid out on his side, supporting his head on his hand, and kicked his short boots off the edge of the bed. I thought he looked more nervous now than when he'd faced eight Scion.

I grabbed the primer and sat up stiffly.

"Let's learn about being a proper Monwyn woman, shall we?" I glanced over my shoulder. How could the little bump of a once-broken nose make me want to rake my nails down his delectable body?

I forced my eyes back to the pamphlet.

I didn't trust myself.

I knew I would use every excuse I could to put my hands on him if he gave *any* indication he'd allow it.

"Monwyn women maintain a certain aloofness." I felt a rough hand snake its way under the mass of my hair and come to rest on the base of my neck. His fingers massaged the muscles there, applying a firm and tension-relieving pressure. "At all times, they remain poised and project only tranquility." Tommand lowered his arm and traced both sides of my spine with his thumb and forefinger. I leaned into his touch. "To present as a Monwyn woman of means, one must command exacting control over one's every physical movement and emotional response... Tommand, you are *not* aiding in my resolve."

"I do not want you to be a Monwyn woman." He tugged gently at my shoulders.

"I'll be whomever I want, thank you."

"I will still like her too... *probably*." He chuckled lightly as he pulled at me more forcefully. I gave in and fell back until my head rested on his hip. The woodsy smell of cedar and the sweetness of cloves rendered me brainless, causing me to lose my place in the primer. *What were the exact words of my vow? Did I leave room for loopholes?*

"Right now, Tommand, I actually *need* to become a Monwyn... and you happen to be the real-life expert I need." I sat up and twisted to my side, lying down beside him. The primer created an ineffectual barrier between us, but at least it was something.

"Is this too much?" I asked, not wanting to add to his discomfort.

"It's good." He reached out across me and laid a heavy hand on my hip. In one solid motion, he pulled me closer, pressing my body against his. "This is better." The primer wrinkled, crushed between our chests.

"Sir, if you keep this up, I will not be able to ensure your innocence remains... *intact*," I said in my best aloof Monwyn persona. I looked him dead in the eyes and raised an arrogant brow like he so often did.

"My innocence was yours the first day we arrived at the temple, ma'am." I melted into him, recalling that day when—

"Tommand!" His eyes shot wide, and he jerked back, smacking his head on the wall. "What do you mean when *we* arrived?"

"When we came into the temple? You were there, knocking on Ambrose like a door." A dimple appeared on his cheek. "I have never seen any woman, or man for that matter, not fall over themselves to give him whatever he wanted... but there you were."

The dots connected.

I could have smacked the innocent look right off his face.

"TOMMAND? Are *you*, the SNIFFER?" I popped up to my knees and pressed my hands against the middle of his chest, flattening his back to the bed. The comical look on his face said it all. His lip caught between his teeth, and he smiled into my eyes, his own dancing in merriment. *Ridiculously beautiful...*

"You absolute asshole!" I sharply smacked a taut pec. "I came close to burning the place to the ground when you cut me off! And then you..." I paused, remembering Cyra Fabias's proclamation. "Tommand... do I smell like fish?"

Tommand had the good graces to look confused.

"Do you smell like fish?" He grabbed my waist and pulled my chest closer to his nose, inhaling a long-winded breath that tickled my collarbone. "Mmmm." He traced his rough fingertips down the gap of my cinched robe and made such an innocent expression when I shivered at his touch.

"Give me a moment." He stuck his nose in my neck and sniffed at me vigorously like a puppy would his favorite meal.

Our combined laughter was perhaps more an aphrodisiac than our closeness.

His sniffs stilled and his face turned serious.

"You smell... clean... uncorrupted. Like the sweet water of a mountain spring." He pulled my wrist to his nose like he had the first time, and his eyes closed, fanning his lashes against his cheek. My feelings were rapidly getting out of check.

"Can I see your chest?" *Oh, that was dumb.*

"Can I see yours?" I bit my lip at the sound of his thickened voice. *What would a Monwyn woman do? Kairus would have had his shirt off ten minutes ago, had she wanted it.* But I was more and more certain she didn't follow the Monwyn mold. Then there was the fact that Tommand was trying to preserve my—

Fuck it.

I gave him no time to react. I tossed my leg over his hips and climbed aboard.

I was *born* to be bold... *like a Nortian!*

Looking down at my scroll-patterned robe, I tugged the end of the silk belt.

Tommand's low murmur turned to a growl in the back of his throat, and I felt him grow hard between my legs. His mouth parted, and I wanted nothing more than to run my tongue over the valley of his top lip.

I let the robe slip from my shoulders and puddle around my hips.

"Fuck." Tommand sucked in a sharp breath like he'd been punched in the gut, and his hands settled almost painfully on my hips. His deep-set eyes were entranced, fixed on the gold ring that adorned my raw, red nipple.

"How bad does it look? Should I cover it up?" His pupils dilated massively, leaving black orbs to swim in wheaten gold.

I reached to pull my robe back up to cover the angry flesh.

"Don't move. I'll spend in my pants like a boy in his sixteenth year," he said through clenched teeth. "It's... gods, those breasts and... and the ring. It's a bullshit archaic custom that that–"

"—you aren't immune to?" I teased while Tommand laughed tightly. He winced as he scooted me backward off the bulge in his pants and took a few soothing breaths. My eyes, which hadn't left his face, lowered, drawn to the magnitude of his response. The outline of his erection did not disappoint. It was a superb sight that made *me* feel more powerful somehow. I'd been the one to garner the reaction, and I reveled in my potency—until I saw the dark splotch that had spread out over his lighter gray pants. My cheeks burned as Tommand's gaze followed my own to the large spot of wetness that my body had left. I didn't know why my natural response should make me feel apprehensive, but it did.

"You are fully unclothed, then?"

"I am."

"Would you be willing to render me senseless with a series of punches to the face?"

"I would be unwilling."

"Would you be able to lay here beside me, reading that ridiculous primer out loud, and not move a single muscle?" he rasped out.

"Are you so opposed to us joining, Tommand? You were my first choice, you know, and it certainly felt like you were amicable to the idea."

"Eira." My name on his lips sent me into orbit. "I don't want you to regret me."

The sadness in his voice sent me crashing back into the present.

Pulling my robe tightly around myself, I moved carefully off his thighs, doing my best to not touch his most sensitive areas. I was unwilling to sever contact with him fully, so I lay at his side and rested my head on his chest.

"At some point, if this continues and you are so inclined, perhaps you will let *me* make the decision about what I will and won't regret." He made no indication he had heard my words and just stared straight ahead. "Would it help if I stayed away from Ambrose while you rein yourself back in? It's not okay to beat on your friends because you're sexually frustrated. So you should figure that out quickly." That was the truth. I didn't want any more dramatics occurring between the two men.

"Fucking Ambrose... I still want to rip his spine out of his asshole for being so recklessly... *descriptive*. But it is completely unfair of me to ask you to do that. I will bring myself under control," he promised.

"Truly, it would be an easy sacrifice for me to make. Zotikos and Evon are still quite available," I chirped like the happiest of birds. Every last muscle in Tommand's body stiffened while I tucked my face into his underarm hiding my smile.

"Nortia, the primer... read it now," he gritted out.

I retrieved the crumpled piece of parchment from under his calf and I settled into what was quickly becoming my favorite pillow.

"Elite Monwyn women tend to favor blue and will wear all shades of the color..."

I didn't stop reading until a peaceful look settled on his face and his arm slackened beneath my head.

CHAPTER TWENTY-ONE

A NARRATIVE OF MY CHOOSING

"Eira, my girl," Nan's voice infiltrated a most pleasant dream where Tommand and I had been swimming naked in a hot spring. "Eira," she whispered loudly while poking a finger into my cheek. "I figured you'd mount the big one... but I can't say this one isn't pretty."

My eyes snapped open.

"Oh my Goddess, Nan... I..."

Tommand's short hair was soft against my ribcage. His head was tucked under my pierced breast, and his mouth had fallen open, a calm contrast to the near turmoil he'd been in last night. His bronzy arm had found its way under my robe and hugged my naked hips snuggly to his chest.

"What was that, my girl? Your tongue still tied from last night's exploits?" Nan bent close as a knowing smile spread across her pink face.

Wide awake, I prayed that the nether would open up and swallow me into the ground.

"We should get him out of here before Tooby arrives. We'd never hear the end of it, love." Nan reached out and grasped my chin between her fingers, moving my head from side to side. "I don't like all that hair, but the brows suit you." Peering over me, she examined the sleeping Monwyn with an appreciative eye.

"Tomwyn," she whispered close to his ear.

I rolled my eyes to the ceiling.

"It's... his name is Tommand, Nan." I inwardly groaned and glimpsed down. Despite Nan's close proximity, the sight of him wrapped around me made my body do things I'd rather it not at the moment.

"Right... TOMMAND!" She bellowed at the top of her lungs.

I jumped hard, and a hand lashed out, biting at Nan's neck!

Tommand shot to his feet, every bit the Protector of Monwyn. In a single movement, he shielded me behind his body, holding me behind his back with his free arm.

Nan, not panicked in the slightest, swung out with an open palm and walloped Tommand soundly on the forehead.

"Tom! Nan!" I shouted from behind his broad back. "Stop!"

The chamber door flew open.

Kairus ran in, huffing and puffing like she'd just run the First Maneuvering all over again.

"Kairus!" I yelled, glancing around a bicep barrier.

"Oh... this is perfect," she chuckled while diving into her bed. Quickly, she pulled the covers up so high that only her flustered red cheeks and temporary cherry-red hair were visible.

"Ignoble actions! Goddess preserve us from such debauchery!"

I hadn't heard the door open again.

Like a trumpet blaring its warning notes, a perfectly pressed Tussi announced his displeasure.

"Ignoble harlot of a Troth! A man in your room while the Lady Monwyn sleeps! I daresay I should report..." he came up short as Tommand stepped off the bed stalking toward him. To his credit, Tussi didn't cower from the beast striding forward, though his eyes did flick back to the door.

"You will report nothing, as there is *nothing* to report." Tommand stood over Tussi, dwarfing the smaller man. His statement was nothing short of a command.

"Emissary Monwyn, my apologies for interrupting your... uh," his anxious eyes darted between Nan, Kairus, and myself, "this—"

"This *nothing*." Tommand's voice dropped to a mincing tone. "You may return to your charge in twenty minutes' time... do leave." Tommand escorted Kairus' advisor to the door before turning to Nan.

"I am not in the habit of sleeping so soundly. I will do what is necessary to make up for your rough handling. Please accept my apologies."

Nan looked him up and down, squinting her eyes while sizing him up.

"She put you through your paces, did she? Nortian women are a lusty bunch. I'd recommend a large meal of salmon and a nap before the next time." Nan collected her apron in her hands and wiped at the footboard of the bed, pretending to dust.

Tommand's mouth worked up and down, trying to find the right words. Were I not horrified, I would have laughed at the sight of his tongue stuck out between his lips. Nan did have a way of rendering people speechless. My eyes settle on Tommand. Normally pristine, he stood in the middle of the floor with one pantleg up around his knee and his rumpled shirt untucked.

"Tommand, please give my hello to Ambrose this morning." Hoping he'd take the hint, I swept my hand to the door.

"I... uh, yes I will, Troth Nortia... oh, uh, my boots," he grabbed his shoes and bowed at the waist, pivoting between us all, no doubt thankful to be given an out. He slipped out the door and left me alone with one woman who had profited off my embarrassment and another who was now cheerfully tidying up the room, acting like she hadn't just left a palm mark on Tommand's forehead.

"Kairus, you can quit looking at me like that." I bit out, looking in the direction of the big blue eyes that were poking out of a shaking mound of blankets. "I can hear you laughing, you shit." She threw back the covers, her dazzling smile at full beam. "I see you sneaking in here after your own little adventures, playing the precious innocent. I should tell Tussi just how many times *you've* been *ignoble* with Amias."

"Now, you just mind yourself little Chulainn." Nan interjected. "Troth Monwyn at least attempted to remain discreet in her dealings. Imagine my shock coming in here to find that man, *an emissary*, wrapped about your naked form." She wagged her finger in my face while Kairus nodded her head up and down, pink lips pooched in agreement.

"Oh, *okay,* Nan... speaking of scarring experiences," she continued polishing the impeccably clean bedside table, pointedly ignoring me, "just how long were you and Kan Keagan an item? Hmm?"

My companion scrunched her apron into a ball with her hands. Her black-and-white day dress swirled around her ankles as she wandered around the room.

"Not nearly long enough, my girl."

I saw her eyes soften when she turned around to re-dust the same table. Her answer hadn't been what I expected, and immediately, I regretted trying to use the information to catch her off guard.

"I'll arrive in the afternoon to help prepare you for the Maneuvering." She bent low and grabbed a pile of laundry. "Your gown will be delivered before then, and remember you have a meet-up with the undersized goblin today."

I bowed my head contritely, worried I'd hurt her by opening up an old wound.

"Nan...?" I searched her gray eyes, worried I'd gone too far.

"Eira, in life, the happy moments should always outweigh the tough endings." She smoothed back the hair that had loosened from the knot at her neck. With a sideways glance at Kairus, she made her way out the door.

"So... did the fey dance around on your heads? Did you reignite Ærta's lost magic?" Kairus asked, pretending to swoon. "You got the Monwyn you wanted... a day after you had the Monwyn you... also kind of wanted." Kairus tugged her knees to her chest and leaned back against the wall. "Well played, Nortia."

I lay down on my bed where the pillows still smelled like Tommand and breathed in his fading scent.

"Nothing happened... well, that's a lie. Stuff happened. It just turns out that along with his sizable anatomy, he has an equally large heart. He said he doesn't want me to regret him."

"Goddess all! It's a *coupling*, not a mating ceremony, not a lifetime commitment!"

"Apparently, it's something to him." I shrugged and changed the subject. "And how was Amias?"

"He's quite well." Kairus looked at me smugly and angled her head saucily. "And we *did* do stuff, but not *the* stuff. The Gaeans are so attached to their purity, but seriously, you can't convince me that there's some sacred difference between the hole in your ass and the one in your twat."

"I... well... " I burst into peals of laughter. "I don't suppose I know!"

"Here's your lesson then. In a pinch, your backside gets the job done... though I recommend working up to it." Kairus outright laughed in my face. I still couldn't get my brows back down from my forehead. "Also, Tussi will be back soon. You may want to make yourself scarce. I think your brute upset him a little."

"The big-hearted brute, you mean?"

I didn't want to leave the cocoon that Tommand and I had created, but I really didn't feel like facing a chagrined advisor either. Rolling out of the bed, I headed to the bathing chamber.

My first mission of the day. A conference with Gotwig.

··· +)⁙(+ ···

Washed, combed, and moisturized, I made my way to the fourth floor. I was running later than planned but had struggled to get my new-to-me mass of curls under control. Until I learned to braid them, I'd just tie it all back using a length of silk ribbon.

I was dealing with an alarming amount of nervousness, all centered around the idea of being alone with Gotwig. But perhaps I wouldn't have to deal with him at all. Already, I'd walked the entire circumference of the fourth level twice and had even stopped a priestess and two acolytes to ask for directions. They were under the assumption, as I had been, that the Devotees and instructors shared offices on the same level. To my growing irritation, however, it seemed like not a single human in this temple knew where the troll kept himself.

Resorting to canvassing everyone I saw, I described Gotwig in exhausting detail to another acolyte who was walking past Mariad Keagan's office. She'd pulled in a fellow trainee. While both of them had heard of him, neither knew how to locate him.

I headed to the fifth floor, and walked its perimeter, stopping at the white door where Gotwig's "class" had taken place and knocking way louder than necessary. No answer. The wings off the fifth floor looked to be devoted to the acolytes' chambers, given the number of them moving about in various states of dress—some shoeless, many without their robes. The sixth floor was off-limits to anyone other than the Devotees, or so Nan told me the day after we arrived, so I didn't imagine his office would be there.

After at least an hour of wandering the halls, I was close to giving up and going back to my room. Perhaps I should have asked him when he requested the meeting, but also, maybe if Gotwig wanted to meet with me so badly he would have given me specifics! It was just like his ornery self to leave out the details.

Just like him.

I sat for a moment to think through my predicament, which also gave my breasts a chance to recover. I'd attempted twice to wrap my binding this morning, but the discomfort of my piercing was unbearable. Today, for the first time in over a decade, I had nothing supporting my chest, and I'd become acutely aware of how awful chaffing could be… especially when bouncing up a flight of stairs. I waved away an acolyte who was kind enough to look concerned.

Just fucking like him.

I *could* go back to my rooms. After all, meeting with him wasn't really on the short list of things I was looking forward to. On the other hand, he was probably eavesdropping on me right now, waiting to see if I'd give up.

Wait… this is exactly like him.

This was probably a scheme of his—a stupid test! He was probably talking to some Scion right now, discussing how I would react to the high level of stress as I searched for him. *Watch how her lip curls above her gnashing teeth...*

Energy renewed, anger mounting, I made my way down the steps, stopping briefly on the third level's landing to think. I wasn't going to be able to run around all day, which he'd known the moment he dreamt up this merry chase. *I bet he's sitting in his office rubbing his boney little hands together, gleefully chortling at the thought of my "repugnant body" running up and down the steps. Or! Wait... slow down, Eira.*

I could do this. I could find him. I didn't think his invitation was disingenuous, and I needed to trust that instinct.

Think back, think back... What do I know about him?

I knew he ran on a tight schedule, checking his watch obsessively. I knew he wanted things to function smoothly, and appropriately—"I expected as much, they tend to be a people who give no thought to protocol"— and, he believed people should take an active role in forming their own future. "What you choose to tell others can be used to create a strong narrative."

What was *his* narrative?

He created situations to make people feel vulnerable. He claimed to have suffered great harm, and I knew he loved watching people squirm... no, wait... I had accused him of liking humiliation, and he'd said, "quite the opposite, in fact." And, then he insinuated he didn't even like the company of the Obligates, and... *there it is!*

"This is why I prefer the company of servants."

I rushed down the grand staircase, heading to the first floor, where the kitchens were located. As I walked across the marble floor, a tiny waif of a girl intercepted me.

"You've almost found it, Troth," she said while bobbing a little curtsy.

"I've almost found it?" I repeated. The stringy-haired child shrugged her diminutive shoulders and flounced away.

Message received. The hunt continues.

The back of the first level had many doors—all of them painted a dark blue-gray. The color blended so well with the polished stone surround, that from a distance, I hadn't noticed them at all. I stood back and watched, trying to discern any patterns in the comings and goings of the different individuals who walked purposely around the main floor. Most people on this level were acolytes or servants, and, on average, they seemed to move around much faster than the pilgrims. The pilgrims were super easy to spot and track, as they wore no temple regalia, only plain clothes. They also tended to stand adoringly, right in the middle of the floor, staring up transfixed by the sight of Verus.

Six doors in total stretched across the back wall. If I put it together right, the door furthest to the left seemed to be an entrance for servants and acolytes. The adjacent door let out only acol—no wait... there was one servant... and another. *That's an exit.*

The middle doors hadn't opened or closed over the last ten minutes, but the two doors at the far right had, and so far, the one nearest the wall had exclusively admitted servants. My hunch was that was the one I needed.

"Troth Nortia?" Marcyn bowed low. "Can I be of assistance?"

"Good afternoon." I inclined my head and smiled at the distinguished advisor. "No, I'm well, unless, of course, you know what the two middle doors are for?"

"As it happens, the door to the right allows companions quick access to the kitchens and laundry, and the left is the exit."

I stamped a foot, confident about the door I'd chosen.

"Ha! Thank you, Advisor." I curtsied and smiled perhaps too triumphantly.

I got only a few paces away before hearing a throat clear.

"Yes, Marcyn?" I turned back.

"How do we find your most charming companion this morning?" He cleared his throat again.

I thought back to this morning's encounter.

"She seemed unusually well-mannered." And that was a fact. Had I known last night she'd come to check in so early, I would have preemptively sent prayers to Merrias asking for extra protection.

"*Ah*, good, good." He clipped out another stiff bow. Was that slight blush I detected spreading out from the crisp white of his collar? Had he and Nan been spending "quality time" together?

"You know what Nortian women love the most, Marcyn?"

"I'm afraid I do not, Lady Eira?"

"Flowers. I'd never seen one not dried until we left home. The person who is able to gift a Nortian flowers... is usually *very* well received. Good day then, I'm sure we'll meet again soon." I strolled away while Marcyn made his second or third bow.

Honing in on my target again, I made my plan. I was sure that slinking around the walls or peering through cracked doors would draw more attention, so I just got right behind a young man who was on his way in and walked right through after him. Now, I had no idea if I was allowed in the servant's domain but figured if I got caught, I could plead confusion or act like a Monwyn and demand something from the kitchen. Either would be plausible.

The servant shot off to his task, and I found myself looking at the inner workings of Verus. A mob of men and women dashed in differing directions, carrying massive bundles and bounding in and out of round tunnels that looked to lead back into the mountain. Not a single person paid me attention, caught up as they were in the hustle and bustle of running the massive temple.

The enormous space was divided into two distinct parts. One side, the closest to where Marcyn had said the kitchens were, had lines of servants carrying silver trays of fruits and confections into a lamp-lit tunnel. Many of the servants wore elegant red livery, but others were attired in incredibly fancy ensembles, no uniforms at all.

The chamber's right side had racks of clothing lining the walls and an army of servants who worked in rows to press what looked like a never-ending mountain of red garments. The laundering area was immaculately organized. The Priestesses' longer robes hung towards the back of the room and the short lengths the acolytes wore to the left side. Other garments were laid out on a waist-height table for a group of seamstresses to repair, and there was an older man hunched over a bright lamp, working to fix a priestess's colorful collar.

Sticking closely to the wall, I made my way around the launderer's side first. It sounded silly in my own head, but my rationale was that Gotwig, being so very thin, probably didn't actually *like* food, so he would locate his offices away from the smell… *or would he?*

I stood still for a moment, allowing a group of servants to move a pile of folded white tablecloths to the other side of the room. In doing so, I noticed a few doors on the back wall. They were ordinary, just wooden panels hung on normal hinges, but I scanned them anyway. I knocked on the first door, and when there was no response, I peeked inside, discovering a giant cache of soaps. *Not here.* I rapped on door number two, and when I opened it, I found it was filled with an array of buttons and sewing notions. As I closed the door, I noticed a glint on the ground. I bent to retrieve a little button that seemed to have rolled into the corner of the third door's threshold. I'm sure Verus kept extensive records, and I'd hate for a servant to be punished for losing track of such a fine piece. I re-entered the storage room and turned on a lamp in order to file it away correctly. *Let's see, little silver daggers.* I looked but could find nothing that matched. *Silver dagger, where are you?*

Then it hit me.

Unbelievable.

I ran out and knocked loudly on the third door.

"Enter."

I pushed the door wide and tossed the button into his outstretched hand.

"Welcome, Troth Nortia." He sat, not behind his desk, but on a cushioned wingback chair with his feet propped up on a wooden table. "One of your ilk has never found my private office, so pardon my informality." He tapped the silver dagger broach that connected the two halves of his shirt. He'd worn the same one during our first session.

Gotwig pointed to the chair across from him with the pipe he held in his hand. At first, I hesitated to move, still surprised I'd found him at all, and then, I found I was incredibly overwhelmed by the space itself. Knickknacks covered every surface of the cramped chamber. Small statues, colorful gold-framed paintings, and vases of feathers all vied for attention. There seemed to be little thought given to any overarching theme, but the effect of the clutter on my eyes was almost unbearable. They were constantly drawn to something for just a few seconds before they moved to the next item and then the next. When I managed to take my seat, I focused on the table between us.

"I realize you imagine me a monster, Troth Nortia, but I shan't bite." He cozied deeper into his chair.

"Says the man who stabbed a Scion? Slashed a Troth's hair? A bite seems an easy jump to make," I retorted.

"It's a shame, you know... that the woman who is thoughtful enough to find her way here... is still unable to see the importance behind how the Maneuvering was carried out." He placed the pipe between his thin lips and drew a match from a box. A tiny fire sprang to life, momentarily illuminating his thin face. "Was it before or after the river incident that you became so quick to provoke?" He puffed smoke rings into the air. "Don't look surprised. By now, you've gathered I make a habit of knowing the movements of every person in this temple, which includes everything that takes place the moment you enter its care. An answer, if you will?"

There was no reason to lie to the man who likely already knew the answer. "I've been easy to rile my entire life."

"And the heightened state of anxiety?" he quizzed.

I didn't answer.

"As I suspected." Gotwig crossed his arms across his sunken chest. "If you would allow me to assist you, I think together we could manage your fear response... it's not an impossible task."

I mulled over what accepting his help might look like. The possibilities made my skin crawl.

"I don't understand why you want to help me, and I don't know why I should trust you," I said plainly.

"Why do you think I'm at this temple?" He asked, smoothing his mustache with his index finger.

"I assume it's because of your ability to read people, something beneficial for the Obligates to learn."

He nodded and lifted his feet from the table to rest them on the floor. "It is partially that, yes, but it is also because of my devotion to this temple and its premise." He drew on his pipe and then lowered it to his knee. "I arrived at the temple a husk. A broken man with an injured mind and shattered body. I saw no value in myself and no value in the life I'd been dealt. It hadn't been fair after all, that I was born into a shit childhood." Gotwig pulled the deep-maroon jacket he wore tighter around his neck. "It took me so long to accept that the notion of 'fair' was a complete fabrication and that horrendous life or not, I *could* overcome what had transpired. I had to let a lifetime of bitterness go. I would never have been able to do it without this place and its support."

Gotwig tapped his pipe in a steady rhythm against his thigh.

"As to trust, there are very few, if any, I would trust in your life as an Obligate, you will have to decide who is worthy of it."

I shifted to the side and crossed one ankle over the other, thinking I still trusted people too easily. "Lord Gotwig, may I ask what happened to you... to break you?"

"As a child, I was enslaved by the people of Baldorva," he began. "I pulled salt from the ground for them, until I caught the eye of a brothel owner who decided my small stature would appeal to his more debauched clientele. For nine years, I saw only chains and a cellar floor and was used as dark amusement for those returning home from pillaging and conquest."

Dreadful. Absolutely horrendous.

I closed my eyes against the sting of tears. I couldn't fathom, couldn't imagine the anguish the young Gotwig had endured. My attack seemed small, so blessedly trivial compared to half a lifetime of captivity and abuse.

"Do not compare trauma, Troth Nortia. It's not fair to your experience or to mine. All people deal differently with their experiences, and all are allowed to feel and interpret those uniquely. What may feel small to me may be defining for you, and that goes both ways."

"I still replay it in my head when I'm not kept busy," I shared.

"And you will, perhaps indefinitely, but if we can frame it in another way—train you to allow the incident to hold less power over you—you may benefit greatly. That is, if you are willing to work... with a monster." His mouth stretched into a twisted smile.

"And will I be subjected to more torture and trials? Made to recreate the incident over and over again?" I was convinced his methods would be steeped in cruelty.

"No, Nortia, we will only talk. If you are willing, I would like to begin now." He pulled his timepiece from the pocket of the cream-colored vest he wore under his coat. "It will not take long, and then you and I will need to prepare for the Maneuvering."

I heard Tommand's voice in my head, telling me I could find someone to talk to here… that it may help.

"I'm ready." I was resolute.

"Then name your fear."

"I… I'm scared of being attacked again, I thought that was rather obvious."

"Why?" He retorted.

"Why? Because it was terrifying!" Maybe this talk-it-out method wasn't for me.

"Why?" He asked again, not looking me in the eye.

"Because… because safety is a delusion. Because the idea of safety is like the idea of fairness: nothing more than an imaginary piece of armor we hide behind. We live amongst predators, and we are prey."

"So feeling unsafe is the crux of your fear, and without ever feeling safe, you expend your mental energy on trying to survive. When was the last time you felt truly safe?"

"It… was… it was last night." *With Tommand.* Gotwig scratched at his chin, and I noticed for the first time he was missing the tips of both his ring and pinky fingers.

"The Monwyn?"

Of course he knows.

"They have presented an interesting pair. The Scion, I believe, puts himself forward, exactly as he is. The Emissary, that is the one you find yourself enamored with, yes? I have yet to gain a full understanding of his motives."

Mossius! The temple truly did have ears.

"Now, with safety being your main concern, I want to ask you… what if? What if your safety is infringed upon again?"

"I want to be able to react. I don't want to freeze. I allowed myself to become a victim at the river by not reacting."

"No, Nortia, there you are wrong. The minute that man chose his path, it was *him* who forced you into the role of victim. You did not choose to become one, and therefore you do not have to designate yourself as such." He leaned forward, placing his elbows on his knees. "It is hard to let go of the guilt, though, even if our part was written for us."

"I do feel that shame, that guilt. I'm so angry at myself for not noticing him. I'm upset at myself for being naked outdoors, for doing nothing when he touched me." Fresh tears stung but didn't fall.

"And why have you not placed your anger at the feet of your aggressor? Why have you taken *his* crime upon yourself?"

I had no answer.

Why *did* I take the blame for his deed? Why did I question *my* choices instead of the ones he made?

"Think about that please, and we will meet again next week. If you need to find me before then, seek out the little one that greeted you earlier." Gotwig stood and walked towards the door.

"Oh, and Troth Nortia, if it's slipped your notice, educated Monwyns rarely use contractions. Clean up your language tonight."

Chapter Twenty-Two

THE THIRD MANEUVERING

Kairus sat staring, lost in herself—I knew what the look meant. She was fighting her darkness.

"We should get ready. I know it will take me at least an hour to figure out these cosmetics, and I can rebraid your hair for you. Do you like the red?"

"Hmm?" She blinked and reconnected momentarily. "The red, well... I don't really know." She drifted off again.

I moved to the bed and sat next to her.

"Kairus, how long have you had these moments? The ones where you're so... down." I didn't look directly at her, not wanting to cause her more discomfort. "You don't have to answer, you know. I'll still sit here with you... if it helps."

I felt her arm shift and slide next to mine. She continued to stare ahead, her turquoise eyes bleak, but just the little contact gave me hope.

"It started around the time of my first menses. It comes on so illogically, and I am unable to think clearly for a matter of days or sometimes just hours."

"Should I check in when they happen? Or..."

"I am not sure it will help... but this was okay," she whispered.

"Wanna skip the Maneuvering?" I said, halfway meaning it.

"We cannot."

A knock sounded at the door. Tussi and Nan came rushing forward, followed by three servants bearing a large chest between them.

Without a greeting, Tussi ushered Kairus into her bathing room, and a tall, well-dressed servant carried a large leather dress box behind them before shutting the door.

"You've so much hair now, I don't think we'll all fit in there, my girl." Nan pulled the servant's stool to the middle of the room. "Sit here for now, I'll air out your gown." She raised the chest's lid and began to sift through the contents. A younger servant began carefully combing through my tresses, smoothing down the ringlets that had slackened to loose curls. The other began rubbing creams into my face while setting out a multitude of jars and brushes that had been stored in the chest's clever compartments. I was thankful to have them here. I thought I'd be the one making up my face for my first public outing as a Monwyn, and the prospect had been daunting.

"Here we are." Reaching in, Nan pulled a cloud of exquisite fabric from the wooden box and held it up for my inspection.

Holy Mother.

"Nan, I…"

"I know! It's magnificent!" she beamed.

The gown she held high above her head shifted from a deep indigo at its top, seamlessly transforming to a light periwinkle and then fading down to its hem in a light, almost white, sky blue. The voluminous skirts were full, made from layer upon layer of fine silk—which had to have been hand-dyed by a master craftsperson. Around the bodice and waist, thousands of glass beads in various shapes glittered, meticulously sewn onto the delicate fabric. They continued to rain down over the outer skirts but tapered in quantity. The lamp's light caught and reflected off the sparkling beads and shot tiny rainbows around the room. With the colors and the placement of the beads, I'd look like a starry sky just before daybreak.

"Troth Nortia, we will need to place your mask before lacing you into your gown." The servant went to the chest and retrieved another box. While another servant applied a thick cream to my lips, I strained my eyes, trying to catch a glimpse of what she had pulled out. I could see feathers dancing from the corner of my eye but nothing more. Finally, after having powders added to my eyelids and cheeks, I saw the crowning jewel.

The half-mask was gold. Tiny glass rounds that matched the ones on my gown clustered across its nose and around its eye slots, and larger pink gems had been interspersed throughout the forehead. Long plumes of white swept from one side of the crown to the other, and curling silk ribbons cascaded down both its sides. It was more finery than it was a face covering. I knew the nobles of Nortia held masked events, but I seriously doubted they'd worn garments as opulent as what had been created for us here. This ensemble made my Congregation gown look like slop clothes.

"What's your name?" I asked the servant who was assisting the other in splitting my hair into two sections.

"I'm called Ness, Troth Nortia." She focused intently on holding together the jumble of curls that currently fell over my forehead.

"And you are?" I asked, hoping the servant standing behind me would hear.

"Netta."

"Ness and Netta, thank you so much for helping me. I wasn't looking forward to doing this alone." Ness placed the mask against my face, and I felt Netta securing several of the silk ties around the part they'd created in my curls.

"There we are." When they deemed it snug, Netta combed the lower half of my hair up the back of my head, which covered the ties and worked to arrange and secure the length on the top of my head. This part took the longest, but finally, I heard Ness's grunt of satisfaction.

"And now the gown." Nan, Netta, and Ness held the sides and front while I disrobed and stepped into the middle of its layers.

The gown was heavily structured in its top, something I wasn't used to in my clothing. The waist nipped in tightly, and the bodice could have stood on its own had you sat it on the floor. The two servants laced me in by tugging on the long ribbon closures found on both sides.

"Of course, I'd prefer the gown be Nortian black, but my girl," in the rarest of occurrences, Nan's eyes swam, "if your grandmother could see you..."

"Tussi, leave it be!" The bathroom door crashed open, revealing a gold-clad Kairus. We all turned, staring at the elegant spectacle that emerged from the room.

From head to toe, she was adorned in a soft, buttery gold. Unlike her preferred formal garments, with their boldly plunging necklines, this gown encircled the column of her neck and clung tightly until it hit her knees. From there, the light silk flared out and spilled around her feet. Thin arm cuffs had been placed above her biceps, and a multitude of dainty gold chains hung from them, with rounds of polished malachite dangling from their ends.

"Lady Kairus, to assume your role completely you *must* have the final piece in place." Tussi chased after her, waving his hands frantically.

"Then make it quick!" she spat back. The tall servant scrambled out from the bathing room, holding an artist's brush in her hand. Tussi pulled Kairus's gold-and-green en-crusted braids over one shoulder, and the servant went to work, alternating painting her with something from a little pot and blowing a fine powder onto her back. We all waited, enthralled by what was occurring.

"It's finished," the servant murmured.

"Are you ready, Eira? *Let's go.*" Ever the Monwyn, Kairus turned angrily and stomped to the door.

"Kairus!" I squealed. The back of her gown was nonexistent, just the circle of silk at her neck and nothing but bare skin until the lower half of the gown fell from her hips. "It's gorgeous." Two entwining flames had been painstakingly painted onto the canvas made from her shoulders and slim waist. They shimmered like a million twinkling stars. Kairus looked over her shoulder and pressed her lips into a severe line.

"It's garish, not gorgeous." She continued stomping to the door and made to leave.

"Lady Kairus? Most devout Troth of *Gaea*. If I may, it would be wise to assume your pious and delicate identity *before* reaching the ballroom."

Kairus glared, her nose flaring indignantly at Tussi for daring to make the suggestion. With an uncharacteristic deep growl, she bolted through the door.

Remembering at the last second to grab the bracelet Mariad had gifted me, I scrambled to follow.

$$\cdots *)(* \cdots$$

The location of the Third Maneuvering was the second-level hall where the Congregation had taken place. Guards were stationed at two entrances, and the plain-dressed Nortian Devotee and a man I didn't recognize stood together, intercepting every person that arrived.

As we neared, the Devotee glanced at the man next to her and inclined her chin. He moved forward and approached Kairus.

"Separate. No parties arrive together," the unidentified man stated.

I was nervous to be walking away from the safety net my friend provided and into a Maneuvering alone, but it was just another challenge in the gauntlet that was fulfilling the Obligation. *Safety is an illusion anyway.*

"Nortia." It was the Nortian Devotee. I moved to her side.

"You have until dawn to learn the surname of Scion Lok's mother. Report the name to me when you have it. If you attempt to speak directly to the Scion, you will be prevented." She waved a hand in the air, dismissing me.

The surname of Lok's mom? How in all of Ærta was I supposed to figure that out?

"This way." A heavily armed guard opened the door, and I entered the hall.

For the third time, the room had been completely transformed to meet the needs of the engagement. The wooden partitions had been removed, making the space the largest I'd seen it yet... which was a good thing given the crush of people already twirling around the dance floor. There had to be hundreds of people here, all dressed in the finest array of clothing found across the kingdoms. I realized now that the servants from below had been tapped to take part tonight. I looked up and watched overhead as an acrobat flew across the high ceiling and landed on a ledge attached to one of the rooms' large columns.

"Oh!" Someone shoved me lightly from behind as they entered the room. "My apologies, sir, I was..."

"Apologies are not very Monwynian, now are they, Lady?" His modifications were incredible, I knew instantly that it was Greggen. Though he'd been transformed into a person of the mountain lands, himself, they couldn't hide the fact that he was one of the tallest people I had ever encountered. His eyes sparkled from under his mask of indigo blue, and the warm blonde fibers added to his normally earthy hair had been flawlessly incorporated. It lay in a heavy braid down his back.

He took my elbow and led me into the crowd. Like myself, he had been dressed in a deep blue, but the overcoat he wore was detailed with scrolling embroidery around its full hem. Small golden beads were clustered at the center of each swirl, giving the garment an appearance of great wealth. A number of gold bracelets encircled his wrists, and large gemstone rings graced several of his fingers—a reminder of the riches found in the Monwyn lands.

"How do you find all of this Eira?" We stood in the shadow of a floor-to-ceiling column.

"This Maneuvering may be the most difficult yet, though perhaps more pleasant than the others." I held my head high, looking up at Greggen but down my nose like I'd seen Kairus do on many an occasion.

"What could be more pleasant than a limp-dicked Amias at your back?" He peered down, the overconfident Monwyn male.

"This isn't the kind of party where I want to be reminded of *that*, Greggen," I said, mustering an ounce of humor.

"This *is not* that kind of a party, and refer to me as *Scion Monwyn*." There was no trace of amusement in his tone.

"Right, fine. Well... I *will* be off, *Scion Monwyn*, good day," I said cheerily, even though his chastisement had rubbed me wrong.

I spun on my heel and walked away.

Greggen was normally quite kind, and I didn't love his Monwyn act. I knew he had to keep it up, however.

It struck me, that though I didn't think of Ambrose, Tommand, or even Evandr as high and mighty, looking back over our encounters and interactions, they totally were. They all ordered people around and issued commands like it was their Goddess-given right to do so.

Alright, I needed a plan. My best idea so far was to seek out Lok's companion, but in this crowd, I didn't know if I would be able to find a person I knew, much less one I'd never met before. Turning in a circle, I recognized no one. Well, that wasn't true. I could point out Greggen, Kairus, and Ambrose, but they would have their own missions to solve so I wouldn't request their aid.

I knew Lok was Solnnan. But besides the fact that their women were hairless, their food was delicious, and they had amazing fabric, I couldn't recall any tidbit to help me out. I knew it was hot there, and of course, I knew their language.

"Do any of you speak Solnnan?" I asked a nearby cluster of masked merrymakers.

They ignored me.

"Pardon me." I approached a woman with hairless legs. "Are you Solnnan by chance?" She shook her head and moved away. Oh right, I'd probably be better off seeking a hairless lady *not* dressed in the colors of Solnna. Unless the non-Obligate partygoers accurately represented their homelands of course. *Hmmm.*

Weaving in and out of the crowd, shoulders back, I tried for all the world to look composed while spying on the legs and arms of what must have been three hundred people. No one stood out. Well, everyone stood out—it was like trying to find a needle in a pile of bejeweled hairpins. For a while, I scanned the dancing revelers, noting how their steps became less precise as they consumed more drinks. That's always how it seemed to go, even at Nortian parties. Spirits seemed to bring out the boldness in even the most timid of people... which gave me an idea.

I laughed loudly, tossing my hands into the air.

"I've prepared myself to be skewered by a happy, stiff man!" I sang out in my most sultry Solnnan.

There! I saw a head jerk in my direction and took off.

"A moment, please!" I slowed and resumed my regal bearings. I reached up to the large-framed person and tapped their shoulder.

"A fair improvisation, little one, but I can tell your tutelage did *not* include the more crude vocabulary of the southern people," said the man. He was resplendent in a mask of feathers in all variations of the color green. The lower half of his face was hidden, covered by a thin gold mesh that draped from the bottom of his eyes to below his chin. Both the voice and the eyes were unmistakable. This was Mariad Keagan, masquerading as a very convincing citizen of Gaea.

"But it worked!" I stared haughtily into his face, not breaking character. "Sir, I have a question that only a devoted man of the great Kingdom of *Gaea* could possibly answer."

"Then ask it, little one." I could see the shadow of his smile behind the fine chain.

"If you so wish, good sir, but before we conduct our business, I'd join you in evening prayers."

"Let us ask the Goddess for her grace then." Mariad's eyes twinkled.

"Most certainly." I inclined my head, taking the elbow he offered.

We walked arm in arm toward the far side of the hall, where I could see several other Gaeans at prayer in the distance.

"What can I assist you with?"

"I need to know the surname of Lok's mother."

"We can't make it that easy for you. Would you like to try again?" he asked.

"Can you give me the name of his companion or a way to find them at this party?" We passed a woman juggling knives and a table loaded with refreshments.

"And what will you give me in return?" Mariad quizzed.

"Wha-what would you have?" The unexpected question made me uneasy.

"Never let anyone name their price open-ended." He laid his hand on my forearm and squeezed gently. "His name is Henric."

We made it to the other side of the room, where carpets had been placed on the floor for the comfort of the devout. Together, we kneeled. After arranging the puff of skirts I sat in, I placed my fingertips to both eyes and asked the Goddess for guidance.

"He's a heavyset fellow... likes his drink," Mariad murmured while bringing his fingers to his chin and then forehead. "Mother Goddess, creator of life, all that we are is through you. Look upon your children favorably so we may know your grace," he prayed aloud. "Good luck, little Nortia, and keep your focus." He touched a single finger to the bracelet he'd gifted me. "In Solnna, it is believed the amethyst provides protection to the wearer." With a final nod, he rose and walked back into the crowd.

My next move would be to plant myself near the refreshment table and watch out for a portly man. I stood up and smoothed my gown, and headed in that direction. Perhaps if I found him, I could ply him with drink, or convince him I had taken an interest in Lok.

The refreshment table was loaded with silver platters of fantastically decorated confections and fruits cut into all manner of shapes. The drinks flowed freely, and the servants were kept busy, filling glasses with bubbly libations and dark wines. A hot drink that smelled bold and earthy also seemed quite popular.

"I do not believe we were done with our conversation." Greggen wrapped his arm around my waist and pulled me to his side.

"Scion Monwyn, remove your hand from me." I stared forward, not willing to break character and be made fun of again.

"You should enjoy my attention, Troth. I've decided we will dan—oof!" The large volume of my skirts veiled my foot stomping on Greggen's.

I'd spotted someone I'd thought fit the description of Henric and had to move quickly.

In front of the drink table was a man who reminded me of Fionn, our guide to the temple. Though not as tall, his belly stood out quite prominently in his Monwyn-blue tunic. Already he swayed unsteadily on his feet, but an easy smile played across his face.

"Lord Henric!" Pretending as if I had known the Solnnan my entire life, I placed a fresh glass of wine into his hand. "Would you care to dance?"

Bloodshot, half-closed eyes, looked me up and down and widened in false recognition.

"Mah Lady Mon"— he hiccupped—"wyn, I would be moth happy." With a wobbly bow, he proffered a meaty hand. Smiling my most dazzling smile, I placed my palm into his sweaty paw and allowed myself to be led to the floor. With unexpected agility, Henric swept me into the steps of a spinning Solnnan dance, one where you held your partner tightly and then swung them out when the drummer banged a three-strike beat.

"You are quite the elegant dancer, Lord Henric." I spoke honestly, enjoying being guided around and twirled about the floor.

"Fank you mah dear," he slurred. "I dare say, in my yoof, I was known to make more than one lady swoon!"

I returned his smile, drawn in by his warm demeanor. "And does Scion Lok share your sure-footedness?" I placed my hand on his shoulder, increasing our closeness.

"Lok? No... he likes to sthpend his time in a corner shlulking at wh-whatever offended him that day." Henric's belly bounced in time to his clangorous chuckle.

"I thought all Solnnans were warm and congenial? Perhaps he got his temperament from his mother?" I followed Henric's lead as he spun me expertly and pulled me back, smacking me soundly against his girth.

"Drellada? No, no. As sthweet as honey, she was."

"Was?" I questioned.

"She passed about a momf before"— he hiccupped again—"we came here."

"Oh, how sad. Her family, her, uh, sister, what was the family name? She must have been most devastated," I said, pressing myself closer, almost wanting to hug the big fellow whose shoulders had slumped in sorrow.

"Shhle was an exemplar of womanhood." Tears welled in his red-veined eyes, and he dropped his head, his gaze catching on my overexposed cleavage. The dress's low-cut *V* was not nearly as revealing as many of Kairus's but it was enough to highlight my abundance.

His head tilted farther forward until his forehead rested on my chin and the tip of his nose came dangerously close to being buried in my cleavage. His hand at the small of my back shifted as well, becoming heavy and pressing painfully into my backside.

"That sweet... thweet Drel-la-la." I felt more of his weight settle in my arms.

"Henric...? Lord Henric?" Any lower and he'd drown in my bosom. I tapped our joined hands to his shoulder, becoming more hopeless by the second.

"Allow me, Madam."

Tommand.

I knew his voice as well as I did his scent.

Hefting the near snoring man from my arms, the emissary—dressed as a Solnnan noble—danced the big fellow to a nearby bench and dropped him heavily into its corner before returning to my side.

"Come with me."

"And go where? I have a task to complete, and it requires *him* to wake." I spared a quick glance at Henric, who was snoring into his own blubbery chest.

"Does it matter where... Nortia?" He stepped into my vision, cutting my target out of view.

Tommand made a devastatingly handsome Solnnan. He wore a sleeveless silk long coat of stark white shot through with gold fibers. The light color, different from the blues and grays he normally wore, contrasted beautifully with his skin and stood out against the deep purple-black of his loose, floor-sweeping pants. Gold bands circled his biceps, highlighting the dense musculature of his arms, and a belt of white leather, studded with sunburst plaques, hung low on his hips.

He took my hand.

"Does it matter?" he asked again.

My body answered before my mouth could.

Already my skin had become more sensitive, and the simmering warmth I felt low in my womb kindled its first small flame.

"I would follow you to the nether, wearing that eye-black." The kohl that had been drawn thinly around his eyes increased their intensity and gave him a roguish look.

"I will keep that in mind, Lady," he said while taking my hand and turning on his heel.

"Where are we headed?" I asked, confused as to why I was being practically dragged behind him.

"My room."

His room.

We passed the stationed guards and a number of partygoers on our way down the grand staircase. Upon reaching the bottom level, Tommand turned hurriedly to the left and propelled us past a group of servants, who bobbed and curtsied as we moved by. Tommand lengthened his steps as we passed into a hallway that looked identical to the Troth dormitories and didn't stop his march until we came to the second to last door on the right.

"Inside, now."

His chamber was bathed in orange firelight and smelled woodsy and warm like he did. A few chairs and a low table sat along the right wall and a bed—larger than my own but less ornate—stuck out from the wall.

Tommand strode toward the fireplace and placed his hands on its mantel before hanging his head between his arms. I heard the hiss of his agitated sigh as I made to close the door, sealing us into his chamber.

"You will need to resist me."

"Come again?" I asked, making sure I'd heard him correctly.

"And again and again—if I am to have my way," he rasped.

Tommand turned, his body silhouetted by a flickering glow. Like a prowling cat, he stalked toward me, undoing the gilded fastener at his collar and popping the second and third buttons of his coat.

"I am to tempt you... make you waste valuable time." His fourth and fifth buttons followed the others, revealing a slice of his decadent chest. "I am a twist thrown into your plot."

His coat parted as he moved forward, and the need to touch him overwhelmed my other senses.

"Are you then?" I stared into his desire-filled eyes and felt my mouth go dry. "It seems the temple chose the right diversion then. I find I'm quite willing to give up a portion of my time for you."

"I prayed you'd say that, Nortia."

Fully unbuttoned, he rolled one powerful shoulder and shrugged off his coat, letting it fall to the floor.

If this is how I fail Trothdom, so be it.

"Tommand?" I searched his face, taking in the strong planes of his cheeks, the mouth that made my legs go weak. "I need to know what *you* want."

"*You* are what I want." He swallowed and took a steadying breath. "I have palmed myself, twice nightly, picturing how you would look below me, about how you might taste and feel wrapped around me." His hand moved low, adjusting the erection that strained against his flowing pants. The loose layers did nothing to conceal his ardor. "Denying myself what you have so freely offered has proven the most daunting of tasks."

Conjuring an image of Tommand stroking himself as Ambrose had—all bunching muscles and moans—made me acutely aware of everyplace my gown touched my skin.

"Tommand, may I touch you?"

"Yes."

Like our tryst at dinner, there was no hesitation in his response, and his assent thrilled me to my toes. To know my desire was reciprocated in kind was almost as titillating as what pressed against his pants... almost.

Why had I ever thought Ambrose the god and Tommand the warrior-king? Seeing him there, bathed in firelight, eyes flashing, unabashedly displaying his hunger. I knew it was he who must have been fathered by a deity.

The slickness accumulating in my passage excited me, made me feel so entirely salacious as I walked toward him. I loved the way my body reacted, a true blessing from our Creator. I bit down on my bottom lip to keep anchored, and still an arm's length away, I jutted my breasts forward, seeking to press the sensitive flesh against him.

His pleased hum was all the encouragement I needed.

Tommand closed his eyes and I brought my hands to his chest.

"I think you're beautiful, Tommand... every inch of you." His breath quickened under my touch. I slid my fingers lightly to his throat. "The speed of your pulse tells me you are quite happy with that knowledge."

I continued my exploration.

He had sweet little freckles on his arms and a tiny whitish mark on the right side of his ribcage. I traced the scar on his abdomen and the line that defined his stomach and hip.

"Tommand? Can I touch you like I touched Ambrose?"

I wanted more.

"I would like you to not mention his name right now, *Nortia*." His mouth tugged lightly to one side. "And you may touch me in any way you please." He stepped closer, pressing himself more firmly into my palms. "If this ends with my cock buried in your tightness, you could shove blades into my nail beds for all I care."

Though shocked by the imagery he painted, I almost believed him.

"Let's just start with this." I lightly scraped my fingertips over his flat nipples. His body shivered at the touch. I watched him clench and unclench his jaw, and the movements in his neck mesmerized me. *I wonder what would happen if...*

Like I'd seen between Cinden and Ozius, I inclined my head and ran my tongue around his areola while simultaneously letting my hand venture low to firmly cup his rigidness.

"Fuck, Nortia," he hissed, gritting his teeth and clenching his hands to his sides. I drew the peaked skin into my mouth and bit down lightly before moving to the other side.

"Tommand, can I see... the rest of you?" I wanted to look upon what my hands had felt, and I was itching to touch him as I had his Scion. I inched closer, ignoring the pierced nipple that pressed painfully against the stiff structure of my gown.

He dropped his hands, deftly unbuckling his belt and unlacing his pants. He let both sides hang free, and I saw the tip of his erection just visible over the waist of his linen undershorts. I wanted, no, *needed* to feel him with no barrier between us. Like tearing into a gift you've anticipated, I pulled the ties of his small clothes, releasing his full length into my hand. I licked my lips looking down at the penis that jerked in my palm. It wasn't as long as Ambrose's had been—his had risen above his navel—but Tommand was thicker, denser than the Scion. It seemed all parts of him were built for power.

My first inclination when sizing him up was to mount him quickly. I was ready. I wanted to feel him slip into, spread me, at this very moment, but... I also didn't want to rush to the end before it had a chance to really begin.

"How do you find 'the rest of me'? Am I to your liking?"

I slid my fingers slowly down him and clasped the base of his arousal. The ring my fingers made closed tightly around him. He sighed and tilted his hips forward into my hand. The thrill of watching him receive pleasure made me slow my impatient self down. I ran my finger up a vein that ran his length and swirled my fingertip around his head. Tommand's hips bucked hard, and a clear bead of moisture released from his tip.

"Quite so, Emissary, quite so." I loved the feel of him in my hands, soft like velvet and hard, made for pleasing my depths. Between my legs, I felt my slickness escape my lips.

"It's incredible how wet you make me, Tommand." I glanced up, truly meaning it. I never lubricated like this for any of the flirtations I'd had. "When I pleasure myself, it's never like this." I closed my eyes, squeezing my thighs tightly under the gown's heavy skirts. Using my fingertips, I smeared his moisture back down his hardness.

"Fuck, Goddess," he bit out while wrapping his hand around my own, stilling my motions. "You talk like a seasoned professional."

I chuckled, rather pleased. "It has been said I was designed to—"

"I am unable to wait."

Tommand pitched forward and clasped his arms around my waist. Impatiently, he walked us backward until the backs of my knees came up against the edge of his bed. He pushed me back onto the mattress and dropped to his knees, where he completely disappeared, hidden by the volume of my skirts.

"You will come on my mouth first, and then around my fingers." He ran his hands from my ankles to my knees. "I want to fuck every thought of Ambrose or any others from your mind." He attempted to push the material around my waist, batting at the layers of netting that created its fullness.

"Fucking stupid dress," he growled while attempting to roll the fabric above my hips. I felt him yank at the material in his frustration.

"Do *not* rip this gown, Tommand." I giggled at his mounting frenzy.

He grumbled irritatedly, fumbling with the ties of the silk underwear he eventually uncovered. Finally, I heard the sound of silk ripping as he snatched the entire front of the crotch into his fist. I felt the ties snap at both sides as the force lifted my hips from the mattress.

"That *wasn't* the gown," he chuckled.

On me instantly, he lowered his head, licking and lapping the wetness that had made its way to the tops of my thighs. *Oh, my gods, all of you... the entire pantheon... this is...*

With strong and sure hands, Tommand lifted my legs and then pressed my thighs back. I laid open to him, not self-conscious in the slightest. He inspected my most intimate area silently. He ran his nose along the crease of my thighs and cupped the soft curls at my apex.

"Am I also to your liking, Tommand?" His extended silence had left me wondering.

"Beautiful," he whispered, his breath warm against my exposed center. Gingerly, he slid his tongue through my slit, gliding through its dampness. I arched into his mouth, reeling from a sensation more incredible than anything I'd experienced so far.

"This is..." My eyes rolled to the back of my head while my hands wrung at the layers of skirting piled above my stomach.

"You taste divine." He parted me further with his fingers and dipped his tongue into my opening. "Sweet and a little salty... like the sea." His voice turned thick and low, and I delighted in the scrape of his stubbly jaw against my skin. "I believe you may become an addiction, Nortia." He dropped his head again and swirled his tongue around my peak, before sucking my most sensitive area into his mouth. He sipped rhythmically on my clit and I felt his fingers at my entrance.

"Jealous of my own hand..." Inch by glorious inch, he tenderly guided his digit into me. "There it is, your pleasure center, is this what you want?"

The need to move against him drove me. I grabbed the blue covering of his bed to keep myself planted while he ever so slowly moved in and out of me.

"Tommand... more, please more." His long sigh tangling with my soft moans filled the small room.

His hand stilled.

I looked down, worried I'd done something wrong.

He was just staring at me—lips gleaming, coated in my dampness.

I wiggled my hips against the thick part of his palm, which pressed snuggly against my overly sensitive flesh.

"Tommand... *Goddess*..."

"You make me feel ridiculous, you know?" He bent, and his tongue darted out flicking at my clitoris, while he stared deeply into my eyes. "A man of twenty and nine years, devising ways to be nearer a destined Troth." Catching his lip between his teeth, he looked down and watched while he slid a second finger into me. The fullness was exquisite. "This should be Ambrose's place"— another flick of his tongue—"but it would seem the Goddess has other plans." He eased his fingers forward, deepening his reach.

"Don't mention his name," I said, arching off the mattress, encouraging him to continue.

"You could not please me more, Nortia." He chuckled low in his throat and increased the speed of his hand.

Then he smiled—his full-on, dimple-flashing, laugh-line-creating smile. There was nothing more I could want in this moment.

"I...Tommand..." I didn't look away from his reddish-brown gaze, I couldn't... I was too far gone, mesmerized by the smoldering golden ring that circled his expanding pupils. I'd never felt worshiped by another human, but somehow this man made me feel like I'd been created for his pleasure alone. I gasped loudly when Tommand dropped his head.

He devoured me with his mouth.

"Tom! Goddess, oh Gommond!" I sank myself onto his fingers while he suckled and lapped, flitting his hungry tongue back and forth against my flesh. His caresses were no longer soft, and the deeper thrusts and mounting pressure made wracking spasms begin to release inside me. I clenched tightly around his fingers and rode their width until, with a powerful thrust of his hand, wave after wave of pulsating pleasure surged through me.

"That. Faster." With every plunge of his fingers, I came harder, loudly moaning and writhing while he consumed my orgasm in his never stilling mouth. I tensed, unable to take more and panted heavily until I floated back to the mortal realm. I had never experienced a release that intense in my life. My passage continued pulsing around his fingers, and when he made to remove them, gently, I bucked hard, yelping at the lingering sensitivity of the drawn-out gratification.

"You are perfect." His voice penetrated the haze of my satisfaction. He stood between my legs, his hardened erection on display. I didn't think it was possible, but the tightening pressure began anew. "You should get back to your task." Tommand winked and offered me a hand.

"But Tommand," I sat up. "What about being buried between my legs?" I raised a brow, curious as to why he would retreat.

"What about your job, Troth?" he teased and made to move.

"What about it, Tom?" I caught his hand and leaned down, taking the swollen head of his jutting erection between my lips. I figured if I enjoyed it so much, he would too.

Tommand's hips jerked so hard that the tip of him slipped deeply into my mouth, hitting the back of my throat. He groaned roughly and I wanted more then anything to hear the sound again.

"I should not." He pushed his hands into the curls at the back of my head, careful not to disturb my mask. I sucked on him lightly and whirled my tongue around his tightened skin, as he had done to me. He pulled himself fully out. His arousal had deepened in color. I lowered my head and adhered my lips to the underside of him and dragged my mouth down his length.

"And yet..." He slowly pressed himself between my lips again when I arrived back at his tip.

I took his base in my hand and traced the crevice at his head with my tongue, tasting his salty response to my ministrations.

"I like the taste of you too, Tommand." I licked at him again, ecstatic to be the cause of his pleasure.

"It's apparent that my self-control ends at the tip of your tongue." He pulled my head forward and pushed in deeply. I took him in as far as I could. I wanted Tommand to give me his everything and not hold back. I tightened around him and gripped him harder, using both my hand and mouth to pump him quickly. "Relax your throat, darling."

I did as asked and his hand tightened on my head.

"Perfect, you're fucking perfect," he growled out. I reached around and grabbed his backside tugging him forward. I kneaded his muscles as he drove himself in and out of my willing mouth.

"I'm going to come, Nortia, let go," his voice strained, but I was determined—drawing on him harder, digging my nails into his sides.

"I—fuck." He jerked one last time before going stiff. A hot spurt hit my tongue and then another and another again. He was salty, with a strong flavor unlike anything I'd tasted before. Not bad. Not good. Just Tommand. With one last pulse he grunted loudly, the unrestrained noise raising goosebumps along my exposed skin.

"Here, gods, it's..." He released my hair and walked over to a chest on the ground to procure a cloth, "It's been a while, and I did not expect you to fuck..." His breathing was ragged, and I found him to be so adorably flustered.

"Spit."

I spat and wiped the corners of my mouth with the towel.

He dropped down in front of me, concern etched on his features.

"Nortia, I was not gentle, I—"

"I wanted you not gentle, Tommand, and I'd like to continue our exploration of each other right now," I stated without hesitation.

He blinked rapidly and chewed on his bottom lip.

"You are nothing I ever expected."

"What? Am I not the sharp-toothed harpy I've been led to believe I am?" I teased.

"You are every bit of that." He traced a finger around my jaw, his eyes focused on my mouth. "And much more, I believe." Tommand rested his palm under my chin holding me gently as his face descended. I'd been craving his kiss since the first time, and I shook with anticipation.

"Troth Nortia!" Someone hammered on the door.

"Go away," Tommand shouted, his eyes locked on to mine. I reached up, stroking the few days of stubble on his cheek, and smiled.

"My apologies, Emissary Monwyn, but companion Nannetta has taken quite the fall."

Flying off the bed with no thought as to my disheveled appearance, I launched myself at the door.

"My Nan? Where is she?" I moved quickly through the doorway and found a livery-clad servant on the other side. I glanced back at Tommand, who was already re-tying his underclothes.

"I'll find you. Go." He nodded toward the door.

"What happened? Please take me to her!" The servant and I took off at a quick pace.

"I was not privy to the incident, Troth Nortia, but her injuries are quite significant," the servant shared. We rushed up the grand staircase, bypassing the second level, and headed directly to the third floor. I prayed to the Goddess that she'd been taken to a healer and prayed to Mossius that her injuries be mended. Hanging a right off of the third-level landing, we worked our way through a throng of revelers that had spilled over from the hall. I picked up my skirt and ran, needing to be with my Nan.

"Just ahead, Troth Nortia." We passed several hallways and prayer alcoves and reached a large entryway.

The double flames of Mossius were carved into the door's heavy wooden surround.

"Just through here, Lady." The servant stepped beside me pushing the infirmary's door open.

I stepped into the darkness.

The room was empty.

"Lady Troth, he... he told me that—" the man stuttered.

"Who told you what?" I spun on the servant, confusion and anger battling for precedence. "Speak!"

"Lady, it... it was..." His eyes widened with fear.

"Before you decide to snub me again, *Nortia,*" a voice came from deep within the room, "you will remember this evening."

A long shadow emerged from behind an apothecary's cabinet, transforming into flesh and blood.

"Greggen?"

CHAPTER TWENTY-THREE

WHAT NEEDS TO BE DONE

"**W**here is Nan?" I didn't care in the slightest that he felt I'd rejected him.

"Did you not hear me, Troth?" He strode forward.

"I heard you, Greggen. But my current priority is Nan and not your ego. You've been acting bizarre all evening and need to stop." I stepped backward, counteracting his advance.

"You didn't think I noticed you ogling me at the Congregation?" He slowed his steps. "Your lust was *palpable*."

"Wait, what? What the actual nether?" I thought back to that day. I had thought him handsome but hadn't made any conscious overtures.

Striding purposefully forward, he pouted, turning his handsome features churlish. He stopped directly in front of me, towering at least a foot and a half above my head.

"The minute I reciprocated, tried to spin you into a dance, you ran, Troth Cocktease," he insulted.

"I'll ask you *again*, Greggen—wait—she's not hurt at all... is she? You sick fuck." There was no number I could count to that would calm me enough to douse the fury burning its way through my chest. The darkness of the room enveloped me, supported me, seeming to understand my need to lash out. "How *dare* you come at me this way—"

"Your nursemaid is fine."

Greggen reached out and raised his hand to my face, tracing the line of my jaw as Tommand had done only minutes before. "I needed some way to get you off that Monwyn's dick." He reached around me and pulled me roughly, connecting his body to my own. "You could do better, Eira... unless you prefer the lowborn."

I spun in his arms and angrily walked toward the entrance.

"Open the door at once!" I shouted, snapping my fingers at the downcast servant.

"No. You will not leave until I've been given my due."

My face met the door.

Dazed by the splitting pain that radiated from my jaw to my forehead, I squeezed my eyes closed, trying to clear the fog that suddenly swam in my vision. A heavy hand tightened on the back of my neck, applying steady pressure to hold me in place.

I feared the man at my back. Why did he want to hurt me? When would he stop? If I ever *had* indicated I was interested in him... would that justify his actions?

No.

No, it does not.

"Get off me, now!" I screamed, my voice exploding around the room.

My need for freedom overrode my pain. I clawed back at the hand that held me and pivoted hard before lunging.

Greggen attempted to tighten his grasp but not quickly enough.

I sank my teeth into the fleshiness of his thumb. I bit down so hard that I cut through his skin, my teeth met and my mouth filled with the metallic taste of his blood.

"Stop! It was my task! Stop it, fucking bitch!" he roared so loudly my ears rang. He swatted at my face, smacking me below my mask. I let go as the third blow landed, finally able to register what had been said. Tears pricked at my eyes as a handful of white feathers floated limply to the floor.

"Your *task* was to assault me, Greggen?" I watched the Scion double over, holding his wounded hand tightly to his stomach.

"No, you dumb whore, it was to make you lose it, Nortia!" He looked at his bleeding hand. "To make you drop character, Gods fucking damn you."

"Well, it looks like you passed!" I yelled, not caring that he suffered. "And *you*?" I wheeled on the servant.

"Here for proof, Lady." His eyes remained downcast.

"Fucking sick... the lot of you! This place is nothing but filth dressed up in silk. You got your proof, now, OPEN THE FUCKING DOOR!"

"Troth Nortia, please, I had to do—"

"I know! Whatever needed to be done, am I right?" I marched furiously toward the exit. "THE DOOR!" I hollered. The servant didn't hesitate and pulled the door wide, unable to look me in the eye as I passed.

"This place can burn!" I screamed to the temple.

I heard Greggen calling my name but ignored him. If he needed proof of my reaction, I'd give them *all* the proof they needed.

Stomping down the stairs to the second level, I set my sights on the Nortian Devotee who stood stalwartly at her post.

"He sure as fuck made me lose it. I failed!" I hurled the words at her. "And if he *ever* touches me again he will WISH, he will fucking PRAY I stop at his hand."

I swooshed past her in a flurry of skirts and was immediately admitted into the fake festivities by a guard who rushed to open the door. The party had continued on, exactly as I had left it an hour or so ago. Costumed acrobats somersaulted through the air, the revelers still danced, and the musicians still played. Henric the drunkard, still sat on the bench, his head sunk into the pillow of his jowls.

It pissed me right off to see him there. I didn't even know why. Maybe because he napped while the Obligates risked injury and a lifetime of trauma to become the hardened servants of Ærta? Maybe because I envied the cozy, stupidly happy expression on his fat face. Well, I was awake, and now he could be too.

"Lord Henric." I tapped the snoring man's shoulder aggressively.

Nothing but a throaty snort.

"HENRIC!" I bellowed while kicking a foot against the bench's wooden leg. Coming to, the advisor blinked the sleep from his eyes, taken aback by the madwoman standing before him.

"*What* was Drelladas' surname?"

The advisor looked around, unable to discern how he ended up on a bench being accosted by a Troth in the first place. "Pardon me, Lady, I d-don't seem to understand." He pinched his nose, pushed his mask up over his eyes, and laid back.

Fucking coward!

I lunged at him, snatching him up by the gold-studded lapels so forcefully that I lost several of the lovely gems from my bodice. I brought my face close enough to his to whiff his alcohol-laden breath.

"Scion Lok's mother. What. Was. Her. SURNAME?" I snapped, batting the mask from his face.

"The Twins be damned, woman! It was uh...uh..." he stammered. "It was Slint." He brushed my hands from his broad neck and sputtered some obscenities.

I should have just done that in the first place. Fuck!

As I made my way out, I snagged handfuls of delights from the refreshment table, piling a plate high with lemon-scented cakes and berries and cream. I snatched three flutes of drink in a single hand and headed toward the door—I wasn't staying in this room for another moment. Still fueled by anger, I kicked the exit, planting my foot so hard it hit the stationed guard, shoving him forward.

I didn't care. He wore armor for a reason.

"Her surname was Slint!" I barked at the Nortian Devotee while reaching down to snatch up a cake that had dropped from my plate.

I don't even remember how I got there, but I reached my room and just stared at the door. My hands were full, the boning of the silly dress was poking painfully into my ribs, and I hadn't brought my key.

Tussi stepped into the hallway, making his nightly rounds.

"Please let me in," my voice cracked as the tears welled.

I waited for his admonishment, knowing good and well there were so many things he could call out—too many drinks, the pile of cakes, having torn up what I am sure was a very expensive mask.

He put the key in the lock.

"Good night, Troth Nortia."

"Good night, Tussi," I choked out, overwhelmed by his kindness.

Chapter Twenty-Four

CAKE FIXES MOST ISSUES

I sat on my bed and stuffed my mouth. The bubbling spirits did nothing to dull the pain in my face or mind. One cake didn't stop the crying and neither did two.

The mask took a half hour to dislodge, and when I finally freed myself, I pulled out all of the Monwynesque hair. I tossed it into the corner before chucking the mask into a drawer. Keeping with the theme of the night, what had made me feel like royalty now lay in ruin. The feathers were mutilated or missing, and the glass disks had come off in several places.

I crawled across my bed and tucked myself into a corner, pressing my back into the cool wall. My beautiful, blood-stained dress lay in a puddle in front of my wardrobe, and looking at it made the tears well again.

A soft knock sounded.

"Go away." I sniffled.

It came again.

I rolled off of the bed and grabbed my robe.

"They would not let me come to you. I am so sorry I wasn't there." A rumpled Tommand, no less handsome than a polished one, looked down at me, holding back what looked like great rage. He came to me and took me into his arms, gently guiding my head to rest on his chest. While the embrace didn't remove my physical pain, the comfort I found folded in his cradled arms was like a healing balm for my spirit.

"Come." He took my hand and led me into the bathing room.

I saw my reflection in the mirror. Black streaks trailed down my cheeks. Blood from a laceration that had been concealed by the mask had dried and flaked in a trail from my forehead to mouth, and my entire chin was stained reddish-brown. A green-and-gray bruise surfaced on my cheekbone, meeting up with another near my eye socket.

I didn't care.

I was beyond caring.

Tommand met me at the mirror with a hot washcloth, and with the gentlest touch, he went to work, wiping off the cosmetics and dabbing at the blood.

"Did you fall?" he asked, drawing his eyebrows together.

I shook my head, too exhausted for words.

He stilled his hand.

"Was this done by someone's hand?" His voice dropped and took on a deadly edge.

"Tommand, it was a task. It could have happened just as easily at the First Maneuvering."

I took the cloth from him and scrubbed the rest of my face clean.

"Eira, tell me who did this."

"Oh, it's 'Eira' now that you've come in my mouth?" I shot back.

I pulled the belt off my robe and let the garment hit the floor before tossing on my oversized linen shirt. The old thing snagged on my piercing, but I found it didn't hurt nearly as bad as it had the day before. I stopped to look at my reflection again and caught sight of a furious and fully-aroused Tommand.

"Ignore it," he said, his eyes narrowed to slits.

I'm not sure how he thought I could ignore *that*, but I could tell it bothered him, so did as asked.

"Is there to be no consequence for the one who hurt you? Eira, I cannot abide the—"

I stopped him with a raised hand. "There most certainly was a consequence." I reached for the jar of mint leaf mixture and scrubbed the powder into my lower teeth and gums, additionally rubbing it over the red remnants at my chin. I spat in the sink, my saliva still tinged, despite having consumed food and beverage.

"Is that...?" he asked curiously.

"It's blood, Tommand, and it's not mine." I reached for the hand he offered and ignored what looked like pride in his eyes. Tommand slipped off his overcoat and tossed it atop the magnificent dress that lay so sadly on the ground.

"Climb in." He held up the covers and laid down beside me, pulling me close. I snuggled tightly into his warmth, inhaling his woodsy scent while he trailed his rough fingertips up and down the small of my back.

"Tommand?"

"Mmhmm?"

"Stay with me."

He tightened his embrace, his closeness doing what the wine and cake could not.

I snapped awake.

I'd been running away, dodging branches and stones, pursued by some nether-bound creature through a densely wooded forest. The beast had Gotwig's face.

To my relief, Tommand was still here, clinging to me like a child would their stuffed polar bear. It was funny to me that a man who knew so much violence could look so innocent while at rest. *Not everything is tainted by last night's insanity.* I'd enjoyed my time with Tommand thoroughly and was thankful he hadn't lied about the part he played in my task.

In the dwindling lamplight, I examined the short stubble on his chin. It was turning more beard-like by the day. His whiskers were growing in deep brown, but lighter golden hairs clustered under his bottom lip. His hair was still somewhat of a mystery but looked fairly dark. *I wonder if it's short because he's graying?* I didn't think he'd be concerned with natural things like aging, but you never could tell what might bother a person. My father hated the little brown spots that had formed on his hands and arms as he had aged. He'd even tried laying naked in the sun to see if the rest of his skin would darken to the same color. It hadn't. I chuckled silently to myself remembering how red he'd turned. If Tommand's hair was a little gray, I wouldn't care. Marcyn, with his salt-and-pepper locks, was quite attractive. Plus, I didn't think even a full head of gray could detract from Tommand's vitality.

I smiled to myself, appreciating how his imperfections made him all the more alluring in my eyes, the way his once-broken nose enhanced rather than diminished his face, for instance. I wasn't sure if noses were widely considered sexy, but I found his to be. Its bridge was prominent and straight, with a bump rising up slightly in its middle, a testament to his rough and tumble lifestyle. Like it often did, the image of his bloodied smile entered my mind... only to be replaced by the euphoric grin he wore when looking up from between my spread legs.

I watched the rhythmic rise and fall of his chest, barely able to control the urge to run my fingers across his scar... and then follow them with my tongue.

I closed my eyes against the impulse. Just the idea made me dampen.

"I asked you once where you would set my price—I never did receive an answer." He opened his eyes and smoothed his palm over my uncovered hip, reaching behind my knee to pull my leg over his. He inserted his thigh into the space he'd made and pressed it snuggly against my vulva. "Having recently had a more thorough inspection of my *specimen*, have you determined my worth?" He bent low and slid the tip of his nose up the bridge of mine.

"Well, you see," I began, "though I've determined your pedigree to be of the highest quality, I do have a couple of doubts... about your talent..."

His eyes went round, forming a little horizontal line of concern on his forehead.

"And what can be done to assuage your uncertainty, Lady Troth?" his eyes darkened as he spoke.

"Well, for starters, I've only experienced this mouth on mine a single time, despite having wanted to try it out on several occasions." I traced his lower lip with my finger.

"Ouch!" I jumped, startled by the sharp nip of his teeth.

"Not enough training for you?" he whispered with a flirtatious half-smile on his lips. I forgave him for the bite, as the little bounce caused an oh-so-delicious friction down below. He must have noticed something in my reaction, because he grabbed my backside with his free arm and began rocking me against the leg I straddled. "That complaint can easily be remedied... and what was the other? You did mention a couple." He continued to push and pull me along his thigh while he used his nose to trace my mouth and tease me with the promise of his lips.

"The other issue is this." I reached between our bodies, and with one hand, began to unlace the opening of his pants. Not able to wait for them to be fully undone, I slid my hand into their opening and grasped his length, excited to find him already thickening.

"And what, pray tell, is the issue there? Too small? Lacking in girth?"

I ran my hand up and down and watched him suck air between his clenched teeth.

"No, the issue has nothing to do with your... stature. I find that especially pleasing. But, Tommand, I'd never be able to properly appraise a mount without first having taken it for a ride."

Tommand reacted fast, flipping me onto my back.

He rolled onto me, laying down the length of my body while yanking himself free from his pants. I spread my legs wide to cradle his rigidness.

His kiss was a demand.

This wasn't a gentle caress between lovers; this was Tommand on campaign. His tongue pushed past my lips, intertwining with my own. He explored every crevice, pulled my lip between his, and ran his tongue along the edge of my teeth.

"Nortia, if you keep making those sounds... I want this to be good for you."

He tore his mouth away and pushed up on his elbows while sliding his length between my labia. He rubbed and slid, over and over, until I was thrusting wildly to meet him. "You need preparation, Eira, or I could hurt you." I knew he saw me roll my eyes, but he'd pounded me with his fingers last evening, and I'd taken the digits of several others besides.

"I want you sunk to the hilt and I want it now, Tommand." I reached between us and attempted to guide his slick erection. My hand wrapped around him, and Tommand's eyes closed. He groaned out his pleasure, the deep guttural sound making me feel every inch the woman I was.

"Now. Fuck me now," I cried, already on the edge of orgasm.

Tommand dropped to one elbow, growling in the back of his throat. He thrust hard into my hand, once, twice, and again, and with a shout that fueled my desire to fever pitch, he came in a series of surges that hit hotly on my stomach. He orgasmed powerfully, stiffening against me, muscles flexing so hard he stopped breathing.

And then he sagged forward, panting into my chest.

"I... you said 'fuck,' and it was... Goddess, and I..." He stopped talking when he looked down and saw my face. I could tell he was embarrassed, but I didn't care. I writhed under him, bucking and pushing my hips into his.

Understanding dawned and Tommand swirled the fingertips of his hand around my Goddess-given jewel—*yes*—and sunk two thick fingers, into me. He set a quick and steady pace and reached deeply, far enough that the palm of his hand struck my clitoris with each plunge—a delightful addition to the already marvelous sensations he was creating.

"I think about you constantly, every hour of the day," he whispered thickly. "Every time I close my eyes, I see your ass filling out those pants, or your breasts pushing against your gowns, and your face... why you honor me with your magnificence, is beyond me," he effused, never slowing his hands. I reached up and pulled his mouth to my lips. The moment our tongues touched, I tightened around his fingers. The pressure built, rising until tiny shocks burst out from my core and the tremors of my release were upon me.

"Tom! TOM!" I screamed his name and raked my nails down his biceps, my completion ripping through me, pulsing and tingling, radiating outward from deep within.

After falling back to Ærta, for a full minute, I continued contracting around his fingers while we kissed like lovers, our meeting soft and intimate. He smiled against my mouth, and my heart flip-flopped in my chest. He kissed my chin, and then sternum. Lower, I felt his lips at my navel. Lower still, he kissed the curls at my juncture. He rolled off me and gathered me in his arms.

"Eira?" Tommand interrupted the silence.

"Hmm?"

"I do not want to cause you embarrassment, and more importantly, I should have mentioned this earlier..."

Derros' Dick, what now? I mentally braced myself.

"I believe you have started your courses, unless you were injured more substantially than you let on during last night's Maneuvering."

Well, that's just great. I stared at the ceiling and inhaled deeply.

"I suppose now we've both been embarrassed... so we're even," I joked, hoping my tone conveyed more amusement than mortification. "Can you refill the lamp?"

With the light at full brightness, I stared at my bed, which looked like the scene of a brutal massacre. Generally, my periods began with a light flow and horrible cramping, but I guessed whatever they did to control our cycles was making something very different occur. I had no pain, and it looked like the entirety of my normal flow had issued during the night.

Together we stripped the bed, and I went into the bathing room to clean up, and change into a clean gown before tying a fiber-filled pad to a fresh pair of linen drawers.

When I entered the room, Tommand turned to face me.

"Your pants!" He was covered in darkened splotches where I'd ridden his thigh. He shrugged, scrunching up his nose, and went about unlacing them and dropping them to the ground.

"They will dry," he said casually. "Also, this is nothing. I am regularly covered in an infinitely greater amount of blood or refuse." He laid them over the footboard of the bed. "Plus I have sisters."

I'd never seen him in full light, so entirely unclothed, in nothing but his long linen underwear. His legs were just as muscled as the rest of his brawny body and just as scarred. Like a winding snake, another long-healed injury roped around him from his ankle to mid-calf. I'd never seen a wound marking as strange.

He pulled the top cover from Kairus's bed and laid it over my mattress and then climbed in to sit with his back against the wall. With a sweet little pat, he indicated I should sit between his legs. My back met his chest, and his arms had just closed around me when it dawned on me just what he'd said.

"Sisters!" I bubbled. "The thought of you playing with a gaggle of adoring sisters somehow makes you even more attractive."

His laughter vibrated through his chest. "And what of my brothers? I played with them as well. Has my attractiveness reached its zenith, or can I further inflame your adoration?"

I leaned back in his arms and twisted my head up to see him. Kindly, he rubbed at the swell of my stomach, I think trying to relieve the cramps I wasn't having.

"Do you miss them while you're here?"

"I do and do not. I haven't seen many of them in years, and... I was raised in a rather isolated environment—I had little quality time with them." He nipped at my ear.

Twisting, I got on my knees and wound my arms around his neck.

"I treasure the childhood I had. I'm sorry yours was not all that it could have been." I kissed him soundly, and he wrapped his arm around my waist, pulling me close. He held my chin in both hands and looked at me like a Gaean who had just found a malachite ring.

"Tommand, why me and not someone else?"

He feathered little kisses along my neck and jaw and then softly spoke, "Because you feel like the home I've always wanted."

My heart. Oh, Goddess. Put a baby in me Tommand, okay don't, but, oh! His hands caressed my arms, and he dipped a finger into the indentation of my clavicle. I could feel him smelling my hair, and I smiled to myself, recalling the first time he'd sniffed at me.

New feelings, ardent feelings, were working in tandem to connect this moment, this man, to my soul. It was exhilarating and unnerving.

"Where do you see this going?" Maybe it wasn't the right time to ask, but I needed to know.

"Where I want this to go can have no bearing on where it *must* go," he said in a regretful tone. His soft lips roamed over my skin and sent shivers down both my arms.

"Tommand? If I were to be placed in Monwyn, we could... could continue... whatever this is." Running my hand along his shoulder, I followed the path of his jagged scar inward, my fingers stilling over his heart.

He captured my hand and held it tightly to his chest.

The silence stretched uncomfortably.

"I don't want you there, Eira."

I couldn't move.

He didn't want me.

"I won't risk you," he said firmly.

Rejection.

This is how it felt. Like the floor disappearing from under you.

"Do *I* ever get to choose what I am willing to risk, Tommand?" Finding my feet, I moved from the bed and walked to the door. Tommand snatched his pants from where they hung and put them on.

"There is so much more to it, Eira," he agonized, "and I will not subject you to it. I would not be able to ensure your protection while working to keep the king safe as well."

"Really? Who's watching him now, Tom? And if you haven't figured it out yet, unlike your king, I'm capable of functioning without a Protector."

He reached for me, and I pulled away.

"My feelings are tangling up in this, Tommand, so it looks like I'll need to protect myself. This ends now."

His eyebrows drew together, and his upturned eyes, those captivating eyes, reflected my pain. He reached for me again and grasped the back of my neck as I stepped back. He pressed his mouth to mine, hard, no room left for nicety.

My body reacted instantly, betraying my brave words, and I melted into him.

But I'd made up my mind.

"It ends," I repeated myself.

I pushed against his chest, and we separated. He nudged his knuckles along my jaw, tilting my head up until our eyes locked. The gold around his irises gleamed.

"And yet... you are *still* mine."

He turned and left.

CHAPTER TWENTY-FIVE

THERE ARE LESSONS WE ALL NEED

AND SOME WE DON'T

I was strong! I was independent! And sitting in the middle of six menstruating Troth, two menstruating priestesses, and four menstruating acolytes, I was right where I needed to be to pull out of the depression that had me feeling otherwise. Together we waited in a quaint, white-paneled room whose perimeter was lined with gold-leafed chairs. Today was day one of Matters of Unity, and my Troth sisters were exactly the people I needed to be with.

"He said you *felt* like home and then uninvited you to... his home?" Luræna shook her head in disbelief, and her bluntly bobbed hair swung around her face.

"Yes!" I blasted, flinging an arm out in front of me.

"That's some shit!" yelled a feisty Cinden. "He said *that* and didn't even put it in?"

I shook my head and stuck my nose in the air.

"And after all that, you're telling me he had the mannish Monwyn audacity to say you were *HIS?*" Yemailrys fumed.

"Yes, yep, he sure did. Gross, right?" I condemned, knowing full well that his outlandish proclamation had tapped some deep, primal vagina magic that had weakened my knees so entirely that I'd found it difficult to make it to the bed from the door.

"You know, if you're just looking for a good time, Evandr is particularly attentive... and Lok, he's super energetic," Kol—who still wore her shiny Monwyn hair—shared, shocking our collective audience.

"LOK?" Yemailrys screamed at the exact same moment Luræna hollered, "EVAN-DR?"

"Keep talking, Troth!" Cinden slid from the chair she'd occupied and took up a seat nearer Kol.

"*Well*... Evandr is a pleaser. He's incredibly empathic and gets off on giving... and giving again." As she tittered behind her hand, Kol's cheeks brightened. "Lok, on the other hand, is built to rut and rut hard. Don't expect any cuddling or sweet words, but do anticipate being speared by the hardest, um, member you've ever encountered. My lady parts were more than thrilled to be on the receiving end of his... I don't think you can call it passion or ardor. It was fucking at its finest, and it was amazing," Kol finished her sentence, and you could have heard a pin drop until all six Troth simultaneously found their voices.

"Well, I never would have thought!" exclaimed Luræna.

"Lok seems so nasty!" Farai chimed in.

"Who else can we talk about?" Yemailrys asked.

"Did Evandr have a nice... *ahem*?" A slender acolyte burst out.

All heads swiveled to the tall woman who asked... and all six exploded into laughter.

"Not incredibly big, no, but I am telling you, he could move his hips better than the acrobats at the Maneuvering." Kol reported, garnering a chorus of chortles and snorts.

"Okay, so I'll be adding him to my list of potentials." Cinden sucked the side of her lip into her mouth and winked at Farai, who was looking decidedly uncomfortable with the whole topic.

I didn't know why Cinden kept up the ruse of wanting other men when she and Ozius had clearly developed a deep relationship. Perhaps it was a consequence of the Gaean purity thing. I could also have been totally wrong in assuming they were lifemates. It's not like they'd said it out loud or anything. And thinking back, twice I'd seen Gaeans have their hair touched by a non-intimate partner, and there were no consequences for those times that I was aware of.

"What do we know about Unity?" Farai asked, looking rather anxious, tapping her toes rapidly on the floor.

"Well, Kairus never told me what happened, but she did tell me it was a unique experience." I left out the part where she'd stared unblinking into the wall.

Scooting her chair closer to the circle, Yemailrys smacked her hands to her knees.

"Kymor told me we would be looking at vaginas and discussing birth," she whispered as if either were a taboo subject.

"I've seen so many babies born, there's not a vagina in here that would surprise me," I said shrugging my shoulders.

"You *have*? You have actually seen it?" Cinden probed. Farai sat wide-eyed in shock.

I nodded. "My mother delivers almost all the babies in the town I'm from. I've seen her put babies into new mothers' arms probably twenty times. She has a true calling in midwifery."

"In Gaea, only trained healers of Mossius can deliver babies, and everything around childbearing is kept quite secretive. I cannot wait to have a child..." Cinden trailed off while a wistful smile bloomed across her face.

"In Monwyn, the woman is put into isolation for the last month of her pregnancy. I have no idea what goes on behind the closed door, but it always sounds atrocious." Yemailrys pulled a lock of hair over her shoulder, twisting it into a tight rope. I had a hard time believing that most of the women surrounding me had never experienced something so natural, or that their kingdoms had so much say over how they gave birth.

A movement at the door caught my eye, and a rather shapeless woman and a gangly-looking man, probably approaching his seventieth year, walked into the meeting room. Both wore warm smiles and matching beige robes.

"Hello, all! Welcome to Matters of Unity!" the balding man beamed. "I am Lord Vaughn and this," he smiled down at the squishy woman beside him, taking her hand into his, "is my dearest Lady Vaughn."

Lady Vaughn walked forward and lifted her arms slightly, palms facing up.

"Today, we will endeavor to teach you the finer points and advantages to mastering the marriage mart... because *unity* is built on robust relationships," she gushed.

Sliding forward to join his wife, Lord Vaughn placed a protective arm around her shoulder.

"We will also be exploring the beauty of our Goddess-given bodies and how and when to use them in your role as an Obligate!"

Farai's eyes darted to where Cinden and I sat. Her eyes were as wide as plums, and she looked like she'd been holding her urine too long. She silently mouthed a word while pointing at her crotch. Her face was so red, her freckles almost disappeared.

"What'd she say?" I asked Cinden.

"Assign us? Maybe? Haven't a clue."

We turned back to our speakers.

"Let us all gather in the next room. You will receive your robes from our wonderful group of acolytes before your examinations."

"Our what now?" Cinden spoke out, rather alarmed.

"We know this may be a little bit uncomfortable on account of Unity falling in the window of your menstruation period, but the assembled emissaries have already begun making their cases to the Devotees. Whether or not you remain intact will be an important determining factor for some of the representatives, though others will not care a bit," Lord Vaugh informed us.

"*Are you intact?*"

"*I'm guessing intact.*"

Tommand.

"That piece of *shit*." The words shot out before I could stop them.

Tears stung my eyes, but I swallowed back the lump in my throat. Had that been his game all along? Is this why we'd never had intercourse? He wanted to keep me 'intact' for some bullshit bidding war. I shook in outrage, feeling unsteady and lost when a cool hand wrapped around my own. Cinden had come to my side. I leaned into her, needing the support.

"I'm a little shocked by the language, dear, but am guessing you're worried about your lack of corona?" Lady Vaughn probed, nodding her head up and down genially.

"*Quite* the opposite," I exhaled, an edge of anger detectable in my voice.

Without pursuing it further, our instructor playfully shooed us into the next chamber.

Cinden and I walked hand in hand into an alcove and were told changing rooms were available to the right and left. We took the robes offered to us upon entry and headed into what looked like the least populated room. Like in the Grooming hall, baskets with our kingdom's names had been set out for our use, and the room smelled of fresh herbs and woodsmoke.

"I've laid my legs open for him twice. I pulled him to me, begged him for it... and now I feel so stupid."

Cinden gathered my hands to her chest.

"Eira, I'm so sorry. I know right now you think he's made sport of you, but I truly don't think that's the reason. Even Ozius has mentioned what a direct person Tommand seems to be. Maybe, for right now, don't let yourself think the worst of him," Cinden counseled.

I let my shoulders fall.

"When did you become the sensible one?" I took the hug she offered, still undecided on if I wanted to scream or cry.

"When I fell in love," she whispered close to my ear.

I pulled from her embrace.

"Ozius?" I asked, keeping my voice low.

She nodded and motioned me deeper into the room.

"We've known each other since we were children. It's not often that Obligates meet before Verus, but we went to the same temple and over the years formed a bond. We were separated when he left to train with the healers, and we met again on the day of the Congregation. It was like we'd never been parted. The day you peeked in on us was one of the happiest of my life." Cinden's eyes glazed over.

"I'm sorry I ruined that for you, Cinden. I just—"

"Eira, the Mantle couldn't have made us stop. You certainly didn't." She wagged her eyebrows suggestively.

We embraced, clinging to each other.

"I won't tell anyone, Cinden," I assured her.

"I believe you, and I'm not just saying this to make you feel better, but, not all things are what they seem at first. Give it time."

We undressed and tossed our clothing into our baskets. The luxuriously soft robes we were given crisscrossed over our chests and had a three-button closure near the neck. I swished the hem around my legs and hoped we got to keep them in the end. They were like wearing my velvet dress inside out.

"Cinden, what's your Primus-King going to think when it comes back that you're lacking your most holy innocence?" I half-joked, inclining my head at a snobbish angle.

"It won't matter, because I will never return to ask his opinion." She smiled, albeit weakly. We walked back into the alcove, and two beaming acolytes ushered us through another entrance. Between them and our instructors, the smiling was getting creepy.

The room we entered looked like a cross between a healer's theater and one used for entertainment. Rows of raised chairs were staggered on risers so that everyone in the audience would have a clear line of vision, and a large raised platform was erected in the center of the room, surrounded by lamps. The room itself was fairly dim but I could make out two groups standing against either of the far walls. An acolyte sent me and Cinden to join the group on the right.

Lord Vaughn, two acolytes, and a priestess waved us over to an area where a thin table and small stool had been set up.

"No worries now, my dears. The practice of inserting implements to test for your corona, or lack thereof, is considered archaic and reveals nothing anyhow. We are all made *wonderfully* different, and it's fine if you've chosen to share your uniqueness with another... I certainly didn't wait after meeting Lady Vaughn." His voice was full of affection. "The inspection itself is simply visual and will be carried out swiftly. When you have finished, our assembled acolytes will provide you with fresh underclothing and paddings."

"Who will be first?" the priestess asked.

Kol and Cinden held back, but with the mood I was in, I didn't give two shits about who saw my twat, bleeding or not. To put my worried-looking Troth sisters at ease, I walked forward and offered myself up.

"Excellent. Thank you. Now, I'll be taking notes throughout." Lord Vaughn smiled encouragingly. "Hop right up."

The crisscrossed robes made sense now. When I climbed the stool and sat back on the table, its sides parted, revealing my lower half, but keeping my upper body modest.

"Scoot toward me, please," the inspecting priestess asked. "More, please... keep moving forward." I wiggled and pushed myself nearer the priestess, who encouraged me like someone would a baby taking their first steps. "Yep, yes, a little more even." At this point, my butt was hanging off the edge of the padded table, and I grew increasingly concerned that if I were to scoot any closer, her nose would meet my anus. "Perfect!"

I started to regret my boldness. It *was* weird to have a fellow I didn't know grinning from ear to ear at my left, scribbling in his book, while the priestess encouragingly clapped her hands an inch away from my lady parts. She and the acolyte who held a lamp between my legs smiled good-naturedly, while a curious Kol and Cinden looked intently at my vulva, their heads perched above each of the priestess' shoulders.

"I've never seen what's inside my own before." Cinden mused aloud. "Yours is very foldy, Eira."

"And foldy is *wonderful*!" Vaughn sang out after taking a quick peek and getting right back to his notes.

Turns out it *could* get weirder.

"And here ladies, look, you'll see her corona right there, the half-moon shape. I don't even need to spread her labia. It's quite visible." She glanced at each of her new pupils. "Now, you see the tissues here? They *have* been stretched, probably from self-pleasure or play with a partner, but there's enough remaining to consider her intact. Would that be accurate, Troth Nortia?"

"It would," I said.

The little group clapped excitedly at the priestess's correct guess.

"Me next!" Kol exclaimed, almost pushing me off the table. Our more mature friend hoisted herself up, wrapped her hands behind her thighs, and pulled her legs back impressively far—her knees almost went to her ears.

"What's mine look like?" she asked, doing her damnedest to look down and see for herself.

"Well used!" Cinden quipped, busting out in loud laughter. "No, seriously," she snorted, still cracked up at her own joke, "yours is lighter than Eira's, and your, I don't know what it is, pokey part at the top is fatter."

"And fatter is just *wonderful*. And by the way, Troth Gaea, you cannot guess at a person's experience based upon what you see here. There is no actual correlation. Isn't that fascinating?" Vaughn interjected, hurriedly taking notes after glancing at Kol's nethers.

The priestess waved Cinden closer.

"The fat part is a happy and healthy-looking clitoris, and you will notice here, at her opening, the corona has thinned out significantly, practically not visible at all. She has most likely enjoyed the Goddess's gifts, so we will mark her as not being intact. Is that commensurate with your experiences?" she asked Kol.

"It is. Thank you." She rolled off the table and joined me behind the priestess.

Cinden's time came, and she stood, worrying her bottom lip with her perfect little teeth. I gave her a quick squeeze on the hand. She walked to the table like a criminal headed to the noose. Of course she didn't regret Ozius, but someone was certain to tell a Gaean emissary and her Primus-King would eventually find out.

"Okay and move down, keep moving down, all the way now... right there," The priestess paused. "Troth Gaea, your inner labia conceal much of your entrance, may I have permission to shift them out of the way?"

Cinden murmured her approval and squeaked when the priestess touched her.

"There we are, ladies. You can see the corona is quite thin, but parts of it are still visible on one side of her passage. I would venture to say not intact but cannot be positive based on what's presented. Troth Gaea, is that commensurate with your experiences?"

The pink-haired Troth glanced down between her knees.

"N-no-it isn't, I'm still pure," she spoke softly, flicking her eyes to mine.

"Excellent, thank you. The Troth is intact, Lord Vaughn."

The priestess made to get up, but Kol put a hand on her shoulder, leaning right over the red-robed woman, closely inspecting the still-exposed Gaean.

"Yours is tidy and bronze, Cinden." Kol grinned.

"And bronze is—"

"*Wonderful!*" Kol and I sang out in unison with our oddly enthusiastic instructor. Our whole group bubbled up in shared laughter. Instead of being offended, Lord Vaughn nodded appreciably and let a massively toothy grin spread further across his already cheerful face. He snapped his ledger closed.

"Please have a seat around the platform. We will begin our lesson momentarily." He turned and met with his wife at the room's entrance, and together they handed off their notes to a collared priestess who was flanked by two guards. I hadn't noticed their arrival and, of course, was unable to tell from their expressions if they'd been there long enough to get a glimpse of the full show.

"Did any of you realize we'd have a say in that?" Cinden whispered when we met back up with our full group.

"Had I known, I would have told them that their guess was certainly NOT commensurate with my experience. But I just *had* to play big and tough and go first, trying to be a fearless example for my two Troth friends." I only half-joked, pointing to my counterparts.

Cinden's hand came to my shoulder, and she scoffed, "Do you not know the value of the label you've just been given? Not only are you one of the Goddesses chosen, but now you'll be able to auction your ass off as an actual treasure. You could become a lesser queen in my kingdom."

"And do you not understand how awful that is, Cinden?" I barked back.

Cinden shrugged and scoffed.

"Given your status, it appears you too could become a Gaean queen." I blinked at her innocently.

"Assembled Troth, take your seats. We are about to begin," Lady Vaughn's voice carried over our chatter.

Together, we sat, facing what we assumed to be the front of the raised stage. Cinden, Yemailrys, and Farai sat directly behind Luræna, Kol, and me on the taller of the two risers. Lord and Lady Vaughn walked hand in hand to the center of the stage that had been furnished with two chairs and a table. They looked for all the world like the most content coupling in existence.

"They are not," Farai gulped.

Facing each other, our instructors reached out and began unfastening one another's robes.

Cinden snickered, and Yemailrys emitted sharp little shrieks. Luræna, sitting beside me, smacked both her hands over her eyes. The couple shrugged off their coverings, and the male Vaughn gathered them both and placed them over the back of the chair that sat next to the wooden table.

Lady Vaughn's pendulous breasts sagged downward, meeting with her flabby belly. Her heavy thighs were striped with horizontal rows of brownish stretch marks and the sides of her rear were dimpled, but she took her seat as regally and confidently as a queen might. When Lord Vaughn walked around the chair, to ensure her comfort, we were given a full-frontal view of his loose-skinned body and droopy ballsack, both of which wobbled and swayed with each step he took.

Seated to my left, I heard Farai's rapid breathing.

"Lady Vaughn is the most precious thing in my life. We met when I was Assigned to her kingdom as Scion," he began. "Now, I won't tell you that your future relationships will be like ours, but together, we very carefully worked to arrange the union that not only brought a large supply of malachite to Gaea but also, through the Goddess's blessings, brought seven wonderful children into the world." He worshiped his wife with his eyes. "We aren't as young as we once were, but when I look at the body that granted me the honor of fatherhood, I know there is nothing greater in my life."

"Damn..." Yemailrys whispered.

"Okay, but what if she couldn't have kids? What then?" Luræna spoke low enough so only we could hear.

Lord Vaughn sat next to his wife and crossed a leg over his knee, letting his balls drop off the chair. Yemailrys did her best to muffle her chuckles behind my head but kept whispering, "Hairy testes!" into Luræna's ear. To her credit, Luræna remained guard-level-expressionless.

Lady Vaughn stood.

"As Troth, you will be relied upon by royalty and Primus to bring about successful political unions. It has been my experience that many a trade agreement can be secured by playing matchmaker. You must, however, always be vigilant in your research and assess all angles when it comes to joining two families. Will an accord bring about strife? Could it work to settle long-suffering feuds?" She paced across the stage, walking the distance of one side and turning about, her head held high like a military officer. "Stay sharp at all times, and watch how young women act around eligible men. If a man is ineligible but the gain will be worth it, for the greater good, determine how their marital status might be changed. For example, as you know, we have the ability to control one's cycle. You will learn the method, and it can be employed to render a woman temporarily infertile—one of the very few justifications for a marriage to be dissolved in the kingdom of Monwyn." She paused and folded her hands together at the small of her back.

A sobered Yemailrys leaned down and whispered, "I really thought she was going to say we would have to kill people... I really did."

"In Gaea," she began again, "plurality is sanctioned. However, should you go about angering the Lead Mate of a family, you will make an enemy of the entire household, whose members, of both sexes, oftentimes wield far-reaching political clout. Always approach the Lead before ever attempting to make a match. Obligates have lost their lives tangling with the wrong kin groups."

The husband Vaughn bounced from his chair, joining his increasingly scary wife. Spreading his arms in an arch like a rainbow in the sky he launched in.

"Babies are another way to cement economic agreements. In Gaea, birth practices are heavily regulated, which is why we have many Obligates hailing from their lands. Despite being the smallest geographically, it boasts the largest population on the continent, and it is mandatory that children be born to a temple-blessed union, so young marriages and matings are encouraged, unlike Solnna. There, children bind families and agreements tighter than marriages. If a couple is childless, the wife is generally given permission, even encouraged, by her husband to choose a male outside of their union in an attempt to produce children. A child conceived would be raised in the husband's home and retain both of their fathers' names. Adoption is also encouraged and welcomed there, and Obligates are often sought out to place children with families or to assist in finding conception partners."

Lord Vaughn wrapped his arm around his wife's waist pulling her close to his side, "In Monwyn, the idea of adoption or allowing one's wife to attempt a pregnancy with another is almost unheard of, though many wives *will* send other women to their husband's beds as a means of lessening the physical burden of their marriage. This is also a custom you may use to your benefit, whether it be providing mistresses who are in your employ or by offering your own body so that you may apply pressure or collect information in person."

"Sex is one of the most wonderful gifts given to us by the Goddess." Lady Vaughn rose up on her tiptoes and planted a kiss on Lord Vaughn's cheek. "And though some would say it only serves the purpose of reproduction, we can tell you that it has played a meaningful role in our lives, even though it took a while for us to get it right. Pleasing your partner and making sure you too receive pleasure takes work. Learn your craft well so you can apply it strategically when a deal is on the line."

"Burl, to the table dear," she spoke just to him then turned back to us. "That is why I will be demonstrating several tried-and-true methods, guaranteed to please a man so thoroughly, he will be quite pliant following. We will then explore how to make sure we, and others with vaginas, may enjoy the process. Life is too short for bad sex, whomever the partner!" she laughed playfully.

Lord Vaughn, with the energy of a much younger man, leapt onto the table, rolled to his stomach, and proceeded to lift up on all fours, showing off his widely spread buttocks, and his exceedingly dangly, dangly bits.

Kol's hand shot out, catching me in the stomach, her grimace so intense all her teeth showed. I doubled over from the impact, Cinden screeched so loudly Luræna covered her ears, and poor Farai... she hit the floor in a dead faint.

"Oh dear, that's never happened before," said a genuinely concerned husband Vaughn, peering backward, head hanging between his legs.

CHAPTER TWENTY-SIX

GODDESS GUIDE US

K airus burst into our bedroom and ran forward, throwing open the door of her bathing chamber. The heaving sounds of violent retching followed soon after.

Right. It was her first day of Matters of the Court. I padded over and peered around the door. She was sprawled out in front of her pot, and the skirts of her lovely sky-blue dress were splattered with a yellow and green mess where she'd missed when taking aim.

"You drank the wine?" I asked tonelessly. She shook her head, bouncing her still slightly red-tinged hair around her shoulders.

"I switched glasses with Chentel after seeing a servant acting shifty with *my* glass." She pulled her dress over her head between dry heaves and passed me the garment, which I hastily folded and tossed in a pile with the other clothing going out to wash.

"You're an asshole." I couldn't help but laugh at what she'd done.

"Why, Eira... why did you not tell me?" she breathed out heavily while laying the back of her head against the stone wall.

"For the same reason you didn't let me in on the fact I'd be watching an old man contort himself into the 'Fourteen *Saggy* Positions of Male Ecstasy,' Kairus!" The sparkle in her eyes was only partially dimmed by the misery I knew she was feeling. She burst out into a grotesque laugh, a mixture of guttural sounds and croaky chuckles. Even if the smell of her was currently turning my stomach, I laughed along. She always managed to surprise me and turn a tough situation right around.

"You're so stinky." I grinned.

I stepped away to grab a ribbon from my drawer as Tussi knocked on the door. He and Nan entered after actually waiting until I gave them the okay before doing so. I waved them over, not wanting the advisor to walk in on his partially nude charge.

"Got-Gotwig said I was awful as well, but co-commended me, nonetheless," Kairus proudly panted, loud enough to be heard from the other room.

Tussi wrinkled his nose and sniffed at the air.

"Nan, she's going to need the citrus water." I looked at my companion. "Tussi, I can take care of her tonight."

"I'll run to get what's needed, my girl—but are you well?" She searched my face. "No ill effects from today's lesson?"

I shuddered, recalling the moment Lady Vaughn lifted her husband's wrinkly scrotum to provoke the 'delectably sensitive skin between his anus and testes.'

"To be honest... I preferred the poison, Nan." I shooed her out the door.

"Hahahahaha!" Kairus screamed-cackled hearing my admission. "I knew it!"

I rolled my eyes to the Goddess and reached for Kairus's bathing room door when the most unladylike grunt, accompanied by a rasping belch met my ears. Tussi turned to me, looking a little green himself.

"Thank you for looking after the Lady Kairus. Send for me if the need arises." He produced a handkerchief from his coat's pocket and covered his mouth. With a clipped bow, he went to the door.

Kairus's flawless skin was blotched with fat red markings, and a fine sweat coated her brow. I braided back her hair and patted her forehead with a cool square of linen. It took a moment to convince her that wearing a towel wrapped around herself would be more comfortable than a new dress, but too weak for debate, she acquiesced.

"My mother never did stuff like this for me. Did yours, Eira?"

"Mmhmm, my dad too if she was out."

"Mine was always out, or well, I didn't see her often except for a few minutes at night," she breathed fitfully.

After procuring the beverage from Nan, I coaxed Kairus into sipping the cool lemon and mint concoction between her bouts of illness, and finally, after what seemed like hours, she drifted to sleep, lying on my shoulder.

I'd never had to care for someone like this before, but knowing now that Kairus was never coddled by her mother made me feel for her. I hoped her father had been able to provide her with love in her mother's absence like mine had. I didn't know if I could truly provide much in the way of comfort, but I wanted to try, even though this was its own kind of exhausting. Every time I laid my head back to sleep, I'd snap awake at the grumble of her stomach or twitch of her head, afraid she'd need her water or assistance at the toilet. I gave up on any kind of rest and let my mind wander to the subject I'd actively been trying to avoid.

I miss Tommand already.

The indignation that had seen me through the morning had faded away, and sitting here, being the best pillow I could be, the grief crept in. I liked spending time with him. Our banter kept me on my toes, and I enjoyed learning about his life. He'd been so thoughtful to teach me defense, to have worried about me at all. And I was *just* discovering how brilliant it felt to be attuned to another person.

Cinden had said maybe there was more to it, but even if that was the case, trying to form anything long-term with Tommand wasn't an option. The possibility of me ending up on the other side of the continent was too close to becoming reality. I was also aggravated by the thought of him just not coming out and saying "we can't *do it* because you're more valuable *with it.*"

My decision was sound, and though it stung to realize he'd been more agent than paramour, he *had* been looking out for the future of his kingdom, and that's really what this was all about. Maybe I should've favored the larger of the two Monwyns.

Eventually, I drifted off beside Kairus until hours later when Nan entered the room.

We'd been summoned to the great hall.

··· +)((+ ···

The room had been changed once more. The enormous panels had been moved between the inner rectangle of columns, shaping the room into an intimate smaller setting. Against the long wall, servants manned stations where treats and drinks were being served, and as always, delicious-looking foodstuffs were piled high on fancy trays, and mugs and glasses were being filled to their brims for the rapidly growing crowd.

A massive table was at the center of the room, and with a cursory glance, I figured it could easily seat thirty people, maybe more. Beautifully woven runners had been laid horizontally across the dark wood, and the four kingdoms' standards fell in a burst of bright colors from the ceiling.

Four Devotees entered the room without any ceremony, but nonetheless, their presence brought the loud buzzing of hundreds of conversations to an end. Wearing their kingdom's colors along with their matching scarlet hoods, Mariad Keagan, the Nortian

Devotee, and two others stood behind four of five large chairs located at the head of the table.

From his sheer size alone, I figured the burly bear standing to the right of Mariad had to be the Monwyn Devotee. He made Ambrose look small in comparison. The towering man had an abundance of stark-white hair that reached the middle of his back and matched his heavy beard. His prominent eyebrows arched so severely that it gave him a permanently sinister appearance.

"Obligates, find your seats on our right, emissaries to the left. We will begin at the top of the hour." The Monwyn's baritone voice cut right through the chatter of the crowd.

Reaching for last-minute items and topping off their drinks, the Obligates made their way quickly through the food lines. I didn't have the stomach or tolerance for making conversation right now. I was feeling too downtrodden from taking care of Kairus and reassessing my barely-there relationship. I circled the table and found the seat marked *Nortia: Troth Chulainn,* two spots down from the head of the table. I waited patiently for a servant to assist me and thanked the boy, who couldn't have been more than fourteen. I peered around and made a show of fidgeting with the embroidery at my wrist, not wanting to catch the eyes of anyone milling about.

The names, *Troth Rayvor* and *Scion Ashdown* were written to my left and right, but I hadn't a clue who'd be sitting there. I didn't know any of the Obligate's surnames barring Kairus, despite the grueling scenarios we'd navigated together.

The vacant seats began to fill.

I eyed the emissaries who sat directly across from me and nodded a silent greeting to the three Gaeans. All older women, they looked splendid in their matching robes of forest-green. Each wore a sizable malachite medallion hanging from her neck and two of the triad had their hair braided with the same gold fibers the Obligates did, their scarlet locks shown brighter then a pair of rubies. The third of the group had only a few whisps of silver-white on her head and was well into her advanced years.

It turned out that Yemailrys was Troth Rayvor, and she sat sandwiched between me and the Monwyn Devotee. Scion *Greggen* Ashdown, sporting a fresh bandage wrapped around his hand, ended up on my right.

"Ouch, Eira!" Greggen hissed. I'd turned to greet Yemailrys and accidentally hit his injured hand. He held the afflicted appendage to my face. "Don't you think you've done enough already? Your tantrum didn't even count for me. It turns out I wasn't supposed to use violence. As if bumping your head against the door was damaging or something."

"So you're *innocent*, Greggen? You *have* seen my face, right?" I pointed to the bruises, incredulous at the fact he was trying to put this back on me. I wasn't about to take the blame for his injury. I had every reason to think he'd been actively trying to hurt me.

"I hardly think your face—" he stopped mid-sentence and stared straight ahead.

I followed his line of vision.

Tommand sat forward, the muscles in his shoulders and neck tightly coiled—he was a bull ready to charge. He squeezed his interlaced fingers together so tightly that his knuckles turned white, and he scowled so intensely I thought he might break a tooth. I'd known I'd have to face him sooner rather than later, but I'd been hoping it wouldn't be in such a public forum.

"*Meerka!* This place is absurd!" fumed Greggen.

Having no clue what he'd just said, I looked from him and back to Tommand, who hadn't let up his murder glare. I waved a hand in front of Greggen and eventually forced myself over into his space.

Tommand's gaze shifted, and his intensity faltered.

"Cut it out!" I mouthed. Tommand dared to narrow his eyes at me but turned toward the other Monwyn emissary, speaking to the man in hushed tones.

"That was all *kinds* of uncomfortable," Yemailrys murmured while elbowing me in the side. "Luckily, I don't think the entire table saw."

"All rise for the Holy of Holies! The High Mantle walks among us," a guard stationed at the entrance bellowed.

Everyone stood, joining the Devotees who had yet to be seated. I'd seen nothing of the Mantle since Gotwig's first lesson, and though Their head was covered by a panel of silk, it felt like Their eyes were upon me. I felt the blush rising to my cheeks, remembering how I'd bungled our first meeting. The Mantle descended like fog rolling down a mountainside. They glided across the marble floor clothed in a cloud of cranberry that swirled behind Them. Two priestesses, dressed in finely embroidered tunics, escorted the Mantle to the chair located between the four Devotees. The priestesses hurried forward to assist Them, adjusting the flowing fabrics as They sat, and remaining by Their side.

"The Fourth and final Maneuvering is set to begin. It is by far the most relevant of the scenarios that you will have participated in and shall be the culminating factor in determining your Assignments. When your destination is decided, you will spend your remaining sessions in intensive conference alongside the emissaries you see before you, to gain a firm understanding of the current issues affecting their states. They are the experts, and you will do well to heed them as such."

I again looked to the emissaries who sat across from me, inclining my head as the other Obligates were doing. As I moved down the line, I avoided eye contact with the Monwyns, skipping over them altogether, and acknowledged the Solnnan emissaries who all wore expressions reminiscent of Mariad: pleasant, like all was at ease in the world. After the Solnnans came—*Holy shit! Is this a fucking joke?*

Nan.

There she was, sitting as straight and confident as a Primus presiding over a contract scrivener.

My Nan. My companion—the one who'd collected my laundry just this evening—was emissary to the glorious Kingdom of Nortia.

I stared at her and willed her lying self to meet my eye, but she ignored me. I knew her better than to think she just didn't see me, and I guarantee she knew exactly how well I'd take being kept in the dark for Goddess knows how long.

"Our assembled emissaries have each been given detailed accountings of your time here," the Devotee of Monwyn said while making eye contact with the Scion and then Troth. "From your arrival onward, we have met in daily council to assess your skills and begin the deliberation of determining where you would be most successful. The Fourth Maneuvering will begin before dawn tomorrow, and we will gather to mete out our final decisions the morning after your ordeal."

I focused on the Devotee as he spoke but knew without looking that Tommand's eyes were on me. Glancing up through downcast lashes, I fought the urge to see if I was correct and failed.

His eyes were heavily dilated, and the visible parts of his neck were flushed copper. I knew the look of his arousal... knew that under the table he grew hard. The pulsing pressure of my own excitement snaked through me and centered itself on that spot deep inside. A lazy half-smile tugged at his mouth, and his tongue darted out to moisten the corner of his lips.

He knew.

I bit my lip hard and turned away, the pain aiding in bringing my focus back to where it belonged.

"Tomorrow, before first light, you will arrive at the fifth-level prayer room. Once the Maneuvering begins, you will only have contact with those we have chosen for the duration of the ordeal," the Monwyn spoke gruffly.

Ordeal. The word echoed in my mind. *We've endured enough "ordeals" for a lifetime already.*

The Gaean Devotee stood, drawing my attention across the table. She was a tall woman with an ample body and a long, black braid. Several of her top teeth had been studded with green gems and others had been capped in gold. When she spoke, her jeweled smile glinted, reflecting magnificently in the light.

"Your new lives will soon begin, and like all new things, you may experience feelings of unease—of fear. But remember, you walk in the light of the Goddess," she said in dulcet tones and placed her fingertips on her brow. "We commend you at this juncture, for each of you has proven capable to take what is learned in your instruction and apply it. I would ask you now, the night before the last Maneuvering, to think about where you see yourself in the future. Do you wish for a life of grandeur, arranging matches and climbing the social ladder? Would you wish to formally join with a Scion or Troth, knowing that any children you bear would be considered as precious as any royal offspring? Do you see yourself working closely with a Primus, ushering a kingdom into a golden age? Think about this, Obligates, and tonight pray to the Goddess that she will give guidance to us all."

I see myself hunting a lying Nortian.

She returned to her seat as the Mantle rose.

"A prayer."

I raised my hands to my brows.

"Goddess, above us all, in your name we move to protect your children. Goddess of all seasons, let us feel your presence in all we do and guide the actions we must take. Goddess of creation, let us live in your grace, and if we are to fall, deliver us quickly to our judgment."

The Mantle rose and left as quickly and gracefully as They'd arrived.

"Obligates, you are dismissed," the Monwyn Devotee announced.

When the Devotees vacated their seats, I saw my opportunity to get to Nan and walked quickly around the head of the table, weaving in and out of the chairs that hadn't been pushed in. I was nearly to her when the triad of Gaean Emissaries intercepted me.

"Troth Nortia. We would speak with you," the wrinkliest emissary said in a wheezing voice. I could see Nan speaking to Kol and Zotikos, only a few steps away, but there was nothing to be done. Decency mandated I stop. The Gaeans pulled several chairs from around the table and placed them in a small, intimate circle. They each sat and motioned for me to do the same.

"Troth Nortia, we are not ones to mince words. Collectively, we have decided that you are the Troth we wish to be placed in our kingdom," the woman said. She looked to be in her seventh decade and had a slight tremor in her hand. Caught off guard by the straightforward proclamation, I worked to shift my expression to one of impartiality, attempting to show the group neither excitement nor disdain. In truth, I was feeling quite a rush, knowing I must have made an impression on them. Most of the merchants I had met back home had been Gaean, given their geographical closeness. I'd be honored to see many of them again. I inclined my head, acknowledging their statement.

"And can you elaborate on why you feel I am the best fit for your kingdom and the potential roles you would see me filling?" Who knew if I had any real say in my placement, but it seemed in my best interests to be just as forthright and ask.

"You have shown yourself to be determined, as the tall Scion found out, and you have demonstrated the ability to intuit and think creatively. You have also proved you can keep your mouth closed when you should." My eyebrow almost quirked in response. *Neutrality in all situations, Eira. Think on that later.*

"There are two responsibilities that you may be called to fulfill. First, Gaea prides itself on our healthy and thriving population. Our people, by the grace of the Primus-King, live on abundant and thriving lands, but as our numbers expand, our lands do not. We require a shrewd Obligate in place to match our strongest families to those from a neighboring kingdom in hopes to expand our borders beyond the rift." There was a long pause, no doubt to study my reaction. Expanding beyond the rift meant moving into what was rightfully Nortian territory. Their suggestion would potentially mean unraveling the maps that were created following the war that almost broke humankind.

"Second," the emissary seated to my left spoke up again, "our Primus-King has taken interest in you specifically. An eligible Nortian woman, whose purity is still with her, would be the ideal mate to help ensure our expansion proceeds smoothly."

The third Gaean, a small woman with wrinkly, teal eyes cut in, "The High Queen lies upon her deathbed and will soon expire from a childbearing fever. You would join with our Primus-King and take her place." The Gaeans' gazes never waned. Three sets of eyes bore into my own, trying to penetrate my thoughts.

The Lead Mate of Gaea, its High Queen. I was shaken. I wasn't even sure what they'd proposed didn't break the continental laws or go against Verus's very purpose.

"Thank you kindly for considering me as a potential Troth for the renowned Kingdom of Gaea. Is there anything further you would like to discuss?"

The faintest smile appeared on the elder Gaean's wizened face.

"You are coming along well in your training, I see. That will be all for now. We look forward to the future."

I stood and placed my hand to my heart, bowing forward slightly.

As I turned to leave, a papery-skinned hand caught my own, holding me rooted while the two younger Gaeans slid from their chairs to the floor, kneeling on the ground.

"To the Goddess's future, child," she rasped and let my hand go.

"To the Goddess's future," I responded, not letting my immediate discomfort leak into my voice. Rising to their feet, the two kneeling women gathered the third from her seat and left the room. I sat back down, needing to be alone with my thoughts. I didn't know which issue I needed to tackle first—Nan the lying stateswoman, Tommand the lascivious, or the conclave of Gaean grandmothers. I shoved it all away temporarily and stood to leave, seeking the comfort of my bed.

"Come on, my girl."

Nan was standing right outside the exit, waiting. Seeing her there tore me in two. I'd always trusted Nan, *always*, but now, I wasn't even sure who I looked at.

She waved me over, and I took her arm.

"How long?" I asked, relieved to be at her side and not looking into her eyes.

"I've trained for two years knowing I'd be coming here with you. The Primus decided that my role here wasn't to be mentioned until it had to be."

"That's ridiculous, Nan. Surely you have a better excuse for staying silent so long." I didn't want to say "for lying" both for her sake and mine.

"It's the excuse I'll be giving, love."

I knew I'd get nothing more.

"Did my parents know?" I asked.

"Of course."

"Then I see no reason I couldn't have been told the truth. Many Obligates are here with emissaries."

"There hasn't been an Obligate from Nortia in years, my girl, and not a single person wanted the focus taken off you. Yes, I am here to assist in choosing something big for the future of the kingdom, but it is not *the* reason I'm here. I chose to come for you, my pup. Not for the kingdom, not for the king, not for the Primus. Know I love you."

What could I say? Was there anything?

"None of it makes sense, Nan." I laid my head on her shoulder while we stood looking out over the balcony.

"I know, sweet. Now—what did those Gaean hags want?" she ruffled like a mother hen.

"Me, apparently." The hand that ran down my braid would normally have comforted me, but tonight, I needed to find my calm in solitude.

Nan walked with me to my door and bade me goodnight.

Kairus wasn't here. She rarely was after determining a room shared with Amias was much more enticing than an empty one, and tonight I was thankful. I sat on the edge of my bed rubbing my temples, the tension of the last hour having turned quickly into a pounding headache.

Three knocks sounded at the door, one hesitant little rap, followed by two harsh bangs.

There truly was no peace here.

The knock came again, more forcefully.

I swung the door open and the little girl who worked for Gotwig came in holding a tray with a covered dish.

"For you, Troth Nortia." She thrust the tray into my hands and scampered off. I laid the silver domed dish on my bed and removed the lid. To my delight, cheese and cucumber sandwiches and a bowl of stew were underneath, and the deliciously herby scent of them wafted its way to my nose and straight to my stomach.

A little parchment poked out from under a few crackers, and it read, *Not Poisoned*. I really wanted to hate Gotwig, I really did, but this kindness softened something inside me. I picked up the meal and inhaled. Nothing smelled off, but what did I know about poison, other than its awful side effects? My stomach growled loudly, so I chose to chance it and deal with the ramifications afterward. Sitting cross-legged on my bed, I tucked into the thick stew, which was rich in flavor and just as filling as it appeared. It was reminiscent of the plainer food I ate back home, and it was just what I needed. After calming my hunger, even my shoulders finally relaxed and the tightness in my chest lessened.

Nan's treachery—*okay, I'm being dramatic*—Nan's freshly revealed role didn't make me angry, but it did make me feel lesser. Did my parents and the Primus think me too much of a child to be told? I was one of the older Troth here. Perhaps being Eira's second mom wasn't Nan's only goal in life, but if she wanted more, as I did, I wouldn't begrudge her.

Kairus had been correct in her assumption that all courts, not *just* Monwyn, worked much less transparently than I had previously assumed. *Gods, the Gaeans offered me a throne.* I knew this was an opportunity that many, possibly *any*, Troth would have jumped at, but I'd never dreamed of being royalty. Especially a queen. Maybe it was different in Gaea, but in Nortia, no one ever spoke of our queen. The Primus never brought her up, and I wasn't sure anyone I knew had ever seen her. To me, being a queen sounded limiting, and I wanted to be out in the world, not shut off in a palace. Also, a joining would require a mating rite, and the idea of becoming a broodmare with a title was in no way appealing to me. I wasn't even sure if I liked children at all.

The Geaens wished to expand their territory into Nortian lands. I could absolutely see the value in having a Nortian Troth as High Queen in that situation, but again, I wasn't sure that boundary lines had been adjusted since the seven kingdoms had been divided. There were no major Nortian cities near the rift, but I couldn't think of anything the Gaean ruler and Nortian king would be willing to trade for something so drastic.

After bathing and brushing and re-braiding my hair, I paced the room. I should have told Nan exactly what had occurred instead of skirting her question. My trust had just been so bruised, despite her having been such an integral force for good in my life.

Gaea *was* a placement I'd been interested in, but all of a sudden, it sunk to the last on my list. My hope at this point was that Devotee Mariad would hold enough sway with their emissaries that I'd be placed in Solnna. I'd even take up the position of go-between he'd offered me. Monwyn was now upgraded to second on my list. I'd just have to deal with having Tommand around, and he'd have to deal with his absurd jealousy.

Tommand.

My body warmed just thinking his name. Those sinfully delectable lips grinning from across the table had almost been my undoing. I supposed you didn't snuff out an attraction like you would a candle's flame... though I wish it was that simple.

Closing my eyes, I willed sleep to find me, but the bed felt too big tonight, too empty, and too cold.

CHAPTER TWENTY-SEVEN

THE DARKNESS

A knock sounded on the door, and I shot awake.

The Fourth and final Maneuvering would soon begin. I prepared quickly and dressed in a simple, extremely lightweight woolen gown of black. My hope was to get out fast and find Nan before being sequestered for three days, and to do that, I had to shove my anxiety about what was to come to the back of my mind.

After debating with myself last night, I woke and *knew* what the Gaeans proposed needed to be brought up to the Nortian Devotee. Nan, as emissary, would surely have access. Hair rebraided and a mauve lip cream applied, I headed to the door. I'd skip breakfast and head toward the companion's quarters on the first level.

I opened the door into an eerily darkened hallway.

I looked to my right, carefully poking my head out, and spotted a servant holding a lit taper inside a red glass dome. The wall lamps had all been snuffed and other than the servant, there were no other sources of light. I rushed to my right, thankful for the stroke of luck. At the end of the Troth's wing, I stepped out cautiously and saw that the faintly glowing path reached around the entire level and up the staircases. It continued up until the candles' flames were tiny, twinkling flickers, and I could no longer make out those that held them.

I groped out into the dark and found the corner wall. Feeling my way as I went, I decided to head in the opposite direction of the servant-lit pathway and take the staircase that would lead me closer to the temple's entry point. I'd have to find my way across the massive first-floor atrium, but I'd avoid the eyes of a hundred servants and whomever else lined the way to the Fourth Maneuvering. I trailed my hand along the smooth wall for guidance and slid my feet forward slowly, never allowing them to fully leave the floor. I knew the stairs would be nearing, and injuring myself in a fall wasn't how I wanted to begin my day.

The wall ended. This had to be the second alcove, the one with the massive statue of Gammond in its recess, so the stairs would soon appear.

The scent hit me before the sound... cedar and clove.

"Nortia," a voice whispered.

I stopped dead in my tracks and waited. Was the dark playing tricks?

"Tommand?" I murmured, "Are you here?"

Two hands came around my waist, and a scratchy cheek nuzzled at the nape of my neck.

"I thought you were afraid of the dark." He ran his nose along the shell of my ear, causing goosebumps to run down my neck.

"Tommand," I rested my hands on top of his. "Was it not perfectly clear to you that our short-lived liaison was over?"

"It was... but then I couldn't sleep," he said. "I missed your back pressed against my chest, the feel of your silken skin under my hands. I thought of nothing but the taste of your lips."

"Well, *Emissary*, you'll be missing those for quite a while longer." Tommand never let go, but turned me in his arms, and pulled me tightly against him. His arousal pressed into my belly and my own desire took root.

"Eira, I want you," he said thickly, his mouth a hair's breadth away from my own. In the gloam, I conjured his face in my mind, the unchecked desire in his eyes, the way he didn't care who saw it. "You make me dream of a future so different from those planned for us." His hand came to my cheek, rough-skinned and warm. The beating of my heart sped to a flutter, his words weakening my resolve.

"Tom?" I felt him stiffen under my hands. "I need to find Nan." The hand fell from my face, and his chest deflated.

"She will be with the Devotees already. I should be there myself, but the thought of three days without even a glimpse of you felt like my version of the nether."

I was cracking with every word that fell from his lips.

Was this what the Troth had been singing about?

She laid her hand upon his chest,
her lover's time grew near,

she whispered of their reunion,
lips pressed against his ear.

"Eira?"

"Yes?"

"Allow me to kiss you before you go?"

"It's not wise, Tommand," I said, my voice stronger than it felt.

He drew back and grasped my hands pulling us deeper into the alcove.

"I should have done my job better, Nortia. I should have encouraged Ambrose to do what he does best and fuck you until you were filled with only thoughts of him. But I failed. Even the rational part of my mind insists you belong to me."

"Let me correct that part for you, Tommand. I belong to *me*, and currently, I need to focus on staying *mine* and not being locked up birthing a dozen Gaean babies for a man who has more than enough willing wives. You will return to Monwyn—where you don't want me to be—and go back to your life. Our dalliance ends the moment I'm Assigned."

His hand curled gently around the base of my neck. "Then we have three days," he replied.

I smiled into the dark, amused at his bullheadedness. "We've shared two instances of fantastic groping, Tommand, and I understand it's been some time for you bu—"

"Goddess, Eira, so brutal." His knuckles brushed my chin and then skimmed the curve of my neck and collarbone until finally settling on the uppermost swell of my breast.

I caved.

"Perhaps one kiss?" I guided my chest into the palm of his hand and he growled roughly in the back of his throat.

I couldn't deny him. I didn't *want* to deny him, and that ludicrously possessive sound was my complete undoing.

"Just one taste, hmm?" His mouth feathered against the sensitive skin around my lips.

"Ju-just one, Tommand."

"Just one," he promised.

Moving fast, he hiked my long skirts, baring my thighs to the dark. He shifted my linen underclothes out of the way, and he tested my readiness with two fingers.

"This is not... oh, Goddess..." I leaned back into the wall behind me. His throaty moan filled the small alcove when he discovered I was drenched—I was undeniably afire for him. I shifted my legs wider and placed my hands on his shoulders while a single digit probed at my entrance, followed by a second. My breath hitched. I waited for him to push into me, to feel the exquisite expansion of his entry. Anticipating what was to come, I dug my toes into the soles of my shoes and planted myself more firmly. I wanted him deep, rubbing against that spot that made me temporarily forget my existence.

"Do you want me, Nortia?" he asked.

"Tommand!" I huffed, wriggling against his hand.

"Nortia!" the ass teased, mimicking my vexed voice. Slowly, he swirled his fingers around the opening of my passage, working them in a little at a time, and then pulling them out till only the tips remained. It was a most splendid form of torture. "I regret not licking your pretty little piercing when I could have, but I suppose if I am never to have you again, your taste is the memory I wish to carry with me."

He rained light kisses from my temple to my mouth.

"Tommand, please." I thrust my hips forward, and finally, he slid his fingers home, sinking himself to the palm. I squeezed him tightly, and the little sparks and spasms began making their appearance.

"Ohhh," I wrapped my arms around his neck and sought his mouth with mine. I wanted more, but he toyed with me, keeping just out of my reach.

"No, Nortia, if I am allowed a single taste, it will be this..." He eased his digits from me, and my skirts fell to the ground.

The telltale sound of him sucking his fingers hit my ears, followed by the satisfied smack of wet lips. I think he meant to shock me, but instead of making me shrink back, it only enlivened me further. I leapt at him, our faces hitting squarely in the dark, but I hadn't missed my target and shrugged off the temporary discomfort. I trapped his bottom lip between my own and swept my tongue into his mouth, tasting the saltiness of myself combined with the exhilarating flavor that was him. I purred my pleasure into his mouth, getting louder when he tugged my hips against his hardness.

"You should undress," I begged between kisses, "Who will see us?"

"I am more concerned with you being heard. You do not love me quietly," he laughed.

My fingers tingled, running over the spikiness of his cropped hair, and his unsteady inhalations were like thunder in my ears. Greedily, I tasted him, twisting my tongue around his and taking it into my mouth. That was, until the kiss turned into something much more intimate.

This kiss was slow... desperate. He pulled me tighter into the cocoon of his arms, and together, in this moment, we memorized each other. I ran my hands down his lightly bearded jaws, over the firm chest and wide shoulders. His hands fanned across my face, and he slid the end of his calloused thumb along my lower lip.

In the distance I heard a noise—another Troth I supposed, making her way to the Maneuvering.

I pulled away, knowing it had to end.

"You are flawless," he whispered to the shadows.

"And you are late." I placed a kiss on his chin. "I will be too if I don't hurry."

"I will tell your companion you are seeking her."

"Thank you, Tommand." I stepped away, needing to leave now before I tried to convince him to walk out of this temple with me.

I found the wall and worked my way back to the line of illuminated servants. I could see the shadows of other Obligates passing in the glowing candlelight. At the fifth level, two rows of priestesses, covered in scarlet from the top of their heads to their toes, watched as the Obligates passed through to our next destination. When I reached the door, the one that I knew eventually led to the prayer room, I was met by the acolyte Lyta, holding a lit taper in her hand.

"We will pass through to the prayer room," she said solemnly. "I will be assisting the priestesses with your daily preparations, Troth Nortia. Each day of this Maneuvering, before sunrise, I will collect you for the rite. You will then be returned to your designated location."

I nodded my grim acceptance.

CHAPTER TWENTY-EIGHT

THE RITE

We entered a chamber cast in scarlet brilliance. Oil lamps, encased in the same glass orbs the servants had carried, dotted the high walls of the oblong room, and from the black-stone vaulted ceiling, three massive chandeliers cascaded almost to the floor. All three dripped with rubies and garnets and reddish-orange carnelians, and hundreds of tapers flickered down the massive metal spirals that were their base structures.

An elaborately carved marble altar rose up in front of a jutting wall that was the canvas for a sparkling, gold-leafed depiction of the Goddess's seven-star constellation. The altar itself was heavily carved in a depiction of the Creator birthing her Twins into her own hands, surrounded by the moon in various stages of its cycle. The most complex part of the carving was her hair. Every coiling ringlet in the halo that surrounded her head had been painstakingly rendered, and the result was astounding. It may have been the most beautiful work of art I'd ever seen.

On either side of the ceremonial space, heavy black curtains hung from the ceiling to the floor. The panels were patterned with massive, golden crescent moons whose outlines had been couched with lines of shining pearls. The lavish drapes hung long, pooling on the cave-like floor where no tiles or finishing had been applied to the uneven natural surface.

The Troth who went before me was being ushered to the left of the altar, and I watched her and her acolyte disappear behind the curtain. Lyta led me forward, and we followed their path. Before coming to the curtains, a movement caught my attention, and as I looked right, I saw the silhouette of a heavily pregnant woman, whose arms were bent in prayer. She faced the starred wall, and at her sides and back, three priestesses sang so softly I couldn't make out their words. Another priestess, facing the opposite direction, was kneeling behind the massive altar pouring a dark liquid from a small cup into a larger vessel.

"Come," Lyta turned and whispered.

I could hear my own heartbeat in my ears. Unknown challenges often felt more daunting to me than facing the dangers I knew. My palms were sweating by the time we reached the cloth barrier, but I assured myself that nothing on the other side would be able to kill me, as nothing had so far.

Lyta paused and swept open the curtain.

The chamber we entered was freezing. Like, standing-on-the-edge-of-the-Penumbrean-Pier-in-the-dead-of-winter-freezing. I could see my breath in the air, and my skin prickled with tiny chill bumps. The earthy smell of soil mingled with a sharply medicinal scent and seemed to sit heavily in the air and in the back of my nose. The walls of the room contained no lamps or sconces, but tall candelabras circled a perfect row of tables at close intervals, illuminating them brightly. Atop each, my Troth sisters were laid flat, as naked as they'd entered into the world.

Lyta escorted me to one of the two remaining tables and assisted me in removing my clothes and unraveling my binding. A servant whisked away both. Had I not been so focused on my surroundings, I would have been mortified at handing her my saturated underwear.

"Lay down, facing up," Lyta said, her voice little more than a whisper.

When my bottom touched the cold leather covering of the platform, I flinched. It was akin to sitting on an ice drift—the Solnnan Obligates were sure to be shivering. Even as used to the cold as I was, the temperature was startling. I waved to my right, and Chentel smiled tightly back at me. She was rubbing her toes together and hugging her arms close to her chest. Cinden was the last Troth to arrive, and after hastily undressing, she laid down and turned toward me. If we had both reached out, our fingertips would have touched. She narrowed her eyes at me, and I shook my head in confusion.

"I'm assuming Tommand's back in the picture?" *Did she see us?* "You have lip cream smeared from your nose to chin," she said, making silly kissy faces.

"And where were you, latest Troth of them all?" I fired back while using the backs of my hands to scrub my face.

"I'll just say... Ozius was likely the last in his line as well." Her tinkling laughter helped settle my anxiety. Something was normal in the world.

"Troth!" A priestess stepped between us. "Remain silent during the rite," she scolded, looking at each of us in turn.

Silence became simple to maintain when my body began to vibrate.

Like the feeling of standing in close proximity to a beaten gong or drum, an otherworldly hum echoed throughout the hall. The low vibrations rose and fell in intensity, changing in pitch at differing intervals. The massive curtains parted, letting rose-colored light filter momentarily into the room, and in marched two lines of priestesses followed by what seemed to be a never-ending line of acolytes. Being nude amongst the Troth and a handful of attendants had been one thing, but as the lines pressed forward and surrounded each table, I became increasingly self-conscious.

Surprisingly, the priestesses who had been outfitted in red weren't dressed in their customary color any longer, nor were the acolytes. They had all removed their garments and replaced them with rough-spun beige tunics that reflected pink or mauve, depending on the density of the glass orbs they carried in front of their chests. I lay enclosed in the circle of women and watched their throats work while listening to their song. The sounds they made seemed to penetrate deeply into my being. My cold body wanted desperately to seek the warmth of the globes that were lit from within. I could see where the heat refracted in little waves in their top openings.

All at once, the song ended, and each of the seven around me placed a single orb-warmed hand onto my chilled skin. I jumped as their heated palms burned me.

"Chosen by our Creator, born under her sign." It was the Mantle's voice ringing out, seeming to come from all sides of the chamber.

The hands that lay upon me pressed into my flesh forcefully.

"From four kingdoms you hail, and in those four kingdoms, your former lives perished. At the culmination of this rite, you belong solely to Verus. There is no greater purpose than ensuring that the smallest live peacefully while the vainglorious are reined."

The four priestesses to my right parted, revealing a shrouded figure.

As the faceless person approached, the seven hands still lying on my body gripped my flesh and held me tightly to the leather-bound table. True fear poured through me, manifesting into a physical need to fight or run, but when I tried to move, they held me firmly. I gulped the air, and my head became dizzy and disoriented as the women holding me captive again took up their eerie melody.

"We mark you now, Chosen of the Goddess, betrothed to humankind," They intoned.

"You are safe within these walls." Like a calming tonic, I heard the voice of Devotee Mariad behind the shroud.

A priestess bearing the multicolored collar came forward, and in her hands lay a scepter whose end glowed red hot. Understanding their intent, I did my best to swallow back my renewed terror and prayed to the Goddess to deliver me from harm. Laying as still as I possibly could, the priestess drew closer as my flesh, of its own accord, tried to shrink away.

I heard the shriek of a Troth. Her scream echoed off the walls and then cut off abruptly. The sound of another becoming sick soon followed.

I closed my eyes and called out to the divine. "Goddess be with me."

When the metal hit my skin, I managed not to make a sound, but tears poured down the side of my temples, and I struggled against the intense pain. Surrounded by the smell of burning flesh, though I fought it, my head swam and my vision flickered, the figure moved toward me again and—

"Wake, little one. The worst is over," said the voice I associated with warmth and love.

Blinking through the haze, I woke, no longer surrounded. Lyta, a priestess, and Mariad, who had removed his covering, moved around me.

"The poultice will alleviate most of the pain, and in a few days' time you will see much healing," the priestess with a nasally but kind voice said, while she applied a sticky substance that cooled the stinging area at my right hip.

Lyta retrieved a large basin while Mariad left and met with Chentel. The acolyte poured warm, lavender-scented water over me and into my hair, which created steam that floated up and around the cold room. Both she and the priestess began scrubbing my skin and massaging my hair until a thick lather formed and ran down my sides and onto the ground. It was not a quick cleansing. Time was taken to see that every part of me was immaculate. The priestess took a tiny spoon and ran it along the folds of my ear and then inserted it in my canal, removing the wax that had formed there. Lyta washed under my breasts and scoured my armpits while the priestess moved to my feet, using another tool to scrape under my toenails and a coarse rag to wash between my toes.

"Turn onto your stomach." The command came from Lyta. I twisted on the now slippery table, doing as she asked. The scrubbing continued, and the cloth passed between my legs and buttocks. A smaller, sweet-smelling basin was brought to treat my hair, which had been draped over the edge of the table. The acolyte moved the bowl up and down, repeatedly dipping my locks in the fragrant liquid. Finally, two more acolytes joined and assisted in rinsing me clean. When they were done, all four moved to stand at the foot of the table.

I looked to Chentel, who stared at the ceiling, and then to Cinden, who looked so thoroughly exhausted, it made me worry. Glancing down the line of Troth, I saw another figure moving from table to table. My heart skipped a beat, and I closed my eyes, preparing again for the worst. I tried to rationalize—if it were to be another trial of pain, I would have heard the yells as I had before. *Breath, Eira, one, two… three.* The counting worked about as well for my fear as it did for my anger. My mind was not convinced.

I was toweled and aided in turning to my back as I watched them approach.

"A child conceived during this Maneuvering will be raised at Verus and seen as the ultimate blessing. It is only those children, sired of Scion and Troth during this ordeal, who can one day shoulder the Mantle."

I opened my eyes, and standing before me was the incredibly pregnant woman who I had seen earlier at prayer. In her hands, she held a long-handled brush and a shallow bowl, and as she spoke, she drew below my breasts and above my pubic bone. As she moved to my feet, I leaned forward and bent my head, looking at the brand at my hip. Four lines intersecting at differing angles formed a rudimentary starburst reminiscent of those that had been painted behind the altar in the first room we'd entered.

Lyta came forward again, with the priestess at her side. The priestess raised her hands to her brow in prayer, and the acolyte lifted a tiny metal vessel above my chest. A thin stream of amber liquid poured out and ran between my breast, and coated my stomach and the curls at the juncture of my thighs.

"The rite is over. Your Betrothal is complete!"

I sat up, taking a moment for the rushing feeling in my head to abate, and scooted my legs off the table. Three attendants moved to stand at my front while one brushed through my hair and another held out a long strip of blood-red cloth that hung between her outstretched arms. The garment, barely the width of my chest, fell to my feet, front and back, while leaving my sides exposed. The priestess and Lyta stood to my left and right respectively and produced two thin metal chains, from which glittering star-shaped medallions hung at differing lengths. Instead of them placing the jewelry at my neck as I had assumed, they pinned one side to the garment near my waist and the other to its back, joining the two sides together. The delicate series of jewel-studded stars fanned out over my rounded hips.

"The Maneuvering begins." Mariad had returned and was motioning for the Troth to follow. Together we proceeded to the back of the room where a door opened, revealing a well-lit staircase. After ascending two flights, he led us into a hallway. Mariad smiled reassuringly and then pointed each of us, one by one, to a doorway.

"In the morning your assigned acolyte will retrieve you. Enter now."

As I turned, I caught Kairus's eye and mouthed *good luck.*

"You too," she replied.

Due to my abnormal level of anxiety, I half-convinced myself I would open the door and enter a tiny cell with no ceiling, where the elements would beat down upon me and burn my skin, all as a trial of fortitude... or perhaps the Gaean emissaries would be waiting behind it, ready to plot and plan my acquisition.

Instead, I walked into a tiny paradise.

The singular room was small, but it was more beautifully appointed than any room I had seen in the Glass Palace. It was even more luxuriously furnished than the ballroom had been.

In the far-left corner, slender columns surrounded a sunken bath that had been illuminated with hundreds of tiny tapers. A sideboard was set along the back wall and topped with steaming dishes and a variety of refreshments. Intricately designed rugs of green and gold covered the floor, matching the coverings of the largest bed I'd ever seen. Gold chandeliers hung from the ceiling, and their dangling crystals cast rainbows on the walls. Walls that were painted with—

"Oh, dear," I said aloud to the empty room. The walls had been adorned with masterful artworks depicting all manner of beautiful people joined in sexual positions I'd not dreamed of.

The door behind me opened, and I leapt forward, startled.

I turned quickly and came face to face with Scion Evandr, who wore a red cloth wrapped low around his waist. Like me, his hip bore a raw brand, the crescent moon of the consort God Gammond. On his pale skin, the burn stood out starkly.

"Huh," the stout Scion said while surveying the room. "This is not what I expected, but rarely has it been in this place." He smiled widely, and I noticed that his two front teeth overlapped slightly in the middle of his short-cropped, white-as-a-snow-drift beard.

"You needn't fear Nortia, though they wish us to screw like rabbits, I prefer to fuck with men." He pointed at the bed.

"With men? What about—"

He cut me off, "Kol? Occasionally I find a woman interesting enough to dabble in."

"Dabble in?" I chuckled, "That's what you call it?" Evandr shrugged and wrinkled his nose. "Glad to know I'm not interesting enough, *Evandr*."

The Scion's eyes gleamed in good-natured amusement. "You hungry?" he asked.

"After smelling my own burning body... I'm famished," I teased, already feeling more relaxed.

"That's disgusting."

Laughing together, we ventured to the sideboard and filled our plates with sausages and fowl, toasted rolls, and a savory vegetable casserole. We sat at a small, round table that had two comfortable chairs positioned closely together.

"Bets on poison?" Evandr questioned.

"If we were brought here to make babies, I'm guessing the odds are in our favor." I stuffed a roll into my mouth. "Plus, heaving takes the carnality right out of me." I pointed my fork at the Scion, who nodded his agreement while managing to shovel an alarming amount of food into his face.

"Evandr, are all the Monwyn men built like you and Ambrose?"

"And... Tommand?" He drew out the emissary's name and waggled his brows.

"*And Tommand.*" I threw a roll, bouncing it off his wide chest.

"For the most part we are," he said between biting off bits of a meaty link. "All males, royal or pauper, are required to work the mines for three years, starting between the ages of twelve and sixteen. We learn to fight there and learn to work together as well. I started at thirteen and worked an extra year to help my father pay a debt. So essentially, for twelve hours a day, we ate, lifted rocks, ate more, and lifted more rocks." He picked up the roll that had fallen to the table and broke it open, then began scooping up the bits of his leftovers into a hodgepodge sandwich. "The priestly class or infirm are exempt from service but must still find a way to serve the state in some capacity." He cracked a previously discarded leg bone in his two hands and sucked the marrow from one end.

"What do you want to do now?" The Scion looked about, pressing his lips in a thin line.

"We could swim in that giant tub, or take a nap, or,"—I spotted a shelf with a few books—"we could read each other stories?"

Evandr didn't look convinced by any of my offerings but went along amicably.

"Okay, let us do all of those things and have a few contests in between."

"Contests?" It was my turn to look skeptical.

"Contests."

Before I could blink, Evandr popped up from his chair and began undoing the moon clasp that held together his crossed skirt.

"I figured we'd wear these in the water?" My eyes widened while I gestured to the red garments.

"Remember, Nortia... not into you." He dropped trou and made a spectacle of showing himself off. He shook his hips wildly and struck poses while flexing his pecs, did a few jumping jacks, and then turned back and slowly bent to pick up his discarded clothing with a flip of his wrist. All I could do was laugh, and then laugh some more—penis thigh slaps had to be the silliest thing I'd ever seen.

"Every man's done it. Now you. Come on, get it out of your system, and then we can cool these burns."

I messed with the clips at my side, unable to budge them.

"Come help?" I asked, and Evandr bounded, literally hopping to my aid. He was able to figure out the locking mechanism in a matter of seconds, and I disrobed hastily, relying on stored-up courage.

"Now hop," he laughed, sizing me up.

"I'm not hopping." I looked him dead in the eye and pointed at his face.

"Come on, it's dumb, but now you are not embarrassed when looking at my massive cock."

"I'm sorry, your very average-sized what? I didn't quite hear?" I joked, holding my hand up to my ear. The smack that came out of nowhere took me by surprise! Evandr, quick as a fox, reached out and slapped the underside of my unpierced breast, leaving it to wobble back and forth between us, and then took off running.

"You better cover anything that dangles, tiny Scion," I threatened. His mouth twitched. He ran to the far side of the table, shuffling back and forth, countering every step I took. I gave chase, but he twisted away and flew across the short distance to the sunken bath. As he stopped short to test the temperature with his toe, I barreled into him and with a sound shove, sent him toppling into the water. I should have anticipated the tidal wave he'd make, but in my hubris, I found myself drenched from head to toe from a splash that sent water flying as far away as the door.

"Well played, Nortia. Now come on in. It makes this feel so much better." He pointed to his reddened hip. The wave had doused many of the candles surrounding the small pool, which toned down the romantic atmosphere. Without the candlelight, I felt much less awkward joining Evandr in the tub, which was twice the size of both mine and Kairus's. He was right. The cool water took the sting out of the brand even better than Lyta's poultice had.

"What about the men in Nortia? What do they look like?"

I thought for a moment.

"Well, they're all shapes and sizes honestly, but on the whole, they don't tend to be stocky, like you, or defined, like Ambrose. The ones who work the boats and docks get incredibly strong, but their musculature is leaner if that makes sense, and most of them are inked on their shoulders and legs." I pointed at the very top point of my arm, where a lot of our menfolk's markings were located. "My father had a blue whale placed across his chest when he became the dock Overseer and a school of fish ringing around his thigh. He got those when I was born." I loved my dad's family of fish. He always told me the littlest one was me.

"Sounds delicious," he crooned.

"The fish?" I asked, confused.

"The father," he cackled back.

"Gross, Evandr, that's gross." Despite never wanting to think of my big ole dad as delicious, Evandr's well-timed jest made me chuckle. We stayed in the water for quite some time chatting about our homes and discussing which kingdoms we'd like to be placed in. Evandr, a food lover like myself, thought Solnna or Gaea would be the most interesting of locations but was open to going wherever the Mantle decided.

When our fingers and toes turned to prunes, we exited the tub and mopped up as much water as two already damp towels could hold.

"Contest number one!" Evandr shouted. "Push-ups!"

"I accept." I raised my head and looked down my nose, striking a cocky stance. There was no way in Ærta I was winning this but was having fun nonetheless.

"Okay, I'll time you. Best in thirty seconds."

I dropped to the ground and assumed what I thought was an acceptable push-up position.

"Go!" Up and down, one! Up and down, two! Up and down... three. Up and halfway sort of down, my arms started to wobble, fou—

"That one won't count. Come on Nortia!" he encouraged. With all the strength left in my arms, I pushed my hands into the pile of the thick rug one last time and sank to the floor before he called time. "We can work on that, but you did it, good job!"

I preened around rocking my shoulders back and forth, happy with the praise I'd received.

"My turn. Sit on me." He dropped to the ground, landing in a much more stable-looking "up" position.

"Evandr. I'm not putting my naked butt on your back."

"Why not? It should be mostly clean now." He looked up in challenge.

"Goddess above, why have you chosen *this* Scion for me to spend the day with?" I dramatically lamented, shaking my hands at the sky... but I also gave in and sat, proudly perched in the very middle of his back.

"Hold on... and go!"

He jostled me and tossed me about but I refused to lose my seat. Laughing my fool head off, I turned to my belly and circled my arms around his neck. Up and down we went at least 10 times before—

"I forgot to count, Evandr!" I giggled, tightening my grip on his now sweat-slicked sides.

"Well, let's call it an even one hundred and seventy-five if anyone asks," he fell, panting to the floor.

Unceremoniously I rolled off his side.

"Alright now, naps?"

"Let's eat again and then you can read me to sleep, eh?" To kick off the next planned activity, Evandr ate another full-sized meal and even grazed on the herbs and lettuces that had been used for garnish.

"Where's the toilet in this place?" I inquired, both meals having settled in.

We both looked around.

There were no other doors, no hidden holes around the bathtub columns, and not even an archaic chamber pot to be found. My stomach rumbled and shifted while the pressure inside me built. I went to the entrance and tugged and knocked but found it locked and unanswered.

"Welp, we're about to really get to know each other." I grabbed a pitcher of juice and emptied its contents into several glasses.

"You are not." Evandr grimaced, his lips pulled back over his teeth.

"If you can shake-slap your penis in front of me and have my asscrack on your back, you can surely be brave enough to hear me go." I dipped the vessel into the bath water, filling it up a little, and grabbed a couple of cloth napkins from the table.

"Look away, Evandr! And close your mouth." I was absolutely mortified, but this was going to happen with or without my consent, so I decided to go with the option I could control and not lose my bowels during his next contest.

I squatted over the pitcher and let my stream loose, sighing in relief. *Easy part done.* I moved the pitcher further between my legs, telling myself it would be okay, but I knew if I heard a plop, or if he did, I very well may never be able to look him in the eye.

"IT'S NATURAL," I yelled while Evandr dove toward the bed. *Sing, Eira, sing loud.*

"If your man ain't pretty,
Goddess hope he's witty.
If your man ain't fine,
just drink a glass of wine.

If your man loves you, but his face makes you blue,
just remember lass, he's mine if he can cast a fishin' line!"

I screamed the Nortian ditty.

"Gammond's balls! Nortia, the smell!"

I cringed, knowing it had to be bad, but finished my business anyhow. I stuffed the napkins I used into the vessel, hoping to plug it up, and next wrapped the entire thing in one of the wet towels by the tub. I ended up stashing it behind a column and topping it with a few nice-smelling soaps, then said a prayer for the servant who'd be the one to stumble upon its contents. *I should leave a note.*

I washed my hands in the tub and wrapped a bunch of dried soap in a cloth. Evandr, the fearless Scion that he was, had hidden his head between the bed's pillows, so I tapped his shoulder and offered him the homemade pomander.

"I'll do the same for you when I have to go," he said sweetly, grabbing the scented package and shoving it and his nose between the pillows again.

"Reading time, are you able to come out now?"

"Yes, I suppose." He turned over and wallowed about, pulling the blankets from under himself. "It's freezing. Get in." It *was* chilly, nowhere near freezing, but I cozied under the covers after grabbing a book from the stand.

"You start. I'm always reading to others."

He took the book from my hand and turned it around in his palm. "I'm not good at this, Nortia. Reading has never come easy," he admitted.

"That's no big deal. No pressure, but would you like my help? I had quite the tutor as a child."

"Yeah, sure. I feel like all the other Scion are better at it than me, but I can fight better than all of them, so..."

"Are you better than Ambrose?"

"Of course I am. Despite my loss on the Maneuvering field, one-on-one, I take him down at least seventy-five percent of the time."

"Are you better than... Tommand?" I questioned, my throat catching on his name.

"No, and he trained me. He throws my ass all over the place ninety... well, ninety-three percent of the time."

"Is he much older than you?" I thought they must have been close in age and found it interesting he would have trained the Scion.

"About six years, but he learned way earlier. He trained before the mines *and* during, and was called back to the palace early to watch the king." He flicked his wrist flippantly and rolled his eyes when mentioning his monarch.

"What's so wrong with your king that he needs this level of protection? The King of Nortia has guards too, but they just stand at doors most of the day. It sounds like Tommand is his personal attendant." Evandr scratched at his bearded cheek.

"I will make you a deal, I'll tell you a Tommand fact for every five minutes you teach me letters."

I chewed on my lip, contemplating his offer. I knew I should be getting Tommand off my mind, but this was incredibly tempting.

"Deal. Let's see where you are. Read this part right here." I flipped open the book and glanced at the title page.

"The Four... tune..."

"Four-*teen*, the two *e*'s make a longer sound. Don't just guess the word, sound it out." I pointed to the letters.

"The fourteen, poe-sit-ons... oh, *positions*," he sounded out the word and then got it correct.

"Mmhmm"

"The fourteen positions of male es-ta—"

"—The *E-C-S* sound combined with the *T* is pronounced more like an *X*, so now what do you have?"

"The Fourteen Positions of Male Ecstasy." He perked up, pleased with himself. I cringed and glanced at the cover—B. Vaughn was stamped in gold onto the leather.

"You know, it just so happens that I am an expert on the subject. I was taught by the very author of this book."

"Nortia?" he questioned while turning to look at me.

"Evandr?"

"You have suddenly become... interesting," he grinned.

"Shut up!" I pulled the covers and shook them back and forth. "It's been five minutes."

"Fine, fine, let's see... Tommand likes the color orange."

"Orange? That's the juicy fact you're trying to pass off? Come on, Evandr!" I pummeled the lumps of his oversized body under the covers.

"Yeah, alright, I guess that's not the most exciting of info... hmm ... remember the day you helped the decrepit old priest say his prayers?"

"Yes, the priest who is literally *dying*?" I chastised.

"Yeah, so when you got far enough away, he was all like, 'Have you ever seen a set of—'"

"A set of what?" I screeched wanting him to talk faster. Evandr poked his head out of the covers and made an intentional sweep from my head to—

"My boobs!" I exclaimed, holding onto my chest, smiling like the besotted woman I was.

"No, you sick Troth, your eyes. He said he thought your eyes were stunning."

I snuggled closer to the Scion.

"That's nice too. Now, you read a page, and I'll help."

We continued like this for who knows how long, and with no windows or timepieces, we had no idea if it was still day or night.

Eventually, after learning that Tommand had always wanted a dog, tried to run away to become a scholar, and also thought mushrooms were disgusting, we, back-to-back, fell fast asleep.

CHAPTER TWENTY-NINE

DAY TWO

There was no warning knock, just two acolytes bolting through the door, shining the light from the lit hallway directly into our eyes. Evandr had become my little spoon sometime while we slept and held my arm tucked close to his chest.

"Obligates, to the door. Wait until you are permitted to step into the hallway."

I shook my heavily sleeping partner awake, and we did as we were told and remained near the entrance.

The two acolytes tossed the pillows from the bed and went about inspecting the sheets like you would lice on someone's head. I turned toward Evandr, and he shrugged.

Lyta walked toward me speaking in her soft tone. "Troth Nortia, dress and enter the hallway. Scion Monwyn, remain in the room until asked to leave."

I re-covered myself in the red scrap and stepped into the hall, watching as my Troth sisters emerged from the various doorways they'd entered.

"Do not speak. Proceed down the stairs and lie down on the first empty table you come to." While rubbing the sleep from my eyes, we retraced our steps to the room in which the rite had been performed. I wondered if each time we did this we had to be rebranded. Just the thought made my stomach queasy. Even now, the spot still felt heated, though it burned less today.

I laid on a table that put me in the center of my Troth sisters, and when the last of us, Yemailrys, sat upon hers, the priestesses made their way to us along with their acolytes. They began to wash us from head to toe with the same foaming soap as before, removing the paint we'd been marked with yesterday. The same mother-to-be who had previously performed the task walked among us again, applying the same red lines. From the look of her stomach and the way she moved, I guessed she had less than a month before she greeted her little one.

After the cleansing, I mentally prepared for the worst but never saw another brand or Devotee for that matter. Acolytes poured warm oil onto our bodies, and placed us into fresh red garments. When we arrived in the hallway this time, an acolyte led me to a different door and bade me to enter.

This room was different, although it had similar elements. Like Devotee Mariad's office, it had a fireplace on the wall and pillows placed in piles on the jewel-toned carpeted floor. The large bed, covered in a lightweight, pink-and-gold blanket, was at the back wall, and to the right, a steaming tub was recessed into the floor.

I heard the door open behind me and turned to see who entered. It was Scion Ozius, who smiled warmly and raised his hand in greeting. His scabbing moon brand showed above the waistline of his skirt and much of the hair next to it had been singed off by the heat he'd endured.

"Troth Nortia." He bowed deeply at the hip.

"Ozius," I replied, barely able to look him in the eye. I remembered exactly what *all* of him looked like.

"Are you well?" he questioned, furrowing his brow.

"Quite, and yourself?" I truly hoped we could move past this formal back and forth so I could feign exhaustion and hide my face under the covers. He knew I'd seen them that day, and I could barely deal with the knowledge.

"I spent a rather loud evening with Kairus last night. She's quite opinionated," he laughed easily.

"She just knows what she's about," I tried to relax, just a hair, the conversation heading to a place I was comfortable with. "Did you all ever find a toilet?" I questioned.

"Was yours not under the bed?" He went to the raised platform and pulled out a large chamber pot, half-filled with heavily scented water.

"Of course, it was..." I smiled sweetly in his direction. *I'll be swearing Evandr to secrecy.*

"And who were you paired with?"

"Scion Evandr of Monwyn."

Ozius nodded in recognition.

This is so flipping awkward. I was trapped in a room with Cinden's lifemate who I'd seen railing my friend, and there was no way to get around the discomfort until I just came out with it.

"Ozius!" I squeaked his name. "I know you know, but I saw you doing... the sex... with Cinden. It turned me on, and I stuck around longer than I should have. I'd like to apologize for intruding on your privacy."

The merlot-haired Scion walked further into the room and lowered himself to the edge of the steaming tub before he answered.

"Troth Nortia, the Goddess designed the body to respond to stimulus. What you saw was stimulating, and your reaction was healthy. I'm not angry and accept the apology." His face was kind and his expression genuine when he waved me over to sit by him.

I was still red-faced but *was* relieved to have just come out with it, had I not, it would've made our day in this small space unbearable. These healer types were so accepting.

I put my legs into the hot water, enjoying the contrast in temperatures between my upper and lower halves.

"Eira, the night of the Second Maneuvering, causing you pain... it was one of the worst experiences of my life. My calling is to take away pain, not inflict it."

I recalled the night he was forced to become my attacker and felt such sadness for what he'd been made to do.

"It had to be done, Ozius." I laid my hand on top of his, "You had no choice, and, in a roundabout way, it allowed me to seek help for something very difficult that I'd been experiencing." We sat in companionable silence for some time, kicking at the water.

"Well," he grinned, "we're stuck in here for a while, what would you like to do?"

"First, tell me about your day with Kairus, and then let's eat. The food has been great so far."

Ozius laid back with his calves still submerged in the water and tucked his arms behind his head. He was a good-looking man, not rugged like Tommand but really quite perfectly formed. His skin was unmarked and unblemished, barring the brand, and I couldn't even see any lasting bruises or cuts from being manhandled by the guards or from the Maneuverings. His features were incredibly symmetrical as well. He had a thinner, masculine mouth and strong jaw, and when he spoke to me from his current position, I could see the gleam of his capped back teeth. His body was mostly covered in dark hair, but I could make out the double flame that marked him as a healer on the side of his chest.

"Kairus... where do I start? I think we want the same things for the continent—health, prosperity, peace. But we butt heads on how that should be carried out. My approach is more healing the souls and bodies of the Goddess's children to make them more productive and content." He held up his hands and stared at his palms. "Her methods include the caid game for all social classes and a program that allows people to travel between kingdoms just to experience something new. I understand where she's coming from, but the problem is, *who* will replace the farmers in the fields when they spend three months across the continent? There will be hunger. Who will heal the infirm if the healers are not in their kingdoms? Any suffering that can be mitigated should be, and sometimes that means sacrificing one's sense of adventure."

I touched the palm he stared at and pulled his hand between my own. He was so thoughtful, so in tune with the Obligation. His concern for the people of Ærta was so great. No wonder Cinden felt so deeply connected to such a caring human.

"Your touch yields power, Eira." He tremored ever so slightly and removed his hand from my own.

I smiled, looking up into his unusual-colored eyes. They were truly amber, a soft, yellowy gold, ringed in the lightest brown.

"I've felt quite powerless here, Ozius, but thank you," I said, meaning every word.

He shifted his head to look at me fully.

"*Here* is not what you were chosen for. It's the *after here* where you will come into your own. This place is but a stepping stone."

His words rang true.

In that single sentence, Ozius made me feel like I could finally take a full cleansing breath. I *could* still be me and follow the dreams I had. I wouldn't be in this temple forever. My shoulders dropped, and my jaw unclenched.

"Go sit by the fire, Troth Nortia." He pointed to the pillows, "I'll bring you something to eat."

"Don't bother, Ozius, I ca—"

"Sit," he said, his grin reaching from ear to ear. "Allow me to wait upon such divinity."

I chuckled and acquiesced to his unneeded kindness. I dried and went to settle into the mound of pillows. The water warmed my legs, but my top half remained chilly, so the fire was pleasant and not overwhelming to be near. This time during the rite, there had been no warm orbs or hot-as-fire pokers, and after we had been bathed, oiled, and toweled, the cold of the room had sunk in quickly.

Ozius joined me on the pillows, sitting closely. He sat both plates on his stomach and laid back with his hands crossed behind his head again.

"You eat and I'll tell you about Gaea." He looked off wistfully. I reached for a plate, but he stilled my hand and moved my fingers to the food. It was strange, but I picked up a sandwich and he nodded his approval. I was eating off an Ozius table, and I laughed to myself, not wanting to seem ungrateful were it a custom in his kingdom. The Gaeans did all manner of interesting things. I'd have to remember to ask Chentel about the practice. I *could* ask Cinden, but she'd just make fun of me like she had the "sexy time" incident. The

Gaeans, though overconcerned with their "purity," were very open about their bodies, which made sense due to their kingdom's long-standing emphasis on healing. I took a bite of the salted fish and fresh dill that had been stuffed inside a crusty bread, and Ozius launched in.

"The Goddess favors Gaea as she favors you, Eira. The land is so rich, so abundant, that the trees there grow taller than anywhere else on the continent. The forest floor is a blanket of lush greenery and floral treasures, and beyond that, near the coast, the sea holly and cabbage palms cover the land for miles." He paused and lifted a carrot to his mouth. "The capital sparkles like a gem. The dome of the central temple is covered with rare stones and precious gold, and the inside... I've never seen another place as magnificent." He turned to look at me while I chewed. You could see the love for his home reflected in his eyes.

"It sounds lovely, Ozius." I reached, still a little awkwardly, for another triangle of bread. He stopped my hand in midair, taking it into his own.

"And could you come to think of it as home, Eira?" As he spoke, he ran his thumb down the palm of my hand. His face looked serene and calm, but his touch confused me. The caress felt more intimate than it should have, but there was no indication he meant it in a forward way.

"Wherever it is I'm placed, I hope to think of it as my new home. I want the people to know I'm there for them, first and foremost, and serve until I'm no longer able to make their existences brighter."

The lounging Scion ran a thumb over the sensitive skin of my wrist, looking somewhere into the distance, completely unaware that while he reminisced, I was growing more concerned by our contact. I wasn't in a relationship, but he certainly was.

"Ozius, your familiarity is confusing to me... considering the mutual friend we share." I was hoping he'd get the point without me having to spell it out. I suspected Cinden would be less than pleased with the contact between us, but then again, she had done some serious flirting with Ambrose. Maybe this was another accepted cultural thing—in Nortia, the married women were too jealous to have allowed it.

"In Gaea, loving two isn't an issue. However, it's not I who is meant to take your maidenhead. You needn't worry about your purity with me. I am permitted to see to your pleasure but will never penetrate you with my phallus," he said.

The atmosphere changed.

"I find pleasure enough in your company, Ozius, but thank you," I tried to settle the matter, "and... my maidenhead is not a topic I feel comfortable discussing as we go on."

He looked up, squinted his eyes, and cocked his head just a hint to the right.

"Your maidenhead—your purity—is most valued and sacred to me. Eira, if you are to be placed in the capacity my kingdom wishes, your corona should be cherished, by you and all others."

"You've spoken to your emissaries, then?" I asked, trying to simultaneously shift the subject and gain more insight. Ozius gazed at me intently and placed his finger to the pulse point of my wrist. With his other hand, he removed the plates of food from his body, setting them on a pillow to his other side.

"They have decided on you, which practically makes you my queen," he said in a reverent tone. "There is no hope for the Lead Mate at this point, and when she passes, your joining ceremony can take place."

I made my face placid. The emissaries could think what they wanted, but I knew the Devotees and High Mantle had the final say.

"My back hurts from the rite, Ozius. I think I'll lie down." I needed to distance myself and think.

"You will let me see to you. I will remove the pain that ails you."

"No, it's not terrible, nothing a little nap won—"

"You have no choice in this matter. If you hurt, I will see you healed," he cut me off.

I shifted to stand, but he seized my wrist and planted his other palm squarely on my chest, pressing me backward.

"There would be no greater honor I could hope to achieve than seeing to your comfort."

His eyes bore into mine. He continued pressing into my sternum, increasing the pressure steadily and rising over the top of me.

"You are a learned healer? Correct?" I threw out the question quickly, trying to think on my toes. He sat back on his knees.

"I am. I studied at Temple Mossius under the greatest thinkers and scientists of our time, and knowing the body as I do... I can feel your apprehension. I can feel your pulse flutter. I told you, I would *never* lay a nefarious hand upon your sacred person," he brought my upturned palm to his mouth as he spoke, "and this I swear."

I clearly remembered the *very* painful hand he'd laid on me once before.

"I still sense your concern." He shot forward again but dropped my hand. It took every ounce of my discipline to remain where I was with his face mere inches from my own. "Listen to me again." He took my chin between his hands. "I will let no harm come to you, do you understand?"

"I'm not recognizing you right now, Ozius. Where is the man who picked me up off the field? The man who fought against the guards... the one devoted to another?" I let my tone become harsh, needing to try another tactic with him. He squeezed my face tighter and clenched his teeth.

"I am all of those men," his eyes flashed a warning, "and I am also much more."

My gut told me not to press him further, not while trapped in a room without another soul to help me. I had no idea if a scream could be heard beyond these walls, or if anyone would respond if it was. I was not his physical equal by any measure, and deflection and flattery had been unsuccessful.

"How would you take away my discomfort, then? Shall we play games? We could read with each other..." I pulled my hand from his grasp when his grip loosened. A smile split his face, revealing perfectly gorgeous teeth like Cinden's.

"Lie back. I'll show you," he coaxed. I looked at him and veiled my concern, trying my damnedest to remain neutral. Laying back would put me in a most vulnerable position, but my options were becoming more limited.

"Eira, you are safe with me. Relax."

Hesitantly, I laid back on the pillows and forced myself to remain calm. He'd know if I tensed again, and that seemed to anger him. I steadied my breathing, slackened the muscles in my face, and dropped my shoulders. He backed up, thank Goddess, and took my foot in his hands. He pressed deeply into its sole, running both of his thumbs from the ball of my foot to the heel.

Oh.

Oh, my.

He bent back my toes and pinched at the bottoms of each, twisting lightly at the same time, then used his fist to work the harder flesh of my heel. His hands were incredible. The sigh that came from my mouth seemed to indicate there *was* a certain amount of weirdness I could overlook if it meant having a skilled set of healer's hands kneading my flesh. Ozius placed my ankle on his shoulder and worked his magical hands along my calf. I closed my eyes, just momentarily, giving in to the profound feeling of relief that washed over my body.

"Just a moment," he said, halting his fingers. I opened my eyes, disappointed that he'd stopped. He hopped up and walked to the bathing tub, only to quickly return with a jar in his hand. He dipped his hand into a thick cream, smelled it, and rubbed it between his fingers before applying it to my thigh. He worked the larger muscles there, and I had to fight myself to stay alert as he alleviated the exhaustion and tension I didn't realize was so bad. His hands became increasingly warm.

Turning his attention to my other leg, he started again at the foot. Tears actually pricked my eyes. *How is he doing this?* It was like he was righting the wrongs in my life with his touch. He worked down to my thigh, and my muscles continued to pour out their grief. All those stairs, all the Maneuverings, the emotional shifts... it had all pent up physically within me.

"Your purity is majestic," Ozius spoke softly.

My purity is wha—oh fuck! Eira, do not freak out! I called back every pain he had taken out and bound them to me again. I opened my eyes, and sure enough, he was peering at my exposed sex. *Had my clothing shifted, or had he moved it?*

Ozius twisted on his knees and squared up in front of me, sitting back on his heels. The movement split open his crisscrossed skirt, revealing his flaccid length. He didn't seem to notice, but like the horns blaring from a ship in the fog, my brain screamed at me to tread carefully.

"Our Primus-King will know such beauty when he claims you. I would be jealous if not for the esteem in which I hold him," he said joyfully. I watched him begin to arouse.

"Ha-have you met the Primus-King?" I attempted to divert his attention.

"Of course. Many Obligates are housed in the palace. I know him quite well. He is a great man and an even greater ruler." He placed the leg in his now hot hands on his other shoulder. Absent-mindedly, like it wasn't anything taboo, he began to stroke himself lightly while gazing between my legs.

"I studied under him for a portion of my training." He reached to my waist and unclamped the gold chain holding my garment together. It made sense to me that crazy and bold went hand in hand, but his undoing of my clothing indicated that he was absolutely willing to take liberties without consent.

My mind was working frantically to figure my way out of this. I didn't want him splattering his semen anywhere near my vagina if the intent of this Maneuvering was to breed the next Mantle, and even though he said he wouldn't harm me, he'd certainly not valued Cinden's purity enough to abstain. I also knew what he was capable of physically... and was now beginning to glean some understanding of the way his mind worked.

"Lust is a much more effective tool when one needs the attention of a target, but not the attention of a whole court. You will all eventually have it used against you. You may even choose to employ it yourself."

I'd never truly given credence to his advice, as I detested the man himself, but now, in the position in which I found myself, I hoped Gotwig's insights might keep me safe. Lust clearly had an impact on Ozius's control, and though I was sure there would be consequences for using his sexual fulfillment against him, I wasn't willing to be subdued by him.

I would play his queen.

"Did the Primus-King speak to you of your pleasure, Ozius? I must remain intact, yes, but where I derive pleasure is in pleasing others."

He considered my words, and I used the seconds to free my legs from his shoulders and sit up on my knees.

"Does this bother you, Troth?" He peered down at the hand wrapped around himself. "It is simply my body reacting to a stimulus."

"They are all manner of pliant after they come," I remembered Lady Vaughn saying. She also cautioned that once a man was spent, it would be some time before there was a likelihood of him becoming amorous again.

"No Ozius, not at all, but I am a person who finds completion when I am able to bring others to fulfillment." *Goddess, would Cinden kill me for this? Should I just try to anger him instead?* I was just so terrified at the prospect of the physical harm he could cause me, and I did *not* want his hands on me again.

"I-I cannot begin to imagine the blessing of your hands on my body," he stammered, dropping his member, "but I am not sure how it would be seen by our Primus-King. I was ordered to see to your pleasure and to ensure you were still as pure as the Devotees have led us to believe."

"If your Primus-King wishes to keep me satisfied, he'll be required to understand how I derive my own satisfaction. Ozius, lie back," I issued the order.

Wide-eyed, Ozius, shifted backward and laid onto the pillows, immediately snapping to action at my request.

"If it pleases you, as it shall me, lay your divine hands upon my unworthy form."

Before I lost my nerve, I reached out and grasped his arousal, and ran my fingertips along its length.

"Put your hands behind your head and keep them there," I demanded, thinking of ways to ensure I'd not be touched. I slid my hand down his erection and he stared at our contact as if transfixed, rapidly breathing, the rising tension evident in his bunching muscles.

"Are you allowing yourself to feel me, Ozius? It is *your* pleasure that will please me, and I would see it and hear it." I made my voice low and husky.

"I am overwhelmed by the generosity of the experience, my Queen."

Twins save me.

I dipped my hand into the pot of cream that he had used on my legs and began twisting and pumping him while using my other hand to lightly stroke his testicles. I remembered the matter-of-fact way our instructor had taught us the technique and how Yemailrys had giggled hysterically through the entire endeavor.

"Close your eyes, Ozius. Just feel." His eyes shut on command, and I allowed myself to pull the briefest of faces. Honestly, I'd stopped feeling some of the ickiness when I took the dominant role in the situation but still needed to remind myself over and over that it was a body. It was going to launch some goo, and when it was all said and done, I would be able to leave this room unharmed.

Ozius began to groan loudly and thrust his hips in time with my downward strokes. He moved his arms an inch, but I scolded him and he quickly returned them, gripping his biceps tightly. His quick reaction to my directive made me think I'd turned the tides of control, and for that I was thankful. He was getting closer now. I felt him stiffen, saw his face tighten.

"Ozius, come now... into the hands of your future queen."

"Divine hands," he moaned. He jerked and spasmed, and with a few more strokes, he poured hotly into my palms. It was a full minute before he opened his eyes, but when he did, I saw that both glistened with tears.

"I will not forget this gift, Eira. You have shown great honor to my temple."

I wanted to yell, "Good! Because it was a once-in-a-lifetime occurrence," but I knew now, I'd do it again if I thought myself in danger. My will to live, and live without violence, overrode any sense of propriety. Ozius stood and sought out a towel near the bathtub. He turned, looking back at me, and lifted the cloth he'd wetted.

"Clean your hands. I won't have you sullied by a lesser-than." I moved toward him slowly, hoping to keep him at arm's length but wanting to communicate that I didn't fear him. He took my hands into his and cleaned them thoroughly with soap and clean water and did the same to his body.

"Tell me about your work as a healer, Ozius." I walked to the table and sat in one of the chairs, putting distance between us. I poured a glass of water and took a sip. He sat on the edge of the bed instead of joining me at the table.

"I've brought many a new life into the world and have ended the suffering of the ill and dying. Were I not born Scion, I would have devoted my life to Mossius. The Primus-King, kind as he is, allowed me more time with the healers than most in my position receive."

"Describe him to me." I wanted to learn more about the monarch trying to claim me.

"He is truly an amazing human. Though he is in his eighth decade, he is the picture of energy and health." Ozius laid out flat on his stomach. "This year, he should sire three new babes. His children are healthy, and his grandchildren and great-grandchildren are as well. He loves his family and is a doting father. Eira, unlike the lesser queens, the children *you* bear will inherit the kingdom."

I almost balked, not at the mention of my future king-babies but at his monarch's age. Luckily I hid most of my shock behind the glass of water I'd lifted to my mouth. I'd imagined the Primus-King to be maybe a man in his fortieth year when speaking to the emissaries, not a great-grandfather. The prospect of a Gaean placement cemented into a hard no in my mind. They wanted me to go sex up some old man, pop out a child, and gain them a piece of Nortia.

The Mantle had to know of their wants, and the Devotees probably did too, Gotwig for sure would know... but Kan, Tommand, they wouldn't stand for this. Nan wouldn't allow a single speck of Nortian snow to be claimed by another kingdom either.

I wasn't doing it.

First, whoever walked through that door tomorrow was going to rid me of my "purity," whether I had to beg or pay them. My hope was that alone would stop Grandpa-Primus-King from wanting to use me as a breeder. Second, I was going to find Mariad and accept his offer of becoming a Solnnan agent and press him into working to place me in his kingdom. It seemed like everyone around me played their games of deception and curried favors, and now, I was ready to play my own hand. This place wasn't about divine mystery; Verus was just as embroiled in the same political bullshit as all the other kingdoms.

"Ozius, I'm quite tired," I lied. I had no intention of closing my eyes with him in the room. I had no trust in the Scion. Though I'd like to think he was a man of his word and would not intentionally set out to hurt me, I had to listen to my gut, and it told me he wasn't stable.

"I'll say my prayers and guard the door. No one will enter while you slumber."

I climbed into the bed and watched him do just what he said. He sat beside the fireplace and positioned himself on his knees, raising his hands to his brow.

For the next two hours, I listened as he sang out his prayers in a gut-wrenchingly beautiful voice. I roasted under the covers, feeling sick to my stomach, trying to sort out what I'd tell Cinden or if I should keep it from her altogether. In all of this, I had made her the victim. I had forced her into a role she wouldn't have chosen for herself. I sat with my shame until the door opened the next morning.

Two acolytes stepped into the room and immediately went to check the sheets.

"You two can keep gazing, but I didn't defile Troth Nortia," Ozius said to the women.

"Is that what—"

"Yes. They are looking for blood or fluids that would indicate your breeching or our potential copulation."

Shocked by what was happening, I somehow still mustered enough courage to turn to Ozius.

"I feel a great deal of guilt this morning, and I'm not sure what to do. It's just... our mutual friend love—"

He took my hand in his and rubbed his finger against my pulse.

"*You* know when to keep your mouth closed."

CHAPTER THIRTY

DAY THREE

T he priestesses couldn't scrub away the stains of my disgrace. The crimson paint
didn't make me pure; the prayers didn't heal my soul.

Any thoughts of the future made my chest constrict, but even that was nothing
compared to the thought of devastating Cinden. This was the deepest depression I'd ever
felt. I'd made the conscious choice to do what I had done, and I didn't feel dirty, I didn't
feel shame for the act itself, but I felt like the worst sort of human because of who it
would impact. I couldn't explain away performing a sex act on her lifemate, even with
the explanation of self-defense, and I wouldn't blame her for hating me.

And then there was the matter of "you know when to keep your mouth closed." I
wasn't stupid and neither was Ozius, but the joke was on him. I'd finish this Maneuvering
and then I'd find Nan, go to Mariad, and if they didn't hear me, I'd leave this place.

I climbed the stairs and opened the third door from the right upon the acolyte's
direction.

I entered.

I would have cried had I not felt so dead inside.

The room was decorated in black and white, gray tones, and creams. The bed covering
was a white fur, and two more buck skins sat in front of the blazing fire pit. It was... home.
Instead of a sunken bathing area, a large tub sat in the corner, and though it was filled to
the brim with piping-hot water instead of left empty with buckets on the side, it was still
a nice touch. Little trinkets and figurines of whales and fish decorated the room, and a
statue of Derros stood in the far corner. The walls were still painted in a sensuous mural,

but I couldn't care less. I made my way into the center of the space where the raised brazier was lit and sat in a low chair that had been padded with feather-stuffed pillows. I could almost believe it would be my mother walking through the door.

I hung my head, contemplating the choices I would soon need to make. None of them ended in my happiness, but I suppose happiness wasn't guaranteed for anyone. Gotwig's life had certainly been proof of that.

The door creaked open.

I couldn't bear to look.

"If it is not the voluptuous little harpy," Ambrose drawled.

I flung myself from the chair and ran into the arms of the big Scion, wetting his bare chest with my wracking sobs.

"This is... not the welcome I anticipated, but I think we should talk, yes?" He didn't wait for an answer, just effortlessly lifted me into his arms and made his way to a chair. He sat down and placed me on his lap, and, like an overwhelmed child would for their father, I poured out all of the tears caused by the last two days. Ambrose patted my back and made sweet little cooing noises until, finally, I was able to quiet. With my head to his chest, I listened to the loud thump of his heart and worked on breathing through my nose and out my mouth.

"Nortia, I need you to tell me what happened to cause you this amount of distress. Was it... Tommand?"

I shook my head no. I didn't want to think about how Tommand would feel about what had happened. He'd have fought back without fear, but that was not an option I felt I had.

"Another Scion? Nortia, I'll fucking kill any miscreant who—"

"No, no, yes... Ambrose, I don't think it's wise for me to say out loud."

"Hang on. Hop up and, go wash your face." He motioned to the tub. The soap didn't smell like it did at home, but cleaning up did help me to feel more put together. While I washed, I heard Ambrose making an awful racket behind me, and when I looked to see what he was up to, I saw he'd piled every skin, blanket, towel, and rug on top of the bed.

"What's this?" I pointed to the massive lump of textiles.

"Come here." He crooked his finger.

I walked to the material mountain, and Ambrose lifted a corner of the giant mound.

"Get in."

"You want to suffocate me?" I quipped poorly, the joke falling flat.

"Nortia, get in." He looked at me in complete seriousness.

I sat on the bed and crawled into the cave he had created, and he climbed in behind me. We were thrown into total darkness.

"Keep your voice to a whisper and tell me what happened." I could barely hear him. I paused thinking about what I should include and what details I should leave out.

"Ambrose?"

"What?"

"Is this how you and Tommand find privacy?"

I couldn't make out his face but heard his chuckle close to my ear.

"I would be a liar if I said it was not."

I continued gathering my thoughts.

"I need you to promise me something. What I need is not action; what I need is advice, okay?" The last thing I needed was his storming out and stirring things up.

"I may not be able to keep that promise, but I can assure you that I will not do anything without thinking the situation through."

"And you won't tell Tommand?"

"Nortia. No. He about had a conniption when you forwent eating at the last meeting. He has *never* once cared that deeply for my well-being. Do you seriously think I could keep something from him that is actually important?"

Tommand had sent the food. My heart swelled in my chest.

"Just... please try," I begged.

"I will make the most valiant effort to... *try*."

That was as good as I was going to get.

Over the next hour, I recounted every detail of every moment, from the time the Gaean emissaries had intercepted me, up until the moment he had opened the door this morning. Only once did Ambrose allow me to poke my head out for air.

"So now, I need you to allow me to have sex with you. Does that make sense?"

Ambrose tossed back the covers, and in the light, I saw the face of a man dumbfounded. His dark eyebrows arched to the top of his forehead. His mouth had drawn into a tight *O* and he tapped both of his hands rapidly against his knees.

"So..." he started, "Tommand may actually kill me if I go through with this, not that his threats have ever stopped me before, but we may have a larger or perhaps smaller issue to contend with if I agree." He chewed on his bottom lip and then released it with a pop. "On Tommand's advice, to prevent conception, I took some herbs. The thought of fathering the next Mantle made me extraordinarily uncomfortable, and well, I haven't had even the inkling of an erection in the last three days... which is a shame because that delightful little cream puff Richelle was offering up quite the menu." *Shoot, Richelle would have been positively chuffed at having a go at Ambrose.*

"Well Scion, it will be up to us to make it work somehow. It's the only way I can see slowing down this wagon wreck."

"It does seem to be a sensible plan of action, but Eira, it is dead-goose-neck limp." He looked down, visibly anguished. "I could just use my fingers aggressively and say we did?"

"Ambrose, I need bodily fluids, maybe some blood, I need my corona obliterated. I... just... it might be enough to save me," I pleaded.

"When Tommand finds out, what will save you will be the mysterious disappearance of four Gaeans and Ærta's most eligible Scion."

I shot him an incredulous look. I didn't want people kidnapped or dead.

He raised his hands up in defeat and took a steadying breath.

"If you can make it happen, I consent to be your first."

The adrenaline surged through my body, and I rose up on my knees.

"At this point, I will stuff that limp appendage inside like a caseless sausage."

"So crass, nasty Nortian." He went to work tossing the pile off the bed.

"*Whatever*. So, what normally gets you going, Ambrose?" I asked, willing to do whatever it took.

"Literally everything, which is why my lack of libido is so disconcerting."

"Let's start with you stroking yourself as you did in the tub. Hurry up and lay down."

He dutifully lay on the bed and flipped back one half of his skirt. Where his once magnificent member had been, sure enough, he was entirely wilted. He took his floppy fellow in his hand and did his best, but it just squished up and down like a piece of raw biscuit dough.

"Wait!" I climbed the Scion's legs, straddling him around his thighs.

Still unable to work the chains at my waist, I ripped one side and pulled the garment over, revealing one mauve-tipped breast—he'd liked it last time.

"It is lovely Eira, truly, but it is—"

"That wasn't the whole thing Ambrose, hang on." I struggled to pull my head out of the red strip of cloth, partially because I was sitting on it. "There," I said triumphantly when the garment pulled free and bared my pierced breast.

"Nortia. I do believe I felt a stir..." A one-sided smile spread across his face.

"I thought you might like it. Tommand did!" I clapped excitedly. "Anything?"

We both looked down.

"I think... maybe a tiny bit of something? Nortia, put it in your mouth."

"Okay, I've only done this once, but I did have a demonstration in one of our sessions, so give me some pointers, and tell me what you like."

I scooted down towards his ankles, willing his lifeless lump to stir.

I didn't even think. I sucked his listless penis into my mouth trying to remember every detail of the pages Evandr had read to me, combined with the tips from both Vaughns. I swirled my tongue, nipped at his head, used my hand to stroke him at the same time and—

"You are doing marvelously! It has to be at least at half-mast," he exclaimed.

"Oh, thank Goddess!" I went back to work, pressing my lips firmly together, while squeezing his base with my hand.

"It's enough, Eira, quick!"

I scrambled on top of him, and though not really very stiff, it looked like it *could* be enough. I rose up and positioned myself over him, quickly sinking down onto—

Biscuit dough.

"This is my worst nightmare, you know," Ambrose said morosely, speaking through the crack of his hands, which he'd smacked over his face.

"Would it help if you did something to me?"

"It's worth a try," he sighed. Ambrose flipped me backward and dumped me onto my back. His head disappeared between my legs and—

Oh.

My.

Goddess.

His tongue spread me smoothly before he ranked his nails down the backs of my thighs. Slowly and softly, he teased, barely touching my flesh. It was a little unexpected, given my pragmatic attitude about our mating, but the featherlight stroking was lightening my mood.

I moaned contentedly, enjoying the delicate caresses.

He looked up, smiling wolfishly. "That helps..."

And then back down he went.

He pressed his tongue against my most sensitive area and then closed his mouth around me and sucked my clit like he was sucking pasta into his mouth.

"Ambrose, Ambrose, how about now?"

He popped back up, and we both looked down. I don't think I'd ever seen the light shine so brilliantly in his eyes.

"Lay back. I'm going to do something that should ensure this stays."

Dutifully, he nodded and lay back against the pillows.

I stuck my finger in my mouth.

"Here we go" I peeked between his legs and found what I was looking for. With a single finger, I entered the tight flesh of his backside, searching for and finding what the wife Vaughn had called the "Queenmaker."

"That!" Ambrose brought his hips off the bed. "Nether, yes."

I didn't wait. I finger fucked his tightness and like the acrobat I wasn't, I fumbled a leg over his hips and around my arm so that my finger could stay lodged in place. For the second time that evening, I rose up and used my thighs to aim him home.

This time I was victorious! I lowered myself down onto a wonderfully stiff penis, inch by uncomfortable inch, until I felt I'd been very neatly speared. Elated, I removed my finger and gave Ambrose a playful double-handed smack on each peck.

"We did it!"

"We did!" Ambrose laughed along cheerfully.

I rose slowly to begin to dislodge myself and felt a stretching sting, not horrible by any means, but I definitely felt that something had changed.

Hmm. On its way out, his erection rubbed that little spot deep inside.

Decision time again.

I'd achieved my goal, but after his little tongue-lashing, the slippery motion of our joining had become quite pleasant. Ambrose, understanding my interest, placed his hands on the sides of my hips and helped me to raise and lower myself on his length, which was kind, as his length was a little too much for comfort.

"This is surprisingly nice, Ambrose." I closed my eyes, letting myself concentrate on the friction delighting my core.

"Just have fun... I'm having fun," he said thickly. I increased my pace, moving a little forward and a little backward, testing out the feel of each position.

Ambrose, reached behind me and pulled my hips forward, which reminded me of the night Tommand had pulled me to him. "*But this is better,*" he'd said when our bodies had touched.

Tommand.

I moved quicker. *So close.* I thought about how much I loved running my hands over Tommand's chest, what it felt like to have his mouth on mine, exploring each other kiss by kiss.

"That's it, Eira. Good girl—"

"Ambrose, I don't mean to offend you, but it's not you I'm thinking of, and if you could not talk, I'd be so very appreciative."

"Fine by me, I don't care who you need me to be, as long as you keep moving."

I clamped my eyes tighter and thought of the evening at the First Maneuvering, that bloody smile, the elation in his eyes, the same look he gave me before he'd buried his head between my legs.

"Tom..." I murmured while arching my back. Ambrose's hand reached out and touched my little gem.

He sped up the swirls.

This was magnificent, I was losing myself in Tomm—

Something in the sensation changed.

I slowed and peeked open an eye.

Ambrose lay below me, his mouth agape. He stared at the backs of his hands, wearing the most crestfallen of expressions, his eyes actually glistening with unshed tears. I raised up tentatively, so close to having reached completion.

"This has *never*... you must promise to give me another chance." With two strong arms, he lifted me off his appendage and looked down. The shock on his features turned to terror. His rock-hard erection had deflated.

"Was it... was it because I said his name? I'm sorry Ambrose, I—"

"No!" he shouted, "I've been used in his place several times before. Shit, I've been called Primus *and* Lord Gammond more times than I can count!"

"Ambrose," I tried to interrupt his tirade.

"Damn Tommand to the nether!" He rendered me impotent not infertile!"

"AMBROSE!" I shouted, taking his hands into mine.

"Do you honestly think he'd maim you permanently?" I said calmly.

"Yes! I... no... but, Eira, promise me," he caught my face in his hands, "you will promise me not to speak to him about THIS!" He gestured wildly at his crotch.

"Wait, so you couldn't promise me to not murder a human, but you want me to keep my mouth closed about your limp member?" I pursed my lips and crossed my arms. "No deal. Not at all. It's the first thing I'm going to tell him when they let us out of here."

"You are a witch, an absolute hag, the nastiest SHREW!" he yelled, shaken by his predicament.

I began to feel a little bad and tried to see it through his eyes. I knew his physical prowess meant so much to him... and I also knew I *needed* something from him.

"Fine, I'll keep that promise but only if you keep mine."

He grumbled, poking at his lifeless penis and then shaking it in his hand, "Fine, it's agreed."

Together, we must have sat on the bed in silence for a half-hour, Ambrose huffing in consternation every other minute, me wondering if the food was still warm.

Fuck!

I scrambled around looking at the sheets, shoving at the brawny thighs that blocked my investigation.

"There's no blood, no... *fluids!* They're going to look for it!"

Ambrose rolled his eyes.

"There is not always blood, Nortia. It's a little wet. I'm sure it will be fine."

"No, it won't be!" I rolled off the bed and headed to the table. There were no knives, nothing stabby at all. I looked around the room, frantically searching for anything I could use to pierce my skin. There was nothing. Everything was blunted or too large to be safe. If I broke a pitcher for shards, they would probably—

There we go! A little narwhal statue lay near the bath. I grabbed the figurine and sent a silent prayer of thanks to Derros. Returning to the bed, I held the carved stone to my finger and closed my eyes.

Ambrose, huffing the loudest of huffs yet, snatched it from my hands. Without needing to steel himself, he dug the narwhal's horn into the bottom of his forearm. He spread a few drops of blood on the sheets.

"More?" he questioned.

I shrugged and shot him an innocent look. "I don't know. I'm a first-timer."

"I try never to mess with the *pure* if I can avoid them, so I'm not in the know." He continued spreading more droplets and smearing them around. "Kol, now there's a woman who knows her way around a man... maturity doth bring wisdom, Troth Nortia." The silly Scion put his hand to his heart and nodded earnestly.

I shook my head. For all his conceit and hypersexuality, I really appreciated Ambrose and was thankful he'd agreed to help me with my current set of predicaments, but he was so dramatic.

Ambrose snapped his head in my direction.

With both hands, he reached out and pulled me into a tight embrace. He laid his lips on my shoulder and worked his way up my neck.

I shoved against him.

"What are you—"

He silenced me by pressing his mouth firmly to mine, and though I struggled, he held tight.

"Stop," he whispered in a cautionary tone. It wasn't a sexual demand or an impassioned plea... something was off.

I stilled while he kissed a path to my ear and captured the lobe between his teeth. "I may be crazy, but I may have also spotted the tiniest movement in the wrinkle of the half-clothed woman's skirt on the wall. I believe we are being watched."

"What if they saw the whale and your arm?" I fretted, thinking the worst.

"Then they will have seen what came before it as well. It will be better for us not to speak any longer on what has taken place with the Gaean emissaries. We will wait until we are no longer in this chamber to figure out what must be done."

I nodded and looked up, kissing Ambrose soundly on the lips, trying to make the effort look as natural as possible.

"What now?" I asked.

"Food?" He patted his rippling stomach.

"Food," I agreed.

We filled our plates and ate the feast of my homeland, a variety of fish and whale meat, a hot and spicy broth, and preserved pickled vegetables.

"Ambrose, your little ear hoop, that means you're royalty, right? Of age?"

"Something like that..." he grimaced.

"You... you don't want to talk about home, though?"

"Not so much."

"Is your family like Tommand's? He said he grew up in a rather cold home."

"Similar, yes, but I had one parent at least who was always there for me." He fingered the moon clasp at his waist.

"And are you and Tommand friends or just Obligate and Advisor?"

"We are friends. We grew up a few hours from each other but went to the mines at the same time."

"What was he like as a child?" I pressed.

Ambrose smiled his lopsided smile and stuffed a chuck of tuna in his mouth.

"He was chubby, and funny, and would try to befriend a rabid wolf—he was so good-natured. He was his mother's favorite and his father's joy, but his father got involved in things he shouldn't have and eventually destroyed the family. That's when he learned to fight and went all caretakery."

I smiled, thinking of what a roly-poly sweet little Tommand would look like. I thought my whole heart would burst.

"And he loved turtles..." I said wistfully. Ambrose glanced at me from the corner of his eyes, looking at me like I'd taken leave of my senses. "And I need to put him out of my mind," I sighed. "Because our futures don't belong to us, and I just had sex with his friend. He doesn't want me in Monwyn anyway."

"I wish things could be different for you and for him. I know he would want that too."

I stared off into the distance thinking of the last passion-charged moment Tommand and I had shared.

"It's been three days... and I miss him," I shared with Ambrose, whom I found very easy to confide in.

"I miss him too."

I had to change the subject. This was getting me nowhere.

"I'm sore."

"Because of the sheer size of my dick?"

"Something like that."

I decided to bathe while watching Ambrose do push-ups on the floor. Sweating from the exertion, he chose to bathe after me, and when finished, we sat near the brazier to let his hair dry.

After spending the rest of the day chatting back and forth and learning to style his hair in the *proper* Monwyn manner, we spent the evening in companionable silence.

"I'm tired, Nortia. Come on."

Ambrose moved to the bed and held up the covers. Without hesitation or any kind of apprehension, I slid into the warmth and scooted to the far side. He followed me all the way over and tucked my body closely into his own.

"Sometimes, just being near someone safe helps us fear tomorrow less," he whispered.

Chapter Thirty-One

ASSIGNMENTS

"**N**ortia!" I could feel Ambrose's breath on my neck. "It's working." I tried my best to focus on what he was saying but was still too groggy from a blissfully deep sleep. "Wake up... mount me!" He shook my shoulder, jostling me awake.

"Ambrose, what in the—"

"Never mind, I can do this from here just the same. Lean forward." He rustled the sheets behind me and before I could wipe the sleep from my eyes, he squeezed his massively rigid erection between my thighs.

"Ambrose." I squirmed away. "What on Ærta! We did what needed to be done yesterday." I chided. I flipped around to face him and poked him in the chest. "So much for being near someone safe." He looked at me incredulously and put a hand to his chest like he'd been wounded.

"You do not understand, Eira! I have NEVER left another unsatisfied and you *must* give me another chance. Nortia, If someone asks you, 'Have you fucked with Ambrose?' and you say something like, 'Yes, but he was all floppy bits and neither of us reached the stars,' I will literally jump off this mountain."

Had he not been so genuinely upset I would have gone to pieces at his high-pitched impression of my voice.

"I'll lie and say you were the best lover north of the Sinnons, Ambrose. Just let me sleep." I begged, knowing I could roll over and immediately be out cold again.

"But it would be a lie. Eira, this is not fair. I will take you to the very peak of pleasure, I will satisfy you so thoroughly you will beg Merrias to take you to the next world!" He grabbed my shoulder and turned me, looking deeply into my eyes.

"Ambrose, I'm tired, and the last two nights I've forced myself into accepting sexual encounters that very well may haunt me for the rest of my life."

His mouth fell open. *Tears again.*

"Which is precisely *why* you need to let me correct this evildoing. This is an actual injustice, a wicked affair!"

"You thickheaded Scion! There was no wrong done between you and I—"

"PLEASURE IS HALLOWED, SHREWISH HARPY!" he hollered, kicking out at the blankets that trapped him.

"SO GO AT IT WITH SOMEONE ELSE, STUBBORN ASS MULE!" I shouted back.

The door swung open

"Obligates, rise." Lyta and another acolyte came forward quickly and directed us out of the bed and toward the door.

"Today will be different. You will be looked over, briefly, and escorted under guard back to your quarters. While there, bathe, and change into the garment that has been provided to you. The same guard will see that you are brought to the meeting hall at the appropriate time. Troth, leave now. Scion, wait until you are permitted to exit."

My last view was of the acolytes examining the blankets.

····◆)(◆····

"That was the absolute best Maneuvering." Kairus exclaimed when the chamber door swung open. "Who did you have? I had Greggen, who is really odd, but I liked him quite a bit; Ozius, who is mega intense, but I think he will be a good Scion; and Castor, who I am convinced I will marry. He's been so quiet these weeks that I barely noticed him, but, Eira, he is everything! He *is* Gaean, but not insanely religious like Ozius or Amias... noble as well. We played a little naked caid," she arched her brows up and down. "No, we didn't go all the way... but Eira, I think that copper-headed cutie is my lifemate."

I finished walking through the door and shut it behind me.

"That is *a lot* to process, Kairus," I declared, surprised at the change three days had made in my friend. "And Amias?"

She shrugged and began removing her chained garment. "Amias is really nice, seriously, a wonderful person, but he's not *my* person if that makes sense?"

"Sure it does," I replied, understanding how different it felt to be around Tommand as opposed to Ambrose.

"Who did you have?" she asked again.

"The first night was Evandr, the second, Ozius, and the third, Ambrose."

"And?" She shifted, moving nearer.

"And what?" I didn't want to divulge much more.

"Who did you like best?"

I acted like I was mulling it over.

"Evandr. I had a really good day with him."

"The short one? Super pale? Real... meaty?" She wrinkled her nose.

"Yep."

"Eira." She scoffed.

"What?"

"You... you picked *another* Monwyn." She looked at me sternly and then cracked. Kairus snorted so hard she flinched, and the laughter that erupted from my own mouth sounded like an old braying donkey. Like she'd broken the surface of a frozen pond, my friend reached right into my battered conscience and broke me free from the misery that'd been holding me prisoner.

"Let us see what we are wearing to this meet-up." She made her way to her wardrobe. "I just hope it's warmer than what we have had for the last three days."

Scowling, Kairus reached in and pulled out what looked like a cranberry-colored sack.

"That is awful." She tossed the offending garment on her bed.

"Well, at least we can be twins, right?"

I retrieved the same shapeless pile of fabric and laid it out.

"Yes, no one will ever be able to tell us apart." Cackling again, she scrunched her little upturned nose and looked me up and down. "Oh, Eira." She turned back to her closet. "I got this for you before the last meeting." She reached into her drawer and pulled out a beautiful black version of the strapped Solnnan binding. "I found a servant with the skill to make one and spent a hilariously long time recreating your boobs from my stockings." She formed a circle with her hands and compared it to my chest, "I hope it fits."

I held the support to my breasts, ecstatic to have been given a gift so thoughtful.

"Thank you, Kairus. This is just the nicest—"

"Hurry, go clean up and put it on."

I practically bounced to the bathing room and spent a little too long washing with the last remnants of my mother's lemon soap. At first, I was hesitant to use it, worried the scent might trigger disturbing memories of that day at the river, but once I opened the lid to take a little whiff, the only thing that came to my mind was the happy memories of home. Today, I began working for myself. It's what my mother would do. She would demand answers, gather advice, and form a plan. This day wouldn't end without me consulting Nan, who could then hopefully access Mariad and the Nortian Devotee. Nan was right; I had the strength of Nortia, and my own strength too.

I met Kairus in our room and modeled my new chest support. Though it made me a little self-conscious having my breasts pushed up, it felt amazing, like I could breathe more freely and move with less restriction. Together we unbuttoned our bags, which turned out to be long robes with deeply pooling sleeves, and put them on. They were tight at the chest, especially mine now that my breasts were cupped instead of smooshed, and flared out quite dramatically immediately below the bust.

"Horrendous." Kairus moved from side to side, holding the stiff fabric wide. She looked a lot like a large ringing bell.

"Troth Nortia, you are summoned!" a voice boomed from behind our door, followed by a heavy knock.

"Here we go," I murmured. I turned to Kairus and pulled her into a tight embrace. She returned the hug and then gave me a gentle nudge toward the door.

I walked in silence next to the armed guard, and as we rounded the hallway that led to the main level, I heard others calling out for Troth and Scion, their voices carrying through the vast cavern of Verus.

Two lines of guards were stationed to the left and right of the meeting hall's entrance, and as I approached, the doors were flung wide.

"The Honorable Troth, Eira Verras Chulainn, born of Ulltan and Vonnie!" The Devotee of Monwyn bellowed.

I walked through the doors and swallowed the fear that abruptly hit me.

The room was filled to overflowing with people. The Devotees sat at the table in the exact spots that they had occupied a few days before, and they wore their ceremonial hoods. However, in addition to the fine garments, coronets of gold and red were perched upon their heads, and massive bejeweled medallions hung from their necks.

The High Mantle was present, and Their chair had been elevated to the point where They looked down over the assembled audience. They were fully shrouded by a veil so heavily encrusted in jewels of all hues, and ropes of pearls, that it lay on Their face almost like a mask, molding to Their form. Today, They were the pantheon incarnate. The atmosphere felt much different than it had before... like the room itself was holding its breath.

"Emissaries Nortia, Monwyn, Gaea, and Solnna, enter!"

Eight emissaries made their way to the table, dressed in finery so grand their costs would have kept my whole village fed for a month. Nan, the first to enter, glittered from her shoulders to the floor. As she closed the distance between the door and her chair, she held her head high, and I was overcome with pride. Her task was not easy and her choices would have lasting impacts for sure, but right now she looked as confident and vital as I had ever seen her. As she came closer, I could see that her gown shimmered with what looked like crystals or diamonds placed upon white silk. It fit her perfectly *and* had a diaphanous piece of material gathered at each point of her shoulder that fell to the floor behind her. It too had been studded in tiny sparkling gems. Upon her chest lay a fat onyx, carved into the shape of a leaping whale. Her hair had been combed straight down her back, but the sides were braided and held together with a stunning ruby clasp. She sat, and the two Monwyn Emissaries strode forward, walking side by side. I only had eyes for one of them.

Tommand was a sovereign in a room of pretenders. Even scowling at the crowd like they were mud beneath his feet, he was the most captivating sight I'd ever beheld. He made the temple seem small and made me feel... happy.

He wore a tailored tunic that hugged him from chest to hip before falling open to the floor, revealing gleaming high boots and fitted leathers. The cloth of his lapis-colored silk overtunic was patterned with muted-gold lions, ripping into the neck of their bird-like prey. The eyes of the violent felines were glittering sapphires and matched those that were studded around a large jewel that hung from his collar. A thin, white belt was slung low on his hips, and from it hung a sword whose pommel was cast to resemble a man's face.

His eyes met mine, just briefly. His harsh expression softened, and I no longer heard the crowd and no longer feared tomorrow. The golden auras in his dark eyes glittered, and when he smiled, ever so faintly, I was sure I'd felt the floor shake. In the three days we'd been apart, his beard had grown in nicely and had been precisely trimmed and shaped.

"You may be seated," the High Mantle spoke in Their soft manner.

The guards, acting as our servants, pushed our seats forward, and our meeting got underway.

"The paths of the Obligates have been determined. None here shall make to infringe upon their destinies or alter the course of their fates. Devotee Solnna."

Mariad stood, regal in his gleaming coronet.

"The following paired couples will travel to Nortia: Obligates Luræna and Castor!"

I couldn't see her, but I immediately felt for Kairus. I'd never heard her speak so excitedly about anyone like she had the Scion.

"Kol and Ambrose!" *Have fun freezing.*

"The following paired Obligates are fated to serve the Kingdom of Monwyn: Zotikos and Cinden!"

If I could have, I would have wept for my friend who was sure to be so thoroughly heartbroken, but at least she wouldn't be near Ozius. She may love him, but did she know him?

"Greggen and Richelle!" *I hope Greggen finds a way to avoid Tommand.*

"The Obligates who will represent the mighty Kingdom of Solnna..."

I stared straight ahead. Two kingdoms remained, and I would only willingly go to one of them.

"Evandr and Eira!" Mariad's voice rang out.

I allowed my gaze to flit to Tommand. He closed his eyes just briefly and nodded resolutely. Bitter tears stung, but I wouldn't let them fall.

I shifted and came face to face with the Gaean emissaries, who did nothing to shield their disappointment.

"Lastly, to the bountiful Kingdom of Gaea go the Obligates Yemailrys and Lok, and Kymor and Amias."

Amias? I understand three of those placements, but I've never heard of an Obligate returning to their homela—Wait! What about Kairus? I sought her out down the table, not caring who thought me ill-mannered. She stared at the hands folded in her lap.

Devotee Gaea stood, and Mariad resumed his seat.

"If we do not try to change with the world, then we will find ourselves obsolete while the world continues to evolve." She looked around, her gaze landing on various members of the audience. "It has been determined that two Obligates will travel across the sea to the land in which Scion Greggen was raised to establish a fruitful trading post. Obligates Ozius and Kairus will serve the continent and travel to Baldorva. There is no greater honor than to be chosen for the task on which they shall embark."

Holy Creator above! I'd only ever heard horror stories about the Baldorvans. They were slavers and warmongers and wild. I was shaken to my core. Kairus, along with *Ozius* were heading to the place Nortian mothers used to scare their children into coming home on time.

Devotee Gaea sat and Devotee Nortia replaced her.

"The Mantle has seen fit to bestow upon Troth Chentel of Gaea and Troth Farai of Monwyn apprenticeships to the Devotees of their respective kingdoms. Grow in wisdom, and serve the Goddess above, for you shall serve her and her alone."

Now *that* was a great privilege for them both. Chentel was the daughter of the Arch Healer and was very much attuned to the temple, and Farai would make an exemplary Devotee. She was kind and fair and wholly devoted to Verus.

Devotee Nortia looked to Devotee Monwyn and inclined her head. She sat, and he rose again.

"The Goddess has smiled upon our group of Obligates. In the coming weeks, we will closely monitor Troth Kol, who joined bodies with Scion Lok..."

Strike.

Me.

Dead.

"...and Troth Eira, who mated successfully with Scion Ambrose—"

A grating screech interrupted the Devotee. Heads turned in unison.

Tommand shot to his feet so quickly that his chair almost toppled over. His hand had gone to his sword. All I could do was stare at the dancing flame of the candle that sat between us—I couldn't bear to look at his face.

"Prayers will be said and fires will be lit. If the Goddess wills it, may the Troth, fertilized by the life-creating nectar released into their bodies, bloom with the promise of a divine child."

The crowd screamed their excitement, clapping and stomping and cheering for well over five minutes.

"Our Troth will be escorted back to their chambers until collected by their matched Scion. After our evening celebration, they will meet with the Emissaries who will guide them through the next weeks," said the Mantle.

"The Mantle has spoken, and the Obligates have been Assigned! To Ærta!" bellowed Devotee Monwyn.

"To Ærta!" the crowd responded amid resounding applause.

Someone pulled out my chair and I stood.

All at once, the collective heads of the audience turned again.

It was impressive how fast a person of Ambrose's size could run.

CHAPTER THIRTY-TWO

THEY CAN ALL GO TO NETHER

"**E**ira, there is little to no chance that what you described would actually result in you being with child."

"I realize that, Kairus, but having it announced to a room full of people, in front of..." I trailed off.

"So what? You will start your courses, they will say another prayer, and you and Evandr will head to Solnna. You got yourself a Monwyn, Eira, and even if by some remote chance you *are* carrying the giant goon's spawn, how sweet of a deal would it be to bear the next Mantle?"

"I'm not sure I want to *bear* anything, Kairus."

"Then next time, you may want to take some sort of precaution," she snapped.

I flipped over angrily and glared at the pacing Troth.

"Yes, Kairus... *next time* I will," I gritted out. It wasn't often that she actually made me mad, but had she known the circumstances, maybe she would have understood my choices. I hadn't shared my reason for having sex with Ambrose, and until things were sorted, she would have to go on thinking it was because I found him attractive. Until I talked to Nan, I was keeping my business mine.

I'd concluded by their expressions at the meeting that my placement and publicly announced deflowering had successfully incited the rage of the three haints of Gaea. I didn't think Kairus would talk, but if any rumors of their "Nortian acquisition" were to surface, it would be traced right back to me.

I guess I do know when to keep my mouth shut.

Kairus had been pacing the floor since we'd returned, asking me all manner of questions and pouring out advice. She was driving me crazy.

"Sit down. In the grand scheme of things, I think your news is much more of a big deal than mine, and that's what we should be discussing. *I'm* not the one traveling to another continent or trying to negotiate peace talks with a country of primitive slavers."

Kairus paused her strides, and her face fell, crumpling in distress. Her blue eyes welled, and her bottom lip quivered.

"If I stop focusing on you, then I have to face my own predicament, Eira."

I should have realized. Though in public she kept her Monwyn mask firmly in place, the truth was, she felt things powerfully, her emotions were big, and her outlets for them were nearly nonexistent. Kairus needed me more than I needed to sulk, and even though I was trying my damnedest to hide from the world, I kicked back the covers I'd wound myself in and went to her side.

"You know, the Mantle is right. There's no one more well-suited for this task than you. You will turn Baldorva on its head!" I clasped her hands tightly in mine and looked her right in the eyes. "They have no clue what they're in for when you step off that boat." What I said was not just for Kairus' sake; I believed it wholeheartedly. "You've longed for adventure, Troth Monwyn, and this is the pinnacle of adventure."

"They are slavers, Eira! Why... WHY would we want any connection to a country whose tenets go so wildly against our own?"

I shook my head. I had no answer.

A hurried knock sounded at the door.

Lyta, along with the acolyte who saw to Kairus during the Fourth Maneuvering, arrived with a group of servants who carried in boxes and linen bags of all sizes. Netta and Ness were among the group, as were three others.

"Tonight you will be presented as custom dictates, according to the traditions of the kingdoms you have been Assigned to serve in," said Lyta, while two servants went to work, setting up a leather-covered table that I was swiftly coming to associate with discomfort.

"Eira, the hair will be removed from your stomach, pubis, and legs," said the acolyte, "and your hair will be gathered and bound away from your face."

"No." I stared at the bald-headed woman, whose mouth fell open in shock. I thought about how red and abused Farai had looked after the Grooming and decided I wanted no part in it.

"But... but Eira, you must..." Lyta stammered, unable to complete her sentence. She was looking around uncomfortably, shifting her eyes to her sister acolyte and then to the servants who had immediately halted their preparations. Seeing her becoming more distraught by the second, my resistance softened... just a tad. She had never treated me poorly and didn't deserve my sharp tone.

"Remove the hair from my legs if you must, but you are *not* ripping a single strand from anywhere else."

The acolyte blinked, and her throat worked up and down.

"This is highly irregular. I must... I will have to consult with the Devotee... and there is the issue of time to consider." She gulped.

"Please, consult with whomever you need." I gestured to the door.

"Begin her cleansing, now!" The acolyte took off at a run.

"Troth Monwyn, we have consulted with Scion Greggen's advisor, Evon. She feels given the circumstances, it would be more suitable for you to present yourself as you are. You will want to stand out to avoid being mistaken for—"

"A slave? Someone forced to call another master?" Kairus blurted.

No one spoke.

No one dared.

It took several minutes before Ness found the courage to break the silence that we two belligerent Troth had forced.

"A new gown has been created for you, Troth Nortia. After you have been bathed, you will lie on the table for... the next steps in your preparations. Lady Kairus, Julanna and Medory will begin styling your hair. Let's begin." The servant clapped her hands at the others, including the acolyte who had yet to pick her jaw up off the floor.

Begrudgingly, I made my way to the bathing chamber and allowed the servants to wash and exfoliate my skin with a rough cream that smelled like the grapefruits we'd eaten during Gotwig's first lesson. The aroma was delightful, but I was still feeling too obstinate to fully appreciate such frippery.

The door of the main chamber opened and closed with a loud bang and in seconds, a red-faced Lyta panted and puffed her way into the room where I was almost ceremoniously being dried by two servants. I stood naked with both arms straight out to my sides while Ness tapped so tenderly at my stomach that I wasn't sure she was actually making contact.

"You will be allowed to keep the hair on your pubis and stomach. The other areas, now including the hair under your arms, are to be removed without argument. A guard will be made present if there is further issue." She cast her eyes down, whispering the last part of her missive.

"Really? A guard? I'll just add him to the ever-growing list of people who've seen my ass. You know, in Nortia, if I went around with my butt out as much as I have here, it'd freeze shut, but it's fine, take the hair."

The telltale snorts of Kairus's laughter filtered into the room.

"The healer said the removal from your pubis may disturb the life growing within... so you were exempted." Her voice shook.

"Maybe they should have thought of that before taking the chance in the first place," I grumbled, leaning into the narrative. We entered my room and I climbed onto the table and checked out the tools Netta had laid out on my bed. A thick green goo that smelled sweet and looked like tree sap was in a large earthen pot, and another pungent cream in a smaller white jar sat to its side.

"Lift your arms, please." I did as asked, and Netta spread the white cream onto my armpits. Next, she reached into the waxy, green substance, and pulled out a sticky mass that she formed into a ball. As soon as she stopped messing with the stuff, it began running out over her fingers, but it solidified again when she smashed it together. She ran the ball down the right half of my calf, rolling out a thin strip as she went.

Without warning, she tensed and violently pulled the wax from my leg.

"Creators tits!" I came up off the table screeching and again heard Kairus's trills. The two young servants shrank back fearfully.

Netta cried out, plainly distraught, "Troth Nortia, Bearer, please forgive me. Is the child safe?" She placed both hands over her mouth, and tears filled her eyes. "We have three more pulls on this leg. It will soon be over!"

Poor Netta. I was more startled than in pain, but I didn't know how Farai had endured this on her woolybush.

"I assure you all is well, Netta," I tried my best to force a genuine smile. I just didn't feel like playing the Troth today. "I was just shocked." I laid back down and grabbed onto the sides of the table, letting her continue. I reminded myself that the sting was nothing compared to the pain of the brand on my hip.

When my legs were finished, she wiped the depilatory cream from under my arms, leaving the skin smooth and hairless. The servant curled my hair, piled it on top of my head, and secured it with ropes of braided gold, leaving a single looping spiral to fall over my right shoulder. Ness applied bold colors to my face to accentuate my features. A bright, plum purple, like the one Luræna favored, accented my lips, and my eyelids were stippled with a fine pink powder.

The two servants, who seemed to go between helping Kairus and myself to prepare, moved to fetch my new garment from a small wooden box. What they pulled out was reminiscent of the spun sugar that topped the cakes occasionally served after our dinners. The front of the gown would bare my legs, but the back swooped down, trailing the floor, even held up high as it was. I was looking forward to trying the style.

"This will be worn without a chest support, Troth Nortia," said Lyta.

"And why is that? Are we all appearing in the nude to celebrate our Assignments?" I snapped. The pinky-mauve material of this gown appeared light and flowy but also semi-transparent.

"Troth Kol will also appear similarly. Until the time something changes, your body is a walking prayer to the Holiest of Mothers and should be shown to all without shame." She paused and placed her hands on her brow. "I promise you, it isn't nearly as sheer when it lays against the skin."

Kairus walked out of her bathing room, stunning as always. She had been styled in red from head to toe, and the gown, which covered her completely, made her pale skin and hair stand out. Her dress clung tightly to her form before falling in dramatically full pleats over her hips. The only adornment to the entire ensemble was a necklace that featured an ornate ornament in its center. Like many of the emissaries, the jewelry didn't sit on her neck but instead attached to her shoulders, spreading the chain widely across her chest and back. The medallion, about the size of my palm, hung from the collar and was the focal point of her outfit. The oval had five shimmering stones embedded into its gilded center: at the top a sapphire and diamond, at the bottom an emerald and an onyx, and at the very middle, a ruby the size of my thumbnail.

She was the continent's representative, and the medallion was a testament to the beginning of her new story.

"I am ready." I knew the tone, where she wasn't ready for the evening ceremonies to begin, she was now resolved in her commitment to her path. I saw it in her proud stance and the stubborn set of her jaw.

While it looked like Kairus had accepted her fate, my need for defiance persisted and grew. After lacing me into the barely-there dress, the servants went to fetch my sandals and the acolytes stood cooing over Kairus. I shoved my chest supporter between my legs and up the back of my gown. The full, fluffy layers would hopefully conceal it, and I had every intention of begging off to the restroom and slipping it on.

My accompanying shoes were brought forward. Brown leather sandals with long straps crisscrossed from my ankles to right below my knees. Purple amethysts studded the leather, and looking down, I actually loved how my oddly hairless legs had become an accessory, adorned with the gems held precious by the Solnnans.

Around my neck, Lyta placed a collar of amethysts and diamonds.

I would have liked to think the white stones were a tribute to my homeland but knew they were also linked closely to Solnnan culture. The last piece of jewelry was placed on my wrist, it was the bracelet Devotee Mariad had given me. It was like he had known I'd be traveling to his homeland, and maybe he had. If he *was* the reason for my current placement, I would be forever in his debt.

I ensconced myself in the solitude of my bathing room, needing a moment alone. Staring at my reflection in the mirror, I waited for a defining moment to hit me over the head like it had Kairus. I twisted from side to side. Lyta had been right. The material did conceal much more than I had assumed; you could just make out the slightly darker ring around each nipple and the flash of my piercing in the light. Peering lower, you could also see the shadow of the hair at the juncture of my legs. I plucked at the curl on my shoulder while considering the consequences of my recent choices. I wouldn't have changed my decision to couple with Ambrose, even with the remote chance of having been impregnated. I wasn't going to be mated to Gaea's king. To avoid that, I'd have gone to the celebration in nothing but these sandals.

I'd just entered our room when Lyta answered a knock.

"Troth Monwyn, you are a vision." Not waiting at the door, Ozius paraded into our chamber, looking as self-assured as Kairus. Wearing a garment to match her, he cut a princely figure. The overcoat, made from a heavy, crimson brocade, had a complex repeating oval pattern in a deeper red hue, and instead of a medallion, he wore a black baldric over his shoulder and a gold ring, studded with the same five glittering stones, on his finger. He bent low over the hand that Kairus raised, and moving only his head, like an owl, he turned his amber eyes on me.

He rose from his bow and stepped forward, allowing his body to come into contact with mine, while he dropped his mouth to my ear.

"Your tear-filled eyes nearly destroyed me when they doomed you to the south." He pressed an unusually hot hand to my abdomen and closed his eyes. "Praise the Goddess... there is no babe in your belly." With that, he turned to rejoin Kairus. His touch left me unsettled, but there was little I could do, other than watch the striking couple walk out the door.

It wasn't long after they'd left that Evandr came to collect me.

"Nortia!" He strolled in with all the manners of a rambunctious piglet and slapped me on the back, "If it is a girl, let's hope Ambrosia doesn't have her daddy's nose."

Lyta blanched at the Scion, and the other acolyte gasped loudly at the ill-mannered jest.

The sleeveless overcoat of lavender suited Evandr's coloring well and elongated his shorter frame. Like Ozius, he wore a black baldric, but instead of a ring or medallion, two amethyst and diamond arm cuffs circled his biceps, giving his thick arms even more definition.

"Whoa, I can see your tits. Solnnan thing?" he taunted.

"No. No, Evandr, this is apparently how it's going to be until tiny Ambrosia makes her entrance into the world."

The servants fell to their knees at my side.

"Can we leave?" I was desperate to distance myself from the devout after having spent just a single day with Ozius. Evandr crooked his elbow and clicked his heels, and together we made our way into the hallway for our first outing as Solnna's newest Obligates.

"We will meet up with Devotee Mariad in his office first and then make our way to dinner together. He has interesting ideas for the future, ones I think you'll like."

"Excellent, I'm looking forward to it. Evandr, how's Ambrose? Have you seen him?" I was wondering how he and Tommand were getting along.

"Yeah, I have. He spent the first two hours after the meeting preening around like a puffed-up peacock, spouting off about the potency of his bountiful seed."

"He... he did WHAT?" The sound of my laughter bounced off the cavernous walls of the temple. I actually laughed myself into a wheezing fit, so I sat on a bench to catch my breath.

"Did I mess up my makeup?" I giggled out the sentence, patting the corners of my eyes.

"I'll tell you if you tell me what's so funny." He squinted curiously and tapped his black shod foot on the floor. Two servants walking by stopped and bowed low before popping up and moving on again. Evandr watched them until they were no longer in view.

"It... uh, must be all that bountiful seed messing with my head." I chuckled.

Evandr rolled his eyes and helped me up. We took a left on the fourth floor, walking past various offices and rooms used by the teachers and Devotees.

"In just a second, I'm going to pull you close," Evander spoke in a perfectly natural tone. "Then we need to act like we're scouting out a place for a quick fuck. We need to head in the direction of the training room. Trust me, okay?"

"Sure Evandr, why the nether not?"

Like dancing at a ball, Evandr spun me outward and twirled me around his arm. Smoothly, he dropped his hand to my waist and hauled me against his body, leaning his forehead against mine.

"Could we not act like we're searching for a place to dance? Or just, you know, walk through the door, minus the charade?"

His answer was to bend me backward so far that one of my legs popped up in the air.

"And here I thought you interesting," the suave Scion crooned.

My mouth fell open, indignant at the jibe. I balled the fist of my right hand, preparing to deliver a sound whap to his chest.

"That will do," he smiled.

Evandr bent his head and swept his tongue between my open lips and slid his hand lower, grabbing my backside. Spinning us both, he pressed me against a wall. *Of course he did... Monwyn.*

"You could at least make it look real, Nortia, or have you forgotten your training so soon?"

I bristled at the comment. He hadn't found Gotwig's office, but I had. Evandr didn't come up with the winning move in a Maneuvering; that was me. I pushed against the stocky Scion and shoved roughly at his right shoulder with both hands. Using the momentum and the surprise of my assertiveness, I pivoted around him and drove him hard against the wall.

"That's interesti—"

Flipping open one side of his coat, I shoved my hand into his waistband and cupped him with my palm. I arched my back and pressed my chest against his while using my free hand to grab him by his thick neck and pull him to me.

"Damn!" he mouthed, with his lip snatched between my teeth. I bit down sharply and felt him stir under the fondling of my hand. Together we walked and gyrated and kissed and groped until he wrapped his fingers around the handle of the training room door, which slammed open behind him. He went in backward pulling me along.

The room was dark, no lamps had been lit.

"That was your plan, Evandr? The best one you had?"

Tommand. He was here. It was his voice coming from the shadows.

"That was the most *fun* plan," the Scion laughed while straightening his rumpled clothing.

Guilt. Instant guilt.

"Eira." He whispered my name like a prayer.

I kept my eyes on his boots as he came toward me and closed them when he reached for me.

"I do not have long." He pulled me into his arms and kissed my temple, "I am due to meet with the Monwyn Obligates." I found the courage to glance up and what I saw reflected in his eyes was not anger, was not blame. "Ambrose filled me in. I will speak to the Nortian Emissary, your Nan, before the celebration. The Gaeans' plans would have resulted in a bloody war. They tried in every possible way to secure you."

I laid my head against his chest, feeling secure for the first time in days.

"Amias?" I asked, curious about his placement.

"His return was a factor in them backing off... that and your dalliance with Ambrose."

"Tommand, I—"

"—have nothing to apologize for." He held my hands. I cherished his warmth, the texture of the callouses, and the scars that crisscrossed his skin.

"Eira," There it was, my name again. Not Nortia, not Troth. "I do not care what you did to protect yourself. There is nothing greater... not my jealousy, my feelings toward you... nothing matters more than your life. You can rely on Evandr. I trust him to care for what is mine," he said thickly.

What is mine.

I looked into his eyes... dangerous eyes. Were I not so drawn to him, that look would have spurred me to run from the vicinity, but like a magnet, I was powerfully attracted to his intensity. I gathered myself closer to his chest and tucked my head under his chin, nuzzling my face against him. I felt the low rumble in the back of his throat before I heard it.

"Tommand!" Evandr barked. "Hey, Tommand, this isn't—"

Tommand wound his hand through my hair and tugged my head backward. He took my mouth roughly with his, and in an instant, I no longer cared what Evandr was saying. I placed my hands on his cheeks, feeling the full beard there, relishing the rough texture against my palms. He bent lower and pushed his tongue past my lips, and I met him thrust for thrust. Lips still on mine, his hand found its way under the short length of my dress and headed straight for my center. He groaned into my mouth when his palm met my curls. I lifted my knee and propped my foot on the stack of straw mats behind him, inviting him to take his pleasure as he wished. He dipped his finger into the entrance of my passage and then reeled back, releasing me.

He began to tear at the lacing of his pants, and not once did his eyes leave mine.

"Eira, I need you to move. Eira!" Evandr yelled.

"Leave, Evandr," I purred, my own gaze unwavering. Blood pounded through my body. I'd been ready for Tommand the moment I'd heard him speak, and now, I wanted my warrior-king to do his worst.

Tommand's nose flared, and his chest expanded to its full width. He reached into his pants and pulled his length free. My mouth watered at the sight of him. I grabbed my skirts, yanking them up over my hips.

"For fuck's sake." Evandr's fist slammed into the side of Tommand's jaw and sent his head whipping to the side. Tommand recovered quickly, but Evandr, having reset, let his arm fly again, connecting so hard it split the Scion's knuckles and felled Tommand, sending him to his knees.

"Evandr!" I gasped and tried moving around the broad body that blocked me.

"He is not in control, Eira. Let me deal with this." I'd never heard the Scion sound more serious than he did now. "I'll send you flying, Cat. Don't push me."

I heard a sharp inhale and could see Tommand shifting around on his knees behind Evandr.

"I'm okay Evan, I am good," Tommand breathed.

I'd never seen him taken down by another, and it frightened me. I ducked under Evandr's elbow and saw the bruise already forming on Tommand's cheekbone. He was tucking himself back into his pants when he looked up.

"Solnna is the safest place for you to be." He ran his hands through his hair. "Evandr." Tommand jerked his head in the direction of the door.

"We need to go, Eira. Give him some time," Evandr said.

"I don't want to leave," I sobbed, and I didn't mean just for the moment.

"Go, Nortia. We will speak again soon," Tommand half-whispered.

CHAPTER THIRTY-THREE

GODDESS, CREATOR, MOTHER...

Evandr, not waiting for me to move of my own accord, hauled me to the door. When on the other side, the Scion went about swiping his thumbs under my eyes and straightening my dress, making me more presentable for the public.

"Maybe if your nips weren't out, he could have dealt." I knew like Kairus, he was trying to lighten what had become an intense situation, but his comment raised my ire.

"Victim shaming, Evandr? That's beneath you."

"I'm sorry, where was this 'victim'? You?" He blinked unbelievingly. "'Victim' my ass! You almost mounted him a foot from my face... my face!" he bellowed while pointing to his nose. "You head to Devotee Solnna, I'll get him out of there and catch up."

"I will *if* you explain to me what all that was about. Who goes around slugging their friends like that?"

"Friendships come in all shapes and sizes, Nortia." I could hear the annoyance in his voice.

"Do they, though?" I turned on my heel and walked away in a huff, heading towards Mariad's office.

I wasn't sure what had gotten into Tommand, but whatever it was, it took my previous lustiness to a whole new level. It had felt a little like the odd possessiveness that Ozius had shown. The difference being, I had wanted everything that Tommand was offering.

Fuck Evandr. Fuck Verus. Fuck the Obligation.

Charging around the corner, I caught a familiar sight. It was the frail priest in his threadbare cloak—the one whom I'd prayed with so many days ago. He kneeled in the same alcove but this time stooped so low that for a moment, I was unsure if he was still with us. I stopped short. Seeing him here gave me a measure of perspective I hadn't felt all day. Getting himself to the fourth floor to show his devotion must have used up all his strength. It was a sobering reminder. It was true I had endured a rough few days, but how fortunate was I to have my health and my new life ahead of me?

"Good Reverend, I... can I pray with you this evening?"

He said no words but nodded his assent.

I kneeled next to the sad figure who shook, unable to control the tremors that wracked his body. His hand barely moved beneath his brown cloak, but I felt its gentle tap against my thigh.

"Divine Mother, Life Giver, Creator of the Realms," his palm rose slowly from where it lay on my bent leg and settled low on my stomach, "be with us now, in us and near us, for we are your essence made flesh." I held the frail hand under both of mine, careful to keep the material of his cloak between our skin. His transparent flesh had been so papery thin the last time, and I feared causing him any more pain. I held his arm to where he had rested it. If it gave him hope or comfort to think I carried a future Mantle, so be it. "Exalted Lord Mossius, Master and Teacher, we beseech you. Enlightened Sage, Healer of Man, we contemplate your teachings, we lean on your storied acumen, to ever guide us on our paths."

He tried but couldn't manage to lift his hands to his brow.

"There you are." Evandr came up behind us. "Mariad is headed downstairs and will meet us at dinner."

I nodded. We were required to attend the celebration, but I couldn't leave the priest here to suffer. I needed to first find a healer to ease his discomfort.

"Help me get our pilgrim back to his quarters. Do we have time?" I asked.

"We do not, no, but who's going to tell Mama Troth she's late?" Evander bent to help the priest stand. "Pilgrims' rooms are on the first floor, correct? Located in the hallway to the right of the emissaries' hall."

Together, with the priest tucked between us, we made our slow descent.

"How's *Cat, Evan*?" I looked over the bent form, arching an eyebrow at Evandr. I thought the nicknames were cute, and for Tommand, especially apropos. Many times I had likened him to a prowling feline.

"Fine. Fully recovered and off fulfilling his duties." He hadn't taken the bait.

On the first level, servants were dashing around us from all sides, passing with trays or disappearing into the kitchen doors. The dinner and celebration had no doubt begun.

"Can you tell us which room?" I spoke soothingly to the priest. "We will see you settled, and I will ask for a healer to be sent the moment we reach the dining hall."

"Th-third door, left," he rasped, while his whole body shuddered.

I took the priest's elbow, helping him walk into the room while Evandr held the door.

His chamber was sparse. A small bed sat in the corner with a gray quilt across its top, and a pot sat near the hearth. I wanted to weep. He lived in destitution, so close to the end of his time. No worldly possessions, no support systems, nothing to see him on his way to judgment.

"Let's get you to bed." We inched our way across the floor, and I heard Evandr follow.

The priest eased himself down to the bed's edge, sinking slowly into the straw-filled mattress. I arranged his cloak around him, covering his body, and reached into the cowl covering his head to smooth his brow. If a fever had set in, weakening him to this point, he was surely experiencing discomfort and wouldn't be with us long. Kan Keagan had passed away soon after the fever entered his body. I pushed the hood back gently to look for the other symptoms a healer may need to be aware of.

I met the Reverend's eyes—eyes as clear as the daytime sky—a man renewed.

There was no pallor to his skin, and though he remained gaunt, there was color in his cheeks.

His hand snapped out and seized my wrist.

Panicked by his miraculous transformation and sudden movement, I twisted away, trying to free myself, but his considerably strong grip held me in place.

I looked to Evandr, who now stood in the middle of the room.

The door shut behind him.

"No!" I screamed.

Goddess, help your child!

Evandr pivoted and made a strike at Scion Ozius, who stood over him, but his fist went off course when Castor jumped in to aid his Gaean comrade. Evandr recovered quickly and sent Castor sprawling with a powerful kick to his hips.

Ozius used the moment to go on the offensive. Throwing all of his weight behind him, he began striking low and repeatedly at Evandr's midsection.

"Ozius stop! STOP" I cried, pulling against the hand that held me.

"Calm, child. We are taking you home."

My mind reeled. *Home? Nortia?*

I watched in horror as a red stream spilled onto Evandr's left boot and splattered the stone floor below. He crumpled, falling first to his knees and then to his side. A bloom of red spread along his abdomen, soaking his lavender coat to its hem.

Ozius, knife in hand, dropped to his knees and assumed a pose of prayer.

"Let go!" I shrieked, clawing at the priest's hand. I kicked out, catching him in his shin and raked my hand across his face. His grasp loosened, and I pried myself free of his grip.

I ran.

Surging toward the door, I knew I had to find help for Evandr.

Castor came into view, and an instant later, all I saw were bright starbursts.

"You fucking idiot, don't hurt her, never hurt her!" I heard Ozius caution the other Scion.

"What did you want me to do Ozius? Let her get out, cause a scene, and alert the entire temple?" Castor bleated.

I tried lifting my feet but fell forward, still dazed by the blow I'd received.

I landed on Evandr, his still body taking the brunt of the impact.

I saw his life's blood, thick and black at the epicenter of the wounds, still flowing. Placing both hands on his abdomen, I tried to staunch its flow but swayed with the exertion. My head pounded like it'd been split in half, and I saw before I felt the trickle of blood fall from my nose, dotting brightly on the light material of the coat he'd worn. While Castor and Ozius bickered and the priest looked out the door, I ran my hand under his lavender lapel and felt for a heartbeat, for a breath, any indication he was still with us.

I felt nothing.

"HELP!" I screamed at the top of my lungs. "HELP!" My voice shredded and tore at my throat.

A hand lashed out, roughly slapping over my mouth.

"Eira, stop now! Stop it!" An elbow wrapped around my throat and squeezed. "My Queen." I fought against him, kicking and digging my hands into his forearm. "Your destiny is not found within these walls. Your future is the amelioration of all Ærta. Calm yourself," Ozius ordered, increasing the pressure around my throat.

"We have to move her, Ozius, now," the priest said. "Put this around her."

My assailants wrapped the brown cloak around my body, and I gulped for air when Ozius removed his arm long enough to allow the hood to be pulled down low, covering my face.

"If you scream, Eira, I will render you unconscious. Do you hear me?" Ozius cautioned.

I nodded. If I were out cold, I'd have no opportunity to find help for Evandr, whose life I knew was slipping away.

"Now," the priest whispered as he looked down the hallway.

Ozius stayed at my back, and Castor and the priest walked at my front moving down the hall and into the wide-open belly of the temple.

"Head through the door and await the oth—"

"OZIUS, CASTOR, CEASE!" Mariad's voice roared from above us.

"Take her!" The priest snapped.

I lunged, wrenching myself from Ozius' hold, and ran, barreling past the priest, who urged Castor to intercept the Devotee.

The hood snatched back around my neck, cutting into my skin.

The adrenaline coursing through me made me impervious to the cruel hands that bit into my sides. Ozius hoisted me into the air and slung me over his shoulder, the impact driving deeply into my chest, knocking the wind from my lungs.

"M-Mar-Mariad," I sputtered, "Evandr..." his name barely passed my lips, not even a whisper. I hammered on my assailant's back and tried kicking my legs free of the arms that bound them.

"Help!" I attempted to scream, but my voice was still too inadequate for the task. And upside down as I was, the blood rushed to my already swimming head, and my vision began blurring again.

I knew this smell, the slight scent of foodstuffs, mingling with an abundance of floral freshness—I was in the laundry.

"Don't let them take me... find Nan..." I said to a familiar-looking shadow.

Then there was darkness.

Was I imagining the yelps and grunts, the thud of fists, the flash of blades?

I came to my senses when Castor flew into a rack of robes, and a massive metallic clattering started me back to consciousness.

The impact caused him to lose his balance, and he dropped.

The warmth of the laundry room floor permeated my cheek while I watched Ozius looming over Mariad, who was down on his knees injured. Gotwig was there too, backed into a corner, holding his own against the priest and—

Marcyn.

Marcyn *was* the shadow I had seen, and he was attacking furiously, landing blow after blow. Gotwig's face remained impassive, but with each strike, deep cuts appeared on his arms and face.

Scrambling to my hands and knees, I crawled to Mariad, who was trying in vain to stand.

"Leave, Eira. Get," he choked, "to Solnna, little one."

I looked to the door and back to the men still throwing punches and circling each other. Castor had joined in again and had surrounded Gotwig. Ozius had vanished.

Mariad got one foot under himself.

"You're too weak." I tried to hold him back as he swayed unsteadily trying to find his balance. He launched forward and grabbed Castor by the shoulders, slamming him to the ground.

"Run!" he shouted, glancing back over his shoulder.

I heard him, but I couldn't, and not because of fear. I took in the violence unfolding before me, the blood running from Gotwig's cheeks, Marcyn's filthy, deceitful face—and I shot forward.

Raising my knee to my chest, I stomped down with all the power I could muster, grinding Castor's outstretched hand into the floor.

"Fucking nether!" Castor cursed, jerking his fingers free.

He bound angrily to his feet and ignoring me, hooked the Devotee's neck from behind. With a violent explosion of energy, he slammed his knee into Mariad's back, and the Devotee sank to the floor again, this time making no attempt to rise.

Castor changed course and stepped in my direction.

He was not Ozius. He *would* harm me.

I lunged hard and ducked out of his path, running toward a nearby table where my fingers curled around a heavy iron. I spun, launching the solid metal tool at him.

He deflected the projectile and drove his arms into my chest, smashing my lower back into the table's edge. The pain alone would have felled me were it not for him wedging himself against me.

Tucked in close to his hips, he drew back his arm and took aim.

"Your blessed womb will bear no Monwyn brat."

His fist collided with my stomach, and I ceased breathing. Saliva poured from my mouth, and I couldn't move or convince myself to react when he grabbed me by the neck.

Goddess, Creator, Mother...

The entryway door burst off its hinges.

Tommand filled the doorway and a little blond-framed face peeked around his hip, only to quickly disappear.

The second blow hit my stomach, and my eyes rolled up. I stayed upright, but vomit spewed from my mouth and ran down my front.

Castor sneered in my face, setting up his next assault.

And then he was gone.

With his body no longer supporting me, I collapsed, busting my knee on the stone floor.

With a brutal twist, Tommand forced Castor's elbow backward, the arm breaking with an audible crack.

Castor's screams pierced my eardrums but stopped the instant the tip of a blade pushed through the front of his neck. In a single swift motion, Tommand yanked free the weapon and hammered it down into the juncture where Castor's neck met his shoulder, and then hurled the lifeless man to the floor.

Whirling around in a blood-fueled frenzy, Tommand headed for the group that swarmed Gotwig. Marcyn spun and swung out, anticipating his advance. His weapon, a small semi-circular blade, caught Tommand across the chest, but the Emissary didn't retreat. He looked at the Gaean Advisor, and the corner of his mouth tugged into an inhuman sneer.

"Monwyn, take her and go!" Mariad cried from his prone position. "This won't stop for her. They know!"

Tommand's head snapped in the direction of the fallen Devotee at the same instant that he landed a kick to Marcyn's kneecap.

"They *know*..." Mariad panted.

Ambrose came running through the door, dressed in the furs and leather of a Nortian. He glanced from me to Tommand, who nodded once. A silent understanding passing between them.

Tommand ran to my side and hauled me up off the floor while an enraged Ambrose took off toward the fight.

Shouting in a language only I would know, Mariad's deep voice followed me into the servant's tunnel.

Chapter Thirty-Four

DESPERATION

"I know you hurt, but keep up, Eira. Push through it."

We emerged from the tunnel on the far-right side of Verus, and Tommand ran ahead past lines of wagons and carts and into a huge stable.

"Emissary, may I be of service?" A young man wiping his hands on a length of cloth stepped into the lamplight.

"Make my saddle ready, Reed. Fill my bags with whatever provisions are on hand. We need them fast," Tommand ordered.

"At once!" The stable hand turned and ran into the dark row of stalls.

Tommand followed him in, leaving me alone. The soft knickers and whinnies of the horses bedded down for the night were a peaceful distraction from my own tumultuous thoughts.

The dread in Mariad's eyes as his head hit the floor... his last words to me, spoken in Solnnan, *keep faith in those who earn it, child.*

Evandr would still be lying on the floor.

Who would find him? Who would perform his rite?

Castor would still be in the unnatural position he'd landed in. Would his eyes have closed, or would his dark gaze still be staring into nothing? Tommand had snuffed out his life in seconds, and the ease and speed at which he severed the link between a man's existence and his end disturbed me.

Tommand emerged from the stable in a hurry, holding the reins of good-sized dun.

"You could have stopped them all," I whispered, frozen in place, staring at the blood stains on the shirt he wore.

"Yes, but there are times, like now, when soldiers are given a more crucial task." He threw a set of double bags over the stallion's rump and glanced toward the door that led to the servant's tunnel.

I turned my face to the darkening sky, wishing I could somehow make time roll backward. Could I have done anything differently?

Was Mariad still alive? Was Gotwig?

"Come back to me, Eira," Tommand spoke softly while twisting an errant curl back up to its hairpin. "You have witnessed Ambrose on the field. Put your trust in him now and—"

"Anything else, sir?" The stable hand returned.

"That will be all, Reed." Tommand produced two gold coins from his pocket. "Give the second one to Mim."

"Yes, sir, thank you, sir!" Reed shoved the coins into his satchel and turned back to his chores.

"Do you ride?" Tommand asked while stepping into the stirrup of the saddle and mounting quickly.

"Yes, but never with another." The thought of not being in control of my own mount made me wary, but my foot replaced his in the stirrup while he simultaneously hoisted me up to sit in the front of the saddle.

"I'm taking you to a healer. Lean back and rest."

At the moment, I didn't have the mental or physical fortitude to chide him about making my decisions for me. By the second, the adrenaline that had kept me going was losing its power to keep the pain of my injuries at bay. I leaned back against the solidity of his chest.

"What do *they know,* Tommand?" I asked, staring straight ahead.

I felt him stiffen under me.

"We have much to discuss, Eira, but right now, we need to put distance between Verus and us, and talking will be difficult in this wind." Tommand clicked his tongue and squeezed his thighs, and our mount responded immediately, moving forward at a light trot, gaining more speed as we covered ground.

We galloped through the archway that had welcomed me to the temple and sped past the road that led north.

"Tell me if the speed causes your pain to increase." He bent to my ear, speaking loudly over the air that whipped around our heads, "Depending on the outcome back there, we could be outstripping a battalion of guards... or no one at all."

I didn't answer, just shivered against him, willing the bile rising to my throat to return to my stomach. I didn't want to think about people giving chase. That would only increase the likelihood that more would be injured... or worse. I didn't want to think at all. I wanted to turn completely off and stop rolling through the multitude of scenarios of what may still be happening at the temple, but it was all I could do.

Would Ambrose be able to take on Marcyn, who was clearly more adept at arms than I would have imagined? And the miraculously healed priest—there was no telling what nefarious dealings he had his hands in, and... what if Ozius had returned? Never in my wildest imaginings would I have thought the healer capable enough to take down a man as powerfully built as Evandr, but he had, and well before any true altercation had gotten underway.

"Tommand?" I shouted.

He slowed our mount.

"Did you encounter Ozius before you found us?"

"No, why?" he questioned.

"He was there, behind the door, and... he... he killed Evandr." I tried choking back the sob that burst from my chest, but fat tears rolled down my cheeks, reanimating the smell of the vomit and blood that had begun drying on the cloak. I doubled over to the side and heaved and gagged but brought up only pungent, yellow bile.

Tommand dropped one handful of reins, and I felt him digging around behind himself. He produced a small metal flask and pressed it into my hand. Thankful for anything to wash the ill from my mouth, I unscrewed the cap and inhaled the sharp, fruity vapors of a fermented beverage. I took a small sip of the strong spirit and was no longer inundated by the odor of the filth at my chest or the acid that had burned the back of my throat. The beverage stung my cheeks and numbed my tongue when I swallowed, and it burned a smooth, cleansing path to my stomach. I swallowed another gulp, followed by one more, and within minutes was relaxed enough to lean back and close my eyes.

Some time had passed when I felt the horse slow. The sky was like pitch and thick clouds covered the moon, but I could make out scattered lights in the distance.

"Many temple servants call Stormridge home. Like Reed, they rotate shifts every few days and make the journey here when they aren't working," Tommand whispered.

"Is it wise to travel where people may know us?"

"It is if we want the right people to know our whereabouts. There is also a wise woman who resides here, and she will be able to assess your injuries. We head first to her and then to an inn on the far side of the village."

We rode slowly into the darkened town, passing well-kept houses and shops, which had been closed up for the night. In the distance, a statue of the Goddess had been erected in the intersection of two lanes. One headed from north to south and the other east to west. Several merchants' stalls surrounded the tall monument and would no doubt be teeming with customers in the morning. We passed a cobbler's shop and a tack merchant's storefront—I could smell the rich, earthy scent of the leather they worked from a distance. There was a haberdashery across the street with a store sign painted with images of mice wearing hats, and a fabric shop with sweet, checkered curtains in its windows.

Tommand turned the horse east, and we moved down the narrow lane until a two-storied structure came into view. It looked to have been solidly built from wooden planks and had three large windows on its top floor. The building was situated quite far from the main drag of town, but considering how bright the place was currently lit up, and the number of people staggering from its door, it was probably located with the peace of the sleepy little town in mind.

"Verrona owns this place." Tommand halted the dun, slipped from its back, and let the animal drink its fill before tying the reins to a covered hitching post that ran alongside the building.

"And Verrona is?" I questioned, keeping an eye on a wobbly patron who'd been trying unsuccessfully to loosen the leather ties that secured his horse.

"The nearest person I *mostly* trust to mend your wounds," he said sincerely. "Come on, and wrap the cloak around you."

I watched the drunkard pet his horse and give up. He just laid down in the hay next to the speckled steed and used his cloak for a pillow. Tommand shrugged and offered me his arms. I slid to the ground with his support, but the woosh of air when I dismounted was enough to bring the wretched smell of foulness back to my nose.

"No cloak, get this off of me, please," I gagged out. "I can't be in it a moment longer, Tommand," I pleaded, unable to undo the closure that had been cinched so tightly. His hands came to my neck and unfastened the metal clasp, and as gently as a mother with their babe, he raised the garment up from my shoulders and moved it back so as not to bring it nearer my face. I looked up to thank him and was struck by how exhausted he looked. He had worry lines on his forehead and dark stains below his eyes and—

"Tommand. Your neck!" I gasped. My heart stopped when I saw the angry-looking gash that had opened up along his collarbone. My head must have been rubbing against it the entire journey.

"It will be fine, Nortia," he said dismissively. "Stay behind me when we enter."

"I will not be ignored or shoved behind you. You need to see a healer as much as I do." I grabbed his hand and took off marching toward the inn's entrance.

"Eira," he spoke softly.

"I'm not hearing it." If he thought I'd sit by and be treated while he ignored a gaping wound, he was sorely mistaken.

"Eira, it's not... listen." He tugged my hand, halting my steps.

"*What?*" I crossed my arms and tapped my foot against the wooden landing.

"Though people at the temple may regard what you are wearing as a perfectly acceptable tribute to the life you may eventually bear, the townsfolk may mistake your near nudity for... something different." His eyes flashed in the light of the lamps that hung on either side of a sign that read, *Taps and Tinctures.*

"Right, you're right." I settled myself and tried to think rationally. The semi-transparent dress *would* catch more than a few folks' attention. I tucked in behind Tommand, doing my best to conceal myself. He pushed open the tavern door, and immediately we were bombarded by the loud and raucous laughter of a large crowd doing their best to sing along with a minstrel who plucked at the strings of his fiddle. The odor of the place was not what I expected. It didn't smell strongly of spirits or drink. Instead, it was filled with the potent aroma of plant life. I picked up on the enticing scents of rosemary and oregano and the sweeter smells of mint and lavender.

We walked through the throng, winding our way through the clearest paths we could find. Luckily, the inn's guests seemed to mostly keep to themselves, though some turned to watch as we made our way to the stairs at the back of the open room.

"You're back!" A tiny little boy jumped in Tommand's way. "Did ya find what ya was lookin' for?" The little one propped his hands on his hips and looked right up at the big man in front of him as confident as he could be. I peeked around Tommand to see him better. He was cute as a little pup with his curly mop of hair and missing front teeth.

"I did, Jenri, is your mother around?" Tommand ruffled the little one's hair.

"MA!" I started when Jenri screeched up the stairs. "YOU AROUND MA? THEM BIG BOYS ARE BACK... WELL, ONE OF EM!" He scratched his chubby little cheek and waited for a reply.

"Jenri! What did I tell you about screaming like that? You scare the daylights out of me—Oh, hello!" A most lovely woman waved from the top of the stairs. She was dressed in a white frilled top that had been paired with a colorful, long, flowing skirt. It reminded me of something Primus Meridett would have had in her collection.

"Is *that* the wise woman?"

"She is. Were you expecting a hag, Nortia?" He let out a short laugh and held his arms out to accept a hug from the lively mother, who, surprisingly, was even shorter than the petite Meridett.

"I see you've brought a friend." She whirled around Tommand and her nearly black gaze met mine. "And you are in need of assistance. Jenri!" She turned, and the little boy ran right to her side. She placed her copper-hued hand under his chin, tilting his head so he looked her directly in the eye. "Tell Sanderson to mind the floor, okay? Now repeat."

"Tell Sanderson to mind the floor." Jenri mimed and nodded.

"Good, now go." She swatted at his bum and watched him scurry away, pushing through the legs of many a confused customer.

"Tommy, head up the stairs and to the left. She needs to disrobe, and you need a new shirt. I'll be along." She walked away, waving to her guests as she went.

The room we entered on the second floor was similar to the healer's spaces I had been in. Three waist-high tables, the length of a tall man, were set about the room. One's short edge was placed right up against the large central window located on the back wall, where the leather curtain that covered it could be rolled up and secured to let in ample natural light. The other two were positioned next to each other along the left side of the room, situated between four wall-mounted oil lamps. A massive apothecary's chest sat in the back corner and a few feet in front of it was a plain redwood desk, covered with stacks of parchment and dozens of potted plants in various stages of growth. There was a bed tucked into the far-right corner as well, but not so close to the wall that the healer couldn't access all sides of her patient. Piles of folded quilts and towels lay out on a table at its foot.

"Go sit." Tommand pointed to the bed.

My legs felt like stone, but I managed to trundle across the floor and hit the bed, just in time for a boisterous group of merry-makers to rush into the room.

"Now fill it, please." Verrona piped up behind the line of men, who all carried buckets of steaming water in their hands. "Hurry up now and then out with ya!" Following her sharply stated directive, each of the men, in assorted states of inebriation, poured their buckets into a large copper tub. "Out!" She shoved at a man who had stopped to play with the fuzzy frond of a large fern. She then turned her attention to Tommand, who had come to stand near my side the moment the first stranger had walked through the door.

"You, go." She pointed her finger at him and flicked it back to the door.

"No. I stay," he said in an authoritative tone.

Verrona squinted, looking me over, and slid her eyes back to Tommand.

"Get yourself gone." Her hands went to her hips, just as Jenri's had earlier.

Tommand stared down at the glossy tresses of the raven-haired woman and shook his head in confusion, then looked at me like he'd come to some quick revelation.

"I have seen her naked, Verrona." His tone softened.

"That's great, but I don't care if you've seen the holy ass of Lykksun, Tommy. Take yourself outside. You can stand by the door and keep guard if you must, and I'll call you back soon."

Tommand rubbed at his darkly bearded chin, considering Verrona's words.

"She may be with child," he said gruffly.

"And nothing will be done to change that, Tommy." The healer nodded and shooed him away. With a curt nod in her direction, decision made, he stormed toward the door and shut it behind him.

"Unless you want it to change." Her voice dropped low when she moved to my side. "Tell me... did he do this?" With nimble fingers, she unlaced my gown and helped me to shimmy it down over my hips.

"Tommand?" I said confusedly, surprised at the suggestion. "No, not at all." I shook my head.

"Good, I don't think I have the amount of henbane needed to render him unconscious." Verrona turned my head from side to side, and pulled lightly at my eyes with her soft fingers. "Lie back and tell me about the type of impacts that caused this mess. Blunt objects? Were they swung? From what distance?"

Pointing to the various bruises and cuts on my body, I told her what I could, leaving out as many details as possible. Verrona palpated my abdomen and grabbed a funnel from the kit at her side, and through it, she listened to the sounds my organs made, as well as the beat of my heart.

"How far along are you?" she asked, still listening to the side of my abdomen where Castor had landed his blows. Panic began to rise in me. Could she already detect something there?

"I... if it were even remotely possible, it would be a matter of two days," I said, louder than I should have. "And I started and ended my courses literally a day or two before that, *and* the man in question was unable to perform to completion."

"Ah, the man was not Tommy then. That explains that." She tossed her head to the door. "I agree with you that the chances would be quite low, but there is no telling what the temple has done to your ovulatory phase. I can give you the herbs to end the possibility, or the ones to keep you from conceiving from here on. The latter will need to be taken weekly, the first will work in a matter of days. Do you have a long road ahead of you?"

"I... I honestly don't know," I confided.

"Then I'll mix up both. It's your choice to take either." She moved to her desk, pulling small paper packages from several of the marked drawers of her cabinet, and went to work mixing and pressing powders and combining them into what smelled like a potent astringent. She funneled the blends into two small bottles.

"The green will end, and the yellow-green will keep conception at bay. Both are yours." She sat the bottles on a three-legged stool next to the bed. Verrona's skirts danced around her ankles, and she took off again, moving around the space collecting bright-green and deep-purple plant clippings. She tossed handfuls of those into the tub and added four heaping scoops of a beige powder, that was stored in a large earthen jar. "I'll help you climb in. It'll sting your skinned knees like the nether but will have them healed up in no time."

I untwisted the leather thongs of my sandals, and Verrona came to my side. I was thankful to have her support as my legs, having finally found rest after the punishments of the day, almost buckled beneath me.

As I sank into the tub, dozens of small nicks and scratches made themselves known. They were mostly concentrated on my legs, but I could feel a few others on my lower back and wrists. The stinging died down after a few minutes, and as it dissipated, the healing heat of the steamy water seeped into my aching muscles.

"What's in here?" I asked curiously, rubbing the milky water that slipped through my hands.

"Clay from Gaea mostly. It's been dried and finely powdered. I mixed in a few healing herbs as well. They come from... one of your homelands. Did you get that at a Grooming?" She nodded at my breast.

"I did, yes."

"And you decided to keep it?"

"I... mmhmm." My cheeks warmed. I didn't want to tell her I decided to keep the damned thing after the reaction Tommand had to it.

"And your hair? Will you let it come back?" she asked.

"I'm not sure. It seemed silly to have removed it in the first place, but I'm from up north. We tend to add on more fur as opposed to taking it off."

Her raspy chuckle brought a smile to my face.

"You seem to know a lot about Verus." I leaned my head against the back of the tub and closed my eyes.

"I should. I trained many of their priestesses," she remarked, "but fell for a boy and chose another path."

I opened my eyes just a smidge and studied the healer, who began bustling around the room. She looked way too young to have trained others at Verus, and also too young to have mothered a child.

"Are you okay with him coming back in? His tapping is driving me mad."

I focused and, sure enough, heard his fingers rhythmically rapping on the wooden panel.

I nodded and sunk further into the tub.

Tommand strode into the room like he owned the entire town the instant the door opened.

"How is she?" He asked the healer.

"She can tell you how she is, Tommy," Verrona scolded.

The look he gave her could have halted an army's advance, but Verrona just rolled her eyes and went back to mixing.

"I'm alright Tommand, really. I'm sore and sleepy, but nothing feels permanently damaged."

"Drink this." Verrona handed me a small glass of yellow medicine.

"Verrona, Tommand's neck is—"

"Fine," he interjected.

"Don't interrupt me." I shot back, making ripples in the foggy water. "It's not *fine*. Can you please look at it?"

The healer circled the tub and stood beside Tommand, who had come and kneeled at the side of the bath. Without asking, she pulled back his collar.

"Needs stitching. Clean him up for me?" She tossed a rag into the tub and went to her desk.

"Of course." I plunged the linen square into the water and kneeled in the tub, reaching to undo the silver buttons of Tom's shirt. The cut ran the length of his clavicle and was deeper on the right side and shallower on the left. It looked like a clean laceration, but I still worried about an infection settling into the opened flesh. I pushed the shirt from his shoulders and let it fall to the floor.

"It'll sting," I warned before touching the skin near his wound. Blood had run over one side of his chest and down his ribs in a smear of rusty red. I closed my eyes briefly, the image of Castor's bloodied body appeared in my mind.

"Tommy!" Verrona snapped. "You will not, and I repeat, will not, put your mouth on that for at least another two days."

I glanced at her to see what she'd been referencing and didn't understand until I looked up and saw the golden auras dancing around large, dilated pupils. His eyes were affixed to my chest.

Tommand grunted in response but didn't look away.

I lowered my lashes and continued to clean around his wound, eventually dropping my hand to remove the blood and grime from his abdomen. I tried to concentrate on the seriousness of the task but felt the tingling and tightening of my nipples, which were hardening to pebbles under his gaze.

"Clean enough." Verrona scraped the legs of a chair along the floor and sat next to Tommand. She shoved him back onto his heels and popped him with a sound smack on the bottom of his chin, which forced him to look up.

"That wasn't necessary, V." He narrowed his eyes at the needle coming toward him.

"I'd say it was. You men are always ready for a fast hump after a scrap... though it looks like your friend here did most of the fighting."

"Oh." It dawned on me we hadn't been introduced. "My manners. Verrona, I am—"

"—Diantha," Tommand interjected, reaching out to smooth a piece of hair behind my ear.

"That's lovely, named after one of my most favorite flowers." The healer looked over her shoulder. I nodded my head and smiled in agreement. I hadn't the foggiest idea of what one looked like.

I sank back into the tub and went under the water, wanting to wash my hair and take a momentary break from Tommand's constant watch.

Evandr.

The water kept me from choking on the sadness... on the shame. His body might still be laying on the cold floor, and ultimately, it was there because of me. The Gaeans were apparently willing to resort to violence if it meant they got their little piece of Nortia, and I should've spoken out the day their emissaries had been so bold as to make their plans known. I should have done everything in my power to get to Nan—*Oh, Goddess, my Nan. When she finds out I'm missing, she'll bring the temple down around the Mantle's ears... unless, please, oh please, gods no. If Marcyn had done anything to her...*

Gasping, I broke the water's surface.

"Tommand, we have to go back!" I cried. I'd left without thinking about who else could be harmed. Not only Nan, but Kairus—what if Ozius had made it back to her? *And Cinden, oh, Cinden... was she a part of this all along?* I grabbed a towel and climbed out, heading toward the bed where my clothes lay over the footboard.

Tommand twisted on his knees and stood up, attempting to follow.

"Hold still!" Verrona yelled. "You'll rip!"

I grabbed the mauve dress and pulled it over my head, wrestling it over my still-damp body.

"Verrona, will you lace me?" I asked while sorting out the mass of thongs on my sandals, doing my best to quickly tie the left one securely under my knee.

"We need to talk, Diantha." Tommand's voice sounded nearer.

"I can't stop stitching now. Give me a few minutes. Tommand stop moving!"

"I don't know if we have a few minutes," I breathed, looking over my shoulder. Tommand, still attached to the thread and needle in Verrona's hand, was making his way in my direction, his skin pulled taut by the last stitch.

"Tommand, don't hurt yourself. I can't stand the thought of any more damage done in my name."

"This is not a level of pain I even register, and before we go anywhere, you and I are speaking—and you need rest."

A booming sound rolled in the distance, the rumble increasing in volume.

The hair on my arms rose, and I felt the desperate need to flee.

"Did you hear that?" The sound came again, this time closer. I looked at Tommand wide-eyed and fearful.

"The thunder?" he said, puzzled.

"That's thunder? Of course it is." I'd never been in an actual storm before. In Nortia, we only ever got snow showers or blizzards, though there were a few times I thought I'd heard thunder snow. On the way to Verus, it had only rained lightly a handful of times.

I went to the window and looked out. The rain was coming down sideways, and a flash, more radiant than anything I had ever seen before, shot down and split the sky. The only lightning bolt I'd ever seen was drawn in *Magika,* and just like the rendering, the bolt shattered in several forking lines. I dropped the curtain and pressed my back to the wall. I knew it was nothing I should be afraid of, but I couldn't seem to drop the shoulders that were now scrunched up around my ears.

"You two can stay here for the night, and I'll check on ya in the morning. Leaving in this storm would do nothing but cause your mount injury," Verrona said pragmatically. "There, done. Have her cut these out in four days' time."

"Thank you, Verrona, for everything. I will leave payment in the morning."

"What you paid last time would cover you for a month, Tommy. Rooms are to the right. I'll send up a few things."

Verrona collected the little bits and bobs she'd left out and deposited them on her desk before leaving. On her way out, Tommand and her exchanged a few words while I stayed planted up against the wall, listening for the next crash that would vibrate the wooden structure.

"Come with me." Tommand held out his hand as he came forward.

I took it and limped my way to the door with him, clutching my other sandal and his filthy shirt.

The room we were to stay in was nothing more than a closet but felt more secure to me, as it was situated in the interior of the building and had no windows. There was a low-to-the-ground bed shoved into the corner, and it was covered with a faded-down blanket. To its left was a small end table with a few books atop it, and—Goddess bless Verrona—folded up on a woven cane chair was a tan nightgown and fresh white shirt.

The walls rattled with the sudden bang of thunder.

I ran the short distance to Tommand, who was turning the dial on a small lamp. The light seemed to cast menacing shadows on the walls, adding fuel to my already anxious mind.

Strong arms tightened around my shoulders, and his rough beard rested on my forehead.

"This building has endured dozens, if not hundreds, of storms," he whispered soothingly. "It will still stand in the morning." I tucked myself tighter into him, and Tommand's lips grazed my earlobe as he rocked me gently back and forth. "I'll keep you safe." Lighting struck again, and within seconds the loudest crash of thunder yet shook the tavern on its foundation.

He *would* keep me safe. I felt the truth behind his words, felt his conviction in his embrace... but I wanted him to feel safe as well—feel cherished, feel supported, and appreciated.

I closed my eyes and took a chance. Seeking to relieve my desperation.

I slid my hands up the plane of his stomach and settled them on his chest.

"Eira, you need sleep."

I shook my head against him and took a step back. A roaring crash of thunder caused me to flinch, but instead of seeking his arms again, I stood before him, slid the mauve dress from my shoulders, and wiggled it over my hips until it fell.

"There is evidence, Tommand, that resting is not on your mind... just as it's not on mine." I returned to him, wrapping my arms around his neck and folding my nakedness into his warmth.

"And though it seems like I have no control over myself where you are concerned, I can assure you that I am an adult and can deal with a hard-on left dissatisfied. I would cause you no more pain Eira... to your body or your heart. We must speak."

I turned my head into his fuzzy chest and trailed my lips down the middle of his sternum. He smelled of cedar and of sweat, and of me. My breasts felt more sensitive the more aroused I became, and that blessed little pulse took up its steady beat deep within.

"I don't want you just for the sake of release, Tommand. I am so bereft, so at the end of my mental endurance, that I'm yearning for connection. I want to share myself with you and have you share yourself with me in return."

I heard not his usual low growl of pleasure, but something softer, different—a faint but contented purring hum.

Cat. I smiled against his chest and conjured a mental image of Evandr.

"I wanted to move in you that first night at dinner." Tommand put a hand on the back of my neck and tilted my head backward to look him in the eyes. "I wanted to shove your skirts past those plump hips and slip my cock into your heat." I let my hand drift down to stroke the arousal that strained against his pants and watched his pupils dilate to double their normal size. He smiled one of his sexy half-smiles, and a dimple appeared on his cheek. "And my want for you has only grown."

I moved both hands to the ties at his waist, noting one side was still broken from our earlier encounter. I freed him from his constraints and took his rigidness into my hand, which caused a drop of moisture to well up from the tip of his arousal. I whisked the bead up with my fingertip and placed it on the tip of my tongue. His eyes danced.

"Sit." He led me to the tiny bed. He lowered himself to his knees and untwisted the leather thong from around my calf. He ran his hands up my smooth legs, starting at my ankles and ending at my thighs.

"Do they feel strange to you?" I asked, wondering how he felt about the hairlessness.

"Your legs? Do you think I give a shit about whether or not you have hair when I am staring at the very evidence of you wanting me? I can see your moisture, your color deepening."

"Was there ever a question of my wanting you?"

Tommand responded by clasping his powerful hands to my hips and pulling me forward, the motion parting my thighs further.

"Will this be my fate every time it rains, Nortia?" He didn't move his gaze from my center.

"Only if there's lightning... *Cat,*" I said softly. Tommand's eyes flicked to mine. The corner of his nostrils flared, and the muscles of his neck and shoulders tensed. I bit my bottom lip, preparing for the warrior-king to emerge and take me as he had in front of Evandr, but Tommand shook his head and took a steadying breath.

"Then I'll pray at the feet of Vikto and beg him to never stop striking the ground."
He rubbed his beard against my inner thigh, and lightly bit my soft skin, being careful to
avoid my scrapes.

I felt the tickle of my wetness when he moved his lips closer to my heat.

"Tommand, wait."

He immediately sat back on his heels and looked up at me.

"I'm ready now. I don't want anything else. I need you in me. I want to feel you,
Tommand."

He exhaled slowly while I looked at his thickness, proudly standing between us.

"And I am greedy enough not to deny myself any longer."

Tommand continued to draw me forward, which dropped me off the edge of the bed.
I was left squatting over the tip of him, with the thick feathered mattress at my back and
my feet planted firmly on both sides of his thighs. He reached one hand between his legs
and jerked his pants below his sac, which propped his arousal up higher.

"Thank you, Tommand."

"You are thanking me for allowing us to fuck? Nortia, I swear to the Goddess, you are
without flaw." My elbows rested on the bed, putting my breasts at the level of his eyes.
Tommand clasped one hand around the base of his erection while the other stayed firmly
attached to my hip. "Take your time."

I poised myself atop his wide head and began lowering myself slowly. His erection
spread my walls, parting them for entry. I pressed my feet into the floor and pushed back
up when I felt the drier skin of his length pulling inside me.

"Damn." Tommand hissed through clenched teeth. I lowered myself again, this time
using the moisture I'd left behind to manage half of him before feeling the tug again.
"Gods, be damned."

I walked my feet out, widening my stance, and locked my gaze to his. I dropped down,
taking him in, inch by broad inch, until he was fully embedded and my tight little gem
pressed firmly into his pubic bone.

Tommand's head fell forward, and both his hands came to my hips, squeezing hard
while he sucked the air between his teeth. I gave him only a moment to adjust, before
grinding my hips against him, eliciting more of the divine contact between us. His eyes
closed briefly, and his lips parted.

"Eira, how ready are you?" He released a needy, impassioned groan, and I wanted to
hear the sound again and again.

I rotated my hips, grinding against him in a circular motion.

"You said to take my time," I breathed, enjoying the feel of my movements against him.

"You will take what I give you." He dropped his hands to my backside, and still within me, he tensed his thighs. I suddenly found myself on my back, sinking into the coverlet. He rested his weight on his elbows and looked down at me.

"Ready to begin?" he smirked. Tommand rocked his hips in the slowest series of strokes.

"Fuck, yes," I whispered, relishing the full, slick sensation. My eyes fluttered shut. I let my thighs fall as wide as they could go and wrapped my arms around his head to tug him closer. I wanted the warlord—the warrior. I wanted him to take my body to slake himself as hard and fiercely as he needed.

"Eyes on me, sweetheart. Let me see you." He pressed a kiss to my lips.

"Tom... use me."

He smiled against my mouth but maintained his steady pace.

"Do you know what I have wanted even more than this?" he said, pushing deeper on the last word. "That piercing, I want to take it in my mouth and draw on you until your flesh turns red."

I thrust my other breast toward his mouth.

"I suppose this one will do." He moved his hips more powerfully but maintained the frustratingly slow tempo.

His tongue flashed out and flicked the tight bud, then re-emerged to swirl ever so slowly around my areola. Now *this* was decadent. My breasts were so sensitive, I thought I could come just by this alone. Tommand sucked me into his mouth and caught my nipple between his teeth before letting his tongue drag across its tip.

"Your eager little cries are my undoing," he said seriously, looking down into my eyes.

I tilted my hips up and watched his brows snap together almost as if he were in pain.

"Put your hand on mine—guide me." I did as told, and he moved them between our bodies, moistening his fingertips in our shared dampness. "Show me." He laid his fingers lightly against my clitoris and slowed the motion of his hips, waiting for me to begin.

"Like this," I whispered. With my hand on top of his, we drew light circles and then I had him slide my tight bead between his pointer and middle fingers and squeeze ever so slightly while moving back and forth. "You take to your lessons well." Tommand repeated the action, and I wrapped my arms around his neck.

With his hand and hips working in unison, I laid my head back and allowed myself to simply feel all of the gratifying sensations he was providing. My passage swelled firmly around his member as if to keep him embedded.

"You feel incredible. Tight... so warm... " The more he said, the quicker I found myself nearer to rocking over the edge. "I knew it would be good, but Eira, it's even better than pushing my cock into your beautifully willing mouth... which up until now was the most outstanding fucking thing I've ever felt."

He dipped his hips and angled himself upward, the little change striking exactly where I desired it most.

I stretched up toward him, ran my tongue along the crease of his lips, and pushed my hips up off the mattress to meet his thrusts.

"Tommand? Will you take me harder?" I was so desperate for him.

"Fucking perfect."

He obliged.

Tommand took me faster, hammering me until all I could do was pant his name incoherently into the little room.

"Tom, I'm... *oh*!" I shouted. My orgasm broke over me swell after swell, cresting in a pure, rushing energy. "Go, go, keep going!" I floated away, lost in the intensity of what words couldn't adequately describe.

"That's it, darling. You have no idea what you do to me," he said tightly, shifting up to his knees and holding onto my hips, which strengthened the magnitude of my completion. With one last powerful drive, he pulled me against his body and sank himself deeply. He was beautiful, magnificent really, and the joy on his face as his fulfillment took hold was spectacular. It was like I witnessed his every tension release, all the pain leave his body. His expression was almost serene.

He pulled from me and pumped himself as he came. I felt the hot, thick streams splash onto my hip bone and watched as he spasmed one last time and fell to one elbow. He covered me with his body.

Breathing heavily, he looked up from where he was nuzzling my neck.

"You have the most beautiful eyes." He lightly kissed the corner of my mouth, "They shift between gray-blue and green," he kissed the apple of my cheek, "and the way your brow arches when you're vexed, it makes me want to destroy all that annoys you." He placed a little kiss on the bridge of my nose. "I could take you twice a day and never tire." He slid a finger down the curve of my cheek.

"Tommand, I—"

"Eira," he paused, his face going grim, his eyes boring a path to my soul. "My name is not Tommand..."

Chapter Thirty-Five

WHO THE FUCK?

I shoved against his chest, bracing myself for betrayal.

"What do you mean your name isn't Tommand?"

He backed away and sat at the foot of the bed. He took his dirty shirt from where it lay and ripped it in half, handing me the cleanest side. He wiped off his hip and hands and then tossed the scrap into the far corner of the room. The hot prickles that came with sudden fear worked their way across my chest and down my arms.

"What do you *mean* your name isn't Tommand?" I demanded again.

He turned to face me.

"It's Catommandus. It's why Evandr called me Cat."

"Catommandus?" The furious boil that gripped me in its angry heat died back to a simmer. "And why are you telling me this now? I really thought you were going to be like 'We just had sex, but by the way, I'm Wiltom Bigtree, a wheat farmer—and I don't come from Monwyn.'"

He didn't smile at my jest, just tossed me the clean nightgown before tying up his pants.

"No, I'm Monwyn," he said bleakly, rubbing his hands back and forth on his forehead.

"And are you the Protector of Monwyn?"

He raised his eyebrows and nodded his head wearily.

"I am," he breathed.

"And are you Ambrose's advisor and the Monwyn Emissary?" I asked.

"Yes."

"Then Tommand, Catommandus, Cat, Tom... Tomcat," I smiled sweetly and crawled next to his side, "why spoil a perfectly wonderful moment because your mother named you so... uniquely."

I pressed my mouth to the point of smooth skin above his scarred shoulder.

"Because I am tired of deception."

"As... as far as lies go, I'm not seeing the real harm here. Plenty of people don't like the name they're born with and go by something else."

I ran my hand across his chest, relishing the feel of him, until he captured it and held it still.

"Were that the worst of my sins," he murmured and stared ahead.

How thickheaded of me. I hadn't once stopped to think about how what happened at Verus might have affected him as an Emissary or as an Advisor. He took a Scion's life, and even a monarch-appointed Emissary would be called to task over the violation. I watched him press his hands to his temples.

"Tommand?"

"Yes?"

"I don't regret you." I swallowed and waited, anxious about what his reaction would be.

He faced me. The tension had left his forehead, but the skin under his eyes was still dark with fatigue.

"Eira, it's about Nortia and Mon—"

It was my turn to cut him off.

"Come here. Lay down." I stood and pulled the nightgown over my nakedness and sat at the head of the bed, crooking my finger at him. He obeyed and sat. I pulled him back by the shoulders and cushioned his head in my lap. "Close your eyes," I said, smoothing my hands over his brows. I leaned over his face, and he let his lashes fall to his cheeks.

"The Gaeans want you—"

"For land, I know, Tommand."

"For you, Eira," he said, drowsily.

I leaned down and silenced him by pressing my mouth to his soft lips while rubbing my fingers down his neck. Stopping before his injury, I massaged the tight tendons on either side, by pressing into the muscles deeply and moving my hands in small circles.

I treasured the intimacy we had finally shared, and despite his bizarrely timed admission, it had been a wonderful experience for me. I felt like he had really taken the time to listen to what I, and my body, had needed from him. I was still smiling, still feeling the high of satisfaction, and I wanted to stay in this afterglow for as long as possible. Tomorrow would come too soon, and we would have to sift through the mess of the day.

Already I'd formulated many questions for Tommand, but right now, after such heinousness, I wanted him surrounded by comfort, if just for a little while. In a matter of seconds, he'd made the choice to drop everything to bring me here. And while I think he knew I was actively trying to avoid his request for a conversation, I think he also understood that I needed some time. I just didn't have the ability to process it all right now.

I kneaded the rock-hard muscles of his shoulder, and he let out a groan of relief.

"Does it still hurt you?" I asked while tracing the bolt-like scar that ran from the top of his arm to his sternum.

His deep and even breaths told me he had fallen asleep, so I continued to run my hands lightly over his body and around his face, taking my time and enjoying the opportunity to do so. I trailed my finger down his proud nose and lingered on the slight bump at its center.

I let my knuckles skim his cheeks. I had been immediately attracted to the clean-shaven man, but so far I liked the way his bearded face felt against me and looked on him. I especially liked how the lighter hairs mingled with darker ones near his mouth. It made him look sun-kissed. The hair on his head was now about the length of the tip of my thumb to the first knuckle, and it was a rich brown with gold undertones. I couldn't be sure right now, but it also looked like it might curl. I could just imagine a severe-faced Tommand with a mass of curls running down his back. Goddess, even his ears made my stomach clench happily. His lobes were rounded and soft, and there was a little freckle on the outside ridge of his left ear and—

Two tiny pinprick scars where two piercings would have gone.

Two.

I bent lower and tilted his head gently, angling it to better catch the light. I hadn't counted wrong. Two tiny holes had been there at one time.

My stomach sank.

We sure did need to have a conversation.

I spiraled quickly out of control, thinking maybe this was why he'd put off joining with me. Did he have a wife back home? Goddess, I hoped not. For her sake and mine. I'd never willingly agree to become the other woman. Ambrose had said he hadn't been with anyone in years... but this little scar wasn't fake.

Yep. I was spiraling. Surely there was some sort of explanation, and I needed to think clearly and rationally to determine what it might be. Tommand had said he needed to speak about Nortia and Monwyn but also spoke of Gaea earlier. *I should have let him finish.*

Gaea wanted a piece of Nortia, and Tommand had said they'd vied for me personally at their meeting. What did Monwyn have to do with it? Their own piece of Nortia? That didn't make sense, but... I thought back to our previous conversations, mulling over every little word we'd spoken. Had there been something I'd missed, intentionally or otherwise? I sat staring at the wall until I landed on something Tommand had said in the dark, the night he had found me before the last Maneuvering: "I should have done my job better, Nortia. I should have encouraged Ambrose to do what he does best and fuck you until you were filled with only thoughts of him. But I failed."

Why would he have wanted me besotted with Ambrose? What had his job been... and how had I been so naïve to brush it off and not questioned him further?

My heart sank. Wife in Monwyn or entangled in some plot like the Gaeans, the reality was I'd left the temple in the care of a man whom I truly didn't know. I hadn't had the time to get to know him. Instead of letting something progress naturally, I went all Nortian woman and found "my man" and sank my claws in deep. Now, here I was, staring at the evidence of his double life. Just the same as the temple wasn't what I thought it was, it turned out that neither was he.

"*Keep faith only in those who earn it.*" Mariad's words.

Had Tommand, or, Catommandus, or whoever he was, earned my faith? Or had he thinly veiled the truth, staying just this side of outright deception the entire time? Had I let my infatuation blind me from seeing what was plainly in front of me? Did this powerful, attractive, and worldly man truly desire me, or was there something else he wanted?

I saw two choices before me. I could wake Tommand this instant and hash out his deceit and try to conclude if I was another pawn in some wealthy man's bid for dominance. But by doing so, I'd risk being subdued by his physical strength. Alternatively, I could leave now and head south on my own. Neither of my choices appealed to me, but I was pretty sure this was another instance of me learning the hard way. This time the lesson of the parable was that the only person I could have true faith in... was me.

My decision was made.

I shook Tommand lightly.

Regret seized me the instant his sleep-hazed eyes opened.

"Verrona gave me a tincture to keep you from getting an infection." I rested his head back on the pillow before walking across the tiny floor.

"Drink this, all of it." I put the tincture to his lips and then tipped the other to my tongue and took a swig before turning out the lamp.

"Eira?"

"Mmhmm?"

"I am in love with you. I have never known such peace."

"Tommand we haven't known each other for—"

"I realize that... but I know my mind and what I feel. And I have *never* been afraid of love—just the consequences that come from loving."

I lay down beside him and pulled him close, the pain in my soul outstripping that of the physical blows I'd been dealt.

At worst the abortifacient would make him severely ill—I hoped—or maybe it would do nothing at all. Whatever his reaction to it, I prayed it wouldn't cause him permanent damage and that it would buy me enough time to put a solid distance between us.

··◆)(◆··

Sneaking out of the inn had been easy. Tommand woke an hour or so after he'd fallen asleep asking for water. His skin had been so clammy and damp that I hadn't feigned my worry over him, and, under the guise of fetching him a drink, I walked right out the front door.

Tears continued rolling down my cheeks even after an hour atop the dun stallion. It was so dark that not a soul could see me, so I let them flow. Besides, they'd be indistinguishable from the sympathetic drops the storm-wetted trees were shedding. I was soaked to the bone.

And I deserved the discomfort.

Tonight, I'd become everything the temple had desired me to be.

When I left the inn, I made the choice to turn left at the statue at the center of town. Even though I didn't follow the traditions as devoutly as others, I'd paused briefly to ask the Goddess for strength.

I wouldn't go back to Verus.

Without knowing the outcome of the altercation, it wasn't safe, so I would head south.

My journey was slow going. The rain had muddied the dirt path to the point where the horse's hooves made a squelching sound when we went any faster than a trot, so I was careful not to let the horse have too much slack. Regardless of the conditions, we pressed forward at a consistent clip.

"Well, horse, it's me and you... and maybe little Ambrosia, though probably not."

Holy shit.

There was another layer I hadn't thought through. Were I with child, I'd need to get somewhere safe sooner rather than later. Then there was the matter of the temple. I'd imagine Verus would spend significant resources to pursue the lost Troth who possibly carried a child who could claim the highest seat of authority on the continent. Though I eventually would want to, right now, I could see no safe way to let Verus know of my current whereabouts or where I was headed.

"You know, horse, this could've been different. I could have let Tommand actually talk like he wanted, but I was thinking with what's between my legs and not with what's in my head."

The dun knickered.

"Right? Not my best moment. And come to think of it, I've thought that way a couple of times. The last man I was with—who happens to be friends with the one I was with a few hours ago—I just needed him for a no-frills, quick in-and-out, but this vagina of mine had her own agenda."

I patted the horse's withers, and water bounced off his coat. He was as wet as I was, and considering the conditions he'd traversed for probably two hours at this point, I wanted to stop soon and let him rest.

"Horse, I may need to reassess how I interact with men." I stroked the mane that I couldn't see very well in the dark. *I bet I could braid it just like Ambrose's.* "He has hair the same color as yours, too." The horse didn't respond. "Do you have a name?" I squeezed a stream of water from the end of his soaked mane. "I think I'll call you Ambrose then. You're both strong and pretty and are both decent company. I just hope you're less dramatic."

I chatted with Horse Ambrose for what must have been a couple more hours, and I began regretting my life's choices once again. I was cold, I was hungry, and I was falling asleep in the saddle. I had to stop soon or I'd become a danger to myself, and I knew the consequences of injuring my mount. Survival meant staying safe and thinking with a clear head.

Eventually, I found a spot that looked promising. In my sandaled feet, I hopped off the horse and squashed down into the thick and shit-smelling mud, which splattered the hem of my long, thin nightgown. I led the horse onto the wet but more stable grass and walked him between the dense pines that lined the road. The morning light was dawning, and the faint outlines of tree trunks and boulders and thickets became easier to see. Ahead, I spotted a short outcropping, and though it wouldn't shield me from another storm if one blew in, it would keep me hidden from riders that might be traveling the road. I tied off Ambrose on a stout limb, with enough slack that he could munch on what was left of the green grass in the area.

With a few handfuls of fallen pine needles, I fashioned what I hoped would be a passable bed. It wasn't. My makeshift mattress compressed the moment I lay on my side, and the moisture of the damp ground seeped through the fabric I wore.

And to think I could have been a Gaean queen.

·····+·)((+·····

My eyes opened and I stared up at a cloudless sky.

Evandr was dead.

Castor was dead.

Mariad, who knew?

And Tommand...

I'd woken often while I tried to rest, startled by every rustling sound or rumble of thunder in the distance. Every time I woke, no matter how much I willed it, nothing changed. I was still here, they were still—I couldn't finish the thought.

My body was stiff from too many days of rough treatment. Sleeping on the ground had only added to my discomfort. My bruises ached, my scratches burned, and another, more sensitive part of me was a little sore as well... but I didn't want to dwell on that for fear of crying my way to Solnna.

I needed to get up and get moving.

"Ambrose, let's see what's in those bags, shall we?"

Both of the leather bags that hung over his sides were stamped with the royal crest of Monwyn.

First, I found a good-sized knife with a sturdy, functional sheath. The blade was about the size of my hand, and I felt like it would be useful in all manner of situations. I reached in again and pulled out... another knife. This one was so small I could almost keep it hidden in my closed fist. I dug around once more, reaching into the bottom of the bag, and produced a length of rope, followed by—*oh, bless Reed*—a package of salted beef.

I dropped everything to the ground and went to investigate the other bag.

My first find was a gray cap. It was a tightly-knit piece of nalbinding made of warm wool and would fit snugly to the head. It could conceal my hair or keep me warm on colder nights.

Next, my hand clasped around a roll of fabric and—

The smell of cedar wafted from the garment. The scent ripped through me like shards of ice, and I had to close my eyes to stave off the despair that settled within me. I buried my head into the dark gray cloth and gave myself just a moment to grieve.

"You know, I poisoned him, Ambrose... and then he told me he loved me."

I rubbed my head on the horse's sun-warmed back.

"Do I love him back?" I looked into the horse's dark, round eyes.

"Well, I might have said maybe a day ago, probably yes last night, but can you fall in love with a man in a few weeks' time? Turns out, I didn't even know his real name."

Shaking out the fabric of the tightly rolled tube revealed a fresh pair of pants.

"Bless you, Derros. Bless you, Mossius."

Shoving my hands in one a last time, the small flask I drank from yesterday fell out of its black linen pouch. I retrieved the vessel to replace it in its bag, but as I did, the bag unfolded, and I stared at the chest support gifted to me by Kairus.

Unable to wait, I tossed off the stained and dirty nightgown, stuffed myself into the pants, and tied the support to my chest. Tommand must have found it during our escape. *Bless you, Tommand.* For a little more warmth and coverage, I used the smallest blade to cut off the bottom of the borrowed nightgown. Removing the last two feet of material lessened the odor of the foul mud that had dried into its hem. Feeling more confident by the minute, I braided my hair into two tight braids that ran down the sides of my head and flipped their tails up into the woolen cap, which I tugged down over the tops of my ears.

I let Horse Ambrose graze for a little while, and then it was time to set off alone into the wilds of Ærta. Together we stepped onto the road and headed Goddess-knew-where. My thought was that if we just kept to the highway, we would eventually land somewhere. I just hoped it wasn't Monwyn. Explaining to the gatekeeper why I had Tommand's horse and yet no Tommand would be an issue. I wanted to avoid that place altogether.

It was another several hours of travel before I began encountering others on the road. None of them were mounted so I assumed, prayed, I would come upon a village soon. I should probably have been more wary of the strangers, but having never spent any length of time truly by myself, I was comforted just knowing humanity was near.

"Good afternoon," I said to a woman carrying an apron full of apples. "Would you happen to know how far it is to the next town?"

She eyed me suspiciously and backed up several feet.

"I'm heading from Verus to Monwyn" I pointed to the crest on the saddle bag, "and need to stop and water my animal." The lies rolled effortlessly off my tongue.

She looked me up and down and narrowed her puffy eyes, clutching the hem of her apron tighter to her chest.

"Y'aint fah," she said tonelessly.

I nodded and went on my way, wishing not to cause her any further distress.

The town I eventually rode into was not as charming a village as Stormridge had been. This place must have been too far from Verus to reap the benefits of the prestigious site. All of the buildings were weather-beaten and dreary. Many had no coverings over their windows or signs that indicated the trade they plied. There was a small stone temple near the center of the town that looked like it had once been cared for, I could see the remains of old dried flowers through its broken glass window and remnants of red paint on its short foundation. But now, its roof was in great disrepair, only one side of the thatching was still intact, and that looked to be held on only by the overgrowth of the moss that covered the longstraw and reed.

Refocusing on my mission and less on the place itself, I searched for an establishment to barter for provisions. I'd gone through half the dried beef on the way here, and furthermore, Ambrose would need something more than grass if I wanted to keep him healthy enough for the journey we were embarking upon.

Up ahead, there were a few stalls lining the road. The first I could see sold gourds and seeds. The second, small blades, in the form of a few blunt-looking knives, and some wooden arrows. The third space seemed to have no wares, but a woman stood behind the wooden counter leering straight at me.

As Horse Ambrose and I neared, the townsfolk glared openly in distrust and shrank back, literally walking to the other side of the dirt street to avoid me. I tossed a leg over the saddle and hopped to the ground, hoping that would put them at ease.

I went to the weapons merchant first.

"May the Goddess bless you today. I'm interested in procuring a bow and some of the fine arrows you're selling."

Just like the woman clutching her apples, the squat lady behind the open-air counter scrutinized me well before speaking.

"It fity fur them arrows, ain't got no bow," she replied, continually flicking her eyes to the horse behind me.

"And would you be willing to barter? I have a well-made hand knife—"

"I gots knives aplenty. It's the king's gold or nuthin," she hurled back, looking insulted that I'd even made the query.

I nodded, making sure to keep my face pleasant.

"Are there any shops around that would take items in exchange for coin?"

She spun on her heel, dramatically looking to her left and then right, and then leveled me with a look that made Nan's harshest stare seem as sweet as a harp seal.

"Don't see none." She crossed her arms over a shawl that she'd kept closed by lacing a thick thread between the chewed moth holes that dotted it.

I nodded and led Ambrose to the next stall.

"I'll take 'at horse fur all me punkins," the grandmotherly merchant hissed through a mouthful of broken teeth.

"I'll pass on the offer, but thank you."

I continued on, surveying what looked to be a multitude of abandoned buildings. There had to be someone in this place who would willingly take something off me in exchange for currency. The tiny knife was better quality than any of the wares I'd just passed.

Another mature-looking woman with thinning hair walked by, giving me a wide berth.

"How far is it to the southern road?" I questioned, praying that there even was one. The thought of trudging through animal-infested forests, or worse, human-infested ones, was daunting. Last night, when mulling over my plan, taking the off-road approach seemed to be my best bet, but today, I kept recalling the speech Tommand gave before the First Maneuvering—Highwaymen who often made their homes deep in the woods were not to be trifled with.

"It be three days on 'at horse." She settled her bug-eyed gaze on Ambrose and then fled at a quick clip.

Three days!

The conviction that had bolstered me this morning was quickly collapsing, and I was left only with a pile of despair. I walked to the far edge of town and sat on a porch that was barely attached to a partially crumbled building. I couldn't go three days without food or a way to procure it. I couldn't even find water for my horse in this place.

Quiet footfalls approached me from behind. I spun, rising fast to my feet.

A striking woman, tall with a broad face and wide, straight shoulders, looked down at me.

"You are in need of coin? We don't trade here, but there is one place where you can earn it." Her voice was lower-pitched and lacked the very noticeable accent the others had shared.

"And where would that be?" I asked, suddenly as cautious as the others had been toward me. I moved closer to Ambrose.

"My place. The Shaft."

"And The Shaft is?"

"Your way out of here," she said, inclining her head to the open road. "There is nothing else between here and the road south—which I understand is your destination."

I stared back, offering no information.

"In about three hours' time, the boys come back. If they find you on the road, you'll wish you had never stepped foot in this town... *and* that horse becomes their dinner for the next month."

I swallowed and studied the owner of The Shaft, looking for any sign that would prove her a liar. I saw no flickering pulse, no sideways glances, no shrugs or ticks... nothing.

"You can stare at me as long as you like, but when the fellas return from their dig, they have gold in their pockets and you will be safe. Nobody, and I mean nobody, messes with Demma's gems."

Oh. Welp. Sex work. It wasn't a crime in any of the kingdoms that I knew of and was seen as a reliable way to make a living for many of the lower classes. And I didn't judge others for their work, but having had sex a whopping two times, I didn't think it was for me.

"You wouldn't have to fuck a single one unless you wanted to. You would be enough of a draw just serving drinks. As you may have noticed, the ladies here are a bit long in the tooth and not so... conventionally attractive. The younger girls tend to leave fast, hoping to catch the eye of a Monwyn or Verus soldier."

My heart sped up.

"I hadn't realized we were standing on Monwyn soil."

She narrowed her eyes and cocked her head to the side thoughtfully.

"You don't stand on *any* kingdom's land. The mountain folk don't answer to any sovereign... even though *all* of the monarchs think we do." She winked. "I have a place to keep him safe and a room that will be yours until you wish to leave. You in?"

I rubbed my palms roughly against my face, attempting to scrub away my growing exhaustion. If what she said was even remotely true, my chances of safety and survival would be better here until I could equip myself properly. Plus, the odds of outrunning a drunken debauchee were much higher than getting away from a gang of filthy lechers on an open road.

"Let's head to The Shaft," I said.

The madam sized me up.

"I'm Demma. Don't trust another soul around here except for me. I'll keep you fully intact... because you're going to make me a fortune."

Intact.

Ugh.

Chapter Thirty-Six

THE SHAFT

That's where you find gems

I followed Demma, who took us around the back of the buildings and walked us right into the forest. I had almost decided to bolt, thinking I'd made a seriously poor decision when I made out a little grouping of itty-bitty cottages about fifty paces in front of me. They'd been blocked from my view by the dilapidated facade of the broken town and sandwiched in between dense trees.

Demma glanced around. "Don't be fooled by what you see. The men here are rough, but if, by the grace of the Goddess, a woman decides to join lives with one of them, he will do everything to keep her in comfort, be it lie, murder, steal... or build her a charming little cabin. The married ones live there." She pointed to the small homes.

"Do all the men work? Are there mines near?" I asked, truly curious about what they 'dug.'

"Nearly all. They dig for copper and nickel about a day south of here, but it's the annabergite where they get most of their money. It's a pretty green crystal that grows around the copper deposits. You can pass it off as malachite to the undiscerning... or those needing to make an impression on the cheap."

We walked back behind the town, staying close to the backsides of the buildings until Demma stopped at a big, yellow door where a young man sat by himself on an old stump.

"Jothaniel, this is our new gal..." She looked at me and paused.

"Diantha," I said so smoothly I nearly convinced myself of the new name.

Jothaniel, a pimply-faced youth, peered out under the brim of his beige flat cap.

"Hi," he smiled sweetly and went right back to whittling down a blank for a wooden spoon.

"Jothaniel, she is a lady... *a new gem*," Demma emphasized exasperatedly.

The young man blinked into the tall madam's face, and like he'd been struck on the head, he jumped up and bent his had-to-be-nearly-seven-foot frame into some awkward semblance of a bow.

"Oh! Hi... Miss! Welcome tah The Shaft. You gots bags?" The gangly, extraordinarily tall youth whipped off his cap, revealing a thin mop of grungy hair.

"Thank you, Jothaniel. I just have Ambrose here." I leaned back and smiled.

"Take the horse and see him fed and watered, put him in with my nag, and see that not a soul gets near either. Tell the new girl the policy." Demma's voice was deadly serious.

"Yep, if a man er woman gets in spittin' distance, I wallop 'em."

"And wallop them soundly. Come on." She turned to me and motioned me through the door.

I handed off the reins.

"Jothaniel, can you bring the saddlebags to my room when possible?"

"Yep..." He stood there just waiting, bobbing his head.

"O-okay, you can go now," I stuttered.

The boy smiled and turned, leading away my only reliable way out of town.

The hallway we walked down opened abruptly into a large room. It looked nothing like any brothel I'd ever imagined. I expected something like the small rooms of the Fourth Maneuvering... beds, nude paintings, dark corners where seedy people could hide their seedy deeds. *Don't judge, Eira. That isn't you.*

Bathtubs had never occurred to me, and yet, as I counted, there were eight hand-beaten copper tubs lined up on either side of a raised stage, much like the one the Vaughns had sat on during their lesson. I followed Demma further in. The walls had been painted burnt-orange, and hundreds of copper mugs hung glittering above a line of casks and kegs on a shelf behind a large counter. I saw a cluster of folks huddled at the bar, cleaning taps and washing down the walls.

"Gems, this is Diantha. She'll be working the floor tonight."

Five faces turned in unison.

"Demma, all them fools'll want to pump their pickles in that 'en." Said a brunette with saggy, pock-marked jowls.

"Look at the fat ass on 'er! I'll have tah stuff my skivvies twice as much tah make a coin!" The tallest of the gems came around the bar and bent over me. "You got teeth?" he asked while pulling at my lip with long fingers that smelled of lye.

A loud *bang* stopped all conversation, and every head in the room, including mine, swiveled to the madam, who'd slammed a copper kettle down on the wooden bar.

"Listen up, the lot of you! *Tonight* her job is to get them up so you lot can get them off. Do you understand?" Demma nodded at each of her employees.

Two of the gems behind the bar smiled widely as the others whooped in excitement.

"Now that changes things."

"It's gonna be busy!"

"I might make enough to get Sed a healer!" said a slimmer fellow with a gappy but genuine smile. Sizing them up, it looked like Demma's gems would cover a wide array of tastes.

"And maybe Lenap would finally say yes! If I got'er a new pot and silverware, she'd polish me ole knob for the rest of mah life!"

"Slow down!" Demma shouted at her crew. "We won't make a bit of gold if she's dressed like a Monwyn military reject. You all tell her the business while I figure out what to put her in." She pointed a finger directly at my chest. "Diantha, I'll shout when I'm ready for you to come up."

The madam took off her hat, which she'd pinned to a white linen cap tied under her chin, and hung it behind the bar. A mass of red curling locks tumbled to her waist. They were the most distinct, bright, flame-red I had ever seen. The Gaean Obligates would have been awash in envy.

"Now get to work." With hands on her narrow hips, Demma smiled at her team and then made her way up the back steps.

"I'm Phillden. Come on over," said the tall man who'd examined my teeth. He led me over to a yellowing couch placed against the back of the stage. I sat dutifully, and the others followed.

"When the fellas come in, first thing we do is strip 'em down. Don't go mixin' up their clothes 'cause they need 'em back. Next, we gotta get 'em in a tub. Ya followin'?"

"Take clothes, get them in a tub," I repeated.

"Then we gonna scrub them boys, 'til they 'bout bleed. They like nuthin' more than gettin' clean after four days of diggin'."

I nodded again. So far this wasn't terrible. I could scrub some people.

"Now here's where *you* come in... ya sing er dance?"

"I don't dance well, no, and the songs I know are, well... I know a few songs."

"Ack! Ya in't got to do nothin' fancy up there!" The pock-marked gem said ear-splittingly loud. "Ya just get up there and act like yur hidin' the gopher!" She laughed and slapped me on the shoulder. "You've boarded the beef, yes? Had yur wheat ground before?"

"Twice... I've had sex twice," I giggled at her hilarious innuendo.

"Thrice? That'll do! The thrice time is about the same as tha fortieth tah be honest. I'm Xillyna," she screamed.

Phillden caught my eyes and tapped on his ear, indicating she was hard of hearing.

I spoke up loudly, "Thank you for the advice Xillyna!"

She smiled merrily, bobbing her head up and down.

A thin gem, the one who had mentioned getting someone to the healer, spoke up softly.

"You'll work them up to the point they are foaming at the mouth. Ply them with drink, *nether*, sit on their faces if you think they'll hand over more coin. Let them remove an item of your clothing, but only if they pay up first. As Ms. Demma said, you don't have to bring none of them to completion. Just know, it's our livelihoods, and we all got loved ones who rely on your performance. I go by Lykksome."

"*Lykksome*? Ha!" The name was a play on that of the goddess Lykksun. It was a bit blasphemous but quite clever. Lykksome smiled and wiggled a fine brow suggestively. They had a thin smile and keen, hazel eyes and wore a silky robe of cream. I could see a red tattoo covering part of the left side of their chest and noticed that, like Demma, they also spoke without the local accent.

"Now yah ain't gonna run hide if a man pops his top down here, are yah? Sometimes they go off like a blown cask before we can get'em up the stairs. Ain't their faults really, depends on how ya scrub 'em— an' how long it's been for em'!" Xillyna pushed her way in front of Lykksome.

The mental images these folks could paint was almost too much.

"How much do you think we can make tonight?" I asked, deliberating my answer.

"After Demma counts it all up and parses it out by seniority, I'd say somewhere in the realm of twenty-five pieces for you being new." Lykksome pushed Xillyna back out of their way.

Okay, I'll stay here for two days, maybe three. I can buy some arrows and a few provisions and pocket the extra for emergencies.

"I won't hide," I said confidently, trusting my temple lessons to see me through.

"Good. Now, that over there is Sed. She don't talk anymore since she started gettin' frail, but if yah run in tah trouble she'll get help. Always looking out, she is." I waved to Sed who waved back and smiled warmly. She did look worn, with dull, yellow hair and sallow skin. "And that's Merton, he's the best of us but has been here the shortest," Phillden filled me in.

"It's nice to meet you, Merton."

"Likewise... are you Solnnan?" asked the heavy-set but easily healthiest-looking person I'd seen so far.

"Yes, I'm headed back home in a few days' time," I half-lied—as Assigned Obligate, it *was* my new home.

Merton blinked slowly.

"The lack of hair under your arms will be another allure this evening."

"Really?" I asked drawing my mouth in a confused grimace.

"Anything differing from the norm will make us money," he said.

"Anything not rottin' will make us money, Merton," piped up Phillden, who scratched at an awful-looking patch on his arm.

"Diantha! Come up," Demma yelled from the second floor.

I jogged up the steps to the upper level, leaving my new companions behind. There were a few beds and several couches covered in thin sheets scattered about, all of them separated by cloth panels that hung from the ceiling.

"In here," she beckoned from behind one of two doors on the right side of the second level.

The room was small and clean and had a little window that let in some natural light. A lamp, holding a couple hours of oil, sat on a small table, and a cane chair sat next to it, opposite a small iron bed.

"You'll not find any bugs here. We keep a clean establishment, and I expect you to go wash before you dress. Pardon my saying so, but you smell like shit."

"Horse shit." I pulled my mouth in a sheepish grin and nodded my understanding. Though I couldn't smell it anymore, I knew it had to be pungent.

"Get undressed and let me see you."

Without hesitation, I pulled off my nightgown and chest support and stood before the madam while unlacing my pants. She was *sure* to have seen more than her share of nude bodies.

"Oh, that's gonna drive them wild." She looked down at my chest, "are you some kinda spoilt royal running away from family troubles?"

"No, I'm surely not," I laughed, amazed at the differing opinions this piercing seemed to garner.

"Well, they don't need to know that. We'll let them think they're getting a chance to plow the field of a Monwyn princess, then look out! I bet I get some old customers back," she exclaimed. Demma began holding up different items of clothing, chucking some onto the bed and others onto the chair. "Don't let them get their teeth around that, though.

They'll rob you blind. You won't even know it's gone." She didn't look up but continued, "I think with your dark hair we'll go with the purple—oh... hold on." Her eyes landed on the brand at my hip, and she froze. "Now, I am clearly not one to dictate how people live their lives, but hun, if they find out you're here, they *will* shut me down. How in all the nether did you get out of Verus?" she said, her voice dropping to a whisper.

"I escaped at the command of a Devotee, and I'm headed to the one place that I'll be safe." Tears stung at the backs of my eyes. For a moment, I regretted telling her the truth, but I needed her to understand how consequential all of this was. "Demma, please don't kick me out... please. I can't say more, but I will *not* cause any issues."

Demma wrung her hands on a blue scrap of lace no doubt pondering the choice between making money or remaining secure.

"I can offer you two days, but no more. You know they'll be on your trail, probably already are, and every time those guards come through here, somebody always gets into a tangle." She paced the floor of the little room, tapping the tip of her elbow with her index finger.

"I understand. Two days, and if you have any type of cosmetics, I'll cover this up and keep it hidden."

"Go bathe and get ready. I'll figure something out." Demma nodded, but her forehead was still creased in concern.

···→)⚬(←···

I sunk down into the copper tub quickly after removing my borrowed robes, hiding my brand under the water. All the gems were bathing as well, chatting happily together about the night to come, except Sed, who of course made her preparations in silence.

Phillden had decided to wear a pair of soft, leather small clothes, with the back cheeks cut out to reveal his best feature. Xillyna had decided on a gossamer dress with feathers around the neck. She said they would "keep her chicken skin hidden." I didn't hear about what the others had chosen because I'd just dunked my head under the near-boiling water.

"Why is the water so hot?" I asked, popping back up and looking at my arm which had gone as red as a boiled she-crab.

"After the fourth or fifth person has their use of it, you still want it to have a bit o' heat or it lessens the chance of more getting in," explained Merton, "cold baths aren't all that relaxing."

"That makes sen—wait, how many people do you expect to be here tonight?" I asked, taken aback at the idea of more than three people per tub.

"About forty, forty-five, give or take." Merton, whose belly rose above the tub's edge, leaned back and closed his eyes.

"Forty-five. That's, like," I counted on my fingers, "nine people each." I'd been under the false impression that ten, maybe fifteen customers would have been a full house for an evening. "So I'm supposed to simulate sex, on a couch, in front of like fifty people?"

I started feeling queasy.

"That a problem?" Merton eyed me out of the single eye he'd opened.

"Nope, not a problem... no problems here." I stood and backed out of the tub butt first, and made my way back up the stairs.

Lying on the creaky bed, I stared up at the ceiling wishing I had some cream to rub into my itchy, dry skin. Before the temple, I'd thought my life boring and average, but I saw now how very fortunate I was to have grown up ensconced in the bosom of means and protection. These people were doing all they could to get by.

"Little Ambrosia... I know you don't exist... but if we make it out... Mama will have some colorful tales about your beginnings." I patted my stomach.

I got up and grabbed the garment Demma had laid out for me. It was in three parts. The first layer was an apricot-colored set of strings. Literally, it was entirely made from flat ribbons that had been sewn to each other. It took me more time than it should have to figure out how to get my legs in, and once on, I felt absolutely silly. One string went down the crack of my butt and split in two under my crotch. On the other side, the two pieces *Y*'ed out, framing my vulva. Both the butt string and the vagina bits met an extremely wide belt of the same shiny material, which sat around my lower stomach and hips. It just barely covered the bottom point of my brand and made it look more like a freckle than a modification. From the belt, a series of strings spread upwards along my stomach, connecting to two hollowed-out, boob-sized circles. My breasts just hung out of the openings, which themselves, were connected to two thin gold chains that slipped up over my head and around my neck.

Layer two was a teal-blue skirt that tied at my waist, just above the hip belt. It was made of two flowy panels that hung to the floor and split at each of my hips. The third layer was a thigh-length sleeveless tunic of the palest sky blue. It had to be some of the finest silk I'd ever touched, it was so soft and transparent. Its hem had been stamped in an orangey flower blossom print, and gold threads ran along each of its seams. Demma had instructed me to keep this layer on until I had the attention of all the bathers. I wore my hair long, pushed straight back from my forehead, and painted my lips pink. I outlined my eyes heavily in kohl and added a little goldy-brown powder to my eyelids.

Demma stepped inside the room with her hands tucked behind her back.

"You look lovely. I used to wear that when I performed, many years ago. Some of the old guys may remember it... well, the two of them that aren't buried."

She brought her hands from around her back and held up two small mugs.

"The house is full, and more people are coming in by the minute—Jothaniel went around when the workers came back and told them all about the new lady with the 'adequate childbearin' hips,'" Demma laughed while I cringed.

"Hey, can I ask you something?"

"Sure."

"Why does everyone seem so sickly around here... so frail?"

Demma compressed her lips, nodding while I spoke.

"It has to do with the mines. Something about what they're pulling up down there, or how they do it. Catches up with all of them eventually, then spreads to those they have contact with. Hardly anyone can afford to uproot or are willing to leave behind their ailing relatives, but those that do get out do everything they can to hitch their horses to richer wagons. This town provides nothing more than a rough life and rougher death." *How awful to have to choose between your future and your family.*

"And no kingdoms, no Obligates have stepped up to help?" I asked.

"They all form their opinions and then look the other way when they get their resources." Demma handed me a mug and two puffy fabric flowers, one blue and the other the color of apricots. I downed the glass in one go, and she pinned the flowers in the hair above my ear. "Perfect. Now get ready to make Mama some cash!" she said exuberantly.

···+)⊃(+···

I heard my audience well before I saw them. I stood still and listened to their deep voices, the cheers, and the bantering of people deep in their cups. If Kairus could sing for a bunch of drunks, I could do this. *Kairus, if you can hear me, send me some of that strength, please.*

Demma began her introduction.

"Fellas!" the crowd cheered. "Have you ever been down in the pits and thought to yourself... 'I sure wonder what it would be like to place my prick in the cunny of some lady's royal rump?'"

The mass of males smacked their copper mugs against whatever surface was near and noises reminiscent of wolves howling at the moon sailed up the stairs.

My stomach got all fluttery, and my heart began hammering. I could feel my pulse not only in my chest but in my neck and hands as well. *Control it, Eira. This is just the next step to get where you're going.*

"Well, we here at The Shaft, are all about making your dreams come true, so would you give a rowdy welcome to the Majestic Mountains of Monwyn!" Demma's voice roared out over the frenzied throng.

Think sexy, Eira. Think about walking into a room and Tommand's there, wearing nothing but his smile... and also that he's not a filthy liar... and also that he wasn't some stupid Protector.

I took my first step down, descending the staircase in my purple-studded sandals.

The roar that greeted me was deafening. I almost ran back up the steps.

This was not forty-five people.

A multitude of stark-naked men were waiting in line for their baths. Most held their clothes in one hand and a drink—or two—in the other.

"Take it off!" one patron yelled before I'd even made my way to the bottom of the stairs.

I stopped and snapped my head around to look the man dead in the eye. *You just helped me choose my narrative.*

The crowd silenced, and only the sound of scrubbing and sloshing water could be heard.

"You will wait until *I* have made that decision, do you understand?"

I flung back the hair that had come to rest over my shoulder.

"Yes ma'am!" another patron called out. I focused in on him.

I sashayed my way over to the rawboned male, whose back Sed was scrubbing. She had dressed in a short leather dress, whose bodice was cut below her small, but pert breasts.

"Oh, how I do appreciate a man with manners, would you assist me?" I batted my lashes and sat on the edge of his tub.

"I'll do whatever yah want if'n I can take a gander at that fine pussy yah got... um, please, ma'am."

"Well, my handsome friend, I simply can't seem to unlace this leather. For a coin, you could help me out," I simpered.

The man hauled himself momentarily over the other side of the tub in order to retrieve a coin from his boots, showing off his boney little butt and brown puckered hole.

"Two coins for both." He returned with the gold in his hand.

"Why you sweet soul... what a man!" I slowly brought my leg up and propped my foot on the tub's edge.

Eagerly, he began unraveling.

I allowed his hands to linger briefly on the still-soft leg before setting it back down on the floor.

"Fellas, she ain't got no hair. Smooth as a tit!" he blurted to the crowd, who seemed to be closing in on me.

"Eh! Leave something for the rest o' us! I gots plenty of coin."

The shouts started to compound.

"Yah want my house? You can have my house if yah walk me up them stairs. Damn it all to the nether! Let me hump yah right here. The boys won't mind if we do it, will ya?"

When Sed's hand started working its way under the water, I patted the patron on the head and walked toward the stage, where the musty old couch had been placed.

"I'll tell you what, gentleman: if you'll be my drums, I'll sing you a little song that I think you might like." Having made my way up, I perched on the rolled arm of the dingy couch and started to clap my hands. The crowd joined right in, minus some of the more inebriated patrons who were off-beat or who currently couldn't lift their arms.

I can make this work.

I opened my mouth.

Nortian girls, they like it slick,
but be warned boys, they'll freeze your pricks!
Monwyn ladies, it's said they're pretty,
but you won't ever see them titties!
Gaean woman, just hang it on up,
you can look, but do not touch!
Solnnan girls will give you love,
but they'll scorch your dicks and burn your tongue!
Lad, get yourself a Nortian gal!

The mob went mad as the ditty—one my friends and I would never have let our parents catch us singing—came to a close.

Several coins landed on the stage.

I had their attention.

"Wait! I have an idea. If a coin lands down my tunic," I pulled the keyhole neckline out as far as I could, "I'll be obliged to take it off."

I hopped up on the center of the couch and tossed back my head.

"Ready? Got them in your hands? One, two, three!"

A metallic rain fell down around me. I felt the plunk of several coins on my chest and others hit my face and arms.

"Well, that was quite a load!" *Oh, Goddess... so gross of me.* I laughed out loud at how ridiculous I'd sounded, but the crowd ate it up. They were stamping and clanking and shouting and carrying on, slapping their buddies on their bare backs.

"You promised!" came a shout, followed by a million voices echoing the same.

"I did, and a Monwyn lady *always* keeps her promises." I watched a new round of men hop into the tubs and others dry off, still staring as they went to stand around the perimeter of the room.

"Have you fellas ever seen what a Monwyn woman gets when she's ready... to be taken?"

"A prize dog?" A drunken voice slurred.

"No, dumbass... a pretty dress?" a portly man suggested.

"A groom?" another shouted.

"No, no, I'll show you." Without missing a beat, I reached to my hem and worked the tunic up until it caught on my breasts. I shook my chest to help free them and swung the blue silk around my head before tossing it to the stage floor. "No boys, we get *gold*... one of my favorite things!"

The room lost control, and the patrons tossed another round of coins to the stage. I brought my hand to my chest and fingered the sparkling hoop and bar.

"By great Gammond's goatee, she's got gold through her titty, right through it!"

"And the finest pair of mountains I've seen this side of Monwyn!" barked out a man who stood deep in the crowd

Laughter erupted all around me.

"Alright, you get a choice now: a song or a show?"

"Show, show, show!" They chanted and hollered.

Great. I was hoping I could keep them happy with the dulcet tones of my wavering soprano, but I didn't figure they would like the Solnnan letter learning song.

"Here's the deal, I need you all to help me out and sing something for me... it just won't be fun by myself," I said cheekily, smiling my brightest smile.

"Ol 'Lim go 'head, sing 'er a tune!" A raspy voice choked out.

"Lim, Lim, Lim!" The chant picked up again.

"Come on up, Lim. Take a seat and get a better view."

I looked out trying to find him in the crowd, and saw the scrawny middle-aged man in the middle of a mob. His face was beet red and the rest of him sunken.

"Don't be shy, Lim. I'll do all the hard work." I tossed my skirts around, which elicited a few more tossed coins. I waited while Lim, who covered his privates with his hat, came up to the edge of the stage and cleared his throat.

"The gong sounds, and the men called to arm—to keep fair love from fadin'.
And the horn blasts—but his banner do fall... to the goddess we all are prayin'

A war song was an interesting choice, but at least it moved slowly. I had fewer chances of making a fool out of myself by not having to attempt some fast-paced gyrations.

I closed my eyes and swayed from side to side while at the same time undoing my skirts and letting them fall. When I thought of sex, of making love, the only person I could think of was Tommand. It was, frankly, the only experience I had to mimic—if I recreated my time with Ambrose, it would have come across just as lackluster as it had in real life.

I spun in a little circle, let myself fall gently to the couch, and slid slowly down its edge, remembering how Tommand's hands had helped me to lower myself upon him. I squatted slowly and came back up, my back braced against the couch, remembering how it felt to finally be filled by him, to have taken him inside.

Standing up briefly, I turned and lay down, raising one of my legs high in the air. I let it fall, hooking over the sofa's back, and placed my other foot on the floor which spread me widely.

"She's right ruby red, she is."

I blocked everyone out and focused on the memory.

"The clangs sound... and the men, they do fall—to keep their foes from invadin',
And they fight strong, but not all make it home... their mem'ries safe with their maidens.'

He'd been so beautiful above me, so serious, and yet so happy, and when he took my hand in his, wanting to know what gave *me* pleasure... I'd known my choice was right. I touched myself, remembering the way his hand moved, and thrust my hips into the air, like he was taking me again. I grew slick at the thought... until I remembered the dry and rasping voice of the man I'd left ailing.

I opened my eyes and sat up. The energy of the room had changed.

The song had faded out, and the men had gone silent.

"Is... is everything okay?" I looked around, where many had paused in their drinking. My eyes found Xillyna, who was the closest gem I could see.

The man in her tub openly wept and patted a tear from his cheek. I looked at him and raised my brows in question.

"There ain't been nuthin' as beautiful in these hills since the town was whole and well," he choked out.

I caught Demma's eyes. She stood in the corner, wildly waving her hands and mouthing 'bring them up!'

I panicked and jumped up on the couch.

"WHO'S READY TO FUCK!" I yelled, using the word all the men in my life seemed to prefer, while raising my arms and jiggling my breasts back and forth.

There was about a three-second beat before the room of men went feral.

Coins rained onto the stage, men shouted offers of marriage, and cups went flying as the crowd moved closer. Men burst out of their tubs and howled with their heads thrown back, the sound swelling to the point it would have drowned out even the closest claps of thunder.

I looked to Demma again, who was now nodding animatedly and signaling me to get back upstairs. I hopped off the stage and grabbed my garments, making a little show of shaking my rear as I walked up each step. When out of sight, I ran for my room and crossed the threshold just in time to hear Merton's voice boom. "Make a line, fellas, make a line!"

I shut the door behind me and tossed the skirt and tunic on the chair, and then as fast as I could, lay face down on the bed and buried my head under the single thin pillow that Demma had tossed upon it. The down-filled casing smelled like bacon fat, but I didn't hear a *single* moan or groan coming from beyond the door. *Thank you, Kairus...*

Later that night, I heard a light tap on the door, and Demma's muffled voice called out. I pulled the cover off the bed to use as a robe and invited her in.

"Here's your share, hun, forty pieces. You did real good out there. The house hasn't seen a day like this in years." She tossed the small bag to me, and I caught it in midair.

"Listen," she came and sat on the bed, "I've been in your spot before, and nothing you did up there was wrong. You made your wage, and I don't want you thinking poorly about yourself. We may not be the courtesans of the courts, but we all share the same feelings, and this *can* be hard."

I didn't tell her that I'd been humiliated twice before, and this wasn't as bad as either of those times. This time I went in fully aware.

"Demma, did they make enough to get Sed to a healer?" I asked, truly concerned.

"Not quite, but a few more good days and it'll happen."

I nodded, happy to lend my hand tomorrow. They all seemed like truly fine people and deserved the same respect shown to those who lived in a kingdom proper.

"Now get some sleep. Morning clean-up comes early, and that crowd left quite the mess."

Stifling a yawn, I opened the saddlebags that Jothanieal had kindly delivered and pulled out the half-cut nightgown. It stank like body odor and horse. I was hopeful that Demma would allow me to wash them in the morning—I couldn't imagine smelling like this all the way to Solnna. I tucked my coins deep into the leather bottom. I was one step closer.

I lit the lamp and lay down on my back. The small window revealed tiny stars dotted through the black sky.

Like I had when I was a child, I made my prayers to the Goddess and hoped maybe my mother was looking up at the same starry sky, saying her prayers as she had done every night of my life.

CHAPTER THIRTY-SEVEN

COMMUNICATION IS KEY

My eyes cracked open. The lamp had gone out, and darkness was my only blanket. I dreamt of Evandr. I dreamt of Castor. I was covered in a cold sweat, caused by the nightmare that had mimicked reality so well. It felt like the air around me was vibrating, like Ærta herself was responding to my guilt.

The clouds shifted outside, and a soft beam of moonlight illuminated my room and the silhouette at my door.

"Did you think I would not hunt you, *Troth*?"

I sat up, screaming out, but the shadow lunged forward and cut me off, sealing its hand over my mouth and nose.

It drove me down into the mattress.

"Did you think you could run and I would no longer seek you?"

My hands were trapped below me, and I couldn't get in enough air. I struggled but it was useless.

"It would seem you prefer the company of filthy kingdom rejects to my own."

I yelled right into his lying face, but my voice was muted by his hand.

"I am taking you back. Now get up."

He pulled his hand from my mouth.

"I'm not going anywhere with you, *Tommand*. Go home to your wife. Figure out another way to pull off your plans—one that doesn't involve me." I said through clenched teeth.

"My what?"

"You're a shit liar! I saw the scars on your ear, you're a pretender!"

Tommand's face changed.

He chuckled wryly, like someone had just fed him a poorly timed joke.

"My wife?" he exhaled.

He bent low and ran the tip of his nose along my lips.

"You've obviously lost your good senses. Get off me!" I hissed.

"Nortia," he nosed me again. "It would be ignorant for a man of my profession to wear the ring, so I do not. And though I quite like the way you look covered in jealousy, the mythical wife that has roused you was a child my father betrothed me to at the age of twelve." He feathered soft little kisses across my cheekbones continuing to chuckle.

I tried again to dislodge him by rocking from side to side. He needed a sound thump on the head, and I was more than willing to deal the blow.

"The contract was broken and the rings both removed when I was named Protector."

"And you want me to just *believe you*?" I said incredulously.

"I do not care if you believe me, I am still taking you with me in the next five minutes. Unless I can beg you for a repeat performance—I too have coins to spare."

He had been here.

"You *are* a *pig*!"

"Yes, well, just a single thrust into your bounty and my appetites are out of control." He dragged his teeth up the column of my neck and nipped at the edge of my ear. "Would it please you to know that watching you on stage made me disgustingly jealous?" He tugged my left arm from under his body and brought my hand to his mouth, biting at my wrist. "I thought to rip off their cocks and set fire to every piece of shit who laid eyes on you. Their screams would have been a comforting lullaby."

My eyebrows shot to my forehead.

"And then... I became remarkably aroused watching my lover bring a room of grown men to their knees. Knowing it was me you replayed in your head did much for my self-esteem."

"I think *lover* is taking it a little far."

"I would like to take it much further still."

Tommand pushed himself up on his hands and crawled back, running his lips over my skin, trailing his mouth from my sternum to navel. He came up on his knees, tightly straddling my calves.

"I have never lied to you," he said.

"But you've certainly hidden things," I rebutted.

"I have," he admitted, "but my mission required me to do so... until my mission changed."

"And if given the choice between me and your mission, which would you choose?"

He remained silent.

"That's what I—"

The door crashed open, and a wailing battle cry pierced the air!

"She ain't for fuckin', rapscallion!" It was Xillyna, screaming loud enough to wake the dead.

"He ain't paid neither!"

"Jothaniel!" Merton bellowed.

More shadows ran into the room, wielding clubs and sticks.

"Yah ain't messin' with Demma's gems!" The last and tallest shadow ran a little behind the others.

Ramshackle weaponry rained down on Tommand, who countered each blow and sent his assailants flying, toppling into furniture, cracking the iron footboard, and splintering the wooden chair.

"Tommand, stop! STOP!" I screamed. He'd kill all the gems who were already so feeble.

Tommand stopped at once, standing stock still in the middle of the floor, even as random bits of projectiles bounced off him.

"Yah know 'em, do yah?" Phillden said from somewhere in the room.

"What in the nether is happening in here?" Demma appeared in her long pink night rail. The oil lamp she carried illuminated the contained carnage of the short-lived scuffle.

"The lady screamed so I gathered up everyone and—"

"Nahhhhhh!" A yowling Jothaniel came barreling through the door.

The towering youth bent low, catching Tommand in the hips, and lifted him off the ground. They went smashing into the back wall, sending dust throughout the room. The very second his feet touched the ground again, Tommand bent and grabbed Jothaniel around the hips and yanked up, causing the kid to collapse and hit the ground face-first.

I scrambled out of bed, worried sick over the too-still youth until he rolled onto his back and rubbed at his nose. He stared up at Tommand.

"Can yah show me 'at again?"

"No. But I am impressed. Take this to the gates of Monwyn and ask for the Marshal if you are ever interested in a life at arms." Tommand reached into his pocket and tossed a glinting disk on the prone youth's chest. "Now, I am taking her, and I will end the person who steps even an inch in my direction—am I clear?"

Seven heads nodded.

"Tommand, the only way I'm walking out of this room without waking up this entire town is if you empty out all of the gold in your pockets... right now." I knew I couldn't stop him from physically removing me, but I wasn't going without being as aggravating as possible. He narrowed his eyes wickedly, and they glowed a strange silver in the moonlight.

"I'll do it too. I'll scream so loud all of my new admirers will come running. Can you handle, fifty... sixty?" I backed up, inching closer to the door.

"Fine." He reached into his pocket and pulled free a leather pouch which he untied and dumped on the bed.

"Ruddy fucking nether!" Demma exclaimed when a small pile of gold coins, a thin gold bar, and a dozen loose gems hit the mattress.

"Now move," Tommand growled, snatching up his pilfered saddle bags.

"Diantha... here." Lykksome shrugged out of the robe they wore and tossed me the heavy woolen garment.

"Thank you." I took their bone-thin hands into my own, "When you can, head east to Stormridge and ask for Verrona. She may be able to help Sed."

I glanced over my shoulder. "Are you coming, Tommand?" I scolded the already angry man and walked out the door.

"Where's my horse?" Tommand asked irritatedly a few steps behind me.

"Ambrose is fine."

Slamming open the door of the brothel, I marched to where I assumed the stable was located to find it nothing more than a lean-to with a heavy wooden board nailed into its front. It took Tommand almost half an hour to pry it off.

"So you know, you will refer to nothing I ride as Ambrose. He has a name and it's Maigremor."

"I'll call him whatever I want when I ride him—just as I did his namesake," I shot back.

Tommand turned and stared down at my upturned face.

"I suggest you remain silent until we reach our destination."

"And I suggest you get *fucked*." I pushed my way around him, shoving him in the chest.

His hand whipped out, seizing my arm, and in a flash he pulled backward and twisted me into his chest. The beltless robe parted, and Tommand's eyes fastened themselves, unashamedly, to where my chest smooshed against him.

"I would like nothing more, Eira. But the next time—and there *will* be a next time—you will crawl to me."

I shook out of his grip and spun on my heel, seeking fresh air.

Tommand appeared leading Ambrose out of the stall.

"You have to close it back. They'll eat the other one."

"Why was *this* the town you chose to make friends in?" he said while helping me push the gate against the structure. He hammered it back into place with a fallen limb.

"Why has your king ignored them?" I tilted my head a narrowed my eyes. "Did you come by horse?" I asked.

"I did."

"And where did you leave *the horse*?" I used the tone my mother did when she chastised my father.

Tommand looked around, clenching his fists at his sides.

"You can now add horse murderer to your ever-growing list of faults."

Tommand swung up angrily into the saddle and without speaking, offered me his hand.

"Where are we going?" I questioned.

"To a rendezvous point. Gotwig and Ambrose are waiting."

"And Devotee Solnna? Evandr? Do we know the outcome?" I flung around to face him, bumping his chin with my head. He pulled back and I watched the corners of his nose flare as he inhaled tersely.

"I have no knowledge at this point. We will ride the full day if possible and try reaching them before nightfall. Your little antics cost us time."

"Did you mean to say that your little lies—oh I'm sorry, your little half-truths—cost us time?"

We rode the rest of the day in silence, but as the evening began to close in, Tommand finally ventured to speak.

"We need to stop for the night."

"But Tommand, we're so close and they will have brought news," I cried.

Admittedly, I was exhausted from a day in the saddle, but if Gotwig and Ambrose were alive, then so many things could be put back in place.

"Nortia, after almost shitting myself to death and then having to track you down to some Goddess-forsaken village of decaying horse eaters, I suppose that falling asleep on horseback and breaking both our necks would end many of our issues."

"Fine, we can stop, but if all you had was horse you'd eat it too." I made to elbow him in the stomach, but he caught my arm sandwiching it between his elbow and waist.

We rode deep into the forest, winding our way around trees and rocks before eventually having to dismount. After some time on foot, we came to a tiny clearing.

"I'll build a fire. When was the last time you had food?"

"Yesterday morning. There should still be dried beef in your pack unless Jothaniel found it."

Tommand moved around quickly, gathering small stones and kindling.

"I swiped a few items from your new friends. Take these and look for water." He handed me three hammered-copper mugs and began constructing a small stone ring.

I took them and my stinky clothes. I couldn't find my cutoff shirt anywhere, but if I did find a water source, the pants and my support might be wearable again. I still had on the ridiculous string outfit under the robe, and I was looking forward to replacing it.

"Eira,"—I glanced back over my shoulder—"there is no place you can run that I will not come for you."

I slowly lifted my hand to my face and even more slowly lifted my middle finger, and then turned, moving on with my business. I roamed around scouting for a source of water, contemplating how quickly a person's focus could change. In the blink of an eye, I went from being intent on getting to Solnna, and now, I couldn't wait to get back to Verus. I needed so badly to check with Nan and Kairus and Mariad. I needed to see that things were going to be okay. I needed to mourn Evandr properly and pray with all the force of my spirit that he lived well in the afterlife.

After wandering around, I found a stream so thin I could easily step over it. I filled the copper cups, set them aside, and began scrubbing my clothes. I hoped the gems would be able to get themselves to a healer now. Though the townspeople were certainly rough on the outside, and I wouldn't have wanted them to catch me at night, they were people living through hard times, just trying to survive. I truly wished them the best.

Until yesterday, I wasn't even aware that there were settlements that *didn't* belong within the confines of a kingdom and wondered if an Obligate could ease their struggles. They'd been forgotten, but they were still people of Ærta.

When I made it back to camp, Tommand had a fire going and had collected an assortment of greenery and mushrooms that he had laid out on a flat rock. A modest fire crackled in a makeshift firepit, and Tommand was feeding it small bits of kindling and blowing at its base. I held up the mugs.

"Sit them on the embers and toss half the beef in two of the cups. It will boil down to a decent broth."

I pulled the waxed pouch from his saddlebags, and my hands brushed against a few new items that weren't there before. I hope he hadn't lifted anything Demma may have needed immediately. I tossed my damp clothes over a branch that hung fairly close to the flames, hoping the fire smoke would cover any of the remaining smells they had collected, and watched Tommand stuff a handful of greens and mushrooms into each mug. He set the remaining mug near the fire and poured a little splash of spirits into the vessel.

"You know a lot about forest survival?"

He inclined his chin. "And mountain and snow and desert... a Protector must prove their ability to withstand all elements."

"Why not just the terrain of Monwyn? Does your monarch travel often?"

"No, no he doesn't. But were he captured, the expectation would be for me to bring him home, no matter the location."

That made sense.

Tommand wrapped my damp chest support around his hand, pulled the mugs off the fire, and sat them near the trunk of a large fir.

"How do you know what will and won't kill you? I know some mushrooms are poisonous."

"For those," he nodded to the steaming mugs, "I had to walk a while to find them growing on an oak. They grow right up the trunk, but you have to check their gills and stems to make sure you are not collecting the look-alike that *could* harm you."

Tommand sat and leaned back against the trunk's rough bark. He took a sip of the hot contents and gave a satisfied nod. Raising the other mug into the air, he motioned me over, with a flick of his head.

I sat next to him but left a large gap between us.

"What did you give me at Verrona's?" he asked.

"An abortifacient. I figured it wouldn't kill you but it might slow you down for a while."

He sat in contemplation and eventually let out a long sigh.

"I will give you the same advice as I do the soldiers I train. If you think the person will continue to harm you in the future—finish the job."

I stared at the fire as if I hadn't heard him but was shocked by the brutality of his suggestion.

"Is... is that why... why... Castor?" I could barely get out the words.

"Yes. I do not think the Gaeans mean to leave you be... but he will." Tommand's voice turned cold.

I finished the salty broth and went to the tree where my not-nearly-dry enough clothing hung.

"Why do you think that, Tommand? About the Gaeans?"

"That is what I wanted to talk to you about before we..."

I dropped my robe and pulled the chain from around my neck and over my head.

"Before we had sex? Go ahead and tell me now."

The stupid garment's string was lodged up my butt, and I had to pluck it free before bending over to push the confounding thing down my legs. I flung it away with my toe and went about wiggling into the chilly pants.

"Go on, Tommand. It has to be important for you to be all mysterious about it, or is this another half-truth situation?" I glanced over my shoulder.

Tommand had come up to his knees but had stopped mid-motion.

I knew that look.

"Uh, uh, no sir." I shook an outstretched finger at him. "There will be none of that. Tell me what you need to tell me."

Tommand shook his head against some invisible force but lost the battle and planted his hand on the ground.

"Look who's crawling to who." I kicked a pile of dry needles toward him. "Now stop!"

He shook his head again and seemed to regain control, blinking a few times and resting back on his heels, like he had when Evandr had knocked him silly.

"Where do you go when you go all warrior-king?" I asked.

It took him a few moments to respond. "I have a few theories."

"Care to share?"

"No. Yes... later."

The unflappable Tommand was breathing deeply through his nose and out his mouth while his eyes were squeezed tightly shut.

I used the time, keeping a watchful eye on him, to finish dressing and adjust myself more comfortably. I really did prefer the support over my old binding, and because its band came down to the bottom of my rib cage and the pants up to my navel, I felt comfy for the first time in days.

"Come sit next to me," Tommand whispered.

"Is it safe?" I said half-joking.

The look he gave me was deadly. His dark brows knit together, and his mouth set in a stern line.

I grabbed the discarded robe and closed the distance.

"Come closer," he said softly.

"I'm not cold."

"You will be when the fire goes out and your wet clothes freeze against you."

"Will the fire not burn through the night?" I asked.

"No. It would increase the chances of our being seen."

I squeezed myself next to Tommand, and his arm went around my shoulders. Only the faint smell of cedar clung to him, but just that little whiff, sank deeply into my lungs. I took the heavy robe and placed it over us both.

"When Mariad fell, he took a risk in asking me to assure your safety." Tommand hugged me tighter. "My guess is he knew one of two things. Either he was aware of our... attachment, and he knew I would protect you—which I will if you stop running from me." Tommand shifted his weight, adjusting his back against the bark. "But more likely, he discovered that Monwyn wanted your placement for the same reason the Gaeans do. That is until I altered those plans."

There it was.

I didn't react.

I'd known it was in the realm of possibility, and I had been right. Hearing it from his mouth just made it all the more ugly.

"You wanted to breed me to your archaic king so you could take a chunk of Nortia, but decided you liked the goods so couldn't go through with it. Is that what I'm hearing?"

"Yes and no. Monwyn wanted you for a different purpose, and Ambrose was to win you over and work to sell the idea of a Monwyn Assignment. My job was to ensure you were Assigned to our kingdom. I was forced to change those plans almost immediately, however. My reaction to you... you've seen it. I made the decision not to let you step foot in Monwyn and was beyond relieved when they chose Evandr and Solnna for you. I knew he would do everything he could to allow you to lead a fulfilled life. But then..." Tommand's voice caught in his throat.

The anguish crushed me.

"Tommand. I'm so sorry. I would never have—"

I choked back a sob. Tommand took my face in his hands.

"It's not your fault. It's not," he whispered. "I will miss my friend, and I will grieve his loss, but the blame lies solely at the feet of Ozius and the other Gaeans who took part." Tommand gently tucked my head to his shoulder and stroked my hair until my tears subsided.

"Tommand, what... what purpose was I to serve?"

He squeezed me tighter.

"The King of Monwyn, for the last twenty years, has been attempting to conjure."

The king has...

I recoiled, trying to dislodge myself from Tommand's arms, but he'd anticipated the reaction and held fast.

"Tommand that's—"

"The most deviant of offenses possible... yes." He laid his head back against the fir. "We had no idea until beasts that had been gone for a hundred years began reappearing. I and my units were sent to dispatch them, but they kept returning. Water would just disappear from the dinner table, after we had all seen it poured. It kept happening, until one day we discovered the king rehearsing an incantation with a set of ancient books laid before him." Tommand paused briefly, staring off into the night. "The king himself became increasingly hostile as the years went by, but we were able to keep him safe from himself until about five years ago. He found a way to practice again, and this time the corruption began consuming him."

"And you wanted me there to what? Run the economy while he raised the dead?" I began shaking. Like a glacier sliding down my spine, dread pulled me to the nether.

"No, for five years we searched for ways to release him from that which he brought upon himself, but we failed. Three years ago, though, I received intelligence from a Gaean merchant who had recently traveled through Nortia. The intel seemed incredibly far-fetched, but we were desperate."

"Whatever it was, it couldn't be more ridiculous than a king of Ærta harnessing witchcraft."

Tommand lifted his brows and sucked in his checks.

"The intelligence was that the Gaeans had located the true descendant of The Child, and that she had given birth in Nortia, and her daughter was born Troth."

I waited for Tommand's brilliant smile.

I counted to ten.

He said nothing more, just sat there as stone-faced as a Verus guard.

"And... and you believe my mother, is like, what? A sixteenth part... goddess? Tommand, she is one of the most humany humans I've ever met."

This was too much.

"Look, I learned to believe in a magic-wielding king, so..." He shook his head softly back and forth. "And you were our last hope for redeeming him."

"Me?" I scoffed.

He really believed this.

"Eira, if your mother, using your words, was a sixteenth goddess, then you would be..."

"Getting the fuck away from you, that's what I'd be." I shoved against him, and he let me stand.

"Where would you go?"

"Anywhere else, Tommand!" I fired back.

"Where? To Verus? To Nortia? To Gaea and your new mate? Do you think they will not pursue you? They murdered a Scion in the sanctuary of the temple, Eira."

"And... and did Mariad know? Wait, no, I'm not believing this."

I paced back and forth in front of the dying fire.

"He had to know, that night he—"

"Stop, so let's say this insanity is true, and I contain a speck of... of god blood. What purpose would I have served you?"

"Surely you know the story. The Magis, his child, *The Child*. She was the only thing that brought him peace and controlled his corruption. We hoped your presence would bring our king back to us."

"And I would... walk behind him all day? Play chess with him? Tommand, this is so incredibly absurd. I really hope you *are* lying to me."

"I am not lying."

"Mmmhmm, but you do know how insane you sound?"

"I am keenly aware, yes."

"Does Ambrose think this is true?"

"He knows it is."

"And Evandr?"

"He did."

"And—"

What had Ozius called me? Divine.

Goddess alive, all of these fools had been led to believe that I was a walking deity.

I pinched my arm. I'd wake from this fever dream soon. I was probably back at Verus right now, under the effects of one of Gotwig's poisoned concoctions.

"Okay, Tommand. Well, I'm going to sleep over there," I pointed across the way, "and think about everything you've said, okay? Okay." I carefully sidestepped the fire and moved away from him.

"Incorrect." His voice carried across the distance. "You will sleep right here," I looked to where he pointed to the ground right next to him, "and you can process this however you need. I realize this is shocking, but I will not let you out of my sight."

"Now you loo—"

"Stop talking." Tommand came to his feet and unsheathed the knife from his boot in the same instant. He squatted low and cocked his head to the side.

"Stay put," he growled.

He shot off into the night.

And I ran.

I took off in the opposite direction, weaving through the tight trees, paying no attention to the twigs that whipped across my face or the pain of the forest floor under my bare feet. I'd hide and run to the furthest town and shave my head like an acolyte, becoming another person altogether.

I ran until my lungs burned, but I didn't stop.

I hopped the small creek with no issue and surged forward, not daring to lose momentum. I stopped being able to feel the soles of my feet shortly after, which was all the better. I passed a large boulder and saw the shimmer of a lake in the distance. I'd have to go around it. Swimming would cost me too much time. I veered left and caught the glowing eyes of a deer family that bounded fearfully away from my intrusion.

Sweat beaded on my forehead.

My panic spiked.

I flushed hotly, and my ears rang. I no longer felt connected to my body.

My numb toes caught something and sent me tumbling, knocking the already thin air from my lungs.

My body rolled toward the bank of the lake until coming to a halt a few feet from the water's edge. Gasping for air, I tried my best to recover quickly. I had to move. I had to keep going. I twisted to my knees and looked up... right into the eyes of a predator.

Even in the twilight, I saw them gleam.

It was the warrior-king.

The fine hairs of my body stood on end as Tommand moved, prowling toward me.

He hunted me. I was his prey.

I lunged to the right, thinking to evade him, but like a flash of lightning, his arm caught me, jerking me against his body.

"You. Cannot. Run. From. Me," he ground out.

The light of the moon, which had just made its presence known in the darkening sky, reflected off the water, bathing Tommand's face in a diffused white glow. His chest rose and sank erratically against me.

Pulling at my loose hair, he bent my head backward. His tongue darted out, tasting the pulse that drummed at the base of my neck. "Will you have me?"

Wild tremors traveled along my chest, bringing every nerve ending in my body shooting to life. The passion in his voice stoked the flames that burned within me. His fingers combed through my tangled hair, and I felt myself yielding. I wanted to use his body like I had begged him to use mine. I wanted to let him conquer me, forget everything except how he made me feel.

I wanted him.

I *still* wanted him.

"Say it, Eira. Who is it that you want?"

"I—" my voice faltered. "I... want *you* Tommand," I spoke to him and to the goddess of the forest who bore witness.

"I have told you. I am *not* Tommand," he growled. "Do you accept *me* as the man who wishes to claim you? To come between your pretty legs?"

The steady pulsing that slickened my passage waged a battle with my mind.

"I want you, the Protector... Emissary Monwyn." I met his gaze with conviction.

His eyes narrowed, and a smug smile spread across his face.

"That will fucking do, clever Troth."

In a single motion, he twisted me roughly and my back collided with his chest. I arched against him, and he ground his arousal into my backside while biting down sharply on my shoulder. I cried out, the pleasure-pain searing a path to my toes.

"Goddess, oh, gods."

"Do those kinds of prayers reach their ears?" he slurred. His hands snaked around my waist yanking at the fabric that kept him from his objective. Losing my balance, I fell to my hands and knees and sank into the soft ground of the mossy bank.

He was on me in an instant, pulling my pants down my hips and past my knees.

"Open," he commanded gruffly.

Encumbered by the material, I parted my legs as much as I could.

Demanding fingers dug into the flesh of my hips and the broad head of him nudged at my opening. I felt every blessed inch of him as he pulled me steadily backward onto his erection, only stopping when he was fully seated. I was filled, stretched beyond what I thought to be my capacity.

My gasp mingled with his groan.

And then he was moving.

The warrior-king was not the man who had loved me before, taking the time to learn my desires, asking me about my own pleasure. He was all hunger, all-consuming, taking what *he* wanted. His hips slammed against my backside, and I met each thrust greedily. I dug my hands into the mud and pushed myself backward, trying desperately to open myself further, to receive each of his plunges more completely.

We slid through the mud as his hammering drove us forward, until he wrapped a demanding arm around my waist and pulled my back flush with his chest.

I could feel his heart pounding against me. He held me securely while pumping into me. I could make no movements of my own in this position, so I lay back against his shoulder and surrendered, letting him take me as he pleased. I felt the cording of his muscles as he shifted his arm and cupped my breast. He rolled my nipple between his fingers, and I looked back and saw his clenching jaw, the ferocity in his eyes.

He caught me... like always.

"Do you like watching me enjoy you, Nortia?"

He slid himself out of me and re-entered, quickly feeding me his length.

"I do," I gasped truthfully.

I found his hand and moved it to the sweet mound of nerves at my apex.

"That's it, love. Show me you want my touch."

I shoved my hips into him.

He released me and planted his palm in the middle of my back, pressing me down until my breasts touched the cool mud and my backside stuck up in the air. He sank lower and his fingers dug into my hips and spread me wide.

"You can't!" I choked. I felt the roughness of his beard push between my cheeks and his tongue flick out over my tightened flesh. He held me against his face and introduced me to a sensation that made me feel more vulnerable, more exposed than anything between us had so far.

"You can take more, sweetling."

I nodded, unable to speak. I would take everything he offered. He got back up to his knees and reentered me from behind.

"I want to know all parts of you." His finger swirled around my sensitized opening and pressed forward. My backside was so tight. The pressure, the intensity, the feeling of being penetrated on two fronts cast me off the side of the mountain.

And then... he fucked. He probed me with his finger and squeezed my rear. His nails bit into me.

He rolled his hips, plundering my passage, and placed his other hand around my waist teasing my clit with two fingertips.

The tension built within me, until I could take no more.

"You're so deep, so deep!" I spasmed and screamed my release, the sound skipping out over the water. My muscles tightened around him, and my mind left this plane. I was flying. I was standing on the outside looking in. My body convulsed and shattered altogether.

The instant I caught my breath, he twisted me to my back, the soft mud and moss making a soft bed.

"Fucking pants."

"Let me help," I raised my hips to aid him in the removal. Within seconds, he was pressing into me again, growling into the night air.

He covered me with his body and brought his face close to mine.

"When you run, it excites me like a dog driven to prey." His eyes bore into mine as he spoke and thrust himself powerfully into me. "I scent you... feel you... must hunt you." He increased the vigor of his strokes. His brows knit tightly, and his jaw worked, clenching and releasing above me.

"I... *oh*," I breathed out, unable to finish. I tilted my hips and clamped myself around him. His skin dotted with goose flesh.

"I worship," he grunted and slid a hand under my hips, "at the feet of your altar." Through heavy-lidded eyes, I watched the corners of his mouth slacken and his eyes close. "Goddess—you are *my* Goddess," he declared to the night. His loud, rough shout sent chills washing over me. He rose to his knees, and I knew he watched where we were joined, watched as he poured himself into my thoroughly sated body.

Knowing he released himself inside of me filled me with a sense of potency.

At that moment I realized, *I* was this man's weakness.

We lay, still joined together, listening to nature's music—the croaks and trills of frogs and the glubs of surfacing fish. He pulled himself from me, and our mixed secretions dripped from his half-erect penis onto my thigh. Though he probably couldn't tell, my cheeks flamed hotly.

I heard a low rumble begin in the back of his throat.

"Tommand, no," I said, recognizing the sound. I was in no shape for a second go-round.

"I'm a damned animal." He shook his head, freeing himself of the haze, and tucked himself quickly back into his pants.

Together we washed in silence.

I stood up and looked out over the lake, watching the white moonlight play on its dark rippling surface, holding my now useless pants together behind my waist.

Tommand came to stand in front of me and, without explanation, grabbed my hand and ducked himself under my arm.

"Hold on to me."

"What are you doing?" I yelled, trying desperately to maintain my balance.

He tossed me over his big shoulder and took off walking.

"Your ass is hanging out, which I very much appreciate, but your feet have suffered. I can alleviate your discomfort with very little effort."

"The effort is appreciated, Tom, it truly is, but maybe ask next time?" I huffed.

"I *asked* you not to run... *and* not to call me Tom," he chided.

"Is that—are you putting what happened back there on me?"

"I am. And because of the volume at which you appreciated my generosity, we have to move camp."

"Tommand?"

"What?" he spat.

"Fuck you."

"Shut up."

"Ouch!" He smacked my ass so hard the sound echoed through the trees.

We moved camp, and by the time we had walked a mile through the dark, I could barely stand on my own two feet. I didn't argue when Tommand laid me down and snuggled into my back. My eyes shut, and I focused on the even rise of his chest behind me.

"Nortia, if there is a baby, will I have hurt the child?"

I thought back to what my mother had told the women she had worked with.

"No, it would be fine. And there's not one."

I felt the nod of his head, his acceptance of my explanation.

"Tommand, does it make you angry, the possibility? I know things got tense at Verus between you and Ambrose."

I felt the rush of air move past my cheek as he exhaled sharply.

"I think... if two people I love create something together... I am bound to love it too."

I bit off the jagged edge of a torn nail. I hadn't expected that answer... or to hear that word again.

"You love Ambrose?"

"Of course. He's my brother." Tommand placed his arm under my head, providing a barrier between me and the hard ground.

"That's sweet."

Sleep came quickly.

Chapter Thirty-Eight

THE CAVE

"Tommand, get up!"

The soundly sleeping warmth behind me jolted to life and got to his feet, squaring off with an invisible adversary.

"Is Ambrose *actually* your brother?" I asked, pulling at the leg of his tan-colored pants.

"Yes," he answered, crouching on the balls of his feet, surveying the area.

"I fucking *hate* you, Tommand." I rolled over, pulling the heavy robe up and around my head. "Hate."

"And what have I done now?"

I kicked out at the cumbersome robe that trapped me and tossed the garment aside.

"So, are you a high society Monwyn too? Or is that all fabrication as well?"

Tommand pushed his hands through the short spikes of his hair and then scratched his beard.

"No, we are both of the lineage, but I don't understand why you find our familial relation distasteful."

"Oh, I don't know *Duke* Tommand... *Count* Tommand... or is it *Prince* Tommand? Maybe it's because you creeps are just a little too close for comfort? You share everything with each other... even me." I came to my knees fumbling, trying desperately to hold my pants together. "What we've done is probably illegal somewhere, and it's just... disgusting—"

"Nether frost, Nortia!" He threw his hands wide, pleading to the sky. "Our father adopted him from a madam's expectant lot when it was clear she would bear an Obligate. We share no blood. He was purchased to further our father's renown."

"Start with that next time. *Shit!*" I hollered, smacking my hands on the ground.

"And what we've done? The former Queen of Solnna *married* her late husband's brother and bore the children of both men... and while we are on the subject, you didn't give Ambrose much of a choice."

"I made myself quite clear when I asked Ambrose." His eyes went wide, and he pressed his lips together so hard you could no longer see their lushness. "You know, we just need to have a sit down at some point and get to know—no, wait! You can just drop me in Solnna and I'll figure my life out on my own, thank you."

"I will not be doing that."

Tommand stomped off to a nearby tree and unzipped his pants.

"Tommand, I'm not sure we're close enough for that." I goaded him further, getting a perverse sort of pleasure from ribbing him. He shook his member and buckled his belt.

His brown eyes glittered dangerously in the morning rays that penetrated deeply through the trees.

"You've had my cock in your mouth, Nortia. You sucked me dry and this—" he gestured wildly at the appendage he spoke of, "is what bothers you?"

"Ambrose had the decency not to relieve himself before or after I 'sucked him dry,' or was it 'got knighted by the king'? I can't remember. Either way, some things should remain private."

I waited for Tommand to start breathing again. Perhaps Kol's favorite terminology had been a little too low-brow, but I wanted the shock value.

Tommand threw his arm up, pointing his finger directly at my chest. "There are three hours between us and the rendezvous point. Be ready in a quarter of an hour." He stomped off between the trees, to where... I didn't really care.

Mommy Goddess.

Brother fucking.

Taking care of my own personal needs, I thought back over the interactions between Tommand and Ambrose. I should have known they were related, sort of, from the way they carried on—the spats, the fights, the laughter.

I inspected my pants and wished for my closet at Verus. The middle seam had been split down the back, and I was trying to discern how I could make them temporarily functional. Fucking, Tommand. Stupid, fucking, delectable Tommand. I replayed the events of last night while I took a knife and rope from the saddlebags and gently, with the very point of the blade, made little circles in the linen's weave.

I'd known the minute I spotted him what I wanted. And Goddess, when he told me he'd be coming inside me and then watched his release like it was the greatest accomplishment of his life? It was like the gods of fertility lit a beacon in my vagina.

I shivered and tried to refocus on my task. It was tedious, but like making lacing holes for a dress, if you didn't cut any of the fibers and just moved them out of the way, they wouldn't fray immediately and would last for some time. I hadn't a clue when I'd be able to find more clothing.

Eight eyelets later and the thin rope laced right through. I stood and admired my handiwork and successfully tightened the lacing that luckily only left a hair's breadth of a gap.

Tommand was waiting atop his horse when I strode back into the small makeshift camp. He'd packed up and covered the area with fresh brush and foliage.

I proudly displayed my ingenuity, twisting around to show him my behind.

"Well done," he complimented. "You have found yet another use for the length."

"The rope? How many uses are there for a rope this size?" I questioned, genuinely curious. I had to think the thin ply would barely make it around my waist once.

He held out his hand and hefted me up in front of him.

"You can tie up a mess of fish with it, you can secure someone's wrist, you can wrap it around the handle of a hot pan, you can strangle someone, you can—"

"Thank you, Tommand. That will do." I didn't want to imagine how many necks it had been around.

"Thank you, *Cato.* That will do," he said.

"I'm not ready for that yet." He was still Tommand to me. Cato implied, just as he had asked of me last night, that I accepted him fully.

"Why Kay-toe? Why not Cat-toe... as it sounds in Catommandus?" I questioned.

"Because that's how Evandr used to say it as a child, and it stuck. My whole family says it that way."

"You grew up with him?"

Tommand handed me the reins while he stretched and bent his fingers.

"Sort of. He was a few years younger than me and followed me around relentlessly begging me to teach him to fight. He drove me mad until the day I agreed to train him. I would have my lessons during the day, and we would train for an hour after dinner. Honestly, it was the only way to keep the scrawny little red-headed rat from hiding out in my bathing room or scaring me in the middle of my studies or shoving himself between me and the young ladies I was trying to win over."

"Red-headed?" I exclaimed. "Evandr is literally devoid of color. His lashes are pure white and so is the hair on his arms and head." I strained my neck, trying to look back.

"That's the corruption."

"From the... the conjuring?" I whispered, still unable to wrap my head around even the possibility.

"Yes. Having trained Evandr from a youth to a man, and having befriended him during that time, I assigned him as the king's personal guard when I became Protector. After a year or so of near-constant contact with the king, his hair began to lighten." Tommand sat his chin on my shoulder and rubbed his beard against my cheek. "We thought it was just a matter of heredity, but then it began happening to the king's door guards and then children."

"Move your head, I'm still mad. And is that why you have lighter hair in places as well?"

"It is, and my eyes. They have lightened fairly dramatically around their centers. As a boy, my eyes were as dark as coal and my hair was not far from it."

"And Ambrose? He was never close to the king? He seems to have no loss of color."

"No, he lived with our mother in the countryside training as a Scion from the moment he could walk. We saw each other infrequently until he came to the mines. We became close while working in the pits and grew into manhood together. Then I went to the palace and he traveled the kingdom with tutors."

"And how were you and Evandr able to leave your posts and come to Verus if you both had to look after your king?"

Tommand straightened and shifted in the saddle.

"Are you sure you are prepared to learn of the corrosion that eats away at so many of Ærta's noble leaders?"

He retook the reins, and I waved a flippant hand.

"Years ago, when we heard of... well, you, Devotee Monwyn created and forged documents and lineage papers for Evandr. He did so on my order. Evan was never born Scion, but the Devotee, well aware of the king's dealings, created a way for him to help me procure you. It gave me another pair of trusted hands and another pawn to play in negotiations. It also gave him well-deserved time away. We have no idea if the corruption stops or reverses if you are away from the source, or if it continues until it ends you."

We rode in silence for some distance while I mulled over the information. Had I known of the duplicity committed by the leaders of the continent a month ago, I would have, in my naiveté, argued their integrity, but since then, I'd come to see rather plainly how the upper echelon got on.

"And then he was chosen as my partner, and together we were Assigned to Solnna."

"It was the best I could have hoped for. You both would have been safe there," he sighed, the emotion heavy in his voice.

"And now?"

"And now *I* will see to your security."

"But what about Monwyn? You are their Protector. Surely you must go back."

I felt the steady rise of his chest and leaned back into him as it fell.

"I left a remarkably skilled battalion to look after the kingdom in my absence and have been receiving regular reports on its functioning. I will see you safely installed in the south, in accordance with the wishes of Devotee Solnna, and if I can manage it, Ambrose at your side. At that time, I will return to my post."

The muscular arms that circled my waist tightened, drawing me closer.

"We are here."

In the perfect imitation of a mourning dove, Tommand let out a low, trilling whistle.

"Where?" I whispered while looking around.

I squinted, trying to make out another person or a small house or any features that would indicate a meeting location.

"Did you hear it?" Tommand spoke softly.

I shook my head and then a sound came, another call that made my ears perk. It was the two-toned call of a bird in the distance.

"It's Ambrose. He's just over there." Tommand dismounted and walked off to scan the perimeter of the glen we had ridden into. Satisfied, he grabbed our horse's reins and led us through a cluster of oaks and bearberries. We walked, making a few turns and twists, all the while following the call of what Tommand referred to as a bobwhite.

"Look up to your right," Tommand said. "Do you see him?"

I looked to where he pointed and strained my eyes, seeing nothing but the leaves, trees, and rocks that I had seen for the last day.

"Watch for what's moving a little differently than it should."

I focused and held my breath, concentrating on the sway of leaves and the light bouncing off of branches, and—there it was! The rise and fall of a man's chest, slightly out of sync with the rest of the gentle movements of the limbs he hid in.

Strong hands found my waist and helped me slide off the saddle.

"Can you control yourself around my brother, Nortia?" Tommand's hand snuck down to cup my rear. He moved forward, wedging me between his body and our mount, his lips teasing at the shell of my ear.

"To be honest, I'm not sure. Our mating was remarkable," I said, innocently batting my lashes. I shoved around him and strode purposefully to where the Scion stood waiting. I thought I had myself under control, but the closer I came to the giant, who had twice made the choice to aid me in this mess of a life, the more I struggled to choke back the tears that stung my eyes.

"Never have I seen a harpy so sad," he said while opening his arms wide. I ran the last few feet and fell into the solid embrace that felt both familiar and safe.

When my tears subsided, Ambrose held me at arm's length and then dropped to his knees, planting little kisses on my stomach.

"Is our little boy safe and snug?" he spoke directly to my belly.

"*Ambrosia* is fine, not that she exists. You will recall your inab—"

Tommand walked near.

"Inability to keep from taking you a third time, I know, I apologize. My prowess in the bedroom can challenge even those with the greatest of stamina."

I bit my cry-swollen lips to keep from laughing and kept them sealed when I saw the desperation in Ambrose's green gaze. I supposed I owed him, first for helping me take care of my pesky corona and again for whatever he had done to be as heavily bruised as he was.

"On your feet, brother," Tommand scolded. "And do better to hide that paunch next time. It exposed you almost immediately."

Ambrose's jaw clenched and released in an action so similar to Tommand's... something else I should have picked up on.

"She is aware then?" Ambrose stood and placed a protective arm around my shoulder.

"She is." Cato jerked his head forward. "Take us to Gotwig."

We walked together, one behind the other, trudging through a forest that looked like it had never seen humanity, it was so overgrown. We came upon a shallow creek, and I stopped to let our mount drink while the men charged ahead. They'd not stopped bickering since we'd set off, and it took them some time to realize I wasn't behind them.

They doubled back, at a run.

"Some protectors..."

"Were *I* a Troth being hunted by a kingdom of cultists, I would, I don't know, keep up and not fall behind," quipped Tommand.

He had a point, but I shrugged and lowered my eyelids. Both of them were on my nerves.

"Horse Ambrose was thirsty, and you should take better care of your pony," I cooed, smooching the soft muzzle in my hands.

"So the baby is Ambrosia... and the horse is Ambrose?" said Ambrose.

He turned and slugged Tommand on the shoulder and was unable to dodge the solid crack of Tommand's retaliatory palm against his cheek. He just laughed it off while Tommand continued scowling.

"Evandr named it, not me."

The mood instantly sobered.

We continued walking for what felt like an eternity. We passed through a grassy field where we were able to see a small band of goat herders high up on a hill, then we climbed into a gorge that slowed our pace and hid the sky again. Eventually, we came to an area where rocky walls rose up on both sides of a narrow path, making me feel incredibly claustrophobic.

"How did you find this place?" I wondered aloud.

"Tommand had every mile between Monwyn and Verus scouted a full year before we embarked," said Ambrose.

"Of course he did."

The craggy walls got closer the further we walked until we finally emerged into an open alcove. There were trees to the right of the opening, and the mouth of a cave to the left.

Gotwig stood just inside the cavern, which was about as tall as Jothaniel and as wide as Merton. He held a knife in one hand, and cleaned the nails of his other with its tip. His face and neck were ribboned with angry lacerations, and I imagined his body would look similar had he not been fully covered in a long gray cloak.

He waved us in.

Our party, including the horse, entered a darkened passageway that forked in two directions. Tommand led the horse to the right, where I could hear the whinnies of other mounts in the distance. To the left was a cavity barely large enough for four humans to fit comfortably. It had been lit with the same small travel light that the guards had used on our journey to Verus—ones made to extinguish themselves if they overturned.

"I'm glad to see you well. Your injuries have healed remarkably fast." Gotwig came closer, inspecting my face and my other visible body parts.

"I would like to apologize for dragging you into this situation. I had no idea how unwell Ozius was."

Gotwig continued to assess me, now using a lamp to see more closely. "Ozius isn't sick. Ozius is a true believer, blinded by his commitment to his Primus-King. He is aware of his actions and understands the consequences they may bring him."

Well, that didn't make me feel any better. It was easier for me to come to terms with everything that had happened when I thought his mind addled.

"Sit and eat. There is no time to waste."

I sat and picked at the offerings of rough oat bread and nuts but found I couldn't stomach anything. It all tasted flat and unappetizing to my anxiety-laden stomach.

Gotwig sat on the dusty floor and drew up his knees. Ambrose came down to lie on his side near him, propping his head up on his elbow, looking as indifferent as he always did.

Tommand returned and sat by my side, taking my hand, which he folded between his own and sat on his lap. I tried to pull it back, but he held firm. Ambrose quirked an eyebrow in his direction but said nothing.

"Mariad is expected to recover, but the healers are keeping him sedated as much as possible. He has sustained blunt injuries to his head and organs," Gotwig began.

I closed my eyes and sent a silent prayer to the Goddess. The relief of knowing he was alive should have fully comforted me, but I knew there was more.

"Evandr is tethered to life by a thread. We assumed him dead when we found his body, but he breathes for the time being."

I squeezed Tommand's hand when he gasped at the news.

"How? How is that possible? He was gone when they took me out of the priest's room. I felt his heart slow. I watched the blood gush from his wounds... too much blood."

"I believe the explanation lies in you." Gotwig's restless blue eyes pinned me. "The priest, who unfortunately took his own life before I was able to more thoroughly question him, went through quite the transformation since he first entered the temple. After the First Maneuvering, Ozius was able to procure a small amount of your blood. Which I believe he gave to the man."

I cringed, recollecting the moment Ozius had so kindly helped me to my feet after I'd fallen victim to my memories.

"Would you allow me to take a small—"

"Wait! You think *my* blood is what reversed the priest's disease?" I questioned as sudden panic flooded through me. A calloused finger caressed the side of my thumb, and mentally I latched on to the touch, trying desperately to ground myself and not flee.

He nodded.

"And perhaps, it's what is keeping Evandr in this realm. Will you allow me to take from you?" Gotwig asked again.

I glanced at Tommand, who looked like he was working through a complicated math problem in his head.

"Before I grant you permission to touch her or not," he said adopting the aloof manner of the emissary, "explain to me your part in this."

Gotwig let the hint of a wry smile spread across his lips.

"I was involved before you were conceived, boy," he challenged.

Tommand remained impassive, not rising to the bait, and gestured for Gotwig to continue.

"A man, by the name of Kan Keagan, another, who went simply by Kennt, and I were charged with the protection of Eira's mother. The previous Mantle had looked after her for a time when she'd sought sanctuary at Verus."

"*My* mother?" I interjected, "My mother has lived in Nortia her entire life. She's never traveled more than a few hours outside of Silverstep."

Gotwig shifted, looking in my direction.

"Your mother was a citizen of Gaea, who was trained in herbs by the previous Arch Healer himself. She surpassed his knowledge before her tenth year and the current king of Gaea was joined with her during her thirteenth year as a reward for her talents."

"I don't believe you," I protested, not trying to keep my voice down.

Gotwig withdrew an aged pouch from beneath his cloak and unfolded the package as carefully as if it held the rarest of gems.

He held the flattened item it contained to the light.

The air became too thin.

My head spun. Everything went black.

I came to after only a few seconds. It was difficult to open my eyes, but I forced them to obey. When they finally focused, three concerned faces hovered above mine.

"Th-that's my mother's flesh," I all but gagged out. "It matches the scar on her side exactly."

There was no mistaking the outline; it had always looked like a pine tree to me.

"It was the mark given to her for reaching the status of a healer. She cut it out herself while you were in her womb. Like you, she healed quickly."

"Were you aware of this?" I asked Tommand through clenched teeth. He leaned in close.

"I was not," he said genuinely, shaking his head.

I looked at a wide-eyed Ambrose, who shook his head vigorously in the negative.

"You can come to terms with this, Eira. You were raised by a strong woman to be a strong woman," Gotwig offered.

How could I believe any of this? It made *Magika and Menagerie* feel tame. But the proof lay in front of me in the form of a leathered piece of my mother, a cloudy green double flame with a four-pointed crown at its top still visible.

"Is there more?" I sat up, aided by Tommand who had moved behind me to support my back. I sat between his legs, which he folded under my backside.

"There is. She fell pregnant in her sixteenth year, but it is unclear whether the babe she bore was sired by the Primus-King or the man who died helping her when she decided to remove herself, and her child, from the king's control."

The wave of nausea hit me so fast that I didn't have a chance to stop the vomit that spewed from my mouth and over the side of Tommand's leg.

"The king, who wished me to become his mate, could be my father?" I retched again.

"Calm yourself Eira. That may very well have been a ploy to get you on board with a Gaean Assignment. There is not a Troth I have known that wouldn't have leapt at the chance to become a queen, and we are working under the assumption that the Gaeans thought you unaware of your lineage."

"Which I was, until only moments ago." Sweat beaded on my forehead, and my palms were hot and wet. I wiped them on the legs of my pants and hung my head between my knees, trying my best to maintain my sanity.

Ambrose, who had left when I'd become ill, returned and handed a flask to Tommand.

"Small sips only." He held the pungent drink to my mouth. I wanted to chug the entirety of its contents but heeded his advice. Using water from another sealed leather flask, Tommand cleaned up the mess I'd made, despite my protests to deal with it myself.

"You mentioned others," I said to Gotwig while pressing my hands to my temples and concentrating on staying upright.

He inclined his head.

"Primus Nortia is aware of your parentage and formed a plan with the current Mantle. It has always been known your placement would be Solnna. Preparations were made early to ensure your success there."

"Was I... am I actually Troth?" I trembled, awaiting the answer.

"You are, yes. And because of that, your value is infinitely more significant to the Gaeans... and if Ozius reaches Gaea with proof of your blessed blood, I fear all of Ærta will be in danger."

"My mother? Is she safe? If her blood is the same as mine, would they not come after her? And who is the man who raised me? And Nan, does she know?" The questions wouldn't stop coming once they began.

"Your mother will have left Nortia the day after you departed, and that man *is* your father. He and your mother fell in love sometime after your birth. He's a good man, and Ulltan has always seen you as his own. Nan was brought on as your guardian, chosen by your parents to see to your safety. She and Kennt, her husband, originally a guard at Verus, were joined for a brief time before he passed."

"And still, none of this explains why you yourself are involved," Tommand interjected.

Gotwig glanced down at his hands and turned his palms over, staring at them like he was deciphering a map.

"After my enslavement, I was stranded in Gaea, severely impaired and broken," blue eyes met mine, "your mother healed my body and reformed my soul." Gotwig looked off into the distance. "When it became clear that her life there was untenable, we were able to see her smuggled out of Gaea with the help of several healers she had mentored. But while running through the night, we were apprehended by the king's guards, and a struggle ensued. After the fight, both she and I were significantly bloodied, and I begged her to run. Were we separated, she knew to seek safety in the only place more powerful than the kingdoms. I would meet her there." Gotwig put the leathered flesh back in his cloak. "I was captured and hung. I remember every blow, the feeling of fire in my lungs, my own neck snapping, my body being dumped in the refuse mound. But I woke. My eyes opened again, and I stumbled my way across a continent in search of her... I am the man who died getting her out."

There were no words.

Only silence.

"We assume it was her blood mixing with my own that reversed my death, which is why I would like to see if the ability has passed to you. May I withdraw a very small amount from the side of your wrist?"

"Very well," I reached my arm out toward Gotwig, who swiftly rose to his feet.

Tommand's hand fired out, halting the arm I offered. I turned to him in question. "If this can provide me with proof, or not, I will better know how to move forward in this madness."

His eyes searched mine, concerned but trusting.

"I will do it then. Don't touch her," Tommand said warily.

"By all means." Gotwig forced an insincere smile but acquiesced and produced a blade that Tommand immediately refused.

"I will use my own. I know its history." Tommand pulled the tiny blade I'd originally found in his bags, seemingly out of the air. "You will barely feel this, just a little sting." He took my hand in his and twisted my wrist to its side. "Here, come close, look at where

I'll make the mark. Is that okay?" I ducked close, and he pointed to a spot below the fatty part of my thumb.

"Yes, that's fi—"

Warm lips settled on mine, a little pleased hum issued from my throat, and I barely felt the swift nick on my skin. My eyes closed of their own accord, and I felt the ticklingly light caress of his mouth to my toes. We remained joined until someone in the tiny room cleared their throat. My cheeks heated as I felt Tommand's smile against my lips. The chaste kiss felt too intimate to be shared in front of the others.

"Here you are." Tommand held his blade out to Gotwig.

Gotwig took the blade and gathered the bead of blood at its edge onto his finger and then swiped it down one side of his cheek and neck. He rubbed the red haze until it fully integrated into his skin.

"We will compare this side to the other after a while, but now we form a plan."

"Can... can I have an hour or two by myself before my future is determined by you lot? By men I barely know."

Gotwig thought in silence for a moment and looked around the small chamber.

"No more than an hour, I'm afraid. I must return to Verus and assist the Scion. We must intercept Ozius before he is able to return to Gaea, and it is the duty of his Obligate brothers to see him brought to heel."

I brought my hands to my face. *How has it come to this?*

I got out of the cave as fast as I could, knowing Tommand and Ambrose both trailed behind me. I spun on them, scolding them both like dogs who'd been told to stay. "I meant it. I need to be alone," I threatened.

"Alone is not an option you have."

I wanted to scream at Tommand, to rage and yell, and tell him to back off... but it wouldn't have made a difference. I knew the stubborn set of his jaw, the determination that glinted in his eye.

"Then you come with me," I pointed to Tommand, "and you go away." I flung my pointed finger to the tree line in the distance and leveled my gaze at Ambrose, who didn't move until Tommand issued the directive that he was to maintain his perimeter surveillance.

I started walking through the tight corridor of stone that had brought us to the cave, and anxiety pressed down on me, making it difficult to pull air into my lungs. When the rock wall became low enough for me to see over, I did my best to scale its side but ultimately needed Tommand's knee to be able to grasp the ledge. He, of course, was able to climb the wall with no issue and was walking before I'd been able to get to my feet.

A short distance away, we came upon a field of lavender, the stalks dry and brittle, swaying in the wind. I breathed more freely here, able to fill my chest with the wind that swept across the wide-open space. The rippling waves of purple plant matter reminded me of the Penumbrean Sea at its most gentle.

Though trying to afford me some modicum of privacy, I sensed Tommand a few paces behind me.

"You know, I've never seen you fully unclothed, and yet you've seen me naked quite a few times. Is there a reason?"

I turned and soaked up the view. He leaned against the smooth white trunk of a birch tree in his borrowed linen shirt. He'd rolled the too-long sleeves past his elbows, showing off the musculature of his forearms, and the buff-colored pants he wore fit him well enough. Even in the clothing of the lower class, he looked like he belonged in the war room of a fortress.

"Other than my inability to divest fast enough before you begin making demands... no," he chuckled.

"And if I *could* manage to wait... would you remove your clothing and allow me to mount you now?" I felt unmoored, and I wanted a connection with him again.

His pupils grew large, and a lazy smile tugged at his mouth. I watched, mesmerized as he hardened. His erection pulsed against his pants as it grew and pointed proudly up to his stomach. My arousal responded in kind, the heaviness, the mouth-watering swell of tension coming on full tilt as I openly ogled him.

He shook his head.

"I need to focus on our surroundings."

I clasped my hands and spun on my heels.

"Is that not what you told Ambrose to do?" I shivered in the cool breeze, which helped to stave off some of my pent-up tension. "I'm sorry, Tommand. I'm just... feeling too much and also nothing at all, if that's even possible. The other night, when I was similarly overwhelmed, being with you, having a release, made me calm... more able to focus."

"And was it in that time of mental solitude that you decided to poison me?" he joked.

I didn't know how Tommand could so easily make light of the situation. I certainly couldn't. The torment I felt when he'd said the word "love" after I'd tipped the tincture to his lips had been excruciating.

"Come here." His velvety voice demanded, pulling me back to the present.

I turned and looked up at him while he stretched his arms wide.

I ignored the musings of my mind and went into his embrace, laying my head in the crook of his neck. When did it happen that another human could make me feel even more myself?

"Forward or backward?" he asked.

"Hmm?"

Tommand kept his head straight and gaze alert, and I watched closely as his eyes oscillated, taking in the environment in front of him.

"Just pick one," he murmured.

"Forward." I smiled into his chest, wondering what distraction he had planned.

"Forward it is." Tommand flipped me around and hugged me to him. I laid the back of my head against his shoulder, doing my best to live in this exact moment and not dwell on anything other than his solid presence. I wanted nothing more than to clear my head and eschew the prospect of what would come tomorrow, or in an hour, or a year. Letting my mind clear, I breathed deeply, in and out, and counted the thumps of his heartbeat.

I didn't know where we were in relation to Verus or Stormridge, but it was lovely here.

"Do you know what is more beautiful than the flowers in the field?"

I shook my head.

"The look you make before you come," he said thickly.

His arms tightened, and I looked down at the scarred fingers splaying across my stomach, watching them find their way upward to cup both of my breasts.

"Your mouth parts, ever so slightly, and you smile the most secretive smile... like you know something none of the rest of us do."

I made a sensual sound in the back of my throat, excited by the turn of events. When he touched me, my mind could focus on nothing other than him.

"Tommand, I don't want to compromise your focus, truly," I said in earnest. I knew he took our safety seriously.

He tugged gently on the gold bar at my nipple, and everything below my navel tightened in response, the flesh there even more sensitive than I remembered.

I rubbed my backside against his hardness, which drew a curse from his lips.

Moving his hands low, Tommand skimmed his fingers under the front of my battered waistband. His knee pushed between my legs, parting them, and I felt him shift his balance while propping a foot against the trunk of the tree.

"*I* have to stay focused, not you," he ran his hand through the curls at my apex, "the mere thought of you riding me for your own enjoyment fogs my brain altogether... but this I can manage."

He split my lips with two fingers and swirled their pads lightly around the damp valley of my inner labia. He knew exactly what I wanted and used my own wetness to penetrate me in a few slick motions. He began slowly rocking his palm against my aching clit, I leaned back, taking what he offered.

"Tommand?"

"*Cato?*"

I ignored him.

"What about Ambrose? Can he... see us? What if he sees us?" I popped open my eyes and looked around.

"I imagine if he can, his cock would already be in his hand."

Heat flared across my face and chest, and a gush of wetness moistened my already slippery passage. My breath hitched in my throat at the thought of Ambrose pleasuring himself. Tommand continued working me, pushing his fingers just a little further each time he pressed into me.

"Does it excite you that another man would take his pleasure while watching you receive yours?" His voice was strained.

"I..."

"Would you like for the two of us to take you together?"

Goddess alive. I'd conjured both their faces in a dream once, but they had come to me separately. The thought of two lovers, at the same time, and how would we— "Oh, I, *ohhhh,*" the extended groan that came from me would undoubtedly disprove the lie I was about to tell.

"I could bear sharing you with another only because I'd be able to witness the amplified intensity of your ecstasy. I think you would rather like taking me into your mouth, while he slid himself into your depths."

Tommand pulled his hand from me, and he went to work unlacing my handcrafted closure. I whimpered and tossed my head back, almost painfully aroused and pressing myself into his knee. He pushed me forward and let the linen drop then repositioned himself.

I felt his forearm moving between my legs but couldn't see or understand his intention until I felt his two longest fingers at my entrance.

"*Ride.*"

It was an order.

Distraught with need, I sunk down onto the digits of his upturned palm and ground my pubic bone into his thigh. Over and over, I rose up and down, impaling myself on the fingers that curved and reached and rubbed against that deep, glorious spot.

"There it is, that little smile. It should be just about... now."

I screamed out and arched backward, continuing to move on him until my passage swelled happily around his fingers and even the smallest of movements against my highly sensitive flesh made me gasp. Still joined, I slumped forward, panting from my exertion.

He gently removed his fingers and studied the moisture on his hand, growling out a satisfied sound. I wiggled down his thigh and bent to retrieve my clothing. Was it silly of me to feel shy about the way I'd moved on him, just wildly seeking my own fulfillment? Or for the pleasure I gained from thinking of him and another?

Leaning against the trunk of the tree, he wiped his hand on his breeches, still fully composed, even with the massive erection at his hips.

"I... uh... thank you," I said stupidly while pulling the rope at my back and securing my clothing once again.

Tommand continued looking over my head, taking in our surroundings.

"Are you embarrassed?" he asked.

"I am... I don't know, not embarrassed, but it was different being the only one receiving pleasure, it just felt so self-centered, if that makes sense, and then there was the... way you talked..."

Tommand came forward and took my hand between his own.

"Never be embarrassed by what your body wants, certainly not on my behalf. Your reactions and responses brought me an immense amount of satisfaction."

I glanced down. I couldn't help myself.

"I practically stay hard around you, Eira."

I pulled away from him and shuffled closer to the tall grass, kicking out at the little clumps of crunchy greens growing along the ground.

"You know, I think that's what I don't understand. I still don't fully get our seemingly strong connection, and you know what bothers me even more?"

"No... go on."

"Well, it's the fact that I should be way more concerned that I may have magic blood, or... or that my father is not my father—but one of two absolute creatures could be—and that my future is, at this point, more up in the air than before I came to Verus. And despite all of that... all I can focus on is what will happen if *we* are parted."

He didn't respond but grabbed my hand again and pulled me out into the tall grass that came up to the middle of my thighs. He sat in the field of withering flowers and tugged me down to lay at his side.

"Can you keep an eye out from down here?" I asked.

"I figured we'd be hidden from the world, so there is less chance of being noticed in the first place." He traced his fingers along the curve of my shoulder. "The thought of leaving you in Solnna makes me feel like my life will end. I am not as immune to my own emotions as many would believe me to be. But the assurance of your safety outweighs any of my personal desires." Tommand rolled onto his back, and I snuggled in close to his side.

"And to answer your first question: There is no 'seeming'. Physically, I was immediately drawn to you, as any other person with eyes would be. You are fairly devastating to the senses." He turned his face to mine. "Your mouth is the most kissable shade of rose, and the way your hips flare out from your waist drives me to fever, and your breasts, my Goddess, if there was ever something made for my hands alone... and you have a great personality, too." He chuckled deeply. "Now, tell me something you like about me."

I'd gone all squishy inside at his admission.

"I like your..." *What don't I like about him?*

"Is it really that difficult to think of something?" he joked, elbowing me lightly in the side.

"No, there is a lot about you that I like, but I'm having trouble not focusing my answer around a certain part of your anatomy at the moment."

Tommand's mouth dropped open, and he gasped loudly.

"Troth Nortia, I do believe your mind is sullied!"

I could have told him that his smile made my problems disappear, or that the sound of his laughter could halt me mid-stride, or even how running my hands over the expanse of his chest made me feel like I could conquer a kingdom.

"Honestly, Tommand, there is nothing about the way you look that I don't find pleasing, but I really value your focus. When we're talking, when we're together, it's like I'm the only one in existence... but mostly I like your penis," I whispered the last part.

"My penis is well pleased then," he outright laughed." I had never entered anyone before that night at Verrona's and it was just as spectacular as I thought it would be."

"WHAT?" I yelled, shocked by his admission. "Why didn't you say something about that?"

"What would I have said? Why would it have mattered?" He shook his head in confusion.

"I don't know. I could have focused on you a little more... or said something nice." I smacked his shoulder. "I don't think anyone would believe you if you told them that, by the way. I don't think *I* believe you."

"Why? Would they see me as lesser? Fuck them. Also, I've gotten off plenty, Nortia," he pursed his lips at me, "but never penetrating someone was the only way to ensure no child would come. I would never be able to see to the safety of Monwyn if my mind was on another—my own blood. That was also the reason I hesitated with you... until I began looking for ways to convince myself otherwise. Also, and I *am* embarrassed to admit this... my immediate thought when I found out you may be with child was, 'Thank Derros, we can finally fuck.'"

"And that's why you pulled from me the first time before you..." I trailed off.

"It is. Though the second time, the whole of the Monwyn army could not have stopped me from spilling inside you," Tommand adjusted himself in his pants, "going forward, I will be more careful."

I crawled onto his body and laid myself out on top of him.

"Tommand?"

"Cato."

"Cato?" The name felt foreign on my lips—but I would use it again if it meant I could continue seeing the massive smile that was currently plastered across his face. Both dimples were visible, even with the beard he had grown, and his eyes squinted into almost nothingness, but it was the joy I saw reflected back at me that compelled me to lean forward and plant dozens of little kisses around his lips and chin. "When you return to Monwyn, you should find someone who makes you happy... have a bunch of children... grow old. Don't live your life devoted to those who have taken it upon themselves to turn a blind eye to the rules of this continent."

I meant it. How much of his life had he already given up for others?

"Were it that simple..." He sighed. "Nortia, what were you like as a child?"

"Me? Well... I was really happy. I had everything I needed and had tutors to teach me things others never got a chance to learn." I ran my finger down the bridge of his nose and over the dip in the middle of his top lip. "I was curious about everything and was probably a little bossy, but I always felt well-liked."

He caught the tip of my finger between his teeth and flicked his tongue over its pad.

"And your mother? Any indication of her... uniqueness?"

"Tommand," he arched his brow at me, "Cato," I whispered. He wrapped his arms tightly around my waist. "When I say she was the most *mom* mom I have ever met, I mean it. I knew not to get out of line, and she called me out on every lie I ever tried to tell. Dinner was always prompt, I was always clean, and I always did my chores. She wasn't oppressive or anything and allowed me many freedoms, but she took parenting quite seriously. Maybe that was her goddess power." I smirked.

"Nortia," he slanted his head to the left, "we've been summoned back."

I didn't bother asking how he knew.

"Time to stop running away from it, I suppose," I said solemnly.

His lips were warm on mine.

"Cat!" The shout came from Ambrose, who sounded nearby.

Goddess, he truly may have had an up-close seat for my unhinged show of self-satisfaction.

"He neared only recently," Cato reassured, reading my expression.

Before I moved away, a warm hand found the back of my neck, and our mouths came together once again, in a desperate mingling of teeth and tongues and moans that ended all too quickly.

"Cato! The captain has arrived." It was clear by Ambrose's tone that our stolen moment was over.

I gazed at my feet as we walked back to the cave. I hadn't come to terms with anything during my hour-long break, but I didn't regret how I'd spent the time either.

Now though, I needed to concentrate on the hereafter.

The captain of the guard, the very man who had put a bolt through my attacker's neck that day at the river, was leading his mount into the cave when we got back.

He wore no temple livery, no red or gold, and his horse could never have been mistaken for the coursers the guards normally rode. The captain was an average-sized man, healthy in appearance with a trim black mustache that began at his lip and rode his cheek downward, ending at his chin. Like every other guard at Verus, I'd never seen him with any expression but the purest detachment.

"Captain." Cato greeted the man with a nod of respect.

"Protector." The guard drew himself up and placed his right fist on his left shoulder.

"Take your ease," Cato ordered.

The soldier, who showed no signs of being at ease, strode purposefully into the small room of the cave, where the trace smell from my sickness still hung in the air.

Ambrose bade everyone sit while he lit the small lamp that he placed at the center of the room. The captain chose to remain standing.

"Report." It was Gotwig who raised his voice.

"Our scouts have lost Scion Ozius's trail but are redoubling efforts to find him. Four bands of Gaean operatives have been discovered: three heading toward the south, presumably to Solnna, and the other rounding the rift, heading into Nortian territory. The groups are small and are moving interspersed with the usual merchants who follow the same paths. They are using the guises of tradespeople and pilgrims. Currently, we believe these pods are solely for reconnaissance but can't rule out future militaristic action.

The Mantle has quarantined the Gaean emissaries and has sent a missive directly to the Primus-King demanding an explanation for the actions of those under his purview."

"And Evandr?" I choked out.

"Little change. The Scion's heart still beats, but the healers are not hopeful."

"Emissary Nortia?"

The captain paused and turned his gaze to Cato, who inclined his head indicating to continue.

"She threatens me daily and has destroyed our barracks."

My shoulders sagged in relief. *A mean Nan was an okay Nan. Had he said she'd wept openly for days, I would be marching right back to the temple.*

"Protector, sir, there is something else."

Cato sharpened his boot knife with a strap of leather as he listened.

"Devotee Mariad has been awake for the past twenty-four hours. He will remain bedridden for weeks, but he asks that you, Emissary, take Troth Nortia to Monwyn for her best chance of survival."

"No!" Ambrose and Cato simultaneously interjected.

Cato bounded up to his feet, knife in hand, and he and Ambrose closed in on the messenger. The captain, in a testament to his bravery, held his position when both Monwyns surrounded him and pressed themselves nearly to his chest.

"If I may, Scion Ambrose, Emissary... his plan is sound. If the Gaeans are to launch an assault or attempt to capture Troth Nortia, your best chances of protecting her are on familiar turf." The men listened but didn't back away. "You yourself designed many of Monwyn's defenses, and the mountainous barrier that encircles your kingdom will make a full-scale attack nigh impossible. Gaea has been in overland trade agreements with Solnna and Nortia for decades; they are very familiar with the topography and defensive positions of both."

The guard finished listing his reasons, and two furious men continued to crowd him, raising their voices.

"Why is it that two Monwyns, so devoted to their kingdom, would not wish to return to their storied homeland with a celebrated Obligate to look over their people, hmmm?" questioned Gotwig. "The Gaean Primus-King undoubtedly believes Troth Nortia belongs to him, and in accordance with Gaean law, he does have a claim. How far would you go to protect what is *yours*?"

Gotwig spoke directly to Cato, whose face turned lethal. He glared down his nose and his eyes gleamed in the dancing light.

"She is mi—"

"She is in danger, Emissary," Gotwig asserted, interrupting him.

He shifted his eyes from a snarling Cato to Ambrose. "Your daughter will be born of two Obligates." Gotwig pulled his blade and looked at his reflection closely. "Beyond that, what will become of her when it is discovered her lifeblood mends flesh. Will the healers ever leave her be? Will the Primus-King seek to bind her to his bloodline?"

Ambrose and Cato talked over each other incomprehensibly and then lowered their voices to whispers, talking closely in one another's ear.

I crawled over to where Gotwig sat and pushed the lamp closer to his face. By no means were the treated gashes healed, but their ends were more closely knit, and wounds that seeped earlier had begun scabbing over.

"I know Mariad's mind, but what do you think I should do?" I whispered to Gotwig.

The captain joined in on the Monwyns' argument, and three voices bounced off the walls in an alarming cacophony.

"What is it you have wanted most in life, Eira?"

"To... to ease the lives of those who struggle. It's all I've wanted. Even if I hadn't been Troth, I think it would have been my calling."

He nodded, and a quiet smile appeared on his face.

"For your mother, it was the same. Be it a wretch tarnished by abuse," Gotwig tipped his fingertips towards his chest, "or a mother unable to bring her child into the world, she devoted herself to those whose innocence had been lost... like hers had been."

I looked down at the hands in front of me. They were so thin, so frail. Locking eyes, I stared into his blue depths and reached out hesitantly, laying my hand into the palm of the man who may be my father.

His skin was utterly frigid and seemed to steal the warmth of my own. It was like his very blood ran cold.

"I bled on Evandr." I kept my voice low, never looking away.

"Then he may yet live. I will find him if he does. I will guide him."

"Did, did you do all of this? Your whole life, has it always been—"

"Dedicated to the possibility of seeing a mother and daughter live well?" His weak smile deepened. "It was the least I could do for the woman who saved me with her love."

Tears threatened again... the tears of the Goddess, of Merrias, and The Child. I shed tears for those who bore their children through pain and blood, the mothers who knew unbearable loss, and the holy mothers who prayed for all children in the temples. I thought of the love of Cato and Ambrose's mother, opening her heart to a child not of her body. I thought of Demma taking care of her gems and Lok, who mourned the loss of the woman who raised him... of Kairus, who knew the pain of being abandoned by the woman who should have supported her most. I thought of the citizens of Monwyn, the children who were no longer protected by the father figure who had pledged them his love and protection.

They needed a mother.

I could be selfless, I could make a difference for them.

"I'm going to Monwyn." My voice rang out around the small cavern and echoed even after the spatting men had silenced.

"You most certainly will not!" Cato blasted.

I stood and snapped my head to face him.

"And you will stop me?" I closed the distance between Cato and myself. "Tell me, Protector, how long can you stay away from your responsibilities while stashing me in some new hideout every other day?" I puffed my chest out and looked down my nose, mimicking the man in front of me. "*Your* job is to protect your fellow man, and they need you. *I* am an Obligate of Ærta and *my* job is to help your *king* and kingdom. These are the laws of Verus, and even you, Emissary, do not outrank Them."

Like two dumbfounded drunkards, the brothers' mouths gaped open. They took turns staring at each other and then back at me.

"*Troth* Nortia, as you know, Monwyn would *be* a dissatisfactory placement for you... even the Mantle felt Solnna a *wise* Assignment," Ambrose muttered, raising his eyebrows at each word he emphasized.

"Troth be wise"? Did he really just use code to say exactly what he meant?

"Fuck off, Ambrose. They can fuck off too."

"Eira, I need you to think," Cato begged.

"I've thought. And what Monwyn needs... is me. You know it, and so do I. I was chosen by the Goddess to maintain the balance on this continent, and I am taking up that banner. I will do what *I* want, whether or not some old monarch thinks he has a claim on my life. He doesn't. And neither. Do. You!"

Cato launched himself at Gotwig, picked the smaller man up from the ground, and slammed his body back into the stone wall.

"What did you say to her?" he bit out, fury seeping from his every pore.

"You will release him and address *me* when talking about my decisions, Emissary," I demanded.

I stood up to my full height and marched myself to where he held Gotwig by his neck. He, of course, showed no indication of pain, but seeing a hand around his neck upset me.

"Release him or I will run from you... every chance I get."

Cato's head jerked back, and he slowly twisted it in my direction. The corners of his nose flared, a primal instinct triggered. That brilliant glow sparkled in his cinnamon eyes, and I... I reared back and slammed my fist into his face so hard I cried out.

The connection of my knuckles to his nose was so shocking that I was still holding my hand rubbing away the pain when Cato shook his head and placed his hand against the wall.

"Thank you for heading that off," he muttered.

"Quite welcome. When do we leave?"

"Tonight."

My heart dropped to my stomach.

I would devote my life to wrestling a madman back to humanity, while trying to avoid being captured by another madman—all the while attempting to appease the very mad man who stood before me gritting his teeth and clenching his fists at his sides.

"Excellent."

I walked further back into the cave and did my best not to hyperventilate.

Chapter Thirty-Nine

IGNITION

L eading Horse Ambrose, I poked my head into the cavern where the men had grouped up again. They were looking even more dour than when I'd left to prepare the mount.

Cato frowned, staring into the light of the traveling lamp in his normal gravely serious way, but Ambrose, always so nonchalant and pleasantly occupied, looked positively furious. He sat perched on top of a rock, bouncing his knee so aggressively that dust clouds gathered around him. His lips were curled into a nasty grimace and his eyes, which were fixated on Cato, were marked with open hostility. I dropped the reins and stepped into the room.

"Eira," Gotwig said in a soft, soothing tone, "we have conferred and developed a plan that will allow for plausible justification for your disappearance. We can disseminate the mistruths throughout Verus and the various kingdoms who, rightfully, will demand an explanation as to the modification of their Obligate Assignments."

"Planning without me?" I said, looking in Cato's direction. He leaned back against the rock wall, arms crossed over his chest, and stayed silent, a quick huff his only response.

"Other than the collective of Scion, and those few chosen by the Mantle, it will be spread that Scion Ozius returned home to put his affairs in order before setting out across the sea. Naturally, he will have traveled with Advisor Marcyn and Obligate Castor, who volunteered to assure his protection. Marcyn, who is still alive for the time being, will remain locked on the sixth floor of the temple, and Castor will befall an unfortunate incident on his travels to Gaea and be laid to rest on the journey."

I rolled my head back and forth, contemplating the plan so far.

"It seems solid, but I'm sure the Primus-King will be able to guess what's actually befallen his Scion... though publicly accepting Castor's death may give him a way to save face when he deals with the Mantle. Also, what about Kairus? Wouldn't she also need to see to her affairs to make it seem more realistic?"

"Women do not have affairs in Monwyn," Ambrose muttered from where he sat.

"*I'll* certainly come as a surprise to your king then... I won't be following that particular custom. My decisions and my dealings are mine."

"You will follow them. Ambrose will see to all the matters that concern you for the duration of your stay." It was Cato who spoke this time.

"Gentleman, I am an *Obligate*. Verus may control aspects of my life, but no other person holds that authority over me."

Silence.

I looked around suspiciously, eyeing each of them. They couldn't seem to hold my gaze... not even Gotwig.

"What haven't you told me?" I asked.

"That you will arrive in Monwyn as Ambrose's betrothed," Cato stated plainly.

Huh, thought I heard something... guess not.

I scooped up Horse Ambrose's reins and trudged towards the cave's entrance, side-stepping some of the larger bits of rubble and kicking away the stones that might have tripped up the steed.

I'd head to Monwyn by my own damn self and figure out their kingly issues. I liked Ambrose, I really did, but there was no way I'd saddle myself to the man in a kingdom where I'd be fighting both a magical monarch *and* a bunch of misogynists.

"Eira." Cato pursued me, his voice echoing through the passageway. "Hear me out."

"Nope, I'm tired of hearing people out. I'm leaving and—"

Cato grabbed Horse Ambrose's saddle and shoved his way between the horse and wall, cutting me off at the pass.

I stared straight into his chest, refusing eye contact.

"There is nothing, *nothing*, I like about this plan... but it makes sense. All of Verus knows of your intimacy, and therefore, it would not be surprising that with the possibility of conception, you would move forward in a joining contract."

"Our non-existent baby makes no difference! It would be born at Verus and remain there to be raised. Besides which, even if Obligates are joined, they don't go back to their home kingdom."

"Yes, I understand, but Ambrose is royal, it would be expected that the betrothal and traditions be carried out in his lands. Any monarch on the continent would see nuptials like these as a boost to the morale of their people and a way to further legitimize their rule—worth disrupting the usual process."

I shrugged off the fingers that ran down my arms.

"Wait, I have another issue. How are you, the man who attacked his brother for fingering me, so calm about the idea of him *marrying* me?"

"At the end of the day, a betrothal to Ambrose would send a message to Gaea, Eira. As a future member of the royal family, with all rights that entails, even *they* wouldn't be foolish enough to launch an attack. If they did, they would face the Protector and *all* of his armies."

I clenched the reins in my hand and sucked in a deep breath trying to get a handle on my churning emotions.

"I understand that, I get it, but... what would become of *us*?" I choked.

I leaned into the hand that came to my cheek, pressing nearer its warmth.

I felt so small, so foolish. When I'd agreed to go to Monwyn, I'd told myself that we could continue on as we had been.

"To make this work, you must convince the kingdom that you and Ambrose are committed to your union. We will *all* have to play our roles convincingly... until a time we know you are safe."

"I do suppose having sex with your brother's wife-to-be would be improper..." My voice shook with emotion.

"Eira, were it not for the citizens... for the king... I would lay you upon my bed and let your screams advertise to the world to whom you belong."

"Mmhmm, well, that will fall to Ambrose now."

Pushing past Cato, I headed to the entrance.

"It is not safe for you to be tied to me. Eira, where are you going?" he asked.

"Monwyn, apparently!" I yelled back.

"So you agree?"

"Tell my beloved to hurry the fuck up."

···✦·)(·✦···

"This is just great, you know, because I wanted to be married... not at all. NOT EVER!" We'd been gone two hours, and Ambrose had yet to stop pouting. "Go sex up some

Obligates. Sure no problem. Want to spend the best night of your life with me in exchange for fur, maybe some oil? Where do I sign up?"

I glared at Cato, who'd forced me to ride in front of his brother "just in case anyone was watching."

"You know what, Nortia—"

"Call her Eira. She's your betrothed," Cato interrupted.

"Fuck off, Cato," Ambrose fired back. "You know what, *Eira*? When I said yes to my brother's original, ridiculous scheme, I thought, sure, I'll nail some Troth and convince her that Monwyn is the best place on the whole godsdamn continent. Shit, I even agreed to start an elaborate affair and convince you to run away with me if that didn't work. Do you know what I *never* agreed to? A wife and kids!"

His big hand patted my stomach as he spoke.

"Freeze in the nether, Ambrose. Is the thought of a relationship with me so revolting? Not that I want to even *think* about being joined with your big, dramatic, stupid self!" I hammered my fist on his leg.

"You? No, you're fine, mostly." My anger simmered down... just a hair. "But marrying at all, being a father? Fucking a single person for the rest of my life? The very idea is revolting. And speaking of, you *still* owe me the courtesy of a solid fuck. That's my price for this bullshit."

"Ambrose!" I shrieked.

"Watch yourself, brother," Cato growled while he rode his horse closer to our own.

"Cat, you know as well as I what a royal bedding entails. They will *watch* me take her. Fuck, *you* will be the one who carries out the rite unless Thierry's in his right mind. And I don't give a shit about your feelings for her; I will not have the whole damned palace thinking I am not the king of my own bed chamber. I will let myself loose upon her!"

"Wait. What? Is that actually a custom? Who watches and what's the rite? The last rite I took part in literally cooked my flesh! Are you telling me there's some backward-ass, consummation rite?"

"You would know if you finished Troth school," jeered Ambrose, who smacked his hand against my outer thigh.

"BOTH OF YOU, STOP!" Cato hollered.

The wind ceased, and even the birds silenced their songs.

"Look, we will deal with what comes... all of us. Betrothals can be long, and if we are successful in stabilizing the king, plans can be remade."

"Plans can be remade," Ambrose mocked his brother as I shot my finger in the air, hoping Cato could see what I thought of him right now.

"I should dump you both here. I should just turn right at the next road and let you figure it out on your own..." Cato grumbled.

"You'd miss this blood-magic *pussy* too much!"

"Mother would actually disown you, Cat!"

Cato's mouth dropped open at our simultaneously screamed insults and rode forward, leaving us behind.

"That was good. Did you see his face when you said pussy?" Ambrose snickered.

I leaned back onto the Scion's large chest, and he wrapped his arms around my waist, using my hips to support his elbows. We ended up riding through the night. I'd have sworn we passed the same landmarks twice, and some of our navigation choices just made no sense. Finally, in the wee hours of the morning, Cato determined that we'd covered enough ground and gone undetected by any potential foes.

We rode up to an abandoned farmstead that looked to have been quite darling in its day. The main house was two stories tall, and I couldn't tell its color in the dark, though I could see where the light-colored paint had begun to peel and chip away from its wooden boards and where the hand-hewn door frame was rotting. The farm, I'm sure, thrived at some point, as barns and sheds dotted the backfields, and there was just enough moonlight to make out the tall cylinder of an old windmill as well. Those had to be expensive to build and maintain.

"We will not sleep in the main house. There is too much risk in doing so. The old smithy out back has three walls and a back stall that can be fully enclosed. The door is also reinforced with metal bracketing. Take the horses there and I will join you later," Cato said before turning to leave.

He handed me his reins, and together Ambrose and I led the horses to their spot for the night and secured them both to a set of bent metal hooks mounted to the smithy's wall beam.

"Come back here." I followed Ambrose's voice and crawled into a small storage space.

Ambrose took my hands and guided me to his side, then shut the heavy door with his foot.

"Nortia?"

"Yes?" I followed his lead, keeping my voice low.

"I want better for him."

As we sat, I wiggled my way closer to Ambrose's side and patted him on his big arm.

"I have had everything given to me, laid out in front of me, paraded around or thrown in my lap," he breathed, "and Cat? All he has ever done is give of himself for the sake of others."

Ambrose leaned back against the wall of the unlit enclosure and led my head to his chest.

"He told me he loves you."

I hid my face in his shoulder and pulled my knees close. "And you should know Cato loves as fiercely as he fights."

The door in front of us slid open on its track.

"It's clear," Cato shared.

"Good. Bed down, she's cold."

"No, I'm fine. I promise it's not—"

Cato shoved himself between my body and the exterior wall, curving himself around me and adjusting Ambrose's arm to use as a pillow.

"When it's cold, Nortia, you cuddle up to whatever makes heat—stinking servicemen, cows in a field... immature Scion."

"Screw yourself, *Tom!*" snapped Ambrose.

Cato's chuckle, his breath against my neck... the tightening of his arm around my waist as I instinctively moved closer. It all made me feel unbelievably calm at a time when I should have been wrapped up in trepidation and anger.

"What's the plan after tonight?" I asked, a little scared to know the answer.

"First, we continue your defense lessons until reaching the palace—if you end up in a situation where one of us is not in the vicinity, you must be able to safeguard yourself." Cato ran his lips up the column of my neck as he spoke, and I shuddered when chills broke out all over my body.

"I told you she was cold," Ambrose asserted.

"Second, we will make a short detour to procure suitable clothing for us all. Our story will not sell if we arrive in the scraps we currently wear."

"That makes sense," I agreed. I couldn't imagine meeting the King of Monwyn with my asscrack partially visible.

"Finally, we must make our way to a Monwyn temple to have your betrothal contract signed and blessed before stepping foot in the capital."

My body *did* go cold at the mention of the contract, until familiar fingers began rubbing light circles on my arm. "Both of you must be prepared for what you will encounter at the palace as well, but for now, sleep. Ambrose, I'll go on first watch. We will trade places in a few hours' time."

I fell asleep immediately and only woke briefly when Cato filled Ambrose's empty spot. Delicate, soft-lipped kisses brushed across my cheekbone, and I smoothed my lips over the scars of the hand I held tightly to my chest.

···+)((+···

Something heavy hit my stomach, and I lurched forward, fearing for my life. I smacked out at what attacked me and grabbed the weight, chucking it against the wall.

"Get up, Nortia. Put those on," Ambrose yawned.

"You know, maybe don't do things like that when we're running from maniacs."

"All a part of your training, my dear. Hurry up."

A pair of dry-rotted leather ankle boots lay on the ground. Normally, I wouldn't have dared to put my scratched-up feet into something that looked like it could single-handedly begin a plague, but this would be the first time since leaving the temple that my toes *and* soles would be covered fully. For that, I was immensely thankful. I didn't care at all that I could smell the staleness of the aged hide or that they looked to be too large. My feet were bruised, the toenails chipped, and one had ripped back to the quick and had been causing me pain for days. I grabbed the pair and left the small room, seeking the scent of fresh air.

The day dawned, a crisp autumn morning, and in the light, I could see the full layout of the farmstead. I dragged my feet through the dewy grass, ridding myself of some of their accumulated gunk, all the while looking up at the leafless treetops above me. Winter would soon arrive, and I wondered what that would look like this far south. I walked toward an outbuilding and could see a red haze playing across the morning sky. I didn't know how it worked inland, but at home, our sailors would have been careful to monitor the sky, as the red hue generally preceded violent weather.

I walked along a partial fence line that rounded the smithy and spring house and noticed little tufts of hair, presumably from sheep that had grazed here some time ago, clinging to the wire. Thinking of my feet, I collected and stuffed the wool bits into the toes of my new-to-me shoes, filling out their too-long length and creating a barrier of protection between their roughness and my damaged skin.

Cato came around the corner of the farmhouse while I was slipping into the leather, scowling at something off in the distance and turning to check behind himself.

My heart flip-flopped.

Even in his ill-fitting clothing and remembering the smell of his unbathed body as he held me closely in the darkness, the fairies took flight. My breaths felt different, fuller, more cleansing. He felt like my person.

Like, he is mine.

As he neared, hands full, I watched his eyes crinkle at the corners as his face lit up.

My tongue went dry, and suddenly, I was overwhelmingly parched.

"The shoes work? I pilfered them from a slop house a few miles away. Got a few other things as well." He held up the small bags he'd lifted from some poor farmer, showing not a bit of remorse for his thievery. "Don't look at me that way. I get it, but this chunk of cheese and delicious-smelling pie mean we don't have to run down a squirrel or choke down nasty fucking mushroom water for the duration. I left them a coin for their trouble."

"You don't have any coins," I smugly reminded him while I ogled the sliver of chest revealed by his half-buttoned shirt.

"Well, *you* did." He pulled the little pouch of my hard-earned money from his pocket and tossed it to me. "I'd be glad to compensate yah fer your loss, ma'am. Simply name yah terms." He winked lasciviously.

Lust. Pure lust rolled through me.

I came to my feet biting at my bottom lip, squeezing my thighs tightly, enjoying the pressure. *Goddess I cherish this body of mine.*

"Why ma'am... I'm not sure I can accommodate them needs in the broad daylight," he joked, talking like the mountain folk.

"And I believe I'll take what's owed me anyhow." I sauntered toward him, pushing out my chest.

His voice thickened as he spoke. "By all means then, by all means."

I pounced, jerking the hem of his shirt from his pants, which knocked him back a half step. I shoved my hands under the garment, and it was like the flesh of my fingertips sparked. I took advantage of his full hands and scraped my nails down his chest, leaving red streaks in their wake.

"Drop the bags," I ordered, desperate to have his hands on me.

He obeyed in an instant, opening his fists and letting the parcels hit the ground.

Tugging at the shoulders of his shirt, I pulled it over his head, exposing that fine muscular chest to my starved gaze.

"Mmmm, I need this," I ground out.

"Growl like that again and you get fucked on wet grass," he promised, jerking me toward him by the waistband of my pants.

"I adored being fucked in the mud, I believe the grass would suffice just as well."

Skilled fingers came to my sides and unlaced the support, which fell to the ground along with the other items now cluttered around our feet.

I pressed my breasts to Cato's chest and sighed, loving the feel of his hardness against my softness. I craned my neck to receive his mouth and palmed the arousal that had grown against my belly.

"To your knees," he said, after dipping his tongue in with mine.

I dropped quickly and yanked at his belt and buttons until my hand found what it wanted. I slid my tongue down his stiff erection.

"Gods above, you favor me," he said while capturing my chin in his hand. He leaned my head back and admired me while I worked my hand up and down his length.

"I taught her well. Beautiful form."

Ambrose.

Cato dropped to his knees and bent over, panting heavily.

Ambrose, not a decent bone in him, strolled over like we'd gathered around the breakfast table and bent to retrieve a discarded bag. He stuck in his hand and pulled out a heaping chunk of pie and bit into like it was an apple.

"Please, do not stop on my account. This is *absolutely* more entertaining than watching the birds shit on the barn."

He didn't leave, didn't turn away, just stood there munching while I scrambled to secure my support.

"You *could* turn around," I murmured, crawling to retrieve Cato's shirt for him.

"And miss the chance to gaze at my almost-wife's perfect chest? Tits are like my third favorite thing, Eira. It's like you don't even know me. Pie?"

I snatched up the offered morsel after dumping Cato's shirt over his head. He'd yet to recover from our encounter and was still doubled over.

"Hurry and eat. We train in ten." Ambrose finally turned and headed toward the old mill, taking the delicious-looking wedge of goat cheese with him.

I grabbed the remaining bag from the grass where it had landed and knee-walked to Cato, who was pulling his hands down his cheeks.

"This is going to prove difficult," he said.

The dew had soaked into the knees of my pants, but I didn't care. My blood was still scalding, and I welcomed the coolness.

"Do you think we could, I don't know... meet up every once and again while in Monwyn, just to lessen the tension?" I asked, licking traces of meat pie gravy off my fingers.

"If you are asking whether it would be wise for us to have secret fuck sessions, the answer is no. You would be condemned for disloyalty to your royal husband if ever discovered, and, Eira, I am very serious when I say there are always those looking for a reason to make me beholden."

I watched him lace himself back into his pants. I knew there was wisdom in what he said, but still, I bristled.

"Would Ambrose be required to remain faithful to a wife?"

"No."

"Then I will bed whom I damn well please," I said sternly, meaning every word of my proclamation.

"Surely, you jest," Cato snapped back.

"Surely, I do not."

A hand struck out, catching me around the forearm.

"If you plan to entertain other men in your time at the palace, ensure I am somewhere far away," he fumed.

"No, that's not fair. I won't stop living in order to appease your jealousy. Do you expect me to remain in a loveless marriage and never seek out the comfort of another's arms? Of your arms?"

"That depends on how far you are willing to go for your citizens, Troth Nortia. If it means saving the people of Monwyn or keeping the corruption from spreading across the continent, I will give up all."

The silence became a chasm.

The Troth in me knew to give of herself. To always put the people before personal gain. But the woman in me... where Cato was concerned, I was entirely selfish.

"We must train." He stood and walked toward the mill. I followed, albeit a few steps behind.

"You will learn to wield a weapon," Cato began when I came to stand between him and Ambrose. "The King's moods are ever-changing. Sometimes he rages and commits violence on those closest to him. At other times he functions like a child, throwing himself on the ground in a tantrum or demanding to be coddled."

"Are you suggesting I use a weapon... against the King of Monwyn?" I asked incredulously.

"I am. He is still physically capable, and, Goddess forbid, if he were to attack you, it would be difficult to thwart him, even if we trained for all the hours in the day."

Ambrose stretched his arms across his chest while Cato bent forward, touching his toes and then the ground.

"He's a big man, taller than me but built less broadly. He is agile and cunning, and the last time I saw him, he had the ability to send small objects flying across the room without touching them, so you must be ever at the rea—"

"He can move stuff without touching it?" I blurted. "That's as terrifying as it is amazing. I figured it was all about controlling the weather or trying to reanimate the dead. I'd never thought there could be a practical side to conjuring."

Cato looked flustered by my interruption.

"He can, and his favorite target is the back of your head. So be alert and always ready to move."

"And does he have days where he's not mad or sad?"

Cato nodded.

"Those are the days you must be more mindful. He will turn sickly sweet, give you gifts, bestow titles on you and your family, tell you how much he values you... and then he will try to put a blade through your back as calmly as we currently speak."

"And you *both* figured the optimal plan to deal with his behavior would be to sexually compel a woman who you didn't know, fuck up all her life's plans, and have her try and suck the magic out of this large and unstable man?"

With an exaggerated frown, I looked back and forth between both men.

"Nortia, it's the only idea we had left. And if you do attempt to suck anything out of the king, I imagine Cato will respond poorly," Ambrose taunted while slapping his brother on the back.

Cato's face turned dark, but he ignored the jab and continued stretching.

"Eira, we have found that His Majesty can be aggressively sexual when in certain moods, which is why he is kept under surveillance and locked into whatever space he enters. He *has* been successful in luring courtiers to him through means we don't yet understand, so a revolving group of trained courtesans service him regularly."

"That seems messed up." I grimaced at the thought.

"It does seem most foul, but he hasn't attempted to prey upon the court since we implemented the use of the workers, who are fully aware of his predilections and compensated beyond that of the salaries given to the state advisors."

"He still sounds disgusting. What was your plan after you decided you would no longer be bringing me to Monwyn? Maybe we should revisit that?"

"I would end him," Cato stated bleakly, locking his eyes on mine.

Regicide. Damn. I couldn't begin to fathom what would become of Cato if he murdered a sitting king.

"Why... why didn't you make that choice before all of this?" I asked, a little afraid to continue our conversation.

"Love." Cato raked his fingers through his beard, combing down the whiskers that he'd mussed. "He is loved, despite his faults and sins. The people still know him as a great leader, benevolent and deeply devoted. It was for them he turned to the dark ways in the first place, seeking to alleviate their mortal sufferings."

"And you think I will not be safe around him, even with my *godly* blood?"

"We will do everything to keep you from harm, but I could never, with full fidelity, say there is not a chance of injury. And if for some reason I am not with you, you must become your own last defense."

"Then let's begin," I breathed. "What weapon will I be training with?"

"A small dagger—sharp, thin, and easily hidden on your person."

"Give it to me." I held out my open palm, serious about this lesson.

"You will not wield a blade for some time yet. This will minimize the chance of hurting yourself while becoming accustomed during practice."

Ambrose stepped into the conversation, adding to Cato's speech, "You must gain an understanding of how violent fighting with blades can be. Expect to be injured, only produce your weapon with intent, and realize that using your weapon to intimidate someone often misfires. Never use your blade to become a hero. Use it to survive the next hour."

Violence. Injury. Intimidation. Survival. It sounded a lot like Verus.

"Today you will work on strengthening your hands and arms. You also need to work on your stamina. Getting away is the true first line of defense, and you are not fast or particularly athletic."

I reminded myself that Monwyn's men were no-frills. It wasn't like he called me lazy, but I didn't feel great about being judged by the person who had so recently referred to me as perfect.

"You will sprint with Ambrose. Ten times between me and the windmill. You can have a break of three minutes after completing your first five counts."

Off in the distance, the body of the windmill loomed. I wasn't sure I could make it twice.

"Go!" Cato barked.

Ambrose shot off so quickly that he was almost halfway to the mill before I took my first step. I looked back at Cato, who stood with his hip cocked to the side, one leg more forward than the other. I wanted to smack the superiority right off of his face.

"Were you going to begin, Nortia?"

"I will. I... I know *why* I need to practice this, but I really, truly, don't want you to watch me." It sounded absurd; I knew it did. I had quite literally opened my body to him and wanted it to happen again, but I couldn't shake how uncomfortable the idea of having him judge my body or abilities made me.

Ambrose, who had finished his lap, slowed to a halt behind me.

"That's ridiculous." Cato looked at me confusedly.

"It may be ridiculous, but I'm serious."

How could I explain to the man whose clothing I tried to shred off minutes before that I was intimidated by his strength and vitality?

"What's the problem?" Ambrose asked, not winded at all from his exertion.

"She doesn't want me to watch her run." He shook his head and shrugged.

"So turn around."

"Ambrose—"

"*Cat*," he mimicked Cato's tone perfectly, "women are odd about their bodies, precisely because of men like you. She doesn't want to bounce and flop and have her physicality critiqued by the man she wishes to mate with... correct?" He turned to look at me, and I could have hugged his big handsome face. "Derros's Dick, it is no wonder you haven't bedded anyone in a decade."

"Yes, he has!" I crowed. "He bedded *this* bouncy, floppy, woman... twice!"

"What?" Ambrose beamed. Strong arms snatched me around the waist, and in an instant, he was spinning me in a wide circle. "I knew he could never resist that slit!"

I staggered a few dizzy steps to the left when he set me a little too roughly back on the ground. His smile was hilariously infectious, and I returned a full beam of my own.

Cato was massaging his temples, probably contemplating our murders.

"And brother, you didn't tell me? Was your performance less than adequate? Did you shoot cobwebs instead of come?"

"Oh, Goddess!" My mouth fell open. I didn't know where to look.

Cato glared at Ambrose, and I swear I saw steam swirling from his nostrils. Ambrose tossed his hair over a shoulder and let out a laugh so loud it scared a flock of birds, who scattered wildly from a nearby tree.

"He's right," I admitted, stepping between the two. Glancing up at Cato, I was surprised to see just how crestfallen the admission made him. His expression almost destroyed me. His mouth pulled down at both corners, and his eyes were frozen wide. He looked so hurt.

Ambrose, the big child, hit the ground crying he was laughing so hard, but I couldn't fathom—

"Oh! Cato, no, no, you were wonderful! Being with you was one of the most memorable experiences of my life. I'm talking about feeling self-conscious in front of you; he's right about that. Get up, you big jackass." I kicked Ambrose in the rear and moved closer to Cato's side, dropping my voice. "I didn't feel this way until Verus. There was so much emphasis placed on what is considered beautiful in one kingdom or another and how we should be able to use our bodies to secure deals or alliances. I know it doesn't make sense that I'd feel this way about someone who has seen all there is to see, but you, you both, all of the Monwyns, just seem so perfect that it's hard to feel... adequate."

Cato stepped over his prone brother, who was still chuckling every few seconds, and took my hands.

"There is *nothing* inadequate about you. I live for the next moment I can feel the softness of your body, and the way you move drives me to distraction."

Behind Cato's back, Ambrose sat up, listening intently to the conversation with a big, goofy grin plastered across his perfect face. "The reality is, you are walking into a den of lions and the thought of you being mauled brings me to my knees—which is exactly the kind of weakness that our enemies can exploit. You *must* learn, but how can I make it better?"

"I'm... well, I'm not a soldier, so I don't suppose I respond like one. Run with us?"

Ambrose started up again. "You expect the general of His Majesty's armies—not one army, no Nortia, twenty-four full regiments—the Protector of Monwyn, the greatest fighter in the realm, *he* who banished the outlaw Sidous, *he* who took the life of not one but seven foreign marauders... to run laps?" The laughter began anew.

I smiled sweetly at Cato, who rubbed his thumb across the top of my hand.

"Let us begin." Cato removed his shirt and folded it neatly before laying it across a stump that bore the deep marks of an ax's head.

"Right now, we just want to increase your stamina. Let's start with five. Ready?"

With a nod, we set out, running to the windmill. We all tagged it at the same time, and I felt triumphant at having kept up the pace.

"Now increase your speed and go!"

I fell back this time, just a few steps behind the brothers, who tried to show up one another. Ambrose pushed toward Cato, who sidestepped the taller man easily but missed the foot that kicked out trying to trip him. While they fought and wrestled each other for the lead, I rounded the stump, passing them both, and headed back towards the windmill, where I leaned on the structure gasping. I watched them, enjoying the sight of their tumbling and tossing each other around. I wished Cato could have more of this in his life but knew once we reached his kingdom he'd need to focus.

A little squeal pulled my attention away from the fun. I tiptoed around the base of the round mill, looked toward the tree line and saw the tiniest little fawn in the underbrush. The little tan baby with spots on his back startled when he saw me but didn't run, just bleated his little sweet sound. I wasn't sure about the fauna of this area, but I didn't think he could be more than a few weeks old.

"Hello, little dear," I giggled at my own pun. "Where is your mama precious one?"

I looked around, hoping to see its mother deeper in the woods.

"Are you hungry, baby? I won't hurt you," I cooed and coaxed as I approached him slowly.

It had the most adorable face I'd ever seen: big, brown eyes and a fuzzy little mouth whose white markings made it look like it had a tiny little smile. My heart just melted over the little innocent who was lost in the woods. I was already trying to figure out a way to tell Cato he had to write "the deer remains with Eira if the marriage is dissolved," into the betrothal contract.

The fawn took a step forward and stumbled, curling up its tiny legs until he lay in a little ball. I squinted, looking closely, and made out a dark spot on the back of his haunch. Attempting to see if he was injured, I stepped forward as calmly as I could, still talking to the babe softly as I approached.

"My poor dove, have you run off from your mama and gotten hurt? I'm sure she wants you home. Let me see if I can help you. I will be so gentle, sweetling."

Despite his more consistent bleats of alarm, he didn't try to take off or flinch, so I was able to push back the branch of the shrub he hid under to get a better look.

What I uncovered was horrific.

I figured he may have had a laceration, but the poor baby had been grievously injured, and the flesh and muscle had been ripped and torn from his back leg.

"Oh." I gasped. "Oh, darling, you must be in so much pain."

The tiny creature struggled but stirred, making it up to his hooves. He stumbled forward as I reached out my hand and brushed my fingers along his soft muzzle.

"I... I... don't know how to help you," I whispered.

I sat and crossed my legs, creating a space for the fawn, who seemed to need a companion. I guided him close, and he curled himself into a little crescent once more.

"I will protect you, my heart."

I cried. Tears rolled down my cheeks as I circled my arms around the poor creature in an effort to bring him more security. I made sure not to press upon his injury.

"I'm sorry little one, so very, very sorry." My teardrops dotted his precious tan coat.

"Eira." Cato spoke my name soothingly. "Eira, he won't survive."

He kneeled beside me and placed a hand on my back.

"I know... I... but, I just can't leave him alone while he goes." I bent low and placed my cheek on the little head that lay on my thigh.

"I can make it quick for him, but, my love, you need not see it."

I turned to Cato, knowing what he offered was the kindest end.

"Do... do you think my blood could give him a ch-chance?" I stuttered.

"I think that nature can be cruel and that it would be impossible and unwise for you to spill your blood as often as it would take to heal life's suffering."

I nodded my head but found I couldn't release the small bundle in my arms.

"Do. Not. Move." Cato's voice dropped.

He rose into a crouch and reached into his boot. I followed his gaze and—

"Don't move!" he hissed.

A large cat had stealthily approached us, coming to retrieve the meal that had gotten away.

My heart sped up and thundered in my chest, and the little fawn bleated in fear.

"Let him go, Eira. Release him and move backward."

I contemplated what he was asking of me. Turn this baby loose and watch him be further mutilated. My insides churned. I'd never felt more desperate, more ill. I could feel myself burning from the inside, and... and shadows, black shadows played around the periphery of my eyes.

"Move, Eira, do it now," he ordered sharply.

I tried, but I was paralyzed. I couldn't move, couldn't turn, couldn't budge. The blackness was taking over my vision, and I was losing consciousness, but the baby... he was safe.

"Move!" I heard the shout through the haze.

My eyes snapped open.

There was Cato, poised to attack.

The cat, its claws out, was suspended in midair.

And I was there, hunched over the little innocent in my lap.

From where I stood, watching the scene unfold from the outside, I saw the cat moving as if it was gliding through water. It reached the zenith of its jump and started the downward trajectory that would lead it directly to me. I watched Cato move forward, as slowly as the cat. Knife drawn, his face frozen in a scream. He moved to put his body in front of—

"*NO!*"

The woman... *me...* her head snapped up, *I* snapped up...

I flew back into my body and saw clearly for only a millisecond before I ignited.

The burning started in my fingertips and toes and scalded a twisting path through my chest.

The pressure built, searing my insides, melting away my eyes and mind.

I screamed for death, and then for life.

And then the world exploded.

The cat flew through the air, and its body hit a tree trunk several yards away. Cato was thrown and laid out on his back.

"Get up! Move!" It was Ambrose.

Strong arms wrapped around me, heaving me to my feet, and the fawn tumbled from my lap.

"Run to the mill," he roared. "RUN NOW!"

I ran, not looking back until I'd reached safety.

Cato was on his feet when the feline pounced. I heard his grunt of pain when the cat latched its claws into his chest and began twisting itself wildly.

The cat screamed and hissed, and I could hear the yelps and sickening thuds of contact as they fought.

"Merrias, *Mother*!" I pleaded with the goddess of judgment. "Spare him!"

Scurrying around the lower level of the mill, I looked for anything to turn into a weapon.

There were little bits and pieces of metal scrap, but nothing substantial enough to make a difference. I ran through the door and back toward the fight, thinking to brandish a stick if it would give Cato a fighting chance. I picked up a fallen limb and ran to the entangled man. I brought the branch down onto the cat's head with enough force that Ambrose was able to tear the stunned animal from where it had gripped Cato's shoulder.

Flying through the air, the tawny cat twisted its agile body and landed on its feet. Immediately, it bolted toward the baby, and snatched the little fawn up by its neck, before rushing off into the woods.

Sobbing and hysterical, I ran to reach Cato.

He'd dropped heavily to his knees.

Slashed and bitten, he breathed raggedly as I wrapped my arms around him but could barely hold on to his blood-slicked skin. Thick, bleeding furrows roped from his chin to his ribcage, pouring freely.

"Ambrose, the knife!"

The Scion blinked, unable to comprehend me. He just stared down at his brother, whose breathing had become labored.

"The knife, Ambrose. Cut me, draw blood *now*!" I barked.

He moved like lightning and picked the knife up off the ground, while I supported Cato's body as best I could. He ran its edge down my forearm.

I felt no pain, no sting or bite.

I held my arm over Cato's back, drizzling my blood over the bite wounds he'd sustained. The punctures near his neck and shoulders concerned me the most.

"How much?" I yelled at Ambrose. "More? I don't know what to do. Cut me again!"

He obeyed and slit my arm.

Lengths of disconnected flesh hung down from Cato's chest. I held up his head and allowed my blood to drip onto his shoulder and run over the slash marks.

His body began to spasm and jerk, and his eyes glassed over.

"Cato, Cato! Look at me," I ordered.

With effort, he opened his eyes, but just barely.

"You love me too," he said shakily before he collapsed and sent me sprawling backward.

I tried rolling him on his back but couldn't manage the dead weight.

"Ambrose, help me!"

He came to his knees beside me and lifted his brother's body, flipping him onto his side.

Dragging the blade across my arm a third time, cutting in deeply, I pressed the arm to his mouth.

"Take it Cato, now!"

He opened his eyes, but they looked at nothing.

"Now!" I grabbed his mouth and pulled at his chin and ran my hand down his neck, encouraging him to swallow. His eyes drifted shut.

"His heart still beats," Ambrose confirmed.

"Then there is still a—"

A violent scream pierced the air.

The noise that burst from Cato's mouth was terrifying... unnatural.

I covered my ears and stumbled back, looking to a wide-eyed Ambrose.

Cato writhed on the ground, contorting and tensing. His jaw clenched and his body shook until finally, with a wracking gasp, he fell still.

Ambrose got to him first, turning his head and pulling up his closed lids, assessing him for signs of life.

"He lives, and—Eira, look." He pointed to the puncture wounds that had stopped their concerning stream.

"Ambrose, I..." I stared at Cato's body. "He needs help."

He nodded, never once moving his eyes from what was occurring in front of him.

"Ambrose, we need to make sure he's safe. I don't know what comes after this." I shook his shoulder. "Can you carry him?"

Again he nodded, lowering himself and scooping his brother into his arms.

"Do you know where we're headed, where we need to go next?"

"Yes." Ambrose's voice was barely audible.

I ran ahead and gathered the items we had brought with us, shoving them into whatever bags had room, and untied the horses.

"Here, hang on." With Ambrose's help, we dressed Cato in the shirt he'd neatly folded and set aside earlier. "That should keep the trail dust out of the open wounds."

Holding the body of his unconscious brother in front of him, we rode hard, only stopping once out of necessity.

The sun was dropping rapidly in the sky when we arrived at the biggest wall I had ever seen. Behind it lay the Monwyn border, and on either of its sides, the massive barrier was anchored to an imposing mountain.

"Is... is this the capital?" I asked, taking in the sheer magnitude of what loomed in front of us.

"No, it's Colpass."

Chapter Forty

COLPASS

We didn't ride toward the main gate but instead struck out to the west, following closely along the walled barrier.

It was fully dark when we came upon a steel-banded door. There was no massive portcullis, no impressive archway, and there had been no road leading us to the entryway. This was the point where the wall met mountain, and the entrance was so close to the natural rocky base that I wasn't sure the door could swing open fully.

"State your business!" From fifteen feet up, a fully armored guard called out.

"Merchant Finarr Mishdall en route from Solnna," Ambrose yelled.

The guard disappeared, and the door swung open almost immediately. Four armed guards and three others came forward. Two men ran out behind us, weapons drawn, and two flanked Ambrose. The remaining three moved fast, relieving the Scion of his burden.

Cato's body was taken through the entrance, and the darkness swallowed him. Ambrose leapt from his mount and came to my side, but I was halfway dismounted before he could lift his hands to aid me.

"The horses won't fit. The guards will see them to safety."

I was too fixated on recalling how Cato's head had lulled lifelessly on his shoulders to even comprehend what Ambrose had said.

Strong fingers threaded through my own and gave a supportive squeeze.

"You are my betrothed."

I drew in a shuddering breath and donned my mask. I would become anyone if it meant I could get to Cato faster.

Entering the hallway, it became clear the brothers were well known to the garrison of this town. Men from all directions were bowing or saluting and darting out of our way as we surged forward, not stopping to make pleasantries.

"Marshal Trenon, Protector Catommandus is to be placed in the adjoining chamber of my rooms. Fetch Imella and see to the comfort of my betrothed."

The Marshal bowed deeply, first to Ambrose and then me, before speeding off in the opposite direction.

"Rickert, see her to the upper-level bathing chamber and wake some shopkeep to find her something decent to wear," he ordered.

The older man, wearing a long tunic of deep blue, bowed shortly and angled his elbow in my direction. Like the most gracious of wives-to-be, I took the offered arm instead of doing what I wanted to do.

"Troth Nortia, it is an honor to be of service. My apologies that you have arrived under such circumstances. We were not expecting the return of His Highness for quite some time."

"That's quite all ri—p-pardon me? I seemed to have misheard you."

"His Highness, Scion Ambrose?" The graying and stooped man repeated. "I suppose with the possibility of the little one on the way, he was eager to return home. We all honestly wondered if he'd travel to Nortia anyhow. He loves his Kingdom, but I can see now why he chose a different route." Rickert patted his soft, sun-spotted hand on my arm, and I returned the sweet smile he bestowed upon me.

His Highness Ambrose.

Prince Ambrose.

That means there's also a Prince "Decided not to mention that" Catommandus laid out someplace. It was good for them both that I was too worried to care at this exact moment.

There were no windows anywhere inside the wall, but the halls were brightly lit with lamps on stone shelves in cages of metal bars. Rickert was chattering nonstop about the history of the wall itself, and we walked past several open entryways where soldiers were in various states of taking their ease—playing dice or bedding down for the night. We walked for a solid stretch before traversing a winding stairway whose steps were so uneven that I had to think about where my feet landed so I wouldn't stub my toes.

"Apologies, they were built with an attack in mind. Much harder to run up when you can't find your footing," Rickert chuckled.

"Very well thought out," I responded. The architect had certainly put thought into the Colpass's security.

"Yes, yes, the king is a wise man and thought of everything we may need when he had the wall built. When you reach the capital though, you will see the masterful defense he and the Protector put into place. Quite the marvel," bragged Rickert.

"No doubt your king is a mighty leader. During my time at Verus, I came to learn about the great wealth amassed under his supervision."

"Indeed, we hold the Monarch in great esteem. He has given us beautiful daughters and strong sons who will lead us into a bright future. That babe in your belly is sure to please him immensely. Can you imagine... a child born to the Monwyn Scion Prince and a Chosen Troth of Verus? He will be elated."

"I am thrilled to be linked to such a magnanimous lineage. I hope to do well by Monwyn, as I have pledged myself to the betterment of all Ærta." I turned on the charm, letting the words fall from my bitter mouth.

"How enchanting you are, my dear. Now, do not hesitate to call out for old Rickert if you need even the smallest of service. Luckily, with the masters having passed through so recently, we are still set up to receive guests. Through this door, you will find everything you need to clean up, and the servants will fetch clothing for you. You won't be disturbed."

Rickert opened a heavy door and held it until I'd fully entered the chamber. The room was warm but not overbearing, and the walls and floors were made of the same buff stone as the outer wall.

When I heard the door shut behind me, I let my entire body slump.

I was exhausted.

The room was not large but had been lavishly decorated with heavy dark-wood furnishings, and the walls were covered in colorful tapestries that depicted hunting scenes—mostly horses and dogs running ahead of mounted riders.

A large, copper tub sat on the far right of the room, and surprisingly, a spigot, just like the one at Verus, hung out over the basin. Flipping that on, I stripped out of the clothing that smelled of sweat and blood and tossed them to the far back wall. The very fact that Rickert hadn't inquired about the state of our party was a testament to his steadfastness. My father would have raised nether had I walked into the house looking like this.

I sank into the warmth of the water before it finished filling. I wanted to remove every reminder of the last day: Cato's blood, the scent of the little fawn, the smell of horse and body. I reached to my side, where a perfectly situated table had been filled with soaps and jars of cleanser.

Letting the dirty water drain, I scrubbed the feet that had been trapped in too-large shoes with no stockings to speak of. My nails were filled with grime, and little bits of wool had snagged on their jagged edges. I ran the sudsy bar of soap over my legs, feeling the little prickles of hair growth there—I wasn't sure I enjoyed that particular sensation but had liked what they felt like smooth. My armpits were particularly foul, and I didn't want to guess what my crotch must have smelled like. It turns out that when you're running for your life, hygiene simply isn't a priority.

I ran fresh water while I rubbed my fingers along my scalp and replugged the drain. Letting wet heat seep into my muscles had been such a luxury at Verus, one that I was so fortunate to have again right now. I dunked my head under the running faucet and dipped my fingers into a smooth, creamy cleanser. My hair was so greasy and limp, and my scalp so tight, that I moaned out loud when I ran my hands down the length of my tresses, pulling the—

Cedar.

Fresh Cedar.

I brought my hands to my nose and inhaled the scent that was him.

The events of the day flashed through my head. I recalled the happily tussling brothers, the agony of the hurt little life, my fear of losing Cato and... and whatever had happened before the cat struck.

Wracking sobs shook me, and the tears I'd not had time to shed ran into the water. I tried my best to stifle the loud wails, afraid Rickert waited nearby, but couldn't manage to mute the sounds of my utter despair.

"Shhh... hush now." Ambrose walked through the door, still wearing the blood-soaked shirt he'd arrived in. "He's okay. I promise you, Eira, he has seen worse and has always made a full recovery."

He pulled his shirt over his head and kneeled at the side of the bath, pulling me close. I went to him like I had the day of the Fourth Maneuvering, crying into his shoulder—praying he was right.

Ambrose helped me out of the tub and found a fluffy towel to wrap around my shoulders before leading me to a chaise that sat near a cabinet full of medicinals.

"Close your eyes for a moment. Rest while I wash."

How could I rest? Cato's scent was all around me, on me.

The spigot turned on and off, and the spicy aroma I associated with Ambrose filled the room, helping to cloak the smell that had set my emotions reeling, like a boat caught in a storm.

Cato.

I lay in a heap of misery. Where had my strength gone? When would I—

"Braid my hair."

"What?" I asked, peeking over the towel I'd pulled up around my face.

"Braid my hair. You need to busy your hands and occupy your mind. And do it well. I can't stand bumps."

"Fine."

I twisted around and planted my legs on either side of the naked giant who sat on top of his towel on the floor. My knees touched his back, but it didn't seem improper. We'd been too close for it to even register as something right or wrong. Richelle would have sold her sibling to be in my place, but, for me, Ambrose no longer held the same appeal he had in the beginning. He was a good man... but not the man for me.

I wondered if the Obligates had heard of my "love affair" yet. I didn't think many of the Troth would believe a word of what they were fed, and of course, the Scion would soon set out after Ozius if they hadn't already. I was sure both groups would go along with Verus's story no matter their personal interpretations... but I shuddered at the thought of the men hunting their brother.

After combing through Ambrose's glossy strands, I braided the mass quickly and secured it with a leather wrap. Gotwig's image drifted through my mind. I wished I'd gotten to talk to him more. I'd just taken the news he shared like I had everything else recently—I locked it up until a time when I wasn't focusing on survival. *Were my eyes shaped like his? Maybe the tip of my nose?*

"Nortia?"

"Hmmm?"

"Are you prepared to experience me at my best?"

It took me a few seconds to register his meaning.

"Ambrose. How could you even suggest that right now?"

"Oh, I don't know, I guess I misinterpreted the verve in which you were shoving your breasts into my back."

He was right. I'd been leaning into him, lost in my thoughts, wallowing against him like I was hugging a comfy pillow.

"I'm sorry, Ambrose. I just forgot myself for a moment. I really do apologize. I promise I'm not aroused," I said honestly.

"You know," he whipped his hair from my hands and pulled its length over his shoulder, "you say the most hurtful things sometimes. You really do."

Goddess, hear me. I can't take dramatic Ambrose right now.

Out of sorts, he stood, penis at half-mast, and strode across the room, flinging the door wide.

"Has suitable clothing been procured?" he barked.

"It has, Your Highness."

"Bring it in."

I snatched the towel tighter around my neck and watched old Rickert enter the room carrying a large bundle between both hands. He placed his parcel on a table and then turned to face Ambrose again.

"Will that be all, Highness?"

"Are my chambers ready?"

"They are, and a fine meal will soon arrive for you and yours," Rickert proudly stated.

"You are dismissed."

With a quick nod of the head, the old man shuffled out of the room, seemingly unaffected by the very visible display of sexuality that was now bobbing up and down as Ambrose walked across the floor.

"Playing the part, *Your Highness*?" I questioned.

Ambrose stopped in the middle of drawing his small clothes up his legs.

"It is your fault the show wasn't better. Get dressed; we will go to Cato."

Snapping into action, I bolted off the chaise, dropping the towel to the floor.

Rickert, by some miracle, had been able to procure fresh linen underwear, as well as a tight-fitting chemise that laced up at the front. Both had been embroidered with dainty, time-intensive, pink and green flower chains along their seams. I rolled soft, woolen stockings, just like those Kairus had worn, up my legs. They were bright sapphire blue and stretched to fit snuggly all the way to my lower thigh, where I secured them with patterned, tablet-woven garters.

The overdress was a thick, woolen gown that, when pulled over my head, fit snuggly right below the bust. The neckline was demure, which suited me just fine, but the sleeves bagged around my arms and then gathered tightly in a band around my wrists. The added volume was already making me warm.

Ambrose tried unsuccessfully to stifle his laughter while watching me dress.

"What?" I held out the dress, thinking I'd put something on incorrectly. It all looked fine to me.

He came to my side and placed his hand through the seam that ran the length of my underarm and pulled it over my right breast.

"It's a nursing gown... normally worn when the baby is already on the outside."

He rubbed the curve of my stomach and patted my head.

"Take me to Cato before I'm tried for treason, *Prince of Monwyn*," I scoffed.

"What a disloyal little mama," he mewled, smacking my backside soundly. "Do you know how long before we find out if we *are* parents-to-be?"

I shook my head and held my arms wide before dropping them to my hips.

"Normally I'd be able to make a rough prediction, but Ambrose, whatever the temple was giving us made my courses unlike anything I've experienced before. And Ozius, when he picked up Kairus, he told me I wasn't. Oddly, I believe him. I *can* tell you, though, I don't feel any differently, haven't been sick or moody or—"

"You *haven't* been moody?"

He walked to the door, looking resplendent in a knee-length silk tunic of dove gray, paired with black breeches. "If that is truly a symptom of breeding, I would predict we are to be blessed with twins," he smirked.

"It would indeed be a blessed miracle, considering the inability of your member to see the task completed," I snapped.

Like an angry little piglet, Ambrose stamped his booted foot and snorted aloud before swinging open the door so hard it squealed on its metal hinges.

"My lady." He bowed low in my direction, putting on a show for the group of men who lined the hallway of the second level.

"Your orders, Highness?" A soldier stepped from the wall, saluting, fist to shoulder.

"Double the night watch and send word to the main gate notifying them of our arrival. The safety of my betrothed will take precedence over all other matters until the time we leave for the capital." He extended his hand to me, "Come, we must see to the Protector."

I laid my palm into his upturned hand and did my best to embody a flawless vision of feminine purity. I passed each of the men-at-arms and lowered my head, graciously thanking them for their hospitality, and apologizing for causing a disturbance so late into the evening.

"No disturbance at all, Lady," a short, red-faced soldier replied.

"You are the embodiment of grace."

"Command us as you see fit, Lady Troth" a guard said with conviction.

We walked the corridor until coming upon a door flanked by two guards. As we neared, the armored men pounded the butts of their spears on the floor, and the door swung open from the inside.

"Leave us."

The chamber servant scurried away in a flurry of black robes.

"He is through there." Ambrose indicated the door to his right.

It was all I could do not to shove him out of the way and into the room.

"Eira," I hesitated, recognizing the serious timber in his voice, "the woman on the other side is our mother. Close your mouth."

Their mother.

"I thought she lived in the country? Wait. So she's the queen, *the Queen*, your mother... is on the other side of that door?" I began to panic.

"This town *is* the country, Nortia. She has made her home here for as long as I can remember. It's my hometown as well."

"And the king is—"

"Abusive, deviant, a sadist? Not really husband material—and I will never blame her for choosing to relocate herself."

I breathed deeply through my nose and slowly let the air blow out across my tongue and felt the mad thumping of my heart begin to slow. Smoothing the skirts of my heavy gown, I pulled my shoulders back and allowed Ambrose to open the door.

My heart lurched and felt wrong in my chest.

Cato was laid out on a healer's table, covered from neck to his toe by a white linen sheet. His mother, sat next to him, smoothing his hair back from his brow.

"When did he cut his hair, Ambrose?" she asked as she rested her hand on his bearded jaw.

"Before we left for Verus. He feared it could be used against him while training the Scion to fight."

Their mother smiled faintly. "Of course his mind was on tactics," she sighed.

I studied the seated figure, the queen of this country. There were no gems hanging around her neck, no tiara upon her brow. The clothing she wore wasn't ornate, and she looked rather ordinary—heavy of frame, broad-shouldered with a large chest that rested on a roundly protruding stomach. Her only crown was her yellowy-white hair, with solid black ends, which was braided into a coronet that wrapped around her head. She had a rich, russet complexion, much deeper than Cato's, that reminded me of autumn leaves.

"And this is the young woman who has captured my boy's heart?"

"Well, I captured something," I murmured, rather incoherently, before snapping back to attention. Like her, my eyes had been fixed on the rusty-red slash marks that had seeped into the bleached linen of his covering.

"Ahhh," she drawled. "She will be good for you, little cub." She smiled knowingly at Ambrose, who arched a dark brow. "Come closer. He breathes on his own, but the healer feels he has yet to wake because of blood loss. I was told this was caused by the attack of a mountain cat. Not many could have withstood the encounter."

She continued to smooth the beard at his chin and cheeks.

"I worry his head was struck, but I can find no lumps or lacerations that would indicate such an injury."

"He's come through worse, Mama."

"Yes, and every time it feels like a part of my spirit is ripped from my soul. I should have done more to discourage him from the life he chose."

"It would have made no difference," Ambrose said while walking to his mother's side. She nodded wearily.

Four servants carrying basins of pungent-smelling liquids and handfuls of fresh linens hurried through the door, followed by a woman who had to have been older than Rickert and possibly even older than the aged Gaean emissary. She moved with ease despite her advanced years.

"He will be bathed first, and then we will apply the topical herbs. Now, repeat the ingredients." The healer turned to a short woman who wore an apron that covered her yellow dressing gown.

"Yes—I have added concentrations of marigold, chamomile, and yarrow. The aloe will be mixed in immediately before application."

"Good. Sit the pots down. Her Majesty will oversee his bathing."

"Please call me Imella. Eira, is it? We are to be family."

I nodded.

Imella went to a servant and took a handful of cloth that had soaked in a basin that foamed with soap.

"Your sisters will be beside themselves when they hear he will bear more scars. Roll up your sleeves and grab your rags." She looked pointedly at Ambrose and then at me.

The wrists of my sleeves were so tight I couldn't get them past the middle of my forearm, but I wasn't about to let that stop me from tending to Cato. I was the reason he was in this condition.

Imella dampened his skin while pulling back the sheet, ensuring it didn't stick to the fibers of the material.

Having never seen him fully exposed, my cheeks heated to the point my face felt scalded.

He'd been inked.

Four blue lines circled his upper thigh, and in the center of them, something had been written in unfamiliar glyphs. He also had another wicked-looking scar located there, and it had cut right through and removed a portion of the tattoo on his outer thigh.

"We will wash and rinse him before he is medicated. His skin already heals at the edges, but he will need to be kept clean and watched closely for fever."

His mother gently but thoroughly began washing the cuts that slashed across his chest, turning her cloth pink.

"Ambrose, I will return home tonight, as I feel he is stable, but I am to be notified at once if there is any change in his condition. Am I clear?"

"Yes, Mama, I will keep close watch."

"Thank you, my cub. I know you will." She smiled up affectionately at her son.

Together, we washed his hair and feet, leaving no surface of his body unclean. I sponged off the beautiful arms that I'd found so much comfort in, making sure to scrub carefully between his fingers and over his nailbeds. Shamefully, my own skin had become more sensitive the moment I ran the soapy cloth down his arm, and I knew the telltale flush would be spreading across my chest. I couldn't believe my body would respond at such a time. I bit my bottom lip between my teeth until I tasted iron, trying to bring myself under control. My wantonness was unsettling.

After spreading the salve over Cato's injuries, I watched his mother procure another clean linen and gently open his mouth. She ran the cloth soaked in mint water over his teeth and tongue.

"Ambrose, moisten his mouth every hour. I will ask the staff to take shifts and remain outside your door should you need assistance." Imella, who stood at least a full head taller than me, rose and walked purposely forward, holding her arms wide open as both Ambrose and Cato had done before. I must have looked like a little lost lamb because she tilted her head to the side and wore an expression that to me read "You need your mother too."

And I did.

I hadn't had a single moment to process the fear I felt for her. To think that she may no longer be in Nortia and that I had no idea how to find her terrified me. I didn't even care that my parentage had been kept a secret. I just wanted her advice; I wanted to hear her voice.

Imella squeezed me to her and patted my back, whispering something in my ear.

"I'm sorry, I didn't quite catch—"

"I said... mind your heart," we locked gazes, "It's apparent who it belongs to."

I stared at her, unable to deny and unable to confirm what she knew.

Was I that bad of a Troth?

She placed a cool palm on my hot cheek and turned to leave, but not before taking Ambrose in her arms and kissing both of his cheeks.

"I love you and am glad you are home."

"I love you too," he replied.

As the door shut behind her, I began the struggle of removing my tight and voluminous gown. The heat had suddenly begun to overwhelm me to the point of fainting. Sweat trickled between my shoulder blades and a fine sheen beaded across my forehead. With Ambrose's help, I tugged at the garment's hem and pulled it over my head.

"Will it be a problem if I stay like this for a while? Nobody will enter?" I breathed, welcoming the cooler air.

"By all means. I will never mind a beautiful woman parading around in her under-clothes... even if she'd rather mount *that*." He waved a hand toward his brother's still form.

The finger I threw up in the air made him chuckle.

He was so inappropriate.

"Come eat and we will watch over him. I am sure you have questions."

"So many questions," I mumbled.

So focused on Cato, I hadn't taken the time to look around the rooms appointed to a prince. The walls of Ambrose's chambers were buff stone, but the floor was covered in a massive hand-woven rug that depicted a Monwyn battle scene with a mountainous background. A bed took up much of the space in the room. Its four posts reached all the way to the ceiling and supported a heavily carved rectangle of lacquered wood from which garnet curtains fell.

"Ambrose, why are there no fireplaces in the rooms?" I asked. All rooms in Nortia had them, our chambers at Verus as well.

"Fire hazard. Though many of the structural elements of our buildings are stone, the roofs and floors are thatch and wood, and smoke can be a more deadly weapon than steel in enclosed spaces." He pulled out a chair from a smaller square table.

The servants had brought in and laid out a formal meal. Goblets and cups and a row of utensils sat before us, along with a stew of goat and onion, mixed with a plethora of spices. Together we ate our fill and drank deeply of fresh water and a bold, spicy wine that was served steaming hot.

"You're a Prince then?" I asked.

"I am."

"And Cato. Prince as well?"

"Nope."

"How does that work?"

"The Protector cannot inherit the throne. He gave that up the moment he took the oath," he said between sips.

"And could a Scion?"

"Could if need be, but we have another brother to fill the role. Our sisters will of course never have the honor." Ambrose tucked in another yeast roll.

"I am certain to hate Monwyn. Next question... Cato said his childhood was rather cold, but your mother seems quite caring."

"She has never been cold towards her children, but being young and watching your parents' relationship deteriorate around you leaves an impression. Mama's people were from Taleer, and our parents felt differently about how we should be raised, and of course, being wed to a conjurer, I am sure she felt bitter. Her entire bloodline was destroyed while fighting in the Awakening. When she left our father, Cato, being our father's natural son, stayed with him at the palace while my sisters lived with our mother and me until they married. And while on the subject of a cold parent, you should know, the last time I heard Cat refer to our father as anything more endearing than 'Your Majesty,' he was, I don't know, nine?"

"No love lost between them?"

"An abundance of love lost, I would say."

My heart went out to his family. My parents' support and love had afforded me a certain amount of privilege in my life—goddess blood notwithstanding—but I hadn't recognized how much until leaving my sleepy town and meeting a more diverse crowd of people.

Pressing his fingers into his head, Ambrose rubbed at his temples and furrowed brow. I recognized the strain and left my seat to stand behind him and knead the muscles that had bunched under his tunic.

"Ambrose, how are you?"

He inhaled and tipped his head back into me while I rubbed down his neck.

In all of this, he was sacrificing the most.

"I am trying desperately to make sense of what I saw this morning." He shut his eyes and I moved my hands to his forehead. I smoothed my fingers over his brow. "Are you mystical like my father or something else altogether?"

I unbound his hair and laid it about his shoulders before massaging his head, working my fingers deep into his scalp.

"I don't know. Something similar happened once, but today it... I can't begin to explain what happened. It was like..."

"You exploded? Because that's what I saw. Did you even realize you were sitting in dirt and not grass after it happened? Everything had been uprooted."

"I... I, no, I couldn't see anything around me. My... my sight had sort of gone."

"Everything near you blew back as if struck by some unseen force. There was no sound; there was nothing I could see. I have no explanation for what occurred." Ambrose reached for my hands and brought me around to face him. I perched on the edge of the dining table, waiting for him to continue, but he remained silent, studying my hands.

"Have you seen your father conjure? Is that like what happened?"

"No, I've never seen it firsthand. Cato has tried to explain, but it seems so unreal."

"I'm so sorry to have frightened you, Ambrose." I clasped his big hands in mine. "The only person who may have answers has fled Nortia."

"It was not fright, my silly harpy," his mossy green eyes held mine. "It was awe."

He looked at me like I was a piece of the finest blown glass. "When Cato wakes, I wish to reevaluate our plans. I am concerned my father would react poorly if you accidentally show him you are much more than Troth."

I agreed with Ambrose. Not only would I like more say in how we'd proceed, but the added stress of trying not to explode while in the presence of others needed consideration.

"Should we check on him? I would like to sleep near him tonight in case he wakes."

He shook his head.

"I will see to his needs for the next few hours while you rest. You remember the First Maneuvering?"

Of course I did, I'd never forget that evening. It was the night he'd kissed me until my toes curled, as well as the same night Cato's breathtakingly beautiful smile became permanently etched in my mind.

"You look *way* worse tonight than you did then."

"Ambrose, if the Goddess had not blessed you with that body, you would be a very lonely man."

"Lucky me. Now get in bed. I'll wake you if anything happens."

"Okay." I yawned widely and climbed onto the big bed whose covers matched the curtains currently pulled back and secured to each post.

Ambrose disappeared into the room where Cato lay.

Before letting myself drift off, I implored the Goddess to watch over both brothers.

···+)((+···

I woke when Ambrose pressed his back flush to mine, and only a few minutes later, he was snoring softly beside me. I couldn't get back to sleep. My mind went straight to Cato.

I knew Ambrose would never have left Cato if he thought him in decline, but I couldn't shake the feeling that something would go wrong if no one was there keeping watch.

Grabbing my pillow, I slipped out of bed, trying my best to not disturb my bedmate. I was barely functional after a few hours of rest and didn't know how he had remained conscious for as long as he had.

Padding through the door, I was relieved to see the steady rise and fall of the recently changed sheet. No more blood seeped through the covering. I pulled the chair that his mother had occupied as close as I could to his face and went about dabbing his mouth and moistening his tongue like I had seen her do.

"I need you to wake, Cato. We have much to discuss."

I laid my palm on his head and chest, checking for fever. "First, I think we should talk about the fact that apparently I can explode. Yes, I think that conversation is quite important. And then perhaps the whole your-father-is-the-King-of-Monwyn business. I would like to yell at you over that little 'forgot to mention,' but it won't feel right if you aren't awake. Oh, and I met your mother. I'm certain she sees right through me... which has made me realize I'm a shit Troth." I moved to his feet, which felt cold, and rubbed my thumbs down his soles until they warmed. "For a while there, I thought I was brilliant at deciphering manipulations, and now I'm discovering that anyone can read me like a book and no one in my life is really telling the truth—"

"Nortia, wrap your pretty lips around my cock if you will... I'd recover much faster if you did."

"Tomman—Cato!"

I tripped over my own feet getting back up to his head, which still rested flat on the table. When I regained my balance, I looked at his face but saw his eyes remained closed.

"Are you awake? Can you hear me?" I whispered, leaning closer.

"Yes, but clearly you didn't hear *me*."

His hand whipped out from under the sheet and wrapped around my wrist.

"Tommand, are... are you well?"

He pulled my hand under the sheet and placed it on his quickly hardening length.

"I feel fucking fantastic," he groaned.

With my hand in his, he stroked his arousal, squeezing hard on the downward motion.

"I can smell that you want me." He breathed fully again and thrust his hips into our joined hands. "Your scent is intoxicating."

"Tommand, you need to calm down—"

"My name is *Cato* and I have decided that every time you slip up, I will fill your mouth with something else." He let go of my hand and yanked the sheet from his body, tossing it to the floor.

His eyes remained closed.

This was unlike any dream walking I'd heard of. Whatever was happening, it wasn't normal.

"If you refuse to suck me off, then wrap your thighs around my face and let me have my fill."

"That's ridiculous. You clearly don't know where you are, and now, as much as I would love to bring you... relief, go back to sleep."

"I know exactly where I am, and after fighting off a mountain predator, I had hoped the woman who tried to fuck me in the middle of a farmstead would be more accommodating."

My mouth fell open. Who even was this?

"And what about keeping up appearances or the fact that you still can't open your eyes? You need to rest, to heal."

"Fuck me. That's what I think about appearances. Seat yourself so deeply on my cock that you feel me tomorrow and the next day."

Head injury. Imella was right to have been concerned.

"I'm afraid, *Cato,* that an incapacitated person can't consent, so that's right off the table."

His hand reached out again, cupping my vulva.

"I have missed her."

Tugging aside the crotch of my underwear, he ran a finger through my wetness, one long motion opening me from clit to passage.

"Do *you* consent?" His two fingers were poised at my entrance, and his thumb laid still, taunting my throbbing mound of nerves.

I trembled against his hand, considering my answer.

"Is that a yes, my love?"

Love.

I reached between my legs and pushed his fingers steadily into me until his palm was flush with my skin. Our combined moans, his harsh and mine helpless, weakened me. The mingling sounds were raw and uninhibited, and my instincts urged me to mate.

"Such a pretty cry," he said.

My legs shook as his fingers worked me to near collapse. Pulling his hand free, I spun around and bent over him, bracing my arms on the edge of the table. His eager hand found me again from behind, and he entered me swiftly, hooking his fingers upward, caressing that glorious spot.

The change in angle sent new, delicious sensations through me that were only heightened when he took his length in his fist and pumped himself to the same rhythm he used on me. Watching him handle himself felt scandalous. The way the muscles tensed in his arms while he moved, seeing what touch pleased him the most, it made me wish I could replace his hand with my body. I wanted to be what enfolded him.

My mouth watered.

I wanted to be the reason for his arousal, and I wanted to be the only one to satisfy him.

I stretched out and leaned forward, sucking his head into my mouth. I groaned at the salty drip that issued when I swirled my tongue around his swollen tip. He held the base of himself tightly, and I took advantage, sliding my mouth down until he struck the back of my throat. My lips grazed his fingers, and I flicked my tongue along them as well.

His growl of approval was loud and drawn out.

"Are you eager for me?" he asked.

I raked my teeth lightly along him and sucked on him so hard my lips popped when I released him. His gasp was all the encouragement I needed.

"I am," I panted.

Cato sat up and twisted, dropping his legs to the floor.

Standing between them, I lowered myself, only for him to catch my shoulders before I hit the wood floor.

"My goddess will never kneel before me," he whispered.

"This goddess will do what she pleases."

I grabbed the pillow and placed it under my knees before continuing to the floor, putting me just below the prize I sought. I tipped his erection to my mouth and slipped him between my lips while rubbing the tip of my finger against the flesh behind his sac. I glanced up and watched the impact of my touch as it played out on his body, gauging what gave him the most satisfaction. The muscles of his stomach contracted, and he pulled the side of his lip into his mouth, biting down every time I made a noise of my own, and his eyes—

I pushed away from him and skittered backward.

"Cato, Goddess!"

His breathing changed, becoming ragged and uneven.

"Your eyes, they are, Goddess, they—"

They were as dark as night, so much so that I couldn't discern any pupil in their blackness.

I spun over onto my knees and hauled myself to my feet, not sparing a glance backward.

I ran.

Hearing a growl so animalistic I thought perhaps a demon had entered him, I leapt over the threshold of the door and continued to flee.

I was hit from behind and thrown into the air. My head struck Ambrose's blanketed hip when I landed on the bed.

Strong hands were on me then, forcing my thighs apart, and then... then I was moaning. Pulling my underclothes to the side with his fist, Cato pushed a wide tongue into my passage and took what he wanted.

"This is what heals me, Nortia," he rasped, lapping at my entrance.

He sucked and bit and teased until I cried, screaming my satisfaction into the room.

"Cato, what the fuck!" Ambrose came up to his knees and attempted to pull me away by the shoulders, but Cato wrapped his arms around my thighs, digging his fingers into my flesh, and continued his feast.

I shouted and groaned and moved against his mouth, gripping Ambrose's arms for support.

Ambrose, unable to dislodge him, thrust his hand against Cato's neck, forcing his head up.

Cato stopped for a single instant and stared at his brother.

"Cato you... you are..."

"In the middle of something," he snarled, pressing two fingers into me.

I feared the drastic change in him, but my body didn't care. My hips jerked, brazenly seeking more.

That was all the invitation he needed.

"Turn away or don't, Ambrose. Regardless, I will fuck your fiancé as I please."

He rolled me roughly by my hip and climbed between my legs, sliding himself into my heat. Nipping sharply at my breasts and shoulders, he glided in and out of my wetness with long, deep strokes. I reached above my head and gripped the blankets in my fists.

Suddenly his weight lifted off my chest, though he remained buried to the hilt.

Ambrose was at his back and had captured both of his arms. Cato continued to fuck, thrusting deeply, despite the restraint.

"I suggested to her that you join us once before. She would be thrilled if we fucked her together."

Cato's hips struck Ambrose every time he sunk himself into me.

"Eira, has he permission to act like this? I will knock his head from his shoulders if—"

"Let him go, let him!" I choked out.

Released, he ripped my chemise in two, baring both of my breasts. I gasped when his lips grazed me and begged him for more when he flicked at my nipples with his tongue.

"Come for me love. Come around me while I fill you. I want to watch my vitality fall from your beautiful opening and streak down your lovely thighs."

I tossed my head to the side, and Ambrose came into view. His face was flushed and his eyes hazed over.

Cato took my pierced breast in his hand and drew its peaked flesh into his mouth, rolling the bar with his tongue, the vibrations of his moans intensifying the already profound sensation.

"Goddess, oh, Gods, don't stop!" My orgasm surged through me so hard I shrieked and screamed until I thought I might pass out. He rode me until my eyes rolled to the back of my head and all of my muscles went slack.

"Who am I, my love, who makes you feel this way?" he demanded an answer.

"C-Cato," I barely breathed, "Catommandus."

Triumph spread across his face.

Locking his black gaze to mine, he shouted through clenched teeth, spilling himself into me, marking me once again.

Breathless, he raised himself up and ran his spread palm the length of my sternum to my navel.

"You are exquis—"

His words cut off.

Black eyes rolled up into the back of his head. He fell forward and his chin cracked painfully against my face.

Ambrose was there in an instant, rolling Cato's body to the side.

"He breathes," Ambrose said frantically.

"Tie him up before he wakes!"

Chapter Forty-One

I GET A SAY

With the lamps fully lit, over the next two hours, we watched Cato from the other side of the room. We'd secured him to the headboard with his borrowed belt.

"Let me make sure I have it right. He was comatose and then you gobbled him down whole thinking it would rouse him, and when it did, he turned into a demon that you allowed to fuck you... a demon. Is that close?"

"No, giant asshole, that is not what happened," I grumbled.

Maybe... that might be exactly what happened.

"And we tied him up because you don't want it to happen again—or because you won't be able to resist endangering the life of a heavily injured man again?" Ambrose loomed over me with crossed arms. "What you did was risky, Nortia."

I threw myself into a chair.

"Get your penis out of my face Ambrose," I snapped.

"I'm sorry, have you suddenly become embarrassed by a public display of sexuality, Demon Fucker? I'll be hard for a Goddessdamn week because of your little show," he complained.

"You know, there's something really wrong with you. Cato's well-being is one thing, but to be worried about the state of your appendage... Don't you have a friend here that could help you out?"

"When would I have time for that? Before seeing you and the demon safely to the palace or after our bliss-filled nuptials? Believe me, if I *have* to marry you, you *will* put out. There will be no infidelity between us."

I did a double take.

"Hold up. You're joking, yes?"

"No, I am most certainly not. Do you know what ruins a marriage? People who cheat and trick and philander. Marriage is a sacred bond, and I don't know how they do it in Nortia, but here, for me, it means we are a unified front. Now, if we are to invite someone or several someones to our bed that is another matter altogether, but I'll not be an adulterer like my father, and I will expect the same from you."

I scrubbed at my eyes with both hands, blinking through the blur it caused.

"And you will... discuss the matter with the demon when he wakes? Share your expectations with the man who just, I don't know, marked me like a fucking dog does a tree!" I hollered.

"Yes, I sure will, and if you thought what he did was over the top, I suggest working on your stamina. I have whole rooms devoted to my pleasure... rooms! And for Gammond's sake, you will cease immediately saying *penis*. What were you, raised in Cult Mossius? Say dick, or cock, or shaft... something that implies strength! Prince Ambrose... married to a prig." He scoffed.

"Is this really the argument we're having right now? Your brother is possessed, like for real, and you want to rant about how I refer to your phallus!"

"Do not shame me for who I am!" he wailed.

"Then don't taunt me for how I speak!" I roared back.

"Untie me immediately."

Our heads snapped in Cato's direction as he lay awake, tugging against his restraint.

"Hold up, Cat," Ambrose said gently, stepping cautiously toward the bed.

"No, I will not hold up. Get over here and get this fucking belt off me, now," he said, deadly serious.

"No. I am not entirely convinced you won't try to have your way with me if I do, brother."

Cato yanked against his restraints so hard the thick wooden post creaked.

"Ambrose, I swear to the fucking Goddess," Cato hissed.

I picked up the lamp from the dinner table and walked around the still-cautious Ambrose. My heart pounded in my chest, beating faster the closer I came. I held the light at arm's length and studied our captive.

"Cato, how do you feel?" I asked, concerned.

"Annoyed, sated, shameful... the list goes on."

"And do you remember... the last time you woke up?" I questioned, trying to discern his state of mind.

"I will never forget even the most minute detail of what happened when last I woke." His eyes darted to my thighs. "I would speak to you privately about the occurrence."

I nodded my head and continued forward.

"Cato, look at me please," I requested nervously.

Without hesitation, he raised his head and held my gaze.

They *had* changed.

"Your eyes are still quite dark, not obsidian like they were right when you woke, but they are now the deepest brown, and... and the gold is almost gone. Just a sliver rings your pupils," I said, astonished by what I was seeing.

He squinted, which made his nose scrunch up.

"Release me. Ambrose, fetch a mirror," he ordered.

Setting the lamp on the side table, I climbed up onto the bed and pulled at the leather belt. Ambrose had cinched it well, but with effort, it finally loosened.

"Cato!" I pointed to his stomach. His eyes followed my finger.

The old scar that should have been peeking above the cover was so faint it had almost disappeared.

He ran his hand over the spot, raising both brows in disbelief.

"But why hasn't the one on your chest faded?" I asked, tracing my finger along its fractured lightning shape.

"Like my eyes, the wound on my hip was caused by corruption. I believe your blood has begun reversing its hold on my body."

He reached out and drew me nearer and lowered his voice.

"Did I frighten you?"

"You did, but—"

"And I hurt you." He reached out and ran his thumb over the bump where his chin had struck the side of my forehead. "My actions were unacceptable, and I will not blame your blood or any unforeseen force—I was aware that when you ran, I should not have followed."

I swallowed back the lump in my throat and continued running my fingers along his old wounds.

"Had I wanted you to stop... I would have said so, Tommand."

His arm wrapped around my shoulder, and he pulled my mouth to his. Delicate kisses pressed to the corners of my lips before his tongue nudged its way past, taunting me until my soft little moans became pleas.

"What was that for?"

"That was me filling your mouth with something else."

I blushed, remembering his promise. I hadn't even realized I'd said Tommand.

"I think, considering how much I enjoy your kisses, your plan may not have the effect you're hoping for, *Cato*," I purred out his name.

All of a sudden, I was swaying on my knees. The middle of the bed nearly collapsed when Ambrose hopped in to join us, tossing blankets and pillows out of his way.

"We need a solid plan. Cato, she can't walk into the palace and explode or turn people into lunatics every time she cuts her finger. I am sure you have already thought of using her blood to cure our father, but can you manage him if he turns into something like you did, considering how far the corruption has turned him?"

"I have thought of the possibility, and no, I am not sure that we could keep him restrained even alongside the others I have trained. Likewise, I do not think it safe to march her in and begin draining her. If you noticed, my eyes still bear the marks. A more subtle approach seems wise."

"I should get to know your father. Spend time with him and learn more about what he is and isn't capable of. Nothing in the story said the Magis fed from the Child or drank her blood. As you had originally planned, it could be that I simply need to exist around him."

"Your existence around him is my most immediate concern. He is completely unpredictable. At this juncture, marriage still seems to be the best option you have, and it will need to take place quickly if agreed upon." He swiveled his head in the other direction. "And Ambrose, we will need to discuss terms. I am unwilling to give her up."

Unwilling to give her up.

That was a drastic shift. It implied a future, a commitment. It is what I wanted, but, it was a decision I wanted to make together.

"I am *not* a Monwyn woman and I won't be treated like I'm one." Both men went silent and faced me. "The two of you can form a plan and discuss your boundaries until the polar bears migrate south, but I am stubborn enough to go against every one of your rules... just so you acknowledge me." I sized them both up. "I've kept my mouth shut and have followed your orders because I thought I needed you to survive. But you are both about *this* close to finding out just how independent I can be. I can fucking explode. My blood heals. I think that just about entitles me to a seat at the table."

Cato reached around my shoulders and dragged me over into the vacant space between him and Ambrose. Emboldened by my own speech, I struggled against him, but together they held me firmly in place, squashed between their two bulky bodies.

"You will be an integral part of planning. I understand its importance to you, but you will recognize the need for our strength."

I wiggled and pushed against their shoulders again, and still not able to gain my freedom, I looked up to Ambrose who just shrugged...

"Fine. You're strong. Cato, you've busted your wounds open. Go clean up and find clothing. Ambrose, I want more of the warmed wine we had with dinner... and I need another chemise to replace the one the demon ripped. While you're at it, I can't wear this wool dress unless Monwyn has seen significant snow overnight. Can you see it remedied... please?" I needed to regain some of my dignity.

Never had I heard so many grunts and sighs.

"Eira, I am fine. There is no need to look at me like—okay!" Cato raised both hands in supplication. "I will go."

"Good, I don't want you to bleed on me the next time you pounce," I derided.

Bolting to his knees, he straddled my legs and leaned low, bringing his face directly in front of mine. His eyes were so different now, still beautiful, but... maybe even more unnatural, the thin gold contrasted so starkly in their darkness. They were the color of the richest earth, like the soil leading to Verus, and that trace that separated the darkness was reminiscent of the solar eclipses I had witnessed twice in my life.

"Cat, cover up that butthole. I'm afraid I'll mistake it for something attractive."

Ambrose, now fully dressed in an exceptionally radiant ultramarine tunic, tossed a small hand mirror onto the bed, which Cato snatched up before I could blink.

"Holy Goddess above," he whispered, sitting back on my legs and pulling at his eyes. "I never thought to see myself again." He angled the glass to catch more of the light, peering at himself from different directions.

"If it keeps fading, I wonder if I will be recognizable at all. No one in the capital will have seen me with shorn hair... or these eyes." He continued to study his reflection, his expression strained. "I do and do not recognize the man I see."

"I think you look beautiful," I breathed.

He swept his gaze over me.

"There is no one more beautiful than she who sits before me."

He dipped down, placing kisses on the swell of my left breast and collarbone before moving off the bed.

The brothers disappeared into the other room to bandage Cato's healing wounds.

Rickert, looking very alert even dressed in his nightshirt, stopped in and delivered a small pile of clothing and sent up a light meal for Cato, which included the requested wine.

Having a few minutes to myself, I laced into the tight-fitting chemise and donned the new dress that I thought would have been more suitable for nursing than the previous iteration. With every movement after I put it on, I glanced down making sure I hadn't fallen out of the extremely low-cut square neckline. The material was much lighter than the wool gown had been, so despite its ridiculous décolletage, it was comfortable, and I was thankful for the provision.

I found the mirror Cato had discarded on the dining table and looked at my reflection while waiting for the men to re-emerge. *Oh, my.* Not even the gown's charming floral silk could make me look less haggard. My piecey, uncombed hair hung loose down my back and the circles under my eyes were a deep purple-gray. Both lips were chapped, and the spot where Cato's chin had hit me was going green—tomorrow it was sure to be a plethora of colors. The arm I had slashed just yesterday was already healing, but the rest of me felt like it was deteriorating.

I examined the eyes that reflected back. My mother's eyes were the darkest green. Gotwig's were blue. I wondered if together theirs could have formed my coloring. Or had that come from the Primus-King of Gaea?

"Deep in thought?" Cato walked in and kneeled in front of me, taking my hands into his warm palms. He wore a tailored long coat of gray that made his shoulders look even wider than they were, and under it a black linen shirt that fastened with dozens of small cloth buttons from the neck down. He wore two rings on his left hand, one with a landscape of mountains carved into its round head, the other a signet ring that bore a crown and shield. A thick, white belt that had been decorated with silver belt mounts in the shape of rampant lions circled his waist.

"Do all of your clothes have cats on them?" I asked, curious if it was a preference.

He dropped his head, looking up at me through lashes that remained tipped in gold. An affectionate little half-grin ran across his face.

"My sisters instructed the tailors and haberdashers on what to include in my wardrobe, so, yes, much of what I own has a feline or two. Which is funny... I actually prefer dogs, but with the nickname and all..." He twisted his hand in the air, leaving the rest unsaid.

I *had* known he liked dogs—Evandr, *bless him*, had told me. I still smiled down at Cato, happy that he wanted to share.

"Now, what was on your mind?" he asked.

Ambrose came through the adjoining room and took a seat at the table.

"My father."

I picked up a goblet from the table and took a small sip of its contents. "If I had to choose, it would be Gotwig. Though I still find him rather dreadful, if it was proven that he sired me, I would have less to worry over in my future. If I am of the Primus-King's line, I'll have no leg to stand on if he demands my return. As tied to tradition as the Gaeans are, I would imagine my mother is still considered his legal wife, and my fear is, whether or *not* he is my natural parent, their marriage still makes me his property. I believe that holds true in all kingdoms except for maybe Solnna."

"Which is why, and please excuse how this sounds, we need to make you someone else's property before he is made aware. A husband is the only one who can exercise authority over a father," Cato said while running a comforting hand along the length of my calf.

"Could we not make it to Solnna or even Nortia, where I would have at least a modicum of personal autonomy?"

Ambrose interjected, "With the Gaeans having sent spies and troops to both those kingdoms, that is not a possibility."

"Eira, this should not be a choice you have to make. Goddess knows I've seen the downfall of a political marriage, but I believe it to be the most effective strategy to ensure your continued protection," Cato reassured as his gaze grew gentle. "Ambrose is your best option, not only because a husband is required, but because, as a Prince of Monwyn, second in line to the throne, he would have the authority to denounce Gaea. His title holds power, and they would think well before attempting to make a claim over his wife."

I stared into the glass of spiced wine that smelled of clove and ginger.

"Ambrose deserves to live as he wishes just as much as I do. We've moved from the idea of reversible betrothal to a contractual union, and it's important to me that he's given as much of a voice as I am in all of this."

Cato looked to Ambrose as did I. He was slumped low in his chair, one leg propped on his knee and a fist balled up under his chin.

"My terms are as follows. I will bed you on the night of our wedding. It is tradition, and I will not have the sanctity of our marriage taken into question. Likewise, you will come to my bed a single time per week, I do not care when, but your marital duties *will* be carried out."

My eyes widened. *Is he actually serious?* I looked at Cato, who stared straight ahead, unfocused.

"You may continue your relationship with Cato, but I will see any others as your having committed adultery, and I am very serious when I say I will publicly condemn you if you make a cuckold of me."

The air rushed out of Cato, and his eyes closed.

"Catommandus, you will have physical relations with no others, I will not suffer some foul disease because you've now remembered what it's like getting your dick wet." He smirked.

Cat nodded, agreeing.

"If I am forced to be married, I will want issue, and those children must be of my body. Therefore, you must take the herbs that render you infertile until the time we are ready to procreate. I already have concerns that he has planted a babe within you."

My eyes were near popping out at this point. I wasn't sure I'd want children at any juncture in my life, and now I had to agree to them if I wished to maintain my security.

"I've had access to a method of control, so that shouldn't be an issue, unless, of course, our brief union was fruitful. But have you considered for a second the implications of siring a child who has the potential of being born of two royal families... who may also inherit whatever makes my blood... my blood?" I asked, unsure if procreation was wise at all given the circumstances of my birth.

"Of course I have, and as the child of a whore and her random liaison, I have found I am not immune to the lure of the position that a child from our bodies would have in this world."

Narrowing my eyes, I felt a fierce need to protect what would be half mine. I didn't want my children to be pawns.

"Perhaps you want to reconsider your plans and consider adoption. It changed your life, after all. You could give a child a loving life, instead of saddling them with the burden that comes with being born a political game piece. I have personally found the experience to be exhausting. Think about it. Here are my terms."

"Do you get terms, Eira? It seems like I am the one making all the big sacrifices," said Ambrose, irritated that I had called him out.

Cato's head snapped in his brother's direction, but Ambrose just scoffed and cocked a brow.

"Continue," Cato grunted.

"You will assist me in locating my mother when you feel it's safe to do so. She's the only person I know who can answer the questions I have about my father and things like... exploding. Second, if Cato would like to carry on his line after I have born your offspring, I am to be allowed to reproduce with him... but the child will take your name." I recalled the night Cato had wistfully looked off while telling me he could never become a father while Protector. Cato laid his head gently in the cradle of my lap, and I smoothed my hand over the back of his head, tracing the dark little flips and curls that were becoming more prominent. "This is done in Solnna, and I think it a fine cultural practice. He shouldn't be denied fatherhood on the sole basis that he is the Protector."

Whereas the thought of bearing Ambrose's children made me weary, trapped even, the image of Cato holding his daughter made me understand what I'd seen in the eyes of new mothers holding their newborns for the first time.

Cato was deserving of that feeling... and so was Ambrose, if I was being honest. Even though at this point I wasn't prepared to give myself up to a passel of children, raising a family still beat out being on the run or being used by the Gaeans.

And I would have, him.

I wanted nothing more than the opportunity to explore what this was between us, and these terms would allow it.

"Lastly, Ambrose, if you ever fall in love, act on it. This is not the union of your mother and father, and I won't shatter if you have your needs met by someone else," I said, softening my tone.

"Thank you, Eira, though I highly doubt the eventuality." Ambrose tipped back his second goblet of wine and proceeded to pour his third. "Cat, everyone else has terms in this bizarre triangle. Let's have yours." He waved his hand in the air dismissively, his speech slurring just slightly. Perhaps this was his fourth refill.

Cato, sitting back on his heels, locked his dark eyes to mine. "If I am allowed only one thing of my own in this life, you are what I choose—if you will have me. If we fail in Monwyn, I will carve out another life for us somehow." His eyes turned glassy while he spoke, and the rest of the world seemed to fall away.

"This is disgusting," Ambrose mumbled. "I accept the terms. Can you hear me beneath the abundance of bullshit you're tossing around over there?"

Ambrose belched loudly and thumped his now empty cup on the tabletop.

Cato cupped my hands between his own, and though I was replying to Ambrose, I felt the promise I was making was to him.

"I accept."

Pulling his expansive shoulders back, Cato nodded curtly to his brother.

"The ceremony can take place a week after the contracts are signed."

"Will your father need to approve the contract?" I asked, wondering if the Monwyn king would be able to fulfill the duty.

Cato leaned over the table and plucked the fourth or maybe a fifth glass of wine from Ambrose's hand, receiving an angry grumble for his intervention.

"I have approved or denied every law, contract, or judgment for the last five years. This will prove no different."

I accepted his answer but found that piece of information to be strange given what I knew of his family.

"You and not your eldest brother? Is he not at the palace? I assumed it was he who would've taken up the reins while you were busy corralling your father or off at Verus."

Cato poured his scowling brother a glass of water and forced it into his hand.

"No, he is not there, and his whereabouts will remain unknown until His Majesty is mended or entombed."

"Can I know his name, or is that also on a need-to-know basis?" I asked, curious about the Monwyn heir.

"Of course you can. Like any other kingdom, royal births are public knowledge. He is called Prince Aberus Tabor—"

"You would have learned that, too... had you finished Troth school," Ambrose declared while saucily weaving his head back and forth.

A knock on the door interrupted my retort.

"Enter!" Ambrose bellowed.

Cato stepped between his brother and the entrance of the chamber, standing at the ready.

"State your business, and for Goddess's sake, stand straight, soldier!"

"Protector! I thought you were... we saw—"

The soldier, who wore a tabard of heavy blue canvas over his splinted leather armor, snapped to attention, saluting his highest-ranking commander.

"The tailors are prepared to see to Troth Nortia, the temple has opened early at your request, and the scribes are drawing up the contracts. They await your arrival."

"And the carriage?"

"Ready within the next two hours, Protector, sir."

"Then leave us."

With a fist to his shoulder, the guard executed a turnabout and moved quickly out of sight.

"And when were those plans carried out?" I asked, irritated that the orders were given *before* our terms were made.

"While you chose to spend your time obsessing over your reflection, Nortia, much was accomplished." Ambrose took off across the room, stumbling over his feet just before crossing the threshold leading to the adjoining room.

"Ambrose, please add a 'don't speak to me' clause in the contract. It will benefit us both!" I shouted after him.

CHAPTER FORTY-TWO

A VERY MODERN MONWYN

After packing up what was deemed essential for the next leg of our journey, our party walked through the wall, heading toward the center of the town. We trekked through the brightly lit tunnel for what must have been half of an hour, passing a few groups of scouts and guards along the way.

Cato explained that strategic exits and entrances had been built into the back side of the wall so that soldiers could move more efficiently to access different parts of the city and that the design decreased the interruption of citizens' lives and eliminated having to skirt around carts or other large objects that might delay their progress.

Eventually, we came to a wide steel door and stepped out into a dismal, gray day. I hadn't heard any thunder while in the wall's confines, but the rain was coming down sideways and collecting on either side of the cobblestone paths. Only a few townsfolk had braved the weather, and they could be seen trying to stay dry by darting between the awnings and covered porches of the businesses that lined the street.

"Shield her." Cato issued the order to the armed escorts who traveled with us.

Four guards lifted an oiled leather canopy over my head, protecting me from the water that poured from the sky. As we pushed forward and walked between the storefronts, the runoff from the covering spilled directly onto the tops of the four men's heads.

"Cato—"

"Protector," he chided, flicking his eyes to mine. *Right, right.*

"*Protector,* is this quite necessary? We could all fit—"

"These men are trained to endure much harsher conditions, Troth Nortia, and are compensated well for their dedication." He stood to my left, staying mostly dry himself, a benefit of his high status.

Ambrose came around me and took his place at my right side. Taking my palm into his hand he raised my fingertips to his mouth and made a show of kissing each one.

"You will know no discomfort as my wife, lovely Eira," he crooned.

I hoped my one-sided smirk read as demure. I doubted it did though.

After a never-ending walk through the deluge, two guards struck out and ran ahead of our contingent to hurriedly fling open the double doors that would admit us into Millanderers Peacock Shoppe, a three-story stone structure that boasted a sign so large it ran the entire width of the building.

Standing under the store's black-and-white striped awning, Ambrose leaned down and whispered, "The couple who owns the place are fairly eccentric, but they will see you dressed in something more sophisticated than the doxies dress you currently wear."

Petulant child. *This* was what I was committing myself to, a lifetime of aggravation.

Plastering a sickly-sweet smile on my face, I shoved a knuckle into his ribs, digging in as hard as I could while still concealing my hand under his elbow.

Ambrose jerked upright, abruptly stopping short of the door. The fury on his face was worth every word that he was about to spit out.

"Oh, darling husband! You shower me with too many fine gifts!" I roughly slapped my hands to both of his cheeks and pulled his face down, planting a dry tight-lipped kiss on his tensed, downturned mouth.

His green eyes glittered behind the calm mask he wore.

"My only pleasure is your satisfaction, *wife*," he effused, every bit the attentive partner.

"Ow!" I yelped, tripping through the shop's open doors.

Ambrose chuckled loudly after he smacked my backside so hard it propelled me across the threshold.

"I can barely wait until the mating night, boys!" He playfully punched at Cato's shoulder while the Protector stared at him stonily.

"You have arrived! A Troth, in our store! Whoever would have thought? And she is joined by our picturesque prince. How divine. Chum, just look at her, so delightfully curvaceous and so absolutely... short," the smaller of the two gentlemen exclaimed.

"No wonder he loves her. She'll look just like his dear mother when she's popped out six or seven," said the other man, whose hair curled in tight silver ringlets around his head.

I stiffened, caught off guard by the wildly inappropriate comments, but Ambrose, who had dutifully marched to my side, laid a hand on my back and pulled me close, acting as if he hadn't heard a word.

"Gentlemen, thank you for seeing us on short notice. The baggage cart moves slowly from Verus and is not expected to arrive at the capital for another week at the earliest. We must arrive at the palace within three days and look to leave in the morning. Are you able to assist us?"

"Your Highness, you ask so much from two aged gentlemen. If you allow us to employ the workers we have locked up in the back, we can most certainly accommodate the lady's trousseau." The one called Chum batted his eyes at Cato.

"I find no humor in the talk of enslavement," Cato grumbled.

"Mmmhmm... I would be shocked to learn you found humor in anything, Protector." The owner laughed behind his hand. "Always so glum."

Tommand—*Cato, not Tommand*—arched his brow and stared at the couple until the air around us became uncomfortable. Chum finally broke the standoff by glancing down at the foot he shuffled back and forth.

"To your posts. No one enters," Cato barked out while surging directly toward the two merchants, who had to hop out of his way to avoid being run down. He disappeared into the shop's backroom.

"How do you stand him?" Chum asked, twisting his lips in distaste.

The taller and much larger shopkeep took a step forward and bowed at the waist, silencing his partner with a pointed look.

"My Honorable Troth, I am Leonard Millanderer, and this dashing fellow is my husband Meachum. Since we got the missive mere minutes ago, we have simply been dying to get our hands on you."

As if to bring his point home, the two immaculately dressed men came forward as Ambrose shoved at the small of my back. Both Meachum and Leonard took me by an upper arm and led me to a leather-upholstered bench, where, for the second time in a matter of hours, two bodies trapped me.

While Ambrose and the owners chatted over payments and particulars, I studied the space whose walls were painted the gray of a dove's wing. The furniture, all matching pieces, were made in a warm amber color, and large, white vases full of—oh! The flowers in the vases were all made of fabric! The roses and lilies and daffodils had been handmade from scraps of sumptuous silks in various hues and textured woolens of all kinds. The floral creations made the most intriguing of arrangements. I had never seen a creation so unique. Even the flower's centers had been hand beaded with pearls and little glass beads. What an absolute delight!

"We need to make you stand out. Something that will be *you*—your personal mark of style, if you will. Prince Ambrose, what do you think?" asked Meachum.

I looked up at the fellow and observed him while trying to figure out what *me* would be in the world of fashion. I studied Meachum as I thought. He wasn't built like the typical Monwyn man who'd spent time in the mines. But I supposed like everywhere else, there would undoubtedly be variation. His shoulders were not particularly wide and rolled inward, and his stomach protruded slightly. His complexion was a glowy light brown and reddish freckles were splattered across the bridge of his nose. He had a head of hair more fantastic than Ambrose, and I have to admit to being a little jealous of the curling nimbus that formed around his countenance.

"Now Chum, not all of us want to be the center of attention in every room we enter. Perhaps His Highness Ambrose would prefer a more muted partner." Leonard reached across my lap and patted his spouse's knee.

He, though dressed just as impeccably as his striped-silk-clad partner, wore a black top with knitted designs that formed chevron shapes from his wide shoulders down to his thinner torso. The effect made him look all the more like an inverted triangle. Leonard was large and, like Ambrose, wore his gray hair in a braid down his back.

"Well, Highness, what do you see your mate wearing? How do you picture her at your side? A shrinking mother figure? A sex goddess that inspires the jealousy of even the most deviant master?" Meachum questioned.

"The only acceptable answer to your questions comes from her mouth, no others." Cato strode back through the main room, interjecting himself in the conversation. "You would do well to remember she is a Chosen Obligate of Verus."

My cheeks flushed hotly when all four men's gazes landed on me.

"Sh-she will decide?" Leonard hesitated.

"She will," came Cato's reply.

"How positively *modern* of you, Protector," Meachum scoffed, fanning his fingers like he was ridding himself of clinging crumbs.

"I think her tits should show," Ambrose lent his opinion to the crowd. The owners nodded merrily in unison. "That's both maternal and alluring, right?"

Cato planted himself next to Leonard, crossing his arms over his chest.

After looking Monwyn's Protector up and down, the shopkeeper's face went a little sour. Like someone was forcing his head to twist upon his shoulders, Leonard turned and with an unconvincing smile, asked, "And Troth Nortia, how do *you* see yourself?"

Naked and on top of Cato if he keeps this up.

I chewed the side of my cheek, thinking of a way I could use this as an opportunity when it hit me.

"I want to dress like Ambrose," I said to the absolute horror of the room.

Like a fish out of water, Meachum's round mouth opened and closed, only stopping when Leonard spoke up.

"What I am hearing... is that you would like to reflect your husband's household colors and perhaps the patterns of your new family crest? Displaying your new connection to your most regal mate would be a wise move."

"No. I want pants," I watched Ambrose's face fall, "and my tits showing... tastefully." I nodded in his direction, letting a winning smile race across my face.

He looked at me with eyes the size of a hoot owl's and clenched his jaw tightly.

If I stood up on the tailors cutting table and freed my bowels, I think I would have offended the couple less. Meachum was wheezing dramatically while Leonard dabbed the sweat from his brow using an embroidered square pulled from his pocket.

This was an absolute riot.

"Yes, I rather fancy the idea of myself in a structured long coat that nips in at the waist and flares to the floor... and pants to go beneath. A skirt would also be nice for when more formality is needed, and please make them of your finest and lightest fabrics. I cannot abide the heat."

Leonard, becoming toasty himself, pushed his sleeves up past his elbows. I looked up at Ambrose, who was doing his best to keep his grimace in check, and to Tommand whose eyes danced with amusement. *Cato, Eira... he's Cato.*

I pointed to Ambrose.

"For my top, do you see how his sleeves tighten from elbow to wrist with all those delightful tiny buttons? I'm rather keen on mimicking the same look, but in a fabric similar to what drapes from your window."

"Lady Troth, that fabric is semi-transparent!" Leonard whimpered.

"Yes, which is why the chest supports I wish you to create must stand out, much like the Protector's belt does with his costume. I rather like the idea of removing my outerwear, as these two so often do, and showing off not only my outstanding cleavage but... I think... embroidered bears. Yes, to represent that fine man I am marrying... and I think to couple them with orcas leaping over their heads. That will link both of our esteemed homelands and show the kingdom that we are not only connected but walk side by side. Oh! And I would like one in orange silk, with appliquéd hounds on its chest... and don't make them look vicious."

Cato spun so quickly on his heel the movement startled me when he left.

Ambrose looked close to succumbing to apoplexy.

"My Goddess. Leonard, I cannot sit by any longer without saying that I absolutely *love* this idea!" Meachum clapped his hands together and tapped his feet in a little dance on the floor.

"It will rattle the ladies of the court so entirely. Can you imagine... pants—on a woman! The men will have to mind their cockstands. And that's your story, Troth Nortia: the most coveted man in the kingdom ensnared by a woman who keeps herself covered like a priggish paragon, but who teases and tempts with glimpses of her tremendous endowments through the shadowy haze of sheerness! Woot!" he crowed.

"And I can assure you if it makes enough splash, Ambrose and myself would surely seek out your designs in the future. And it would only be right to pay you triple for today's rush. Am I right, my love?" I looked up shyly, twisting my hands in my lap.

"How could we possibly not?" Ambrose bit out, letting a blinding smile spread across his face, even as his nostrils flared in obvious aggravation.

"Then it's settled! Leonard, my honey love, I'll take her back while you pull fabrics. I haven't been this excited since Lord Muncy brought his mistress in to be fitted for her bridle and barding. Come on, dear." Meachum popped up and pulled me along.

"A bridle? Truly? Well, measure her for a muzzle. I think it will only enhance our time together." I heard Ambrose say to Leonard from the hallway we walked down.

"Troth Nortia, go behind the curtain and remove everything but your underwear. We will need to measure every inch of you to ensure perfection."

Meachum's measuring tape unrolled with a snap.

"Go on then." He pushed lightly at both of my shoulders, forcing me to take several steps backward before pulling the heavy drapes closed right in my face.

Ambrose had not been wrong. They were certainly a pair.

"*Oh*!" I squawked, turning around in the small room.

"Is everything alright, dear?" Meachum asked.

Cato leaned back against the corner of the front wall, holding a finger up in front of his lips.

"Quite!"

He prowled toward me letting a seductive grin slide across his face. "I simply love your décor." I lied.

Cato bent low and pulled the hem of my dress over my head, leaving me in my underclothes and stockings. He twisted around, coming to stand at my back and nudged the thin straps of my chemise over my shoulders.

"Alright dear, find the robe, and when you are ready, pop outside," Meachum said.

"You know," Cato grazed his lips along my bare shoulders and whispered, "if running away to suppress my laughter becomes habitual, I will lose my credibility as Protector. Can you just for a second imagine me, a fully armored warrior, giggling atop his horse all because I can't get Ambrose's stupefied face out of my head?" His hand went to my laces. "Pardon me, Outlaw MacOgre, my lady told me the most amusing anecdote. Do you mind? It gave me quite the chuckle."

I had to stifle my own laughter at the high-pitched tone he used.

"Oh, that's funny, is it?" The chemise glided over my head. "Do you know what else is funny? Watching that smug brother of mine having to keep his exhausting mouth shut. I could do with you kissing him less, however," he pouted teasingly.

"I'm afraid you'll have to grow accustomed if we are to make this convincing, Protector, but I can owe you two for every one he gets if that will soften the blow."

Cato came around and stood at my front, cupping my breasts in his hands.

"Nothing is likely to soften if you plan to prance around the palace in pants all day," he laughed.

"Well, I have plans for Monwyn. Pants will only be the first stance I take."

Cato crooked his finger and beckoned me to follow as he sat in a corner chair.

"You remove the rest while I watch?" he crooned while sitting back.

Channeling the woman who tossed her robe off while straddling him once, I did a little spin.

Cato let his legs spread apart and rested both his arms along the rounded top of the chair, behind his head.

I placed a foot on his thigh and found my balance before I began to roll the bold-colored stocking down a single leg, bending so low when I got to my ankle that my chest came parallel with his mouth.

"What happens to the credibility of a consistently aroused Protector?" I asked while tending to the other leg.

"I can't wait to find out," he rasped.

Looking me in the eye, he patted his leg. I swallowed deeply.

Standing in nothing but my too-small underwear, I closed the short gap between us and lowered myself to his lap. He lifted my legs and let them hang over the arm of the chair, running his hand along their length.

"Cato," I whispered, still unaccustomed to using the name he preferred, "why did you change your mind concerning you and me?"

He titled my chin, urging me to look at him.

"Because I've prayed to the Goddess every night begging for her permission to be selfish just once, pleading with her to find a way for me to remain near you. Because the thought of you with Ambrose is far less painful than the thought of never seeing you again." He placed his rough-skinned hand over my heart. "Because I've never known anyone who wanted to keep me as safe as I did them."

I felt his chest expand and watched his cheeks dimple.

"Lady Troth! You must be ready by now."

"Oh, I am! Just a moment!" I gasped.

Shocked into action, I leapt off Cato's lap and grabbed the robe, but stopped short before going through the curtain.

Cato cocked his head to the side.

Fingertips to my mouth I blew him a kiss and waved goodbye.

Dramatically, he flung his hand to his forehand, pretending to faint.

"Why, you've gone all pink, Bride Nortia, but surely your betrothed has seen you in your skin before. And dear, no worries where myself or Leonard are concerned. The mere mention of a lady's puss makes him nauseous," Meachum assured me. "Leonard! Leonard! She's pierced *and* branded!" he yelled to his partner. "How would you feel about leaving that breast bare? No! Don't speak, don't decide yet!"

Chapter Forty-Three

PERFECTLY ORCHID

A weary-looking Ambrose and I sat together in a quaint tavern not far from the Peacock.

I was quite pleased with the concepts the Millanderers had come up with despite the fact that our entire day had been spent having textiles tucked, pinned, and remeasured. Though the idea behind my creations stemmed from the intention of upsetting Ambrose and the entire Monwyn patriarchy, wearing something that appeared so regal and lovely gave me a distinct feeling of power, and I was grateful I didn't leave the shop in the dress I'd worn in. The spouses and their workers were happily banding together to work through the night, despite gnashing their teeth about the brief time they'd been granted. A few more coins in their pockets and we were ensured the rest of the wardrobe would be sent before we departed.

What I wore now was nothing short of fantastic.

The tailors had altered and reshaped a much too-large man's coat to fit me. The fabric was a mixture of light gray and black woven into tiny stripes. I was thrilled to wear the stark color in honor of my Nortian roots, even though Ambrose insisted that my colors should be the blue of Monwyn and red of Verus. The wool it was made from was so fine it had to be lined with a gorgeous silk, which featured red rosettes on a gold background. Though you didn't see the fine fabric immediately, when I moved or kicked out, it appeared as though small swirls of fire licked at my knees and ankles. Wide and voluminous black pants floated around my legs all the way to the ground. The amount of yardage they included gave the impression that I was wearing a skirt, but because they turned out to be quite comfortable, I didn't press Leonard to make them more masculine. Due to time constraints, I wore a simple black chemise underneath my coat that had been created to be laced up on both sides, allowing me to adjust the fit to meet my needs. Currently, the tops of my breasts swelled over the coat's scooped neckline per Ambrose's request for a "dinner look worthy of my husband."

Flanked by two guards, Cato strode into the tavern and joined us at our table, tucking into the food that had arrived earlier.

"The contracts are secure, and the horses are equipped and prepared," he said, never looking up from the leg of poultry he tore into. "We leave immediately."

"Immediately as in tonight?" I croaked out, disappointed I wouldn't have a single night of proper sleep. The pace at which we'd been traveling and the nocturnal interruptions had been catching up with me for days. Whereas the Monwyns were used to the misery, I was certainly not. I didn't want to complain, though. They were uprooting their lives for me.

"Immediately, as in, the moment I finish my meal."

He tossed the cleaned bones onto a plate and grabbed a bowl of fish stew, to which he added both my and Ambrose's leftovers.

"And the carriage... is it ready? I thought with the—"

"We will not be traveling in the carriage... though the highwaymen and scoundrels who prey upon that leg of the road won't be the wiser."

"And we will ride... through the night?" I asked, keeping my voice level. In truth, I was close to sobbing.

He nodded while polishing off the bowl of stew and extras.

"Correct. We will stop for a few hours of rest this evening and then continue on our way." Cato swiveled his head around and gestured to the tavern keeper. "Wrap up another bird and basket of bread. I can continue my meal on the road."

"You will be fat as a sow before we reach the capital, Cat," Ambrose said, glancing in my direction and then back at his brother in concern.

"I think it has to do with the blood. I've been this way since I woke. All I want to do is fuck, eat, and fight," he raised his eyes to mine, arching his brow suggestively, "in that very order... let's be off."

···+)(+···

We rode at a fast pace, only a few minutes behind two scouts who had gone ahead of us. Though confident in my horsemanship, the speed we maintained as we traversed the unfamiliar terrain was daunting and made me constantly aware of my form. No leaves clung to the trees that stood between the two mountains, probably due more to the wind that howled fiercely through the pass than to the changing of seasons. Already, my hair had dislodged from its braid leaving strands to whip around my face.

The moonlight filtered through the swaying branches, casting eerie shadows that danced along the ground and protruding rock faces that appeared frequently along the path we followed.

When Cato finally halted our party, I was so exhausted I almost asked for help in dismounting but managed to slide off the horse's back and find my feet.

"Tye, you will take the first shift to our front. Decka you will watch from above. Scale up as soundlessly as possible," Cato looked pointedly at both scouts, "start no fires, cover anything reflective."

Both the men nodded their understanding and faded into the night.

We couldn't easily hide the horses as the trees were not as densely packed as the forests in southern Nortia had been, so they were tied off a ways from where we camped.

"Come snuggle your almost-husband," Ambrose said after locating a tree trunk wide enough to suit him. He sat down and leaned back holding his arms wide. "After today I deserve to nap while cozied up to your succulence."

Cato, timing it well, plopped down into his brother's lap.

"Here you are then, brother. Hold me as tight as you please."

Even as tired as I was, I smiled at the two.

"You know, I'm afraid the unconventional relationship we are about to embark upon will inevitably become problematic. Scoot apart." I waved my hand back and forth until they separated. I sat between them and they both inched closer, squishing me firmly into place. "I'm not kidding; I'm really fearful of jealousy or bitterness coming between the two of you."

"I am not the jealous type. I do not care about you and Cat fucking, so long as you never make it public. And I simply need you to be a warm and willing vessel for my pleasure once per week while acting like the proper wife for the remainder, maybe occasionally snuggling at night."

Wow... a vessel. That was a sobering description of my role in my impending marriage.

"But Ambrose, how long have you gone without sex, or... snuggling?"

"No more than two days I would imagine, but I've never been a committed man before... and I do intend to heed my vows."

Ambrose's arm came around my stomach, pulling my hips snugly to his.

"Cato, when I am being used as Ambrose's *vessel,* you will be doing what?" I asked.

Silence.

"Cato, what is your expectation for how often you and I will be able to see each other?"

"Nightly, every evening. Unless I am detained with work, most mornings."

"That poses a problem. Do you all *see* the problem?"

Neither of them spoke.

"No? No problem? Alright then, well, I will require a bedroom of my own with a working lock unless we work out some sort of schedule for Ambrose nights and Cato nights."

"You will have an adjoining chamber that leads to my own, and there will be no lock. I've only been to the palace proper a handful of times over the years, but I have my rooms there and I will want access to you at all times—as will Cat. The capitol is rife with vulgar courtiers who will try to seduce and sway you. If we are to protect you from them, you can't be where we are unable to get to you."

"You should know, being their ringleader," Cato murmured.

Ambrose snorted loudly. "If they attempt to lay a finger on my wife, I will remove the offending appendage from their body." Ambrose nestled his face into the back of my neck and wriggled until comfortable.

Cato turned his body to me and moved closer to my side. He didn't say anything but lifted my hand to his lips and ran my knuckles across their softness. Placing our entwined hands on his chest, I closed my eyes and tried to drift off listening to Ambrose's rhythmic breathing.

"You are unable to sleep?" Cato asked after a length of time.

"Mmmhmm," I hummed. "I have too much on my mind."

The hand that still held mine released and drifted to my face, skimming the bridge of my nose.

"It seems like, since the last Maneuvering, you have begun to question your strength."

"Well, of course I have. Since then, I've had to commit sex acts with a lunatic, watch a man die inches from my face, run for my life, fear every little sound, and subject myself to public scrutiny... I could go on, but giving it voice makes me fear my future even more." I swallowed.

Cato pressed his body nearer mine and patted his shoulder. I laid my head on him, thankful for the cushion and closeness.

"That is what you see." He bent and pressed his lips to my hairline. "I see a woman who made the choice to preserve herself, one who faced those who would commit violence against her," he chuckled and continued, "one who poisoned a man she thought false, and one who fled to the forest and survived. Promise me you will try to recognize your own worth and see what I do, love."

Like the morning glories I'd seen at dawn, tenderness blossomed in my chest.

"Eira, your power may not lie in your muscles, but it certainly lies in your cunning and creativity, both of which can be mightier than all the swords in a kingdom. It is that which will see you through your next chapter," he said with certainty.

I brought his hand to my mouth now, kissing each of his knuckles.

"I adore it when you touch me. It has not been often that anyone would even dare."

How can anyone not want to touch him?

"Cato, will you truly be able to cope with this arrangement?" I asked, worried by his earlier silence.

"You will bear your burden, and I will bear mine," he replied.

"I promise, I will take no enjoyment in it."

"No, that should not be how this works. Your discomfort will never bring me pleasure. If I knew you went to him feeling shame or distress... *that* is when I would not be able to cope."

"This is all so strange," I fretted.

"Wait until you meet the magical-mad-king. Our situation will feel tame when he tries to smother you with throw pillows while dancing a jig joyfully at the far side of the chamber."

I snorted, trying not to laugh at something so awful.

"He does that?" I asked, surprised.

"He tries to kill me every time we meet, sometimes twice. He's fond of pillow asphyxiation but has also tried to drown me in old vase water. He can move liquids like a big bubble and somehow stick it to your face."

I laughed at the image of a water-encapsulated Cato running for his life.

"Are you really laughing at my misfortune, Lady Troth?" he chided.

"No, no, I would nev—yes! It just seems so comical, so outrageous... like dealing with an all-powerful two-year-old."

I could sense his smile and felt the shake of his broad shoulders.

"It is actually a lot like that, *and now,* we get to deal with him together," he joked.

"It's like you've made me an offer I can't refuse. A phony marriage, the constant threat of death, a father-in-law who may kill me, and... absolutely mind-blowing sex. The sex makes up for most of it."

"The sex, Goddess alive. I have devised all manner of objectives for the couplings I plan to impose upon you."

"Have you then?" I asked breathily.

"I have had a long and unfulfilled stretch of time in which to visualize the ways in which I could use a woman's body. You should prepare yourself."

"Prepare myself?" I questioned, all of a sudden looking forward to the future. "And how would you suppose I do that?"

"By working on your grip strength."

I batted at his chest, thankful for the darkness that covered my blush.

"I will give you a couple days' rest before seeking you out again," he promised.

A couple of days? I would accept him now were it not for my eyes closing of their own accord.

We sought each other's mouths in the night. I would have stayed awake for three days straight if it meant he would continue showering delicate kisses along my collar bone.

"You need to get—"

He stiffened and went quiet, placing his finger on my mouth.

I nodded, understanding the command to keep silent.

Slowly and soundlessly Cato made his way to stand. He tapped Ambrose's foot with his own, and I felt a change in his breathing pattern instantly. Both men squatted low to the ground and without words began to communicate with each other through a series of touches and hand signs.

I caught Cato's shadow reaching into his boot but was surprised when he turned and pressed the dagger into *my* hand.

Still keeping low, he moved around the tree at our backs and re-emerged with a much longer blade that glinted in the moonlight.

Ambrose, whom I could make out fairly well, removed a weapon from under the cloak that he then unclasped and dropped to the ground. Though not a blade, it was about the length of his forearm and had a fist-sized spiked ball at its top.

Cato leaned into his brother's side once more and then the larger shadow took off and headed through the trees toward Colpass.

Crouching on bent knees, Cato moved in our horses direction.

Fear being a strong motivator, I got to my feet quickly, and positioned myself behind the tree trunk, and peered around it to scan for danger. The suspense of not knowing why both men had left meant my brain was churning through a host of scenarios, every new one more alarming than the next.

I clutched the dagger tighter, keeping my hand as far away from the blade as possible without weakening my hold.

A horrible screeching pierced the night. Was it horse or man? I couldn't tell, but I was hit with the most profound urge to run.

The sound of snapping twigs came from behind me.

Goddess, protect us...

I held my breath and leaned further into the tree, trying to become one with its knotty bark.

I willed myself to freeze.

There was movement in my periphery.

And then I smelled it.

Like a foul rot or decay, the stench was so intense that fluid rushed to my mouth, threatening to spew forth the contents of my stomach. I let the saliva flow down my chin, aware that choking could give away my location.

From what I could see, the man, who would dwarf Ambrose in height and weight, moved slowly and leaned from side to side like he was trying to make a decision on which way to go.

My burning lungs were thankful when he resumed moving forward, though I didn't dare exhale until the stinking behemoth was a couple of horse lengths away. Gradually, I let the air slide through my lips and willed my heart to slow its rapid pace.

As if it sensed a change, the giant stopped dead in its tracks and sniffed at the air.

My knife hand trembled.

The man turned and fear coursed through me, but just as I'd convinced myself I was its target, it continued walking, following the path that Ambrose had taken.

Ambrose was certainly strong, but I wasn't sure he'd be a match against someone so beast-like. I dared to glance around the tree and watched the fur-clad being walk away on its massive unshod feet.

I had to get to Cato. Their combined strength would be necessary to take that thing on.

I squatted low like I had seen the brothers do, and though the muscles of my thighs weren't used to the position, I did feel as though I could pivot faster than if I were standing upright. Moving quickly from tree to tree and doing my best not to jump at every branch that rocked in the wind, I returned to the road.

Cato was there. Surrounded.

He stood in the middle of a horseshoe of bandits, so completely unaffected I expected him to bend over and stretch his legs like I'd seen him do often.

Cato's voice carried over the distance.

"The choice is yours, gentlemen: tell me who sent you here and die with a clean conscience or don't. Either way, your lives are forfeit." He kicked at the tip of his downward hanging sword as if bored. "Who knows, perhaps Merrias will tip the blade in your favor."

"The mighty protector thinks he can take us," sneered their leader. The taller man leaned forward and hurled a ball of spit, hitting Cato on his cheek.

I saw the flash of steel but must have blinked when Cato thrust forward, running his sword under the bandit's ribs.

The man fell to the ground with a pained grunt when Cato extracted his weapon.

The remaining six backed up and drew blades. From my hiding spot, I saw two others step just past the trees at the edge of the clearing. One of the cloaked figures kneeled almost directly in my path. At his side hung a crossbow, loaded and ready. I saw the partner on the other side of the trail loading his weapon, cocking its string back against his hip.

I was leaning to the left, searching for Cato, when the burglars began their attack. They all headed for him at once, swords drawn and daggers unsheathed. One smaller bandit held a spear in front of him.

They meant to kill him.

The clang and clash of weapons met my ears as dawn approached. I knew Cato could handle himself, but watching the speed and style of his combatants, I couldn't help but think these highwaymen seemed more versed in combat than a roving band of outlaws should be.

The figure in front of me moved quickly when he saw an opening.

He raised his bow and took aim.

It took two steps for me to reach him. He spun on his knee, realizing he wasn't alone.

He wasn't fast enough.

I brought my dagger down on his chest, piercing him in the hollow of his neck, just above his collarbone.

I expected screaming and spurting blood, but the man toppled calmly, almost peacefully—no sound coming from his mouth, no thrashing of his limbs. It took me a few tries, but I was able to slip the knife from his still form. The exit wound was little more than a thin slash. I looked around to see if anyone had noticed me. Thankfully the bow in his hand hadn't discharged or shot erratically when it hit the ground.

I'd never held a crossbow, but I knew the basics of its mechanics—you aimed at your target and squeezed the rod that ran the length of the bottom. Across the way, I spied the other bowman pressing forward, moving closer to the battle. I raised the bow and let loose the arrow which shot well above the assailant's head and off into the woods.

I withdrew another bolt from the dead man's quiver while glancing to Cato, who was now facing only two others. I didn't have the arm strength to span the crossbow, even using my hip as support, so dropped to the ground and tried again using my stomach while pushing my foot into the prod for more leverage.

"Fuck!" I bit down on my lip to keep silent. The string had pulled back just enough but jumped out of the slot that should have contained it. My thumb had caught in its whip and momentarily felt like it had been put to flame before going entirely numb.

I couldn't stop, I tugged again at the cord with both hands as I braced myself. My arms shook and the string bit into my skin, but this time it sank solidly into place, fully secured.

"Aren't you—"

I jerked the bow upright and fired.

The force of the bolt leaving the bow caused the heavy stock to hit me solidly in the solar plexus, knocking the wind from my lungs.

Fired so closely, the feathered shaft embedded itself into the woman's face, near the side of her nose. Her unfocused eyes looked into mine when she fell forward, and the projectile's end bit painfully into my shoulder when she came crashing down. Hot and viscous blood oozed from the wound and made its way down my neck and into the bodice of the coat I wore. Frantically, I pushed against her body but only managed to lift her high enough for me to see the bloody mess of her sunk-in face.

"Eira? Eira!"

The body rolled off me and a wide-eyed Cato stared down.

"Respond to me. Are you hurt?"

He came to his knees.

"Ambrose needs you. There's something out there Cato. I'm okay."

To show him, I sat up, ignoring the little flashes of light that danced in my vision.

"Are you sure?" he questioned while checking my head for injury.

I nodded. I could deal with the pain later.

He held out his hands and hoisted me to standing, and together we moved out.

"I'll catch up!" I yelled, remembering that I had dropped the dagger nearby. I didn't want to be without it.

Cato continued on as I quickly backtracked. When I retrieved it, I cleaned off its sticky handle using the bottom of my coat and ran to catch up, to make him aware of what he might face.

"He's bigger than Ambrose, seriously, and is wearing a bunch of furs, and... he smells, like, like decaying meat."

"Troll."

"TROLL?" I shouted back, stunned to the core.

"Troll," he repeated just as blandly.

"Trolls exist? You're telling me trolls are real?" I screeched.

"What do your eyes tell you?" He inclined his head and jerked his chin forward. I looked around him and saw Ambrose, wailing on a creature who took no notice.

In the light of morning, I could see that what I had encountered was no man. Its face looked to have been built from potatoes. It was all bulbous and ill-formed. What I had thought was a fur mantle was actually a pelt of the beast's own fur that trailed heavily down its back.

"His morning star isn't enough unless he can get to its head. Did you bring the crossbow?"

"No."

"Always take an extra weapon if there is one to be had. Never go into a fight with only a single method to kill if it can be avoided. Switch me." He put his sword in my hand and took the dagger.

Cato took off at a sprint, headed to the battleground where Ambrose and the giant faced off. The troll, who I could smell from where I stood, wasn't quick, but he pressed on relentlessly, obviously unaffected by the blows Ambrose kept dealing.

Having seized a thick branch, the troll reared back and took a tremendous swing, forcing Ambrose to dodge and spin to avoid the branches and shrapnel that went flying. Nothing in the troll's trajectory remained standing. The force uprooted saplings, and dried-out limbs cracked loudly as they busted in half.

I flicked my eyes between Ambrose and Cato. This was not a fight I could enter.

Cato took a running leap and wrapped his arms around a medium-sized tree. He squeezed the trunk with his knees and pushed off with his feet, successfully climbing up, until he stood on the first substantial limb he came to. While balancing himself with both arms spread wide, he shuffled slowly toward the fighting pair.

As though sensing Cato's plan, Ambrose ran around to the troll's backside and released a torrent of blows. The troll swung in a massive arc, and when his weapon crashed to the ground, Cato leapt from overhead and landed on its back. He wrapped his arm around its thick-skinned neck and worked to pull himself over the top of its head. The troll flailed about and gnashed its teeth at Cato's arms.

Cato squatted atop the troll's shoulders and drove his dagger repeatedly into its eyes. A pained roar burst from its mouth, sounding something like a cross between a bear and a screaming sow.

I covered my ears, stricken by the sound of its cries.

While it teetered on its feet, Cato hopped from its back and motioned Ambrose forward. The second the blinded troll hit the ground, Ambrose held his mace above his head and drove it down, crunching into the troll's head. He struck over and over until the creature's face was no longer discernable. Nothing but brain matter and crushed bone remained.

I covered my eyes and staggered behind a tree where I bent and heaved, leaving the contents of my dinner on its twisting roots.

"We must go," Cato said softly behind me. "If there are more they will attack the horses."

Balking at the thought of seeing Horse Ambrose mauled, I straightened my spine and wiped the back of my hand across my mouth. Every breath I took smelled of carnage or rot.

The three of us made our way back to where our horses remained tied off.

"These were not thieves. They didn't touch the horses after bringing down Decka, and when I emerged from the wood, they waited to attack... Highwaymen don't wait."

"Gaeans?" I asked Cato.

"Maybe, but would they be so bold as to walk straight into Monwyn under no guise at all—"

"If they thought they could get their goddess-princess back they would," Cato cut in.

Cato wiped down his blades and returned one to his boot and the other to his waist.

"With the addition of the troll, we have no time to search the bodies." Cato waved to Tye, who had come in from his rounds. "My guess is His Majesty has been able to dabble in his trickery, with or without his guardians' knowledge."

"He creates trolls?" I asked. If he could animate life, he was far more powerful than he'd been given credit.

"No, we have never had one running the halls of the palace, but there are more oddities sighted when he is able to conjure," explained Cato.

We mounted our horses. My thumb was still so numb it didn't yet give me any issues taking up the saddle, but my shoulder was beginning to throb the more I jostled.

"Ambrose, had you seen a troll before?" I asked.

"Never, but on the way to Verus, Cat briefed me on what to expect from the creatures he has dealt with so far, just as a precaution."

"I should like a briefing myself. You both smell horrific." I rode out in front of them to stop myself from gagging.

"If our father is up to no good, how do you suppose we introduce his daughter-in-law-to-be. Walk her straight in?" asked Ambrose.

"Absolutely not. Until I have assessed his condition, she won't be subjected to him."

"She could wait at an inn, I suppose."

"No. I will not want her out of my sight for long."

"You don't think they could have been interested in the second heir to the throne?" Ambrose asked while dusting off his pants.

"Did they come after you?"

"Well, no but—oh… I can take her to the palace through the Den…" Ambrose said, letting his voice trail off.

"You would take your betrothed, a *literal* Troth, through Monwyns's own nether? Have you lost your fucking mind?" Cato shoved Ambrose in the shoulder, hard enough to make him sway in his seat.

"The Den is?" I butted into the conversation curious as to what kind of place riled Cato.

"It is just a lovely little place where a group of like-minded men go to unwind from time to time," Ambrose said in a sickly-sweet tone.

"Do not let him fool you. It is where the most depraved of Monwyn men take their mistresses to show them off while they lock their wives up at home."

"If I took her through, our betrothal would seem less fictitious. My appetites are well known."

"And you would allow them to paw her?" Cato glowered.

"Of course not… I would do the pawing to make it look real. You know I have no need for pain to be mixed in with my pleasure. It's about the show for me. I would keep her safe, and *they* would be sent a clear message that she is not to be added to their list of potential conquests."

"I will come and stand guard," Cato fumed.

"Absolutely not. The last time you stepped foot in the Den you almost tore the place apart. The lady's partner was very lovingly choking her if I recall, and we were kicked out before either of us had the opportunity to get someone to suck us off. Not sure I have forgiven you for that…"

I raised my eyebrows but kept looking forward. I don't think I would ever understand their dynamic.

"I was barely sixteen. I didn't know that was a thing some people liked."

"Regardless, you won't enter. It will be hard enough to keep your relationship with her private. They will need to be convinced, and you won't be able to remain calm when I expose her."

I tugged on the reins gently, halting my mare and cutting off the two horses behind me.

Ambrose correctly interpreted my scowl.

"Honestly, it is nothing you haven't done already. Men go there to show off their wealth and prowess. Maybe they have tempted a high-status woman to their side, a pierced royal, a deliciously all-gender partner... a male with a particularly grandiose appendage. They show them off, fondle them a little, and the others get a look. It would be no worse than the Second Maneuvering, and I would make it a point to send the message that you were not to be trifled with."

"That's fine," I answered, not overly concerned with the thought of being exposed.

"Is it?" Cato asked, sardonically.

"If it gets me to a bed quickly, I don't give a damn. I can't feel my thumb, my shoulder has gone all tingly, and I am utterly exhausted. Oh, and I killed two people and yet I feel more remorse for the troll that died. That feels problematic, but here we are. So show them my tits, smack my fat ass in front of their stupid noses, I don't give a shit."

"You were hurt?" Cato asked, trying to take my hand.

"I'm fine." I shot him a pointed look.

"I am so proud of your proper usage of the word 'tits,' lady wife," Ambrose said.

"Look here, be prepared for me to bring every troll I ever encounter into your bedroom if so much as another man's finger touches me tonight," I challenged.

"That wouldn't be much fun. I've already seduced most of the trolls that hang around the palace." He laughed louder than was warranted, quite pleased with himself.

I looked at Cato.

"How do you stand to claim him?"

"By beginning all introductions with 'This is my brother; we share not a speck of blood,' Mother never let us call him 'the adopted one.'"

"He doesn't lie, it is how he introduced me to his first little love interest."

"Whom he fucked not a week later," Cato murmured.

Ambrose let out one of his manly giggles.

"She wasn't right for you. Anyhow, it is settled, we need to bathe and procure a change of clothing from the carriage. I would imagine it should be rolling through in a few hours' time. By nightfall, wife, I will tuck you into my bed, and you can sleep for the next three days."

I nodded curtly and turned, resuming our ride.

···✦)(✦···

"The spring is up ahead. We will each take turns bathing while the other two serve as lookouts. We don't want man or beast to surprise us."

We had ridden at a leisurely pace for another couple of hours before stopping. Cato, familiar with the area, led us beyond a row of leafless trees. Due to the lack of foliage, we would be able to see the carriage from a distance with no issue.

"Cat, I'm not going to fit in that," a lighthearted Ambrose said in a singsong voice pointing to the trickle of water that Cato had referred to as a spring.

"That's not—I know." Cato dismounted and waved us around a boulder that jutted from the ground.

A perfect little well hid behind the rock. Its water was clearer and more pristine than any river I'd seen.

"After a rain, the water here is recharged. You can drink from it, too, as long as nothing dead is floating around."

A stark-naked Ambrose strolled happily past my side, heading toward the natural bath.

"I suppose we take the first watch."

"Let us go up," he said while pointing to the top of the tall rock. Together we climbed up the side that angled deeply toward the spring. I lay back, taking in the blue sky.

"Let's see it," Cato said.

He slid his fingers up and down each digit of my injured hand, palpating and pinching certain points.

"The tip of your thumb is broken right under the flesh that's missing."

"I'm sure my heal-y blood will take care of it soon. It's not overly painful," I assured him.

"It *will* be unless your blood can reset small bones. If it is not set, it may heal crooked and cause you future issues. Let me set it back into place?"

"Okay, I—damn, Cato!" I sucked the air through my teeth, trying to not yank back the hand. He worked the tip of my thumb between his fingers. "Ow! Ow! Oh!" I struggled to keep my volume in check until he finished. The numbness, though still apparent in some places, gave way to a pain unlike anything I'd felt. It was deep and pounding and radiated back into my hand when touched.

"If you are having fun without me, I will consider it a slight!" Ambrose yelled up from below. We both ignored him.

"There. You did better than some soldiers do. We need to find something to keep it straight, but for now, try not to use it. If you shift it again the pain will be much worse."

Ambrose climbed atop the rock, smiling merrily.

"Your happiness is actually offensive to me right now." I scowled at the naked man that laid himself next to me. He flung his wet hair out and arranged it to dry on the sun-speckled rock. A secretive smile played across his face as he looked in my direction, shielding his eyes with his hand.

"What? It's obvious you want to share something."

"Is it just?" He feigned confusion. "Well if you must know, you will be the first I have ever shown off at the Den. I've been planning which parts of you to show first. The piercing will get them going, but the big reveal will be that saucy little brand at your hip. What should we wear tonight?"

"I don't care." And I didn't. I just wanted to be on our way so I could lay on a giant bed in a dark room.

"No? Perhaps we should match. How do you feel about red, as we are both returned from the temple?"

"I'm going to wash."

I scootched down the rock on my butt but didn't escape quickly enough to keep from hearing Ambrose talking to his brother.

"What color do you think best sets off her divinely tight—"

"Ambrose..." Cato warned.

"You are being immature, Cato. We have both had her and will again, and I—"

"I will permanently silence you if you speak another word, brother."

I made it down the rock and chucked my clothes on the ground. The pool of water was cold but did a lot to soothe my pains. I dunked myself under and with one hand scrubbed at my hair and scalp. Then I paid special attention to my chest. Blood had dried to my body in a path from clavicle to hip.

I'd taken lives.

I was still waiting to be hit by the guilt of my actions, but so far it hadn't come. With the baby fawn and the troll, there was a physical response to their deaths, and they stayed with me even now. The archers, however... the archers knew what they did, and my perception was that they were a threat to Cato. But did that justify my actions? Did I care if it didn't? I scrubbed the rest of my body as well as I could manage without soap and winced when I made contact with my shoulder.

"What the nether." I looked up just in time to see both men's heads disappear from the overhang, where they had obviously been spying on my bath.

Stomping around the rock, the brothers charged toward me. Cato tossed his clothes aside and chastised me from the bank.

"Deity blood or not, when I ask if you are hurt, I expect you to answer honestly," he scolded.

"I was *honest*," I threw back. "I didn't know of its extent until now."

"Bullshit!" he raised his voice, shocking me with his tone.

Both men came trudging through the water. Ambrose pulled my hair back and then positioned my shoulders to look at my wound in the more intense rays of the early afternoon sun.

"How am I to show them this? You have gone purple and green. The puncture looks like it could fester in the next moment."

"Tell them I like being stabbed."

Ambrose's mouth pulled down in consideration.

"The carriage," Cato said, still holding my gaze.

"See to her. I will stop them." Ambrose stomped back out of the water, displacing an impressive amount of the spring's volume.

Cato prodded at my shoulder, sending searing pain through my arm and chest.

"Are you so ready to die?"

I raised my chin and glanced up at him. Anger was written plainly across his features. He clenched his jaw, working the muscle, and scowled down at me.

"You're being dramatic, I told you—"

"A lie," he hissed.

I rubbed at my temples, trying desperately to tamp down my own rising emotions.

"You know more about lying than I do and—"

"When you are hurt, you will tell me. This is not negotiable."

"Quit cutting me off!" I shoved my hands against his chest, knocking him backward.

His head went under the water, and his legs flailed comically above the surface.

Oh, Derros, Protector of the Sea.

When finally his head emerged, Cato was in a full-on rage. He hung his head low and stared at me from under his brows, reminding me of a bull before it charged. He narrowed his dark eyes.

"I bet it's been some time since you were last dumped on your ass. You were due."

He rose straight out of the water and streams flowed down his face and body... his rugged and beautiful body. Goddess, I couldn't think when confronted with that powerfully built chest, all that substantial brawn. I dragged my eyes downward and was hit with the fierce need to run my hands through the soft hair that was sprinkled across his taut stomach.

"You will NOT defy me when it comes to your well-being," he thundered, clenching his fists at his sides.

The intensity of his voice snapped me back to attention. I curled my top lip in defiance and shrugged. I wasn't here to be treated like a soldier. I turned on my heel and stepped up to the bank, making to leave the spring.

"Don't. You. Dare," he growled.

"Ooh, a contraction. You are mad."

His fingers locked around my wrist and I was whipped around. My chest met Cato's ribcage with a solid smack.

"Where has your fear gone, Troth? Why do you challenge me?" He forced my chin up, making me look him in the eyes.

Like he'd placed me under a spell, a heaviness settled between my legs, followed by that wonderfully tingling pulse. I bit at my bottom lip and dragged my nipples up to his torso.

"You... are you aroused?" Cato bellowed. "Goddess be damned, you and Ambrose undoubtedly deserve each other."

I moved my hips against him, and a soft whimper escaped me.

Cato released me, and stumbling backward, my thighs came up against the edge of the well. I breathed in deeply in an effort to calm my libido and reached back to steady myself. I closed my eyes, shuttering the view.

"Open your eyes. Do not shut me out."

I lifted my heel to the ledge of the spring and hoisted my bottom up onto the solid ground.

"Cato, I can't."

"What do you mean you can't? Open your fucking eyes and communicate like an adult."

Like a WHAT? My eyes snapped open, primed for a confrontation.

"Take that ba—" The word ended in a deep, throaty moan.

The thick base of him, nodded in and out of the surface of the agitated water. My tongue darted out to wet my dry lips. I was consumed with the thought of how descendant it felt to have him push himself inside me.

"I... can't focus... with...that." I pointed, backing myself further onto the bank.

"Ridiculous! Will I be required to fuck you before we spat?"

"Yes. I'm waiting." I laid back and spread my legs wide. "Please, Cato..." I let my hand drift between my legs and swirled a finger around my peaked flesh.

"*No,*" came his impertinent reply.

I moved my hand lower, slipping my finger into myself. I was desperate for him.

"No?" I cried, whimpering in frustration.

He moved and stood between my legs.

"Thank Goddess." I removed my finger and looped my hands around the back of my thighs, pulling them back as far as they could go. I watched his body stir to life before my eyes. His erection filled to pulsating, its thick head poised at my opening.

I waited, writhing below him.

"I said, no. And I will not enter you again until I know you won't make a habit of hiding the truth from me." He laid his dense shaft along my cleft but gave me nothing. I arched and rocked my hips, seeking any friction I could. "You aren't the only one with wiles, Troth. I'll have your promise and then I will take you."

"Fine, yes, fine, I'll tell you if I'm hurt... put it in now."

"No. You are to promise me you will hide nothing from me, Eira. Then you may choose how you come. Perhaps I guide myself into you. Perhaps you ride my mouth. It would be the perfect position for me to further accustom you to the feel of my finger in your backside. Eventually, I will replace it with my cock. Are you aware that is another way we could play together in the future?" He stroked himself.

I thought briefly to tell him that Ambrose had sure enjoyed it while getting blown, but my defiant streak was currently being drowned out by my screaming sex drive.

"I want you in me, everywhere," I panted, grabbing for his erection.

"No! No, no, no. We have no time for that," a voice interrupted from above.

"Fucking Ambrose!" I yelled while pummeling the ground with my uninjured hand.

"Cat, you still smell of troll. Eira, save that for the Den. Do you two always angry fuck? I do not think that's healthy."

I covered my eyes and snapped my knees shut.

"I believe I've won this round," Cato whispered while backing up into the water. "Ambrose, did you locate the healer's bag?"

"Of course, and clothing for us all. Eira get up. Your hair and face will take time."

I remained as I was.

"Now!" he snapped.

"Will you be doing my hair and making up my face? If you haven't noticed, I'm down a hand." I threw my arm in the air, waving my hand in his direction.

"Yes. Unlike you, when I send a lover from my room I make it a point to *allow* them to dress and refresh."

"Ambrose, get over yourself!" I yelled.

Cato's head snapped toward his brother, whose arms were full of garments.

"Anyway, I went with red for you. Paired with your blue undergarments, it will make your perfectly orchid-hued cavern look amazing... I think. Spread your legs again?"

CHAPTER FORTY-FOUR

THE DEN

If Scion or prince didn't work out for Ambrose, he'd have a solid career in the Grooming room at Verus. As we rode together on his mount, he held up a small carved bone hand mirror and once again assessed both of our reflections.

He'd made up my eyes to look smokey and seductive in shades of brown and gold, and with powdered kohl, he'd drawn a thick line along my upper lash, creating sharp points that winged out just slightly at their corners. The look was bold and built up my confidence ahead of what I was positive would be a harrowing evening. He'd gilded my eyelids by mixing a creamy argan oil into a powder he called mica. The mineral, which was mined in the western region of Monwyn and exported to both Gaea and Solnna, must have been the same powder used to create the masterpiece on Kairus' back for the Third Maneuvering. As her skin had, my eyes and lips shimmered gold and reflected the light when I turned my head from side to side.

To intrigue the Den's patrons, he'd styled my hair in a traditionally masculine manner, the only difference being Ambrose plaited my hair in a five-strand braid instead of three and wove in several lengths of bright-red silken fiber.

"How did you think to bring all of this?" I asked, wondering how and when he was able to procure hair accessories and face paints.

"I was considering the fun parts of having a wife when I made my list. As to how… I'm a prince. I wrote it down, and it materialized," he said while practicing a few faces in the mirror.

"That's awfully thoughtful of you," I replied. He really had made the experience a good one. We laughed and chatted while he made me over, and told me a few things to expect in the Den. If someone was crying, they were probably okay. If someone was screaming, they were most likely having fun. If someone touched me, they would die slowly.

"Yes, well, if I find myself tiring of you, I figured the ability to alter your face would be a viable way to enliven our relationship."

I reached up and twisted the mirror out of his hands. He could ruin a moment so fast.

"That is. Just. Wow, Ambrose." I reached back and tucked the mirror into the first flap I could reach on the horse's bags.

The fine embroidery on the sleeve of the dress caught my attention. Little green scrolls and blue flowers circled the wrists, and at the center of each needlework bloom was a ruby cabochon or pearl. The red overdress was lined in a sapphire-blue-and-red shot silk. It sheened a lovely purple, which I thought appropriate, as I was still technically a Troth assigned to Solnna. Of course, my cleavage was a focal point of the ensemble's deeply plunging neckline.

"You know what we should have done? We should have painted my nipples gold, too."

I let my head fall back and appreciated how Ambrose had skillfully added kohl to his own eyes, giving himself a more daring look for the night to come.

"Goddess, yes. Unbutton. I do not know how well it will stay, but we can reapply right before you go in."

I went to work on the dress's tiny gold buttons. They only ran the length of my chest to hip, but there were a ton of them. On one hand, they helped give my stomach a nice cinch, but on the other, it made me realize how reliant I'd become on the servants at Verus. Another unanticipated perk to the dress was that though it looked like any other full-bottomed gown, the front of the skirts split, and glimpses of my flowy semi-sheer pants were visible with any exaggerated movements.

"I am increasingly troubled by your encouragement of him," Cato murmured as he rode up beside us on a freshly brushed mount.

I glared at Cato from the side of my eyes, still aggravated by his antics at the spring.

"If it gets me to a bed quickly, I'm all for it. Be glad I didn't suggest the other idea."

"Which was what?" Ambrose asked while poking at my ribs.

"Painting your lips gold and having you leave kiss marks all over me. The Den's all about possession, right? And making everyone covetous of your most recent plaything?"

"Let's do it! We have a little while until dark." Like two maniacal co-conspirators, we cackled atop our horse and plotted several more ridiculous ideas. Finally, I made it through the entire line of buttons and pulled down the top of the support I wore.

Ambrose, like a master tailor, had removed the straps from the garment, citing the need for "prompt accessibility."

"Gracious! Before you publicly fondle me, do me a favor and warm your hands." I flinched against Ambrose, who applied the sparkling paint with little dabs of his ice-cold fingers. I popped my top back up and started the task of rebuttoning what seemed like a hundred little closures.

Cato scowled at the two of us but said nothing. Just flicked his reins and rode forward.

"How are we going to do this without hurting him, Ambrose?" I asked, instantly concerned by Cato's sullenness.

"I am sure you will think of something, wife," he sighed, once again having located the mirror and holding it up to his face.

"You are actually awful, almost-husband."

"And *you* are the one person who can make him feel differently in all of this. Might I suggest you figure out how in a hurry? I abhor seeing him sad."

"Awful," I grumbled and shook my head.

"You are welcome for the advice, my heart. Dove? My soul's song? What should I call you in front of others?"

"Don't care. Ouch! Ow! Watch my shoulder!" I yelped, trying to shelter my wound from Ambrose's attempt at smoothing the wrinkles from my gown. "I don't want a repeat of Cato's side-of-the-road care. I think he tried disinfecting my bones."

Cato had used the tools in the healer's kit to thoroughly search for and remove bits of feather and a sliver of wood from my wound. I was extremely grateful for that and the salve he applied, but not for the alcohol he poured directly over the area. Ambrose had held me against his chest, where I wailed until Cato doused me with clean water.

"You will be happy for it when you aren't smelling of gangrene."

"I didn't say I wasn't thankful, my ass. My goon of a spouse. My narcissistic bun-bun."

Ambrose smacked at my lips playfully and rubbed the sticky gold that stuck to his hands along my neck.

"Shut up and sleep, *my nagging hag*. We have an hour before we arrive."

···+)(+···

I should never have closed my eyes. The short nap seemed to sap every ounce of the remaining energy from my body. When I woke, the sun was in its descent, and though bleary-eyed, I had expected to be greeted by the scenery of monumental buildings or a wall that rivaled the one at Colpass. I looked about but saw nothing. No kingdom, no city, just jagged rocks and steep crags.

"Remember—your job is to present yourself as humble, unpretentious, and above all, in love with me to the point you can think of no other." Ambrose reminded me for at least the fourth time.

"I know," I yawned. "Where are we?"

"Well below the city," Cato said while offering to aid me in dismounting.

"You know I can get off my own horse."

"I know. You have proven yourself a competent horsewoman, but this allows me to touch you without suspicion." I reached for him then, and both his hands slid from my ribcage to waist and settled there for longer than would be appropriate.

"I will check the path, see if they have maintained it," Ambrose informed us as he turned and walked off into the distance. I followed him with my eyes until he disappeared between two huge rocks, one of which looked—"

"You see the head?"

I nodded, astonished by how the stone formation could look so uncannily like the profile of a wolf.

"It's how the Den got its name. The entrance is just on the other side. The woman who runs the place pays a handsome fee to have guards stationed there both day and night."

"And as Protector, this doesn't seem like a way to invite people into your city?"

"Yes and no. We attract many visitors seeking its special brand of entertainment, and they always seem to overshare with the workers... who also work for me."

"Oh, I do see." Of course he would have eyes and ears all over the capital. "Cato, let's talk." I took his hand in mine and led him to the most private alcove I could find. It was unlikely anyone was near, but it was a known entrance and I wouldn't chance someone spying on us. My eyes wandered to his, and the fatigue I'd felt all day faded. There was a weariness about him and a sense of sadness that tugged at me.

"What would you speak of?" he asked.

The one thing that mattered more to me than magical kings or crazed kidnappers.

"Of us."

He swallowed deeply and closed his eyes, looking as forlorn as a man headed to the gallows. I dropped his hand and wrapped my arms around his neck, and he buried his head in my uninjured shoulder, holding me like it was the last time we would touch.

"The moment we walk into the city, everything changes. I go back to my life, and you will start yours," he breathed.

"Have you given up on us already?" Fear threatened to take hold of me.

"I will never give you up," he growled. "But I have dreaded the day you and Ambrose begin living your life together—even knowing it is for the best."

I held him tighter and twisted the little flip of dark hair at the nape of his neck around my finger.

"Cato... I don't want Ambrose. I don't think about him as I do you. His presence can't bring me calm or turn my body to flame. When he walks into the room, I don't forget to breathe. He's not the one I love."

He lifted his head. The last rays of fading light illuminated his dark eyes.

I love him.

A smile pulled at his lips, making his adorable dimple appear.

"You love me?" he asked, pressing me further into the rocky nook with his broad-shouldered body.

"More than anything, I think." I ran my hands up the planes of his chest.

"Do you love me more than... books? You seem to like those an awful lot," he purred, stepping in closer.

"Mmhmm, more than books... and more than maps... I like maps, too."

My back met the cold rock wall, but Cato slipped his hand behind my head, cradling it comfortably before it touched the rough surface. He surrounded me entirely.

"More than... a table of scrumptious Solnnan treats..." he rasped, leaning his head down to my ear, letting his lips graze its sensitive lobe.

"Even more than *two* tables of treats." I tilted my head to the side and stretched my neck, urging his lips down the column.

"But not three?" he feigned concern and stood upright, looking down at me with a grimace and his brows drawn tight.

"I... can I think about that?" I giggled while seeking his mouth with my own. He avoided me handily.

"Will you tell me then?"

"Tell you what? That... I love you?"

"Yes," he whispered reverently and smoothed his hands down my arms.

"I love you, Catommandus of Basilia, Protector of Monwyn. I wish it were your name written in the contracts binding us for life. The thought of bearing *your* child fills me with an emotion I am unable to describe. I would give up the entirety of Nortia for you. I would give up Verus, the Obligation, all of it, to be yours alone."

Cato dropped slowly to his knees and laid his head against the softness of my belly.

"Eira, may I come to you tonight? I know I said I would—"

"You should take me now and then again tonight, and you told me once what would happen if you had me in your bed. I'm ready for you to make good on your promise."

His drawn-out groan sparked something deep within. Like being driven by thirst or overcome by hunger, I craved not only the comfort and pleasure his body could give, but also to be always near the person he was.

The head held between my hands shook back and forth.

"Now we must focus... but tonight I will seek you. My need for your body has me bordering on insanity."

Cato pushed his hands into the opening of my overdress and ran them up my silk-covered legs, finally splaying them across my rear.

"I still need to hear a specific promise, but following that, I will not be rushed." He squeezed my backside in his hands and jerked my hips forward. "I plan to test your limits." I jumped when he bit at the soft skin of my hipbone through the sheer silk. "I must know how far we can take our lovemaking—and spend my time discovering how every inch of you responds."

Dragging himself against me, Cato stood until the rigid evidence of his excitement was cradled against my stomach. "I will master the technique of making you come in minutes, and learn to keep you on edge until *I* have had my fill."

Eagerness snaked through me. The anticipation of the night to come renewed my vigor.

"Nortia?" Ambrose's voice sounded in the distance.

A cold breeze wafted into the alcove, cooling my flushing skin.

"We are here," Cato replied.

He let his lips graze lightly against mine, just a feather-light contact, and smiled warmly when I couldn't contain the whimper that issued forth.

The crunch of footsteps on gravel signaled our time together was dwindling.

"Ambrose, if any harm comes to what is mine, I will raze this city. I will burn it to ashes and piss upon its remains."

Cato took my hand and placed it over his heart, covering it with his calloused palm.

"I am yours," he vowed, pressing my hand into his chest.

In the distance, the sound of rolling thunder announced an approaching storm.

···◆)(◆···

We faced the entrance to the Den.

"Now, assuming you don't become incredibly turned on by the whole affair and want to continue the fun, just tell me you are 'ready to be taken to bed,' okay, then we will leave. But please to the Goddess, not before you are mostly naked. Or maybe all the way naked. Can I slap your ass if I feel the clientele is not responsive to my handling of you? I just need this to go as well—"

"Are you nervous?" I cut Ambrose off, detecting an unfamiliar level of apprehension in his voice and stance.

"I think not!" he shot back, entirely offended.

"Come here." I turned him around and hammered on his back percussively until his shoulders lowered a hair. "You have to stop blabbering and turn on that near-perfect Scion charm. Go all Gotwig on the place because, what you're giving right now isn't going to sell."

He shook his upper body and let his arms flail about.

"I'm not used to being the power person. It's not what I'm into. I prefer the stand, all the eyes on me, people passing by and coveting all of this... reaching out to—it doesn't matter. I want to out-dominate the alphas, make them lust uncontrollably for you, for us. I want them beholden to their prince." He turned on his heel, his eyes flashing in the lamp's glow.

"Alphas?"

"Think of it like a pack of wolves. There is an alpha couple who leads the way—sets the standards, the pace. The betas follow their lead, look up to them, and, most importantly, stay in their place. There are also the omegas who will do everything we ask to be allowed to chew on the bones we cast off, thankful for our leftovers."

"Good Gammond, Ambrose, that is *not* how wolves work. You want us... to rule the Den?" I questioned. *Matron of an unconventional sex pack is a position I haven't thought to add to my list of titles.*

"*No*, I want them to understand that if we desired it, we could walk in and take it."

"And this is how important to you?"

"So much so," he said as his eyes took on a far-off look.

"Enough to spare my uterus from housing your child for... let's say, two years?"

Ambrose's eyes refocused and settled on me.

"Cunning harpy. Yes, I do think it is that important to me, but I will only promise a year and a half. And does this mean you know we are not currently expecting?"

"I'm still not absolutely positive where that is concerned," I admitted truthfully.

"Play this right, and you will have one year and a half before I get you with child... even though it goes against my better judgment. After we are wed, many will expect us to procreate sooner rather than later."

"Are you ready? I'm ready." I smiled sweetly, prepared to do what was needed to ensure Cato and I would have more time without additional complications.

At his knock, a rectangular window slid open at the top of the iron door, and behind it, a guard looked us over.

"Who enters?"

"You know exactly who enters. Open the door at once." Ambrose snapped as he slipped on a pair of fine doeskin gloves.

He looked every part the Monwyn heir this evening, having chosen to wear a dark-blue silk-and-velvet vest embroidered with muted-gold crescent moons. He covered the stunning garment with a tight-fitting, floor-length overcoat of dark burgundy. Mounted at each shoulder, two gold-cast bear heads held in their mouths a length of chain that ran across his chest. From the middle of the chain hung a red ruby surrounded by tiny pearls and malachite rounds. I wasn't sure he could have flaunted his wealth more. He'd even done his hair differently for the occasion, braiding just the top in a complicated style that looked like the vertebrae of a fish and letting the rest hang down to the middle of his back.

The heavy door opened with a creak, and together, we walked into a darkened room that smelled heavily of spirits and tanned hide.

"How far underground are we?" I whispered, noticing there were no windows and the room had a distinctly earthen odor.

"Not far. The staircase to the right leads up to the quaintest of eateries. By now, though, it has closed to its regular clientele. Most of the buildings in Monwyn have a cellar built underneath them like this, by the way."

"That's an incredible way to achieve more livable space for your people. In Nortia, our shovels would break before we could remove a foot of soil, so everything must be built up and out," I remarked, appreciative of the clever design.

"Ever the Obligate. Let this not be your only topic of conversation when you are introduced to the others, hmm?"

"Fuck off," I murmured under my breath.

"Better. Now, wrap your hand around my arm and drop your gaze to the floor. Remain that way until I have indicated otherwise."

Ready to get this over with, I complied, dropping my eyes, irritated that I hadn't taken a more thorough look at my surroundings. It was rather dark in the underground chamber, and the lamps cast a light that washed everything in a faint blue hue.

We walked together to the far side of the room, all the while receiving greetings and accolades. All I saw, of course, were the fine leather boots and shoes of the kingdom's gentle class.

"She is a prize, Your Highness. Will you be showing her this evening?" The voice that spoke was a deep, masculine bass. The owner of said voice wore a fine pair of tall boots that buttoned tightly with silver clasps that ran from right below his knee to his ankle.

"If I choose to, Lemder," came Ambrose's lazy voice. *Okay, this is how he's chosen to play it. Indifferent. Aloof.*

"It is my fervent hope that you do. She appears to be more ample than the Monwyn mistresses we normally get to peruse."

"She is indeed built abundantly in the most divine of places. Leave us." Ambrose flicked the wrist of the arm I held. He wore a stunning ring of sapphire and diamond on his middle finger.

"A drink, Your Highness?"

"Yes, Heveret."

"And the lady?"

"Will drink only what I offer."

This person wore black half-boots, recently shined but the soles were heavily worn. Maybe a lesser noble or a servant with a different day job.

We walked forward in between platforms raised a hand's width from the ground.

"Your newest pet is most fetching, Your Grace," Ambrose addressed a pair of red leather low-top shoes that were embossed with geometric designs and cutouts. They reminded me of the ornate half-walls at Verus.

"Show your face to my dear friend, Ethens."

I inclined my chin, keeping my expression neutral. Ethens was a plain-looking man with no truly stand-out features. Average in all aspects—lackluster hair, medium build, medium height. He made up for his basic appearance in his attire, however. Paired with his stand-out footwear, he had donned a short coat of fuchsia and wore a tight pair of leathers that—oh. He was not average in all aspects.

"She is unique, Ambrose. She doesn't have the look of a local girl. Have you put those plump lips to proper use?"

I stared past him, my eyes settling on his "pet." He stood on the raised area, along with several others. I couldn't see the man's face at all, he'd been covered with a bright pink mask, all but his mouth. It was gaping open, having been forced wide with a meal ring that fit behind his teeth. Saliva was running down his chin and falling to a chest covered in red welts.

"Drink," Ambrose commanded, pressing his glass to my bottom lip.

I took a sip of the strong liquid, almost choking on its fumes.

"Make her continue, pretty please," the overly eager noble begged.

"Drain it, my heart, and lick the rim clean."

I let my tongue dart out, tracing the edge of the long-stemmed vessel, repeating to myself "one and a half years" over and over in my head.

"I could teach your slave a few tricks if you but say the word Highness. By my hand, she would learn quickly."

"My *betrothed* will learn from me alone."

"Ahh, my mistake, please forgive your humble servant. You have my congratulations on such an acquisition."

Acquisition? The alcohol I'd consumed burned its way through my veins and made my arms and legs feel slack. I hoped it wouldn't loosen my tongue as well.

I was relieved when finally Ambrose steered me away from his acquaintance.

"I saw you staring at his dick," Ambrose murmured while placing a finger on the crown of my head and applying pressure, forcing my head further down.

"And? It looked like he'd hidden a cask of wine in his pants. Anyone would have looked. Also, no more spirits—that made my head spin." I closed my eyes against the effects momentarily.

"Noted."

Many pairs of feet walked in and out of my limited field of vision as we moved along, until a set of ridiculously ornate chair legs became visible. They were carved into the shape of a naked man lifting his arms above his head, and below him, a woman and man clung to his heels. I chanced a peek, glancing up just a hair. The chair itself was overstuffed and covered in a blue brocade. Oddly, it only had a single arm.

Ambrose sank down into the chair at the same time the noise in the room picked up exponentially.

"Fantastic," he muttered under his breath. "Stand to my side. Place your hand on my shoulder. Do not look up."

The swelling noise of the crowd grew and seemed to head in our direction.

"Ambrose, we haven't seen you here for some time. Your absence was refreshing," a gravelly-voiced man said while approaching us with a group of others. I couldn't tell which pair of boots was talking, but I could see pairs of smaller and more slender feet mixed into the crowd, as well as one set who wore only beige stockings.

"I had an important event to attend, or have you forgotten of my blessed status of Scion?"

"Right... the Scion son. Unlike your lineage, I suppose you *can* rightfully claim that."
Laughter, punctuated by a few gasps, broke out all around us.

Who would have the audacity to walk in here and insult the second heir to the throne? His adoption didn't make him any less the child of the king and queen! Heat prickled at my face, but I clamped my jaw shut, staying faithful to my character. Even though he drove me crazy much of the time, there was a fierce need within me to protect the man who had rescued me on more than one occasion and with whom I'd indelibly bound my life.

"And have you visited your precious cow of a mother since your return, or have you come straight here to play at being prince, child?" the voice sneered.

Shit! One, two, three, breathe—Nope, not happening.

"We are here at *my* request." I lowered my voice and mimicked the way Cato clipped off his words when making his point to others.

"Your mistress speaks for you, then? Had you come from the king's loins you'd be no weakling."

I lifted my eyes, knowing I shouldn't, and peered into a face that rivaled Ambrose's beauty. *My Goddess, he is positively divine, bordering on otherworldly.* White-blonde hair, luxurious and unbound, flowed down his back. His jaw was strong, and his beard was as light as the hair on his head, and his lips were sensuous and perfectly formed. He practically exuded authority from the top of his blessed head to the bottom of his brown-booted feet.

This was the pack leader.

"I am not his *mistress*..." I threw the term he used back in his face, pinning him with a look that nakedly displayed my disdain.

I waited for his reply, knowing he wouldn't be one to back down, but surprisingly, he stared back at me, remaining absolutely still. I didn't dare let my eyes drop or look away. I stared into his icy-blue gaze, not willing to lose the battle.

"No... you are not." His pupils dilated massively in his eyes, which is when I noticed that he, like Cato, had a small golden ring surrounding the black spheres. "Whose most captivating presence am I in?"

He reached his upturned palm toward me and bowed at the hip, his eyes never leaving mine.

"Do not touch my betrothed. Am I clear?" Ambrose warned, his tone unmistakably blunt.

"Your—but Ambrose, you were always one to share," the man crooned, still holding his hand in my direction. "Who is she that has incited this transformation?"

"*She* is Lady Eira Chulainn, Troth of Nortia, Chosen of the Goddess, my mate in the Rite. The contracts have been drawn, and we have chosen to join for life," Ambrose boomed, loud enough for anyone standing in the vicinity to hear.

"My, my... two Obligates, one an enchanting Troth, the other a false prince... surely you must—"

"—feel particularly powerful," I interjected, still holding his eyes. A low wave of laughter oscillated through our audience. "I would wager that the children I bear him will outrank everyone in this room."

"Indeed." The impeccably dressed courtier smiled, showing off a row of perfectly white teeth. "You know," he took a step closer, "if the contracts have been made up but not yet signed, would you rather not ally yourself to a true royal, a man from a pure line?"

The crowd silenced and pressed closer, while others strode over from the outskirts of the chamber.

"Are you insinuating yourself? Are you not still married, old man?" Ambrose mocked. He took my hand from his shoulder, pressing the flesh of my inner wrist to his lips.

"Nothing that cannot be remedied," the man retorted, unfazed by being called out. Finally dropping his eye contact with me, he instead focused on the wrist that Ambrose continued nuzzling.

I walked behind the one-armed chair and slid my hands down Ambrose's chest, letting my cleavage push upward. *If I spill out, I spill out.*

"Your offer is refused. Ambrose provides for me in ways that others simply can't measure up to," I drew the hand that held mine to my lips and kissed the tip of his middle finger before sucking it briefly into my mouth. I slid my gaze back up to the beautiful irritant that seemed content to stick around and insult my future husband. His face remained impassive, but there was an uptick in the pulse at the base of his throat. I was sure Ambrose would notice it as well.

"I do enjoy a defiant partner." His gold aura glittered just as Cato's always had when excited or emotional. "She may prove too much for you and need a stern hand to bring her to heel."

I moved to the armless side of the chair and ever so slowly lowered myself into Ambrose's lap, ready to play my hand against our adversary and hoping my suspicion was correct. I reached behind me and gathered Ambrose's hands, then led them around to my breasts as I leaned back and laid my head against his shoulder. Ambrose took the hint and began to pop the buttons of my overgrown until he was able to pull both sides apart, bearing my shining undergarments in their beloved Monwyn blue. Even the triangle I wore on my bottom half stood out, visible under the sheer fabric of my pants.

"Come Ahdmundus, she is nothing but a Nortian peasant. I was sure it was whale I scented the moment w—"

"Silence yourself, woman." His hand lashed out, and his knuckles struck the small lady to his side. I was ready to rush him like I had the Verus guard but remembered the story of Cato causing a scene. I kept my mouth closed and my focus where it belonged.

"I would see more of her, Ambrose... if only to establish her suitability for joining with a mock Monwyn heir."

"You go too far—" Ambrose growled.

"Certainly," I interrupted. "Looking out for the fitness of your kingdom is a noble act. My heart, please forgive my interruption."

"I will deal with you later," Ambrose snapped while letting his hands wander back to my breasts, cupping them and lifting them as if gauging their weight.

"No doubt she will provide well for the children I get on her."

I let out a throaty moan to see how this Ahdmundus reacted. Sure enough, the corner of his nose flared just slightly.

"Show him how you marked me *permanently*, my love."

Ambrose understood and went to the lacing on my support, making a show of slowly pulling the ribbon through each eyelet. Like opening the most precious of gifts, he pulled back first the material of the side where I wasn't pierced. I almost laughed, having forgotten the oil we had applied. My nipple glittered like a coin in the sunlight. He then revealed my pierced side.

Hums of approval echoed through the crowd, and a few grunts rent the air when Ambrose plucked the bar of the piercing, causing my breast to sway in front of them all. Naturally, both nipples stiffened with the sensation.

"*You* pierced the Nortian Obligate?" Ahdmundus jeered, acting as if Ambrose wouldn't have had it in him.

"She was more than willing. I pierced her moments after piercing her maidenhead. If you find it hard to believe, you can check the records. They observed it happening. And mine will be the only cock she knows from that moment on."

"Mmmmm." I turned my head and bit Ambrose smartly on the base of his neck. "Yours is the only that *can* fill me." I felt him begin to harden underneath my behind.

Ambrose splayed his hands across my chest, rubbing at my nipples with his pointer finger, pulling the gold glimmers in lines across my chest.

"I paint her in the morning and check her in the evening. If a speck is out of place, she is punished."

"But that's only happened once." I shrugged my arms fully out of my overdress, exposing my injured shoulder. "His play is rougher than mine," I giggled, going along with his ruse.

"*By Derros!* How much will it cost me to have her for the night, Highness?" A tall man in a finely tailored black tunic pushed through the crowd.

"She is priceless, I'm afraid," he sighed.

"To squeeze her magnificent breasts until she cries? Name it, land or gemstone."

"Her tears are so lovely, as is this..." Ambrose replied. His hands went to my pants and unbuttoned the three buttons that held them secure. He ran his fingertips over my brand, tracing the starburst at my hip. "You should have heard her screams."

There it is! I saw Ahdmundus's quick intake of air, saw the corners of his nose flare. It was so similar to how Cato reacted.

"A taste of her, Ambrose, name your price." Ahdmundus shivered, and his eyes bored into my own. I felt the entirety of Ambrose's torso tense. *A taste?* I knew exactly what he meant, and it wasn't a kiss.

"On your knees," I said before Ambrose could reply. "Drop to your knees and bow down to my betrothed, His Highness of Monwyn. Do so, and I will feed you from my own fingers." His breathing deepened, and his eyes flicked to Ambrose, who'd moved his hand below the waistline of my silken underwear, cupping my most intimate area.

"She tastes like nothing I could compare her to. What is it worth it to you to sample the Troth who I've bathed in my semen?" Ambrose pulled my multi-hued braid over my shoulder with his free hand and trailed his tongue along my neck.

"Do you think him worthy, my love?" I questioned coyly. "Or will you frighten me and give chase as you did when a man neared me last?" I fixed my eyes on icy-blue ones. "He's caught me every time I've tried to run. Would you be able to catch me before he did?"

There is the transformation. It was like the man in front of me swelled up to twice his normal size, and his eyes dilated so profoundly that you could barely see the cool blue of his irises. What was it about the corruption that made them react this way? Would Cato's father be the same? I kept my face a perfect mask of blatant wantonness even as the thoughts ran through my mind. Ahdmundus shook his head, trying to snap out of the state he was in.

"Go ahead then. Drop to your knees and tell me who I am," Ambrose replied from behind me.

Ahdmundus fell so fast that his knees cracked on the flagstone floor. His hand shot forward, grabbing at the seat of my pants, and again he shook his head as if trying to clear his mind of some possession. Ambrose reacted quickly and blocked him from being able to make contact with my body but ended up ripping the superfine material's seam.

"Say the words, Septimus."

Wait.

Time slowed.

I remembered the leather-bound pages of Kairus's lineage papers. *Septimus* had been written across its top. *Is this her brother or perhaps cousin?* I blinked back to the present.

"Your Royal Highness, Ambrose of Monwyn. If you tire of her, I will hand over my southern lands to have her in my possession," Ahdmundus Septimus panted out while his chest rapidly rose and fell.

"I will take the life of any who dares touch her... until the day she or I meets Merrias," Ambrose's voice rang out.

"I will pray as ever for your speedy demise then, child."

"Try again." I placed my foot on the kneeling man's shoulder and tugged him closer between my legs, where Ambrose was steadily drawing delicious little circles, enticing all the nerve endings that I didn't need awakening at the moment.

Perhaps I shouldn't have let myself become so aroused earlier, but Cato—*nope, I can't think of Cato right now, I'll climax in front of everyone here.* I beat the image of him back into the recesses of my mind.

"'I will pray as ever for your speedy demise...'" I paused, waiting for him to finish the sentence.

"Your *Highness*," he choked out the last word. I knew he was seething, but if this was even a bit like what Cato went through, he would remain focused on me. "Let me drink straight from your well, Troth Nortia, and I will be satisfied."

"You will not be," I said coyly. "You may take from my hand or my future husband's." I tried to deal with the sensations Ambrose was all too skillfully foisting upon me.

Ahdmundus laid his palms on the floor and inched his head nearer me. He flicked his corrupted eyes to mine and in a too-familiar gesture, sniffed at me as a canine would. *Oh, dear Goddess.*

"From your fingers, then," he said in an almost reverent tone.

"Ambrose, will you please?" Understanding, he removed his hand from me, thank goodness, and ventured down to the opening of the ripped seam, shifting the triangle of my underwear to the side.

A feral growl came from the head between my legs, and I could feel his breath on my damp and exposed flesh.

"You are never that wet for me. Is that some bitch's trick?" A shorter but broad man said to a slender blonde, who he shoved away from his side.

More and more, I loathed Monwyn males, and more and more, I was thinking about destroying their male-centered dominion.

Ambrose ran two fingers down the slit of me and spread my labia. The pricking sensation of self-consciousness threatened, but I stifled my fear and focused on the power and supremacy this would bring to Ambrose and as an extension of him, to me.

"I have done your bidding. Give me what I desire," Septimus all but yelled.

I wanted this over. I reached down and swirled my fingers around my tightened clitoris, then looked up at Ambrose and silently urged him to take my mouth. He held my chin tightly in one hand and jerked my face up to his before running his tongue across my lips. Bending his head, he claimed me with his demanding tongue and went so far as to bite at my bottom lip and chin. There would be no misunderstanding for those who viewed it. I belonged to Ambrose.

I let out a groan, much less fabricated than I wanted it to be, and Ambrose let go. He moved his hand behind my palm and then guided it to the genuflecting Septimus's mouth. He licked his lips in anticipation. I wondered what would happen if I shoved my finger down his throat. Watching him gag would probably be amusing, but not nearly as gratifying as making him kneel had been.

A smooth, moist mouth sealed over my fingers. A warm tongue circled around their tips before gliding in between them. A long-winded and guttural hum vibrated the digits which he sucked further into his mouth, working them until I pulled against the suction he'd created.

"That's *enough*," Ambrose commanded in a manner that said he was not to be trifled with.

He loosened slightly, and I'd just began to withdraw my hand when his eyes shot to mine. A wicked smile tugged at the corner of his mouth, dimpling his cheek.

Oh, no.

The bastard clamped down on my finger and bit me so hard I saw red.

I clamped my teeth tightly and stayed silent.

"I wanted to hear you cry. My Goddess, you are a fucking force wasted on the likes of... *His Highness*," he laughed as if he were demented, and then went momentarily silent.

I watched his face change. His jaws slackened, and his eyes closed. Like someone in the throes of orgasm, he shouted and groaned and wailed until I kicked out with my foot and sent him tumbling to the floor. He lay there on his back, all beautiful and deranged, smiling and panting with an impressive erection pressing against his clothing.

"How ridiculous you look upon the floor, uncle. You are embarrassing your friends."

Uncle?

Ambrose looked down his nose while righting the buttons of my pants and then overdress. The support was lost, stuck in my garment somewhere, and would have to wait until later.

"Get up Septimus. You give us a bad name by acting as you are!" someone shouted.

"Take yourself to a corner, man!"

Ambrose patted the side of my thigh, and I stood up and moved to his side, placing my hand on his shoulder.

"It was a pleasure to meet you all. I hope you have found me satisfactory," I said, lowering my eyes.

"You are a gem, my dear, obviously trained to the highest degree for the pleasure of our heir." Came a voice that I matched to a pair of shuffling shoes.

"Were you ever interested, my companion and I would be open to joining you for an evening of entertainment," a pair of blue boots offered. "I've never known anyone to drive him to such a pitiful state, but I am more than willing to follow in his footsteps, with His Highness's approval, of course."

I allowed a blush to play over my features and placed a sweet smile on my lips.

Kill me now.

There was no way the man on the ground was—"

"Ambrose, *love*, I find that I am ready for you to take me to bed." And I was... three times over. I was ready to sleep, ready to greet Cato and hold him in my arms... and then prepared to sleep again.

"Gentlemen, it will be a few hours or more before she is fully sated. I bid you good night."

Rising to his feet and tugging at the bottom of his vest, Ambrose straightened while I let my hand fall to his elbow. I watched my feet carefully as I walked up the steps, not wanting to end our performance by falling on my face.

Together we drifted through a small restaurant that looked like a place you would take your grandmother for a dessert and lute concert. Little dried thistle flowers and lavender stalks lay on each table, and the floor was so shiny and clean you could see your face in its reflection. Ambrose led me to the door, and we walked straight out and into a pod of at least eight armed guards.

"Cato?"

"Undoubtedly," Ambrose smirked, looking right at home in the center of the unit. At least he could see over their heads. My first look at the capital of Monwyn was limited to staring at the straps that held the metal breastplates on each of the men, who stood at least a head taller than myself. I did my best to crane my head and weave left when a guard inched right, but it was too dark to successfully catch a glimpse of my new surroundings. Instead, I settled myself and listened to Ambrose hum a jaunty little tune under his breath.

"We are currently at the back of the palace. If all is well, tomorrow, the Protector and I can show you around if you are up to it," Ambrose said as if sensing my need to know more about my new home.

We stopped briefly at a guard tower, and they admitted us through a spike-tipped gate that closed heavily behind us. The path of the courtyard we came to was softly lit with covered lamps, and I was able to see a few stone benches and beautifully intricate tile mosaics under my feet as we passed. We came to yet another gate, and while stopped, I was able to look up and see hundreds of multi-colored glass windows lit from within the palace. What a marvel it was to behold the rainbowed panes rising into the sky, even at the darkest hour of the night.

"Who goes there!" The shout rang out from somewhere in front of us.

"His Royal Highness Ambrose Burchard Berra Odel Ricard, second heir to the throne of Monwyn!" heralded the guard positioned at the center front.

I squeezed the arm I held tightly, pressing my face into the muscular bicep.

"Do not laugh, betrothed. Our firstborn, no matter their gender, will bear the name proudly."

"I don't believe naming our future daughter 'Burchard' appears anywhere in the contracts... my sweet *Odel*,"

The guards ushered us into the palace and led us down a dim corridor, four of our guards peeled off, stationing themselves to our back. With less of a human wall obstructing my view, I could finally size up the seat of Monwyn power.

It did not disappoint.

All of the walls were built from massive, sand-colored stones, and the floors were the same marbled white and gold found in the study at Verus. Every door we passed was arched, not squared, and each door frame was surrounded by thick, white tiles that shimmered ever so slightly. The halls we walked through were open and airy, and the magnificent windows that I now saw from the inside, were even more impressive up close. They were not haphazard patchworks of color like I had thought they were from a distance. They were each distinct works of art; the masterfully placed shards of color forming different depictions. The one I passed to my right was a scene of snow-capped mountains in the background and small glass flowers in the foreground.

After walking the long hall, we climbed two flights of stairs and headed down another long corridor.

"Our rooms are just ahead."

Ambrose held out his hand and smiled down at me. The guards at our front parted and flanked a set of double doors. As they had at Colpass, the men pounded the butts of their spears on the ground, and the sound echoed in the massive hall. Both doors opened, and two liveried servants stood at the ready.

"Leave us. Everyone," Ambrose commanded. The two doormen plus another four servants scurried from the room. Without warning, Ambrose scooped me into his arms, strode through the entryway, and kicked back, sending a door closed with a bang. Peering around his big shoulder, I watched as a guard reached soundlessly into the room and closed the other with a soft click.

"Brilliant harpy!" Ambrose shouted before throwing his head back in a full belly laugh. I held on to him tightly and squealed aloud as he twirled us around in fast circles and then charged through another short hallway.

"Open the door!" I bent low in his arms and obliged, laughing along with his infectious cackling that had yet to cease.

"You were like, you wanna taste this? Bow down to my man! How did you even think..." he trailed off, and tears sprung to his eyes and ran down his cheeks. "Take it from my husband's hand or mine, oh my Goddess!" He screeched mid-cackle. "I will *die* happy."

Nudging the door with his foot, we entered a cozy room with a large, roaring hearth and an even larger bed covered in fine white linens. The room was breezy, not stifling, despite the large blaze, and there was a window located above the bed that depicted a blue-clad woman with her hands raised to her face in prayer. An oval, representing the womb, was set above her head in the sky.

"Ambro—!"

My back hit the bed with a thud, and before I could recover my senses, his big body followed, jumping into my view. I threw my hands up to protect my face, but the impressively agile dummy rolled to my side, pulling me along with him. We lay facing each other like Kairus and I would when discussing the most recent Troth drama.

"Make him grovel again and I will throw a yearly allowance into the contract. Ahhhhh, that felt so good!"

"He was a real asshole. Is the rest of your family like that?" I asked, happy to have assisted him in bringing his uncle down a notch. It would have crushed me if Ambrose had been made to cower before him.

"On my father's side, yes. On my mother's, not at all. But he is by far the most vocal in his disapproval. Wait until you see him around Cato, though. At least with me he has an excuse of sorts. He treats Cat like a pile of shit for having given up the chance to rule."

"And is he... does he happen to be related to Troth Kairus?" I asked, wanting to know more about their relationship.

"Mmhmm, her father. I'd never met her until the Obligation. Ahdmundus never allowed our association growing up."

Well, fuck me.

"And he's corrupted like Cato? Approximately how many others are? I'd like to keep them at arm's length until we understand more about my effect on them."

"You think he is?" Ambrose asked turning serious.

"You think he's not? He acted just like Cato when he's, um, the warrior-king. And the blond hair and gold around his pupils."

"He's always looked like that, seriously. And according to Cato, he has severely limited supervised access to the king himself."

"That's fine and all... but I'm telling you, he's corrupted. How often do you fall on the floor in spasms after sampling lady parts?"

"Nortia."

"So you may want to consider—"

"Nortia!"

Ambrose grabbed my hand and held my finger up between us.

"He got your blood, didn't he?"

Sure enough, a minuscule, rusty-red clot had dried on my nail bed.

"That jerk bit me hard. I hadn't realized how hard, though. I'm guessing that's what caused the reaction, but such a small amount?" I turned my hand and examined the pad of my finger. Two pinkish, crescent-shaped marks were there, but no skin had broken.

"Fuck! Cato will be furious. I need to tell him before someone else informs him of our masterful performance." Ambrose pointed to the tall side table that rose up slightly higher than the bed, "Looks like he wanted to tell you something as well."

There was a folded parchment with the letter *E* written on its outside. My heart filled to bursting.

"Ambrose?"

He stopped at the door and looked over his shoulder, arching a perfect brow.

"I would like it if Cato and I could be together first before we... I... take on the role of your... vessel." I scrunched my nose up at the term.

"The mood you've put me in... I'll deliver him tonight with a silk bow tied around his balls. You can wash in there. Check my closet for something to wear to bed."

The door shut out the elated prince's grinning and I made myself count to three before scrambling over the white-on-white embroidered bed cover and snatching up the letter. I brought it to my chest and shut my eyes just for a moment before popping off its seal.

Make a list of every desire and every whim that has ever crossed your mind. I will happily spend my life making every last one of them a reality.

Until tonight,

With my legs dangling over the side of the bed, I reread his words. Maybe it would be different tomorrow, but right now, I couldn't think of anything I desired more than him. I wanted him in this bed, above me and beneath me. I wanted to rub the tension from his back and smooth the line of concern from his forehead and plant kisses along his stomach and chest.

For the umpteenth time, my waning energy miraculously restored itself, revived by the thought that tonight, I could tuck myself into Cato's side and let the even sounds of his breath lull me to sleep. I looked around, taking in the room while heading to the door Ambrose had indicated. It was like the architects had taken a look at Verus and decided to create its antithesis. Down to the furnishings, it was more elegant than ostentatious.

In the bathing chamber, thin, white marble columns reached from floor to ceiling, one at each corner of the *T*-shaped basin that was sunk into the floor. Centered behind the bath, two arching windows surrounded by fine marble tiles would allow sunlight to shine down on the water and the two overstuffed chaise lounges that flanked the tub. A silver tray inlaid with green gems sat within reach and was filled with a variety of soaps and cleansers and scrubs.

I turned the water on, thinking it would be hours before the basin would fill, but when I flipped the silver handle, water poured from all sides of the bath in a glorious cascade. I grabbed two rolled linen towels from the stack in a large woven basket and sat myself down on the marble edge dangling my feet into the rising warmth while smelling all the available scents. A few were the distinctly Ambrose smell of spice and sweetness, but others were floral and musky or citrus-inspired. I settled on a cheerful green jar whose lid pull was cast into the shape of a delightful golden frog. The sunny-yellow soap smelled of a spice called saffron. I had fallen in love with it the moment I had tasted it at Verus. It was both honied and earthy, and combined with the sweetness of vanilla, it created an intoxicating scent.

The hot water soothed my shoulder and briefly made my finger sting. I cleansed my hands, hopeful that no infection would set in. After washing the rest of my body and scrubbing my hair clean, I laid my head on the edge of the tub and let my arms and legs float freely.

Out of the bath, I dried and sat on a low, cushioned chair, watching my yawning reflection in a wide mirror framed in a shimmering abalone shell mosaic. Ambrose was right. I looked worn. My eyes were dull and dark, my skin was dry and there were bruises peppered all over me. For many of them, I couldn't recall what had caused them. I picked at the few remaining pieces of faux red hair and rubbed them into a ball between my palms. I'd have to fish the other bits out of the tub, but right now... I didn't have the energy. The bed was what I needed, and to the bed I would go. At this point, given the news Ambrose was taking him, I wouldn't be surprised if Cato were held up. How they didn't see the corruption in their uncle was beyond me. *Maybe that will turn out to be another of my powers...*

I walked across the carpet-strewn floor, turning off lamps and squishing my toes into the extravagantly deep piles. Slipping between the crisp sheets felt like being cleansed yet again. *Oh, my Goddess.* I sank into the soft feather mattress. I curled up and closed my eyes, picturing Cato arriving in nothing but a bow. No matter how tired, no matter the hour... I would welcome him.

··· +)((+ ···

It may have been minutes or it may have been hours when I heard the door open. I came awake and watched his shadowed profile as he moved toward the bed. I reached out to take the hand he offered, my heart overflowing.

And then the smell hit me: pungent... wrong, but familiar.

"I am told you are quite fetching... daughter."

SNOW ON THE SUMMIT

Eira, Cato, and Ambrose will continue their journey in the mountainous Kingdom of
Monwyn in:

Snow on the Summit—Coming February 2024

For updates and opportunities, join E.A. Fortneaux's newsletter!

Sign-up at www.Fortneaux.com

FOLLOW E.A. FORTNEAUX ON GOODREADS, AMAZON AND MORE!

Made in United States
Troutdale, OR
08/24/2023